EVERYMAN'S LIBRARY

EVERYMAN,
I WILL GO WITH THEE,
AND BE THY GUIDE,
IN THY MOST NEED
TO GO BY THY SIDE

THE
TRANSYLVANIAN
TRILOGY

VOLUME II

For my dear children, for whom I first started on this translation of their grandfather's greatest work so that they should learn to know him better, he who would have loved them so much.

K. BÁNFFY-JELEN

In loving memory of
PATRICK THURSFIELD, 1923–2003

BOOK TWO

THEY WERE
FOUND WANTING

'And the first word that was written in letters of fire on the wall of the King's palace was MENE – The Lord hath numbered thy Kingdom.

'But none could see the writing because they were drunken with much wine, and they called out in their great drunkenness to bring out the vessels of gold and silver that their ancestors had laid up in the Temple of the House of God, and they brought forth the vessels and drank wine from them and increased in their drunkenness and madness.

'And the Lord's vessels were wasted among them as they abused each other and quarrelled over their own gods, each man praising his gods of gold and of silver, of brass, of iron, of wood and of clay.

'And as they drank and quarrelled among themselves the fiery hand wrote on in flaming letters upon the plaster of the wall of the King's palace. And the second word was TEKEL – Thou art weighed in the balance and art found wanting.'

PART ONE

CHAPTER ONE

ONE DAY IN the autumn of 1906 the Budapest Parliament was unusually well attended. In fact the Chamber was packed, with not an empty seat to be seen. On the front benches, the government was there in full force. It was, of course, an important day for that morning the Budget was to be presented and everyone knew that, for the first time since 1903, it was bound to be passed and, more important still, passed by a massive majority. For the previous three years the country's finances had been ordered by 'indemnities' – unconstitutional decrees, which had mockingly become known in pig Latin as '*exlex*' for the sake of the rhyme, and which had had a disastrous effect on the economy.

At last, and this had been the great achievement of the Coalition government, the nation had put its house in order.

Pal Hoitsy, the Speaker, ascended the podium, his handsome grey head and well-trimmed imperial looking well against the oak panelling behind the platform. In stilted words he commented on the importance of this blessed situation in which confidence had been restored between the nation and the King, the Emperor Franz-Josef in Vienna.

A few meagre 'hurrahs' came from a handful of enthusiastic members, though the rest of the House remained silent, stony-faced and stern. None of the political groups – not even the minorities party whose leader, the Serbian Mihaly Polit, was to propose acceptance of the Budget – gave the smallest sign of believing the Speaker's words. The reason was that that morning, September 22nd, an article had appeared in the Viennese newspaper *Fremdenblatt* baldly stating that this much-vaunted harmony was nothing more than a cynical and dishonest political fiction.

The article concentrated on the resolution which had been drafted on the previous day by the legal committee of the Ministry of Justice and which, so everyone had been led to believe, would be incorporated into law at today's session.

It was a delicate and disagreeable situation.

The difficulties had started two days before when a member of the People's Party had proposed that the recently resigned government of General Fejervary should be impeached. The new government, much though it would have liked to do so, could not now avoid a debate on the proposal (as it had done the previous July when similar propositions had been put forward by the towns and counties at the time of the great debate on the Address), especially as the proposer was a member of Rakovsky's intimate circle. Naturally the government suspected that the latter was behind this latest move and it was believed too that the whole manoeuvre had been plotted in Ferenc Kossuth's camp of treachery and was intended to breed such confusion and doubt that the newly achieved harmony of the Coalition would be endangered. This was indeed a direct attack just where the new administration was most vulnerable. Everyone now professed to know that one of the conditions of the recent transfer of power had been that no harm should come to members of the previous government. The leaders of the Coalition had accepted this condition since their object was to restore good relations between the nation and the ruler and the government of General Fejervary had been appointed by the King. That this agreement had been made was not, until now, public knowledge and indeed had been expressly denied during the summer when Laszlo Voros, Minister of the Economy in Fejervary's so-called 'Bodyguard' government, had first announced the existence of the *Pactum*, the settlement of differences between the royal nominees and the elected representatives. These denials had then been in somewhat vague terms, but now the matter had been brought out into the open. The new government's problem was how openly to face the situation provoked by the People's Party representative, offer a solution that would content the opposition, and at the same time keep their word to the King.

Everyone's face was saved by the intervention of Ferenc Kossuth, who boldly risked his reputation in the discussion in the committee when he declared that no *Pactum* existed since secret agreements of that sort were unconstitutional. This was a dangerous statement to make since everyone knew that for the King to have made the new appointments, agreement must have been reached on specific points such as this; but it sounded well and so dignity had been maintained by oratory. As a result it was planned that the House would reject the impeachment proposal and instead give its approval to an official statement which branded Fejervary and his cabinet as 'disloyal counsellors of the King and nation' and delivered them to the 'scornful judgement of history'. It was further decided that this official statement should be everywhere displayed on posters.

The formula was a good one and all the committee members had left the meeting satisfied in their own ways; the radicals because the hated 'Bodyguard' government would be publicly degraded, and the new cabinet because they were no longer faced with a constitutional obligation to initiate an impeachment which would be most embarrassing to them.

But now, when everyone had breathed a sigh of relief and thought that the difficulties had been solved, the bomb had been exploded in the leading article of the *Fremdenblatt*, which was known to be the semi-official mouthpiece of the Court in Vienna. Here it was declared that, 'according to well-informed sources in Budapest', the previous day's committee decision would not be presented in its agreed form since it was unthinkable that those who enjoyed the ruler's confidence should be put publicly in the pillory. It was further declared, and this was said to have come from someone 'close to Fejervary', that the former Minister-President would himself speak at the next session of the House of Lords and that he would then explain the full details of the *Pactum*.

No more. No less.

There was an atmosphere of gloom in the Chamber. The weather outside was grim and autumnal and little light filtered down through the glass-covered ceiling. The lamps were lit that illuminated the galleries on the first floor and the seats reserved for the press, and these too added to the lack-lustre effect for, although here and there faint reflection could be caught from all the panels of imitation marble and the gilding on the capitals, there were great areas of shadow which made the vast hall seem even darker than it was. Even the painted plaster statues could hardly be seen. Only the Speaker's silvery hair shone on the platform.

Out of bored good manners the members remained seated in their places; but everyone was preoccupied with their own thoughts and they hardly heard the Speaker's rolling phrases. In many parts of the Chamber five or six heads were bent towards

each other as little groups discussed in whispers the new turn
of events revealed by the *Fremdenblatt* and the menace that
lurked between the lines of the article. Only Minister-President
Wekerle leaned back calmly in his chair, his handsome face,
which was so reminiscent of that of an ancient Roman emperor,
turned attentively in the direction of the Speaker. As the architect of the Budget which was everywhere acclaimed he was, no
doubt, contemplating the triumph of its acceptance; but his
manner was that of a man who has weathered many a storm and
whose nerves were firmly under control.

How the world has changed, thought Balint Abady who, as an
independent, sat high up in the seats opposite the Speaker. What
storms would have raged here a year and a half ago! How everyone would have jumped about shouting impromptu phrases,
raging against the accursed influence of Vienna and the sinister
'Camarilla' that ruled the Court. Then even the Speaker would
have made some reference to the 'illegal interference by a foreign
newspaper!' Perhaps they saw things more clearly now that they
knew more of what is really going on . . . perhaps at last they were
beginning to learn.

With these thoughts in his head he listened to what the
Speaker was saying.

As the speech was coming to an end someone from the seats
of the 1848 Party came over and sat beside him. It was Dr Zsigmond Boros, the lawyer who was Member for Marosvasarhely.
Dr Boros's political career had started well. After his election in
1904 he had become one of the chief spokesmen for the extreme
left and when the Coalition government was formed he had been
appointed an Under-Secretary of State under Kossuth. After two
months of office, however, he had suddenly resigned without
giving any reason. Gossip had it that his legal practice was
involved in some shady dealings, though no one knew anything
specific about the matter. Nevertheless, he found himself cold-
shouldered by many of his fellow members for, in those days,
while any amount of political chicanery would be tolerated,
people were puritanically strict about personal honesty. Boros
had only occasionally been seen in the House since his resignation from office and it had been assumed that he had been busy
putting his affairs in order. Two days before the present session
he had reappeared. Abady had noticed that since his return he
had held little conferences with one group or another, obviously

explaining something and then moving on to talk to other people. Now he had come to Abady and sat down next to him. He must have some special reason, thought Balint.

After some ten minutes had passed in which he had seemed respectfully to be following the closing phrases of the Speaker's address, he turned to Abady and said, 'May I have a few words with you?'

They got up and went out through the long corridor outside the Chamber where members were gathering in heated discussion and into the great drawing-room, which was almost as dark as the Chamber itself and where little groups of chairs and sofas were separated from each other by columns and heavy curtains as if the room had been designed for conspiracy and intrigue.

As they sat down Boros started the conversation. 'I would like to ask your advice,' he said, 'on an important matter which affects the whole nation. I really am extremely worried as I don't know where my duty lies. If you don't mind I'll have to start some time ago, with the circumstances of my resignation.'

Balint tried to remember what he had heard, but all he could recall were some half-expressed insinuations. Now, sitting next to the man, he wondered if they could be true. It was hard to believe.

Zsigmond Boros was a handsome man with a high forehead, smooth as marble. He looked at you with a straight clear eye and a calm expression. His pale complexion was set off by a well-groomed beard somewhat reddish in tinge. His clothes, which were exceptionally well-cut, only accentuated his air of reliability. His voice was melodious and he chose his words carefully and well. Firstly he spoke about the time when Voros had made the statements about the *Pactum*.

'I don't think you were here then?' he asked.

'No,' said Abady in a somewhat reserved tone. 'I was abroad.'

'Ah, yes. I heard that you were in Italy. You don't mind if I go over again what happened then?'

Boros then repeated what, as a Minister in office, he had stated at the time. He said that during the preliminary discussions there had been talk of an *ad hoc* cabinet which would take over the administration and introduce general suffrage and that this temporary government would consist exclusively of members of the 1848 Party and members of the former government. The presiding Minister had to be Laszlo Voros and, so Boros said, the proposition had been accepted by Ferenc Kossuth.

'But that's when I went to see Kossuth. I wanted to know exactly what was in his mind. I needed a clear picture and I felt, as one of his confidential advisers, that I had a right to know. Kossuth admitted that such a plan had been discussed but that he personally took it only *ad referendum*, as a basis for discussion. He said that as the other two parties of the Coalition in opposition, the Constitutional and People's Parties – which had formerly been against the universal suffrage proposals – now seemed to accept this reform, it had seemed to him that any other combination had become superfluous. He then showed me the actual text of the *Pactum*. That is the reason why I handed in my resignation. It had nothing to do with the slanderous stories that I hear were circulated about me as soon as I had resigned my ministry. As they did not know the truth I suppose it was inevitable that some people would believe the worst of me!'

Boros paused for a moment as if he were expecting some reaction from Balint. Then he went on:

'So, you see, the *Pactum* really does exist. At the committee meeting yesterday Kossuth – well, to put it mildly – made a statement that hardly accorded with the truth. The question which worries me is this: should the matter be hushed up? Should we allow the country to believe in a lie? Is it, or isn't it, our duty to intervene and stop the people from being misinformed? Is it, to be specific, my duty to tell the truth as I know it? I don't know where I stand. On the one side I am not bound to secrecy by any promise: on the other I was in office at the time. Of course this is a political matter, not merely a question of professional discretion. But if I tell the House what I know the government will collapse like a house of cards.'

Boros looked questioningly at Balint.

'Why do you turn to me, of all people?' asked Abady.

'Because I know that you accept no party whip and that you look far further in these matters than do most of our colleagues. I know all about your work in establishing the co-operatives in Transylvania and I much admire what you have achieved. Therefore allow me to explain how I view the present situation and why I believe it to be so serious, even, perhaps, fatal.'

As he spoke a new Boros appeared, quite different to the man Abady had known up to this moment. Until now Balint had seen only the elegant, somewhat bombastic orator who had a talent for the well-rounded patriotic phrases which were so appropriate to popular meetings. Now he talked from the heart, to the point, and from a totally unexpected point of view.

He spoke with bitterness and hatred in his voice.

'It is clear,' Boros started, 'that the present government is based upon a lie. They have made the public believe that the Coalition has won the battle. But the truth is just the opposite. It is the King who has remained on top and who has proved that the so-called road to progress, the controversy about army commands and all the other slogans we have brandished for so long, is altogether impracticable. But no one will admit this. And to maintain the lie, to keep up their pretence, the public is fed with all manner of nonsensical rubbish. All through the session Parliament has been discussing Rakoczi's so-called re-habilitation laws. Slush, just slush! This new decree – slush again! Other proposals will follow, anything which will ensure the government's continued popularity. More slush! And they will have to, because they dare not admit that everything they promised before the elections is impossible to realize. So what do they do? They go trudging along after more and more tasty-sounding carrots to disguise the fact that their programme is an utter fiasco. This is very, very dangerous, if only because only pretend-laws and pretend-decrees will be passed, things that the press will acclaim and write about. And since we are powerless to alter our relationship with Austria our incapacity will be disguised and dressed up in all sorts of false colours. It will be just the same with the banking question, with the Austro-Hungarian customs problem and with the military "quotas". Oh, the Austrians are clever enough! They'll make us pay for our little gestures towards independence with the jingle of silver and gold and we'll pay the price for the sake of being able to name the filthy bargain a "customs contract" instead of "integrated customs", or some such meaningless phrase! And this will be so in all things because all our beloved government wants is to be able to maintain the show of progress towards national independence; so they'll do it in all matters not subject to the *Pactum*. As I understand it Apponyi is now planning a new law for the State schools – which will cost a great deal of money – so as to have a show of Hungarian language teaching – on paper, of course – and Kossuth is working on a plan to bring new order to the Croatian railroads. They are already drawing up the plans for a decree to ensure that all railroad employees should use the Hungarian language even there. Can you think of anything more stupid and ill-conceived?'

'Surely that's not possible,' said Balint. 'Doesn't the law already state that Croatian is the official language in Croatia?'

'Of course! While I was in office I did all I could to speak against the idea. Especially because it was our fault that the Khuen government collapsed and thus ensured the majority of the Serbian Coalition. But this was exactly what Kossuth wanted because the Serbs were the only party who backed him on the Personal Union issue.'

Abady felt that this was really going too far and he answered, with some heat, 'I'm sure they didn't do that just to please us. The immediate consequence of Hungary's personal union would have been Croatia's right to the same autonomy, leading sooner or later to the formation, with Bosnia and Dalmatia, of a new sovereign country within the empire. Triality instead of duality. It's already an idea dearly beloved in certain circles in Vienna!'

'That is a matter for discussion. But one thing is certain and that is that it is absurd to foster a movement and later on to strike down what we have laboured to create. And, if this government remains in power, that is exactly what will happen. My problem is this. Is it or is it not my duty to try to overthrow the govern-ment before it is too late?'

Balint thought quickly about the discussions he had recently had with various Ministers about the development of his co-operative and housing programmes in Transylvania, discussions which showed every sign of leading to official support for his plans, and he did not want to do anything which might put these plans in jeopardy. At the same time he was extremely reluctant to have any part in an intrigue which would lead to a new crisis in the government.

'What you have just told me,' he said, 'is certainly very, very serious. It is indeed dangerous, and harmful, if the government gives too much weight to individual nationalistic aspirations without regard to the well-being of the whole nation. I am honoured,' he continued, feeling himself getting more stilted and pompous with every word he uttered, 'that you should have trusted me and told me all these things. However, I don't really know how to advise you. I imagine that you have talked over these matters with others as well as myself?'

'Not from quite the same angle, at least not in such detail. In fact, I didn't really expect advice from you. I really only wanted the opportunity to talk over the matter, to try to clarify my ideas, with someone whose opinions I respect. I also wanted to explain that I had resigned office for important national reasons and not just because of some dubious financial dealings as some of my so-called friends have been pleased to suggest!'

At this point Dr Boros returned to his usual orotund manner. The bitter note disappeared from his voice and the velvety politician's baritone took its place as he went on '. . . because I, who have given my life's blood to work only for the salvation of my country, with no other notion, no other intent, than to make our nation great and prosperous and powerful, ready at all times to face undaunted the villainy and craftiness of . . .'

In the corridors the bells rang shrilly, the sound echoing throughout the domes and vaults of the vast building.

From all directions members started to run back into the Chamber to regain their seats. A young member of the 1848 Party dashed past the sofa on which Balint and Boros were sitting.

'Apponyi's going to speak. Everyone to their places! Apponyi's on his feet . . .' And he ran on.

Abady was thankful for the interruption. He felt annoyed that Boros should have spoilt the effect of his apparent sincerity by returning so abruptly to his usual affected politician's manner. Somehow it diminished the seriousness of what he had just been saying.

They walked back to the Chamber together.

It was some time before Balint saw Zsigmond Boros again and so the question of the *Pactum* was not again discussed between them.

The public condemnation of the Fejervary government did not, after all, take place. The committee of the Department of Justice met again on the following day and five men were nominated to draft a new text. The matter was thus neatly buried and forever after forgotten.

The leading article in the *Fremdenblatt* had told nothing but the truth.

CHAPTER TWO

IT WAS ALREADY half-past two in the morning when the members of the gypsy band collected themselves together and set out in the calm spring night. March had been unusually mild that year. Laji Pongracz, as befitted the leader of the band, stepped smartly out ahead of the others, his fur collar turned up on each side of his fat cheeks and with, carefully swathed in a wrap of soft silk, his precious violin under one arm. The last of the group was the cymbal-player, limping as he carried his heavy instrument on his back. Behind the musicians followed an open wagon on which had been placed a table and six chairs. The wagon moved slowly, driven by a coachman beside whom sat a waiter holding on his lap a basked filled with glasses. Between the waiter's knees was a box in which some ten bottles of champagne and a couple of bottles of brandy rattled together, and a bucket of ice. The procession was closed by two policemen. These had been sent over from the Town Hall, since the city's regulations demanded that all serenades should be officially announced in advance and must be provided with a police escort.

As the group of musicians turned into University Street, out from the hotel's main hall came the gentlemen who had ordered the serenade. In front were two men, arm-in-arm. One was large and good-looking, the other was much smaller: they were Adam Alvinczy and Pityu Kendy.

These two were now always seen together since for more than a year they had both been helplessly in love with Adrienne Miloth. No doubt they felt that a sorrow shared was the easier to bear and so they spent all their time in each other's company. When they had both drunk enough they would explain their sadness and grief to each other. Each felt increasingly sorry for the other and when at last they felt they could drink no more they would return to their respective homes, only to meet the following day to repeat the pattern, day after day, night after night. On this day they had already been at their favourite pastime for some hours and both were in full flood of woe and commiseration.

Behind them were two other men. On the right was Gazsi Kadacsay, who was on leave from his regiment of hussars that was stationed in Brasso, and who was therefore not in uniform but dressed in a short jacket with a sheepskin hat askew over one ear. On the left was Akos, the youngest of the four Alvinczy brothers. Between these two strode Ambrus Kendy who, though older than his companions, was still the leader of the *jeunesse dorée* of Kolozsvar. The two younger men were assiduous in their attentions to 'Uncle' Ambrus, for they felt that it was a great honour to them that he had interrupted his evening of drinking and carousing with the gypsies to join them on this serenade. They also knew that if he had not agreed to join them they would never have been able to get the gypsy musicians away from him. Indeed they had hardly known how to ask the favour.

To their great joy Uncle Ambrus had agreed at once.

'Devil take it!' the older man had shouted. 'I'll join you myself, though I can see from your faces you'll be going far afield tonight, pack of young rogues that you are! What? Right out there? To the lovely lady herself! To the Uzdy villa, what? To Adrienne Miloth, no less? Oh, yes, I'll come with you. Why not? I'll come along though I'm far more used to pursuing women indoors than squeaking away outside their windows!' And he let out a long drawn-out cry 'Aay-ay-ay!' and rubbed his great hands together just as peasants do when they dance the csardas.

Uncle Ambrus's presence was one of the reasons why they had brought along the chairs, for they knew that he did not much care for standing about, and if one chair why not several others and a table and some champagne to set upon it? Of course they had done all this before, but tonight they all felt it was a special occasion.

The sixth man to join them had been Laszlo Gyeroffy and his presence was by chance. He had just been loafing around in the street, as always something of an outsider. In the darkness he seemed very elegant, for in the dimly lit street no one could see how threadbare and worn was his well-cut coat nor how shabby and damaged his once expensive hat that had come from St James's Street in London. He still looked as handsome and as proud in his English clothes as he had been a year earlier when he was still the *elotancos* – the leading dancer and organizer of all the smart parties in Budapest – before he had been ruined by gambling too heavily and had been made to resign from his clubs in the capital. Laszlo's good looks had not changed but there was something in his manner that had not been there before, an awkwardness, an infinitesimal air of servility that was only apparent when, for example, he would go to the end of the table and sit down only when expressly invited, and how gratified he seemed if anyone deigned to speak to him. When he had had too much to drink this new-found timidity would desert him and then he changed completely, wrapping himself in a strange exaggerated pride and carrying himself with dignity. Then he would stand exceptionally straight, tilt his tall hat on the back of his head and, with an air of disdain and infinite distance, speak scornfully as if all the world were beneath him. On this evening he had not yet reached this state as, even at that late hour, he had not yet put enough alcohol beneath his belt. Modestly, therefore, he hung back and quietly followed the others on their way.

The first stop was on the Torda road where the widowed Countess Kamuthy lived with her grandchildren in an old house which had been built against the ancient walls of the town. Here the procession entered the courtyard, because the windows of the family's rooms all opened onto it, and at once Akos Alvinczy ordered the musicians to play the tune that the youngest Kamuthy girl had chosen as her own, then his song followed by a couple of waltzes. As there was no answering sign from the windows Akos told the musicians just to play some mood music. All at once there appeared behind one of the windows a lighted candle. This symbolized the fact that the serenade had been accepted and so the band broke into a swift and merry csardas. As soon as this was brought to an end the party left the house and headed for the Monostor road. Here they stopped in front of Jeno Laczok's house, lifted the table from the wagon, set it up on the sidewalk and placed the champagne, glasses and ice bucket upon it. Around the table sat Uncle Ambrus and all the rest of them, except Baron Gazsi, drinking heavily and toasting each other. Gazsi remained standing by the gypsies because here it was he who had ordered the music. Although it never entered his head when he was sober, a little drink always convinced him he was madly in love with Ida Laczok. One sad lovelorn song followed another as Gazsi gazed up mournfully at the almost instantly lit window, his woodpecker nose tilted on one side in the very attitude of the despairing lover.

Nearby the cook from the house next door was saying goodbye at the wrought-iron gate to her soldier lover. Hearing the sweet music they remained discreetly in the shadow, hiding behind the stone gatepost. The policemen were just about to ask them to move on, but seeing that they were merely standing quietly in the dark and were not making any trouble they let them be.

At the end of Gazsi's serenade the little band continued on its way down the Monostor road. They had between three and four hundred metres to go before they reached the Uzdy villa. At Kolozsvar this was considered a great distance but there is no sacrifice a loving heart will not make to tell his beloved of his devotion, and in this party there were three of them who felt that way about the beautiful Countess Adrienne, wife of Pal Uzdy. Adam and Pityu had been her devoted slaves for a long time, and everyone knew it, but now they had a new recruit in Uncle Ambrus, though he himself had kept very quiet about it.

Until recently Ambrus had concentrated on more facile conquests. With his hawk-shaped nose and bristling dark brown moustaches he had the sort of good looks that made servant-girls catch their breath when they met him on a dark staircase. He was usually in luck even though his conquests rarely lasted more than half an hour and were the result of a casual and laughing request for a 'quick rough and tumble' for which nothing more was needed than the opportunity and an available sofa. Since he had been a boy Ambrus's heart had never beat the more swiftly for any woman, and he was convinced that they were all there for the taking whenever he was in the mood.

It was also true that he never made a move towards any girl who had not already shown him that she was ready for it.

He had never previously taken much note of Adrienne's existence. Of course they had moved in the same social group for several years. He had danced with her countless times, often dined at the same table and met in the same houses, but Adrienne, with her girlish appearance, thin neck and undeveloped body, and with the air of icy disapproval with which she kept at bay any conversation that seemed to be heading towards *risqué* subjects or lewd innuendo, had held no interest for Ambrus. Subconsciously he had felt that she was not yet really a woman in spite of having a husband and a child. In some way she was different from the women he was used to. When Adam Alvinczy and Pityu Kendy had openly avowed their love for her he had laughed at them and told them they were a pair of donkeys. But everything had changed, quite suddenly, when he saw her again this carnival season in Kolozsvar.

It was difficult to explain what it was in Adrienne that made her seem different. She was cool and flirtatious, but she had been both before, and she had always loved to tease the men who were in love with her, even tormenting them a little. The truth was she played with them as if they were amusing automatons, dolls without hearts. This play was totally instinctive, like that of the fairy tale giant princess who tossed the dwarfs in her pinafore, never for a moment reflecting that they might have human feelings. Adrienne kept her playthings in strict order. No words with double meanings were ever allowed; and no reference, however veiled, to sexual desire or contact, to kisses or even innocent compliments to her beauty, complexion or colouring were allowed to pass their lips. All this remained unchanged ... yet there was a difference, subtle but definite. Now she played her game with compassion and with a softer, wiser understanding than before. Though, as before, all references to sex were forbidden, now it seemed as if her veto sprang not from a lack of knowledge or from unawakened ignorance, but rather because she held the subject so holy that she felt it would be too easily profaned.

The men who continued to pursue her were still her playthings, but she no longer treated them as unfeeling objects, rather, perhaps, as lesser beings who knew nothing of what they wanted to discuss and who, if they suffered at all, suffered only lightly with no risk of serious wounds. If they desired something it could only be trivial, minor yearnings with which she could sympathize and feel sorry for, listen to gently and even try to ameliorate by a kind word ... but as for taking them seriously? What did they know of love, of what she had experienced, of what *she* had lived through?

What she had lived through ... It had been the previous summer. For one short month she had escorted her sisters to Venice and, during those four weeks, every dawn had brought her one step nearer to self-destruction, to a death towards which she went with head raised, happy as she had never been before, as if she carried her red beating heart in her two hands in joyous sacrifice, glorying in the magic of her own fulfilled womanhood. That she did not kill herself before returning home, as she had planned, but came back to the husband she loathed and dreaded and must continue to live with, was for her the real sacrifice. This was the price she had had to pay if she was to save her lover from taking his life too. She would willingly have accepted her own death, but she could not bear to be responsible for that of her lover. He would have killed himself if she had, and that was the reason why she had come back. With this memory deep within her, with the knowledge that she had already lived through all the pain and bliss of life, experienced every pleasure and faced the reality of death, with this secret in her heart, everything else in her eyes seemed grey and drab, cheap and poor. It was because of this that she listened with sympathy and understanding, and with a tiny pitying smile upon her lips, to Adam Alvinczy or Pityu Kendy when they poured out their woes to her and tried to tell her what sorrow she caused them. She treated them like children who had to be comforted when they had fallen and bruised their knees.

No one knew anything of the drama she had lived through in Venice: no one, that is, except perhaps her youngest sister, Margit, who was an observant girl and who may have guessed, but only guessed, a little of the truth. But even she knew nothing for certain and the others nothing at all.

Adrienne's appearance had hardly changed. Her figure was as tall and slender as ever, like the Greek statues of antiquity, but her arms were perhaps a little rounder and the hollows above her collarbone, which had given her such a girlish undeveloped look, had now filled out. And her ivory skin shone even smoother, as it does when women leave their childhood behind them, and glowed as if lit from inside. Adrienne no longer pulled her wraps or boas tightly round her shoulders as young girls instinctively do when some man glances at them. Now she allowed herself to be admired, though she did so with the somewhat contemptuous air with which beautiful women use their desirability as a form of armour, which would itself hold an enemy at bay.

No one saw this clearly, though Adam and Pityu were more hopelessly in love than ever, but Uncle Ambrus had felt it instinctively and so he too started to pay his court. He believed that it would take no time at all to reach his goal. At first he started with the same approach he used to peasant girls, but when Adrienne reproved him sternly he became all submissive and tried other ways of attracting her attention with humbleness and sentimental looks and phrases. In Countess Uzdy's presence the formidable Ambrus became quite a different man. When he was with her he played the faithful guard-dog – but only in her presence; when he was with the other men he felt obliged, so as not to lose face, to maintain his former role of the all-conquering seducer and every now and again would let drop hints that he wasn't hanging around that 'pretty little thing' in vain!

The Uzdy villa was a large building that stood alone surrounded by a vast garden. On each side of the main house were wings which had originally been designed as servants' quarters and in one of these wings were Adrienne's apartments. The musicians entered the forecourt and stopped in front of the glazed veranda behind which they knew was Adrienne's bedroom. They all walked on tiptoe as quietly as possible, and exchanged only a few words in low whispers while the double-bass player took extra care that not a throb should be heard from his instrument; for it was an unwritten law that serenades should come as a surprise and that the music alone should awaken the sleeping inmates of the house. Everything was carefully done and the table, chairs, glasses and wine were all in place – and the men seated round the table – when the musicians started to play.

On the way the young men had drawn lots as to who should have the first turn with the musicians. Thus it was decided that Uncle Ambrus should be first and the others would follow. Ambrus stood facing the windows in front of the table on the side nearest the house, the others further back on the other side. The band started softly, playing his own tune: '*Do come when I call you . . .*' and then, somewhat more loudly, Adrienne's song. After these two there followed some mood music and, as soon as they could all see a glimmer of light from the window giving onto the glass veranda, Ambrus began to sing. He had a good baritone voice, even if it was by then somewhat vinous in quality. The other men sat round the table drinking their champagne in the background. Song followed song until, after a rippling csardas, Uncle Ambrus signalled to the gypsies to stop. At this point he should have stepped back as it was the turn of Pityu's serenade. However he did not do so but had a chair brought forward to the place where he had stood in front of the window and sat down, glass in hand; and there he stayed.

Ambrus was in an awkward position, because if he had retired to the other side of the table, as he ought to have done, he would have had to abandon his pose of the triumphant successful lover. So he stayed where he was, playing the Devil-may-care wooer in front of the other men, but only showing to Adrienne, who might have been peering unseen through the window curtains, a face less ferocious than the others would ever have imagined.

So he stayed there, conscious – as it was a clear moonlit night – that he was in full view of the window, and every now and again he would sing again with the musicians, even though he no longer had the right as it was not his music that was being played. As their leader, Ambrus assumed more rights than the others, but even so Pityu did not like it. He said nothing because he was a modest young man, a weaker bough than most on the strong ancestral tree of the Kendy family. This could be seen in his appearance. He was thinner, frailer than other members of the clan and in him the famous Kendy nose which so resembled the beaks of birds of prey, eagles, falcons and hawks, had dwindled in Pityu's case to the less ferocious but none the less exaggerated beak of some exotic jungle bird. With Pityu's weak chin his face seemed to consist entirely of a huge hooked nose and two sad-looking black eyes.

The serenade was nearly over when there was heard behind them a loud clatter of horses' hoofs.

A carriage drawn by a team of four horses raced into the forecourt and drew up barely an inch from the back of the cymbal-player. The first two horses snorted but remained otherwise motionless but the gypsies quickly scattered.

Uncle Ambrus started to swear in his usual masterly and complicated fashion but he was forced to break off when he saw that it was Pali Uzdy, Adrienne's husband, who jumped down from the high travelling carriage. So he rearranged his face into a smile of welcome and cried out, '*Servus*, Pali! Where do you spring from at this late hour?'

Uzdy walked over to the serenaders with his usual measured tread. His thin figure, like a dark tower, seemed even taller than usual in his ankle-length double-breasted fur coat and, as he was narrow-shouldered as well as exceptionally tall, he somehow gave the impression of having been whittled away the further up you looked. With his elongated pale face framed in the fur collar, long waxed moustaches and goatee beard he looked for all the world like one of those tall bottles of Rhine wine whose wooden stopper has been crowned with the caricature of Mephistopheles.

Towering above the others he replied, 'I've just come from home, from Almasko. I like to come and go without warning . . .

and sometimes I get quite a surprise, as now, though this, of course, is a very agreeable surprise!' Pali emphasized each last word in his usual ironic manner. He shook hands with each in turn.

His slanting almond-shaped eyes glinted with private amusement as he sat down at the table. 'You don't mind if I join you?' he asked, the polite words barely masking the mockery of his tone. The serenaders were extremely put out, for they had chosen that evening only because they knew that Uzdy was away. Now he had turned up and spoilt everything.

'So? A serenade? It is a serenade, is it not? For Adrienne, of course! Very good! Very good! You are quite right! I am most flattered that you should honour our house in this way. I am only sorry I disturbed you, but I must say in my defence that I knew nothing about it. You will forgive me, I'm sure,' went on Uzdy without giving the others any chance to reply, '... but go on! Please go on, and, as long as you don't object, I'll just sit here and listen. It's a great joy to me to hear such beautiful music. I never get the chance at home.'

This was more than Uncle Ambrus could bear. Angrily he burst out, 'Only an idiot would serenade a lady when her husband's at home! Perhaps you'd like us to come and play to you when...' Ambrus broke off when he saw that Uzdy was looking at him with a strange gleam in his eyes.

'When ...?' he enquired icily, raising his long neck from the fur collar.

'Well ... when you're asleep, or, or ... when ...' stammered Ambrus. 'Anyhow, it isn't the custom!' Then, to bring the evening to an end as quickly as possible, he turned to the musicians and shouted, 'Well, you dolts, get on with it! Play Master Alvinczy's song, are you daft?' Turning once more to Uzdy in explanation he said, 'It's Adam's turn. That's what the boys agreed.'

Again song followed song, but more swiftly now as if the gypsies wanted to get it all over with and run.

Though the music continued the festive mood round the table had been extinguished. While Adam Alvinczy stood near the band-leader, all the rest remained seated, Ambrus still nearest to the veranda, Uzdy at the upper end of the table, Kadacsay and Pityu on the courtyard side and, at the other end of the table, rather apart from the others near to the wooden gates at the end of Adrienne's wing which led to the garden and the Szamos river

that flowed beyond it, sat Laszlo Gyeroffy. While it was obvious
that Uzdy's arrival had spoilt the evening for the others, Laszlo
seemed quite indifferent. He sat very straight, staring into the
night, drinking tumbler after tumbler of champagne, laced with
brandy. He sat so still he might have been a robot.

Alvinczy told the gypsies to play 'A hundred candles...'

Up to this moment Uzdy too had sat quite motionless in his
chair, his long narrow eyes fixed on the glimmer of light that
showed from behind the shutters of Adrienne's room. His lips
were drawn back, showing his broad teeth as if he were about
to bite. Now, however, he straightened himself up and his hand
disappeared into the folds of his coat. When the band came to a
climax with the words 'a hundred pints of wine', his arm suddenly shot forward and, at the *fortissimo* of 'wi-i-ine', fired his
Browning directly at the gate-post leading to the Szamos, not
twenty yards away.

It was lucky that the gypsies, intent on their playing, did not
hear the noise of the shot; but all those seated round the table did,
as well as the bullet's impact on the gate-post. They all jumped in
their seats, Ambrus belching out 'God damn it!' as he snatched
his head sideways.

Uzdy burst out in a roar of laughter.

Only Gyeroffy remained unmoved, even though the bullet
had whistled straight past his nose. Without appearing to notice
what had happened, Laszlo continued to look dispassionately in
front of him as he raised his glass once more to his lips.

This unexpected calm seemed to impress even Uzdy.

'Your nerves are good,' he called to Laszlo.

'My nerves?' said Laszlo, his voice seeming to come from a
great distance. 'Why?'

'This is why!' cried Uzdy, and fired two more shots in quick
succession past Laszlo's head, but the latter merely reached for
his glass and drank down his wine as calmly as before.

This brought the serenade to an abrupt end. The gentlemen,
all of them now in a chastened mood but delighted to get away,
hurried back to town grumbling among themselves about what
a strange, unpredictable fellow that Uzdy was. The only exception was Gyeroffy.

He walked now with a proud air, his previous diffidence
completely gone, his head held high, his tall hat at the back of
his head and, below those eyebrows that met so menacingly

across his face, his aquiline nose was lifted in proud disdain. Laszlo's lower lip stuck out, giving his whole face an air of arrogance. 'Don't stumble about like that,' he said to Pityu Kendy when they were about fifty yards from the villa. 'You're in my way!'

The others whispered among themselves because they realized that he was extremely drunk.

And drunk he was, so drunk that he no longer remembered all the humiliations that he had suffered before returning to Transylvania the previous spring. Then, when he had been sober he had never been free of a nagging sense of self-accusation, never free from the knowledge that the cousin with whom he had been so in love, Klara Kollonich, had married someone else because he, Laszlo, had shown himself to be too weak of character to deserve her; never free either of the disgrace of being forced to resign from all his clubs in the capital because he could not pay his gambling debts. When sober he could never escape a nagging sense of being inferior to others. He had convinced himself that he was worthless and that he wore on his forehead a visible brand that advertised this worthlessness to everyone he met, even if they were kind to him and pretended not to see it. And if anyone showed signs of being friendly, he took it for pity.

At the moment when he had had such terrible losses at the gaming-table, he would have been able to settle if he had not thought it more important to repay his mistress the money she had paid out for him on a similar occasion some months before. He had felt himself more dishonoured by being indebted to a woman, even though no one else knew of it, than by the public scandal which had put an end to his being accepted in the high society of the capital. And at the time he had felt that there was something noble and uplifting, cruel but at the same time triumphant, in choosing social death over private dishonour.

It was not long before the exaltation, the sense of the spiritual strength which had then given him such support, began to wither and die. Soon the recollection of his folly and weakness came back more and more strongly, to the point that he could only banish these gnawing regrets by getting drunk. And when he was drunk he went at once to the opposite extreme. Then he would become arrogant and scornful, letting everyone see that he thought himself infinitely superior to them. At these times he would believe himself to be a great artist, which indeed he could have been if he had not squandered his time and neglected his talent. But of this he never spoke. Even when drunk he would tell himself that they would never understand; and so confined his boasting to telling tales about his social success in grand society as if that were the only thing that would impress 'those country bumpkins'.

His drinking companions noticed at once what was happening and so, as soon as Laszlo began to hold his head high and look haughtily down his nose at them, they would start quite consciously to tease him, which is, and always has been, the favourite pastime of the men of Transylvania.

Today, it was Baron Gazsi who went up to him and said, apparently quite seriously, 'You did very well to tell off Pityu. He needs a lesson in good manners!' And Pityu took him up by saying, 'Indeed I'm most grateful for your telling me how to behave. You, who have always moved in the most exalted circles!' Whereupon Adam Alvinczy said, extremely solemnly, 'We should all follow your commands, naturally!' and his brother Akos chimed his agreement.

Then it was the turn of Uncle Ambrus who, taking Gyeroffy by the arm, bellowed out, 'All these young fellows here are as raw as bear-cubs. Of course they've not had your advantages. They've never been anywhere or seen anything, unlike you who was used to hob-nobbing with all the big-wigs in Budapest!'

And they all crowded round Laszlo, bowing obsequiously and winking all the time at each other. Then someone said, 'It must have been marvellous, that court ball you told us of – the one for the King of Serbia!'

It never occurred to Laszlo that his friend had mentioned the wrong king on purpose.

'It was the King of Spain, not Serbia,' said Laszlo. 'Alfonso XIII, who is nephew to the Archduke Friedrich. You really should know these things and get them right . . .' and he launched into one of his favourite subjects, waving his arms with the unsteady but self-important gestures of the very drunk.

Dawn was beginning to break as they approached the main square. They had almost reached the Town Hall when Gyeroffy stopped the whole group with a peremptory wave of his hand.

'Now we're here, it's my turn to give a serenade!' he said, and called to the gypsies to get ready and have the table and chairs put on the sidewalk.

Ever since they had left the Uzdy villa Laszlo had been think-ing of ordering a serenade himself, regardless of the fact, which never even occurred to him, that he only had some twenty crowns in his pocket. Now he felt himself to be a *grand seigneur*, high above everyone else, and this was his chance to set them an example and show them all how these things should be done. The problem was to decide where, and to whom. It was not as if he were paying court to anyone in the town, either to a young marriageable girl or to a married woman. On the days that he happened to come to town from his home at Szamos-Kozard, with a few coins in his pocket from the sale of some cucumbers or lettuce, he would put in an appearance at whatever festivity was going on, dance if it were a ball or pay calls and drink coffee and whipped cream at a house where there were young girls on the market, play the piano if anyone asked him; but he would do all this mechanically, hardly noticing where he was or what he was doing. Although he was still so good-looking that more than one girl would try to make eyes at him, he took no notice and indeed was barely aware that he had made a conquest and had an opportunity for flirtation. It was all the same to him whether he sat next to one girl or another. When invited to sit down and talk he would do so partly because good manners demanded it but mainly out of torpor. Now he had no idea to whom he should offer a serenade.

As they happened to be in front of the small town *palais* of the Gyalakuthys, which stood just across from the road from the Laczok house where they had been earlier, he decided on impulse that this must be the place.

Dodo Gyalakuthy was a nice little thing, a good girl who loved music and who, when he called at the house, always asked him to play. Now, as he tried to collect his thoughts and concentrate, he remembered that she always talked to him very nicely, asking him all sorts of questions about many things, about music, for instance, and his life in the country. Why not Dodo? Yes, he would play his serenade for her!

It was about five o'clock when Dodo was awakened for the second time that night. How odd! she thought. The Laczok girls are getting two serenades on the same night. They *are* lucky!

Dodo never thought the music might be for her, for the simple reason that it never was. None of the young men would dare to be thought to be courting her as she was known to be so rich that no one wanted to be branded as a fortune hunter by paying the slightest attention to her. In Transylvania such a thing – God preserve us! – would have been thought very bad form, indeed dishonourable.

Knowing this, she automatically thought it was for one of the Laczoks that the gypsies were tuning up again.

Dodo turned over, trying to get back to sleep. There would be no reason to get up again, as she had before, tiptoeing to the window and peering down from behind the curtains. She was sure it must be the same band, the two Alvinczys, Pityu Kendy, Gazsi and Uncle Ambrus . . . and Laszlo Gyeroffy.

Yes, he had been with them. Well, in a sense with them, though he never seemed to be much with anybody. He just tagged along. Poor Gyeroffy! How hurt and bitter he had been when he came back from Budapest! Of course it was all the fault of that cousin of his, Klara Kollonich. What pain she must have inflicted to poison the heart of such a sweet dear boy! How could she have done such a thing? How could she? Oh! thought Dodo, I could kill her for it! And she tried to get to sleep.

Somehow the music seemed to get louder . . . and nearer? She listened hard, sitting up in bed. Indeed the music came from under her window; it was not on the other side of the street at all! And the music? Why, it was that fast csardas that Laszlo had played to her the last time he had come to tea. It was that music, *his* music.

Dodo jumped out of bed and ran barefoot to the window. Through the closed shutters she could see that it was already light outside. A table stood on the broad pavement outside the house with the men sitting round it. On the table stood champagne and glasses, and on each side there was a policeman who shooed away any early passers-by. And under her window the band of Laji Pongracz played, and by the side of the band-leader stood Gyeroffy! The serenade really was for her, for the girl whom no one came to court.

And it was him, Laszlo!

Dodo stood quite still beside the window, too mesmerized to move. She pressed her hands to her round little breasts as if by so doing she could still the excited beating of her heart and control the joy which throbbed in her throat. Then she remembered that she had forgotten to light a candle and that if he didn't see an answering light he might think his offering was not accepted. She had to be quick as the second song was already coming to an end.

Quickly she ran to the bed and returned with a lighted candle to the double windows. Opening the inner panes as hurriedly as she could she placed the candle behind the curtains. Then she realized how foolish this was, for as it was daylight outside such a tiny flame would hardly be seen. Pulling the outer lace curtains aside she put the candlestick on the sill between the inner linen drapes and the outer window. There it was sure to be seen, and what did it matter if someone had had a glimpse of her round bare arm? Anyhow, what else could she have done? And it wasn't as if everyone outside had not seen her naked arms when they danced with her at a ball. Surely no one would find fault with that and think her immodest? Feeling chilly, she went to find her feather-trimmed wrap which would keep her warm, as by now she certainly did not feel like going back to bed. What she really wanted to do was to go to the other window and there peep discreetly out to gaze and gaze upon the young man who serenaded her, that young man who at long last had noticed her, who had, perhaps, seen how interested she was in him . . . and who, maybe, even returned her love. Oh, even a little, little bit of it would be enough! How wonderful that would be!

Around her waist Dodo tied the sash of her silken wrap which fitted closely to her slightly chubby but well-formed body and, leaning against the inside of the window, let her dreams float with the memories the music conjured for her. Some of these memories were quite old, going back to the day, a year and a half ago, when she saw Laszlo at the Laczoks' ball. That had been the first time they had exchanged more than a few polite phrases. The following two seasons had been filled with vain longings, for she had only seen him occasionally and by chance. Still she had always had news of him: the news that he was courting Klara Kollonich and that he had become a tremendous gambler and then, almost a year ago, that he had resigned his membership of the Casino Club. 'And it was only because of his grand relations that he escaped being thrown out!' Dodo was told, with mocking laughter, by several people who never knew how much they hurt her. But it was not only hurt, because this last news also gave her a tiny secret joy as she realized that it would mean that Laszlo would be forced to leave that cursed Budapest and come home to Transylvania ... and when that happened, when he was near at hand, she would somehow contrive to see him, be near him, perhaps even console him, and then ... maybe then?

There were also newer memories, souvenirs of this last season when Laszlo occasionally was to be seen in Kolozsvar. When Dodo had heard that he was in town she had got her mother to ask him to tea and to dinner, always of course when other young people were present. She had thus been able to see a little more of him, even though Laszlo never stayed in town for more than a few days at a time.

Always they had talked of music and, with the instinct of a woman in love, she had found just that form of expression and manner that echoed the young man's artistic yearnings.

During their talks she had also come to learn many other things about him. From a word dropped here and there – which she carefully pieced together afterwards – she had gradually learned all about Laszlo's financial problems. She discovered that he had leased his property to Azbej, who acted as agent for Countess Abady's estates, and that ten years' rent had been paid in advance. 'It was really very good of Azbej,' Laszlo had said. 'I owe him a great debt of gratitude', and Dodo realized that this meant that he had to live on what his gardener could raise from the sale of apples or vegetables from the garden. Of course he no longer had any credit, only debts, and for this he was grateful to that trusted steward! Naturally Laszlo did not tell her these things all at once. He did not even notice that he had told her anything. Dodo knew because she had listened assiduously to what he would say – a fact here, a fact there, some little hint – and later she would carefully put it all together until these little fragments of information, as in a jigsaw puzzle, formed a complete picture. Already she had thought that somehow she must come to his aid and now, as he stood under her window and serenaded her, now that at last he showed some signs of being interested in her, what had only been a vague intention crystallized into a firm resolve.

Looking down from the other window, through a discreet gap between the curtain and the window-frame, Dodo had a clear view of the group on the pavement below. Ambrus, Pityu, Kadacsay and the two Alvinczys sat sleepily around the table while a waiter who could hardly suppress his yawns continued to fill their glasses with champagne. The cymbal-player leaned dozily against a rubbish bin. It was now full daylight, an hour when all carousers are overcome by sleepiness. The two police-men were still making passers-by cross to the other side of the road. These were mostly peasants from the village at Monostor bringing their produce to the market – a few chickens, onion-chains or other vegetables. Some of them stopped for a moment to listen to the music and then went on their way.

But Laszlo played on. A little while before he had taken over Laji's violin and started to play himself. From his bow flowed a rich stream of impassioned melody. He seemed to have forgotten everything, time, place and occasion, and was conscious only of the music he created. He stood very tall and straight, his hat tilted on the back of his head. His eyes were shut even when, as now, he turned to the musicians and started a new song – *'They put new tiles on the soldiers' barracks . . .'*

Dodo could not take her eyes off him.

In the middle of the song everyone round the table suddenly jumped up. Uncle Ambrus shouted something, the music stopped, and everybody, even the passers-by on the other side of the road, stared up at the window where Dodo had placed her candle just inside the outer glass and in front of the fine linen curtains. The material had caught alight and long flames were curling up to the eaves. Smoke was already filling the room. There was a sharp crack as one of the window-panes split in two and fragments of glass fell tinkling to the street below.

Dodo swiftly pulled the bell-cord and then, regardless of her-self, grabbed both sides of the burning curtains and tore them down. Then she ran to the washstand and seized the water jug.

By the time the frightened maidservant rushed into the room, Dodo was already pouring water over the smoking remains of the curtains on the floor and in her light slippers was stamping out the little flames that still occasionally burst forth.

It was lucky that she had acted so swiftly for if the fire had reached the voluminous lace curtains that hung inside the room it might have been much more serious. As it was the only signs of the near-disaster were some black marks on the parquet floor. That was all; and the soles of her slippers were almost burned through. There was no other material damage.

While her maid, and two others who had run to help, were swabbing up the water from the floor and removing the charred remains of the curtains, Dodo took another look at what was happening outside.

Only the two policemen were still there and she called down to them that the damage was only slight and that they could go home. For a while she stood silently by the broken window.

Now Dodo felt sad and heavy-hearted, feeling it to be an evil omen that, just when she was feeling so happy, the serenade should end in disaster. Then she shook her head vigorously as if thereby to dispel such foolish thoughts and turned back to the room.

You silly! she said to herself. There are no such things as evil omens. Sheer foolishness!

And she jumped back into bed, noticing only now how cold the room had suddenly become.

CHAPTER THREE

IT WAS COUNTESS Roza Abady's birthday, a day she liked to celebrate and when nothing pleased her more than for a succession of callers to visit her little *palais* in Farkas Street.

Only one thing was forbidden – nobody was supposed to mention which birthday it was.

No one ever did, of course, although they all knew that she had been born on April 12th, 1854. One there was who was bold enough to break the rule, and he had lately taken to annoying the countess by sending her a card on which he wrote 'My congratulations to the Gracious Countess on her fiftieth birthday' (or whichever it happened to be).

This bold fellow was Boldizsar Kozma, the son of her father's former estate manager.

The elder Kozma had five sons; Dezso and Aron were the oldest, Geza and Jeno came last and the middle son, Boldizsar, was the same age as Countess Roza. When she was a little girl all five boys had been her playmates until they left Denestornya when old Kozma decided to set up on his own as a farmer, left Count Abady's service, and rented a substantial property near Teke. Since then the Kozma family had prospered and become rich. They had bought up estate after estate until today they were the owners of the entire districts of Ormenyes and Teke in the Kolozs county. These they had acquired from the former landowners who could not compete with five such hard-working, knowledgeable and unpretentious young farmers.

Countess Roza had not seen any of them since her thirteenth

birthday. She would hear, for example, that one of them had been to Denestornya to buy the yearling colts, or the lambs or fatted pigs; but though it was always one of the sons who made their purchases and never the father, not one of her former playmates ever came up to the castle but remained instead below in the farm buildings with the estate manager. Only Boldizsar used to write to her every year on her birthday from somewhere in the meadow country. Since she had celebrated her fiftieth anniversary he had sent cards never failing to mention which birthday it was.

Why he did this Countess Roza never discovered. She was sure that it was done to tease her, perhaps as a belated revenge for some forgotten offence, and it caused her great annoyance. This was now the third birthday on which the arrival of Kozma's card had put her in a bad mood.

In the morning her son Balint had arrived from Budapest and until after lunch she was happy and gay. In the afternoon, however, the fateful card arrived and for Countess Roza the brightness faded from the day. As a result she, who was usually too good-natured to permit malicious gossip in her presence, said nothing when her two housekeepers, Mrs Tothy and Mrs Baczo, who always took their lunch with her, started to spice the coffee with ill-natured tales about the Abadys' friends and neighbours.

Never stopping their knitting the two elderly women sat at each end of a long table, perched on chairs disproportionately small for their short fat bodies, and kept up an unending stream of malevolent calumny. Although they were in the countess's presence they knitted away and chatted rapidly as if they were talking only to each other. And when they related some exceptionally shocking tale they would stab their needles into their half-finished work as if despatching the culprit in self-righteous virtue. This went on for a long time. Balint listened in silence.

At last it was half-past three and the first callers arrived to offer their congratulations. The two housekeepers rose and discreetly disappeared.

As the afternoon progressed more and more visitors were announced until both the large and small drawing-rooms were filled with people. In the larger room the hostess sat in the usual place in the centre of the sofa. In front of her, grouped around the tea-table, sat the older ladies; the mothers, countesses Gyalakuthy,

Kamuthy and Laczok, and with them was the ancient Countess
Sarmasaghy, Aunt Lizinka to almost everybody in Transylvania,
tiny, shrivelled, amusing and malicious, who talked unceasingly
both of politics and of the failings of all her friends and relations,
and who was never afraid to use a coarse word, though in a most
refined way, if she felt her stories needed emphasis.

Deploring the general wickedness of the world she covered
much the same ground as had the two housekeepers an hour or
so before. The chief target that afternoon was Adrienne Miloth,
wife of Pali Uzdy, who, declared Aunt Lizinka, was an incorri-
gible flirt who had set her cap at every man in their circle ever
since she had come to town for the carnival season.

'. . . and she's not content – oh, dear me, no! – to turn the head
of my poor nephew, Pityu Kendy, as she did last year, or of that
great dumb Adam Alvinczy – and they are just two among a
whole throng of others,' croaked Aunt Lizinka in her guinea-
fowl voice, '. . . so she's now seduced my other nephew, Ambrus.
Of course I haven't seen it with my own eyes but Ambrus isn't
the sort of man to be satisfied by sweet talk alone. Oh no! I'm
sure she's put more in his mouth than honey-covered words.
No doubt of it. Maybe they're careful but it's well-known that
a stallion like Ambrus doesn't stop at neighing. And what's more
– and I know it for a fact as my cook told me – that when poor
Uzdy's away Ambrus is always hanging about the house even if
no one sees him.'

The other ladies just listened, hardly uttering a word. Even
Countess Laczok, whose sister was Adrienne's mother, did not
dare defend her niece since she too had marriageable daughters
and was afraid of what Lizinka might start saying about them if
she appeared to disagree. Eventually it was Countess Gyalakuthy
who tried to put a stop to it.

'All that's as it may be,' she said, 'but it's surely over, especially
now that Akos Miloth's wife has got so much worse in that clinic
in Vienna. I hear her daughters have all gone to be with her.'

'They left last week,' Countess Laczok hastened to reply. 'I'm
afraid it's bad news.'

Countess Abady's bulging grey eyes looked round the group
from Aunt Lizinka to her son, who was sitting silently among the
old ladies. There her glance lingered for a moment before she
turned and spoke to the kindly, plump Countess Laczok.

'I had heard that the poor thing's not been well for some time.'

'That's for sure. And this time it'll be the end!' interrupted Aunt Lizinka who was dying to get back to her favourite theme. 'And what'll become of poor little Margit Miloth without a mother one can only imagine! Then she'll only have Adrienne's example to guide her!'

A new visitor was announced. It was old Daniel Kendy who, in his old-fashioned and slightly worn morning coat, was still an impressive figure. Only his red nose showed how partial he was to the bottle.

He bowed over Countess Abady's hand.

Balint seized the opportunity to offer Daniel his chair and walked swiftly into the adjoining room, his mouth set in a bitter line from all the innuendo and gossip he had been forced to listen to since lunch.

In the smaller drawing-room were gathered all the girls and young men. The butler and a footman were serving coffee and whipped cream and handing round cakes on crystal plates. Every now and again the Countess's two housekeepers would bring in more delicacies – Viennese *Kuglhopf* cake, éclairs and almond pastries – and would put on hurt expressions if everyone did not sample each new dish at least twice. Even so an obsequious, ingratiating smile never left their fat faces.

Balint exchanged a few polite words with each of the guests in turn and was just answering someone's question when Dodo Gyalakuthy came up to him and touched his arm.

'AB!' she said, for Balint was known to everyone in Kolozsvar by his initials. 'I want to tell you something.' She spoke urgently and quite loudly for the others were making a lot of noise. 'Let's sit somewhere in a corner where we won't be disturbed.'

Balint led her to two empty armchairs that were at the far end of the room and looked enquiringly at her as they sat down. Now Dodo seemed to hesitate before starting to speak in broken, disjointed phrases.

'I know it really isn't any of my business, but still, I think I must tell you ... I think it's my duty to tell you ... he, he *is* your cousin...' She paused and then, suddenly determined, she turned to face Abady. 'It's about Laszlo Gyeroffy!' Now she spoke fluently and in a down-to-earth manner. She was quite specific and related succinctly what she had picked up from Laszlo during the last few months, and which she had cleverly reconstructed to form a true estimate of the situation. She explained how advantage had been taken of Gyeroffy's lack of interest and apathy and of his total indifference to worldly matters, and that he had been persuaded to lease his entire property for an absurdly low sum that had been paid in advance and how, as a result, he now had practically nothing to live on. Advantage had been taken of his need and it was absolutely vile, what had been done to him. It was a wretched matter which shouldn't be tolerated. No! It simply shouldn't be tolerated!

'But this is very serious,' said Balint when Dodo had told her tale. 'I suspected something of the sort but I didn't know what was going on as for some time Laszlo has taken care to avoid me. However, if it's all been done legally and Laszlo accepts it, I don't see how it can be put right.'

'But it can!' interrupted Dodo triumphantly. 'Don't you see? The one who's done all this to Laszlo is *your* agent. He's called Azbej, or some such name. That's why I've come to you. If *you* intervene, if *you* threaten him . . . why, he could go to prison for such villainy!'

'Kristof Azbej? You really mean him, my mother's lawyer? There are lots of people of that name.'

'Oh, yes, it's quite certain! They met at your place, at Denestornya.' Dodo laughed: '. . . and that stupid Laszlo has even been led to believe that Azbej has made a great sacrifice to help him. Look, I've written down all the details as Gyeroffy related them to me. I think I've got them right!'

She handed him a folded sheet of writing paper.

'Something will be done about this. You can be sure of that,' said Balint as soon as he had read Dodo's notes, all his natural instinct to help others, that instinct that had caused him so much trouble in the past, now fully awakened. 'I'll send for the fellow at once. It's unheard-of – and to one of our own relations on top of it all. I'm deeply grateful, Countess Dodo, that you've told me all this.'

'It's I who will thank you, if you do something!' replied Dodo, blushing deeply as if she had inadvertently said something indecent. Then she got up abruptly and hurried into the big drawing-room.

The young man remained for a moment standing in the centre of the room. Through the wide-open double-doors he watched the girl go up to her mother and put her hand on her shoulder.

The old lady got up at once and the two of them said their fare-
wells and left.

'That Dodo is a nice, clever girl,' thought Balint. 'How good
she would be for Laszlo! She'd keep him in order all right!' Then
he turned his thoughts to Azbej, deciding that he would send a
telegram summoning the man to come and see him. Then he
would question him and if he discovered that what he had been
told was true, then, and only then, would he tell his mother. It
was unthinkable that one of her trusted employees should do
such a monstrous thing. The man should be thrown out at once.

The same afternoon he sent a wire to Azbej at Denestornya:
'COME IMMEDIATELY'.

In the morning there was no sign of the man but after lunch
Countess Roza asked her son, 'You have sent for Azbej? May
I ask why?'

Balint was somewhat surprised by the question, wondering if
someone was spying on him by reading his telegrams. His tone
in replying was therefore rather more short than was called for.
'Yes, I have something to ask him.'

'Well, what is it? Is it about the forests or about your constituency?'

'Neither, Mama. I want to ask him about something quite
different. I'm not even sure it really concerns us at all.'

'And I would like to know why *you* have sent for one of *my*
employees. After all, I think I have a right to know,' interrupted
Countess Roza coldly, and turned on the sofa so that she was
facing her son. Clearly she was expecting a full account, and so
Balint found himself forced, contrary to his instinct and intention, to tell her what he had heard about the lease of Gyeroffy's
property.

As he was telling the story to his mother he glanced at the
two housekeepers, thinking that it was really rather a mistake to
discuss such matters in front of them. Tothy and Baczo, however,
sat tightly in their seats, stiff and upright as two large wooden
idols, knitting away furiously with downcast eyes. It looked for
all the world as if their attention was totally concentrated on their
work as they changed needles with dizzying speed.

'That would certainly be a vile thing indeed, if it's true! But
how did you come to hear about it?' asked Roza Abady when
her son had completed his story.

'I'm sorry, but that I can't tell you.'

'From that good-for-nothing Laszlo, I presume?'

'No. Not from him.'

'From whom then? Some anonymous mischief-maker?'

'You must forgive me, Mama, but I cannot betray a confidence.'

'So it's a confidence, is it? And you can't even tell me! All right, but I must tell you that your dear father taught me never to listen to informers. I never have, and I never shall!'

The old lady did not speak for some moments. Then she lifted her head with the gesture of an autocrat, and gave her orders: 'When you have finished speaking with Azbej, send him to me.'

So the matter was closed for that day.

Balint spent the rest of the afternoon visiting Staniszlo Gyeroffy, Laszlo's former guardian, to find out details of the Kozard property.

The next day towards noon the round little lawyer bowed his way into Balint's study.

'At your Lordship's most humble service, and begging your Lordship's pardon for not coming here at once, but the telegram was only put in my hands late last night on my return from the county court in Torda where I was attending a matter of great importance for the most Gracious Countess. I am indeed ashamed for the delay.'

The words poured out from his little red-lipped smiling mouth, which looked surprisingly soft and melting in the middle of his bristly hedgehog face. His large plum-shaped eyes looked balefully at Abady who was sitting behind his desk.

'Sit down!' ordered Balint curtly.

Azbej went to fetch a small chair from beside the wall, even though there was an armchair nearer at hand. Moreover he only sat on the edge of it, though it was not clear if he did this out of respect or because he was forced to by the shortness of his legs. He placed his two hairy hands on his knees like an attentive pupil summoned to his teacher.

'A year ago you took a ten-year lease of the Szamos-Kozard property from Count Laszlo Gyeroffy?'

'Indeed that is so, your Lordship. Or, to be strictly accurate, it was not I but my wife. I used her dowry to pay ten years' rent in advance. I myself, if your Lordship pleases, would not have possessed such a large sum. Where would I have found it? His Lordship Count Gyeroffy needed a substantial sum in a hurry and I could think of no other way to solve the problem and to be of service to the Noble Count's family. It was a pleasure to be in a position to do it.'

'I can readily believe that! You made a fat profit on the deal! For those 90,000 crowns you obtained not only 1,800 acres of prime farm land and 300 acres of grazing but also the entire stock and farm equipment on top of it all, did you not?'

What could be seen of Azbej's cheeks between the tufts of black beard reddened visibly. He was not prepared for Balint's being so well-informed.

'That all had to be bought in if we were to give the Noble Count what he wanted . . . and, if your Lordship pleases, as I was managing my wife's little property, you see, this . . . and in any case, the stock and farm equipment were hardly worth mention-ing, with respect to your Lordship . . .' And he started to explain that most of the bullocks were old, that there were very few cows or young calves in the herd, hardly a pig, that the flocks of sheep were all mixed breeds. He spat out figures and sale prices with ever-increasing speed and then added: '. . . and most of those were so poor they had to be sold or replaced. That too was a terrible expense!' Then he added and subtracted more figures in a confused rush, his technique being to dazzle by a display of acrobatic mathematics. And all the while he was closely watching Abady's face to see if there were any signs of his relenting.

Balint's expression remained hard. He let Azbej speak on until at last the little lawyer himself became muddled by the rush of his own eloquence and brought his monologue to an end, wiping his forehead which by now was dripping with perspiration.

A short silence followed. At last Abady spoke. 'You will please provide me with all the figures. I wish to have an exact account of the whole transaction . . . in detail. I warn you that I will check every single fact. As it is I must tell you that I have no doubt, no doubt at all, that my cousin Gyeroffy made a very poor deal and that you made a very good one. And I find it intolerable that you should speculate in this way, especially with a member of our family. However, we'll see when you produce the figures. One thing more: what you have said about the farm equipment is not true. During Count Gyeroffy's minority, which ended only a year and a half ago, Kozard was a model farm and the equipment alone was worth more than you paid for the whole deal. I have proof of that.'

The fat little lawyer jumped up, gabbling, 'I beg of his Gracious Lordship please to believe that I only wished to be of service. I really . . . and recently I haven't had a minute to look into the lease since every moment of my time is spent in his Noble Lordship's service, indeed all my life . . . But I'll look into everything at once. It was all done so hurriedly that the figures were only approximate . . . just to help out the Noble Count. I'm not sure of the exact figures, all I've said is from memory, but I'll check it all at once . . . and I'll be glad to hand it all over to who-soever your Lordship desires. Indeed I wouldn't mind giving up the lease altogether if my wife can have her money returned. Oh, I'd give it up willingly!'

It was obvious to Balint that the lawyer had had a good scare.

'Very well. In a week's time you will provide me with full details, a clear picture of the whole matter. Now go to my mother. She too wishes to see you. Good day!'

'I beg his Lordship to accept my humble farewell!' The hirsute little man made a deep bow, bending almost to the ground, and backed to the doorway. As he bowed again before going out a little hopeful glimmer might have been seen in his half-closed eyes. 'I go at once to wait upon the gracious Countess!'

And he disappeared.

'That deal with Azbej was not at all as you related it,' said Countess Roza severely to her son after lunch. 'He didn't only pay the sum you were told about, but far more and at several different times. And he only did it to help that unfortunate Laci. He even borrowed from his brother-in-law as he didn't have enough himself.'

'His brother-in-law? That's the first I've heard of it!'

'Yes, his brother-in-law provided the money. Azbej said so.'

'My dear Mama, are you going to believe what that man says? He tried to tell me lies too, but I don't believe a word of it!'

'And why not, may I ask? Why not?' said Countess Roza angrily. 'I've dealt with the man for years and I've never caught him in a lie. Though I did put him to the test once or twice!' Then she turned to the two housekeepers, who were sitting opposite her, busily knitting as usual. 'You two know all the facts. Didn't we check up on Azbej's deals, several times? Well? Speak up! Isn't it so?'

'Indeed we did, your Ladyship!' said Tothy.

'Yes, indeed!' said Baczo. And they continued their knitting in silence.

Balint shrugged his shoulders, but before he had had time to open his mouth to reply his mother turned angrily towards him. 'And I will thank you not to shrug your shoulders at me, young man. You have accused one of my employees on mere tittle-tattle; and you don't even dare to say where it came from.'

'It's not that I don't dare, it's merely that I cannot break a confidence.'

'That's quite enough reason for me not to take any of this seriously. As I told you before, I never have and I never will, as your dear father taught me! I wish only to say this: I am deeply hurt that you give more weight to the word of some secret informer than to that of your mother. I would never have expected it of you, never!'

Countess Abady fell silent. Then she stretched out to the Chinese lacquer bowl in which she kept her needlework, her white, chubby little hands scrabbling around in agitation. Balint got up.

'But, dear Mama, there's no question of that! I don't mean that I don't believe *you* . . . !'

He tried to take her hand to kiss it, but she drew it away. 'I don't want to hear any more about it! Now go away; this whole affair has upset me deeply. We will not speak of it again!'

For several days relations between Balint and his mother were icy. Several times the young man tried to broach the subject, but his mother always refused to listen. Therefore, although he continued to take his meals at home it was only out of a sense of duty, and he went out as soon as he was able to get away. He found it unbearable to look at his mother's withdrawn expression, and even more unbearable to have to suffer the continual presence of the two fat housekeepers who, even though they spoke only when spoken to, sat constantly with Countess Abady like two female prison warders. So every day, when released from the bondage of mealtimes, he would wander round to the Casino Club and play Tarok for pennies with old gentlemen out of sheer boredom. Every day the town grew emptier.

It was on one of these days that the news arrived that Countess Miloth had died in Vienna; it was the only social news that interested Balint. On the other hand the political news did arouse

his interest. Apponyi had presented his proposals for a new compulsory education law. Several minority members did all they
could to obstruct the measure and it seemed that the debates were
degenerating into mere inconclusive bickering. It was while
reading these accounts in the newspapers that Balint, on the spur
of the moment, decided to go back to Budapest. I can't stay here
any more, he said to himself. It'll be better for everyone if I go
away!

As it happened, when he announced that he would be leaving
in a couple of days, relations with his mother improved at once.
Countess Abady enquired tenderly when he would be back and
then, as though to underline that peace had been re-established
between them – though without any sign of her yielding – she
started to talk about Balint's management of the forest properties.

'I really am very pleased with all the reforms you've put in
hand in the mountains,' she said. 'You've obviously got a thorough grasp of it all now. I'd like you to start managing our low-
land forests too. You know, the oak and beech woods near
Hunyad. You can take full charge. No need to consult me except
when there's something really important to decide.'

Balint took her hand and kissed it.

Countess Abady went on, 'Old Nyiresy is really no use any
more as forest superintendent.' She paused. 'You see I do know
who is useful and worthy of our trust. I'll let the other know . . .'
thus avoiding mentioning Azbej by name, '. . . that you are the
master there. But do tell me when you'll be coming back?'

'Unfortunately I can't be sure; but I feel I should stay as long
as the education debate goes on. I might even speak. But as soon
as that's over I'll come back at once.'

'That's good. That's very good!' murmured Countess Roza,
and as a token of peace she rather distantly stroked her son's face.

Though the two housekeepers for once had not been present
when this conversation took place, they had spent so many years
by her side that from half-expressed references dropped by their
mistress they soon were aware of what had been decided. No
time was lost in passing on to their old ally, Azbej, that he should
now practise a little caution.

Consequently it was the very next day that Azbej came post-
haste to Kolozsvar. He was clever enough to realize that though
the countess had backed him up in the matter of the Kozard leases
it would be just as well, if one was wise, not to forget that he still

had to reckon with Count Balint. It was important, therefore, in some way to humour him in this latest dispute, because – who knows? – one day it might come about that the countess sided with her son. It would be prudent to make some concessions in the Gyeroffy affair, and so he begged Balint for an audience.

Azbej's manner was even more humble than it had been before. He told Balint that he had made a full check, re-thought the whole situation and made some provisional plans to so force production that the estate would yield more. Also by re-estimating the value of the equipment he found that he would be able to increase the rent by 2,400 crowns each year. He said that he had made his wife accept this extra charge . . .

Abady interrupted him, asking ironically, 'And your brother-in-law? Did he agree too?'

Azbej smiled, not in the least disconcerted. He knew well that he had never mentioned any brother-in-law to Balint, and indeed that he had merely invented a brother-in-law's participation for the benefit of the old countess because he thought it sounded better. Such inconsistencies never bothered Azbej, so he merely skated over this obvious crack in his story by blinking and saying, 'Of course! Naturally! With him too; though, as he had never paid my wife's dowry in full, all he had to do was to sign a draft.'

He went on talking volubly, bowing whenever he could and swearing that his only desire was to remain in his Lordship's good graces; and all the time he kept a fixed smile on his little red mouth to conceal from the noble Count how much it hurt that some of the fat profit he had planned for himself was now to be plucked from him.

Well, thought Balint, it's just as well that I did intervene. My mother may still be annoyed but in time she'll forget about it. When Azbej took his leave Balint sat down and wrote a few words to Dodo telling her what he had achieved, thinking that if she was so concerned for Laszlo she would be made happy by his news.

Later that afternoon he heard that the Miloth family had returned and that Countess Miloth would be buried on the following day.

He left for the capital that evening.

CHAPTER FOUR

IT WAS THE beginning of May and spring was at its most beautiful. There was not a cloud in the clear blue sky which covered the whole mountainous landscape like an azure dome.

Far away to the south, behind the bare peaks of the Korosfo mountains, there started a dark wavy line high up in the sky, which marked the highest and furthest ranges. This continued to the south-west past the triple summits of the Vlegyasa and the steep crags of the mountains closing the gorge of Sebesvar, crags that were crowned by thick forests of oak, until, in the west and north-west, it merged with the towering Meszes range which, stretching far into the distance, ridge after ridge, descended gradually into the bluish vapour above the river Almas. Then to the north, there appeared the bare clay slopes and leafy beech forests of the Gorbo country. Finally the circle was closed to the east by the strange mushroom-like cone of the Reszeg – or Drunken – mountain. All around the horizon there was a pale shimmering almost grey radiance which became more deeply blue as it rose into the clear azure of a sky so clear, so immense, so virginal that it was as if it had never known the sign of a storm cloud. In the silence and stillness the earth seemed to vibrate slightly as if the whole world were throbbing with the expectation and desire for the great re-birth of spring.

On the wide plateau at the heart of this panorama, whence rose the springs which on the one side fed the Almas river and on the other the Koros, in the centre of a gently sloping little circular meadow shaded by the low hanging branches of the surrounding trees, stood Balint Abady. With him were Geza Winckler, his newly-engaged forest manager, and, a little way off, the estate forester 'Honey' Andras Zutor and a small group of other men who carried red-and-white painted poles, compasses, measuring tapes and a set of binoculars on a tripod – all the tools of forest-planning.

Winckler, a highly qualified forester, was explaining his plans. Firstly, he said, he had made himself familiar with the Abady holdings by himself walking all over them. Now, he suggested, the plantations should be laid out on each side of a main drive which, starting from where they stood, would run from one end of the property to the other right to where, just east of Count

Uzdy's holdings, the Abady forests marched with municipal lands. On each side, north and east, smaller drives would separate each stand of timber into fifty-acre plots. All this he explained to Abady, showing him detailed maps that he had drawn up himself. One problem remained to be decided: should they now let each plot follow the contours of the valleys on the side of the plateau until they ended naturally on the crests of the surrounding hills, or should they disregard the lie of the land and plan the separate plots on a strictly geometric basis which, of course, had certain administrative advantages but which would entail reckoning with different soil conditions. The first proposition was more complicated to administer but, from the point of view of husbandry, might well prove the more profitable.

Abady was trying hard to pay attention to what the manager was saying. It was important to him, as the whole future profitability of the holding depended on what was now being decided and so he made every effort, mentally, to take in what was being suggested. His mind was with it. His eyes were not.

Abady's eyes did not see the maps. They looked elsewhere, into the distance, where, far away through a gap between the young foliage of two great oaks, just visible behind a lacy curtain of pale green leaves, could be seen two vertical lines, the colour of newly churned butter, which shone in the early morning sunlight. They were the two remaining walls of the donjon of the ruined fortress of Almasko. From where he stood these two distant lines were only tiny strips but one felt that they must in reality be very high indeed, standing like two exclamation marks reaching into the sky demanding attention. At their feet lay the forests, wave after wave, until at length they ended at the two oak trees between which the ruins could be glimpsed. It was like a window, just large enough for the two massive walls to shine through from the far horizon, from the distant past . . .

Balint moved his position: one single step and the forest closed up, the ruins disappearing. Now his whole attention was given to the forest manager.

By the late afternoon they had walked to all the more important parts of the forest, returning at last to the sloping meadow from which they had set out. Here Abady's tent had been erected as, although the meadow was by no means at the heart of the property but was close to the eastern border only a few hundred metres from the Uzdy forests, it had an excellent water supply which was always important to the people of the Kalotaszeg.

The sun had already disappeared below the Kiralyhago – the King's Pass – but, high above, the light clouds which had started to gather during the afternoon, shone brightly in the distant sunshine.

The foresters were busily occupied in bringing wood and building a fire and preparing their beds. Winckler was writing up his notes.

Balint set off to walk in the forest, following a narrow deer track.

Now that at last he was on his own Balint walked slowly, and his thoughts returned to the time he had just spent in Budapest and to the violent debates in Parliament which had arisen only a few days before.

Discussion had raged about Apponyi's proposals for a new schools law which, while bringing substantial financial help to the minority schools (and incidentally adding a heavy load to the State budget), would at the same time have exacted an even more intensive instruction in the Hungarian language and increased State control of the teaching profession. The motion represented a radical change, especially for the ecclesiastical schools, because it gave the State school inspectors the authority to suspend teachers if their teaching of Hungarian was felt to be inadequate. Previously such sanctions had been the privilege of the church authorities alone.

From the start Apponyi broke with tradition because in the past any motion that affected the powers of the clergy would have been preceded by discussions with the church authorities and would have then been presented with their tacit, if not open, consent. Apponyi ignored this procedure, relying directly upon the legal obligations concerning the ethnic minorities.

At the beginning of March the minority members declared that they would revert to that policy of obstruction which formerly had been the favourite tool of the present government when it had been in opposition. At this moment the heads of the Romanian church handed in a protest memorandum demanding that Apponyi should pass it on to the King. This last action made it clear that discussions on Apponyi's motion would lead to the reopening of the Romanian question since, of the twenty-five-strong minorities group in Parliament, only three were not Romanians.

On April 4th, Polit, the leader of the minorities group, had presented his own deposition and he was followed only by Romanian members who all made lengthy speeches. This policy had been decided upon as their numbers were insufficient to insist upon endless vote-taking, the classic method of stopping or delaying parliamentary business. Instead they embarked on a policy of talking out the debates with speeches lasting several hours, speeches which often consisted largely of reading out lengthy extracts from previous debates and pleadings, until the rest of the House, the majority, was dying of ennui.

There had been the occasional lively moment when some government member would shout out some colourful phrase or slogan – as they had in the past, when in opposition, inveighing against that 'cursed Vienna' – though now their invective was directed at the cursed minorities. Discussion raged one day when government members read in their newspapers that during the previous day's debate the Romanian Vaida had read out a poem defamatory of Hungarians which no one, not even the shorthand recorders, had even noticed, so general had been the boredom.

The debate was not really taken seriously until one day Istvan Bethlen made his first speech. Until then, though everyone knew that Bethlen was one of the leading figures in Apponyi's section of the Independence Party, he had worked almost exclusively in committees. When it was known that he was to speak the House suddenly began to fill up until not a seat was empty. They were rewarded by a most powerful intervention, hard-hitting and aggressive, which instantly transformed the farce of the previous proceedings into a serious battle on more fundamental issues than had until then been discussed.

Bethlen, ignoring the petty matters of school laws, went straight to the heart of the whole problem of the large Romanian minorities who, of course, actually formed a majority of the population in the province of Transylvania. This had the shock effect of bringing out into the open what everyone had until then refused to discuss. At once there were accusations of chauvinism, of disloyal contacts in Bucharest, and hotly contested statements about the increasing power and influence of the minorities. From that moment on the Romanian members found themselves on the defensive.

Abady had now felt that the time had come for him to speak up too. He had realized that he might not be able to say anything that was new, interesting, or previously unknown but he had felt nevertheless that he should now rise and say what he thought. Accordingly he had set to work to prepare himself and when he had gathered his material together he sent in his name as a speaker in the debate.

When Balint rose the House was half empty, probably because he was unknown and owed allegiance to no party. This last was important because each party always ensured that there was an audience for its own members, who would be encouraged with applause and loudly vocal support. But a member who belonged to no party, who had no declared policies, was heard only by those few enthusiasts who would listen to anything and everything, and, of course, by the Ministers whose motions were the subject of debate.

And so it turned out that while Abady was speaking there had only been a bare ten or fifteen of the majority party members present in the Chamber. Only the minority listened carefully to what he had to say; and sitting at the end of the minority bench was the lawyer, Aurel Timisan, who had been one of the defendants in the Memorandum Trial.

Balint spoke about the carefully planned and politically motivated policy of agricultural loans which the Romanian-owned banks, under the leadership of the Union Bank, pursued among the peasants in the central plain and mountains of Transylvania. Certain persons in the confidence of the bank would receive cheap loans and they, in turn, would lend this to the Romanian peasantry through intermediaries. With each transaction the loan would get more and more expensive until the peasant borrowers would find themselves paying staggeringly high usury rates.

'I know cases,' he said, 'where the original twenty-five or thirty per cent has risen to two or three hundred per cent. Of course no debtor can cope with such sums. When compound interest is added to the loan the debt soon exceeds the borrower's assets and he is forced to go bankrupt. The bailiffs are sent in, the lenders foreclose and the land passes into the hands of those "men of confidence". The peasant proprietor is ruined and the best he can hope for is to become a tied worker on what used to be his own land. There are thus two major effects: human rights are violated and political resentment is fostered. And who are these "men of confidence"? They are the Hungarian notary, the Hungarian bailiff, and the Hungarian judge. All the poor Romanian peasant can grasp is that the very men who should be his protectors against injustice are the same men who enforce that injustice! Can anyone wonder that he considers these men as much his enemies as their intermediaries who have furnished these monstrous loans? Can anyone wonder at the sense of injustice felt by the hard-pressed borrower and the dispossessed small farmer when at the mercy of the very men whose authority they are forced to accept? This state of things is endemic in the poorer regions. It is a carefully planned operation which is swiftly moving our under-privileged minorities into dependency while at the same time building up rich and powerful estates who owe their existence to Romania.'

The House listened in bored indifference until Balint had felt that everything he was saying was futile and devoid of interest or significance. He also had an uneasy feeling that he was not presenting his case sufficiently well, that his voice was monotonous, his manner dull. Only the Romanian members paid any attention and they, shrugging their shoulders at everything he said, showed clearly that they did not believe a word of it, that it was all untrue and the product of an overworked imagination.

Of all his hearers, only old Timisan gave the impression of really listening to what Balint said. He leant forward, one hand cupped to an ear, clearly intent on not missing a word. Under his bushy white eyebrows his watching eyes were full of suspicion as he took in every sentence. He was waiting to see if Balint would mention his name.

The reason for this was that Timisan had been the man from whom Balint had learned all about the Romanian bank's carefully laid plans, about the systematic policy they had been employing. This had been when Balint, a year and a half before, had gone to seek his advice when he had found out how some of the former Abady dependants were being ruined in this way.

Balint never referred to Timisan by name. To do so would have caused a sensation but he refrained, speaking only in general terms and not revealing his sources.

When Balint had finished explaining the situation and had begun to suggest ways of putting matters right Timisan's obvious interest vanished. Now Balint proposed co-operative societies as an antidote to the individual peasant's dependence on bank loans. He said that such co-operatives should group together people of the same region regardless of race or religion, that smaller centres should be established where the population was sparser, that teachers and trained accounting clerks should be posted to country districts and that bigger credits, at lower interest rates, should be available to the communities. He also proposed that free legal aid should be given to those who were already entangled in the money-lenders' clutches.

Carried away by his own enthusiasm Balint spoke warmly and urgently, with colourful phrases that reflected his perennial urge to help others. Even so there was very little applause when he sat down and the next speaker was called upon to rise.

Balint gathered together his notes and left the Chamber. At the end of the corridor he was met by Timisan.

'My congratulations on your Lordship's maiden speech!' he said, holding out his hand. Then, smiling slyly under his grey moustache, he said, 'Do you remember when you honoured me with your visit? Was I not right? Now you can see for yourself: the Hungarians are too busy with other things to bother with such matters!'

He turned to go. Then, looking back over his shoulder, as if it were an afterthought, he said, 'It was kind of you not to have mentioned my name! Thank you!'

Then the old man stumped heavily back into the Chamber.

The spring was so beautiful in the forest that gradually these disagreeable memories faded from Balint's mind. His footsteps made no sound as he walked slowly over the carpet of fallen leaves now softened by the melting of winter snow. Tiny bell-like flowers glistened on the red-brown loam that lay below the giant beeches whose pale grey trunks towered high above him. In the clearings between the trees cornelian-coloured cherries were in bloom and the hazel bushes were tasselled with catkins. Orange-red 'Bleeding Hearts' glowed beneath the white stars of blackthorn and here and there wild cherries were festooned with cream-coloured bouquets. Looking up through the lacy green trembling foliage of the trees one could see that the sky, though flecked with a few barely moving clouds, was still brilliantly blue; down below the shadows of dusk were just beginning to blur the outlines of the magic forest, giving it a dreamlike quality of unreality.

In the trees the evening calls of those day birds who would break into full chorus at dawn were dying away, to be interrupted by the first tentative notes of a nightingale whose broken roulades seemed to suggest that he was only waiting for darkness to fall before breaking into full song.

Balint's path took him slightly uphill to the eastern edge of the forest. Already he could glimpse the line of the ridge that marked the boundary and in a few moments, without planning or even consciously thinking where he was going, he found himself standing on the summit. It was as if his feet alone, automatically, instinctively, had carried him to just that place from which he could see, across the valley, an open clearing sloping towards him.

Here he stopped.

He looked across to the hills opposite which were covered with oak saplings, clad in pale green and standing in fields of lush grass. Above them there was a wall of tall young trees. To his left the valley twisted sharply away so that the vista was closed by a ring of small hills whose tree-covered crests concealed the world beyond. Everything was green, green of all shades, sprinkled with the cool freshness of young shoots, some so pale as to be almost yellow, nature's renewal triumphant.

Balint looked around. He was at the place where the Uzdy forest began.

It seemed to him that he had come to the very spot where he had stood a year and a half before. And yet perhaps it was not quite there but a little further up, for there near the path was the giant beech tree at whose foot he had stood, one morning last November, waiting for Adrienne. It was from there that he had seen her, crossing the ridge opposite and emerging from the trees by the bend in the valley, hurrying towards him with her long even strides.

She had worn a grey homespun dress. He remembered it well.

Even now it seemed to him that he could see her. Then everything had been golden-bronze in colour, purple and flame; now it was all emerald green. Yes, surely it was there, just a little way away where the huge tree's forking branches towered above the shrubs beneath, that he had waited so anxiously on that autumn morning when they were to say goodbye for ever. And how much had happened since!

Spontaneously he started to walk towards the tree, still without thinking, as one does when going to meet a friend at a familiar rendezvous.

To reach the great beech he had to get round the trunk of a tree felled by the wind which lay across the path, and to do so he was forced to fight his way through thick undergrowth, breaking off shoots as he went. By the time Balint emerged once more onto the path it was getting dark. He stood there, alone. Before him, barely twenty paces distant, was the old tree, its vast trunk like a tower, its spreading roots covered with velvet moss.

And between the roots, leaning against the tree, was a woman, her grey dress melting into the dove-grey of the bark. Only the pale oval of her face, framed by the dark aureole of her hair, stood out against the shadowy background. She stood quite still, her amber eyes gazing straight into his, wide open as if she were seeing a vision.

It was she, Adrienne! And she stood there, melting into the tree, just as if she knew he was coming and was waiting for him.

As a gust of wind will seize a leaf and make it fly so the young man stormed forward. In a second he stood before her and in another they were in each other's arms.

Thirsty lips searched for thirsty lips, their arms held their bodies in tight embrace while their hands grabbed and tore at each other's flesh all the more fiercely for after many months of enforced separation and suppressed longings they were both overcome by a storm of desire, an elemental force that neither could withstand. For Balint and Adrienne it was like an earthquake or typhoon, a destroying power which no words could express, sublime and irresistible, annihilating everything in the world but their need for each other. The only words they could find were each other's names, endlessly repeated and half swallowed by the eagerness and desperation of their kisses as they pulled themselves to the ground and sank tightly entwined into the deep carpet of moss and leaves, abandoning themselves to their mutual passion . . .

In the twilight sky above a few bats flew ever upwards barely visible between the forest and the deep violet of the heavens.

At length Adrienne sat up and raised her hands to tidy her tousled hair.

Balint looked up at her, hesitant and worried. After the joy and daze of their unexpected meeting had subsided he was suddenly assailed by terrible misgivings, remembering Addy's baleful words in Venice nearly a year before when they had parted at dawn and when she had said, 'I will try to go on living . . . provided we never meet again.'

That had been their agreement, and he had accepted it to save her from the despairing self-inflicted death she had determined upon if ever their love were consummated and to which he had again agreed after they had become lovers and then been forced to part. The threat of death had long been with them, not only her own freely chosen suicide but also from outside, from Adrienne's husband, Pal Uzdy, the mad son of a mad father, who, burdened by his own baleful heredity, always carried a loaded revolver and delighted in the fear he inspired. During Balint's long pursuit of Adrienne he had paid little heed to the menace of Pal Uzdy's unstable temperament, but it had haunted them both when, a year before, Adrienne had travelled to Venice with her sisters.

It was then that, at long last, Adrienne had summoned Balint to join her. It was just to be for four weeks, no more, just four weeks of joy and the fulfilment of their dreams, four weeks of paradise for which she had decreed she would pay with her life. At the time it had not seemed too high a price to pay.

On their first night together they had been on the point of drawing back but, overcome by their love, they had been carried away until no withdrawal was possible. At the end of their brief month it was only fear for what might happen to Balint that made Adrienne's determination falter.

Long before they finally had come together they had been haunted by the Angel of Death when Adrienne, at last conscious of her love for Balint, had written to him imploring him to go away rather than make her surrender to his passion, saying, '. . . *if that would happen I would kill myself . . . I am his wife, his chattel. How could I live . . . if with him and with you too? I would rather die. There is no other way!'*

What happened later, until their sad parting in Venice, was now only a memory, but the words of Adrienne's letter had remained with him as an ever-present threat. What would now happen? What *could* now happen? To part again was to him unthinkable, nothing would make him leave her again; but his heart missed a beat at the thought that this unplanned meeting might not have released Adrienne from her promise and that, as before, she would never accept a double existence with her husband and with him.

From where he lay he could not properly see her face. He sat up, his hand on Adrienne's knee. He said only one word, but in it was framed the only question to which he needed an answer. 'Addy?' he said.

She looked at him smiling faintly with her mouth and more frankly with her eyes. She gave him her hand, her long supple fingers gently caressing his own.

'I don't mind anything any more . . . not now,' she said slowly.

Adrienne had also been thinking back to their parting in Venice and to what she had then said.

When, after Balint had left her and she had stood at the window gazing sightlessly over the great lagoon, she had felt that she had already died, that her life was over, and that in promising her lover that she would not now take her own life she had merely done so to comfort him. In reality she had decided that she would do nothing for some weeks, or even months, so that no one would make any connection between her death and the man in whose arms she, for the first and only time in her life, had been made happy.

Afterwards she had not changed her intention.

When her husband arrived in Venice she had greeted him with as much interest as if she were walking in her sleep. She had been kept busy with arranging the details of their return and above all with caring for her sick younger sister, Judith.

It was concern for Judith which had kept Adrienne sane in the first days after Balint had gone away. Poor Judith! What a sad fate hers had been! The trip to Venice had been arranged by the family to give the girl a change of air and to take her far away from the place where she had been shocked into mental withdrawal when her lover was proved a villain and ran away without giving her a thought. Maybe, the family had hoped, the change would help bring her to her senses.

As it had turned out Judith had already been nearer to a complete breakdown than anyone had realized; and the final blow that thrust her over the edge had come in Venice, at the Lido, when her own love-letters were sent back to her by an unknown woman in whose house Judith's lover had left them. Until then Judith had not realized the full extent of the betrayal, thinking her lover as much sinned against as sinning, and the shock of this new knowledge had completely unhinged her. Her mind, already disturbed, had then become so totally withdrawn that she was hardly conscious of her surroundings and had to be tended, with great gentleness, as if she were a backward child.

Afterwards there had been the trip to Vienna to consult nerve specialists and also to visit the sanatorium where her mother had been for some time. And when they had returned at last to her father's home at Mezo-Varjas Adrienne had found that it was she who had to take charge of everything, for her father, though full of good will, was capable of little more than shouting at the servants and creating confusion wherever he went. The responsibilities had helped Adrienne to get through the first five weeks after Balint had had to leave her.

All this time Adrienne had lived only for other people and it had seemed to her that her own life did not exist, that she had become a mere abstraction, a will, whose only function was to keep her family from breaking up.

With these burdens upon her shoulders Adrienne had spent almost all her time at her father's house where she had found herself obliged to manage everything. It was to her that the estate manager came for all decisions, discreetly and without letting Count Miloth see that he was doing so; and it was Adrienne who had seen to it that the heavy cost of her mother's stay in the Austrian sanatorium was paid promptly and in full.

As for Judith, it had been obvious that she could no longer continue to share a room with her younger sister, Margit. Accordingly Adrienne had decided she would be better off isolated at the far end of one of the wings of the old one-storey manor house where she would not be disturbed by the noise of her father shouting at the servants.

Adrienne had chosen two unused rooms, furnished them, and installed Judith in one while in the other she placed a kindly old serving woman who had lived at Varjas all her life and who had known Judith since she had been a child.

One day Adrienne had noticed that the sight of some small domestic animals had awakened some sign of interest in Judith's muddled brain and she had, accordingly, arranged for her a little domestic poultry yard at the corner of the house with a few hens and some rabbits. This had been a great success. Judith had seemed overjoyed when she was first shown this new toy and ever since she had spent much of her time here, feeding and tending her new pets.

All this at last made Adrienne more independent of the authority of her mother-in-law and of her husband. This was a duty, and before such a duty her husband and his mother had had to yield. Furthermore it had provided a wonderful excuse to escape frequently from her husband's house, Almasko, where Adrienne had had nothing to do and where it was as if she were a guest in her own home. There it was the old countess who ran the household and supervised the upbringing of Adrienne's little daughter – and in both she brooked no interference from Adrienne. For the rest, Pal Uzdy did everything, himself attending to the smallest details of the running of the estate and the forests. Adrienne had tried to interest herself in the gardens and orchards but it had soon become obvious that the others despised her for it, tolerating such activity with condescending smiles as if it were a mere pastime, the futile and meaningless games of a child.

But now everything was different, for Adrienne's family responsibilities were real. Until now Pal Uzdy had always treated his wife as if she were some sort of bought slave who had no other function in his house but to look beautiful, act obediently, and be there whenever he desired her. Now it was as if some new recognition had dawned in Uzdy, as if, however dimly, he had become aware that she might just be human – and it even appeared, in some strange way, as if he took pride in her being of use to her family.

This, however, was only upon the surface, for their marital relations remained the same as before. Adrienne still felt only fear and disgust when Uzdy came to her bedroom, and, with the blissful memory of her nights in Venice with Balint, she felt that she had stepped back from heaven into hell, a hell to which she had sentenced herself.

As the weeks – and then months – had gone by Adrienne thought more and more of what she had denied herself when she had banished Balint from her life. As she did so it had seemed that the arguments by which she had convinced herself she was doing right had dimmed into pale insignificance.

Whatever she did she was haunted by the memories of those weeks of joy and happiness, and hardly a day passed without her mentally reliving the love they had known together.

At Mezo-Varjas she would return again and again to the garden bench where Balint had first told her of his love and where she had been angry and offended by his passionate words of love and by the kiss he had implanted on her arm. How childish all that seemed now!

In her rooms at the Uzdy villa at Kolozsvar, where Adrienne often spent the night on her way to her father's house, there were memories in every corner. There everything was the same as it had always been: the deep-piled white carpets in her sitting-room, strewn with soft cushions where, in front of the fire, Balint and she had lain so often in an embrace as chaste as if they had been brother and sister. How many times they had been there together in the first days of their love! It was there that Balint had first taught her to kiss and where he had once, on a dark evening as dusk was falling, tried to take her by force. How she had rebelled! It was in the same room, much later, when she had just started to become aware of all that true love entailed, that she had written him that terrible letter, the letter that was to have put an end to their friendship, in which she had explained that she did not want to become his mistress, that she could never ever become his mistress for 'if that were to happen' she felt she would have to kill herself...

It was there, in June the year before, that it had been decided with her father and younger sister Margit that they should go to Venice and where, when she had obtained the necessary agreement from her husband and mother-in-law, that she had first known, even though she hardly admitted it to herself, that she had taken the great decision to ask Balint to join her believing that she would never return alive.

In those days her desire had been stronger than anything she had previously known.

Even at Almasko it had been the same. Here, too, everything reminded her of her love for Balint: in her bedroom, when she had been ill and Uzdy had left the house at dawn, Balint had come to see her; in the forests where they had walked, their arms enlaced; and, above all, here under the great beech which had been the only witness of their secret meeting.

Adrienne had come here often since her return from Venice. And almost every day she had stood there, alone and forlorn.

Tormented by her memories, there arose in her one over-riding desire – to see Balint again. During the long, long months of separation she had been assailed by all sorts of conflicting emotions, emotions that seemed to have only one thing in common and that was that they all led to one conclusion: nothing that she had previously thought sacred and unchangeable was valid any more.

Adrienne had had little news of Balint. Occasionally she had heard that he had been in Budapest, or at Denestornya with his mother; but these had been mere geographical facts – of his life she had heard nothing. She longed to know what he was doing and above all what he was feeling. Did he still remember her or had he already found some other woman with whom he could console himself? When this thought came to her the pain of jealousy was so sharp that she nearly cried out in despair.

Naturally she had blamed herself for these pangs of jealousy, for was it not she who had sent him away, giving him his freedom and insisting that he resign his place in her life?

Why, she wondered, had she ever done this?

Why? Because she had had to do so. It had been impossible to divorce her husband while he, in turn, would never have let her go but would coldly and ruthlessly have killed both her and her lover. She had felt then that she had no choice, for she knew that if they were to meet again she would never have been able to resist him or deny herself to him ... and, then, when her husband came to her, it would be a defilement impossible to bear. This was the moral argument that Adrienne had then felt to be ineluctable. Slowly, however, as the months of longing and lone-liness went by, as she suffered and jealously waited she knew not for what, this argument had somehow lost its force.

Adrienne's once strong will had been eroded. Surely, she had begun to reason with herself, nothing had changed. Wasn't everything always going to be the same? Could she really go on living like this? Was it not madness to banish from her life the only man she ever had or ever would give her heart to, to throw away the only chance of bliss she had ever known, she who had even seen her own child removed from her?

It was her mother-in-law who had done that and even here her husband had not taken her side. For Uzdy, she knew, she was merely an object with whom he could satisfy his desires, no more real than a whore. Her whole relation with her husband was a disgrace to human dignity, and so what would it matter if, in her slavery and subjection, she was to take what life might offer her?

What difference would it make to her life? Why not? Why ever not? And it was now that she had come to believe that it was only pride and conceit and meaningless love of self that had led her to reject a double life, a rejection for which she was now paying with such anguish – and to what purpose? Surely this suffering was all for nothing?

These thoughts, so contrary to everything she had formerly held sacred, chased themselves in her brain and, though she tried hard to banish them, returned with ever-growing force, stronger and stronger. Having only herself to argue with she fought with her memories and her desire. And all the while her whole being cried out to be with him once again.

It was almost dark when they parted, but both of them knew that far from being a dismal farewell, it was the beginning of future happiness.

Balint stayed by the tree until Adrienne looked back from the edge of the woods across the valley and then disappeared along the forest path.

Then he too started back to his camp.

On the way he was thinking of what they had now agreed. Over and over again he went over in his mind the code by which they would arrange their meetings – any four numbers that might be found in their otherwise harmless letters would signify the hour and day they were to be together.

Balint decided that he would build a little shooting lodge in that meadow where his tent now stood, and from it a path for the forest guards would be cut to where they had just met; Adrienne would be able to use that whenever she could get away from her husband's house.

Later that evening, when he gave his orders, he told them to cut several other trails as well, all of them leading to where salt blocks would be provided for the deer. This, he felt, would serve to veil his real intentions.

That night, for the first time in many months, Balint fell asleep happy and contented.

CHAPTER FIVE

BALINT WENT BACK to Budapest at the end of May. Parliament was still in session and it was only out of a sense of duty that he attended the debates, although as an independent he was not subject to any party whip. He was still keen to do what he could to make his plans to enlarge the co-operative movement a practical reality, and in this he had the support and help of the president of the Co-operative Centre, who had recruited to their side one Daranyi, a Minister in the government. The other members of the cabinet were not so easily convinced.

At this time the government had enough troubles without risking anything new or controversial. The debate on the schools proposals and the controversy about the minorities problems had hardly died down in the capital (though echoes of protest still rippled through public meetings in the country towns) when a new and more serious storm threatened.

Everything that Zsigmond Boros had predicted the previous November now came to pass. The discussions about Apponyi's increasingly chauvinistic schools proposals had barely come to an end when Ferenc Kossuth dropped a new bombshell with a motion proposing that employees of the State Railways should henceforth be subject to specially stringent conditions of employment as theirs was a service of national importance. The object of the proposed reforms was to prevent any possible repetition of the recent rail strike which, though it had only lasted a few days, had caused general consternation. The trouble lay in the fact that the motion did not only contain disciplinary measures but also laid down new rules about the official language to be used. The State Railway company, M.A.V. – Magyar Államvasutak – was to be instructed to employ only Hungarian-speaking workers.

Since the national railway network also operated in Croatia, this new law would apply to Croatian employees and, according to them, it would be in direct contravention of the Hungarian-Croatian compact which had permitted the use of national languages. Naturally, for them, the national language was Croatian and even though the proposals specified that anyone in contact with the public on Croatian soil must have a knowledge of the Croatian language, the Serbo-Croatian Coalition which had risen to power with the help of Kossuth, immediately turned against him. Accordingly, when the debate on the motion got under way on June 5th all the Serbo-Croat members exercised their long-neglected right to make their speeches in their own language, thus producing a new method of obstructing the business of the House. As there were now more than forty Croatian Members of Parliament the situation became much more serious than in the previous debates on the national minorities. Ironically enough the Hungarians now found being used against them all the tools of obstruction whose use they themselves had formerly brought to such a fine art.

These tactics were bitterly resented, especially by the Independence Party which, two years previously, had backed the Serbo-Croatian Coalition at the time of the common law debates on the Personal Union issue and on the question of the Fiume Resolution, and who had considered the Serbo-Croats their allies. Now, they cried out angrily, what traitors these allies were proving themselves to be!

Needless to say, there was hardly anyone among the Hungarian legislators who even attempted to listen to the lengthy speeches in Croatian since only two or three of them understood the language. Instead they filed out into the corridors of the House and stood about in groups – sometimes all day long if their presence was required for a vote – grumbling and quarrelling with each other. This went on for days, and the days lengthened into weeks. Accordingly it was a great relief if some former leader took it into his head to visit Parliament and then a sort of pseudo-debate would be arranged in his honour.

The day that Samuel Barra put in an appearance he was immediately surrounded by a crowd of admirers. Without delay Bela Varju started off with a provocative remark designed to bring out Barra's talent for invective. More members joined the group knowing the spectacle would be worthwhile – or, at the very least, would serve to pass the time.

'It's my view,' said Varju, 'that we're all fools to put up with this nonsense. We've sat here for two weeks and those louts are still drivelling on in their absurd language! If I were the government of Hungary I'd soon crush that lot!'

The great Barra opened his mouth, which was so huge that it seemed to be wider even than his face as if it had been stretched by all the speeches made by its owner during his life in politics, that mouth which seemed to have a life of its own between the sweeping moustaches and the heavy chin.

'What do you mean – "crush"? If you're suggesting that the government should act against the Rules of the House, I'd fight you all the way! I've fought for the sanctity of our House Rules all down the years, even against the bum-bailiffs of the Camarilla. Oh, yes! I was the first to see what they were up to, as you must know – and the time may well come again when the freedom and independence of our country will be saved by the citadel of those very Rules. Let me tell you: the Rules of the House are sacred!'

Old Bartokfay lifted a finger in agreement and then, speaking as always in the strongly accented dialect of the Maros country in Transylvania, said, 'That we could never allow. Not to Ferenc Kossuth, nor even to Lajos Kossuth himself. Never! Never!' And he stuck his hand majestically behind the lapel of his old-fashioned Hungarian dress, just as he had done back in the sixties some forty years before, to show that even then he had been a person of importance.

'Indeed, we must never infringe the House Rules, even if they try to use them against us,' fluttered some young member eager to keep in well with Barra.

'That is not so!' interrupted the great leader, who dearly loved an argument. 'Remember that we represent the country's will, the country's good faith and liberty; that is why we use all the weapons we can lay our hands on! But think where we'd be if the whole thing goes too far! Just ask yourselves that! Parliamentarianism would be finished, our age-old constitution a dead duck! What *we* have to do, my dear Sir, is to find some way by which the only obstruction possible remains in the hands of the party, our party, which truly represents our national ideals!'

'But you've just said,' stammered the young member. 'At least, I understood . . .'

'You understood wrong; but I said it right! The Rules of the House are sacred. Nevertheless our national and moral aims and those alone – give us a moral right . . .' and he went into a flood of high-sounding phrases to expound a theory which sounded magnificent but which no one understood. More and more people clustered round, and Abady, hearing Barra's voice booming away from some distance off, joined them too.

Balint was in high good humour for his plans all seemed to be bearing fruit. While the surging tide of Croatian oratory stopped all business in Parliament and gave an opportunity for the general run of members of the three principal parties to indulge in their own disputes, the government had time for other things. Balint's appointment as chairman of the co-operative project had already been decided, and all that was now needed was for the Economics Minister to have an opportunity to announce the details in Parliament.

Abady joined the group round Barra just as one of his listeners had made some obsequious remark about Ferenc Kossuth, saying how wise he was, what a great statesman, etc. Barra did not like this, since he had been on bad terms with the Minister ever since they had been adversaries in debate.

'He a statesman? Of course! Ministers have to be statesmen, do they not? It goes without saying!' shouted Barra, his mouth wide with ironical laughter. 'But we should ask ourselves this: was it wise – statesmanlike, if you wish – to bring in this controversial language decree at this moment? Remember this, and what answer do you get? Our poor government has so few friends that it seems a pity to have offended their only allies.'

Balint intervened. 'That, surely, must depend on the value of the alliance – and of its sincerity. Personally I'm convinced that the Serb Coalition never supported the Fiume Resolution out of love for us, but only because they were ordered to do so by Belgrade. Very cleverly they'll give their support to anything that tends to the break-up of the Dual Monarchy. Perhaps Kossuth put in the language conditions expressly so as to find a way of breaking with his Serbian friends!'

For a moment the great Barra stared at Abady in silence, baffled by the intervention of a man he hardly knew and who rarely opened his mouth. He was just about to answer, to slay this troublesome stranger who had dared to interrupt, when Zsigmond Boros, who had been standing on the other side of the group for the last few minutes, got in first.

'That is a highly intelligent observation,' he said in his velvety politician's baritone, 'but I can assure you that Kossuth didn't even think of it. It just didn't occur to him that the decree would cause all this trouble, which just shows how ignorant he is!' Then, to build up his own reputation and public image, he said, 'I warned him, when I was still in office and the matter was discussed, but he would not listen to me. That's why I resigned.

I couldn't say anything about it then, of course, but now it's different. I mean, now it's a matter of my country's well-being and nothing else means anything to me or ever will!'

The great Barra now found himself in a dilemma. He hated Kossuth, but he also hated anyone who drew attention away from himself and stole his thunder. Angrily he went on, 'I'm not here to defend the Economics Minister, even if he is ignorant, uninformed and often weak too, but I must say that patriotism will always find a way, through no matter what obstacle — nay, through hellfire itself — to defend the nation's best interests. It is this flame, burning away always in our breasts, which lights the way to the future, and which has guided my way all down the years . . . and remember this — our country, our nationhood, our constitution, everything that we hold dear, draws its inspiration from that one word alone.'

At this moment an usher came up to Abady and tapped him on the shoulder. He had been sent for by the Minister. He turned and hurried away to the private office and, even as he reached the end of the corridor, he heard the meaningless phrases thundering on: '. . . because, I declare to you all, that I shall never falter nor waver in my view that what this country's welfare demands is . . .'

Half an hour later Balint left the Houses of Parliament with the Minister's appointment in his pocket. The same evening he started for home and, for the first time since he had entered politics, he was returning happy with a sense of achievement. At last he would be able to be of use; at last he would be able to put into effect some of his plans to help the people in the country districts he knew so well.

Before falling asleep he wondered in which district he should start his new organization. The choice was between the rolling prairies near Lelbanya or the mountain villages of the Kalotaszeg. He was still going over in his mind the merits of both when he dozed off. His last thoughts had rather favoured Kalotaszeg because there, at the foot of the mountains, were Hungarian communities where he would be able to recruit the necessary local leaders who could help him forge a link with the Romanian villages high in the forests. Yes, he thought, that was where he should start; and, faintly echoing in the deep recesses of his consciousness — now almost overcome by sleep — was the thought that there, between the valleys of the Koros and the Almas, was the ridge with a little log-cabin waiting in that clearing in the forest where, hidden from the rest of the world, protected and in secret, he would soon be able to relive the joys which had so stirred his blood a year before in Venice.

Roza Abady was overjoyed to welcome her son back at Denestornya. She had been prouder of him than ever before when she heard of his speech in Parliament and this she had read aloud several times to her two housekeepers, Tothy and Baczo, who nodded vehemently and marvelled over it at each reading; and once, too, to Azbej, who bowed his veneration, doing so with added fervour as each sentence came to an end. After that she locked it in her desk. Sometimes, when she was alone, she would take it out secretly and read it again to herself. Now, when Balint was himself there and explained to her in detail what his plans were and how he had been appointed by the government to carry them out, she was deeply touched. 'It's as if I can hear your dear father speaking again,' she said, laying her head against his shoulder. Then she asked where he would begin.

'I've been thinking of two places to start with. One would have Lelbanya as its centre, where the co-operative is already working and only needs to have the neighbouring villages tied in with it. The other should be one of the settlements at the foot of the Kalotaszeg, where later we could bring in some of the people in the mountains.'

'Which will you do first?'

'Kalotaszeg, I think. So I've written to the Prefect of the Hunyad asking him to call the local notaries to a meeting to discuss it.'

'So you'll be leaving me again, as soon as you've arrived?'

'I'm afraid so. The meeting is to be the day after tomorrow. At the same time I'll take a look at the forests.'

Countess Roza's face clouded over. She looked hard at her son, showing in her slightly protuberant grey eyes that there was something else she would have liked to ask him. However, all she said was, 'So you're going there again? So soon?' There was something pensive in her tone.

A month before two letters had arrived for Balint with the Nagy-Almas postmark.

Countess Roza, to whom all mail was brought at Denestornya before being distributed to the household, knew well Adrienne's slanting handwriting. Several years before, when Balint had been abroad in the diplomatic service, Countess Roza had always taken special note when envelopes addressed in a woman's handwriting arrived for her son. These caused her great pleasure as she was secretly proud that he should have his conquests. But it was different when, two years ago, letters had started coming from Adrienne. These filled Roza with anguish. The previous summer, when these letters had stopped arriving, she had been reassured. But lately two envelopes addressed by Adrienne had come within the short period of three weeks, and the anxious mother realized that the affair had started again and feared that that dangerously wicked woman had managed to re-ensnare her beloved son.

She was thinking this, and inwardly was boiling with rage while Balint, self-consciously talking rather too much, was trying to explain his plans to her. 'Winckler has made all the measurements . . . painted posts indicate the parcelling . . . the nursery for young trees . . . huts for the foresters, maps, tripods . . .' He went on until he sensed that his mother was not even listening but was thinking only of one thing, as he was himself, and that was of when he was going to see Adrienne again.

'So I'm to be left alone as much as when you were abroad *en poste*! I suppose I must accept my fate!' said Countess Abady when he was about to leave her.

Balint took the old lady in his arms and kissed her face and hands.

But his mother pushed him away coldly, saying, in a cool voice, 'Well! Go, if you feel you have to! Just go!'

The meeting seemed to go quite successfully. It was held in the office of the Prefect of Banffy-Hunyad and attended by the four notaries-public of the district where Balint intended to begin his co-operative movement. Three of them, while accepting Balint's orders, expressed the gravest doubts as to whether the plan would work, saying that they would be more than surprised if the people of any mountain village would co-operate with those from another by whom they were treated as strangers. These three thought that the idea would never work and that the people would not even understand it. But, naturally, they said, if that was what the government wanted then they would do their best.

Only Gaszton Simo from Gyurkuca took a more positive view. He was now riding even higher than he had been before.

He was on terms of intimacy with the Prefect, who was his cousin, and he never let anyone forget that his uncle was a Court Chamberlain. It had only been due to an unlucky stroke of fate that he himself had never risen above the status of a country notary – just before his final examinations there had been some little difficulty, some prank, concerning the debating society's petty cash, but it had all been hushed up and smoothed over by his family. So here he was, a gentleman, independent, doing the job of a notary in a country district where such a man, in such a post, could be a real pasha. And this year his sense of his own importance had been further swollen by his election as chairman of all the notaries in the district. Simo was no fool.

All his life he had given his allegiance to whoever had been in power. After the days of Kalman Szell it had been Istvan Tisza. Now he bowed the knee to Ferenc Kossuth, just as recently he had done to Kossuth's one-time sworn enemy, Gyula Justh.

'I'll see that this gets done all right!' he said confidently, his little button-like eyes gleaming shrewdly beneath his bushy eyebrows. 'I'll round up as many people as you want for the co-operative! How many do you think will do?' he asked Abady in a familiar tone.

Balint found Simo every bit as antipathetic as he had each time he had met him in the past.

'It's not a question of what I want. The people must come in voluntarily, because they want to. We have to explain to them that it's to their own advantage. We must start with some of the more intelligent among them. It doesn't matter if they are poor or in debt because that's why the whole movement has been started – to get them out of the money-lenders' clutches. It is this that we have to make clear to them. If one approaches them with understanding and kindness we are sure to have results. Look what happened last year. One of those money-lenders on the mountain got himself killed during the winter. What was his name? Rusz Pantyilimon, wasn't it? Such a thing would never have happened if all the villagers had joined together.'

Gaszton Simo laughed, but his expression was surly enough. 'Yes, yes. That Rusz got himself beaten to death.'

Simo's expression clouded over, not, however, because he was thinking of the Rusz's fate, but because he knew Balint had alluded to the matter only to remind him that Abady suspected he had been implicated in the money-lending traffic which had led to the hated usurer's murder. As a disciplined civil servant, however, he did not allow himself to be upset by the allusion but merely signified his agreement with everything that the government had seen fit to command. Discreetly he winked at the Prefect.

By the time the meeting ended it had been decided that the first co-operative would be started in three villages where there were Romanian as well as Hungarian farmers, and that it would also be open to those living in smaller settlements in the mountains nearby.

That afternoon Abady drove up to the forest. It would be the first time that he had come to his newly built log cabin in the meadow near to where the Abady lands marched with those of Count Uzdy.

In the evening he sent his men away and remained alone.

He dined at a little table set in front of the cabin, sitting there for a long time afterwards and watching the night fall. Hardly a sound could be heard except for a soft rustling of leaves as if, in some mysterious way, the forest itself were breathing.

Finally he dragged himself to bed, knowing that he could not expect Adrienne to come before morning. Maybe as early as dawn?

Had she received his few formal scribbled lines ... would she be able to slip away ... perhaps she had changed her mind ... would everything go as they had planned it?

As he waited every nerve in Balint's body was racked with yearning.

'I'll have to go back now,' said Adrienne. 'It'll look strange if I'm out in the forest too long.'

She walked across to the little window which opened to the east and flung back the shutters. A golden shaft of sunlight shot into the cabin and marked out a clearly defined square on the beaten clay floor until, all at once, the inside of the little cabin, previously so mysterious in the half light, lost its magic in the sober glare of morning.

It was the simplest and most ordinary of dwellings. It was exactly like any other refuge built in the mountains for the use of the hunter. The sides were made of round logs while the crevices between them were filled with a mixture of earth and moss

to keep out the wind and the light. It contained only an iron
cooking-stove in one corner, a zinc wash-stand and a simple
wide bed of planks on which had been thrown a mattress filled
with sweet-smelling hay instead of the usual coarse straw. Hooks
had been fixed into the walls so that Balint could hang up his
clothes, gun and cartridge bag. There were no luxuries, but it
was all they wanted. Careful not to do anything to draw attention
to themselves, Balint and Adrienne cared little for what their
refuge contained or looked like, provided it was somewhere they
could celebrate their re-found love. For both of them the real
world was to be found only in this humble little cabin.

For some time before Addy started for home they sat side by
side on the wooden bed holding hands.

Finally she started to say something, her golden onyx-like eyes
not looking at him but staring straight ahead. Very slowly, almost
heavily, she said, 'You will have to come over to see us at Almasko
soon. Uzdy heard that you were in the district in May – but you
didn't come then – and as soon as he returns home he'll get to
know you're here again . . . and it won't look right if you don't
come over. He'd find it strange.'

Adrienne was deep in thought, thinking what she had not told
Balint, about the way in which her husband had already mentioned the subject.

About two weeks before they had been having coffee in the
drawing-room after lunch, the Countess Clémence in her usual
place on the sofa, Adrienne sitting in an armchair nearby and
Uzdy walking up and down the room with his usual heavy
affected tread. Suddenly he had stopped.

He had been directly in front of Adrienne's chair. Looking
down at her from his great height he said sharply, 'Did you know
Abady was in the neighbourhood?'

Adrienne had not known how to answer. For a moment she
considered the alternatives: if she said 'No' and then Uzdy later
found out she had seen Balint it could lead to his death; yet if she
said 'Yes' it might lead to so many embarrassing questions about
who had told her and where and when she had seen him, that
she was sure to get entangled in a web of untruth from which she
could not escape.

Better deny it, come what may! She looked up and met his
eyes and at once said, 'No, I didn't know.'

'Just so! Just so! Of course, of course! But it seems he was here
in May and spent several days in the forests quite close to us without so much as honouring us even once with his august presence.
Honouring my mother and myself, and you, of course. Mainly
you, but the rest of us too.'

Adrienne made no reply. Then her husband walked slowly
once or twice up and down the room again before stopping once
more in front of her.

'Don't you find it strange?' he asked. 'Almost insulting,
I should say, according to the normal rules of politeness, not
that I care much for such things; but he was one of your admirers
long ago, was he not . . . oh, *en tout honneur*, of course?' And he
laughed, his long moustaches somehow seeming even longer as
the chuckle rumbled in his throat.

Soon Uzdy had returned to the subject. 'Don't you find it
odd? Yes, very odd, that's the word for it, odd! Last year he
called on us twice but since the autumn, after you had returned
from Venice, he hasn't been near us. You see why I find it odd,
don't you?'

Adrienne shuddered, her skin like goose-flesh in sudden
alarm. The reference to Venice was unexpected and menacing.
However she managed to answer with apparent calmness, 'Well,
I've hardly been here since Venice. Remember how much I've
had to be at Mezo-Varjas!'

'Of course, of course! True enough! I beg your pardon,' said
Uzdy, waving his arms about in agreement. Then once again he
walked down the length of the room several times before finally
stopping near the door. 'I still think it's very odd!' he called back
and though he laughed as he said it Adrienne seemed to detect a
menacing glint in his slanting tartar eyes. 'Yes, indeed. Odd!'
Then he opened the door and stepped out, very slowly, and
without making a sound closed the door behind him.

Adrienne glanced at her mother-in-law. Countess Clémence
was sitting bolt upright, absolutely immobile. She was looking
straight ahead of her with the intense expression on her face of
one who suddenly hears faint echoes of some ancient memory.
It was as if she had heard nothing of what had actually been said.

All this was in Adrienne's mind when she spoke to Balint, but
she had said no more than she felt to be absolutely necessary.

She told him nothing of how worried she had been when,
later, she had wondered what her husband had really meant by

those sinister words. Why, she asked herself, had he mentioned
the subject at all? Did he know anything of what there was, and
had been, between her and Balint? Why should he, who never
wanted visitors and never invited anyone to the house, suddenly
want to see AB, of all people? Why just him? And the talk about
Venice? Did he really suspect something or had it been just a
chance remark? If he did suspect then everything he said must
be part of some plan of his own, some sinister private game in
which she would be used as a mere pawn to lure her lover to
Almasko. Perhaps it would be wisest to prevent his coming, to
keep him, at all costs, away from her husband.

For a long time Adrienne had wrestled with this dilemma.
In the end she had decided that Balint should come, no matter
what the outcome might be. There was no way by which she
could keep them from ever meeting each other again and so it
seemed best to go forward and confront what Fate had in store
for them. Adrienne's nature, so frank and full of daring, could
accept no other course, no unworthy little game of marital hide-
and-seek. And, after all, she reflected, they only had one death
to fear and that they had already faced in Venice.

Even so, when she had said, 'It is necessary that you come . . .'
Adrienne had not dared to look at Balint, lest he should read in
her face something of what was in her mind.

They agreed that when Balint heard that Uzdy had returned
home he would present himself at Almasko at noon on the
same day.

A few days later, dressed in shooting clothes and with a shoulder
bag containing a change of linen and a pair of shoes, Balint
turned up at the Uzdys'.

As he arrived in the forecourt Balint again thought how
sombre and gloomy it all looked. The outbuildings that flanked
the main mansion were hidden behind carefully trimmed yew
hedges. The lawn at the centre of the carriage sweep was circular
and all the window shutters on the main façade were tightly
closed as if no one was in residence. The very neatness of everything seemed to underline a certain unfriendliness, a lack of welcome. Nothing had been left to chance, there was no disorder,
everything was carefully and meticulously under control. At the
base of the walls, for example, there was no hint of moss on the
carefully dressed stone of the great uniform blocks that made up

the foundations. And on the surrounding gravel not a single weed was to be found, any more than there was a flower to spoil the virgin symmetry of the lawn.

Everything had the perfection of ice.

Balint stopped at the huge front door. No one was to be seen.

He wondered what he should do. In any other country house he would simply have opened the door himself and gone in search of his hosts. Somehow here that was something he could not do. It would be wiser, also, he thought, not to risk meeting Adrienne before he had greeted Uzdy or his mother.

He had been waiting for a few moments when the great oak door swung silently inwards and the elderly butler, Maier, stepped out.

'The ladies are not in the house, your Lordship,' said Maier after making the appropriate greetings to a visitor. 'The Dowager Countess has gone for a drive with her grandchild and Countess Adrienne has gone for a walk to the ruins. If your Lordship would care to walk in that direction he would be sure to meet the Gracious Countess.'

'I would prefer first to pay my respects to Count Pali if he is in the house. Would you tell him that I am here?'

Old Maier shook his head.

'His Lordship is at home but I am afraid he is working and has given orders not to be disturbed.'

There was something so infinitely sad in the old serving-man's voice that Balint looked up at him sharply and asked, 'Busy with the estate accounts, I suppose?'

Maier lifted one of his powerful arms in a vague gesture which suggested the rolling of the ocean's waves. He looked at Abady as if seeking sympathy. 'Nowadays his Lordship is on to something else, some indexes, or something like that ... a lot of indexes. Your Lordship must forgive me, I really don't know. But please come in.'

Balint decided he would prefer to wait in the garden. He went round the house and down to that bench on that side of the mansion which faced the view. There, far away on the horizon, he could see the two butter-coloured walls of the ruined castle's donjon with, below them, firstly the dense oak forests and then, closer to where he sat, the grassy park on the sloping mountain-side below, that park which was dotted with dark green box and thuya but on which no flower was allowed to bloom.

The bench was placed between the pillars which supported the elaborate rococo balcony which led from the main drawing-room. Balint had only been sitting there for a few minutes when, from one of the windows of the strangely inappropriate Swiss chalet-like wing which projected at right angles from the otherwise classical building, came the voice of Pal Uzdy. A few seconds afterwards his face too appeared at the same window, pale and oriental-looking, framed in the darkness of the window's small opening.

'Well! Well! Well! So here you are. I *am* pleased to see you, very pleased indeed. You can't imagine how pleased I am!' From under his wide-spreading moustaches Uzdy's teeth gleamed as he looked down on his visitor and let out a peal of laughter. 'Wait there! I'll be down straight away.'

The wooden gallery creaked under his measured steps and so did the stairway at the corner of the projecting wing.

Uzdy emerged from the stair and walked slowly towards Balint. His manner was far more amiable than it had usually been in the past; not only did he shake hands but he also patted Balint on the shoulder.

'It was good of you to come, good of you to come!' repeated Uzdy. Balint had never known him so welcoming. As his host plied him with questions as to where he now was and what he had been doing, all sign of his habitual cold ironic manner had vanished. Only, from time to time when he turned in Balint's direction, his small slanting eyes seemed to have a peculiar glitter.

They talked for a long time just as if they had always been good friends.

At length Adrienne returned from her walk and the three of them strolled across the flowerless lawns making polite conversation. Then the butler announced that luncheon was served.

Nothing exceptional occurred during the meal nor afterwards in the big oval drawing-room, which seemed as oppressive as ever with its cold grey walls and closed shutters. Everything was as ordered, as dull and conventional as it always had been, with heavy formal furniture symmetrically arranged with no sign of anything personal left lying casually where someone had left it. Everything was in its carefully planned position as if no one had yet come to take up residence.

The conversation at table and afterwards was also stilted and formal, mere words being forced out to fill a vacuum while each person's thoughts were far away. Sometimes the hesitant flow of words faltered, but it was never allowed to stop altogether, for the old countess, who had been brought up to 'make conversation' lest a dinner table should be forced to endure the social solecism of silence, deftly introduced new subjects to keep things going in a proper manner.

This went on for some time. As always when he came to Almasko, Balint sensed a floating menace in the air; it was as if the cold petrified atmosphere concealed something unspoken, mysterious and menacing.

An hour was passed in meaningless insipid talk which was carried on principally by Abady and the old countess. After the meal Adrienne sat in silence, her amber eyes open wide as if she were expecting something. Uzdy, as so often, walked up and down the room, but did not speak. He went backwards and forwards between the fireplace and the long French windows which gave onto the balcony, and as he did so his slanting eyes turned more and more in the direction of Abady. From time to time his mouth contracted spasmodically. He seemed to be on the threshold of some important decision.

Suddenly he stopped in front of Balint and spoke: 'Come to my room!' he said in a commanding voice. 'Come! I want to talk to you!'

He turned and walked towards the door. Balint got up and they left the room together.

Adrienne thought that she could not bear to remain another moment with her mother-in-law and so after a few minutes she too left the room and hurried down the corridor to her bedroom which was at the end of the house and just above her husband's study.

Adrienne went to the open window of her room and leaned out listening. The window of the room below was also open, but she was unable to distinguish what Uzdy was saying. She could just hear his voice, but the words were unintelligible. All she could make out was that he seemed to be explaining something and that his voice rang with controlled passion.

Her heart constricted. What could he be trying to explain? Was he telling AB to his face that he knew all about them? Was he accusing him, spelling out their guilty behaviour in Venice and their illicit meetings in the forest? And would he, when he had finished, turn on Balint and shoot him as he would a dog?

Adrienne was filled with a dreadful premonition. She waited, terrified, believing that the awful workings of Fate were about to end in a death.

While all her attention was riveted on the mysterious happenings in the room below, her mind went back to a string of seemingly inexplicable events in the past weeks, the oddnesses – some ominous, some reassuring – in her husband's recent behaviour, his sudden sharp glances so full of menace, and strange disconnected utterances. She tried to recall everything that he had said and done.

Only now, as she began to put it all together, did she begin to glimpse a pattern which had eluded her at the time. For several months Uzdy had shut himself away in his study for periods far longer than he ever had before. In the past he only used to disappear into his study in the morning to bring the estate account books up to date, but recently he had taken also to vanishing for most of every afternoon, frequently not even emerging in the evenings. Sometimes he would remain there for most of the night. She had often heard him walking up and down for hours at a time. Then there would be silence, and then, after a while, she would again hear him pacing up and down, and the light from his window would stream out onto the lawn below almost until dawn. Up until now she had hardly given a thought to what he might be doing, and she certainly had not objected, but on the contrary had rejoiced in the fact that her husband had taken to shutting himself mysteriously away only allowing old Maier occasionally to come in to clear up. As long as this went on he very rarely came to her room and so she had been spared the sinister sound of his heavy tread on the creaking wooden stair, a sound that filled her with terror and loathing for what must inevitably follow.

All this had been a great relief to her, indeed it had seemed like her salvation, especially now that she had been able to give full rein to her now liberated passion in Balint's arms.

Consequently she had not looked for any explanation of the odd behaviour which had kept her husband away from her. Now she began to wonder if, during these long weeks, Uzdy might not have been planning to kill the man she loved. The more she thought about it the more she convinced herself that Uzdy had merely been waiting for the right moment to settle the account once and for all; and now, when all she could do was to wait and listen, listen and wait, wait, wait, now that moment of decision had arrived.

There was still no sign, no movement, only the sound of Uzdy's voice, talking on and on with an occasional interpolation from Balint. Uzdy showed no signs of stopping, just endless, endless sentences, half-heard and totally incomprehensible. Adrienne's nerves were so strung up that sometimes she even imagined that she heard the sound of a shot and then she could almost see the figure of her husband standing triumphant and mocking as he laughed over the dying body of her lover . . . but nothing happened. It was only her imagination working her up until she had terrified herself.

Two hours went by, two long hours of agonized waiting.

After the two men left the drawing-room Uzdy had led his guest in silence out of the house and then climbed the wooden stairway that led to his study above. There he had taken out his keys, opened the door and, when they were both inside, locked the door again behind them.

At this moment Balint also believed that a final reckoning was about to follow.

He wondered if Uzdy planned to shoot him at once or whether he would first be subjected to a litany of accusations and interrogation. He looked around him to see if he could lay his hands on some heavy object with which he could defend himself if Uzdy should suddenly attack him, but there was nothing to be seen. All around the room were hung clip-boards carrying long sheets of paper covered with columns of figures. At one side were two large architect's drawing-tables covered with more sheets of paper bearing columns of figures and complicated diagrams. Near the window was a shelf carrying some heavy agricultural books and Balint thought that perhaps he could protect himself with one of these if Uzdy reached for his gun. He quickly placed himself within reach of the shelf, his back to the wall, his body in shadow. It was a strategic position from which he could watch Uzdy's every move. Now he was ready for anything.

However, all Uzdy did was to seat himself in a chair in the centre of the room and at once start to explain something. It was a most unexpected subject.

'Do you know why we use a decimal system, basing everything on multiples of ten? Tell me! Why is it that we count up to
ten, and then ten times ten, followed by ten times a hundred and
a thousand times a thousand to a million? Do you realize that this
is just a legacy of barbaric times when man could only count on
his fingers? And mankind has gone along with this, despite the
fact that all science is based on units of twelve, and has been
forced to carry on this nonsense? The year has twelve months, a
day has twenty-four hours, the circle has three hundred and sixty
degrees . . . and yet we still go on with a decimal system, counting
everything in tens, just because the world is full of fools too
cowardly to touch what has been for so long established! They're
afraid, that's what it is, afraid! Do you grasp what I'm saying?
Well, I'm not afraid. Oh no! Not me!'

He slapped the drawing-board sharply with his long hand, his
eyes glinting. For a moment it seemed he was about to jump up
in his excitement, but then he controlled himself and went on in
a more dispassionate voice, 'The decimal system has other serious
drawbacks. Ten is divisible by only two other numbers, the two
and the five; all others produce a fraction. But twelve can be
divided by three numbers, by two, three and four. For any mathematical problem this is an incalculable advantage! Yet we've
thrown this away, ignored the possibilities until now. It's incomprehensible. You understand that, don't you? You understand
that this is of world-shaking importance?' And he leaned forward, his lips drawn back showing his teeth tightly clenched, his
normally grim tartar face alive with eager expectation.

'Everything you say is most interesting, but I don't see any
solution.'

'But I have the solution!' cried Uzdy, leaping up, his long
narrow-shouldered figure almost majestic as he flung his arms
wide apart, the very picture of one of the prophets of old. 'I've
solved it! Yes, I! And I'll tell you – but only you, mind you,
because you're the only man I know who could grasp how
universally important this discovery is!'

Suddenly he burst out laughing.

'The solution is utterly simple, as all great natural things are.
Look! Sit down here and I'll explain it to you.'

Balint came forwards and sat down at the table close to Uzdy.

'I call the twelve ten. From one to nine the numbers remain
as they are, but ten and eleven need new names and signs to fit

the new numerical order. It may be childish vanity but I've named the old ten and eleven Uz and Di, after the two syllables of my name. I had to think of something and of course these two syllables can be pronounced in any language. It follows naturally that the new numbers are written as U and D. Now the secret is this: according to my system, in the old value of one hundred there are one hundred and forty-four units, in a thousand three thousand and thirty-six units. It's so simple, ten times ten is still a hundred, and ten times a hundred still a thousand – so we keep all the advantages of the decimal system as well as the Arabic figures! On the other hand the year has ten months, the day twenty hours, and the circle three hundred degrees.'

Balint felt his head reeling. He said, 'Then according to this all historical and astronomical data will have to be altered.'

'Exactly! That's just what I'm saying!' replied Uzdy enthusiastically. 'And that's what has scared off anyone who's thought this out since men discovered how to write. Oh, I admit this is going to be the biggest hurdle when I finally reveal my system to the world. That's why I've worked it all out alone, by myself. I know I'll still have to work on it for years, but it'll be well worthwhile. Look how far I've got already!'

They went together to study all the data clipped to the boards on the walls. There were five or six long sheets, all covered with figures, attached to each board. Uzdy went on, the words pouring out of him as he set out to explain, 'Here we have the historical lists! All the most important dates of antiquity – well, not all, for the Babylonian ones haven't yet been done – here are the Greek ... and here the Egyptian ...' The paper rustled as he turned up the sheets with his thin fingers, showing Balint all he had done. 'Now, here are the mathematical tables, every number up to billions. Maybe that number of figures will satisfy those idiots ...' and words poured from him as he talked of eclipses, comets, quoting figures and numbers sometimes according to the old system sometimes to the new. He seemed to have it all by heart or be able to find what he wanted as soon as he needed it, waving his arms, pointing, stabbing at the sheets with his bony tapering fingers. He did not wait for an answer, for any questions that his hearer might want to put, but talked on and on, his sentences crowded with facts and dates and theories until his hair seemed to stand on end and the veins on his forehead bulged and his mouth widened in joyful fanatic enthusiasm.

This lasted for a long, long time. Abady listened, marvelling at all that Uzdy had learned and studied in the pursuit of his strange mania. As he did so he became deeply saddened.

Dusk had already fallen but Uzdy did not stop. Now this obsessed monologue became ever more confused and rambling as Uzdy paced the room, his long arms flailing as he hurled curses at Archimedes or Newton, abusing their memory and praising himself.

All at once he stopped and sank into a chair, silent. He wiped the sweat from his forehead and then remained there for a moment, immobile and spent. Then he turned to Abady and, with an unusually sweet smile, said, 'I hope I haven't bored you. I've talked far too much, but you see I am so full of it and it was wonderful at last to be able to tell somebody!'

And when, finally, they went back out onto the lawn Balint saw that his host's face wore an expression of calm fulfilment.

At dinner that night the conversation was as cold and meaningless as it had been at lunch, perhaps even more random and impersonal. Uzdy, worn out after the excitement of his afternoon with Balint, sat silent and withdrawn and Adrienne hardly spoke. Those two hours that she had spent at her window, suffering endless tortures of anxiety and terror, had filled her with renewed hatred for this house and its inmates. It had been, of course, a relief when she had finally seen her husband and Balint pass below her window calmly talking together, but the release had come too late to make her calm too, too late to wash away the effect of those terrible hours of waiting.

Adrienne found herself filled with a mad desire for vengeance, for the chance to pay back what she herself had been made to suffer, and this longing for retribution strengthened her will. She already knew how she would do it for after dinner she had once or twice seen on Uzdy's face the tell-tale signs, the constricted mouth, the facial spasms like an animal about to bite, the strange glittering light in his eyes that meant that that night he would come to her room.

It was quite late when everyone rose and said goodnight. For once Uzdy accompanied his wife along the corridor to her room and as he did so he put his arm round her shoulders as if he would press her to him, but Adrienne coldly shook herself free.

When they arrived at her door Adrienne would not let him in.
'No! Not today! Not today!'

'Why? What is it? Darling Addy, what silliness is this?' said
Uzdy, all honey and sweetness. Then, abruptly, he changed his
tone and with all his old menace he asked slowly, 'Any special
reason today?'

Adrienne longed to tell him how much she loathed him but
she knew from experience that any such words only excited him
the more. She knew that any opposition only whetted his appetite, provoking his desire and stirring up his conquering instincts.
Accordingly she merely said in a cold voice, 'None. I just don't
want it today, not today. That's all!'

Uzdy towered above her, his hand clenched into a fist against
the door, but Adrienne stepped quickly back, pushed him away
with a sudden thrust against his chest, closed the door and locked
it from inside.

This happened in the fraction of a second.

Inside Adrienne leaned back against the door, her heart beating wildly as she wondered whether in his rage he would hammer
on the door and try to break it down. But nothing happened.
Both remained motionless, she in the dark room and he in the
corridor divided from each other as if by a wall. For a long time
neither moved. Adrienne could just hear the sounds of old Maier
closing the main door of the house and then his footsteps on the
gravel outside as he crossed the outer court. Then once again
there was silence. Neither moved . . .

A long time later Uzdy turned and went away. Perhaps the
fulfilment he had found that afternoon had deflected his usual
determination but, whatever it was, he went and he went so
softly that the only sound Adrienne could hear was the gentle
creaking of the wooden stair that led to his rooms below.

When Adrienne heard this noise, which had always before
been the herald of such horror for her when he was coming to
her room, she was filled with a sense of triumph and her amber-
coloured eyes opened wide with joy at the knowledge that, at
last, and even if only for once, she had been able to protect herself
from his hated love-making.

She was as dazed as a slave unexpectedly set free.

For a long time Adrienne could not sleep. She lay still and
triumphant in that great wide bed where she had so often
cried herself to sleep, humiliated and defiled among the ravaged

sheets, and the sense of her victory kept her awake until, at long last, as the cocks were already crowing, she feel into a deep untroubled sleep.

Abady did not leave Almasko as early as he had planned. It was about nine o'clock when he strapped up his bag ready to return to the forest, but even then he was hanging back hoping against hope to see Addy again, even if only to exchange a word or two and to arrange when they should next meet. Still hesitating, he went out into the forecourt, moving slowly towards the circle of lawn in the centre. All at once Adrienne was beside him, cool and radiant, her eyes bright and shining.

'I'm coming with you,' she said. 'We have to talk.'

When they had gone only a few steps a window from the corridor was flung open and Uzdy appeared. Adrienne and Balint stood for a moment petrified, for both of them were surprised that Uzdy, who always slept late, should be up so early. 'I had to say goodbye,' he called. 'Out of politeness, of course! It's proper for the host. Wait for me! I'm coming down!' He disappeared and Adrienne and Balint looked wonderingly at each other, asking themselves what this could mean. Had he been spying on them? Could he have heard how familiarly they spoke to each other?

Uzdy came out towards them dressed in a long dark-grey flannel robe like some ghost advancing slowly across the lawn.

'I wanted to ask you to be so good as not to tell anyone about what we discussed yesterday. Not to anybody, anybody at all! This whole thing is so universally important – and, of course, so simple, so elementary – that somebody might well try to steal the idea. Then it would get written up and all my work would be for nothing. It's just the idea, that's it, just the basic idea that counts. That's what matters – the idea!' He barked out the words and tapped at his forehead as he almost shouted once again, 'The idea! That's what matters!'

Balint assured him he would keep it all deathly secret and they shook hands. He started to move away, and Adrienne went with him.

'Darling Addy, you are going with our distinguished friend?' asked Uzdy in an exaggerated drawl.

She turned to face him, her black hair seeming even more alive than usual in the slight breeze. Her head was held high, her aquiline nose as sharp as a knife-edge and her whole attitude one of challenge and defiance.

'Oh, yes! I'll go with him. I always walk at this time. Do you object?'

'No! No! Not at all. Go ahead . . . of course, of course. Do go . . . of course.' He spoke each word more slowly than the last, but stayed where he was, motionless on the lawn in front of the house, as Balint and Adrienne started to climb the hill.

Before they reached the trees they both turned and looked back.

Uzdy was still standing in the same place and to the young man at least it looked as if Uzdy's oriental features were distorted with rage and his mouth open as if he were about to call out after them. The tall elongated figure silhouetted against the butter-yellow building was like an exclamation mark after a cry of menace.

'You must tell me! What happened yesterday, all the time you were in his room? Why that awful time?' asked Adrienne as soon as they had reached the shade of the forest. 'I was so afraid for you. It was hours . . . I was terrified!'

Balint laughed.

'So was I, when he issued his summons. I was sure we were in for a showdown and that, as soon as we got to his room, or shortly afterwards, he'd pull his Browning on me. But it wasn't for that or anything like it. I don't think it even entered his head!'

Adrienne wanted to know what they had talked about.

'He wanted to explain some abstruse mathematical theory that he had invented and was working on. I can't really explain it – it's very peculiar, brilliant in its way but quite pointless. He wants to change our way of counting and proposes that ten should not contain ten units but twelve.'

'I don't understand.'

'No more do I, not now when I have to explain it! But when Uzdy talked about it I seemed more or less to follow him, even though it all seemed completely crazy. It was really very interesting; he's got the most extraordinary range of knowledge – but to spend so much time and energy on such a pointless idea – it's just not normal!'

'When was he ever normal?' cried Adrienne. 'Never! Never! Never!'

Now they emerged from the trees and found themselves on a bare ridge. The view from where they stood was beautiful and in the valleys the morning mist was bathed in sunshine until it looked almost liquid, vibrating and surging like a vast sea which submerged even the farthest mountains.

Back among the trees they continued along the forest path and, as they did so, the feeling of liberation in Adrienne grew stronger and stronger. When, after the traumatic afternoon of waiting on the previous day, she had finally seen Balint emerge unscathed from the lions' den and in quiet conversation with her husband, the release from those two hours of terrified waiting had come as more than mere escape from a dreaded threat. It was as if she were now released from all obligations to her husband. Now, at long last, she had found the strength to resist him and when, the previous evening, she had at last shut her door on him it had left her with a sense of triumph, of long-awaited freedom. She was still engulfed in the shade of the prison-house, but now, for the first time, Adrienne felt that the doors to freedom were opening before her.

Beneath their feet the dust of the forest floor rose as they walked, and to Adrienne it was as if they floated weightless over clouds of heavenly vapour, returning unharmed from the gates of Hell, ready now to defy the whole wide world. Balint had braved Uzdy in his lair and walked away free. She had at last denied herself to him and also walked freely away, and it was as if the fetters were melting away. Drunk with a sense of victory she walked on light and she knew where she was going. Putting aside all their previous caution Adrienne did not stop when they reached the boundary of her husband's properties but strode on confidently at Balint's side, heedless of the fact that when they reached the giant beech tree from which led the track to Balint's hut she could be seen and recognized by the peasants using the same road on their way to market.

As soon as they arrived she flung herself into his arms, hungrily accepting his love . . . and only much later did she tell him what had happened the previous night.

PART TWO

CHAPTER ONE

DODO GYALAKUTHY'S MOTHER bought her an automobile.
It was a handsome open car with a canvas hood of American
design and it was capable of cruising at the then amazing speed
of seventy kilometres an hour. At the same time she engaged a
sensible and trustworthy chauffeur, old enough not to be too
irresponsible, and gave her daughter permission to use the car as
she liked, even for going alone to visit friends in the country.
This last had not been easily granted but Dodo was a determined
girl, strong-willed and sure of herself, who would have done
whatever she wished regardless of any parental ban; and so Countess Gyalakuthy, the kind-hearted chubby Adelma, who realized
this, had yielded to her daughter's pleas all the more as she knew
her daughter to be a sensible and clever girl who could be trusted
not to do anything foolish.

Naturally this caused a great deal of talk when the older ladies
got together for a gossip. 'A young gel like that traipsing about
alone God knows where! Did you ever hear anything so dreadful!' cried the wizened old Countess Sarmasaghy, everyone's
Aunt Lizinka, when she first heard about it, and immediately
ordered up her ancient pair of big-bellied carriage horses and
drove over to Radnotfalva saying to herself that she'd put such a
scare into that foolish Adelma that that would be an end to the
matter. What she really wanted, of course, was to be the first to
know all the details which she would then circulate, adorned and
embellished, to her little clan of scandal-mongering old ladies.

Nothing she could say could remove the smile from Countess
Gyalakuthy's good-natured face.

'My daughter is no longer a child,' she said calmly. 'She is of
age and there is no need for me to watch over her all the time.
Dodo is quite capable of looking after herself.'

And so Dodo proved herself. Nothing she did provided any
food for the ladies' scandal teas. There was nothing very dreadful
to be inferred from the fact that she drove over to Var-Siklod or

Mezo-Varjas to play tennis – and as it was well-known that none
of the young men was paying court to her the harvest of sly innuendo was meagre indeed. Aunt Lizinka soon dropped the matter
when she found that there was nothing scandalous there for her
to get her teeth into.

So Dodo went where she wanted and no one thought any the
worse of her for it. Sometimes she made quite long trips simply
for her own pleasure, driving up the Maros valley or up to the
mountains of Torocko. She loved speed and when at the wheel
herself would drive as fast as she could.

One cloudy morning in late September, her cobalt-blue sports-
car could be seen rushing down the slope of the Felek. There was
hardly any sound on the mile-long stretch for Dodo had turned
off the engine. Occasionally there was a slight whine as she
braked at the corners. Then she slowed down only to speed up
again when she reached the straight road ahead. Dodo drove
calmly and with great concentration, touching the horn only if
it were necessary to warn others on the road of her approach.
She had learned well how to assess the space between the carts
she might want to pass and she drove as if she were thinking of
nothing else. In fact, the car and the road occupied only one part
of her mind, the practical, active part. The other was far away as
she went over in her mind some of the things that had recently
happened to her and what she had now decided to do.

Since they had moved back to their country place in May she
had only occasionally been able to see Laszlo Gyeroffy. With
much cunning she had lured him over to Radnotfalva, having
organized a tennis tournament with the sole purpose of having
an excuse to invite him. Then she had kept him there for several
days talking to him about music and getting him to play for her.
It filled her with joy that she could get this normally withdrawn
and shy young man to talk freely to her, his reticence melting away
as she encouraged his confidences. She knew he did not love her,
but she also knew that he found her sweet and sympathetic.

After he had gone home they had exchanged letters. Dodo
wrote asking questions about music, sending him scores and asking for his opinions. And Laszlo always answered her letters,
though not always at once, and when he did so Dodo seemed to
sense something behind his words, something deeper that suggested some emotion other than mere polite interest. A week

before he had sent her a little song, somewhat roughly put down on the page, a sad little melody that could hardly be thought a song of love. He had written that it was quite old but she wondered if he had said that only because he had not dared to admit that, maybe, it was new and that he had written it for her.

The thought of this filled her with hope and joy.

The blue car speeded across the valley, crossing the river at Apahida and turning off at Tarcsa. As Dodo got nearer to Kozard she began to feel a little scared at her own temerity, wondering how Laszlo would respond to what she was going to propose.

Very carefully Dodo had gone over in her mind everything that she knew about him and every word that he had spoken to her. She knew that he had loved Klara Kollonich, his cousin, but that she had thrown him over a year and a half before and married someone else. Now, thought Dodo, surely there had been time enough for the hurt to wear off. The last time Laszlo had been to stay there had been no sign that he still gave any thought at all to his old love. Then, for once, he had seemed light-hearted, even jovial, and had said things that could only encourage her in her hopes, phrases like, 'You're the only person I can talk to like this. Only you understand these things.' That sort of remark must mean something, even if they were only talking about music. Dodo was sure that he meant more than he said, that he was trying to hint at his feelings; and she believed this because she wanted to.

The village of Kozard consisted only of a few small peasants' houses and one larger old building in which was a grocery store. When Dodo's elegant car drew up in front of the store the owner, Mor Bischitz, looked out with joy in his heart. Anyone who owned such a wonderful vehicle must surely be great and important and noble indeed! Quickly he stepped out, respectfully doffing his wide-brimmed hat and revealing the little skullcap on the crown of his head from which no practising orthodox Jew would ever be parted.

'How can I be of service to your Ladyship?' he asked in a rich plummy voice.

'I am looking for Count Gyeroffy's house. Can you direct me?'

As Bischitz was explaining that Dodo would have to drive on past a little vacant plot, turn off by an abandoned labourer's cottage and follow the road until, on a small hill ... he was interrupted by a little Jewish girl, barefooted, who stole shyly up to the car. She was about nine or ten years old, very dirty and unkempt, but she had a most lovely face. Her uncombed hair was thick and lustrous and Titian-red in colour and her eyes were large and black.

'I'll show you! I know the way!' she said eagerly.

Her father turned on her and shouted rudely at her, 'Regina! Get away with you! You stay where you are. Back to the kitchen!' and he menaced her with his fist.

By now the car was surrounded by a group of urchins all offering their help. When Dodo put her foot on the accelerator and speeded away they all ran after the car until it was out of sight.

The little lane wound itself up the hill and finally led to a handsome building in the French style. Above substantial foundations the raised ground floor had a long row of tall French windows fitted with square window-panes, most of which were missing or broken. It was clear that no one lived in those rooms. The windows of the first floor projected from a mansard roof.

It was obvious that the house had been the whim of a most individual man. It had been built by Laszlo's father at the time of his marriage to the artistically-minded Julia Ladossa who greatly admired the French taste. It was truly beautiful, pure in style and so elegant that it would have seemed entirely at home standing somewhere on the banks of the Loire. But for this very reason it looked out of place in Transylvania. 'Long windows in this climate!' people had said mockingly. But it had been Julia's wish, and to Laszlo's father that was all that mattered.

As it turned out they had never moved into the grand rooms on the ground floor. Beautiful French marble chimneypieces had been fitted but the walls had only been whitewashed because, long before the silken wall-coverings had arrived from Lyon, the lady for whom all this was being prepared got into her carriage and drove away. She had escaped. A week later Mihaly Gyeroffy was found dead in the woods shot by his own gun.

Since then no one, except a sort of guardian, had lived in the house.

Everything had been kept locked and untouched until the day came that Laszlo returned home, ruined by his losses at cards and, as he thought, a social outcast.

* * *

'Would you take a look at the spark plugs? They don't seem to be working quite right. Oh, yes, and better check the carburettor too, please,' said Dodo to her chauffeur, who had been sitting beside her. This was her pretended reason for stopping at Kozard.

The man looked a little surprised but Dodo took no notice and went up the steps to where the front door stood open and straight on into the house.

She found herself in a large and beautiful entrance-hall, the unpainted walls stuccoed in the style of Louis XVI. In front of her was a pair of large doors which presumably led to a drawing-room. She was wondering what to do when an untidy elderly man shuffled slowly forwards coming from an unnoticed service door. It was the guardian, Laszlo's only servant.

'Where can I find Count Gyeroffy?' she asked.

'Upstairs in his room, my Lady, that's where! You go up there!' said the man roughly, pointing to a stairway at the end of the hall.

Dodo hesitated for a moment not knowing if she should go up or tell the man to ask Laszlo to come down. But the man shuffled off and disappeared and so Dodo started upstairs herself.

The stairway had no banisters or rails, for the ornate wrought-iron work still lay rusting in heaps beneath the curve of the stair. It had never been installed.

Upstairs there was a long corridor and Dodo would not have known where to go if she had not seen a pair of shabby riding boots near a doorway in front of her. Quickly making up her mind Dodo knocked and went in.

Her guess had been right. Laszlo was indeed there, sitting in an armchair near one of the windows, dressed in a soft open shirt and trousers: he was busy filing his nails. When he saw her he jumped up, saying, 'You! You here! What's happened?'

'Nothing much,' said Dodo. 'I was passing on my way to the Kamuthys near Des and there seemed to be something wrong with the car. So I thought I'd drop in on you while they fix it.'

She blushed a little at her lie but went on lightly, 'I hope I'm not disturbing you, bursting in like this?' and then laughed to cover her confusion.

'Not a bit! It was very nice of you. But this room is awful! I'm ashamed you should find me in such disorder,' said Laszlo, looking around him in distress. Then, suddenly noticing how casually he was dressed, he slipped on a jacket that had been thrown on the floor.

It was true that the room was in a mess. Laszlo's bed, which was in one corner, was unmade, the covers in a heap on the floor and the pillows none too clean. Next to it on a bedside table was a half-empty bottle of brandy and a dirty glass. Quantities of cigarette ends littered the floor and there were innumerable burn marks on the parquet. The remains of the previous day's evening meal had been left on a commode which stood between two of the windows, the dishes stacked one on the other and coated with congealed grease.

'Oh dear,' said Dodo laughing. 'I suppose this is how bachelors always live!' and she looked round the room indulgently.

It was a large room with three windows on one side. Laszlo's parents had used it as a sitting-room while they were waiting for the main rooms below to be finished and some of their best furniture had been put there. Since Laszlo had moved in the carefully contrived harmony of the room had been spoilt. His father's ormolu-mounted desk had been pushed aside to make room for the piano that Laszlo had brought from Budapest, and an Empire sofa had been shifted so that a bed could be brought in. An elegant vitrine that had held a valuable collection of porcelain now half covered one window and its place had been taken by a plain white-painted wardrobe. Only the family portraits remained in their places. Alas, not all of them, thought Dodo as she looked round because, right in the middle of the room there was a space where one was missing, a slight rectangular mark on the wall showing where it must have hung. The long shape of the frame was indicated by a cobweb or two which had presumably once attached themselves to the picture and had not been brushed off the tattered wallpaper behind. Everything looked old and dusty. Below where the missing portrait had hung Laszlo had placed the coloured photograph of his father in Hungarian court dress, which he had brought with him from Budapest and now returned to its original place.

For something to say, Dodo, somewhat rashly, asked, 'What used to hang there, in the middle?'

Laszlo frowned.

'They tell me it was the portrait of my mother, allegedly by Cabanel who was well-known in Paris in the eighties. I don't remember, of course, for I believe my father threw it out of the window when, when my mother left ... when ...' and he broke off.

'Poor Laszlo! Do forgive me for evoking such a sad memory!' and she put her hand comfortingly on the young man's arm.

'I don't mind, really I don't! When I was still a child, perhaps, but it doesn't mean anything to me now.'

'I know what you mean. You see I understand it very well. My father died when I was very young, so I'm half an orphan too. It's horrid when you're young, but when you grow up it's still sad but it doesn't hurt any more. We've got our lives before us ... and life is beautiful!'

'Not for everybody,' said Gyeroffy with a bitter smile.

'Oh, yes! For everybody! It's only a matter of will power. You have to want it,' said Dodo and sat down on the window-sill. 'Look how beautiful the view is from here! Isn't it a joy to see something so lovely?' and she pointed to the gently sloping garden down below.

Laszlo sat down next to her, and Dodo went on chattering away, asking questions, listening to the young man's answers; asking more questions, interested, charming. 'It was gardeners from Schloss Laxenburg who planned the park! How cunning they were, it seems twice as big as it really is! You'd never know we've only got twenty acres!' he said, and Dodo replied, 'I'd never have believed it! And what sort of tree is that? I've never seen one like it before. And that one over there? What is that? It's very exotic.' She went on to ask how far they were from the Szamos river and commented on the hills in front of them and the three peaks of the Cibles shining in the distance. As they talked they were sitting very close to each other and her soft arm brushed Laszlo's face each time she leaned forward to gaze from the window, and her chubby little hand grasped his shoulder for support.

When Dodo tossed off her motoring cap, her dark hair hung free giving forth a subtle sweet female scent and her neck rose smoothly from the open blouse like the throat of a dove. As they chatted easily together Laszlo felt himself gradually being overcome by some magic spell. The girl's wide-open eyes were filled with tenderness.

Outside it started to rain, a few drops spattering the window-sill.

Dodo jumped down and went over to the Bösendorfer.

'Are you still working at the piano?' and when Laszlo shook his head, she went on, 'No? What a pity!' For a while they turned over the musical scores that were lying in untidy heaps on the piano top and then Laszlo started to look for some of his own manuscript works and showed them to her and Dodo leant against him; so interested was she, it was like some comradely game of love where words and actions have no real meaning but serve only to tie the two of them together, close to each other, their shoulders and hips touching, and their young blood racing beneath the skin.

Outside the rain was now falling hard, drumming on the window-sill like a prelude of Chopin and forming a curtain of close-knit threads separating them from the world outside. Once again it was Dodo who broke away. Still not quite sure of herself she went first towards the sofa, but it was covered with books and clothes carelessly thrown down and that, perhaps, was why she moved over to the bed, pulled straight the eiderdown and sat down on the edge. Laszlo followed her almost unconscious of his movements and sat beside her.

Dodo leaned towards him, slipped her arms round his shoulders and without a word offered him her mouth. At once they were welded together in a long kiss until the sound of the rain-drops seemed to echo the throbbing of their desire for each other.

After a while Laszlo pushed her gently away, shook himself, got up and went to sit down on a chair a little way away. It was as if he were fleeing from the passion within him. Then, very softly, he said, 'We shouldn't . . . we shouldn't!'

Dodo looked at him, smiling. 'Why not? You know I love you. I've loved you for ages, for ever. I've always loved you. I'm yours if you'll have me. Why don't you marry me? I'd be happy to be your wife! You'll see how happy we'd both be!'

'But that's impossible!' said Gyeroffy, though there was no con-viction in his voice, only slight protest against the unexpected.

'Why impossible? There's nothing to stop us. We're both free. We can do as we please. Isn't it enough that I ask you?' and she repeated softly, sweetly, 'Well, isn't it?'

As Dodo said this she presented a charming picture sitting on the edge of the bed leaning forwards towards him, her light raw-silk dress emphasizing the contours of her body, her round breasts, her smooth round neck. Her lips were reddened from their kiss and her eyes were beseeching. Laszlo's first impulse was to jump up and take her in his arms; but the impulse lasted only a fraction of a second before something stopped him, though not before he had started to move towards her.

In the last few weeks more and more writs had been served on him, writs for the payment of long-standing debts. The bailiffs had been twice to the house and maybe they had even now fixed a date for selling all his belongings. Laszlo never understood these things. Azbej arranged everything for him, postponements, arrangements for amortizations – how and with what Laszlo had no idea. All he knew was that he was submerged in debt and that any day might find him thrown out onto the street.

It was the sudden memory of this, the consciousness of his bankruptcy, which had stopped him. He looked at Dodo from where he sat and in his distress answered her, 'I, I have nothing, only debts. Even now this place may not be mine. I'm a beggar.'

If at this moment Dodo had taken him in her arms, pressed her young body to his and had said she didn't care, or that it didn't matter, or even if she had said nothing but just pressed her mouth to his without another word, then perhaps all would have been well and their fate would have taken a different turn. It was one of those moments in life when destiny is determined by a single word and what happens thereafter can never be reversed. But Dodo, alas, did not choose either of the ways that would have ensured her happiness. Quite unconsciously it was she herself who undid everything that up until now she had planned with such care and success. She said, 'What does that matter? I know all that already. Everything can be arranged. I'm quite rich enough to take care of all that!'

From where she sat, facing the window, Dodo could not see how Laszlo's face crumbled as she spoke.

At those few short words all Laszlo's recent past surged back into his mind. At that moment he was faced with everything that had happened to him. It was all there in front of him. There stood his former mistress, the lovely Fanny Beredy, who had loved him and without his knowledge pawned her famous rope of pearls to settle his gambling debts. He could think of nothing but his shame when he had found this out, a shame that had been with him for months until he had freed himself by redeeming the pearls, leaving his new debts unpaid, an action which he had known would lead to his being thrown out of the Casino Club. There too stood the phantom of Lieutenant Wickwitz, his handsome face contorted with mocking laughter, whom Laszlo when drunk had insulted by accusing him of living off rich women, when all the time he had known that he himself was guilty of the same sin. The Austrian officer had been disgraced and had fled abroad but he, Laszlo, he had sat in judgement over this scoundrel and over himself, over all men who lived off women. Never! Never! Never again would anyone be able to accuse him of that! Never! Never! Never!

Laszlo jumped up and backed behind his chair, using it as a barricade between them. He flung out an arm, pointing to the door. 'Go away! Never! Never that!' and his voice was filled with menace as he shouted; 'Go! Go! Go!'

Pale as death Dodo got up. Then the blood rushed to her face. Picking up the motoring cap that had fallen to the floor, she ran out of the room.

Once outside she flung herself into her car. 'Drive!' she muttered to her driver. 'Drive!' and when they reached the main road and he asked where she could only just whisper, 'Home . . . home . . . home . . .'

Dodo pulled the thick motoring cap tightly down over her hair and put on the heavy thick driving goggles. The rain ran down her face and clouded the lenses – but it was not only this that misted her vision. Inside the goggles tears poured from her eyes until they too seeped down onto her cheeks.

It was as if her eyes and nature both competed to weep over her sorrow.

CHAPTER TWO

AT THE BEGINNING of October there was a large family gathering at the manor house of Mezo-Varjas. Since Countess Miloth had only died six months before, in February, this was somewhat unconventional; but it was what Count Akos (known to all as 'Rattle') wanted. He had told his youngest daughter, Margit, to summon Adrienne and their cousins, the Laczok girls; and his son Zoltan, who was now at college, to round up some young men because his god-daughter, the child of the Miloth estate overseer, was getting married and it was only right, however he might mourn his wife, that Count Miloth should see that the marriage was properly celebrated by the family.

'I know the man's a fool,' shouted old Rattle to his children, 'and probably a thief as well, but since he's served us for so long, and the girl is goose enough to take that good-for-nothing son of the Lelbanya chemist, I don't see what else we can do!'

Margit said nothing. Her brother was not so sensible.

'Who do you want me to write to, Papa? Who do you want?' he said.

'How do I know, you dolt?' shouted Count Akos. 'It's all the same to me. Do you think I care, after losing your mother? Anyone you like! Now get out of here or I'll hand you one you won't forget!' and he aimed a kick at the boy, who jumped nimbly out of the way, quite unperturbed by his father's apparent anger. At the door he turned, smiling, and said, 'I'll talk it over with Margit!'

'Do that, you dimwit!' growled his father and then stumped off to the stables whistling quietly through his teeth. In a few moments he could be heard shouting again, this time abusing the stable lads. It was what he called 'keeping order'.

Margit arranged everything just as it should be. Forty-eight hours before the marriage Adrienne arrived with one of the Laczok cousins and the next day they were joined by two of the Alvinczy boys – Adam and Akos, the second son and the youngest – together with Abady and Gazsi Kadacsay.

Abady arrived in his own carriage, as did the Alvinczys who came over from their nearby estate at Magyar-Tohat. Gazsi, as might have been expected, rode over from Kolozsvar. Slung across the pommel of his saddle was a large dead fox, because Gazsi's latest pastime was to chase after any wild animal he saw on the road, and try to shoot it with a huge double-barrelled shotgun he had had made just for that purpose. Usually he was unsuccessful but, occasionally, as today, he would make a kill.

'It's a great sport, my fr-r-riends!' he cried out on arrival, 'because you can't look where the horse is taking you. You've got to keep your eyes on the hare or the fox, and follow wherever he goes, no matter where! I've had some staggering falls, I can tell you. Once I nearly br-r-roke my neck!'

As he was explaining this to the girls who were standing on the veranda that ran the length of the house, Gazsi held his head sideways tilting his raven's beak of a nose in a most comical fashion. The girls' admiration only lasted the fraction of a minute. As Gazsi held up the fox they all let out a scream for a myriad swarm of red fleas were seen jumping about in the fur and falling in a rust-covered heap on the ground below.

Kadacsay was chased away from the house and Count Akos

shouted for the servants to bring a broom and sweep away the nuisance. The girls fled indoors.

Away from the house, and holding his unwelcome booty in his hand, Gazsi stood forlorn not knowing what to do. From the windows the girls scolded him for being so thoughtless, but they hardly knew how to do so they were laughing so much and, after all, it was not very serious.

Only one of the Laczok girls had come with Adrienne. This was Ida. If anyone had asked Margit why she had arranged it that way, she would have given no reason. Perhaps she could have, but that was not her way. Why give reasons? Why explain? Margit always knew exactly what she was doing, but telling was another matter.

There was a reason, all the same. One Laczok girl would be quite enough, for it never did to have too many girls. Ida had been chosen because, when Gazsi had had enough to drink, he was always convinced he was in love with her. There was nothing wrong with that and, given the opportunity, he might propose to her. Margit would make sure that there was plenty to drink. Then, of course, this meant that Kadacsay had to be invited too. Of the four Alvinczys two would be enough. Farkas, the eldest, had been ruled out as, since he had been elected to Parliament, he had become far too serious; and the third son would only be an embarrassment because, copying Uncle Ambrus, he always got drunk very quickly and then used the most obscene language – and it only needed a glass or two to set him off. The youngest boy, Akos, was necessary as someone was needed who would listen to old Rattle's oft repeated reminiscences of the past; but Adam's presence was absolutely vital. Adam had to be there because, as he had for a long time fancied himself in love with Adrienne, who would have nothing to do with him, he used to confide his sorrows to Margit and that, Margit thought, was a step in the right direction. Of course AB would have to be there too. And if one asked why she chose Balint Abady she might have explained it was only correct, as he was the member for Lelbanya, that he should attend the wedding of the Lelbanya chemist's son. When Margit thought about Balint a tiny secret smile might have been detected on her face; but if anyone had looked at her at such a moment that smile would have vanished, for Margit was nothing if not discreet.

The day of the marriage came and all the guests gathered in

the afternoon in the estate overseer's office where the ceremony was going to be conducted. It had to be there because the little Protestant church in the village had disappeared many years before. The pastor from Lelbanya came over to bless the young couple.

Also from Lelbanya, to act as best man, came the squire himself, the ruined old knight Balazs Borcsey of Lesser- and Greater-Borcse.

This had been brought about after much diplomatic manoeuvring. The original suggestion had been made by the village doctor, the innkeeper had been in favour and the mayor had managed to organize it. The gift of a cow in calf had clinched the matter and the animal's upkeep had also been provided for since Borcsey was so poor that otherwise the cow would have died of hunger. Even this would not have sufficed to conquer the pride of the old squire who was puffed up with a sense of his own importance. The decisive point had been the fact that Count Akos Miloth had consented to give the bride away. Though old Borcsey considered that the Miloths were greatly inferior in birth and breeding to the Borcseys of Lesser- and Greater-Borcse, the old man, himself a hero of the 1848 uprising, was told that Rattle had fought by the side of Garibaldi and so could almost be thought of as a comrade-in-arms.

The overseer's office was small. At one side was a sofa covered with oil-cloth and, between that and the simple painted pine-wood table, the space was entirely taken up by the priest, the young couple, the parents and the two important witnesses, old Borcsey and Count Akos. The other guests remained outside beneath the tile-roofed portico whence, through the open door, the ladies could admire the bride's white gauze dress, the groom's new if somewhat oddly cut black coat, and the imposing presence of two such grand witnesses as the local landowner and the old knight. Of the two it was perhaps the latter who made the greatest impression, despite the fact that not one of the chemical formulae invented by the chemist could remove the ancient stains from his coat. Nevertheless he cut an elegant figure in his tight-fitting breeches; and with his long grey hair and waxed moustaches he looked like an engraving of the sixties.

By the time the pastor had finished his address, which was extremely long, it was almost dark. Although it was late in the year the weather was still so mild that all the guests were quite happy to stay out of doors in the grassy courtyard where some light wine was served and the gypsy band from Ludas was playing. Stable lamps were brought out, and a supper was to be served later in the evening.

Sitting round a long table were Borcsey, Count Akos, Abady, the chemist and his bridegroom son, and the father of the bride, the Miloths' overseer, who sat a little back from the others as a mark of respect in the presence of his employer.

Borcsey had seated himself in the place of honour at the head of the table, and so forceful was the old man's sense of his own importance that no one thought to dispute his right to do so. Wine was brought to them as soon as they sat down and, as the wine flowed so did the talk. Their subject, naturally, was politics.

Just as if he were chairing a meeting the old revolutionary lost no time in asking Abady to take the floor, questioning him about the latest problem facing the government.

'Tell us, honourable member for Lelbanya, what is the news about the Quota?' This was the annual contribution made by Hungary to the Austro-Hungarian army budget. 'Is it true that our government has come to an agreement with Vienna?' And he pointed a long finger at Abady and then, folding his hands over the knob of the long stick he always carried, he leant back in his chair as if waiting for a young subordinate's report.

Balint at once felt that he was being called upon to account for himself and the actions of the government. He explained that there had been lengthy discussions in Vienna and that, as Budapest had thrown over the existing agreement, all the negotiations about the Quota and the formation of a national bank had to start again from scratch. It was rumoured, however, that agreement had been reached though, as far as the bank question was concerned, there was only, for the present, to be some form of 'declaration of intent' which would leave the details to be settled later. As to the Quota, the government had agreed to increase Hungary's contribution by two per cent over the next ten years. This was the price they had had to pay to obtain recognition for their independent customs proposals and for the future acceptance of the bank reforms.

'Do you mean to say that the Independence Party will accept this?' asked Borcsey in surprise.

'In all probability, yes. Though it is possible that we shall see a few resignations – Barra, perhaps, and Apponyi. But the majority will certainly vote with Ferenc Kossuth who has already given his ministerial approval.'

'To think that Lajos Kossuth's son should sink so low! So this is all we've got after two years of nothing but talk, talk!' cried the old firebrand and he turned to Rattle and said, 'It's just as I've always said: cut the cackle and march on Vienna. That's what we did in my day!'

Count Akos, himself the most peaceable of men, made suitably belligerent noises and, out of sheer politeness, the others murmured their agreement.

Abady went on to tell how Andrassy had presented new proposals to strengthen the independence of county districts, and this at once led to a discussion of what they were pleased to call 'cleaning up the civil service' – by which was meant getting rid of anyone who had too faithfully served under Tisza or, more recently, given their allegiance to the government of General Fejervary. Already there had been witch-hunts in the counties of Fejer and Maros-Torda – as a result of which many former government officials had been dismissed – and everywhere people were dividing into opposing party groups. The tranquillity of country life had been shattered, duels were being fought, women joined in the fight with their own weapons of evil gossip and slander, and in some country towns things had gone so far that members of one party would use one side of the street so as not to encounter their political opponents who used the other.

Then they began to discuss what would happen to Peter Beno Balogh, the official notary of Maros-Torda, whose behaviour at the inauguration of the Prefect appointed by the Bodyguard government had been, to say the least, equivocal.

'Oh, they'll kick him out, for sure. At least that's what I've heard,' said the chemist. No more could be said for at this point the overseer's wife called from the house that supper was on the table.

So the stormy waves of politics were stilled and forgotten as everyone went indoors for the feast.

No one was disappointed. The meal was sumptuous. The table was laden with a multitude of dishes, fattened geese and capons, enormous ducks and, what was exceptional at that time of year, sucking pigs roasted crisp and golden. Then there were French breads, stuffed cabbage, brioches, coffee with whipped cream, sugared doughnuts and *strudl*. With all this were served several different kinds of heady local wines and, of course, toast followed toast. As the heavy food and copious draughts of wine began to take effect, there followed ever coarser allusions to the wedding night and heavy jokes floated in the air, itself now thick with the aroma of food and wine and cigars and the presence of so many people in a none-too-large room.

Finally everyone got up and went into other rooms or out under the portico while the table was removed to make space for dancing.

Old Rattle had not eaten so much rich food for years. During her lifetime his ever-ailing wife had allowed no fat at the Miloth family meals and their cook had become so accustomed to this that even though the countess was no longer there the meagre food remained unchanged. Nor, for some time, had he had so much excellent wine, which, as he roundly declared in ringing tones, he fancied was the fruit of his own vineyards picked up 'by that rascally overseer' from the manor house cellars. He said this to the chemist's wife in what he firmly believed to have been a whisper, but it was overheard by everyone, including his other neighbour at the table who was the overseer's wife. No one minded because he said it with such a good-humoured chuckle. After dinner Rattle remained in a good humour because old Borcsey showed much interest in his tales of Garibaldi, tales for which Count Akos could now find few listeners.

He had just got to the battle of Palermo, which he was describing with outflung arms, when Adrienne came up to him and reminded him that the dancing would soon start and that as they were still in deep mourning it was now time to leave. At once old Rattle assumed an expression of the profoundest grief, his white bushy eyebrows and giant moustaches drooping with sadness.

'Ah, my dearest daughter, of course you are right!' he said mournfully. 'This is not the place for a broken-hearted widower. My days of merry-making are over.' And he started at once for the door, followed by his son and daughters and by the other guests who had come down from the manor house.

They were all outside when Rattle stopped in his tracks.

'Go on ahead, all of you! Old fool that I am, alas, I have to stay on just a little while. I've just remembered I promised the first dance to the bride. It would be too churlish to break my word. Painful though it'll be I'll just tread a few steps and come on after you ... after all I'm almost a sort of best man, aren't I? Go on, you lot! Go on!' and he turned and vanished into the bustling crowd indoors.

It was a long time before Count Akos came home. After he had danced a slow csardas with the bride he whirled her mother round the floor in a swift one. Then he danced a polka with the agility of a billy-goat and, in between dances, he would lean against the door-post mopping the sweat from his face, his eyes brimming with tears, and murmur, 'My poor Judith, my poor dear wife!' to whoever happened to be near him at the time. Then he would leap up again and bound away with some girl, hopping about and leaping in the air with all the energy of a twenty-year-old, before once again stopping for breath and his little moment of misery.

The light of the full moon shed such a milky radiance over the mountainside and farm buildings below it that the shadows cast by the barns and stables seemed as dark as soot. The night air was cool and invigorating, and it was either that, or the fact that all the young people had had more than enough wine at dinner, that led to the mischief.

'Let's all do something crazy!' suggested Adrienne, who, back home here at Varjas, felt just as she had years before when it was she who led all their childhood pranks. Here she became a girl again, forgetting her deranged sister, her own unhappy marriage, Uzdy and Almasko; here she was carefree and filled with the joy of being alive and young.

'Come on!' she cried. 'Back to the village. If we look around perhaps we'll think of something.'

Young Zoltan, who spent most of his time with the estate workers during his holidays at harvest-time, at once had an idea. 'Everyone says that the night-watchman doesn't make his rounds any more but sits up at the shop because the Jew pays him more. Let's go and see if it's true!'

This would do to go on with, so they all trooped off down the deserted village street where the high pointed roofs of the houses cast cone-shaped shadows on the unmade road.

It was not long before they arrived at the shop, which was dark and silent and firmly closed by iron-bound shutters. They looked around but there was no one to be seen, neither on the steps, nor in the ditch which surrounded the building. So what they had said about him was not true. Then someone suggested that maybe the man went home to sleep and cheated both the village and the shopkeeper.

'If only we knew where he lived!' said one of the others. Zoltan knew that too. The night-watchman's house was at the far end of the village close to the gypsies.

The little band turned and went in search. At the foot of the hill, where a rough track led up to behind the manor house, they found a little house just across the road from the first of the gypsies' huts. This too was in darkness but the watchman's house was brilliantly lit by the moonlight. Under a towering thatched roof there was a veranda with wooden pillars, in the middle of which was the door. Against the door-post was leaning a giant stick as thick as a man's arm with one end thickened into a club. There it was, sure sign that the village watchman watched no more but had simply gone home to sleep.

Everyone was delighted by this bizarre discovery; it was more than they had hoped for. Someone said, 'Let's teach him a lesson!'

'What shall we do? Steal his stick?'

'That'd give him a surprise in the morning!'

'It's not good enough. We must think of something else.'

The little band stood in the road huddled together, talking in whispers and giggling, all of them trying to think up some prank that was worth playing.

'If he's got a cow we could steal it. That would be a lark!' This bright idea came, most unexpectedly, from Balint, the serious legislator, Member of Parliament for Lelbanya and hard-working apostle of the co-operative movement, who was as much carried away by the infectious merriment of the others as any of them.

The cowshed was close to the house. There appeared to be no one keeping watch; and if there was a dark shadow in front of the gypsy hut on the other side of the road, it did not move and so no one noticed it.

The two Alvinczys opened the door as quietly as possible and Balint and Gazsi tiptoed inside. It was very dark and they could see nothing but, groping their way, they found the cow. Kadacsay quickly untied the halter while Abady grabbed the horns and pulled the animal out of the shed. On the road they were greeted by the others with half-stifled laughter and then they all joined in to drive the beast up the road and away from the watchman's house.

It was a bizarre procession, the women in silk dresses and high-heeled shoes and the men in thin patent-leather evening pumps and evening clothes and, in their midst, the skinny little cow, sickly and dirty and with her backside crusty with dried dung, being urged on as quickly as possible so that she would not start to make a noise too close to home and thus wake her rightful owner. All went well and the little band was already halfway up the hill and well out of earshot when the cow recovered from her surprise and started mooing pathetically.

Everyone broke out laughing, pleased with their adventure. They were wondering what to do next, discussing where they should hide their prize and what they should agree to say in the morning, when the little cow started to run away, not, as might have been expected, in the direction of home but off the road and straight towards a field of clover that she must have smelt was nearby. Still laughing they all watched her as she fled, lurching awkwardly with tail twisted up and udders swinging right and left and flapping against her hind legs.

The laughter quickly died on their lips as they realized what a catastrophe could follow if the cow was allowed to remain free and started to eat her fill of the dew-soaked clover. If that happened then, like as not, she'd overeat and get all bloated and die of a colic; and that would be a sorry end to the prank! At once they realized she had better be caught again before she did herself any damage.

At first it was just the men and young Zoltan who set off. The first to reach her was the long-legged Adam Alvinczy and his brother Akos, but no sooner had they caught her up than she was off again changing direction and running downhill. After some twenty metres she found herself face to face with Zoltan, Gazsi and Abady but before any of them could catch the rope which trailed from her halter she was off again, racing down towards the reed-covered lake only stopping every now and then to gulp down a mouthful of rich grass.

The race was now on in earnest for the pursuers quickly realized that once she reached the reeds in the lake they would never be able to get near her and prevent her eating her fill of such dangerous food. This had to be prevented at all costs and so the men, running hard, formed a half circle to drive the now terrified animal back up the hill. Lowing dreadfully, she seemed quite wild as she searched for a means of escape.

Now it was the turn of the women to join in the chase for if they did not close the circle at the top of the field the animal would certainly get away again.

Adrienne, Margit and Ida Laczok quickly formed a battle-line at the top edge of the clover field and as soon as the little cow came towards them they danced about, jumping up and down and waving their evening wraps like great furry bat's wings so as to scare her back. The animal stopped and stared at them. Quickly Gazsi saw his advantage and, creeping up silently behind her, seized the trailing cord. Taken by surprise the little cow, finding herself caught, jumped crazily sideways and rushed down the hillside dragging Gazsi, who had fallen on his stomach, across the wet clover. Gazsi, who had the presence of mind not to let go, soon slowed down the animal until she ran out of breath and stopped. It was this heroic deed which ended the battle. Everyone now crowded round, petting the little cow and letting her have a few munches of clover as a reward, for a little could do no harm.

Then they stopped and looked at each other, laughing because of the state they were all in, muddy to the knees, great smears of earth on the women's silk dresses, silk stockings soaked and torn and fine leather shoes unrecognizable under the dirt. The men stood there sweating, hair on end and collars awry. The oddest-looking, and the funniest, was Gazsi, whose stiff white shirt and waistcoat were so smeared with green from the clover that even the patches that were still white also seemed to glow green in the moonlight.

'Just my luck!' he said ruefully, in his old mock plaintive manner. 'First the fox and now the cow! Why, I might be a fr-r-rog,' and he started to croak away sadly. Everyone laughed because the contrast between Gazsi's great beak-like nose and the frog-like croaking was so absurd.

Still laughing, and with the little cow in their midst, they moved on uphill until they reached the garden door of the manor. Then they led their prize up the shadowy paths to the coach house and put her in one of the empty horse boxes. Zoltan, who knew where everything was kept, threw in a bushel of fodder and they all stole out taking care not to wake the coachman who was asleep on his own bed of straw. They went so silently that not for a moment were the man's healthy snores interrupted.

*　*　*

'What on earth can the time be?' asked Adrienne, as they all stood together in the moonlight in front of the house. And when Akos Alvinczy replied that it was half-past eleven, she glanced at Abady and said, 'Time for a good sleep! Goodness, I'm tired after all that running about!'

They said goodnight on the veranda that ran the whole length of the house and, still laughing at their adventure, started to go to their rooms. Under the vine-covered trellis it was so dark that only Margit noticed that when Addy arrived at the door of her room she stopped for a moment and looked back briefly before disappearing inside. By this time the only ones left were Adam, whose back was turned, and Abady. Then they too turned as if to go to their own rooms.

In a few moments all was silence, mysterious and profound. All that could be heard, from far, far away, was an occasional note from the gypsy band's bass viol whose distant rhythm sounded like a man's heart beating in joyous expectation.

It was ten o'clock before everyone started to gather at the break-fast table and the news from the village of the bizarre consequences of the night's adventure had already reached the house.

The dining-room was between the main living-rooms and the kitchen quarters. There were doors at each end of the room and as a succession of servants – the footmen, the butler and maids – passed through, so each of them brought more news until by midday the full story was known.

At dawn the watchman's wife had risen to milk the cow and, finding that it was nowhere to be seen, had rushed back into the house to wake her husband and give him the dreadful news. Dumbfounded, they had together stared into the empty shed and then the curses began. 'Stolen, God damn it! Stolen! But who did it, in God's name?'

Chacha, the gypsy potter whose hut was just across the road, was the first to hear the news and the first to bear the brunt of the watchman's wrath, who at once accused the poor man, with horrible curses, of being responsible for the theft. Chacha just shrugged his shoulders and laughed. Then the watchman's wife remembered that it was market day in Sarmas and that there would be another market, in two days' time, at Regen. Perhaps itinerant salesmen, who often drove their cattle that way as it was a short-cut across the mountains, had passed in the night?

They could have stolen the cow! Surely it must be them! So she urged her husband to hurry after them so as to catch them before they arrived. The man grabbed his stick and rushed off to Sarmas which was ten kilometres away; the woman, sobbing and whimpering, limped up the crest of the Ormenyes in case she could see something, but she came back crestfallen and it was noon before they had both returned empty-handed.

By then the news of the theft had spread throughout the village and, as it was Sunday and there was no work to do, a group of villagers had collected in front of the watchman's house, bewailing the loss and eager to be the first to hear what had happened.

Why, they lamented, their cattle were not even safe in their own houses! This was a dreadful thing, unheard-of, appalling! Everyone at once thought of their own possessions and this made them ever more sympathetic to the watchman who was sorrowfully repeating his sad tale, over and over again, to each newcomer who arrived. Meanwhile his wife, keening as for the dead, kept up a continual wailing chant: '*Vaiii! Vaiii!* My poor Jambor! *Vaiii!* You were so beautiful, so lovely! My poor Jambor!' calling out the beast's Hungarian name because even in Romanian villages in Transylvania all animals were given Magyar names.

From his hut the gypsy then called out softly that of course he didn't know but that it was possible that the cow was up at the manor house. Chacha had been the dark shadow that Adrienne and her friends had not noticed.

General astonishment. What was this the man was saying? What on earth could he mean? The watchman bellowed out furiously, 'So now you tell me, you bastard?'

There was a roar of laughter for everyone at once grasped that the whole affair was nothing more than a joke, a trick played on the watchman to show him up as being so lazy that he whose job it was to guard the village could have his own possessions removed from under his very nose, indeed from his own backyard! And the more they thought about it the more they laughed. And at this moment their mirth got completely out of hand for just up the road the cow itself appeared, led by Zoltan and driven from behind by one of the Miloth stable lads.

Up at the manor old Rattle, who always got up late, had just heard about the affair and stormed into the dining-room, roaring like a bull and shouting, 'So my house is turned into a nest of thieves and robbers, is it? Shame on you all, to bring dishonour on my grey hairs! My honest house a receiver's den, a dirty receiver's den!' he shouted as he rushed into the dining-room where his daughters and their guests were still chuckling over the news that the watchman had run all the way to Sarmas while his wife had climbed almost as far as Ormenyes. 'Off with you, you rascal!' he bellowed at his son. 'Go hang your head in shame and take the poor beast back at once. Yes, you, at once I say, or I'll break every bone in your body!' and he lunged at young Zoltan with his stick – just as the boy was making for the door. Then he turned back, shaking with laughter, and said, 'All right, you blackguards, how did you do it? Tell me all about it, my dears. Come on, tell me!'

He sat down at the table, spread a thick slice of bread and butter with honey and, his moustaches dripping, munched away as he listened eagerly to their tale. Still eating, he nodded and swallowed and let out great roars of laughter as they told him what had happened. This went on until it was nearly time for lunch. Only old Mademoiselle Morin, the sour-faced old governess, sat grimly at the end of the table and, every now and again, repeated, '*Oh, ces enfants! Oh, ces terribles enfants!*' because even after more than twenty years in the house, her spinsterish nature, soured by a bad digestion, had never learned to appreciate the pranks of her former charges.

After lunch everyone went their own ways. Rattle, tired out by the previous evening's dancing, decided to have a nap. Zoltan, Akos, Gazsi and Ida went down to the lake to look at the wild duck, and Margit and Adam, with Adrienne and Abady behind them, went walking in the garden.

Since Countess Miloth's death the garden had been almost abandoned; the lilac bushes were untrimmed and the lawns were covered in weeds. As they followed a winding path Adam, to his disappointment, found himself once again alone with Margit whom he still thought of as a mere child. He was angry because he had only come to Mezo-Varjas to see Adrienne and had hoped, during his afternoon walk, once again to pour out to her all his adoration and love. Perhaps, persuaded by his eloquence, by the beautiful phrases he had planned in advance, she might at last be persuaded to take him seriously.

He looked sadly at Margit. 'You see,' he cried. 'She's avoiding me. She won't even hear what I have to say. Oh, I'm the unhappiest man in the world. If only I could tell her all my sorrows!'

Margit put her hand on the young man's arm. 'Well, you can tell me, you know. I'm your friend, a good friend, and I'm a very good listener,' and she led him away from the garden, through the park and up to an old wooden bench on a hilltop which overlooked the village and the abandoned Protestant cemetery.

Adam now poured out his heart as he once more went over all that he felt for Adrienne, how in the past she had seemed to listen to him sympathetically. Of course it was true that she had always teased him and joked about his declarations of love, but that had not mattered because his feelings for her were so true and beautiful and all he had wanted was to be allowed to adore her, to kneel before her without touching even the hem of her skirt. He knew he was not worthy of her but all he wanted was the chance to talk to her and show her what was in his heart. And now not even that was possible for she always cut him short and stopped him before he had got a word out. She wouldn't even give him the chance to speak – even though that would be the only consolation possible for his hopeless sorrowing heart.

Young Margit was a wonderfully sympathetic confidante. She seemed to understand every nuance of what was in Adam's heart as she cleverly led him on to bare his soul to her. And she seemed, too, to share his sorrow, saying how cruel it was of Adrienne and asking how she could possibly allow herself to be so cold and merciless. Adrienne was beautiful, of course, oh yes, very beautiful, but she could have no heart if she could so torment someone like Adam, someone so true and lacking in guile or deceit. Oh, how could she cause so much pain? And so she went on, comforting the lovesick young man, stroking his shoulders and lending him her minute lace handkerchief when he had to brush away his tears.

They sat on the bench until it was almost dark and for Margit it was time well spent. Adam felt happier than he had for days because at last he had been able to tell everything that was in his heart to such a sweet, selfless girl. It was like talking to the sympathetic sister he had never had, whose hands he could squeeze in sympathy and with whom he could share his tears and his sadness. Although they had often talked of all this before it had never been so good as today on the bench on the hilltop. As they walked back to the house Margit suggested that perhaps he would like to write to her, especially if he was far away and needed some relief for his aching heart. Wouldn't that be a help to him, she said, a comfort in his loneliness? And he agreed that it would.

Adrienne and Balint, in order to escape from the other two, turned off the path at the angle of the manor house and continued to the end of a long side wing. This was where Judith Miloth had lived since her mind had become clouded and they had brought her home. Next to the house was the wire fence of the poultry yard that Adrienne had had made for her sister when she discovered that the girl took pleasure in looking after small animals.

On the sunny side there was a double row of chicken coops and next were several separate little houses for broody hens. A little further on was a low hut to house the rabbits in front of which a clay floor had been laid. Further on still there was a pile of sand which was renewed each month by a cart sent up from the Maros. This was necessary because no sand was to be found in the high prairie-lands and the health of the chickens depended on it. Once, before Adrienne had organized this, some epidemic had broken out, the hens had died and Judith had cried for days on end.

There was a narrow path between the fence and the lilac bushes and along this Adrienne led Balint in single file. From here he caught his first sight of Judith whom he had not seen since she had been brought home from Venice a year and a half before.

The girl was sitting on the ground. A black kerchief covered her hair and was tied under her chin like the peasant girls'. She wore a wide blue cotton apron which was spattered with whitish chicken droppings as were her hands. On the ground beside her was a metal scraper with which she had just cleaned the clay floor of the chicken run. Around her was a cluster of rabbits greedily munching on the lettuce leaves she had just given them. As she sat there Judith with one hand flung out handfuls of feed to the chickens while with the other she nursed a crippled chick which had been born lame.

'Eat, my little one,' she was murmuring. 'Go on, eat! No one will harm you here. It's good, isn't it? Eat, little one, eat!'

Judith only spoke to her animals; to people she hardly opened her mouth.

The old maidservant who looked after her was standing at the door of her room and, as Adrienne passed by, she called out, 'Kiss your hand, my Lady.'

As the old woman spoke Judith looked up. Seeing only Adrienne at first her expression did not change; but the moment she saw that Abady was with her, and lifted his hat in polite greeting, her face was contorted with horror and she looked at him with a mixture of surprise and terror, her eyes opened wide with shock. Her thin lips opened, as she straightened up, hands hanging loosely at her sides. She only looked at him for a few seconds but it seemed to him that perhaps she was, however uncertainly, recalling the moment when he had brought her home after she had been abandoned by the man she loved.

Abady too was thinking of that moment when he had found her alone at the railway station at Kolozsvar, waiting for the man she loved, that scoundrel Wickwitz with whom she had planned to elope to Austria but who had fled across the Romanian border the night before without even troubling to send her word. He remembered well the terrified expression on her face, like some caged wild bird, when he had stepped up to her just after the Budapest express had already left and told her that she was waiting in vain. Today, for a brief instant, he saw in her face that same expression, but it remained there only briefly and then the vacant look returned, empty and blind as it had been ever since that second shock which had broken her completely, when an unknown woman had sent her all the letters she had written to Wickwitz.

Now Judith lived shut away in these rooms in a remote corner of her father's house. She lived there like a shadow. She was alive but she might have been dead. She was still beautiful, but she was paler than before, and thinner, and her glance held no more meaning than the unblinking stare of a wild animal.

Adrienne and Balint walked on without speaking. They had both been upset by the sight of Judith.

When they had been wandering in the orchard for a while Balint started to speak, and as so often happened between them, he said exactly what was in her mind too.

'Ever since I left Almasko I've been thinking that if Uzdy is now so wrapped up in his new hobby, and if he doesn't seem so jealous and possessive as he was, surely a divorce might now be possible?'

Adrienne answered very slowly, 'Yes, maybe. I often think about it, especially when I'm with you. But he isn't always the same, you know. Sometimes . . . well, sometimes he seems to . . . oh, he's completely unpredictable . . . and . . . and, well, demanding!' Her face clouded over and she shut her eyes tightly. It was clear that her victory over him was by no means certain.

'I use every excuse,' she went on, 'to go away. Now I'll stay here for a week or so; then maybe go to Kolozsvar for the hunting at Zsuk. I really ought to do that for Margit's sake and of course I'll say it's for her, to give her a chance of meeting some young men. I may not be able to pull it off as of course we can't go to balls as we're still in mourning. Anyhow I'm doing all I can to get him used to my being away.' They walked on in silence. Then Adrienne tried to sum up her feelings: 'This is what I'm working on, but I can't make a final decision yet. The time isn't ripe and I feel it's impossible just now. If I raised the matter I'd have to tell him why. Even if I didn't tell him and he didn't already suspect the reason, he'd soon find out . . . and then . . .' She shuddered. 'No, it's impossible now.'

Balint thought he caught a note of fear in her voice, even though she had not told him everything that was in her mind.

The day after she had last been with Balint into the forest she had returned to take a walk in the same direction, westwards, towards the Abady holdings. On that day she had not gone as far as the boundary between the properties before turning to go home: and then a most unexpected thing had happened. She found herself face to face with her husband. There, on the path, was Uzdy who never normally walked more than a hundred paces away from the house and who ran his estates by studying the agents' reports in the comfort of his own study. But there he was, standing in front of her!

He must have been spying on her, she thought. That could be the only reason why he had got up so unusually early. She could only imagine that he had been secretly watching to see when she left the house and then, wearing noiseless rubber-soled shoes so as not to be heard as he stole after her, he must have followed wherever she went, presumably at some little distance. And he, who never took a shot at any living animal but only at targets set up in the park or in the castle shooting gallery, was carrying a precision rifle on one shoulder. He surely would not carry such a thing for no reason – he must have brought it either for her, or for Abady.

All these thoughts passed swiftly through her head as she saw him on the path in front of her. Everything fell into place. It was obvious! And how lucky it was that AB had left the day before and was nowhere near. Quickly she walked up to Uzdy and stood before him. 'Whatever are you doing here?' she asked belligerently with her head held high.

Uzdy laughed somewhat awkwardly. For a moment he looked like a young boy caught out in some minor misdeed. 'Why, I wanted to see for myself how nice a morning walk could be. Don't you approve, dear Addy?'

She shrugged her shoulders. His words seemed hardly to warrant any reply, so she merely said, 'And the rifle? Are you going shooting?'

'Shooting? No! But I thought maybe I'd find some convenient target here in the woods, a tree, or a stone . . . something like that!' He laughed again, somewhat maliciously, Adrienne thought; and for an instant his eyes flashed dangerously. 'I thought it might be interesting to try some target without measuring the distance beforehand. If I could hit it accurately . . . That's the important thing, accuracy . . . accuracy. The whole beauty is in accuracy, to hit accurately, just that. Accuracy,' and he repeated the word several times.

They had walked home together without speaking; and afterwards the incident was never again mentioned between them.

Adrienne was thinking of this incident when she again said, 'No! We can't do it yet, not yet. We can't bring it up now.'

After dinner at the Miloths' everyone remained in the dining-room, the ladies leaning their elbows on the wrinkled table-cloth and the men drinking their wine and dropping cigar ash on the table just as if they had been in a tavern. The footman and the maid leant against the wall scarcely troubling to conceal their yawns. This would never have happened while Countess Miloth was still alive but since her death what little order she had contrived had vanished. Everybody did as they pleased and young Margit, who was trying to run the household as best she could, followed her own instincts and pursued her own goals which were, simply, that the young men who came to the house should feel themselves at home and be able to talk as they pleased and drink what they wanted. Even if anyone had questioned her she would probably just have replied that it was best that way.

The first person to get up from table was old Mademoiselle Morin, who retired to the drawing-room as soon as the meal was ended, offended and sighing deeply, to continue knitting the eternal woollen stocking on which she seemed to have been engaged for the last twenty years. Later on old Rattle dragged the youngest Alvinczy there too so as to have a captive audience for his tales of the Garibaldi campaigns. The others had stayed in the dining-room for, with peals of laughter, they rebelled at the idea of hearing all that again. What they wanted to talk about was the previous night's adventure and what it had led to. Nemesis, it seemed, had caught up with the night-watchman, for the village council had met and dismissed him; and so the drama of the cow, as in a Greek tragedy, had had its inexorable effect.

Although everyone was laughing and joking the evening was not entirely carefree; a shadow lurked behind the mirth for no one could quite forget that poor Judith, their former companion and playmate, was living there, at the end of the house, her mind clouded. A few of them, like Abady, had caught a glimpse of her, and the others had been told by Ida Laczok. The knowledge that she was there afflicted them all and gradually the jokes and laughter died away. One or two of them occasionally glanced at the glazed door that led to the veranda and even fancied that they glimpsed there the face of a young girl with death in her eyes.

As their mirth faded so they began to talk about more serious subjects, about people who were lucky and those that were not, about the disappearance of Laszlo Gyeroffy, about Dinora Malhuysen who had signed bank drafts for Wickwitz and who had everywhere been ostracized when the scandal became known; and about Fate who distributed good and bad luck with total indifference and how some people were destroyed without apparent reason while others, who might not deserve it, had joy and success thrust upon them.

'You can't measure happiness equally; everybody is not the same!' said Adam Alvinczy sadly, as he looked at Adrienne. Then Gazsi thumped the table loudly.

'That's just not true,' he shouted. 'Everybody is the same, neither happy nor unhappy. It's the same rotten deal for us all!'

Everyone looked up at him in astonishment for Gazsi had never been known to think about anything but practical jokes and horses.

'Oh, yes,' cried Gazsi. 'I've thought about it a lot. I've often noticed that in company...'

'The company of horses?' interrupted Adam, who resented having his own pessimistic attitude adopted by anyone else, especially by Gazsi.

This made Kadacsay angry. Adam's scornful tone seemed to touch some deep wound within him, some sorrow of whose existence even he may have been previously unaware. Always before he had reacted to such mockery with such comic self-deprecation that everyone laughed. Today, however, perhaps because he had had a lot to drink, the mask of comedy had dropped and everyone could see he was offended.

'I suppose you think that just because a man knows how to ride he must be a complete dolt? Of course I spend a lot of my time with horses – perhaps too much; but I can still think when I'm in the saddle, and that wouldn't be easy for you even standing still!'

Balint sensed that the conversation was getting dangerously out of hand and decided to intervene. 'Well, Gazsi, let's hear what you do think! Tell us!'

'Yes! Yes! Do go on, Gazsi!' cried the ladies, 'and then we'll tell you what *we* think.'

Kadacsay leaned his head on one side and his plaintive eyebrows rose even higher than usual. With his long nose he looked like a raven contemplating some strange object. Fixing his eyes on the table-cloth, as if he could read something there, he started to talk, though at first in broken phrases. His manner was dream-like, but his logic did not falter. Using rather too many words and often repeating himself, he said that no matter what one achieved, no matter what joy came one's way, it was never enough; there was always some further goal before complete happiness could be won. No one could ever say, 'Now I wish for nothing more!' Whatever Fate sent one's way, somehow it was never enough. It was not a question of wanting more of the same thing, it was just that there was always something else, something one did not yet have but which was or now seemed necessary for complete happiness. It was this constant desire which kept human joy in check, for everyone felt that if only he could achieve just this one little thing more then all would be well. It was the same with unhappiness. No matter what terrible sorrow came one's way there was always some tiny grain of hope to be one's consolation and which kept one from despair. It didn't matter what one called it – duty, a debt to be paid, a moral obligation – there was always something more to be done despite the shattering blow one had just suffered. When someone very dear to one died, there were things to be done and people to be cared for. And in every other sort of sorrow there was some compensation which provided its own joy, something that could not be left undone, some work to be concluded, some person who needed care and help – be it a relation or a friend or servant, or even an animal. It did not matter who or what it was but there was always someone or something for whose sake one must accept the sorrow and bear it with fortitude, for that someone or something had no other person to whom to turn. Even the profoundest mourning had its compensations.

'It is like a giant scales,' said Gazsi. 'One side of the balance holds happiness, the other sorrow. And they are always there in equal measure, no matter if one side seems full and the other almost empty!'

Kadacsay was gesticulating with fingers that were stiff from so much riding. Some of the others tried to laugh, but Gazsi's eye looked gravely at them with something of the fixity of a fanatic.

'Well,' someone said. 'What happens if one side of the balance is completely empty, if all the weight is on the side of happiness?'

'Then whoever it was would dance and sing all day and would soon be locked in the madhouse!'

'And if it were all unhappiness?'

'He'd shoot himself!'

As Gazsi had been talking old Rattle came back into the room. He listened with growing amazement. Now he said, 'Do you think I'm not grieving for my beloved wife? Why, I think of nothing else, day and night! Where on earth did you read all this nonsense, my dear boy?'

'Nowhere!' said Gazsi. 'What with the army and the horses I've hardly had time to open a book . . . unfortunately. I've lost a lot of time but I'm trying to make up for it now. I just hope it's not too late.'

'The Devil take all that reading, dear boy! I had a chum in Italy, such an ass, a real bookworm, never had his head out of some work by goodness knows what idiotic philosopher; he'd even read by the campfire! I'll tell you a story about him; it's really very funny.'

He pulled up a chair facing Gazsi and, despite the united protests of his daughters, started off his tale with gusto.

'Listen! This happened when we were in camp after the battle of Calatafimi. This chap was there with us and, for some reason, the kindling wouldn't take. Now there wasn't much wood to burn – and very little else – so I said why the hell do we need a fire anyway? And then I said . . .'

Abady looked at Kadacsay as he sat facing the old soldier. Sometimes he inclined his nose to the right and sometimes to the left but all the time, though he seemed to listen, a tiny smile lurked under his moustache, a bitter, slightly mocking smile, and his forehead was lined with a deep furrow which Balint had never seen before. It was now that he recalled that when Gazsi had stayed at Denestornya the year before he had asked for a volume of Schopenhauer from the library and he wondered what deep hunger for learning and self-knowledge possessed this man who everyone believed thought of nothing but horses and playing the fool.

Rattle never finished his tale, though not for want of talking. He went on and on, occasionally bursting into loud peals of laughter, until the guests started to get up and his daughters suggested that it was high time for everyone to be in bed and asleep.

'All right, my dears, let's go!' the kind-hearted old man agreed at once. 'Tomorrow I'll tell you the rest. You'll see, it's absolutely priceless!'

As they went towards the guest-rooms Balint touched Gazsi on the shoulder saying, 'What you said was very interesting.'

Gazsi shrugged off the compliment.

'Oh, it's nonsense really. Old Rattle was right,' and he laughed awkwardly as if he were ashamed of having unwittingly revealed something of himself.

CHAPTER THREE

AFTER THOSE FEW days spent in the high grasslands, Balint
returned to Denestornya. He only remained there a short time
for he had to attend the Szekler congress which was due to open
at the spa town of Homorod a week later. As he had already told
his mother about this more than once his rapid departure did not
cause any surprise, but it did not lessen her resentment even
though he was not going to be away for long.

Relations between Balint and his mother had recently become
increasingly strained. In vain Balint tried to explain what he had
already achieved in the Kalotaszeg, both in the management of
the Abady forests and in the new co-operative movement; but
neither the fact that he had doubled their income from the forests
nor the news that the experimental farm and smallholders' club
at Lelbanya were doing well, removed the frozen expression of
disapproval from his mother's face. From time to time she would
ask him some question, but it was clear that she took little interest
in his replies. No matter what subject Balint tried, all Roza
Abady thought about was that wherever her son went it always
brought him closer to that accursed Adrienne Miloth.

There was little that Countess Roza did not know about her
son's affairs, for Azbej had organized an efficient spy service to
check on all his movements.

Old Nyiresy, who had managed the Abady forest holdings for
many years, could not stomach the reforms that Balint had
brought to what the old man had come to look upon as his own
domain. Until quite recently Nyiresy had been omnipotent,
smoking his pipe with the air of a squire and able to do whatever
he liked. Now a young, and highly qualified, forest engineer had
been appointed to supervise the running of the forests and
Nyiresy could do nothing without consulting him. It was unbearable. And that was not all; the new man, on Balint's instructions, had moved into the spacious Abady estate house at Beles,
which for thirty years the old manager had come to think of as
his own property. The man had been given two rooms, both of
them formerly guest-rooms; and the loss of these, and of the
room reserved for Count Abady himself, meant that Nyiresy had
nowhere to put up a friend for the night. Beles was so remote
that now he could only be visited by those two close friends who

lived in the mountains close by – Gaszton Simo, the notary from Gyurkuca, and the manager of the nearby sawmills. No one could come from further afield as there was nowhere for them to sleep. He couldn't even have an evening of cards, let alone throw those wild parties which had been such a solace in his lonely life. So he asked to be allowed to retire, and he asked also, in recognition of his long service, that he should be allowed to live in the Abady house at Banffy-Hunyad which until then had always been let. This was really asking too much, but Balint agreed because he was anxious that the old man should go and did not want any more ill-feeling to spoil his departure.

Accordingly Nyiresy had now been installed for some time at Banffy-Hunyad, where, as it was a market town, everyone for miles around gathered once a week to exchange news and gossip. And what could be more interesting than to chronicle the comings and goings of young Count Abady? Though he did not much relish writing letters the old man wrote a note to Azbej every time he heard something that sounded interesting.

That was one source of information; the other was the inn-keeper at Lelbanya, who was a distant cousin of Azbej and who, greedy and self-seeking, hated the farmers' club that Balint had founded, for although it was true that no wine was served there it still took customers away from the inn. Furthermore the inn-keeper did not like the fact that their Member of Parliament came so often to the town and poked his nose into everything that went on there. To him Balint was nothing but a nuisance. The innkeeper was an even better informant than old Nyiresy, for Lelbanya was such a tiny place and there, up in the lonely prairie-lands, everybody was so bored that if there was any gossip they all, peasant, minor civil servant or shopkeeper, would always think it worth a two-hour walk to spread it around.

With these two informers beavering away Azbej was quickly kept up to date with everything that Balint did; and he saw to it, through the housekeepers Tothy and Baczo, that Countess Roza was also kept informed. Every day, after lunch and dinner, the two old women took their places at either end of the table in the drawing-room behind which Roza Abady sat to do her needle-work. As always at this season all three were knitting warm clothes to be given to the village children at Christmas.

If Balint was not there one of the fat housekeepers would start off by sighing deeply. Then the other would ask why; and so, like a game of question and answer, with many 'Indeed!'s and 'Not possible!'s, and much nodding of heads and pregnant silences, they would relate the gossip they had heard. Not that they ever addressed the countess directly, their tales were directed only at each other. In this way Balint's mother learned that her son had again been in the forests at Hunyad and that he had had a lodge erected there, a lodge that was – guess where? Just where the Abady holdings adjoined those of Count Uzdy. And where did the young master go? To Almasko, of course. And in the same way the drama of the watchman's cow at Mezo–Varjas and Balint's part in it, quickly reached Denestornya and was related with much drawing in of breath and self-righteous disapproval.

In this way Baczo and Tothy laboured hard to poison their employer's love for her son; and it was no wonder that, however hard Balint worked to improve the family fortunes or whatever he achieved in the public interest, the old lady believed none of it and imagined that her son was making it all up just to cover his godless relationship with the hated Adrienne.

And so it was that when Balint announced that he would soon be leaving for Homorod, his mother fixed him with a glassy stare and said, 'Surely the season's over now, at the end of October?' in a mocking tone which meant, in her roundabout way, that she supposed that Adrienne had gone there to take the waters, even though it was late autumn. Balint knew instinctively what his mother was thinking and so took pains to explain that Homorod had been chosen for the Szekler congress for the simple reason that as the spa was closed there would be plenty of rooms in the hotels – and even villas to let – and so all the two hundred or so delegates to the congress would be able to find a bed.

'Strange place to choose, Homorod! Very unusual!'

'Yes, it is unusual; but I believe that Samuel Barra wanted it. And, of course, there will be plenty of room, much better than in most country towns.' And though it was obvious that his mother did not believe a word he said, he went on to outline the project he was going to present, hoping that he could convince her that it was true that he was going only for political reasons.

But Countess Roza merely looked in another direction and began to talk about something else.

The congress had been called to discuss a problem that was beginning to grow to alarming proportions. The districts inhabited by the Szekler people were becoming dangerously depopulated as a result of emigration. Daranyi, the new Minister-President, had proposed giving aid on an unprecedented scale so that the afflicted areas would be re-populated by the very people who were now seeking their fortunes abroad. Among the new proposals were free distribution of breeding stock, free technical advice on modern farming methods and the appointment of a special delegation drawn from the Szekler people themselves to help direct how this aid should be organized.

The plight of the Szeklers was indeed grave. They were a prolific people and their inheritance traditions exacted that each child should receive an equal portion of the family holding. As a result the Szekler smallholdings had been divided and subdivided into such tiny strips of often very poor land that even the thriftiest farmer could hardly glean from them a fraction of what was needed to feed a family. At first the Szeklers had tried to find a living working in the forests or on the railways, or even in small businesses; but wherever they went there was never enough work for their rapidly increasing numbers. Then they started to go to Romania, and now more and more were heading for America and there, save for a few, they stayed.

Istvan Bethlen, realizing that this growing emigration and the depopulation it left behind were a serious blot on the reputation of the Hungarian government as well as being damning proof of a careless economic policy, had encouraged successive agricultural ministers to take some measures to reverse the trend; but instead of searching for cures to the reasons why so many were leaving, all that the government had done so far was to organize the emigration. Though this was done so as to prevent exploitation of the poor emigrants the only real effect was to contribute to the evil itself. Daranyi was the first national leader to tackle the problem seriously.

The official delegates, together with Mihaly Koos, the lawyer who had been elected chairman of the Szekler representatives, took a slow train from Budapest to Kolozsvar. They could have travelled by the express but Samuel Barra, shrewd politician that he was, thought that it would be better to take a train that stopped at every station along the way so that delegates from country districts could join it anywhere on the route; and then they would all arrive at the same time. It had not escaped him, either, that slow trains always stood for some little time at each stop thereby giving time for the politicians to greet welcoming committees and make themselves better known.

By courtesy of the Hungarian State Railways a restaurant car had been attached to the train and so they all travelled in high good spirits. At one end of the car Barra held court, revelling in one more opportunity to argue with, and upbraid, his own supporters – and the more he insulted them the more they loved it; while at the other end the journalist-turned-politician Marot Kutenvary kept the Transylvanians in a roar with the latest Jewish anecdotes from the capital. Kutenvary had just managed to scrape into Parliament for some district in Gyergyo by making the most of his resemblance to Hungary's great patriotic poet, Sandor Petofi, who had died on a Transylvanian battlefield, and so felt obliged to attend the Szekler congress. These two were the opposing poles of the restaurant car. Loud political discussions at one end, loud peals of laughter at the other.

Balint joined the train at Aranyos-Gyeres. Seeing that although most of the compartments had been taken very few passengers were actually in their seats, he walked down the corridor hoping to find some interesting company. In one compartment he saw Mihaly Koos and his two secretaries with Istvan Bethlen, but as he presumed they were discussing the organization of the congress and had covered the seats of their compartment with papers, it did not seem the moment to join them.

Instead he too went to the restaurant car.

When Balint first came in the two groups, the serious and the jovial, were still fairly evenly balanced, with as many men surrounding Kutenvary as were grouped round the great Barra. This was all changed after the train had stopped at Kocsard, for all the newcomers at once joined the Barra group. Among them were Zsigmond Boros, old Bartokfay, Bela Varju, Jeno Laczok and the banking baron, Soma Weissfeld. Laczok was attending as a great landowner in Szekler country and Weissfeld because, as a director of the bank at Vasarhely and chairman of the company which exploited the Laczok forestry holdings, he was one of the principal employers of the Szekler people.

The newcomers were all in gala dress: Bela Varju in a brand new black traditional outfit and Bartokfay in a short mulberry-coloured spencer-like jacket covered in braid and embroidery, and tight trousers. More magnificent than either, however, was

Soma Weissfeld who had put on the traditional Hungarian costume that he had had made a few years before when there had been rumours of imperial manoeuvres on the banks of the Maros. Though the King never came the costume remained and so, ever since, the banker had seized any opportunity to wear it. Made by Grünbaum and Weiner in Budapest, the outfit had cost a great deal of money and was in the most exaggerated old Hungarian style. The dolman was of snow-white silk, the trousers deep carmine and the boots of yellow morocco leather. The bright blue cape with its wide 'Zrinyi' collar was trimmed with rabbit fur dyed to look like marten; and the whole was richly decorated with clasps and buckles all large as pigeon eggs and made of gilded copper. To top it all he wore a gold-plated sword. Ill-natured gossip said that the banker looked like a cross between a chimpanzee and a cockatoo, but the man himself was quite satisfied with the vision he saw in the looking-glass. That the pince-nez clipped to his nose were not entirely in the manly Hungarian tradition was unfortunate; but the banking baron could hardly tuck them away in a pocket for without them he could see nothing.

The politicians now so outnumbered the others that the men round Kutenvary fell silent and left the floor to Samuel Barra.

Soon the train drew to a stop at the Tovis junction, and here it had to wait for a while until the connecting train from Deva should arrive. The station was decorated with flags and on the platform stood the station-master and all his men drawn up as if on parade to greet the monarch himself. Behind them were a crowd of onlookers, the railway employees' choir, the local gypsy band and the town judge with a group of white-clad schoolgirls who recited a poem and then presented a beribboned bouquet, not, however, to the representative of the Minister but to the famous Samuel Barra whose face was the only one they recognized.

As the weather was clear and sunny and it seemed the halt would continue for some little time, everyone got out of the train. Barra, Bartokfay, Varju and Kutenvary all took the opportunity of making speeches explaining what they were going to do for the poor Szeklers; and when they finished the mob cheered wildly even though Tovis was not in Szekler country and most people present were either ordinary town-folk or railway employees. At each pause the gypsy band played a flourish just as they did at official toasts.

Balint walked down the platform and by the last carriage he

found a small group that had descended from a third-class compartment and were stretching their legs on the platform. There were six or seven Romanian *popas* dressed in shabby grey priests' robes and among them were some laymen dressed equally shabbily in grey. Slowly they walked up and down hardly exchanging a word and when one of them turned round Balint recognized the old lawyer and politician, Aurel Timisan, who was one of the Romanian minority Members of Parliament.

When Timisan came up to greet Balint his companions turned away and left him.

'What a celebration they are having today!' said the old lawyer in a faintly mocking tone. 'It's a joy to see! And may I ask where you gentlemen are all going?'

'To Homorod. The Szekler congress opens there tomorrow.'

'Very right and proper! Most wise to think about the people's problems. And how beautifully you Hungarians organize these things. All these excellent speeches, all this cheering. Nowhere in the world do they do it so well.'

At that moment the train from the south rumbled into the station and many more festively dressed men jumped out. At once the cheering started again, with more singing, more speeches on the platform, and the choir started on the Kossuth song. Hats were waved, handkerchiefs and banners fluttered.

'And who is that magnificent gentleman in Hungarian costume?' asked the old deputy pointing at Soma Weissfeld. Under his thick moustaches there was the hint of a mocking smile.

'He is the director of the bank at Vasarhely,' said Balint drily, sensing the old man's mockery. Not wishing to seem to share it, he went on, 'Where are you going? I see you are not alone.'

'To Brasso. We have an unimportant little meeting there ... just church affairs.'

'Then perhaps we could have a talk on the way? Which compartment are you in?'

'Naturally I should be most honoured by your Lordship's company, but you see I am travelling third class with my friends and I could not very well leave them. And where I am neither the place nor the company is worthy of your Lordship. They are very simple people, very simple indeed.'

With his last words Timisan waved his hand in farewell and chuckled as if amused by some inner meaning the other could not share.

* * *

The two trains were soon linked together and, as the band on the platform played the Rakoczy March, the much lengthened train pulled slowly out. During the wait at Tovis the carriages had all been decorated with flags and so it was with a mass of bunting fluttering in the wind that the delegates were transported across the bridge over the Maros and, leaving the rich flat grasslands, entered the gorge that led to the mountains.

Soon they arrived at Balazsfalva, the seat of the Romanian Uniate bishop. It was from here that all the pan-Romanian movements of the last century and a half had been initiated.

At Balazsfalva the train was joined by the delegates from Dicso, led by Joska Kendy who was now Prefect in Kis-Kukullo. As always, Joska himself, pipe firmly clenched between his teeth, remained silent, but his companions soon made up for this. As at Tovis there were more white-clad schoolgirls, more bouquets and speeches of welcome; and here it was the banker Weissfeld who was cheered, for they all imagined, from his elaborate dress, that he must be the Minister's representative.

Balint was watching all this from the window of his compartment when he caught sight of a young man dressed as a theology student hurrying towards the back of the train. He looked neither to right nor to left and clearly knew exactly where he was going. Balint was sure that he knew his face, and wondered where he had seen him before.

The youth was very slim, almost gaunt in appearance, with an olive-skinned face whose cheekbones showed the telltale red spot of tuberculosis. Balint watched to see where he would go.

Eventually the student stopped in front of a third-class compartment. As soon as he did so a large hand shot out of the window into the palm of which the youth pressed a small piece of paper. Then he turned and stepped back on the platform, gazing back at the richly decorated engine. His glance met Abady's and at once Balint recognized him: he was the son of the *popa* at Gyurkuca in the mountains whom Balint had seen when his father Timbus had asked for wood to enlarge the village church. Balint well remembered those burning eyes as full of hatred then, when the boy was lying covered in fur rugs on the veranda of the *popa*'s house, as now when gazing at the train full of Hungarian delegates. Balint had heard that he had recovered sufficiently to study for the priesthood and he remembered, too, that the notary Simo had said that while the *parintie* Timbus was a reliable man his son was a dangerous pro-Romanian agitator.

Young Timbus stayed where he was on the platform, rigidly upright, as the Hungarian delegates crowded back to their seats. And he remained there, still without moving, as the gaily decorated train clattered noisily out of the station and finally disappeared in the cloud of its own smoke.

The congress at Homorod opened at ten o'clock in the morning under the joint chairmanship of the sheriffs of Maros-Torda, Csik, Udvarhely and Haromszek, each taking their turn to preside in order of seniority of service. This had been planned by the government so as to recognize the loyalty of these regions which had remained faithful to the Coalition party all through the time of the government appointed by the King. These four men therefore sat together at the presidential table which had been placed in the centre of one of the long walls of the hall where the congress was to take place.

During the spa's high season this room was used as a general place of assembly and amusement. It was built of wood and the outer walls were mostly windows. At one end there was a platform where gypsy musicians would play every afternoon and evening and where visiting theatrical companies would erect their stage. The hall had now been filled with rows of chairs where the delegates took their places, automatically following the rules of social precedence so that the more prominent and important had the better places. Between them and the presidential table was a space where the various delegations could come forward to present their points of view. There were not many of these because, although the Szeklers were an enterprising and vigorous people always ripe for new experience, they were also essentially practical folk who were reluctant to leave their land just at the moment when their fields should be ploughed and winter sowing begun. As a result there were not many of them there. Those who did attend quickly retired to places at the back as soon as they had delivered their formal speeches of welcome, and from there they listened somewhat suspiciously to what all these lords and great folk had to say.

The largest group was that of the charcoal-burners, and this was because they felt they had serious grievances to be laid before the congress. There were some sixteen of them and instead of approaching the presidential table they went immediately to find places at the extreme back of the hall.

They were stern-faced, serious men who all seemed to look much alike, perhaps because of their unceasing work in the forest where, day and night, the success of their work depended on unrelenting attention to the fires. They were dressed in the same clothes; black in colour, with black boots, and their skin too was darkened from the wood-smoke that had stained their foreheads, faces and hands with indelible little black marks.

The charcoal-burners sat in silence, waiting while the formal speeches of welcome were made, and while all the other delegates were greeting each other, exchanging compliments and somewhat vaguely outlining a rosy future for everyone present. Then someone read out the agenda for the discussions, followed by an explanation of the Minister's proposals.

Balint was sitting at one side of the hall studying the notes he had made of his proposal that the Szekler land inheritance should be by entail and not by general division of property. At one moment he looked up and saw to his surprise that one of the faces among the charcoal-burners was familiar to him; it was Andras Jopal, the young Transylvanian mathematician who had discovered how to make a flying machine at the same time as the Wright brothers and Santos-Dumont, but who had not had the means to present it to the world before they did. He had missed his chance not only from lack of money to complete the model and build the engine, but also because he was so suspicious of other people that he had refused help when he most needed it. Balint had come forward with an offer of aid but Jopal had rejected it angrily, believing that Balint merely wanted to steal his secret from him. It must surely be him, thought Balint, as he looked at that very individual face, broad shaven skull and domed forehead, and those small bright piercing eyes. But what was he doing here among the charcoal-burners, seated at the centre of their group, holding in his hand the paper on which their complaint was written and apparently being treated as their leader?

The debate started with discussions about the Minister's proposals for the free distribution of breeding stock and the choice of which cattle would be most appropriate to the different types of farming land.

Although there was general approval of the overall idea an argument soon started between the government expert and some of the local authorities. Whereas Daranyi's man proposed Simmenthal cattle, one local man stood out for Pinzgau stock and another for the established local breeds. Both were talking in vain because the Ministry of Agriculture's men, having studied the situation, had already made up their minds what was best and were not going to change their view, especially as the experiment had already been made with success in northern Hungary. While reluctant to argue about a free gift the local men were determined to have their say, if only to prove that they knew what they were talking about. The same thing happened when they started to talk about stallions at stud, poultry and pigs. And when pigs came to be discussed a self-appointed 'expert' from the Szilagy district, which was far removed from any Szekler settlement, got up to champion the 'Baris' pig which was popular where he came from even though everyone else knew that you could feed it for five years without it ever getting fat. 'The Baris has no equal!' cried the man from Szilagy in the tones of a religious fanatic.

When all these discussions came to an end the Minister's proposals were unanimously accepted. Everyone was delighted – even those who had argued the most fiercely – for it was recognized that if Daranyi had initiated the programme then he would see it through; and also because it was well-known that the congress had been convened only for one purpose, which was that the public should know what was being done for the Szeklers. And, of course, there would always be those ready to declare that it was their personal participation at the congress that had had a decisive effect on what would have been done anyhow.

At the end of the morning session the meeting was adjourned for lunch. Abady waited until Jopal should come forward with his companions. Then he went up to him and said how glad he was to meet him again, though it was a surprise to see him with the charcoal-burners.

Jopal stopped. A faint smile lit up his smoke-grimed face. 'But I am one of them,' he said. 'I've lived with them now for two years. I work with them. They are very nice people.'

'Don't you think it is a waste for a man like you, with your knowledge and skill, to bury yourself like this? Even if the basic problem of flying has been solved and others have got the credit, it's still very primitive and there are many more problems to be solved. And flying isn't the only field for a mathematician like yourself.'

'It's all foolishness,' replied Jopal. 'Vanity and foolishness. And to what purpose? There's more satisfaction in hard physical work among good and simple people. Only that is really worthwhile. To live out of doors, in the forest, chop wood, cut trees, build the ovens ... to learn how long the charcoal must smoulder inside, and when more air must be let in and when the fire extinguished. To watch over it, guard it, care for it ... it needs a lot of care, and knowledge and strength. And it's beautiful, too, to live naturally, to be free...'

How different Jopal had become, thought Balint, from the time they had last met on the crest of the Ludas hills a month or so after Santos-Dumont had flown for the first time. Then he had been so bitter, while today he radiated peace and serenity.

'Come and have some food with me,' suggested Balint. 'I don't at all mind missing the official feast.'

The inventor-turned-charcoal-burner shook his head. 'Thank you, but I can't leave my friends. I belong with them now.' And he said goodbye and went off with the others who had been waiting for him a few yards away.

As Abady walked over to the restaurant he was thinking over what had happened to Jopal. How strange it was, the destiny of Hungarians! How many there were like Jopal, as full of talent as their greatest rivals in the world but who, once they had reached their goal, would give it all up as easily as it had been obtained. Such people would never fight for the recognition they deserved; it was as if they would soon lose all interest if everything didn't go their way from the beginning, and that they had striven so far only to prove to themselves that they could do it if they wanted to, and not for worldly success. Several names at once occurred to him. There was Janos Bolyai, one of the outstanding men of his generation, who gave up everything at the age of twenty-one; Samu Teleki, who had explored so many hitherto unknown parts of Africa and discovered Lake Rudolf, but who never bothered himself to write about his travels; Miklos Absolon, who had been to Lhasa but who never spoke of his travels except obliquely and as humorous anecdotes. Then there was Pal Szinyei-Merse, the forerunner of the Impressionists, who gave up painting and did not touch his brushes for more than fifteen years; and, of course, Tamas Laczok, who earned fame in Algeria where he could have made history but who abandoned it all to return to Hungary and work on the railways as a simple engineer.

There seemed to be a sort of oriental yearning for Nirvana, a passivity as regards worldly success which led his compatriots to throw away their chances of achievement, abandon everything for which they had striven for years, sometimes justifying themselves with some transparent excuse of offence offered or treachery on the part of so-called friends, but more often offering no explanation at all. Perhaps it was the other side of the coin of national pride which led them to throw everything away as soon as they had proved to themselves that they could do it if they wished, as if the ability alone sufficed and the achievement counted for nothing. It was like an inherited weakness transmitted from generation to generation and, of course, it had been epitomized in Janos Aranyi's epic poem about Miklos Toldi, who under appalling difficulties conquered all his country's enemies in a few months and then retired to till his fields and was never seen again until extreme old age.

The government's plan for bringing back the emigrants and re-populating the deserted areas was announced at the afternoon session. Only the general idea was put forward because there were so many legal and economic aspects of the plan still to be worked out that no detailed discussion would have been possible at a public meeting.

All the same the announcement gave Abady the opportunity to put forward his suggestion for modifying the inheritance laws.

He started by saying that if the re-colonization of the land was to be successful it would have to be carried out on a massive scale. There were too many Szeklers for the land available to them and traditionally theirs. He quoted statistics, birth-rates, emigration figures, and laid special emphasis on the ever-diminishing size of the Szekler smallholdings, showing how it was impossible for most of these holdings to support a family. The only legal solution was to establish a system of entail by which properties could be handed on intact from generation to generation. He cited the example of similar situations in foreign countries – Canada and the United States, among others – where a single heir could inherit everything. He followed this with more statistics and explanations, quoting from books such as those of Lorenz von Stein; and added that such a system as he suggested was by no means unknown in Hungarian law which for centuries had established a minimum size for serfs' holdings which could not further be divided. The Szeklers, he said, should be enabled to preserve their existing land by entail to the oldest son, the other children's future being secured by the state providing them with re-colonized land.

Such was Balint's intervention; and though it might have had some effect at a legal conference it fell extremely flat at the Szekler congress, few of whose delegates were sure where Canada was and even fewer of whom had ever heard of Lorenz von Stein. As he was speaking Balint knew that he was boring his audience – and this knowledge robbed most of what he had to say of any conviction. The audience stopped listening.

Only one man paid attention. This was Samuel Barra who jumped up almost before Abady had finished. His powerful voice booming across the hall, he cried, 'It is absolutely scandalous that anyone should dare to put forward such an idea, especially here in the very temple of the people's liberties! Suggesting that the Szeklers should love and favour one of their children over the others, to keep one and throw away the rest. It's a monstrous idea!' And he waxed emotional over the sacredness of a father's love for his children, over solidarity between brothers, and over the fate of widows and orphans. Grabbing hold of Abady's reference to division of serfs' properties, he shouted that the noble member for Lelbanya apparently wanted to push the Szeklers back to serfdom and that it was obvious to him at least that Abady's real purpose was to abandon the liberal achievements of the twentieth century, and return to the Middle Ages, to forced labour and public floggings! 'Never!' he cried. 'And anyhow the Szeklers were free men even in mediæval days. Why, even all the armies of Hell could not defeat them, neither the Bashi-Bazouk Turks nor the satanic Caraffa.'

Though Caraffa had had nothing to do with Transylvania and by the Bashi-Bazouks he presumably meant the Turkish gendarmerie, the words sounded good and, as Barra hurled them at the delegates, general cheering broke out. People clapped wildly and many ran forward to shake his hand and praise his patriotic outburst.

Balint, shocked and bitter, sat down. He knew he should rise again and explain, but then, he reflected, it would be to no purpose for there was nobody present who would understand and to whom it was worth defending himself. Even the Minister's representative hardly opened his mouth, while Bethlen, who after all had initiated the whole idea of saving the Szeklers, did not speak at all. While he hesitated another speaker rose to his feet.

It was Jopal. He had a good voice and he spoke well, in short easily-understood sentences. Calmly and with great precision he described the miserable situation of the charcoal-burners. He spoke with conviction that lent weight to his words but he remained matter-of-fact. He asked that they should be able to sell their own produce rather than be forced to do so through middle-men who made all the profit. Though they were an established union neither the state nor private enterprises recognized their existence or had any direct dealings with them. In this way they were being reduced to misery.

Balint listened carefully. It was extraordinary how nothing in Jopal's words or manner revealed his educated scientific past. If one knew nothing about him one would take him for a simple workman who had grown up in the forests and who knew all about charcoal-burning but nothing else.

When Jopal had finished he descended slowly to the centre of the hall, laid his memorandum on the presidential table and went back to join his companions.

Later, when Jopal once again got to his feet to answer some questions put to him by the Minister's representative, Balint was wondering what would have happened to him if he had not refused to allow himself to be helped. Would he now be in London, Paris or New York, the chairman of some great international company, a leader of industry and a power to be reckoned with in the world of science and big business? And just as Balint was thinking of these things Jopal sat down once again in the centre of the little band of stern dignified smoke-grimed men and immediately became just one among sixteen other men, indistinguishable and unremarkable.

A banquet was held in the evening with much wine and drinking of toasts, gypsy music and speeches praising the great patriotic civic virtues of everyone present. No one was left out, no one left without a word of praise or some flattering adjective. The government emissary and the man who wanted the Baris pig above all others were awarded the same laurel leaves of praise.

Only the charcoal-burners and Balint Abady were absent. While the forest men had rumbled off to the Hargita on their small carts, Balint had hired a vehicle and drove away, hoping to get as far as Segesvar where he knew there was a good inn. He minded bitterly that he had made all that effort for nothing. He realized that his speech had been inept and ill-thought-out, and it had perhaps been naïve of him to imagine that his un-familiar ideas could have been understood by such an audience who had not the faintest notion what he had been talking about. He would have been better advised, he thought, to have written a pamphlet several months in advance and seen that it was properly distributed; and then followed it up by some articles in the news-papers rather than jumping in and throwing such a revolutionary proposal at people totally unprepared for such things. Perhaps if he had given the matter more thought someone would have appreciated what he was trying to achieve – but would they? As it was he could only blame himself for the fiasco of his speech. How stupid it had been of him to recite all those boring figures, to quote at random from abstruse legal precedents. Of course it served him right. But he was still very hurt, especially by the cheap mockery of Barra, to whose effrontery he had been too ashamed even to attempt a reply. To think that in Hungary such people passed for honest men!

Balint's carriage drove slowly through the country villages, which were now silent and seemingly deserted in the growing darkness with only the occasional gleam of light from behind shuttered windows. Now everyone was safe at home and mostly fast asleep. No doubt they would all wake up again when some great man was to be cheered on his way home, perhaps even the famous Barra?

Half dozing as he lay back against the cushions of the carriage certain images floated into Balint's mind. They were fleeting impressions of incidents only half taken in on his way to the con-gress. For instance, at Balazsfalva there had been the Romanian theology student, his glance full of hatred for the travelling Hun-garian delegates, who had clearly been waiting on the platform for the arrival of the carriage full of Romanian priests. He had obviously known that they would be on that train; and it was equally obvious that they had known too that they would receive some sort of message, for as the young man handed up his little paper a hand had reached out and taken it without a word even of greeting being passed from carriage to platform. The *popas* had travelled discreetly in their third-class carriage, grey, modest and unobtrusive as they went on their way to Brasso where only a little mountain ridge separated them from Romania. To cross the frontier was a matter only of a few hours' trudge across deserted rocky tracks. After that a few more hours' walk through gently sloping woods led to Sinaia ... just a few hours' walk, that was all. Balint was wondering if he was just imagining things, that it was all nonsense. After all, had not old Timisan said, 'We have a little meeting there on parish matters!'

On reaching Udvarhely Balint dined early, as it was still some way to Segesvar, but when he had finished his meal he found that the last train had already left and that he would have to find another hired carriage. This was not easy as the best were still at Homorod but eventually the innkeeper rounded up a rickety old fiacre with two tired-looking nags in the traces. Despite Balint's misgivings the young driver confidently swore that he would soon get the gentleman to wherever he wished to go.

The carriage passed through country quite unknown to Abady, for he had come to Udvarhely by train and what one could see from the train windows seemed quite different when looked at from a slow carriage.

They had been travelling for about an hour and a half, and it was already quite dark, when one of the horses which had been limping for some time now became too lame to go on. By a lucky chance they appeared to be close to a village so Balint walked ahead until he found a post to which was nailed a rough signpost with the village name. After lighting several matches he found it was Kis-Keresztur, where, he recalled there lived his distant cousin, old Sandor Kendy, known to everyone as Crookface, and whose white-columned manor house he had glimpsed through the now leafless lime trees as he had passed by in the train. The house must be at the other end of the village, he thought, so he went back to the coachman who was vainly prodding the lame horse's hoof and shaking his head hopelessly.

'Well,' said Balint. 'What's the matter?'

'The Devil knows,' said the young Szekler driver.

Abady took a look himself; the whole underside of the hoof was inflamed, the frog untrimmed and badly overgrown. 'We won't get anywhere with this one,' he said, and when the driver continued to shake his head, he went on, 'You'll have to get the shoe removed at the nearest smithy and put a compress on it as soon as possible.' Balint knew about such matters as he had been well taught by his mother and the grooms at Denestornya.

'I have nowhere to tie him up,' said the youth sulkily. Balint had quickly to make up his mind. The obvious thing was somehow to reach the Kendy house, yet for some reason he was reluctant to try this. It was well-known that the gruff old man was not inclined to be hospitable and never asked anyone to come to his house in the country. Also to arrive at this late hour would be awkward, especially as Balint had never met Crookface's wife.

Some ten years before, when Sandor Kendy was already well advanced in age, he had suddenly and unexpectedly found a wife in Sepsis-Szentgyorgy. She had been a stenographer, or something of the sort, the daughter of an employee in the tax office and was called Alice Folbert. Crookface had never taken her anywhere with him, never introduced her even to his closest relations, but had brought her home at once to Kis-Keresztur and kept her there ever since. All this was strange enough, especially as rumour had it that Alice Folbert had been quite deaf when Crookface had married her. Apart from this the gossips had been unable to find out anything more about her and soon, as no one ever saw her since she never left her husband's country house and as he led the life of a bachelor in town, she was soon as forgotten as if she had never existed.

The coachman walked the carriage slowly through the village and then down a road on one side of which was a wooden paling set between stone pillars. Eventually they reached an open gate open because in those days life in the country was so secure that a closed gate signified either unfriendliness or else that the owners were away from home. A short avenue of lime trees led to the stone-columned portico of the house.

Balint got down and stepped into the dimly-lit entrance-hall. From above he could hear the sound of a piano. Someone was playing a nocturne by Chopin, accentuated perhaps with rather too much emotion but brilliantly executed all the same. How amazing, thought Balint, that the deaf lady should be a musician. It did not occur to him that anyone else in the house could be playing.

A footman appeared now from somewhere. Abady explained who he was and was at once led through the large entrance-hall that divided the house in two halves and up a wide staircase at the far end.

At the top of the stairs he found himself in a corridor that was closed on the hall side by a glass partition that had been

constructed so that people could go from one side of the house
to the other without entering the hall. This corridor was in darkness, but from where he stood the brightly-lit drawing-room
could clearly be seen through double glass doors. The walls were
white and on them was hung just one large portrait. The furniture was of stiff dark ebony upholstered in blue and white striped
chintz, of a style much favoured in Transylvania at the beginning of the nineteenth century. On a large round table in the
centre of the room stood a lamp and by its light the young Countess Kendy was busy working at her tapestry-frame. Close to the
tall dark windows, seated before a giant grand piano, was old
Crookface. It was he who was playing.

Balint caught his breath, so taken by surprise was he that it
should be the coarse-spoken, rough-mannered, hard-eyed old
roué who was playing Chopin with such delicacy. Balint felt that
he had been vouchsafed a glimpse of some forbidden secret, for
he was sure that no one else could know that the much-feared
old man would pass his evenings in playing sentimental ballads
and nocturnes.

And yet there he was, his powerful torso motionless, his bald
head a faint gleam in the semi-darkness, his hooked eagle's nose
barely visible. He was looking straight ahead, into nothingness,
the notes singing under the light touch of his fingers, and it was
as if he himself were a thousand miles away. He must have played
these melancholy tunes a hundred times; and he played only for
himself, for his wife was stone-deaf and could hear nothing. Just
for himself; this sweet old-fashioned music, the music of his
youth, played by memory at the dark end of a vast but sparsely-
furnished room.

Balint touched the footman's arm. 'We'll wait until Count
Sandor finishes,' he murmured.

When Crookface had played a couple of preludes he got up
and walked with a heavy tread towards where his wife was sitting.

Balint and the footman now came in as if they had just arrived.
Kendy turned towards them in welcome.

'Where the Devil have you sprung from at this time of night?'
he cried, and gave a big good-humoured laugh with his lop-sided
mouth. Then he turned to his wife, smoothed his moustaches
upwards, and, making no sound but merely mouthing the words,
said, 'This is my cousin, Balint Abady!'

Countess Kendy rose dutifully and shook hands with the

visitor. There was something essentially humble in her manner. It was as if she were not in her own house, indeed as if she were not even the wife of the noble Count Kendy but was still no more than a little typist. Very softly, in the hardly perceptible whisper of the deaf who have no means of judging how loudly they speak, she murmured, 'Welcome, I'm sure. So pleased!' Her face was lit by a serene smile.

It was a beautiful face, interesting and pale-complexioned, with full red lips and grey eyes that were fringed with thick dark lashes. Her black eyebrows nearly met over the bridge of her nose and this gave her glance an unusual and mysterious look, as if she were peering at one from a great distance. Her hair was light-brown in colour, wavy and very thick, with two great tresses wreathing her head in the same manner as one saw in portraits of the beautiful Queen-Empress Elisabeth.

She looked at her husband with the unspoken question as to whether she was doing right and then, with a slow, solemn, almost lazy movement, gestured Balint towards an armchair beside her.

He sat down. He told how it was that he came to be there, how he had been making for Segesvar so as to catch the express train home and how the carriage-horse had fallen lame just as they reached the outskirts of the village. Crookface interrupted him once or twice with brief questions: Where was the carriage now? Was the horse being cared for? Had Balint dined on the road? Then he rang for the footman and gave orders for Balint's coachman and his horses to be properly looked after. When this was done he turned once more towards his wife, again brushed back his moustaches and mouthed something silently to her. Immediately she rose and started to leave the room. Balint involuntarily watched her as she went. She had a beautiful walk, like that of oriental dancers, whose hips and shoulders swayed to an individual rhythm, a rhythm that ought to be accompanied by slow syncopated music. Like a mirage she disappeared silently through the doorway.

She did not return, but in a few moments servants brought in two more lamps, a small table and a cold supper. Balint ate ravenously, for his dinner at Udvarhely seemed a long time ago.

Crookface asked about the meeting at Homorod and Balint told him what he could, but the conversation dragged as the host was a silent man by nature who normally only let drop the occasional four-letter obscenity from the corner of his mouth and the rest of the time merely sat puffing at his cigar.

As he was eating Abady looked up at the large picture on the wall in front of him. Only now did he begin to notice it and realize that it must be a portrait of his host's young wife. It had the same figure, not tall but well-proportioned, and the same face. There were the mysterious grey eyes in their frame of black lashes, the same eyebrows, the same lustrous hair wound round the head in the double crown made famous by the wayward Empress. Only one thing was different, startlingly different. The dress in which she had been depicted was nothing like that of today, or even of the recent past, but was in the style of the seventies, with long narrow sleeves, plunging décolleté and a bell-shaped skirt decorated all over with different coloured little ruffles and bunches of artificial flowers in the rich confusion of the fashion of those days. It was beautiful and harmonious, but strange.

'What a wonderful portrait!' cried Balint enthusiastically. 'And what a superb likeness!'

Crookface did not answer, but merely puffed more smoke from his cigar.

'Who is it by? I never saw such exquisite work,' he went on, looking at his host.

'Oh, some Frenchman or other,' he murmured.

'But what an interesting dress! I suppose the Countess had it for some costume ball?'

The old man sat back, but he said nothing. Balint got up to look at the picture more closely. Standing slightly to one side he noticed that the lamplight revealed a long scar across the picture all the way from the right shoulder down to the left hip where the carefully concealed blemish was hidden in a cluster of little painted nosegays. There had obviously been a most skilful repair, probably from behind the canvas, but the long rip was still just visible. Balint was about to ask his host about this, but something held him back. He knew that Crookface would not take kindly to cross-questioning – indeed no one ever dared ask him anything – and so he held his tongue, sat down again and just went on staring at the picture.

There was something else mysterious about that painted face, Balint thought, noticing now what a sensuous mouth the lady had, something he had not really remarked when she had been in the room.

* * *

For some time neither of them spoke: both were looking at the picture on the wall in front of them. Then suddenly old Crook-face said, 'How is Laszlo Gyeroffy?'

Abady was amazed. Whatever could be the connection, he wondered? Why, out of the blue, should the old man suddenly mention Laszlo?

Of course there was a connection, and a most intimate one, though Balint could hardly be expected to know what it was. The portrait was not of Crookface's wife, but of Julie Ladossa, Laszlo's mother. Her portrait had been painted in Paris by the celebrated Cabanel, then the most fashionable of contemporary portraitists. For barely a year it had hung in the hastily arranged temporary drawing-room, upstairs at Szamos-Kozard, where cobwebs and a rusty nail still showed where it had been placed. It was the picture at which Laszlo's father had struck and then thrown away in his rage and grief at his wife's desertion . . . and that was why it had that terrible tear from shoulder to hip.

How it had found its way to Sandor Kendy's was never revealed. It was a mystery to which nobody but he knew the answer. Was it mere chance, or was there a history of secret searches and even more secret deals? Was the torn masterpiece rescued by the local store-owner, only to be sold, discreetly, later? No one knew.

There were many other secrets tied to this picture too; old passions, yearning desires, misunderstandings, the conflicts of pride and disappointment, and, above all, the gnawing regret for what ought to have been but never was.

Many years after the scandal of Countess Gyeroffy's flight and her husband's death in the woods Sandor Kendy had had some business with a lawyer at Haromszek. There he met the lawyer's niece, Alice Folbert, who was the living double of Julie Ladossa. When Crookface saw the young Alice it was as if he met again the woman he had loved twenty years before. He did not mind that the girl was already extremely deaf and was likely to become even more so; indeed, it was rather an encouragement for him, for it made the girl seem all the more impersonal. She did not need, or want, to be spoken to. Indeed it was neither necessary or possible. All he had to do was to watch her, to gaze and wonder, and observe how she held herself, how she walked, how she moved her shoulders, how she bent over her needlework, how she looked and how she smiled, always without a word. She was there, and yet she wasn't. She was a symbol, a dream, a ghost; and yet she was flesh and blood and real and he could play for her the old tunes which he never could for the other one – and never, never, could she destroy the illusion by some unfortunate remark which would shatter the spell.

As for that other one, the proud, faithless, uncompromising one, to whom he had so longed to play Chopin during those long winter evenings, had she ever seen, or glimpsed, the delicate mimosa soul behind the rough armour of his reserve?

For the rest of the world Sandor Kendy was a hard, hard man who might have been hewn from rock.

'Laszlo Gyeroffy?' answered Balint at last. 'The poor fellow is in a bad way. It seems that he's granted a lease on his properties in return for ten years' rent in advance, though maybe he still gets some paltry little sum each month. But I've heard that many of his old debts have never been settled and so he's gradually being sold up and now, apparently, what he's still got is to be auctioned. The trouble is that he's drinking and doesn't care a damn what happens to him.'

Crookface said nothing for a moment; he was still looking at the picture. Finally he said, 'What an idiot! And no one can make him see reason?'

'He won't listen to anyone. I've tried, several times, in vain. And he's avoided me ever since. It's a sort of suicide, what he's doing to himself. His only hope is to be made a ward of court. That might save him, but there's no one to do what's necessary as he doesn't have any parents or brothers; and no one else has the right to act.'

'Bloody fool!' said Crookface, and fell silent again. After a little while he got up and said, 'Time for bed. It's late. You'll have to get up early to catch the morning train. I've ordered the car for six. That'll get you to Hejjasfalva in time to catch the express.'

Old Kendy showed Balint to a guest-room which was near the drawing-room just beyond the corridor. There he said goodbye, turned away and left quickly. There was no question of continuing their conversation.

Balint found it difficult to sleep. On the other side of the wall of his room he could hear heavy footsteps walking to and fro, resounding in the empty space of the great drawing-room: it was old Kendy, cigar in mouth, pacing up and down the room from the glass doors to the windows and back, again and again.

CHAPTER FOUR

EIGHT PAIRS OF perfectly matched Lipizzaners trotted down the arrow-straight country road.

They were splendid horses, all dapple greys which could have been cast from the same mould, the only difference being that the older ones were slightly lighter in hue and the younger darker with more pronounced shading. They all had the same prancing movement, with their forelegs bending up well in front of them. This, of course, they had been trained to do, not for speed but for beauty and elegance and in fact their progress was comparatively slow. The eight carriages they drew were also identical, painted black with yellow roofs and upper-work. The coachmen wore grey livery and black top hats and they were all of similar build, broad-shouldered and clean-shaven. They too kept perfect rhythm and the fifteen-metre distance between each carriage was never varied. Inside each carriage there was one male guest, who was one of the guns invited to the shoot, and in several there were also some ladies. And so, in stately procession, they passed along the acacia-lined country road. When one of the carriages reached its destination – which was marked by a bale of straw whose prominently displayed number corresponded to that accorded to the guest in the carriage, and where that guest's loader, cartridge carrier and game collector were already waiting – then it pulled aside and stopped and allowed the other carriages to go on their way.

A great hare shoot was about to begin, and it needed over three hundred people to be properly organized.

Where the carriages stopped was the start. Between each gun, well spaced out, were six or seven peasant youths. The main band of beaters were nearly out of sight, divided into two halves, those on the left flank being nearly a mile apart from those on the right. These were mostly made up of girls who were more disciplined than young men and did not jump about so much but who remained well in line, their full skirts spread wide, crouching close to each other so that none of the hares should pass between them. From where the guns were placed for the start their multi-coloured blouses and head-scarves looked like an endless row of field poppies disappearing into the distance.

All the beaters were Slovaks, for the shoot was taking place at Jablanka in Slovakia, a country estate belonging to Antal Szent-Gyorgyi, which was situated just where the valley of the Vag opens out onto the Lesser Alfold, the northern part of the Great Hungarian Plain. The landscape shone in the wintry sun. In the east could be seen the peaks of the smaller Carpathians while to the west the Tapolcsany range closed the great horseshoe-shaped ring of mountains to the north of the plains which stretched away endlessly to the south. In the centre of the horseshoe there was a row of gently undulating hills and there, right in the middle, was the snow-white square of the great castle of Jablanka, its windows, though more than a mile away, shimmering in the sunshine. Far behind, on a jutting outcrop of rock, the ruined fortress of Jablo was silhouetted against the shadowy outlines of the far-off Trencsen mountains.

The shoot had been arranged so that the guns advanced towards the castle, finishing just at the edge of the park, where the two long lines of standing beaters converged. This was carefully thought out because the host was anxious not to over-tire either himself or those who had had the honour of an invitation to shoot with him. Unlike his brother-in-law, Louis Kollonich, whose ambition it always was to set up record bags, Antal Szent-Gyorgyi merely sought elegance and style. For him a shoot should be a pleasure, not a competitive chore. It should not start too early; and it should not last too long. The guests invited to shoot should have room to shoot as they pleased – which is why they were placed so far apart. It was for this reason that he never had more than eight guns and he only invited enough guests to make up this number. As both his sons were at home only five others had been asked this year. It was considered a great honour to be invited to shoot at Jablanka, and all the more so because Antal Szent-Gyorgyi was known to be extremely choosy as to whom he might ask. Apart from his own relations hardly anyone was held worthy of an invitation. Count Antal's group of accept-able guests was like the very smallest of concentric circles, like the monarch's own chosen group of shooting friends whose composition was forever frozen in immutable categories of which only the innermost could ever hope for an invitation. As in Dante's Purgatory the ever-rising floors finally dwindle into the narrowest, uppermost circle and there, right at the top, the peak of the whole envied structure, was Paradise.

Szent-Gyorgyi's reasons for exclusion, starting from the outer rings, were quite clear. Ruled completely out were the bad shots; these were utterly unacceptable. Next were the bad-mannered, people who were known to be querulous or irritable or bad-tempered if they missed a shot: they were not to be thought of either. These were followed by anyone with decided political opinions, for Szent-Gyorgyi loathed politics – and politicians – and though such subjects were by no means banned in his presence, and indeed he would from time to time speak of such matters himself, they had to be discussed dispassionately as if the speaker were infinitely distanced from his subject. The fourth criterion was birth and here Count Antal had his own special individual standpoint. With a rich knowledge of history and genealogies, he was capable, if he thought their ancestry ignoble or unworthy, of placing ruling princes and families closely connected to royalty, in a lower category than some simple country nobleman whose ancestors had been 'nice people' since time immemorial. For Count Antal, anyone who was able to trace his descent from the days of the Arpad kings, especially if they had earned no black marks by unfortunate behaviour in the ensuing centuries, took precedence over all others, provided always that they fulfilled his other requirements. A fifth category, which was totally excluded, was composed of anyone of Czech origin no matter what rank he might hold. Whether it was because in the fifteenth century the lands of the Szent-Gyorgyi and Bazini families had been overrun by the army of Giskra, or because he believed that anyone even remotely connected with the ever growing pan-Slav movement had to be pro-Russian and was therefore automatically the enemy of the Habsburg monarchy, was not clear: but all Czechs were automatically banned from Jablanka. For the sixth group, which was composed of anyone who had had any kind of connection with the Heir, the Archduke Franz-Ferdinand, he had more personal reasons for antagonism. As hereditary Master of the Horse to the King of Hungary, Szent-Gyorgyi gave his entire loyalty to the old Emperor and he classed all those who grouped themselves around the person of the Heir (and who were clearly only waiting for the demise of the old monarch to be shown in their true colours) as greedy, unacceptable opportunists. The seventh category, those who were eligible for invitations, therefore had to pass unscathed the severe requirements of the first six.

This year, however, there were some surprises as there had been included two guests who would never normally have qualified at all.

The first was Fredi Wuelffenstein, who was not important but who was well-known to be a party man, ferociously partisan, loud-mouthed, outspoken, argumentative and always knowing better than anyone else. It was hoped that here at Jablanka he would be sufficiently in control of himself to keep quiet, especially as he owed his invitation solely to the influence of his sister, Fanny Beredy, the only female guest who was not herself a relation of the host or hostess.

More important than Fredi was Count Jan Slawata, whose presence was indeed astonishing for according to the rules he should have foundered on all counts; firstly at the outermost circle because he was such a bad shot, secondly because he was a politician, thirdly because one of his ancestors, in 1618, who had never drawn his sword to defend himself, was flung out of a window in the fortress of Hradčany in Prague and, instead of being killed honourably on the flagstones below, landed on a dungheap and lived (thereby falling inevitably into the category of 'unacceptable behaviour'), fourthly because he was a self-declared Czech nationalist which he proclaimed by signing his name 'Jan' instead of 'Johann'; and finally because it was well-known that he belonged to the group who clustered round Franz-Ferdinand in the Belvedere Palace and indeed was rumoured to be the Heir's confidential adviser on foreign affairs. And yet he had been admitted to Eden, to that Paradise of sportsmen, a shooting party at Jablanka.

It was such an amazing thing that even such a self-assured man as Antal Szent-Gyorgyi felt impelled to offer some explanation to the other guests – Balint, Imre Warday and even to his nephew, young Louis Kollonich – as to why Slawata had been invited.

Szent-Gyorgyi had ordered a pedigree pointer puppy from Germany. The dog had been sent in a specially constructed cage by the Orient Express but at the frontier post at Passau the customs officers found some reason to object to the animal's importation into Austria and wished to take it off the train until some obscure difficulty as to its legal status could be cleared up. As it happened Slawata was on the same train, learned what was causing the delay, and used his diplomatic position not only to keep the dog on the train but also to free it from its prison cage and take it into his own private compartment (though it wasn't yet house-trained). Such a personal service had to be properly rewarded.

It was one of Antal Szent-Gyorgyi's guiding principles that he would never accept a favour, except from a close personal friend, without returning it in full measure. And if the donor was a stranger, or someone socially inferior, then the recompense must be all the more generous lest there be the slightest suspicion that Count Antal remained in their debt. Since it was not possible to offer Slawata a tip he had been invited to the shoot. Szent-Gyorgyi would far rather have paid out any amount of mere money!

However, having once decided to do it, it was done in style. Slawata was treated as the guest of honour and given the best position, at one of the ends of the line, for it was one of the peculiarities of hares that they would run along the line of the beaters, out of range of the guns until they reached the end of the line where they would come straight towards the last gun. This place was therefore the most sought-after for here there was always more game to shoot. Slawata was known to be a weak shot and so young Louis Kollonich, who was very good indeed, had been posted next to him as *Eckhalter* – or corner guard – with strict instructions to 'help' the guest of honour by shooting first at anything that came that way.

'Don't let anything past!' called the host to his nephew as he passed by in his carriage and winked at him from an otherwise expressionless face. Then he drove on past his son Toni to his place at Number Four. Countess Beredy, who had been sitting beside him in the carriage, started to get down when he did but Count Antal, speaking in English, called back to her, 'No! No! You go on!' and gestured to the coachman to continue. Fanny smiled back indulgently. Many months after Laszlo Gyeroffy had left her she had started an affair with Antal Szent-Gyorgyi. For Fanny this was an innovation since hitherto her lovers had all been young men. However, after the shock of her desertion by Laszlo, who was the only one she had truly loved, she did not feel like starting a new relationship with anyone else young and unreliable. The few words that Laszlo had sent her – 'Thank you for everything . . .' – just that, scribbled on the back of a visiting card – still made her heart contract with pain each time she thought of them; and it was for this reason that she had finally responded to the silent courtship of this man of fifty. Szent-Gyorgyi was tall and elegant, like a well-bred greyhound, a man of the world who would hold no surprises for her. She needed someone in her life – for she and her husband had led separate lives for a long time – and she had been almost a year without anyone when she decided to accept Szent-Gyorgyi as her lover. It was a calm relationship which brought both of them solace and joy with none of the pangs and complications of a passion. Count Antal was a careful man, for he still lived in friendly companionship with his ageing wife Elise; and for both of them caution was necessary, not the least for Fanny since she knew only too well that 'my lord Beredy' – as she ironically called him whenever she happened to think of him – would be only too happy to throw her out and divorce her if she gave him the opportunity. He had made this perfectly clear to her many years before, and ever since she had been very, very careful. Only with Laszlo had she taken any risks, but then she had been a little light-hearted . . .

'At least with this one I won't have to worry about causing any scandal!' she thought, and smiled to herself.

This was the third day of Fanny's visit to Jablanka. When she had first arrived she had thought that she had been asked so that her host would be able to come to her at night. This would have been easy and agreeable and such a pleasure to be able to make love freely and at leisure instead of going through all that performance of stolen meetings, dressing and undressing and watching the clock in the little *garçonnière* in Budapest! But it was not to be. She was mistaken. On the first night he did not come, nor on the second, and when she had asked him why, he had replied that it was too dangerous, someone might see him . . . the servants . . . the risk . . . ! Who knows what might not happen? 'No! No! It's no good, not here!' he had said in English, whereupon Fanny had decided to become better acquainted with the lie of the land. She started to make a tour of the vast house. If anyone had asked her what she was doing she was going to say that she was looking for her maid.

The castle of Jablanka had been built round a huge sym-metrical square courtyard on all four sides of which was a two-storeyed vaulted gallery off which opened all the rooms as in old monasteries. And this, indeed, is what it had once been. The Szent-Gyorgyi family, who then still lived in the now ruined fortress on the crags above, had had it built for the Pauline monks in the first years of the eighteenth century. In 1780, when the order was dissolved, the Emperor Joseph gave the building back to its original founders as they were considered *gut gesinnt* – well disposed – to the Habsburgs, of course. It was at this time the ancestors of Count Antal decided that the vast monastery would make better living quarters than the mediæval fortress and moved in. The monks' oratory, now the castle chapel, was situated on the first floor directly opposite the main entrance and to this day the wings on each side were known as 'on the right of the chapel' or 'on the left of the chapel'. The reception rooms were all on the first floor on the front of the building, looking south over the plain. The exterior of the great house had been left exactly as it had always been, austere and plainly whitewashed. Inside a few smaller cells had been joined together to make larger rooms and the corridors had been lavishly decorated with the heads of roe-buck and other game.

Fanny started off from her room which was the furthest from the chapel in the left-hand wing. The next door led to her bath-room and after that there was a little staircase. Then followed door after door, each carved from precious woods, inlaid with the sort of elaborate motifs beloved of ecclesiastics. On each door was a little brass frame holding a card with the name of the guest to whom the room had been allocated. After two that were empty Fanny found that the third bore her brother's name, Wuelffenstein, and after that Abady. Round the corner the first name was Warday's and then Slawata. After this there was a double stair and at its head the monumental doorway which led to the chapel, then more doors which opened on the Szent-Gyorgyi boys' rooms and that of the young Louis Kollonich. Round the next corner the rooms were family apartments – this was the 'right of the chapel' side and finally, with windows that must be on the eastern façade of the building, to Countess Szent-Gyorgyi's own apartments.

Fanny did not go as far as this but turned back.

As she did so she noticed Klara Kollonich's name on one of

the doors. So she did not share a room with her husband, thought Fanny, who wondered for a moment until she remembered that Klara was in the last stages of her pregnancy and that she had heard her hostess say that they would put her in her old room so as to be where her aunts and cousins could look after her properly. Nothing very interesting here! thought Fanny and she went back to where she had started and descended the small stair near her room. Here too was a wide corridor hung with antlers and other game trophies, hundreds of them clustered on the whitewashed walls.

Fanny walked slowly and cautiously along towards the main staircase, cautiously because she had heard that Count Antal's smoking-room was to be found somewhere there. She did not have to go far. The second door was open and she saw at once that this was the host's bedroom. On the vast bed several different sets of shooting clothes had been laid out for the count to choose from, and his valet was now busy putting them back on their hangers. Luckily he was standing with his back to the door and so did not see her looking in. As the second door was the bedroom Fanny at once assumed that the first was probably that of the adjoining bathroom, as on the floor above. Therefore if Szent-Gyorgyi wanted to come up to her all he had to do was to slip out of his rooms and up the little stair beside them; and it would be the same if he wanted her to come to him. No one would be likely to notice them. Why! she thought. Nothing would be easier! All she had to do was to be careful while in the corridor for no one could possibly catch sight of her on the little stairway which had walls on both sides. She decided that as soon as she saw him she would suggest coming down that night. That would certainly be the best. Perhaps Antal was afraid of catching cold in the corridors – men were so delicate! – and that perhaps had been why he had not come to her. Fanny's mouth widened in a knowing smile.

The carriage in which Fanny was riding passed Wuelffenstein's place and arrived next at the place allotted to the elder Szent-Gyorgyi boy, Stefi. Here she told the coachman to stop, for further on there were only Imre Warday and Magda, the daughter of the house, and finally, at the corner stand, there was Balint Abady.

Also there was another young girl, Lili Illesvary, a young niece of Count Antal who was barely out of the schoolroom. Just turned seventeen, Lili was still chubby with a rounded face and a teenager's rather plump arms. She was also shy and timid, unsure of herself, as if she knew that she was like a picture that was almost finished but still needed the finishing touches. Her femininity was still a little uncertain. But that she would soon be a beauty no one who saw her could doubt. Her eyes were exceptionally large and azure-blue in colour, and the line of her mouth and profile was as finely etched as in a Greek cameo, though the determined chin inherited from her Szent-Gyorgyi grandmother was still partly hidden by baby fat.

Lili had wanted to stay with her cousin at Warday's stand but they had made her go on to Abady who was alone in the corner. 'It's a bore to be too many!' Magda had said. 'Go on to the last gun. The ground will be better there too, the beaters will have trodden down a proper path.' Lili had done as she was told.

'Can I stay here, with you?' she asked timidly when she came up to Balint and just smiled shyly when Balint greeted her in a friendly manner, her eyes opening even wider with astonishment at finding herself accepted so naturally in the great grown-up world she was now entering for the first time. Her companion thought: what sweet fresh youthfulness!

At this moment the horns sounded. First at one end of the line of beaters and then at the other and then – in the distance from the invisible ends of the two flanks – came the cry: '*Vorwä-ä-ärts* – forward march! Advance!'

The shoot began. In front of Balint lines of peasant girls, led by Szent-Gyorgyi huntsmen carrying a gun, stamped their feet in a regular rhythm. Behind him was his loader, a man carrying his cartridge-case, and four men with long poles, whose job it was to collect what Balint had shot. On each side of him were the male beaters who were given a stream of orders from the estate's mounted foresters. '*Pomali! Rovno!* – Slowly now! Straight ahead!', while some distance away the country lanes were filled with a rearguard of farm wagons to carry the day's bag drawn by enormous *Pinzgau* horses like a baggage train following an army.

And suddenly there were hares everywhere. Some were small, the colour of lightly baked buns, not at all like the hares of Transylvania which gave such sport to the mounted huntsmen at Zsuk. Only city-dwellers think of hares as all being alike. Quite different from the long-legged mountain hares, those of the plain came in all sizes, great and small, and they behaved differently too, from one district to another. In the great plain they ran powerfully before the line of beaters, invisible to the guns for nearly an hour, so that it was only at the end of the drive that they all swarmed together in a rush to escape. Here in the valley of the Vag, on the other hand, they rushed about in front of the advancing beaters and all the guns sounded off from the first steps of the drive.

There always seemed to be at least two or three, and often five or six hares running wildly about no more than a hundred metres in front of the guns. And a charming sight it was. On the beautifully tended fields of rape or young green corn the animals seemed to be dancing, kicking up their tails with every leap they made and sometimes sitting down and apparently gazing unconcerned at the fluttering line of the peasant girls' gaily coloured skirts, before again running forward through the furrows left by the plough. They always kept the same distance, only occasionally dashing further away when Stefi or Fredi shot at them from the centre of the advancing guns. The only times the little animals went at full speed was when they found themselves close to the openings at the end of the line and then they ran for their lives. A few there were that waited until the beaters were almost upon them and then, instead of racing forward they would double back and try their luck by darting swiftly through the line. Most of these were females and the order had been given to let them go, at least for the first half-hour. Even Wuelffenstein did not dare attempt a shot as he was walking next to his host. Some of the hares would run in a wide circle only to be shot as they approached the centre, but mostly they would run for the corners and so Abady, at the end of the line, and Warday next to him, were kept busy. Behind them the game collectors walked proudly two by two carrying long poles on their shoulders from which, like tassels, hung ten or fifteen dead hares.

Each huge square field was divided from the next by hedges planted with *gleditschia* trees – the honey-locust – in which openings had been left for the guns to pass through. As they did so each had to wait until they had been joined by the beaters who then reformed the line as the horns sounded and there came the order: '*Virovnajte clapci!* – Line up, lads!' Then the horns sounded again and they moved relentlessly on.

Balint and little Lili Illesvary had just passed through one of the hedges and entered a field of young clover when with a sudden strident whirring a dense cloud of partridges rose up and flew over them at high speed. They turned away to the left as the wind from the north made them fly at a great height towards the centre of the line.

'How beautiful they are!' exclaimed Lili as she gazed up at them.

It was an exceptionally large covey, and they flew straight towards Szent-Gyorgyi who always chose this place as it was here that the late winter partridges always came. With the speed of a hurricane they flew towards him. Four shots were heard, and four little specks, two in front of him and two behind, fell from the sky rolling along the ground from the force of their own velocity.

This happened several times and Abady, who was never more than an average shot himself, was so lost in admiration of his host's skill that more than one hare found its way safely past him.

As the long line of guns and beaters passed steadily from field to field through well-tended hedges or avenues of trees – occasionally passing neat little groups of farm buildings all surrounded, after the Austrian custom, by low stone walls – great herds of Electoral-Negretti sheep, which were reputed to produce the finest wool, stared stupidly up at them and then went on contentedly chewing the rich grass.

Until then the drive had been much like any other at a well-organized shoot. Now the picture began to change. Instead of the simple well-tended fields of a great agricultural complex, there began to appear clumps of fir trees, standing like islands in the wide paddocks, lines of tall Lombardy poplars on the banks of little streams, and thick plantations of oak at the edge of each meadow, all so cunningly planted that the game would run in the most diverse manner possible and the birds fly at even dizzier heights. And so it was: the hares stopped running predictably and darted unexpectedly in every direction, disappearing into thickets of undergrowth and vanishing from sight round the edge of each plantation; and the partridges and pheasants got up as if shot from catapults and rose high in the sky over the lines of the tall poplar trees only to take refuge once again in the next block of covert. Every shot was different and every hit a triumph.

A little further on, while at the corners there were still open fields, the six guns in the centre found themselves deep in a long and narrow wood where cock-pheasants rose in confusion, whirring back and forth in every direction, while on the ground hares and little wild rabbits darted about like lightning. The beaters put up a tremendous show, all shouting at once: *'Zayac! Zayac! Nalevo! Napravo!* – Hare! Hare! To the right! To the left!' and then: *'Kohut! Kohut!* – Cock here! Cock there!' The noise was tremendous as it seemed that all the guns were shooting at once. All this, however, was as nothing compared with the hub-bub a few minutes later when, after traversing another field of barley, the line entered a plantation which stretched right across the line of the shoot. Suddenly the cry was heard: *'Liska!* – Fox!'

It started on the right not far from Balint, firstly by the baritone voices of the male beaters and then taken up with a high shrill cry by the girls, hopeful and triumphant, joyful and at the same time surprised, for the Szent-Gyorgyi estates were so well patrolled and kept by the army of keepers and forest guards and carefully laid traps that to put up a fox seemed like a miracle.

It was not difficult to keep track of where the quarry ran for, shrewd and swift though he was, each time he was sighted, at the centre, to the left or to the right, everywhere he was followed by the cry of *'Liska! Liska!'* And the cries never let up until, as the guns were emerging from the densest part of the thick plantation, there came the sound of two shots in quick succession followed by a long-drawn-out shout of triumph of which all that could be distinguished was the long double vowel 'aa-aa' of the word *'spadla* – he's fallen', as the girls at the edge of the beat passed to the moving line the happy news that the fox, that enemy of every poultry-keeping peasant, was no more. When the line stepped out into the open, there, at the far left-hand corner, was one of Slawata's game carriers holding high his master's booty for all the world to see and admire.

Now they passed through a gently sloping and rather damp meadow in the centre of which there was a plantation of plane trees. Beyond this was a hillside covered in shrubs which marked the boundary of the Jablanka parkland. After barely fifty paces, when the party was only halfway towards the trees, the horns sounded to tell everyone that the official drive was now over and that the guns should stay where they were so that the two wings of girl-beaters could join up and drive any game that remained back towards the mile-wide line of guns. The head-keeper now galloped down the line, stopping his horse as he reached each invited guest, lifting his hat and saying politely: '*Belieben Euer Hochgeboren, hier auch Hennen zu schiessen* – If your Excellency pleases, here we will also shoot hens!'

Though said with the greatest respect, the phrase could perhaps a little later, with the knowledge of hindsight, have been taken as the gentlest of mockery, not because there were no hens to be shot but because all the birds, cocks and hens alike – and there were tremendous quantities of both – now flew so high and so fast that only the most skilful shot could bring them down at all.

Most of the birds started their flight from the top of the hill ahead. They took an arrow-straight line back to the woods from which the guns had just emerged, and they flew straight over the 100-foot-high plane trees. With dizzying speed, they streaked through the sky, only one or two darting through the highest branches or swerving diagonally with wings spread wide, hundreds of them, brown hens and green and reddish cocks, and with them some strange birds with tails more than a yard long, crosses between the Amherst and silver pheasants, with exotic crests, which Szent-Gyorgyi bred specially to add variety and colour to the game in his forests. In the bright sunshine they glittered in jewelled splendour.

On the floor of the meadow hares and rabbits were milling in untold numbers, falling over each other as they tried to jump the water-filled ditches which had cunningly been dug on each side of the trees. As they did so coveys of partridges rose and flew through the lower branches as fast as a hail of gunfire. All this had been carefully and masterfully planned so as to ensure that the last minutes of the day's shooting should be the best and also the most taxing. The wide spacing of the guns and the purpose-dug ditches were placed, as were the trees and shrubs, with knowing care, so that suddenly the sport was more difficult, required infinite skill, and was much, much more exciting.

Where the guns stood there raged an inferno. Nothing could be heard but the continuous rattle of gunfire and the shouts of the beaters: '*Kohut! Kohut!* – *Zayac! Kohut!*' while all the time the loaders frenziedly changed their masters' guns and the game collectors rushed in every direction to pick up the birds and beasts which died all around them. Sometimes a hit was made only by chance and then, in the sky, a few tail-feathers flew or a bird was winged and fluttered slowly to the earth. The two young Szent-Gyorgyis and Louis Kollonich were excellent shots who rarely missed their aim but now even they did not always hit their mark. And still, all around, could be heard the shouts of '*Nalevo zayac!* – Hare to the left!' and '*Napravo!* – Look to your right! – *Zelanka!* – Partridge!' and then, over and over again, '*Kohut! Kohut! Kohut!*'

Amongst them all only one man remained absolutely calm; it was Antal Szent-Gyorgyi. His tall figure seemed to move no faster as he took each of his three weapons in turn, fired twice, once in front of him and once behind – always killing cleanly with a shot in the head so that each bird fell dead to the ground with folded wings dropping in a gentle arc and propelled only by the velocity of its own flight – left and right, left and right, left and right! with unfailing precision. Count Antal's calm and uncanny skill were indeed imperial.

It was some time before the line of the girls in their multi-coloured skirts emerged from the shrub-covered hillside. At the end of the beat only hares were still running, plenty of them. These were males and had to be shot – just as at the beginning the females that had darted back through the line were spared – because the breed would suffer if too many were left alive.

When the sound of gunshot finally died away the guests' carriages were already lined up to take them back to the castle.

The beautiful dapple-grey horses moved slowly and rhythmically between the double rows of beaters who were lined up on each side of the road. All the young men now had long pheasant feathers stuck in their caps and, as Slawata's carriage passed by, they waved these hats in the air and cheered loudly, for was he not the Great Lord who had slain that wild beast the fox? It was possible that some there were who cheered him for other reasons; for while Louis Kollonich had been busy shooting hares for him in his remote place at the end of the line, Slawata too had been busy, busy talking politics with the beaters who accompanied him, if not in Slovak, their own tongue, at least in Czech. The anti-Hungarian movement, called Sokolist in Moravia where it was spreading fast, was beginning to take hold in North Nyitra, where Jablanka was situated, and here its partisans were clamouring to be heard.

Sitting back in his carriage, his eyes glittering behind the thick lenses of his spectacles, Slawata responded to the men's greetings with genuine satisfaction; and it was for more reasons than the killing of the fox. He was pleased at the thought of a day well spent. Often, as the drive had halted while it was being reformed, or if there had been some obstacle to be overcome before everyone lined up again before once more moving forward, or if someone had lagged behind, Slawata had found time to talk politics with some of the local men and, while not concealing his subversive ideas, what he had mostly discussed were the effects of the Rozsahegy case.

This had been a particularly disagreeable affair which had upset many people. Since the last elections to the Parliament in Budapest, during which for the first time there had been many candidates of Czecho-Slovak blood for this predominantly Czecho-Slovak province, there had been growing political unrest, resulting in that year alone in thirty-three prosecutions for sedition. Most of these had been, juridically speaking, justified. Politically, however, they had been disastrous, for their principal effect had been to create martyrs for the cause of the ethnic majority. The government's policy was far from clever for, though each condemned man spent a few months in a not uncomfortable state prison, everyone felt he had earned a martyr's crown on his release. The government, having once embarked on this campaign of repression, found itself hoist on its own petard, helpless in the face of an ever-growing political movement of opposition, fostered and encouraged from where no one knew.

It was when this impassioned situation was at its height that there occurred the uprising at Chernova.

A priest named Hlinka had been suspended by his bishop from the care of the parish of Rozsahegy and a local tribunal had found him guilty of making treasonable statements in public. Hlinka's birthplace was the neighbouring village of Chernova where he had built a church out of his own money. This he wanted to consecrate himself, but he now found himself forbidden by the bishop to do so, while other priests were sent to Rozsahegy to do this office for him. The people of Chernova were at once up in arms, hid the sacred vessels of their church and sent furious threatening letters to the bishop, whose chosen priests took fright and asked for an escort of gendarmes, even though the local sheriff had told them that this was not wise. What happened was that, when the priests arrived to consecrate the church, they and their escort were met with a hail of stones. The gendarmes, to defend themselves as well as the priests, opened fire. Nine men fell dead and many others were wounded, of which several died later. It was a sad, unnecessary and bloody affair.

Sad it certainly was, and nothing to smile about; but Slawata saw it in a different light. He knew only too well the secret links between this sort of commotion and the planning office of the Archduke Franz-Ferdinand, the so-called '*Werkstatt* – Workshop', as the followers of the Heir called it. This sort of thing was just what they wanted, the more trouble there was the better! And when the new ruler ascended the throne – and this must be soon now – he would spread joy everywhere by putting all such matters to rights, after his own fashion, of course. It was just as well that the Hungarian government had not intervened between the bishop and his parishioners, for this was just one more problem they must work out for themselves. So, as Slawata reclined comfortably against the cushions of his well-sprung carriage, which swung gently from side to side as it progressed in stately fashion along the winding road, he thought of the words of Goethe: '*Blut ist ein ganz besonder Saft* – Blood is a very strange liquid!', for Slawata was nothing if not well-read.

CHAPTER FIVE

IN THE LAST carriage were Countess Beredy and the host. Though the short journey to the castle only took just over a quarter of an hour there was plenty of time for Fanny to outline her plan. She spoke in English so that they would not be understood by the coachman.

She had made a survey, she explained. Using the little side-stair she would easily be able to come down to his room that night – no one would see her, for she would wait until everyone was already asleep – really, it was quite simple, she never caught cold anyway and of course she'd wear a well-lined kimono – it would be so amusing, far better than his coming to her – such fun and much more enjoyable too! So she chatted on, showing him every reason why it would really be so much better and of course she had quite understood, the previous night when he had not come to her, that he had been afraid of catching cold and didn't like to admit the real reason . . .

Count Antal's lean greyhound face never moved a muscle. He looked straight ahead, his expression oddly cold if not icy as he said, like her in English, 'Oh no! That would not do at all!' and he gave an almost imperceptible shake of the head.

'But why not?' she asked, astonished, and started once again to explain how she had looked carefully at the layout of the rooms and the corridor and the stairway just next to their bathrooms. It would only take a moment, and she'd be very, very careful.

'No!' he repeated. 'No!' and when Fanny, in an attempt to arouse his desire, told him how she had watched him at the end of the drive and had admired him so much that she had wanted to take him in her arms right then, he turned towards her with an unusually stern expression on his face and said, 'I wouldn't dream of doing such a thing! Here, in my own house, my wife's house. This is my home, this is not . . .' and he broke off leaving the word unspoken.

'No!' he said again. 'This is not the right place!' and perhaps to soften a little the effect of what he had just said he gave a little almost apologetic laugh: but his voice had lost none of its decisiveness when he added, 'I'm such a fool, you know. I have principles!'

The eyes of the beautiful Countess Beredy narrowed until only two long narrow slits could be seen, catlike, between her lashes. Then, her mouth a thin line too, she made an effort to chatter on as if nothing had occurred. 'Oh dear! What a charming fool you are!' she said in English; but inside she knew immediately that she would lose no time in finding a way to be avenged of that barely veiled insult.

When the carriages arrived at the castle they were driven one by one through the giant gateway and into the courtyard, drawing up at the foot of the great stair to discharge the guests and then turning and backing up to stand in line facing the entrance. They waited there until all the sixteen horses were standing in line apparently quite motionless except for the occasional soft rattle of a curb-chain. They remained like this for a few moments and then, one by one, starting on the left of the line, they moved slowly off, out through the gates and down the hill to the stables.

No one, alas, saw this elegant and precise manoeuvre which was performed with all the precision of clockwork. The guests hurried up the stairs to their rooms while the accompanying throng, loaders, game carriers, keepers and forest guards, all heavily laden, streamed away through doors at the rear of the courtyard which led to kitchens, game larders, gun-rooms and servants' living quarters.

The hostess and her widowed sister-in-law, Countess Illesvary, received the returning guests in a small corner room which was the only one of the castle's drawing-rooms to be furnished in a style later than that of the Empress Maria Theresa. While all the others were decorated in the delicate rococo popular in Vienna in the second half of the eighteenth century, this little room had been completely refurbished from Paris at the time of the Szent-Gyorgyis' marriage. It bore the unmistakable hallmarks of the Second Empire.

Every armchair and sofa was covered with a red repp material, as were the innumerable footstools, and each was bordered with heavily patterned black and red ribbon. The walls were covered in the same stuff and the same ribbon had been used as borders for the artificial panels.

On the walls were hung a multitude of family portraits in oils, most of them fairly recent in date and many representing Countess Szent-Gyorgyi's Transylvanian relations. There was a group of Abadys with her grandfather; there was Balint's dead father with her uncle, Balint's grandfather, Count Peter; Gyeroffys, her parents and their children including poor Mihaly, Laszlo's father, who killed himself; and a double portrait by Barabas of her sister Agnes, later Princess Kollonich, and herself as children. On the many velvet-covered little tables were placed miniatures on tiny stands and many, many photographs of her husband and children at various ages from their infancy to the present day. Everywhere, too, there were vases filled with flowers, and the floor was covered with a thick pile carpet.

Although the little salon was filled to overflowing with all these objects and heavily over-stuffed furniture, it was still warm and harmonious, as cosy and welcoming as a soft all-embracing down-filled nest.

This was where Countess Elise was always to be found, sitting between the windows, from which she was protected by two screens – for she was extremely sensitive to draughts and always caught cold at once if she sat in the other rooms. In autumn and winter she would only emerge at mealtimes or bedtime, returning immediately afterwards to her chosen place. Today she was sitting, not only with her sister-in-law but also with her niece, Klara Kollonich, wife to Imre Warday. Klara was in her sixth month of pregnancy which is why, instead of joining the shooting party, she had lunched quietly at home with her aunts.

As the other guests came in one by one they greeted their hostess, kissed the ladies' hands, made a few appreciative remarks about the morning's sport and then strolled through to the adjoining dining-room where they sat down informally at a large table laid with platters of cold meats and hot bread, decanters of sherry and pots of tea. This was a light meal designed just to tide over the guests' hunger because they had all had a huge, rather late breakfast before setting off for the shoot. After all the walking they had done that morning even this light meal was received with pleasure.

Szent-Gyorgyi alone stayed for some time in the little sitting-room with his wife, telling her in detail everything that had passed that morning, who had been placed where and what they had shot. They chatted together speaking, as well-matched couples do, in a sort of private language of their own that had been developed by years of intimacy and fondness and understanding.

'But you haven't told me what *you* shot? More than all the others, I'm sure?' she said, interrupting him, but smiling at the same time.

'Oh, no! I think that Balint on the right got more than I did.'

'Balint? Pheasants and partridges too? Come on, tell the truth, don't lie!'

'Ah well, perhaps not those; but then there are always more birds at the centre, you know,' and Szent-Gyorgyi gave a little laugh as if mocking his own modesty.

When at last the host went into the dining-room he only took a cup of tea which he started to drink still standing. Imre Warday came over to him and said, 'Would you allow me to look at your Jersey cows before it gets dark? I'm sure I could learn a lot from seeing how you look after them.'

'Of course! Naturally!' said his host and gave orders that some-one should telephone to the stables for a carriage and then to the dairy farm to expect a guest.

'Yesterday the sheep, the day before the Poland-China pigs! Proper little farmer you are!' called out young Louis Kollonich in careless mockery.

'And what's wrong with that?' answered Warday. 'It's quite natural, and nobody but a fool would miss an opportunity to look at the Jablanka farms. It's rare enough to get a chance to see model farming on this scale; it costs a fortune and few people can afford it.'

'Of course, that's true,' said his host, 'but, you know, it's abso-lutely vital. At the time of the great innovations of Szechenyi...' and here he started to talk in an impassioned manner unusual for the man who affected to despise all forms of enthusiasm, 'we started to import thoroughbreds from England, then we experi-mented with Rambouillet sheep and Simmenthal cattle. Now we must look further afield. All this is much easier on the big estates, easier even than for the State itself. Of course I find it a fascinating hobby as well as being...' Here he let the sentence trail off with an indefinite gesture of the hand for Antal Szent-Gyorgyi could not bring himself to pronounce the revealing word 'duty' and, besides, he found the phrase too pompous.

Countess Beredy looked across the table at Warday. She said nothing, but when he started to get up she too rose from her seat and said, 'I think I'll come with you!'

'Wouldn't you rather come with the rest of us to see the brood-mares?' asked Szent-Gyorgyi as he walked with her to the door.

'No! *I* would like to see something different!' said Fanny, smil-ing as she moved past him. Then, laughing softly, she added, 'And I did ride with you in the carriage this morning!' before gliding swiftly out of the room.

Szent-Gyorgyi shrugged his shoulders and turned back to the others.

The Jablanka breeding stables were a sight not to be missed. The buildings themselves were extraordinary and had been designed by Count Antal's grandfather who had had them built after a model he had seen in England.

They stood in the middle of a great meadow in the park. The

central building was higher than the others for it contained, on the ground floor, a large drawing-room furnished in Early Biedermeier style, with parquet floors and a wide-open fireplace. It was lit by long French windows and above was a vast hay loft. All around were blocks of ten loose-boxes, five and five back to back, each the size of a room, with enormous doors split in the middle so that the upper parts could be left open to let the brood-mares and their foals get enough air even in the worst of bad weather. From each block of boxes radiated white-painted pali-sades dividing the great meadow into segments which ended only at the edge of the surrounding woods. In some of these paddocks there grazed a single pedigree mare followed by her foal. These were the dams of famous racehorses, winners of great filly races.

Szent-Gyorgyi showed them round explaining exactly why everything was laid out as it was. As he did so Wuelffenstein knowingly interjected as many sporting phrases as he could, Balint and young Louis gazed at everything with admiration, Slawata pretended an interest he did not feel, and the two girls fondled the muzzles of those mares that were in their boxes and fed them sugar.

From there they went to the paddocks where the recently weaned colts had been placed, and then on to see the two famous stallions that Count Antal had brought from England.

It was a pity, thought Szent-Gyorgyi, that Fanny had not come to see all this. Though he never said so, he was especially proud of his thoroughbreds.

But the beautiful Fanny was far away, driving from farm to farm with Warday in an open carriage. She listened patiently to the explanations and reports of the farm overseers who were eager to show the visitors the milking charts, explain the chemical pro-cesses of butter-making, and outline the statistics of percentage yield and cost of transport. Everything produced here was, of course, sent to Vienna. Fanny kept quiet, standing, walking from place to place, turning, stopping again; and again walking on dutifully, always close to Warday, while from time to time she would nod in agreement as if she understood what was being talked about. And always she moved with that peculiar, indi-vidual walk, like a cat who placed one little paw directly in front of the other, lightly, in a single line.

It was already beginning to get dark when their carriage left the third farm and turned towards home. The evening sky was clear and beautiful but it was a trifle cold and this was perhaps the reason why the couple in the carriage sat so close together.

'Imre, tell me, are you happy?' Fanny broke the silence between them.

'Oh, yes!' he replied. 'I can say that, but it isn't such a great . . . I mean . . .' He paused and then went on, 'Well, that doesn't exist anyway. Klara is really very nice, and she's got some money of her own which comes in handy, and now we're having a baby. It's all wonderful, really.'

'I'm very happy to hear it,' said Countess Beredy. 'I knew this was the right thing for you to do, and that's why I made you do it. Remember?'

'Oh, yes! You threw me out at the right moment, just the right moment!' and he laughed good-humouredly.

Fanny turned to look at him. She opened her eyes slightly. They shone green in the evening light.

'Though it was so good with you I knew you ought to start a family, and . . . and Klara was just right, a good match. It wasn't easy for me to give you up, you know, a real sacrifice!' The lie came easily from her lips: she knew she would have sent him packing anyway as the love between Laszlo Gyeroffy and Klara had just gone inexorably wrong and so if Imre was out of the way she would at last have the chance to get Laszlo for herself.

'Sacrifice?' asked Warday, astonished. 'But, my darling, you told me . . . I remember the exact words, "you have to stop when you are still hungry". That's what you said, isn't it?'

'Yes; that's what I *said*,' agreed Fanny, but she did not pursue the question of sacrifice, but went on, 'and wasn't I right? But we, we still have our appetites, don't we? And if we wanted to . . .'

Warday looked up in startled surprise and pleasure. 'Do you really mean that? Really?' He looked down, straight into her eyes. Their faces nearly touched.

Fanny now opened her eyes wider than ever, the green flame shining ever brighter, filled with an appeal, a message, a command.

'I still ache for you as much as ever!'

A long kiss followed, a familiar, breathtaking, overpowering kiss that left them both panting when they drew apart. Neither spoke; only her hand searched for his under the fur rug that covered their knees, her fingers, at once so small and yet so strong, clutching at him. They still did not speak; but when the carriage reached the wide lawn before turning into the castle gates she looked up at him and murmured, 'When everyone's asleep. The door after the little stair; it's my bathroom, the first door!'

On one side of the castle's great quadrangle, between the chapel and one of the corner towers on the south side, two rooms had been thrown into one to make the dining-room; while on the other side was the library which led off Countess Elise's private sitting-room. Between them the vast old former refectory of the Pauline monks had been turned into the castle's principal drawing-room.

As was the custom when there were guests, everyone gathered in this drawing-room before dinner. Balint arrived early and, when he first entered the room, he fancied that he was alone. However he had barely crossed the threshold when from an arm-chair in the middle of the room opposite the fireplace, there got up a short plump elderly priest. Clean-shaven, well-groomed, pink and shining, he had very small piercing eyes set beneath bushy eyebrows. His rather short nose was thin and pointed. With his well-cut ecclesiastical dress he wore a wide red sash. He walked swiftly over to Balint and introduced himself. 'I am Father Czibulka,' he said with a slight Slovakian accent and, when in turn Balint had introduced himself, he went on, 'Ah, indeed! I have heard a great deal about your Lordship, especially about how you have been promoting co-operative ideas in Tran-sylvania. All that is very good, marvellous work!'

Balint was taken by surprise.

'Oh, I hear about all sorts of things,' the priest went on with a slight smile. 'I often come here to stay with your cousins. And when I am home at Nagyszombat I always come over to say mass on Sundays. I'm really part of the furniture, as I was once Count Antal's tutor. They call me "Pfaffulus" after the comic character. He gave me that name, impudent brat that he was! Didn't you ever hear of it? All the children here call me that; behind my back, of course, because only Count Antal has the right to say it to my face!' And he wagged his finger humorously at Balint.

'I've heard it, all right,' said Balint, laughing. 'And always with great affection.'

They chatted for a while, walking up and down the huge room in which, although there were any number of red and gold brocade-covered sofas and armchairs – and also a large concert grand piano and a quantity of potted palms – there was still plenty of room to move about. So large was it that despite all these furnishings there was still an air of emptiness in that huge room.

When they had exchanged a few sentences the priest looked about him as if to make sure that no one was there to overhear what he was about to say and then turned to Balint and asked, 'Please tell me. Do you have any news of your cousin, poor Laszlo Gyeroffy, the Countess's nephew?'

Abady started to tell the story of Laszlo's unpaid gambling debts which had led to his resignation from the Casino Club and exile from Budapest society, but Czibulka stopped him. 'Oh! I know all about that, perhaps a little more than you might guess. I was very worried about him the last time he was here. No! What I want to know – is how is he now? Has he been able to pull himself together? Has he found any consolation for his sorrows?' and, hardly waiting for Balint to reply, he went on, 'I feel so sorry for him and think of him often. Look at this,' and he paused, fished in the pocket of his soutane and brought out a tiny parcel wrapped in silk paper before going on, 'I brought this for him from Rome. It's a little medallion, blessed by the Holy Father. Do please give it to him. It may help the poor fellow. And tell him I pray for him. Of course,' he went on, 'this must be a secret between us! You understand, don't you?' And here he broke off because they could hear the door opening and footsteps approach from the direction of the library which was situated between the drawing-room and the dining-room.

'Pfaffulus!' called Antal Szent-Gyorgyi across the dinner table. 'I'm sure you've brought some secret plot with you from Nagyszombat. I can see your nose twitching from here!'

The priest felt his nose in pretended alarm.

'Oh, dear!' he said. 'What a dreadful give-away!' and he laughed. However he went on at once to relate what he had come to tell them.

It seemed that the neighbouring constituency of Szerencs was vacant and there was to be a by-election soon. Two-thirds of the people in the villages there were of Hungarian origin – and all of them fierce adherents of the radical separatist 1848 Party – while the remaining one third were Slovaks and rabid socialists to boot. The former member had been a constitutional-minded adherent of the Conservatives and he had only been elected because formerly all such 'elections' merely followed meekly what had been ordered by the ruling party in Budapest. Now the situation was different and it was rumoured that a really independent candidate would stand and that, if he did, since the Conservatives had no backing in the district, he was sure to get in.

'And that, I fancy,' murmured the little priest, 'might not be – er – entirely desirable, eh?' And he turned to his hostess with a gesture that seemed to be asking her opinion. Countess Elise merely smiled; she was not one to embroil herself in any argument, and certainly not a political one. Instead it was her sister-in-law, Countess Illesvary, who was sitting next to her brother and who loved nothing better than discussing politics, who replied, 'But that would be dreadful!'

'It could still happen! Especially if no socialist candidate presents himself and if the Constitutional Party doesn't withdraw! Even then it wouldn't be easy unless the clergy and all the white-collared employees banded together. And this could only come about if – how shall I put it? – the High Court of Jablanka was known to approve and support such a move.'

Now Wuelffenstein thought he should put his oar in, though moderating his usual vehemence as he knew Szent-Gyorgyi considered any sign of enthusiasm to be a breach of good manners. Even so his voice trembled with emotion as he said, 'It's really too much to ask this of us. Why, the Constitutional Party suffered enough last year when the district boundaries were redrawn; and what's more it's entirely against the movement towards party unity.'

The priest turned his well-shaven face in the direction of Fredi. Pfaffulus's antenna-like eyebrows were lightly raised as he took out the long-handled lorgnette, which was kept stuck between two buttons sewn to the red sash round his waist, looked hard at the young politician, and said, 'In my modest opinion, I feel that the voters' feelings must be allowed to count for something, don't you think?'

'As far as the voters are concerned, it doesn't really matter which party or coalition they vote for. We're all in the same camp and everyone's got more or less the same programme!' was Wuelffenstein's cynical reply.

'How right you are!' said Szent-Gyorgyi coldly. 'There's not a pin to choose between the lot of you!'

This was an acid reference to the mutually incompatible

policies which had recently led to the dissolution of the pact which had resulted in an uneasy alliance between the ruling 1867 Party and those who supported the complete independence of Hungary from Austria. Fredi, however, did not grasp the allusion.

'I'm glad you agree!' said Wuelffenstein, entirely missing the point and believing his host to be on his side. 'Neither Kossuth nor the People's Party should put forward a candidate. They've absolutely no right, no right at all! Why should we be forced to surrender a district? Never, as far as I'm concerned!'

'*En politique et en amour il n'y-a ni jamais ni toujours* – in politics as in love there is no never and no always!' quoted Countess Illesvary, laughing at Fredi's insistence.

'And what about the legal aspect? Could the law remain as it is?' asked Pfaffulus in a low sweet voice.

'Well, it's an old adage that a law respected will live on but a law ignored will soon die of its own accord.'

'And the union of our ruling parties? Can it survive no matter what happens? Will today's Coalition endure even when the franchise has been broadened? Even now, are the parties really united on, for example, the Croatian question? I can hardly believe that Andrassy agrees with the dismantling of the Unionist Party which is, after all, our only real support?'

Countess Elise also found any sort of wrangling or dispute bad manners; and for her it was particularly bad form to disagree about Hungarian politics in the presence of strangers. She therefore turned to the only stranger present, Count Slawata, and, so as to make everyone understand her meaning and speaking rather more loudly than usual and in German, she said, 'Do forgive us, Count, for this little discussion in Hungarian about domestic affairs which can't possibly interest you.'

The counsellor to the Foreign Ministry in Vienna turned to his hostess and, in his most diplomatic tones and smiling through his thick lenses, said, 'Oh, but I do understand a little Hungarian, you know, and what *Seine Hochwürden* – his Reverence – has just said is very true. It's all a great pity for the Croatian unionists who are, they say, the only party to be truly *Kaisertreu* – loyal to the Emperor – and they say . . .'

At this Szent-Gyorgyi intervened.

'*Königstreu!* – loyal to the King, if you please!' for in spite of his Viennese sympathies and personal devotion to Franz-Josef

himself, he would always strictly maintain the niceties of etiquette of the Dual Monarchy. Also he was not sorry to administer
a gentle rap on the knuckles of the secret envoy of the Belvedere
Palace.

'*Natürlich! Natürlich!* – Of course! Of course!' said Slawata with
a bow before continuing, 'Rumour has it that the Ban is seeking
new elections in Croatia too. That would be most aggravating,
and could end in untold disaster.'

The conversation continued for a while and the Croatian
situation was considered, in all its aspects, with many details, for
Szent-Gyorgyi owned a considerable property in Szeremseg
(which, of course, Pfaffulus knew) and the host was therefore
eager to hear what the well-informed priest could tell him.
However all of this was discussed in measured, somewhat subdued tones, following the ancient tradition by which the most
radical of opposing opinions could be expressed providing that
it was done with gravity and finesse.

Though Balint took no part in this conversation, for the Croatian problem was not one of his fields of interest, he still found
it useful to listen to what was being said. However his neighbour
at the table, young Magda, found the subject boring. With a
sudden little bird-like movement of her head she turned to
Abady and asked, 'Well, how many did you bag this morning,
in your corner?'

'I really don't know. I didn't count exactly. Perhaps a hundred
and fifty . . . or a hundred and sixty or so.'

'That's not very much! Last year we didn't have a real shoot as
we were all in mourning for my uncle, though Papa and the boys
used to go out whenever they could – just walking the fields,
you know; but the year before that the corner gun shot 237 hares
alone.'

'Who had that place? He must have been a better shot than
I am!'

'Oh!' she paused, embarrassed. 'I don't remember!'

'Nonsense!' said Balint. 'Whatever can you mean? You know
he shot 237 hares, but you don't know who did it?' He laughed.
'Come on, out with it! Who was it?'

Magda's voice was very low when she replied, and her manner
suddenly seemed oddly frightened.

'It was poor Laci, that's who it was . . .' and she lifted her finger to her lips and looked across at her father. 'Papa has forbidden us to talk about him. Even his name is never to be mentioned in the house ... but we're all so sorry for him!'

Coffee and liqueurs were served in the great drawing-room by an army of silent footmen.

The hostess only stayed in the room for a few moments. In spite of a roaring fire in the great open fireplace and two white porcelain stoves heating the far ends of the room, Countess Elise still fancied she was cold; and so, with Fanny Beredy and Klara, she quickly retired to her own cosy little sitting-room. When she had gone most of the men of the party, with Countess Illesvary, gathered round the fireplace in the centre of the room while Magda and Lili Illesvary, with Louis Kollonich and the two young sons of the house, sat down at a round table near one of the porcelain stoves and played a game with chips called 'Hoppity' that was fashionable that year.

Back in the centre of the room politics were once more being discussed. In the previous summer, in August, Edward VII, King of England, had visited the Emperor Franz-Josef at Ischl. Officially it was merely a visit of personal friendship with no political significance whatever. But rumour held otherwise. It maintained that it *was* a political visit and this view was strengthened by the fact that King Edward, as soon as he had returned to Marienbad where he was taking his annual cure, was visited by some other important international statesmen; first Clemenceau, and then the Russian minister Izvolsky. It was more than anyone was prepared to believe that these two gentlemen had come, just at that moment, merely to take the waters.

The Franco-Russian alliance had been in existence for some time. It was also a matter of common knowledge that the Belcassé pact – the *Entente Cordiale* – had been agreed between France and England three years before. This pact brought definite agreement between those two powers regarding their colonial differences in Africa; and even the friction that had grown at the time of the Boer War had gradually been worn down and the old friendly relationship re-established. The way that both powers handled the Moroccan situation had made this clear to the rest of the world. The French had been allowed a completely free hand there to do as they wished and, to everyone's surprise, they had been encouraged in this by Germany who hoped that adventures in Africa would tie down the French army for many years to come. In Berlin they forgot, or ignored the fact, that most Frenchmen had never forgiven Germany for their defeat in 1870 ... and never would.

But that summer had also brought an unexpected turn to international affairs.

After settling the African disputes Edward the Peacemaker had turned his attention to matters further east and further north. One Asian problem was quickly solved. The centuries-old rivalry between Russia and England had been brought effectively to an end when England, taking advantage of Russia's preoccupation with the Russo-Japanese War (which she had lost most ignominiously), achieved an impregnably strong influence over both Tibet and Afghanistan, which formerly had been real bones of contention between the two countries. The new-found accord between England and Russia was to be celebrated, it was announced, by an official visit of the King of England and the principal units of his enormous fleet to Reval in the following spring.

And having achieved all this King Edward turns up at Ischl just before having even more discussions with French and Russian leaders.

Any outsider might well be pardoned if he looked at the King of England's movements and then decided they could have had one purpose and one purpose only – the encirclement and isolation of Germany.

It was this that was being discussed in front of the fire at Jablanka; and in particular what had really taken place at Ischl.

Irma Szent-Gyorgyi, Countess Illesvary, sat in an armchair close to the fire. She was tall and thin, like her brother, and in her long fingers she held a medium-sized Havana cigar, which was then unusual for a woman. Countess Irma, however, again like her brother, held herself to be above criticism and so felt no compunction in braving public opinion. When she spoke of some facts of which she was certain she would underline the words with extra-strong puffs of cigar-smoke.

'I don't believe a word of all this gossip!' (she used the words *toutes ces blagues* as she habitually spoke mostly in French). 'One of my friends who was staying with the Emperor at the time said it was merely a friendly visit, an act of politeness – *une visite de politesse*. After all, it would be only natural to call on Europe's oldest ruler if one found oneself visiting his domains!'

Pfaffulus, rather cautiously, tried to interject a note of contradiction. Surely, he said, England possessed similar watering places
to Marienbad? If King Edward was so anxious to rid himself of
his excess weight why, he dared ask, was it necessary to go all the
way to Bohemia?

It was now Slawata's turn. He embarked on a lengthy exposition feeling that he should in some way sing for the supper to
which he, as did his host, felt he really had no right, by revealing
something of the secrets of the Ballplatz, the foreign ministry in
Vienna. He decided to let drop a small secret – nothing that could
be thought of as *streng geheim* – or 'top secret' as it would come
to be known in later years – but something that could be told in
confidence to reliable people of standing knowing it would go
no further. Even so he still spoke cautiously, mincing his words
so as not to get himself into trouble.

'According to reports from London,' he said, 'the King of
England certainly had the intention, if possible, to wean the
Emperor away from the German alliance. He was going to offer,
in the event of a war between England and Germany, to support
the Habsburg monarchy on condition that Austria-Hungary
remained neutral. That, of course, would have been tantamount
to suggesting the automatic dissolution of the Tri-partite Alliance. However it never came to this for, before any such offer
could be made, his Majesty made it quite clear to King Edward
that he would never desert his old friends. Of course we can't
know exactly what was said, word for word, between the two
monarchs, but this is the gist of the communiqué that we at
the Ballplatz sent round to the German ambassador. Berlin had
been understandably nervous, as you can imagine, for if Austria-
Hungary had joined up with the other great powers then
Germany would indeed have been encircled.'

'Why on earth,' cried Wuelffenstein, 'should the King of England wish to destroy the Emperor Wilhelm, his own nephew?'

Slawata smiled.

'When relations don't get on, their dislike of each other is far
stronger than that for a stranger! However the real reason has
nothing to do with that. What has led England on is nothing less
than the build-up of the German fleet. That is something that
England will never accept.'

'Unfortunately,' murmured the priest in his modest manner,
'the real risk is ours. In the event of war, we could easily lose

not only our provinces in Italy but also our friendship with that country. Italy could hardly do otherwise than side with England. She is surrounded by sea – and the English rule the seas. I heard talk of this when I was in Rome recently. So the danger is not just the encirclement of Germany, but the encirclement of both central powers – in other words, *us!*'

Behind his thick glasses Slawata glared.

'*Dann müsste man eben Prevenire spielen* – then we must play our cards so as to prevent it!' he said mysteriously.

The fat little priest turned towards him, his face as always calm and enigmatic, and all he did was to raise his bushy black eyebrows. He was about to speak when Countess Illesvary sighed deeply and said, quite quietly, 'Perhaps, after all, it was a mistake not to listen to King Edward?'

Her brother interrupted her before she could say any more. 'Surely his Majesty knows best what is right for us all?' he said in a hard decisive tone that brooked no argument.

Slawata quickly grasped this heaven-sent opportunity to agree with his host. He said at once that the situation of the Dual Monarchy itself would be impossible if ever it were to turn against Germany. They would then be the first victims of any war for whatever might happen elsewhere in Europe the far-flung boundaries of Austria-Hungary were untenable, even indefensible. Bohemia, where the Skoda Works, their only ordnance factories, were situated, would be in German hands in a matter of days and then their only defence would be the Moravian hills! All Bohemia would at once be a battlefield. Up until this moment Slawata had spoken with professional restraint, objectively, as became a diplomat. Now his voice rang with personal conviction, deeply moved by the thought of the possible fate of his own homeland. As he said himself, he was, first and foremost, a Czech.

Only two people had not taken part in this discussion. One was Warday, who smoked his cigar in silence and smiled quietly to himself, thinking of the sweet experience that awaited him later that night. The other was Abady. Everything that he had just heard was new to him. Of course he had read the newspapers, and, as he had formerly been a diplomat himself, he had not been able to avoid such thoughts as everyone had so openly been discussing that evening. But he had been so wrapped up in domestic Hungarian politics, in his co-operative projects – and

above all in his love for Adrienne – that he had paid little heed
to what was going on in the world.

How different life was here, he thought, from that in Transylvania, where everything was on such a tiny scale. All that
mattered there were only little quarrels, minor disagreements.
There it was important to know what would happen to Beno
Balogh-Peter, the former chief notary of Monostor who had
collaborated with the Bodyguard government and tried to instal
the nominated Prefect. This was the sort of issue for which his
native Transylvanian brothers started blood-feuds and hates that
endured for generations, while all the time, in the real world outside, the threads were being spun of some giant tragedy to be
enacted in the unpredictable future. On the other hand, here at
Jablanka, in North Nyitra, these people were living in the centre
of world happenings, aware of what was going on around them,
so familiar with it all that they need discuss only the consequences, not the facts that led to them. And all this lightly, even
politely.

While thinking about this Balint was watching Antal Szent-
Gyorgyi, who stood, upright and slender, in front of the stuccoed
fireplace. Far above him, set in the plaster-work, was a life-sized
portrait of his great-grandfather, he who had been palatine to
Queen Maria-Theresa. He had been painted with the insignia
of the Order of the Golden Fleece hanging from a heavy gold
chain and was wearing a heavily embroidered cloak of purple
velvet and on his head was a powdered wig. And suddenly Balint
saw that it was the same man who stood there today, in front of
the marble and stucco fireplace, dressed in a velvet smoking-
jacket, just like any of the other men in the room, but, unlike the
others, with the tiny emblem of the Golden Fleece on his watch-
chain and that worn not out of pride or vanity but because it was
the rule of the Order that it was always to be worn no matter
what the dress or occasion. There, below the painted portrait,
was the same narrow face, the same proud self-sufficient glance.
Even the living man's greying hair made the similarity the more
pronounced. Antal Szent-Gyorgyi was the very archetype of
those men of family who had lived for generations close to the
throne, who in Hungary had controlled the country's destiny
since the end of the Turkish wars, who had looked empirically
at their country's needs with all the knowledge of what else was
happening in Europe, and who yet still remained essentially

Hungarian, like Ferenc Szechenyi, Gyorgy Festetics or the Eszterhazys.

In the meantime Slawata had begun to sound more cheerful.

'Izvolsky, of course, came on to Vienna when he left Marienbad, and so we were able to settle the Macedonian question. That little nest of thorns won't give us any trouble for years to come, I'm glad to say.'

He was still explaining this reassuring news, while from time to time bowing from his seat towards his host as if he was laying all this confidential information as homage to Count Antal's patent-leather pumps, when the butler came in, went over to Abady and spoke softly to him.

'Her Ladyship would like to see you in the small drawing-room, my Lord.'

Countess Elise sat in her usual place between the windows, protected by two silk-covered screens. She lay in an armchair, her feet on a footstool, for there it was a great deal warmer than close to the little onyx-inlaid fireplace. The secret was that close to her chair were two little latticed openings from which a stove outside the room blew gusts of hot air.

On her left sat Fanny, and near the fireplace was Klara. Balint was shown to a place near his aunt, a strange little low upholstered chair which seemed almost to embrace him as he sank into its cushioned softness. He was facing Klara.

'That's right, just beside me, my dear Balint! Now tell me about Transylvania and all the dear people there,' said Countess Elise, taking the young man's hand and keeping it imprisoned affectionately in her own. A series of questions followed.

'First of all how is your mother? I haven't seen her for more than a year and a half, since she last passed through Budapest. I suppose she's now at your beautiful Denestornya? I often went there to visit my uncle Peter, your grandfather. And how is Aunt Lizinka? Is she still rushing about all the time? And dear Countess Gyalakuthy, that good-natured Adelma? They tell me her daughter has turned out to be very pretty. And how is Countess Jeno Laczok and her husband? And Ambrus Kendy, who used to dance with me? And Sandor Kendy?'

It was incredible, thought Balint. She knows everybody and

still remembers exactly what relation they all are to each other. When Balint recounted the latest news, she would turn to Fanny and Klara and tell little anecdotes of them all, girlhood memories and funny little half-forgotten things so that they too might know something of this – to them – unknown world, of which she was obviously still very fond. And, of course, she often spoke of Szamos-Kozard, the former home of the Gyeroffy girls.

While he was answering her questions, or listening to her reminiscences, Balint's eyes would wander to Klara Kollonich. As she sat there near the fireplace in a richly frilled house-gown covered in lace which showed her shoulders like a ball-gown with a deep décolleté, ruffles and ribbons tumbling all around her, her advanced state of pregnancy could hardly be seen. With her beautiful bare white shoulders that sloped ever so slightly, those eyes the colour of the sea, and her fair wavy hair, she was still as enchanting as she had been as an unmarried girl. Only a faint weariness, which one felt rather than saw, gave an indication of her condition. There might, he thought, be just the hint of a tiny wrinkle at the corner of her full lips which spoke of tiredness, or, perhaps, disappointment. And this, thought Balint, is the girl for whom Laszlo threw away everything he had! For whom he gave up music and his studies at the Academy even though his masters had predicted a great future for him; for whom he had plunged into the great social whirl of the capital, which in turn had lured him to the gaming-tables and then coldly thrown him out of the world he had wanted to conquer for her sake and left him ruined both morally and materially. As Balint gazed at Klara now his mind went back to the day, three years before at Simonsvasar, the Kollonichs' great country place, when he had discovered Laszlo's fatal love and realized, oh so clearly, that his cousin was rushing inevitably to his own destruction. Like a vision he saw Laszlo's face before him, that face so passionate and impetuous . . .

Perhaps it was because of the road down which his reflections had led him that Balint now began to answer his aunt's questions in a somewhat distracted manner. Whatever the reason, the conversation died and there was a sudden silence as if everybody's thoughts had suddenly turned to a subject which must not be discussed and a name which could not be mentioned.

Countess Elise grasped her nephew's hand more strongly than

before as she turned again to him and asked, 'How is Laci?' and her voice held a deeper note than was usual for her. There was a catch in it for she was deeply moved.

Balint was not taken entirely by surprise for he had already sensed that the memory of Laszlo was floating in the air around them, waiting only for the right moment to be expressed in words, challenging the silence and the dying questions, ready to blaze out in open rebellion. At last his name had been spoken, but Balint still answered, slowly and with hesitation, 'Poor Laszlo, I'm so worried about him. I see him so seldom, almost never, in fact.'

'Tell me, please tell me!' cried Countess Elise. 'I know absolutely nothing, and I've heard nothing since, since . . . since it all happened. I've written to him twice, once just after – you know . . . and again last year; but he didn't answer. And Antal, well, Antal's so severe about these things. But I love him so much, just the same as always, and I would like to help him if I could.'

At the first mention of Laszlo's name Klara had got slowly to her feet. She rose with difficulty and at Countess Elise's last words she went silently out of the room.

Fanny Beredy, however, stayed where she was, and this bothered Balint who would have preferred her to leave too. He looked over towards her. The beautiful woman's long catlike eyes were almost closed but he could just make out between her lashes a little gleam of moisture. She sat quite still, but for one hand that moved up to her throat and touched the string of giant pearls that encircled her bare shoulders, dipped down between her breasts and fell into a pool in her lap, a pool of frozen tears, a fabulous jewel that somehow had a life of its own – and a past. Apart from this faint movement as Fanny caressed her pearls she was as motionless as a puma in a cage, oblivious of her present surroundings as she dreamed of life in a long-lost wilderness.

Balint had to answer, so he told all he knew about everything that had happened to Laszlo. He told it, perhaps, in a slightly toned-down version, for how could he speak frankly in front of a stranger? Still, he did tell everything and behind the bland phrases it was not difficult to sense the distress, the spiritual hurt. One felt, he said, that Laszlo believed himself to be a pariah and somehow this obsession never got better, only worse. He told them of the financial situation at Szamos-Kozard, which would probably soon have to be put up for auction and then Laszlo would own nothing, not even the roof over his head. Then Balint remembered his talk with Sandor Kendy who had said that the only solution would be to make Laszlo a ward of court, and so he told them about this too, hoping that maybe Countess Elise would be able to do something on those lines.

Balint talked for a long time, and when he came to the saddest parts, like the ruin and impending loss of the Szamos-Kozard estate, which of course had been her childhood home, the old lady pressed his hand with a force he would never have believed her to possess. It was clear that she was very much hurt and moved even though she had not been back for more than thirty years.

'I will write to him again,' she said when Balint had finished his tale. 'That business of guardianship . . . I don't know anything about such things, but perhaps that's just as well. I'll recommend it anyhow. I'll write at once and you'll take it to him yourself, won't you?'

'I can't take it until after Christmas, Aunt Elise, because I have to stay in Budapest until then.'

'It doesn't matter. Perhaps things aren't too urgent, but I still want you to deliver it personally.' And she got up and went over to her little desk where there was hardly room for the morocco-leather letter-case, so covered was the tiny sécrétaire with little *objets d'art* and photographs of the countess's father and mother, husband and children. Once at the desk she sat down and switched on the table lamp.

Fanny and Balint left the room.

They walked in silence through the vast library which, in contrast to the cosy luxury of Countess Elise's friendly little sitting-room, was furnished only with great ecclesiastical oak manuscript chests on which the gilded baroque carving was cold and impartial.

They had almost reached the doors of the drawing-room when Fanny suddenly stopped. She turned towards Abady, her lips slightly parted and her eyes closed shut. They stood like this for just a moment, but it was a moment of eternity, for Balint, like everyone else, was quite unaware that Fanny and Laszlo had been lovers. So he stood there surprised, expecting at every moment that she would say something; but nothing came, not a sound emerged from her lips. At last two huge tears forced their way through her closed lashes and rolled slowly down her face to her bosom where they joined their sisters petrified into ropes of pearls.

Slowly Fanny walked into the drawing-room and over to the piano. She opened it and sat down, running her fingers over the notes in soft *roulades*. Then her host came over and stood near her, suggesting that maybe Countess Beredy would honour them with a few songs, as she had often done on previous evenings.

'Do sing us something! It would be so nice of you,' he said.

But she only shook her head, turning her face away, and once more her hands just wandered four or five times over the notes before she jumped up saying, 'Oh, no! It's far too late! I for one will now go to bed!' and as Szent-Gyorgyi bent to kiss her hand, she murmured, with a sad and somewhat ironical smile, 'You were quite right ... what you said about this house. Oh, yes, quite right!'

CHAPTER SIX

LATER, WHEN ALREADY dressed for bed, Magda and Lili came to see their cousin Klara. This was quite easy as her room was next to theirs, 'right side of the chapel', in the family apartments, the same room she had always had as a child. Her aunt had wanted her here, rather than on the other side in the guest-rooms next to her husband. Aunt Elise was anxious to have her near her so that she would be able to go to her room and look after her without having to pass along those freezing corridors.

The two girls slipped out of their adjoining rooms just down from Klara's. They wore light dressing gowns, and both wanted to have the intimate girls' gossip for which they had had no opportunity during the day.

Magda wanted a chance to give rein to her annoyance. For a long time she had kept up a flirtation with Klara's older brother, Peter; and then this dreadful thing had happened – her father had invited one of her younger half-brothers, Louis, but not Peter.

Lili came too, partly because she was no longer a child and shouldn't be treated as if she were, and so, though she was already in bed and half asleep when Magda came in to suggest they visit Klara's room, she jumped up at once – for wasn't she grown up and able to stay up if she wished? – and anyhow she felt like a

good talk. What about? Well, that didn't matter; just to talk
would be enough, talk a bit, listen a bit. She might learn something . . . about that Abady, for example. Who was he, always so
serious and somehow different – well, different from the others
– and how strange he was!

So they sat by Klara, Magda on the edge of the bed where Klara
sat up supported by a mountain of lacy pillows because she found
it easier to breathe that way, and Lili in an armchair at the foot
of the bed.

An alabaster night light spread a filtered glow throughout the
room so that the silken wraps of the girls melted into the pink
satin which covered the walls, the bed and all the upholstered
furniture.

Magda was pouring out her sorrows without drawing breath.

'It's really too bad of Papa. He could easily have asked Peter,
but he said that it was Louis's turn since he hadn't been for
years as he had been at Oxford with Tony. I told him that was no
reason since Peter was the eldest and anyhow was a far better shot.
All Papa said was, all the better then, Louis needs a chance to
improve and get in some practice. Then I said, why not make an
exception and invite a ninth guest, and all he said to that was
that there wasn't room for nine, only eight! Not room! Here!
To which I said, what about that bespectacled booby who
doesn't know anything about anything and Peter would do far
better in the corner where a good shot was needed and all Papa
replied was that a guest couldn't be put in a less honourable position! So I said that Peter wasn't like a guest, he was a near relation
and wouldn't mind anyhow. Isn't that so, he wouldn't have
minded, would he?'

She turned, twisting this way and that with little birdlike
movements, first to Klara, then to Lili, and then back again to
Klara. Of course she only expected a reply from Klara as Lili was
too young to know Peter at all well. Klara's voice was tired and
lazy as if she had dragged her thoughts back from somewhere
far away.

'Why? I suppose not. It's all much the same anyhow . . .'

'You see!' cried Magda triumphantly. 'I knew it! Of course he
wouldn't have minded and he was dying to come, I know it, and
for my sake, too, of course, but don't either of you tell that to a
soul!' and she turned to Lili, saying, 'It's a secret, you know!'

'I wouldn't dream of it! Never! Not to a soul!' the young girl promised fervently in her deep rather slurred manner of speaking. She was very flattered to be let into something so private and important. Imagine, a family secret!

'And there was no reason to ask Balint. He could easily have been left out as he isn't even a good shot, not like . . . like . . .' but she faltered, not being able to bring herself to mention Laszlo's name.

Klara opened wide her sea-grey eyes and looked angrily at Magda, and it was, perhaps, lucky that Lili interrupted excitedly, 'Oh, but why leave out Abady? That *would* have been a pity!'

'And what do you know about such matters, you little brat?' laughed Szent-Gyorgyi's daughter. 'Has he caught your fancy then?'

The still chubby teenager blushed deeply.

'Oh, no! I only meant . . .' but Magda was not listening, she was far too full of her own thoughts.

'And you know I've just realized something quite different. Father didn't ask Peter on purpose. I'd make a bet on it! He didn't ask Peter because he's found out there's something between us. That's why! And what's wrong with that? Plenty of people marry their own cousins,' and she started to count on her fingers some of those she knew who had done just that. She started off with her Viennese friends, because that is where she had come out, 'Why, there's Mitz and Trudi, Titi and Momo . . . and in Budapest there's Marcsa and Ili, and Marietta – though she married her second cousin. Anyhow it doesn't matter, the whole thing's too absurd and Peter's not a blood relation anyway, we're only *angeheiratet* – connected by marriage – after all's said and done!' And now she really went too far, not noticing how ravaged with pain Klara's expression had become as she plunged into a discussion on love between cousins, gabbling on more and more on the same subject, until suddenly out the words came: 'And surely you too, Klara, weren't you in love with . . . ?' when she realized what she was saying and fell silent.

In her embarrassment she turned to Lili. 'And why don't you say something, instead of just sitting there like a stuffed dummy?'

'What should I say?' stammered the young girl and blushed again. She blushed, not at what had been said to her but at her own thoughts. She had been thinking about Abady. When they had been together at the shoot, each time that the drive had stopped he had always talked to her; and he had talked as if she were grown-up. She was remembering how his dark-grey eyes turned up slightly at the corners and how he had looked at her in such a natural, friendly and encouraging manner. And how his moustache was lighter than his hair, yes, much lighter. And that afternoon, when they went to see the brood-mares, he had talked to her again, saying, 'I can see that you too love and understand horses! I can see it from the way you stroke their noses.'

Yes, that's what he had said – 'I can see it from the way you stroke their noses!'. Then he had told her that in Transylvania he too owned a stud farm. That had given her extra pleasure because he wanted to talk to her even when he wasn't obliged to by common manners. Out there in the paddocks it hadn't been a social duty – and this new acquaintance was a grown man, and she was still almost a child!

Influenced by this train of thought, and since they were talking of relationships and genealogy and Magda was almost insulting her, Lili felt bold enough to ask, 'What relation is he to you, this Abady?'

'*Cousin issu des germains* – second cousin,' said Magda.

'Then he must be my cousin too?'

'Not at all! It's not on the Szent-Gyorgyi side, but the Gyer-offy. My mother's mother was Kate Abady, sister of Count Peter, Balint's grandfather. She married my grandfather on my mother's side, Laszlo Gyeroffy . . .'

Now they were interrupted by an angry voice. From deep among her pillows Klara said, 'Please go away, both of you. I'm getting a headache from all this chatter.' And when Magda tried to kiss her goodnight she merely pushed her away and buried her head in the pillows, saying, 'Go away! Please, just go away!'

After saying goodnight to the others in the drawing-room Balint and Slawata had walked together along the corridor to their rooms.

'May I come in and talk to you for a while?' asked the diplomat when they arrived at Abady's door.

As soon as they were inside Slawata started to pace up and down, for which there was plenty of room, for Abady's was one of the larger apartments made out of two of the original monks' cells. Then he took off his thick glasses and polished them carefully. He had the air of somebody who liked to tidy his thoughts before speaking.

Abady sat down and waited.

At last Slawata spoke. He started off with a few compliments saying: '*wir* – we' (meaning the Belvedere Party that supported the Heir rather than the Ballplatz where he was officially employed) 'have been watching you. We have observed the path you have been following. We observe and we remember. We find it admirable that you have not entered party politics, not taken sides!' and two or three somewhat flattering remarks followed about Abady's obvious abilities. Finally, after all this preamble, Slawata started to come to the point, almost, if not quite, making a definite statement. 'What I tell you now, and what I will ask of you, you must understand is said only by me, Jan Slawata. I have not been instructed to do so, and I must make it absolutely clear that anything I say comes only from me and that I say it because I have faith in the soundness of your judgement and in your discretion. Any answer you may make is for my benefit alone and for no one else! *Also ganz unter uns* – just between us!'

He stopped, readjusted his glasses upon his nose and then began again. 'Now give me your opinion. If the monarchy should become embroiled in a war with one of its neighbours, what attitude would the Hungarians take?'

Abady was startled. At that time no one believed in the possibility of war in Europe. Everyone accepted that the race for armaments was just a device of the great powers which was nothing more than a safety-valve used to save everyone's face. The compliments just lavished on him by this former 'colleague' at the Foreign Office made Balint suddenly cautious. Therefore, before giving a direct answer, he felt he needed more information.

'A war?' he said. 'But I thought you were saying after dinner that the Macedonian question had now been settled by Izvolsky?'

'That is so. And in any case Russia is in no state to make war today. All her supplies have been used up in the Far East and the revolutionary movements are keeping her busy at home. That is why the question is becoming a real threat.'

'What threat? There is general peace. If Russia can be counted out for some years to come then surely the Serbs too will keep quiet? Romania and Italy are our allies. Which neighbour could possibly attack us?'

Slawata had quickly grasped that he would get no answer from Balint unless he gave him some more information. He paused. Then he pulled up a chair and sat down.

'This is the situation. Father Czibulka interpreted the problem quite correctly when he analysed the consequences of the Anglo-Russian Agreement. Undoubtedly Italy is already lost to us – and in my opinion Romania too, their sympathies are far too close to St Petersburg. And so we have to think of what will happen in a few years' time when Russia has been re-armed with French gold. Then the Dual Monarchy will have to face a coalition compounded of Russia, Serbia and Montenegro that will, of course, be backed by Italy and probably Romania, since they all hanker after different parts of our territory. There'll always be some reason for a war in the Balkans. All this means that the monarchy's 7 million citizens will have to face a quarrel with 182 millions all around them. It is obvious that we could never survive unless someone came to our aid. And if Germany comes galloping along to the rescue they'll find themselves attacked at once by France and England – France because it would offer a marvellous chance of *revanche* for 1870 and England because it would be in their commercial interest to destroy the German fleet. It would be a terrible risk for the German *Reich* to take, especially because of the great resources and remarkable toughness of the English. There is only one solution, and it would have to be put into effect immediately without any hesitation. This is the opinion of Conrad, the Chief of Staff. Germany's enemies – and our own – would have to be put out of action one by one, starting with Italy who has no fortifications and whose military equipment is far too antiquated to be any use. Ours is too, for that matter,' added Slawata with a wicked smile, 'largely owing to Hungarian obstruction, of course; but the Italians are even further behind than we are, so it's certain we would have an easy task. Therefore my question is this: Where would Hungary stand in these circumstances?'

'Certainly I assume that Hungary would stand by her obligation, her duty if you will, to contribute to the defence of the monarchy. However it may appear, loyalty to the King is strongly rooted. Of course sympathy with Italy exists too, in no small measure – but as long as our people understood that they were merely fighting a defensive war . . .'

'That is most interesting – a *defensive* war!' interrupted Slawata. After a moment's reflection he went on, 'You are quite right, of course! The incident to be used for declaring war would have to be provoked in Fiume, inside the lands of the Holy Crown . . .' and now his voice took on a mocking tone and he emphasized his words with clownish gestures as if to underline the cynical nature of the farce he was proposing. '*Die Länder der Heiligen Krone*, of course! That's it! That's how it will be done; and then it will at once become a matter of *Hungarian* honour! A defensive war in Hungary's interest! That's how Hungarian opinion will see it! *Sehr gut! Sehr gut!*'

Abady's expression darkened. It hurt him to hear such a low opinion of his countrymen coming from a foreigner. He cut in, making clear his displeasure, 'These ideals are sacred to me too. Therefore please do not mock them if you wish us to discuss this calmly!'

'I'm sorry! I beg your pardon!' the other said hurriedly. 'Please do not misunderstand me, I did not mean to mock. Far from it, I picked this out only to show how well I understand the political ideology that is so dear to the Hungarian mind!'

Neither spoke for a little while. Then Balint broke the silence between them. 'A preventive war? Isn't that a truly terrible idea? Didn't Bismarck once say that he would never recommend starting a war only because the enemy might become stronger if he waited – though, of course he was not a sentimental man!'

Slawata shrugged. 'If you know that you are being stalked by bandits who are eager to kill you, would you not shoot one first before they could surround you and make sure of killing you? It's just the same situation!' He paused for a few moments before saying, 'All Hungary's problems would be solved by a little war such as I've described. Then we would have time really to prepare for the inevitable attack from Russia. And if such a war were to be declared then the Hungarian Parliament would surely pass every estimate for bringing our joint armies up to date?'

Balint did not answer. Slawata's reasoning filled him with horror even though he recognized its logic. Once again he was felled by his fatal capacity to see both sides of the question. Even when he disagreed from the depths of his soul, he could understand his opponent's standpoint and his reasons, no matter how alien they might be to his own way of thinking. He had often suffered from this, especially during all the obstructions and upheavals at the time of the Fejervary government; and now, as then, he felt it all with an almost physical pain.

'And when is all this planned for?' Balint just managed to get the words out and still remain civil to his guest.

'Nothing is settled yet. *Hoheit* – his Highness (he referred to the Heir to the throne) and Conrad both believe this to be the best way. Aehrenthal does not agree. And our revered Lord and Master? Well, of course, he is for peace at all costs. But we'll prepare the ground, you can be sure of that! Mayor Lüger will raise the subject in his speech at the Radetsky dinner, and his tone towards Italy will be nothing if not belligerent!'

After this they exchanged only a few platitudinous phrases and then Slawata got up to go.

'Well!' he said. '*Vedremo* – we'll see. *Und ich danke für den wert-vollen Tip!* – and I thank you for a most useful hint!' Then he disappeared through the door.

'Thanks for a most useful hint!' Balint was particularly an-noyed by this remark as the fellow seemed to imply that he, Balint, was offering sympathetic advice to the agent of the plot-ters surrounding the Heir. He was so angry that for a moment he nearly followed Slawata out into the corridor. But he stayed where he was. What would be the point? Slawata was only trying to be polite in his own fashion and the difference between Balint's bald statement that Hungarian public opinion would only give support to a defensive war and the way that Slawata seemed to interpret this as a useful piece of information and an informed warning, was nothing for him to worry about. And when you studied the matter the difference between them was so slight that even to explain it was almost impossible.

As he stood there in the middle of the room, upset and angry, it seemed to him that everything that had happened that evening somehow formed one cohesive whole. While the other guests had exchanged words in the drawing-room that could be inter-preted in many different ways, Balint's whole attention had been riveted on what they were saying. Now, later on, he found him-self shocked by Slawata's cold cynicism. Alone in his room he was horrified by the thought of war, by the dreadful possibility that a war was not far off in the future, a real war, here in Europe, not just some struggle for a remote colony but a war which could toll the death-knell of nations and which, if lost, would certainly bring about the break-up of the Dual Monarchy. And what price would be paid by his own country, by Hungary, and by his beloved Transylvania which had always stood as a proud fortress on the road from Russia to Constantinople?

This last thought so constricted Balint's throat that for a moment he found himself breathless.

He went to the window and opened it. The icy air came in with a blast. It was good, it was real, and Balint for a moment felt soothed and soon started to breathe again normally. He leaned out, his elbows on the window-sill. There was no moon and he could see nothing outside, only a myriad stars high above in the sky, the unchanging stars that had gazed down on human misery for a million years and more. They were like huge signposts which no one except a few eccentric magicians could ever attempt to interpret, claiming that they foretold the fate of men and of nations.

As if mocking the limitless oceans of space in the sky above, somewhere down below in the valley of the Vag a tiny light appeared, moving slowly northwards, crawling along the bed of the valley. Just behind it was a minute red spot – it was, he realized, the Berlin Express, for now he could even hear the faint chugging of its engine. Balint's heart missed a beat. If there ever were a war with Russia it was through this pass that the troop trains would make their sad way to the north. This would be the road down which would go so many of the flower of the nation's youth to the horrors of war, to their death in battle . . . and against such a vast enemy their sacrifice would surely be in vain . . . in vain . . .

Warday had been lodged in the third room away from the chapel. He made careful preparation for the blissful moment when he would steal into Fanny's room. After much application of lotion and frantic brushing he decided that his hair shone sufficiently brightly. He had carefully anointed his face, neck and shoulders with scented cologne and his silk dressing gown was just as it should be. He listened to be sure that no one was still about, and then, hearing nothing, he opened the door a crack and peered out. He had almost put a foot outside when suddenly Slawata walked by. Again he waited until everything was once more quiet. Then he stepped out.

Just as he did so the second door along from his was opened and Pfaffulus appeared. Warday drew swiftly back, but he had not been seen for luckily the priest moved swiftly, his breviary under his arm, towards the chapel door. He was wearing only his black soutane and had left off his red sash and crucifix. Then he disappeared and the chapel doors clicked shut behind him.

Again Warday waited for a few more moments, for perhaps the priest would come back. But no, he had his breviary with him and that surely meant he had gone to pray and so would be inside for some time to come. Warday was now so impatient that he quickly let himself out of his room, glided softly along the carpeted corridor as if he were skating – not that his heelless slippers would make any noise – until he reached the door to what had to be Fanny's bathroom, the door next to the stair. It was open, and inside there was darkness.

Now he recalled what Fanny had taught him when two years before she had first taken him as her lover. 'It is far more sensible to turn up the light for a moment and find out where you are than to bump into something and wake everyone up!' He smiled at the memory and his hand reached for the light switch. When he did so he realized that he was at the door of her room, and that all he had to do was to turn the knob and go in to her. Quickly he turned out the light again and, his heart beating hard with joy and anticipation, put his hand on the door-knob in front of him.

The door did not yield. It was locked.

He knocked lightly. There was no answer. He knocked again, louder this time, and then waited. He fancied he could hear some soft panting inside. What on earth had happened? Was she playing some sort of joke on him? Angrily he knocked again, quite loudly, and called out in an annoyed voice, 'Fanny! It's me, why have you locked the door?'

But all he heard was some sort of stifled sob and finally Fanny replied faintly: 'Go away. I've got a headache, I can't . . .'

Warday was not a bad man. He felt sorry for the poor girl whose voice had sounded almost stifled as if she could hardly speak.

'Poor Fanny, what rotten luck! Perhaps in Budapest we might . . . ?'

'All right! All right! But go away now, please!' and as the young man moved cautiously back to the corridor he heard again that soft panting that had so disturbed him before.

How the poor girl must be suffering! he said to himself as he hurried back to his own room.

He was right, of course, but not in the way he thought it. Countess Beredy was lying face downwards on her bed, her hair spilled carelessly over the pillows and she was sobbing her heart out in great racking spasms. Her nightgown was torn and every now and again she would arch her back and plunge down again into the soft coverlets as if thereby she could smother herself and find oblivion.

* * *

Finally there was peace in all parts of the great castle of Jablanka.
Of the hundreds who lay down there at night only four were still
awake, two men and two women. Klara, in her old room, lay
motionless against the high pile of lace-covered pillows, gazing
up at the alabaster hanging lamp; and on the other side of the
castle, Fanny was drowning in sorrow and misery, her hair and
pillows wet with tears.

Pfaffulus was in the chapel, kneeling in front of the candle that
burned there perpetually. He was praying for that foolish and
wayward young man, the same for whom one woman wept and
another gazed silently at the night-light in her room.

And Balint, too, kept vigil. Still at his open window he might
have been staring into the face of destiny, the inexorable destiny
that would in time overwhelm his beloved country.

Now the Berlin Express reached that curve where the valley
of the Vag narrows into a mountain pass. The engine shrilled a
loud warning, its whistle, screaming in the dark, echoed through
the cloisters of the former monastery.

PART THREE

CHAPTER ONE

BALINT RETURNED TO Budapest. There he found a stormy atmosphere in parliamentary circles.

The most noise was being made by the Independence Party. Kossuth had had to work hard to keep its members sufficiently in order to get the new commercial agreements with Austria ratified. Obstructions were being made by all those who had left the party in protest over the increases in the Hungarian contribution to the joint Austro-Hungarian army and so, with these problems in mind, the government put forward a proposal that consisted only of a single paragraph which laid down that, once accepted, all budget proposals would remain in force for ten years from the following January 1st.

Never before had any government dared to ask Parliament for such a mandate; and it was all the more surprising that this measure should come from those in the Coalition who formerly, when they were in opposition, had bent over backwards and split every hair to maintain the supremacy of Parliament in the passing of laws, and the freedom of speech of all members. However the government's hands were now bound for they had sworn to follow a certain programme and this was the only way this promise could be redeemed.

It was in these circumstances that the party rebels took especial pleasure in attacking their former leaders in the Independence Party who, they claimed, had gone back on all their former promises! It was in vain that Apponyi, with his honeyed speech and well-known eloquence, should rise and defend the party's actions. And so the discussions and arguments became more and more personal and venomous. Things reached such a pitch that the Minister-President found himself obliged to fight a duel with Geza Polonyi. Even though both were elderly men and none too agile, their seconds still insisted that they fought with sabres.

As it turned out no great harm was done; and no blood was shed since both men were soon so out of breath that the physicians stopped the fight declaring mutual exhaustion. Though this was nothing if not accurate, it was the source of many ribald jokes throughout Budapest – and none of them were to the government's advantage.

This was the only sort of news to which the general public paid the slightest attention. The anti-Italian speech in Vienna, made, as Slawata had told Balint, by Mayor Lüger, aroused no interest at all in Budapest. There people were only concerned with the proceedings in Parliament and so it was remarkable that no one seemed to notice or comment upon Andrassy's cunning ruling that all civil servants must be able to speak the language of the people they served. It had been expected that the extreme chauvinists would have a field-day haggling about the details of this measure, but the storm about the army quotas overwhelmed discussion of all other issues.

Unfortunately the Croatian situation was getting worse daily. The congress of the Starcevicz Party passed a resolution declaring their firm intention to break away from their allegiance to the crown of St Stephen. Although the session of the Zagreb Parliament opened on the appointed day it had immediately to be adjourned, so revolutionary was the mood of the people who were making demonstrations daily throughout the city.

Balint was even more upset by the news from Croatia since he had listened to the talk at Jablanka.

He went home to Transylvania for Christmas in a dark and depressed mood. The awful threat posed by the rivalries of the great powers, the sinister plan for a 'little war' with Italy, and the upheavals beyond the Drava, all weighed upon his spirits and seemed to him only to emphasize that the political unawareness of all those in Hungary whose self-indulgence, preoccupation only with such internal issues as affected themselves, and whose self-centred conviction that only such trivial matters were of the smallest significance, was leading his country to isolation and ruin.

When Balint reached Kolozsvar he thought it would be nice to surprise his mother with a small gift which just might help to soothe the tenseness that had recently developed between them. It was difficult to know what to choose because Countess Roza had a rule that she never accepted anything personal, but only gifts intended to adorn her beloved Denestornya. Little objects such as ashtrays, antique clocks, or pieces of china would do, but little else. It had to be something which would look as if it had always been there. This gave her pleasure because for her the house was like a living person and to make it more beautiful was her daily preoccupation.

Since he had not thought about this before leaving Budapest Balint went at once to see an antique dealer in Kolozsvar who always had good things.

Old Mrs Bruckner did not keep a shop; she dealt directly from her apartment on the first floor of a building in Belmagyar Street. She was a small woman, rather fat, and entirely trustworthy. She never knowingly sold imitations or fakes, even though she was entirely uneducated with no knowledge of styles or period. If she believed something to be truly old she would say, '*Das ist gotisch* – this is gothic!'

Mrs Bruckner knew everyone in the town. She led Abady through her rooms, merrily showing him a host of every imaginable sort of object piled one on top of another or hung all over the walls; commodes, chests, tables, clocks and statuettes, ornaments, pictures, lampshades, embroidery or church vestments, everything everywhere in apparent confusion.

'I've just got in a lovely cup!' said the old woman enthusiastically. 'It's new in, so no one has seen it except you!' and she took her customer to a shelf on which stood three beautiful *Alt Wien* cups among a host of rubbish. Balint was immediately struck by the one in the centre for he recognized the painted portrait on its side as that of his mother's great-grandfather, the Abady who had been Governor of Transylvania. It had been fashionable at the end of the eighteenth century to give such cups as souvenirs to friends or relations, especially to relations, rather as at a later date people would give signed photographs. At Denestornya they already had two similar ones, and this would make a third.

'Where did you get it from?' asked Balint, marvelling at his luck. But Mrs Bruckner just gave an enigmatic smile and said, 'From a very good place, I can assure you. I can't say where, but it's a very good place indeed!'

The price was sixty crowns and Balint paid it without question. As the old lady accompanied him to the door she said,

'Come again in a few days, if you like. I may have some things from the same place. *Alles prima, alles hochprima* – everything of the highest quality, of course, and from the same place.'

Though Balint again asked her she would not say where it came from.

Christmas Eve at the Abadys', whether at Denestornya or in Kolozsvar, was always a somewhat solemn occasion with nothing cosy or intimate about it. While Balint had been away at school in Vienna he had always had to spend Christmas in his rooms in the college and so for many years Countess Roza had spent the holiday alone with her servants. As the years passed, the ceremonies at home had frozen into an occasion of cold convention. Always, as now, there was a small tree in the centre of the dining-table. This, as always too, was bought, for to her it would have been unthinkable sacrilege to uproot and bring anything from Denestornya or from the forestlands in the mountains. On the sideboards were high piles of woollen shawls and waistcoats that the countess and her two housekeepers had spent much of the previous year knitting just for this occasion. At Denestornya they would be distributed to all the children of the village on Christmas morning itself. Now, as they were at the town house in Kolozsvar, the estate manager would collect them on Christmas Eve and travel at dawn to the country so that the children would receive their presents after church the following morning. Around the little tree, which was ablaze with a multitude of candles, was a cluster of presents for the household servants and their families, all useful objects carefully chosen and marked with the names of the recipients.

Each servant was called in turn, with members of their families, and in turn they were handed their gifts by the countess, kissed her hand and made room for the next in line. Countess Abady sat in a large armchair in the middle of the room and, as each man, woman or child came up to her, she extended her chubby little hand to be kissed, exactly as if she were a queen receiving the homage of her people. Balint himself was given two silk ties and a silver cigarette case, the tenth of its kind, since Countess Roza had little imagination when it came to choosing presents and so gave him the same thing each year.

When the ceremony was over Balint produced the governor's cup. He had been quite right, the choice had been perfect and his mother was overjoyed. Then they went back to the drawing-room to have the tea and stewed fruit which Countess Roza always liked to have served in the evening. She carried the cup with her and sat down, still holding and caressing it and examining the inscription.

Balint told his mother all about the visit to Jablanka, and especially about Aunt Elise's solicitous enquiries about her and about all her former acquaintance in Transylvania. They stayed up for a long time and Balint had the distinct impression that his mother now thought of nothing but the news he brought her. The thunderclouds seemed to have passed, and Countess Abady was all smiles and sweetness the whole evening.

Balint was thinking about this when he finally found himself alone in his room. It was possible that the old lady had come to believe that he had found a new distraction at Jablanka, at the Szent-Gyorgyis', for when he mentioned little Lili Illesvary, his mother had even smiled, with no sign of disapproval or that sharp nodding of the head which always signified anger or disbelief. Of course it was more than two months since he had seen Adrienne and no doubt his mother knew this and rejoiced because she believed that his infatuation was over. In fact the link between him and Adrienne had grown ever stronger, even though they had recently met so little. Until recently, since they had renewed their love, hardly a week or ten days had passed without their somehow contriving to meet either in public or in private, or even in some secret place where they would not have risked discovery. Since his last visit to Almasko Balint had decided that he did not dare visit his little lodge built where the Abady forests marched with those of Adrienne's husband, for it would have seemed strange to go to the cabin in winter-time, when the Uzdy mansion was so close, and therefore he would be forced to stay in that hated house knowing what happened there between Adrienne and her unhinged husband. Adrienne too, though she never told Balint that her husband had followed her through the forest with a hunting rifle on his arm, had written saying that he should not come to Almasko. It was only because of this that they had not seen each other for the past two months.

Time and again Balint said to himself that this cat-and-dog existence was no life, no life at all. Now, on Christmas Eve, he felt it even more strongly and made up his mind, which had been strengthened by these endless weeks of separation, that somehow this sterile, frustrating, bleak existence must be ended; and he thought once more of his mother's obstinate resistance and of Pal Uzdy's madness and total incompatibility with his wife.

Finally he decided that as soon as Addy came back to Kolozsvar they must definitely arrange her divorce.

However, days and weeks went by and they brought no change. In the middle of January Adrienne wrote and said that she would not be able to move from Almasko for some time to come. Her daughter had developed measles and even though old Countess Uzdy took entire charge of the sickroom and practically denied Adrienne access to her child, she was still unable to get away.

Balint wrote to Gyeroffy at Christmas time and, in his own name and that of his mother, asked him to spend the New Year with them. He also mentioned that he had a letter for him from his aunt, Countess Elise. Laszlo did not answer and did not appear; and so Balint decided one day to take a hired sleigh, drive to Szamos-Kozard, and take his cousin by surprise. It would be better that way for if Laszlo saw one of the easily recognizable Denestornya carriages on the road he might take fright and vanish before Balint could find him. It was not far, only about five miles.

There was thick snow everywhere that year and it took nearly three hours for the heavy covered sleigh drawn by three horses to reach the village of Kozard. It was a good sleigh, for at that time there was no lack of excellent vehicles available for hire, and it drove merrily along with a happy jingle of silvery-toned bells. They arrived at midday and drove straight up to the little country house on its hilltop.

'His Lordship is not at home,' said Marton Balogh, Laszlo's old manservant. 'He went down to the village. Perhaps you might find him at the village store. I'm afraid I don't really know.'

'When do you expect his Lordship back?' asked Balint, but the old man merely shrugged his shoulders, thinking that maybe his master had gone down for some country brandy and if that were so then his movements would be totally unpredictable.

Balint decided to walk down the hill and see for himself, and so he started off down the slippery snow-covered slope. Halfway down he met a young farmer, who was also the local civic deputy and who carried an official-looking paper in his hand. Balint asked him where he should find the village store and the young man pointed out the way.

Laszlo was indeed there.

He stood with his back to the shop door and on the other side of the counter was Bischitz, the owner of the shop, who was standing just in front of the glazed door which led to his private rooms behind the shop. All around them were the thousand different items which made up the stock of a village general shop – by the doors were bunches of harness and tack, scythes, hoes and spades tied together with twine; on the shelves were tobacco, vinegar, spices, sugar, rice, bottles of raw and refined alcohol, glasses, a pyramid of salt-blocks, a barrel of salted herrings and some stiff planks of dried cod leaning against it. From all this came a strong and rather disagreeable odour compounded principally of vinegar and tobacco with a strong dominant smell of the local aniseed-flavoured brandy.

When Balint opened the door of the shop a bell rang loudly above his head and Balint just had time to see the shopkeeper seize some bit of porcelain from Laszlo's hands and whisk it out of sight. Only a bottle of plum brandy, and a single used glass, remained on the counter-top.

'Well! And what brings you here?' said Gyeroffy as soon as he saw who had come in. Balint could hear no sign of pleasure or welcome in his cousin's voice, but rather a strong note of annoyance.

'I came to see you. As you wouldn't come to us it has to be a case of the mountain and Mohammed!' Abady laughed good-humouredly. 'So you see I've come to you.'

'That old fool at the house could have come for me,' growled Laszlo as he offered his cousin a glass of plum brandy. This Balint refused, with some impatience, saying, 'If you've no further business here, we might as well leave, don't you think?'

Gyeroffy looked hard at him.

'No! I've nothing more to do here; and what there is can wait until this afternoon, can't it, Bischitz? However I'll have another dram even if you're too grand to join me!' and he swung himself round leaning on the counter in an obviously sulky temper. Bischitz refilled Laszlo's glass, which the latter drained instantly before demanding another. When that too had been despatched the young man turned back and muttered, 'Well, we can go now!'

Even so they did not leave at once for at this point the civic deputy came in. He too was looking for Count Gyeroffy.

'This has come for you from the County Court,' he said, handing Laszlo a sealed letter. Then he opened the book of receipts and said, 'Sign here, please!'

'Sign for me, Bischitz,' said Laszlo, throwing down the official letter and refilling his glass. Abady glanced at the writing on the document which had fallen on the counter in front of him. He picked it up and looked inside. A man called E. Leo Kardos, resident of Budapest, had asked the court for a writ of seizure and the auction of Count Gyeroffy's house and possessions.

'But this is very serious!' cried Balint. 'Look! Everything goes to auction on April 15th!'

'I've had lots of those,' said Gyeroffy, before turning to the shopkeeper and saying, 'Send it to Azbej, you know, like the others.'

Balint shook his head. He could hardly credit such fecklessness. 'Perhaps it would be better if I took it to him?' he suggested. 'I'll be seeing him tomorrow or the day after when I go to Denestornya.'

'What for? You'll send it, won't you, Bischitz? It won't be the first,' said Laszlo in a mocking tone.

Now they really did start to go back to Laszlo's house.

They did not say much to each other on the way. Balint was racking his brains as to how to get Laszlo out of all his trouble and how, too, to wean him from this solitary drinking. Only when they reached the house and had gone up to the former salon of the manor house, which now served Laszlo as a bed-sitting-room, did he take out Countess Elise's letter to her nephew. Before he handed it over he told Laszlo how lovingly they all thought about him at Jablanka, Aunt Elise, Magda, Pfaffulus, everybody ... but he did not mention either Klara or Imre Warday.

A little stove had been installed in front of the French marble chimney-piece. A fire was burning in it and the smoke and fumes were led into the chimney by a rusty black metal tube. Laszlo stood beside the stove without saying a word, his eyes fixed upon the window and on the grey wintry sky beyond. He said nothing during Balint's long story about his cousins, and he still said nothing when Balint came to the end of his tale and handed over the letter. For a moment he held the envelope in his hand, then he waved it twice in the air before his face before grabbing it with both hands and tearing it to pieces unopened. With his boots still covered with snow he kicked the bits of paper into the fireplace surround.

This was such a surprise that Abady jumped up in protest, only to find that Laszlo was quite calm, saying, 'I've done with that world for ever, do you understand? I don't want anything from it and I don't want to hear anything from it. Nothing! Nothing at all! For me those people no longer exist. For all I care they may be dead, or they may never have existed. Never! Never!'

'Why do you reject everyone who loves you and wants to help you?' asked Balint gently.

'I don't *want* anyone to help me! Why can't you all leave me in peace? Especially all those, those . . . there in Hungary!' Laszlo was shouting now, and getting increasingly agitated as he whirled about the dirty, untidy room where every piece of furniture was piled with filthy unwashed articles of clothing and the ragged sofa covered in old books and papers.

His cousin felt deeply sorry for him and so he moved across the room and joined him. 'All right! All right! Nobody's forcing you to anything,' he said, and then, so as to give Laszlo time to simmer down, took him by the arm and started walking up and down the room, chatting trivially about a number of other subjects. As they did so they passed several times the corner of the room where there stood a delicate old glass-fronted vitrine. Its dusty velvet-covered shelves were now almost empty. In one corner there was an old chipped Meissen coffee-pot and beside it a matching sugar bowl with a long crack on one side, things no one would buy. In several places imprints on the velvet, less dusty than elsewhere, showed where other objects had once been placed. So this is where the governor's cup came from! thought Balint, and realized why even today the shopkeeper had been in such a hurry to hide something. With his usual instinctive urge to help others Balint, without thinking, stepped over to the vitrine and said, 'You've been selling the china, haven't you?'

Laszlo did not reply.

'Look, my dear fellow, if you really have to part with family things it's absurd to give them away for practically nothing to the village store. My mother and I would be only too pleased to have a valuation made and give you the proper price. Far better than let it go to waste!'

Laszlo screamed at him, 'Leave me alone, all of you! I don't need telling how to run my life. If I want to go to hell, I'll go to hell. And I'll sell what I please to whom I please and when I want to. As for you, you can stop sticking your nose into other people's business!'

Now it was Abady's turn to get angry. He turned away and left the room without saying another word.

Laszlo followed him out slowly. Only now did he realize how offensive he had been to the only man who had been a faithful friend to him as long as he could remember. He wanted some-how to make amends, but was not quite sure how. By the time Laszlo reached the head of the stairs his cousin had almost reached the bottom, so he called out, 'My love to Aunt Roza! As soon as I get some money I'll come over to pay my respects. Do forgive me, Balint, please. I've become such an ill-tempered bear these days,' and he turned and went back to his room. Despite the implied olive branch he still could not resist the temptation to slam the door behind him.

CHAPTER TWO

WEEKS WENT BY and it was the end of March before Balint was able to get back home to Kolozsvar. Parliament had now been adjourned after a winter session made monotonous by a series of futile verbal battles, mostly about the proposed new House Rules. The only serious piece of legislation to receive the assent of the House was the motion concerning land reform in Tran-sylvania. This was the first tangible result of the Szekler congress at Homorod. It was only a modest beginning to what Balint was anxious to bring about, but at least it was a first step. The rest of the debates were given over to meaningless obstructive measures put forward by those who wished to embarrass the government; or resentful echoes of matters the Hungarian representatives had discussed in Vienna, particularly a proposition made there by the Hungarian Minister of Defence concerning army officers' pay.

There seemed to be some connection, though no one was quite sure what, between these events and the reappearance on the political scene of Kristoffy. At the beginning of March his banner arose again when he presided over a political meeting called to announce the formation of a new so-called 'Radical' party. Since his resignation from office Kristoffy had been in close touch with the Heir and the party which surrounded him. When he had been a Minister he had, of course, been a faithful servant of the old King, but now he had transferred his allegiance.

The Radical Party itself existed only on paper. It was a sort of slogan to be brandished only by those few university professors, do-gooding intellectuals and the recently-formed Galileo Circle made up of cranky university students who described themselves as 'citizens of the world' or 'superopeans'. The group was of thoroughly bourgeois character and as it included neither socialists nor anyone of the working class, it was not taken seriously by the general public, particularly as Kristoffy, as a former member of the unpopular Bodyguard government, was generally thought of as politically tainted. Nevertheless, though of course it was not then realized, it was from these sources that flowed the current that, ten years later, would lead to revolution. Neither, of course, was it then known that Kristoffy had sold his soul to the Belvedere Palace.

For Balint these weeks passed slowly. He went to meetings, to sessions of Parliament, to dinners and evening parties, but he felt his life to be meaningless and empty. He tried to take up once again the half-philosophical, half-doctrinal treatise that he had started to write under the spur of his love for Adrienne but which he had dropped when it seemed that this love was doomed never to be fulfilled. Then it had been a song of love, for Addy had not yet been his and his yearning for her had inspired every line.

Now that he had not seen her for several months his desire for her had in some way been strengthened and he determined not to put off any longer serious plans for their future life together.

While they had been able to meet frequently this thought had not been so compelling. Even when they had had to take extra care in planning their secret meetings – and days had often gone by without any opportunity of seeing each other – the intervals of separation had never been prolonged and this gave them both the feeling of belonging to each other, almost indeed of their living together with his absences caused only by his work. The previous spring, summer and autumn had passed in this manner. Balint had often had to absent himself for political reasons, for his work for the co-operative projects or simply to look after the Abady lands and interests at Denestornya and in the mountains;

but all this time, because they both knew that they would soon be together again, these absences did not seem to matter. But for the last three months, three long months, things had not been the same. They had had no opportunity to meet at all and their situation was far from happy. There was no way now that they could meet; they were inexorably shut off from any contact. If Adrienne had fallen ill he would not have been able to go to her or help her in any way. He could only wait in the hope of perhaps hearing something by chance gossip just as if he were a stranger. It was dreadful and deeply frustrating. Adrienne managed occasionally to write and this was how he learned that her daughter's attack of measles had developed complications, that the girl's convalescence would be slow and that she could not leave her side until the child was completely recovered. Waiting ... waiting ... waiting...

As the days passed into weeks and the weeks into months Balint's determination grew ever stronger: he must somehow force Adrienne to seek a divorce. They had to marry.

There were only two obstacles in the way, and from a distance both now seemed to him far less formidable than they had previously. The main problem was Uzdy, and Adrienne always insisted he would never let her go. Although she never said it, behind her words lay the conviction that he would rather kill both her and the man she dared to love. But was this really so or merely a fantasy of hers, an imagined nightmare? It was true that he was a deeply confused, unstable man, who was obsessed with firearms and always carried a revolver ... and whose father had died insane. She knew that none of this constituted proof, for he had taken it quite calmly when she had refused to sleep with him. Balint had taken heart at this; but what he did not know, for Addy had not told him, was that the following day Uzdy had followed them like a hunter stalking his prey. So for Balint it seemed that all they had to do was to face the situation, confront Uzdy, and tell him openly...

The other seemingly insurmountable problem was his own mother. She hated Adrienne and would certainly oppose any plans they might make for a life together. Her hatred of Adrienne was unreasoning and senseless and, thought Balint, quite unfathomable. Aware of his mother's dominant and intractable character he knew that it would be far from easy to get her to change her opinions, all the more so since in every other way he had, until now, done everything to please her and avoid giving her pain. And if now he were to defy her and challenge her authority? He was deeply sorry for the sorrow he was bound to cause her and, until recently, had thought that their relationship would be destroyed by such a marriage. Now, however, he tried to make himself believe that the inevitable rift would heal, that his mother's anger would fade and that, in time, she would come to love Adrienne as soon as she had allowed herself to get to know her. Balint, in his loneliness, went on weaving new dreams. He convinced himself that the coldness would pass, that the first grandchild would come, that grandchild for which Countess Roza had always yearned and to whom she constantly referred, and that when there was an heir, a boy, of course, someone to carry on the line ... but here Balint's arguments would dwindle away to be replaced by his yearning for a home-life of his own, for a woman who was his companion in life, who would be a mother to his children – who was a mother already – sitting by a peaceful fireplace, a life without problems, a life of occupation and love and lightness of heart and children for whom it would be a joy to toil.

Wherever he found himself Balint was obsessed by these fantasies: in his seat in the House when surrounded by noisy argument and endless speech-making, at the rooms in the Casino Club where all his acquaintance were still arguing about politics, at formal dinners or at evening parties while languidly drawling sweet nothings to whichever lady happened to be sitting next to him: wherever he was he was like a sleep-walker. Young Magda Szent-Gyorgyi, with her quick-sighted birdlike eyes, had noticed it at once and said to him outright, 'Whatever have you been doing to get so absent-minded? I suppose you've been out carousing with the ladies of the town, what?' for Magda liked to talk in this way so as to show off how knowledgeable she was about relationships between the sexes. 'You've lost weight too!' she added laughing. 'Tell me, do tell me, is all that very ... very ...' and she broke off not quite able to put into words the rather uncertain ideas that were floating around in her inquisitive little head.

Finally, in the middle of March, the long-hoped-for message arrived. Her husband's mother was going to take the child to Meran where it was hoped she would recover more quickly, and this meant that in a few days' time Adrienne would be free to come to the Uzdy villa just outside the town. Her young sister Margit would be with her and they would both be there in time to run their own stall at the charity bazaar which was held each year for the benefit of the orphanage. At last they would see each other again.

The bazaar organized annually by the Archduchess Maria-Valeria Circle was a great event in Kolozsvar. Every lady with any pretensions to a position in Society joined in the preparations, the older matrons acted as official patronesses and the younger ones, and the unmarried girls, manned the stalls and, for one day, pretended to be salesgirls. At each stand there were two or three of them, at least one from an aristocratic family, the others from the prosperous middle classes.

There was much jockeying for position in the days that led up to the bazaar itself, for there was considerable rivalry as to who should sell what and in what part of the hall their tent-like stands should be erected. It was not only important to have one of the best positions, it was also hotly disputed who should be placed next to whom and important to make sure that no one was displaying the same merchandise as their neighbours. It was not easy, either, to invent something new and original which might therefore lead to that great triumph of receiving more money than anyone else. The decoration of the stands was therefore also extremely important. It had to be at the same time striking and sufficiently open to attract buyers while being discreet and intimate enough to make them sit down, chat, and open their purses to be milked of every penny they had brought with them. To ensure this was the job of all the prettiest young girls.

The hall in which the bazaar was held was known as the *Redut* – a local corruption of the Viennese *Redoutensaal* named after the masked balls which were held there. The Kolozsvar *Redut*, which was built in the eighteenth century, had once been the seat of the Transylvanian Parliament. Now it was used for balls – and for the great charity bazaar. It was very large and had an immensely high ceiling.

On each side of the main hall there were other rooms. On the occasion of the bazaar, one of these was used as a changing-room for the amateur artistes who would later give a theatrical entertainment, while the other was made into a sort of drawing-room where the older ladies could withdraw to rest and have some coffee or other light refreshments. Near the door of the first room was a raised platform where there were placed chairs for the Lady Patronesses and which would later serve as a temporary stage. Down the full length of the hall were placed the tent-like stands which were so close to each other that it was difficult to pass between them. Each was different. Some of the stall-holders had used Persian carpets as decoration, others were hung with long streaming ribbons, or peasant embroideries, or bales of silks in a myriad brilliant colours. And as to the goods on sale they were as varied as the colours of the stands themselves. Everything was there from home-brewed liqueurs to delicate needlework. It was a vivid scene suggesting an oriental market which happened to be taking place not in the open air but in a rococo ballroom. And in the centre of each stand there was an elegant lady and some smiling girls ready to tempt the cash out of anyone's purse.

A large number of men were strolling up and down the wide alley between the open stalls.

The bazaar was attended not only by the townspeople but many country folk too who had crowded into Kolozsvar for the great annual agricultural meeting. The ladies of the organizing committee planned this date on purpose because they knew that thereby they ensured the presence in town of all Transylvania's leading citizens. It was considered an unwritten law that everyone must attend the bazaar, not only to make an appearance but also to buy; and this applied to young and old alike. Therefore at the Maria-Valeria Bazaar you would meet not only the young men but also the old ones such as Sandor Kendy, Stanislo Gyeroffy, and even Miklos Absolon and old Daniel Kendy. Young Farkas Alvinczy and Isti Kamuthy had come specially from Budapest and as both of them were now in Parliament they were treated as important personalities. Even Joska Kendy had put in an appearance, not because of anything to do with horses (which was all that really interested him) but because he too had become a prominent public figure since his appointment as a Prefect of his county. Only old Rattle Miloth had failed to appear. 'It's not for me, my dear,' he had said to his youngest daughter Margit, 'not for one whose heart is broken like mine! And don't forget there's the place to be run. Someone's got to supervise the ploughing and sowing, and I can't trust that idiotic farm manager of ours!' Margit did not insist for she knew that he had recently made friends with their neighbour, the elder Dezso Kozma, one of those brothers who had been childhood playmates of Roza Abady at Denestornya. The previous Michaelmas he had bought some 2,000 acres of land not far from the Miloth estate and, if the road was not too muddy, old Rattle had taken to visiting his new friend almost daily. Kozma listened contentedly to Akos Miloth's stories for, being a commoner and a newcomer while Count Akos came from a long line of aristocratic landowners, he was flattered by the old man's attentions.

All the men visiting the bazaar were happy to let the bevies of pretty girls cajole them into parting with their money. They carelessly bought anything put before them, some of it useless junk of no value but offered for many times the price they would have paid at one of the town shops. And they bought with such recklessness because these inflated prices included the right to a little mild flirtation. The girls were not ungenerous with their favours for it was exciting to see how much more than its worth the lovesick male could be induced to pay for a one-crown pot of flour, a necktie which usually fetched three crowns or a completely useless paper doll. If she smiled a little more than he had expected, if she leaned towards him so that he could catch the scent of her perfumed shoulders, or if – just by chance of course – a lock of her hair brushed his cheek, if she sold just a little bit of herself, then the money came raining in and the sense of triumph made eyes shine brighter and added a touch of real sensuality to every laugh. Even the most upright and straitlaced of women can occasionally succumb to the lure of trying a little hint of seduction without ever realizing that it was perhaps tantamount to prostitution ... but by this process the most natural of instincts was satisfied by knowing exactly how much money each girl's charms were worth to their eager male customers.

Some of the stands were more popular than others and around one or two there was a positive crowd. Some of the customers were real buyers while others, after making some insignificant purchase, just stayed to chat. The bar this year was in the charge of Isti Kamuthy's pretty older sister, Countess Szentpali, who had recruited the two elder Laczok girls to help her. They were busy encouraging everyone to sample their flasks of French brandy and Benedictine. The only one of their customers who needed no urging was old Daniel Kendy who made straight for the bar

on arrival and settled down for the duration of the event, though
he was absolutely penniless and did not have the means to buy
himself anything let alone spirits at three times their normal
price. It was a well thought-out move, for all his friends who
passed by found themselves obliged to offer the old man a drink.
Daniel had a wonderful time, which he remembered for a long
time to come; and it was made even more memorable for him
when Laszlo Gyeroffy turned up, sat down beside him and
started ordering double-sized drinks for them both.

In the stand across the way Mrs Bogdan Lazar was selling
honey, the product of her own bees, in attractive specially
designed little jars. She was being helped by Dodo Gyalakuthy
who had brought her own home-made honey-cakes to complement the pure honey. At this stand, too, there was someone who
never moved away. He was a large, sturdy red-haired man with
a long bony face covered in freckles; and he was a foreigner, Ugo
von der Maultasch, who came from Pomerania on the Baltic
coast of Prussia. What brought him to Transylvania no one
knew, unless it was the mysterious scent of money which was
apt to reach penniless Teutonic barons, no matter how far away
they lived, and tell them where marriageable heiresses were to
be found.

He had arrived some weeks before the bazaar and had been
courting Dodo assiduously ever since. Now he was not buying
up the whole stand, as an ambitious Hungarian might have done,
but was making himself discreetly useful, always at hand to help,
wrapping parcels and praising the merchandise seemingly unconscious of the fact that few people could understand his outlandish north German accent. He was presumably working hard
to show what a helpful and useful fellow he could be.

Adrienne Miloth's stand was not far away, a little nearer to the
Patronesses' platform where the dowagers sat enthroned.

With her was the attractive young wife of Dr Bela Korosi, the
elderly university professor who was a prominent member of the
Opposition in Transylvania and a power at the provincial assembly, where he led the Independence Party. Mrs Korosi was a
pretty dark-haired woman with large eyes and a sweet slightly
plaintive expression which seemed to say, 'Oh dear! Politics and
public affairs! There seems to be so much of it! My husband's
entirely wrapped up in such things, and in his teaching . . . why,
he hardly has time to notice poor little me!'

Their stand had been made to look like a toy shop that specialized in dolls of every sort. There were giant ones from Italy, the size of a six-month-old child, and tiny ones made from a single little cotton tassel, many of them hanging in rows along the front and the sides of the stand, all sorts of Punchinello dolls, comic dolls and baby-dolls; and the largest sat on the counter staring up at the customers with their huge glass eyes.

From a distance it was hardly possible to see what Adrienne's stall held for the crush of buyers crowding around. The pretty little Mrs Korosi was a general favourite and all the young men from the Miloths' circle of friends, the Alvinczys, Pityu Kendy, Kadacsay and many others, kept on coming back even if from time to time they strayed briefly to other stalls or to the bar. Only Uncle Ambrus never moved. He brought up a chair, placed it beside Adrienne and never ceased, in his noisiest manner, to pay court to her across the bonnets and silken hair of the dolls and puppets. He was trying to show by this proprietorial manner that he had some sort of prior right to Adrienne's attention and so he played the part of a sort of host. He interfered when customers were bargaining, shouting at the young men who clustered round, 'Don't be so stubborn, you ass, let's see the colour of your money!' or else, 'Don't fool around, young fella-me-lad, do as I do! For this lovely lady I'd let them skin me alive!' And so he thundered on; and he was as good as his word, himself buying the largest doll on display for many times its proper price. He kept the thing on his lap, rocking it in his arms and crying, 'What a lovely baby! But I could make a better one!' leering at Adrienne as he spoke. For Ambrus the opportunity was worth every penny he had spent, especially as Adrienne was so busy that she could not answer back.

Business was good, but there was a problem. As soon as a sale had been made someone had to take the sold doll down and wrap it for the purchaser. This was the job of the two young girls on the stand, Liszka Laczok and Adrienne's own youngest sister, Margit. Liszka was rushed off her feet, unable to cope with the rush as for most of the time Margit was nowhere to be seen. Each time she was wanted they had to call and call, often as many as eight or ten times, and a few moments after she had reappeared she was gone again.

In fact she was not very far away, only a few feet in fact, hiding in the little space between the stand and the wall.

In that little narrow space she was sitting, not alone but with
Adam Alvinczy, and it was from there that she reappeared when
the calls became too insistent. 'Why! Here I am!' she would say,
wide-eyed and innocent; but she wasn't there for long. Margit
had something on hand that was for her far more important than
merely wrapping parcels at a charity bazaar; she had to cheer up
poor love-sick Adam.

Adam was more forlorn than ever, parading his sorrow at
length and finding beautiful love-sick words with which to do
so. It was, of course, the old story of his yearning for Adrienne
who now would not even look at him let alone speak to him.
Why, she even seemed to favour old Uncle Ambrus while hardly
noticing Adam's existence; it was truly depressing.

This was a familiar subject between Adam and young Margit,
and, as far as Margit at least was concerned, it was well worth
talking about, as would have been anything that kept them
together. And together they certainly were, huddled closely on
a narrow chest where there was hardly any room, the long-legged
Adam and the little round Margit. In such a constricted space
they were obliged to sit closely together, their arms linked, not,
of course, in an embrace, but simply because otherwise one or
other would have fallen to the floor. And if they were whispering
into each other's ears, so closely that the mouth of one might
have been caressing the ear of the other – that, too, was not kissing, not at all, for it was merely by chance that their nearness
entailed such intimacy. Merely one of life's little hazards for
which no one could be blamed.

The main subject between them, either in conversation or in
their letters, was Adrienne's heartlessness. But more and more
there was another aspect of the matter which had come to the
fore: this was Margit's great capacity for understanding. And this
was what they were discussing at the bazaar. Margit, they agreed
between them, after she had first rather shyly made the suggestion, was quite different from her sister. She was warm-hearted,
understanding, compassionate, even merciful, and she could so
well understand what Adam was suffering. She was, unlike the
other, sympathetic . . . so sympathetic indeed that it was increasingly in vain that Adrienne and Mrs Korosi called for her, for
how could she leave poor Adam alone with his great heart and
his great sorrow? And this, no doubt, is what she would have
replied if anyone had taken her to task for neglecting her duties.

* * *

Roza Abady sat on the Patronesses' platform among the other dowagers, not because she liked it or had wanted to be there, but because on this occasion she felt it was her duty. Countess Abady's presence was important and conferred an honour upon the other ladies because it was well-known that she never went out and only saw her friends in her own home. As it happened Countess Roza was already beginning to regret that she had come because she had been forced to have Aunt Lizinka sitting next to her and Aunt Lizinka, as always, let out a stream of poisonous gossip without drawing breath for an instant. Today it was worse than ever, especially for Countess Roza, because Aunt Lizinka had chosen Adrienne for her special target, to which she added pretty little Mrs Korosi, simply because their stall seemed particularly popular with the men. This hurt all the more because it was only that morning that Balint had returned from Budapest, having only now, it appeared, finished his business there; and the old lady found it hard to believe that Adrienne's move to Kolozsvar had nothing to do with it. Of course, she thought, he had come only because of that woman – and here she was, flirting with all the world in front of the man who thought only of her. If only Roza could believe that Adrienne really loved her son; but no, there she was, leading everyone on, even that terrible old peasant Ambrus Kendy just as if she were in love with him! Of course she must have had an affair with Ambrus – or rather shouldn't she say 'with him too!' These were the thoughts which were upsetting Countess Roza so much that her tired old heart constricted with pain and hatred. Meanwhile Lizinka did not let up. Now she was whispering.

'You see, my dear Roza, that is how such women are today. One man isn't enough! Oh no! They want a dozen of them, all at once. Look over there, I beg you, just look! You see how Adrienne Uzdy is bending over my nephew Ambrus! Shameless! Why, she might just as well be sitting in his lap before our very eyes!'

It was true that Adrienne was making it obvious to everybody that she was flirting with Uncle Ambrus. She was doing it on purpose because she knew that Balint had returned and would no doubt come to the bazaar to search her out and it was important that this at least should attract no notice and, therefore, no gossip. It was particularly important because Uzdy was strolling about the hall and every now and again looking over towards her, staring from his great height over the heads of everyone else to check on what she was doing. If only, Adrienne thought, he would notice what she was up to with Ambrus for then he would be less likely to take any notice of Balint.

Countess Roza sat stiffly upright in her chair, her eyes constantly on the main entrance watching for her son's arrival. She made no reply to what old Lizinka Sarmasaghy was saying. She merely prayed that the old gossip-monger would start attacking someone else and drop a subject that she found infinitely distressing.

But nothing deterred Lizinka.

'What I'd like to know,' she was saying, 'is how she manages to keep them all? No one used to be more of a womanizer than Ambrus, running after a different woman every day – but she's kept him at her skirts for more than a year. Maybe she has some hidden secret, like the witches of old; but what it is, my dear, we'll never know!'

Seven o'clock had come and gone and now the crowd was beginning to thin out. There were still plenty of men, however, who were staying on so as to take out to dinner the ladies who had worked so hard at the stands; and there was plenty of time before that, for there was still the theatrical performance to come; and for this all sorts of new people would arrive.

It was at this point that Balint came in. He did not go straight to Adrienne's stand but went first to several others before mounting the Lady Patronesses' platform and greeting his mother and the other ladies, most of whom were now profoundly bored, especially as they had been joined by old Sandor Kendy and the retired Major Bogacsy who was telling them for the umpteenth time all the details of some long forgotten duel. Balint first of all kissed his mother's hand, then he greeted all the others in the same way, suffering a wet kiss on his forehead from Lizinka, and then sat down beside Countess Gyalakuthy and pretended to listen politely to what Bogacsy was saying.

The presence of Balint on the platform which was normally used only by the older people soon prompted two of the other young men to come up too. These were Farkas Alvinczy and Isti Kamuthy who, since their election to Parliament, had become imbued with a sense of their own importance and thought it only right to show it by separating themselves from the noisy laughing crowd that was milling about below them.

Since Farkas had become an elected legislator he had totally changed from the happy-go-lucky young man, who was kind to everyone, danced beautifully and who laughed and joked and went on light-hearted drinking bouts with the others, to a pompous and conceited young politician anxious only to show how important he had become – though in reality his only political function was to attend the House and meetings of the Independence Party and vote in the way he was told to do by the party leaders. Farkas himself barely realized that in Budapest he was merely one of a faceless crowd, and back at home in Transylvania he was anxious to cut a dash in front of all his relations. Nowadays his handsome Grecian face – all the Alvinczy brothers looked alike – rarely wore a smile; and he refused to discuss anything but politics.

Budapest had had an even worse effect on Kamuthy, who had become a slave to what he thought was fashion. Some enterprising tailor had taken advantage of his vanity and convinced this essentially provincial young man that he had a naturally English appearance. This statement had had the effect of a revelation upon young Kamuthy, especially as he already had a natural lisp which he hoped sounded like the English 'th' and which he now used relentlessly even when it did not come naturally. Isti also started dressing in what he fondly believed to be an English manner, but it was more that of the Englishman in a French farce, with a hound's-tooth check grey morning coat, grey tie, top hat and white spats. To top it all he had taken to sporting a monocle and side whiskers to frame his pink baby face.

The two politicians came straight over to Balint and at once embarked on their favourite topic: 'What have you to thay about the thituation in Parliament?' asked Kamuthy. Then, without waiting for an answer, he went on, 'Perthonally I find it motht alarming. I told Gyula Juthth that hith Houth Rulth reformth are motht untimely!'

'And why?' interrupted Alvinczy. 'Kossuth is perfectly right! It's the only way to maintain any sort of order. The country needs something different from what we've got.'

'The Anglith conthtitution,' said Kamuthy, making the 'e' in English sound like a flat 'a', 'doethn't allow for Houth Rulth. At Wethtminthter only tradition counth.'

Old Crookface growled his disgust at the young men's foolishness, but as he could hardly use his habitual filthy language in front of the dowagers he rose noisily from his seat and fled.

The bored and long-suffering Lady Patronesses also found the intrusion more than they could bear and gradually melted away. So did Balint; and eventually the only two left on the platform were the tall Alvinczy and the short Kamuthy, who continued their argument for all to see – which both of them no doubt thought was an impressive and improving sight.

At length one of the organizers came up and asked them to move elsewhere as the platform was now needed for the entertainment.

As it turned out the entertainment ended sooner than had been planned because one of the star attractions had to be cancelled: this was Laszlo Gyeroffy playing the violin. Laszlo, like old Daniel, had become so dazed with drink that both had had to be helped out of the hall before disaster struck. When the entertainment came to an end the public melted away and the bazaar was over. Now the great hall looked quite different. Whereas at the beginning it had had all the air of an oriental market-place, now it looked like a gypsy encampment after a pogrom. The stalls had all been stripped of their wares; for not only had everything been sold but many of the decorations had been sold too. Some stands were lacking parts of their decoration and were now showing the bare wooden laths of which they had been constructed.

Now all the organizing ladies handed over their takings to the honorary secretary of the charity and at last everyone could relax and have supper.

The original plan had been that everyone should now retire to the *Redut*'s restaurant, where a cold buffet had been laid out for them, but as no one seemed to want to move the men went to the buffet and brought back plates and glasses, dishes of food, napkins and knives and forks and spread the supper over the empty shelves of the stands and even on the floor.

Many of them formed little groups, sitting down on carpets or cushions robbed from the stands with, in front of them, great dishes of cold roast turkey or galantine or a ham garnished with all sorts of delicious savoury specialities. In a few moments Laji Pongracz and his gypsy musicians appeared, grouped themselves a little way off from the diners and in an instant the violins began to play.

Adrienne and her friends took possession of the Lady Patronesses' platform with its wide steps where, as theirs was the largest group, there was room for them all. They were joined by the two other Laczok girls, the young Countess Szentpali, by Dodo Gyalakuthy, and finally by young Margit, who by now was somewhat dishevelled, and Adam Alvinczy whose right jacket shoulder was covered with greenish whitewash from the walls of the hall, not that anyone seemed to notice. Mrs Korosi and some of her women friends occupied the other side of the platform along with some young men who had come with them from Budapest for the occasion. This group was joined by Joska Kendy, the new Prefect of Kukullo, who, in his silent manner, was paying court to the professor's pretty young wife.

The effect was bizarre enough; the women in their elaborate silk dresses reclining like Turkish houris on the floor and close to them their equally elegantly dressed escorts all sporting the objects that they had bought from the ladies they courted, whether this courtship was serious or merely in fun. Most of the men were carrying dolls and though Uncle Ambrus had already taken his leave, there were still plenty of others carrying their symbols of gallantry. The smallest was a tiny tassel doll which Joska Kendy had attached to the stem of that pipe which was never out of his mouth. Others peeped from Adam Alvinczy's pockets, a giant Mr Punch was suspended from around Pityu Kendy's neck and Abady had sat his Pierrot doll on the ground beside him. In the other group on the platform a further multitude of dolls advertised the success of Adrienne's stall. Ugo von der Maultasch, on the other hand, had somehow pinned a large gingerbread heart on his waistcoat. Odd though all this looked, no one was quite as ludicrous as young Kamuthy.

In the course of strolling elegantly up and down the aisles of the bazaar Kamuthy had found himself at one point in front of the Stamp Collectors' stand and there the ladies greeted him with cries of joy as if he had been a visiting Englishman.

'But we were sure you were English!' they screamed, and made him repeat 'Anglish! Anglish! Anglish!' over and over until he was so overcome with joy and flattery that he allowed them to stick a whole sheet of ten-cent stamps on his forehead. All Transylvanians, be they men or women, never cease to take pleasure in making fun of themselves and of other people – and so it was now with young Kamuthy. By the time the stamps had dried to his skin he had entirely forgotten they were there.

Laji's musicians played on, but not so loudly as to drown the conversation or prevent the exchange of anecdotes.

Much of the talk was being led by young Akos Alvinczy, who had become a sort of honorary aide-de-camp to the new Prefect of Kukullo, Joska Kendy. Despite the fact that Joska was sitting only a few feet away making sheep's eyes at Mrs Korosi, nothing would deter Akos from telling a series of stories which all had Joska as their hero. *Ad majorem Joskam gloriam* – to the greater glory of Joska – might have been the motto of Akos's tales.

In Joska's office, Akos related, there was a young trainee who did not turn up for work for several days. The Prefect had a notice printed which he distributed round the town. It read 'A TRAINEE HAS GONE ASTRAY – TEN CROWNS REWARD TO THE HONEST FINDER' exactly as if the youth had been a stray animal. Within minutes the young man had reappeared at the Town Hall from which he hadn't budged since.

Not far away, he went on, there lived a retired Austrian army officer, who owned some land and who had bought a threshing machine from the government agricultural store. It had the Hungarian national crest fixed to the side. The Austrian somehow laid his hands on a little metal double-headed eagle and pinned this over the Hungarian emblem. So what did Joska do? He asked the man if he had obtained permission from the Emperor to sport the Habsburg crest? If he had, then all was well; but if he didn't then he'd first be prosecuted for usurping a foreign emblem, then he'd find that his water-pail was too far – or too close – to the engine and, whatever fault had been established, woe to him as all threshing would be prohibited for three months!

There were roars of laughter as each story came to an end, for Akos knew well how to tell a tale to good effect. Only Gazsi Kadacsay, who was sitting nearby, seemed to grow sadder and sadder as he listened. In the past Joska had been his hero, the ideal man, who knew more about horses than anyone living and who held the reins better than any other amateur driver. Ever since he had been a small boy Gazsi had done all he could to imitate and emulate him, and if he couldn't surpass him as a driver at least, perhaps, he might excel as a rider. It was, of course, true – as he knew to his cost – that it was not advisable to buy a horse from Joska; but then in that world cheating when selling horses was accounted almost as a virtue, a skill to be admired! Later it had seemed to Gazsi that Joska had not seemed unduly troubled by his conscience in other matters either, but then, as long as he was merely an amateur sportsman, such failings could be overlooked.

The death blow to Gazsi's hero-worship had come when Joska accepted the post of Prefect, for now his lack of conscience came as a real disappointment. Gazsi felt somehow deceived and started to look at his friend with new eyes, and judge him ever more harshly; for this revelation of his old hero's real character coincided with a new spiritual hunger that, had he known it, had been growing in him for several years past. More and more it was borne in upon him that all those years spent in trying to be like Joska were wasted years, years squandered in pursuit of a foolish, vain and useless dream. Gazsi, though basically intelligent, had not done as well at school as he should have. Though a volunteer for army service he had remained a soldier principally because in those days young officers in hussar regiments spent most of their time, like Joska, either riding in steeplechases or resting while their collarbones, broken at point-to-point races or in training sessions, had time to mend. Now he began to realize that he was ignorant and knew nothing of things that really mattered. Accordingly he had left the army, started buying books and studying in a mad desire to catch up on everything that he had previously disregarded. His reading was haphazard and indiscriminate. He would read anything, particularly works of philosophy. But the more he read the more bewildered he became. He would puzzle out one problem only to be faced with another; and when he had started to tackle the next subject the more complicated and puzzling it would seem. And the more he read the more he developed a deep resentment for his former neglect of himself: and with it almost a hatred for Joska Kendy on whom he had squandered ten long years of hero-worship. And when he drank too much, as he had on the day of the bazaar, these thoughts became so strong as to become almost an obsession.

Akos Alvinczy was telling a new story. This time it concerned a landowner, one Todor Racz, whose property was situated in a remote country district. He was a passionate but singularly unskilful gambler and, of course, he usually lost. The new Prefect,

Joska, was one of his regular poker school. One night, after the usual disastrous session, Racz told everyone that this would have to be the last time he played because in two days' time the bailiffs would come to take possession of all he owned. For years, Racz explained, he had managed not to pay any taxes, not a penny, but now they had caught up with him and everything he owned would have to go to auction. What, asked Akos, did Joska do? Why, he sent for the village headman and ordered him to declare an outbreak of cholera in the district and to mark every other house with a red cross, thereby in effect putting the whole district in quarantine. When the bailiffs arrived on the following day they were chased away by armed guards from the village itself.

'And so Todor Racz's absence didn't spoil their game after all. He went on playing and to this day the bailiffs haven't dared set foot in the place!'

At this Gazsi could no longer contain his anger. 'I don't think that's at all funny. No humour in that little stor-r-ry!' he growled, rolling his 'r's as usual. 'A Prefect isn't appointed to ensur-r-re that a fellow ar-r-ristocr-r-rat can welsh on his taxes!'

Whatever, they all wondered, had come over Baron Gazsi? He had always been such a joker, a fellow never known to take anything seriously. Abady, however, remembered the little speech that Gazsi had made that evening at Mezo-Varjas when, though less tipsy than tonight, he had talked about the non-existence of true happiness. Something is troubling this man, he thought, as everyone else looked at Gazsi astonished.

Joska Kendy merely took his friend's words as the introduction to some joke or other and so, from where he sat near to Mrs Korosi – having until now behaved as if he had heard nothing at all of these flattering stories about himself – he called out, pipe in mouth, 'When four-legged animals form a government you too can be a Prefect!' in the sort of bantering tone they had always used with each other.

'Not even then!' retorted Gazsi in an angry tone. 'I'd never accept a job I didn't know how to do. I'm a fool, a donkey, and I know it!'

'Fancy admitting it! That's most interesting,' said Joska in a tone of unconcerned mockery.

'And even if I were made Pr-r-refect for four-legged animals – as you so cleverly put it, meaning donkeys I presume – I'd still feel I had some obligations and not tr-r-reat it all as some kind

of joke!' Turning to Balint, Gazsi went on, 'Aren't I right? You
talked to me once about this. Do you remember?' And then, not
waiting for an answer, he shouted over to Joska, 'At least I admit
I'm a donkey.'

'And what does that mean?' asked Joska drily, pipe in mouth,
but with a serious expression which showed them all that the
argument was about to get serious. Gazsi hesitated for a moment,
obviously searching in his mind for the appropriate insult.

At this point a tall lean figure stepped up between the place on
the platform where Joska was sitting and the stand, a yard or two
away, where Gazsi had sat down. It was Pali Uzdy, tall as a tower,
who was dressed in a long travelling overcoat. Totally disregarding everyone else he stopped in front of his wife, put one booted
foot on the steps leading up to the platform and said, 'I'm leaving
for Almasko! Do you have any messages, dear Adrienne? Is there
anything you need from there?'

'You're going now? At this time of night?' asked his wife,
somewhat taken by surprise.

Uzdy's slanting eyebrows were raised even higher than usual
as he asked, 'Surely, my dear, you are not still surprised by my
comings and goings?' And his tone was as ironic as ever. 'My
carriage is at the door. So there is nothing you want? Good! Well,
I just asked. Well, well! Goodbye then! Until we meet again!'
and he swept his beaver hat in a wide gesture of general farewell.
'Goodbye to you all!'

He turned and stalked out with the same silent measured tread
as when he had walked up a few moments before.

When the doors had closed behind him Adrienne's and
Balint's eyes met for a brief second.

Young Kamuthy now decided to take advantage of the sudden
silence to return to his favourite theme. 'In Angland,' he said
with even more self-importance than before, 'no one expecths
national figureth to be experths in their jobthe. On the contrary,
they feel that too much expertithe destroythe all objectivity.'

'Well, nothing'll destroy yours!' shouted Joska, who was all too
glad of the diversion because he would have hated to have been
obliged to have it out with Gazsi as this would have meant
making their dispute an 'affair of honour' with the inevitable
duel to follow. Everyone, in fact, was happy that the laughter and
the joking had started again and they all joined in with gales of
mirth when Pityu Kendy went for Kamuthy and said, 'You'd do

better to go and wash those stamps off your face, young man! Someone might try to shove you in the post-box!' At which the stage-Englishman touched his forehead and, horrified, screamed out in English, 'Oh, my God! Oh, Lord! Oh, Lord!' and ran shamefacedly away.

Kamuthy's going prompted others to leave too.

'Goodness, how late it is! Time to go home!' said someone; and at these words, as if by magic, everyone started getting their things together.

'Only now, when the party's over, does one notice how tired one is,' said Adrienne as she walked towards the door.

Balint stayed on for a few moments, barely seeming to notice Adrienne's departure. He appeared to be absorbed in something that the Prussian baron was explaining – though it might have been that he was merely fascinated by Ugo's Pomeranian accent.

'*Das ist man so, wie ich soeben Ihnen sagte, mein lieber Graf; bei uns und auch in Ost-Preussen ist es wohl nicht anders* – that is how it is, as I've just explained to you, my dear Count; with us and also in East Prussia, it is never otherwise ...'

CHAPTER THREE

ADRIENNE'S BEDROOM WAS in almost total darkness. Only a single candle was burning and this she had placed on the floor beside one of the bedside tables. The light was therefore indirect and cast strange shadows on the walls, transforming the outlines of the table-legs into weird lines that broke disconcertingly at the angle of the ceiling. The outline of the bed threw half the room into shadow as if it were filled with dark clouds. The unusual source of light gave a sense of fantasy to a room whose appearance was normally quite ordinary, indeed almost banal. There were a few upholstered chairs dating from the 1860s, a chest of drawers indistinguishable from countless others, and, in front of one of the windows, a dressing-table. On the walls was a faded wallpaper: nothing more. If it had not been for the bed the room would have been like any of those furnished for occasional guests. Adrienne's bed was exceptionally large, had no headboard or tester, and was covered with flounces of flowing ivory-covered lace draperies. In the grey, ordinary, otherwise cheaply-furnished room, it was like an exotic foreigner. Indeed this bed was the only thing in the room which was Adrienne's own; all the other pieces had been put there originally by her mother-in-law. There it was, an alien object, as out of tune with everything else as were, in the adjoining drawing-room, the white woolly carpets strewn with multi-coloured cushions that Adrienne had placed in front of the vast chimney-piece and which contrasted so strangely with the severe lines of the despised Empire furniture which Countess Uzdy had thought fit for her daughter-in-law's use.

Everything that Adrienne had brought to these rooms had a curiously temporary character, as if they were a nomad's possessions put down wherever their owner should lay his head. The great divan set haphazardly in the centre of the room, pillows, blankets; they had come with her and should she go away and remove them then the rooms would not change but merely revert to their original appearance. It was as if their owner had merely chosen the rooms to camp in, rather as Bedouins might set up their tents between the columns of some classical temple.

The only definite colour in the room was the triangle of black on the pillows where Adrienne's hair lay fanned out like an ancient Egyptian wig.

She was awake; and waiting, for she was sure that Balint would come to her that night. They had not discussed it, indeed they had had no opportunity, and besides Uzdy had been in Kolozsvar and no one had known of his imminent departure until he himself had announced it so abruptly and unexpectedly at the end of the bazaar. Adrienne's and Balint's eyes had met, just for a brief instant, but it had been enough. Their meeting that night had to be, must be, after so many months of waiting and aching for one another.

It had been a long, long time. Ever since Adrienne had returned to Almasko from her father's home at Varjas they had not been able to meet. That had been the beginning of November and now it was the end of March. Endless days, endless nights of absence and yearning and waiting. It had been the same for both of them, obliged to live apart and only from time to time getting a brief note one from the other; for a regular correspondence would have been too conspicuous and drawn attention to them. For Adrienne it was as if she were a prisoner in her husband's and mother-in-law's house without even the consideration offered to a guest. There had been dreadful weeks of worry over the health of her little daughter, and of struggle, too, with her mother-in-law who ever since the child had been born had taken full charge of the girl and done everything to exclude the mother. When the child was well Adrienne had not seemed to mind so much and, indeed, after the first few confrontations with Countess Clémence, had given up the unequal struggle. That had been eight years before, when Adrienne herself had still been very young. She had had to give in; and slowly she had got used to the fact that they had stolen her child from her, though this had been somewhat if not entirely alleviated by the growing knowledge that little Clemmie herself was so different from her mother, so passive and unresponsive that she might have been someone else's child.

But Adrienne's own passive consent had vanished the day that the child had fallen ill. By nature all women are nurses. It is one of the immutable laws of motherhood and it is doubly true when it is the woman's own offspring who needs care. Adrienne's first outright revolt came when the old countess, without even telling the child's mother, had a trained Red Cross nurse sent out from Kolozsvar. There had been an appalling scene between the mother and grandmother made all the more bitter and distressing because it had been conducted with the greatest politeness and in calm, smooth words whose meaning was impregnated by mutual hatred. Her husband had not helped her but had merely sat by and listened in silence to the embittered dispute between the two women. It was almost as if he were amused by the scene. As it turned out the younger woman won, but her victory was far from complete. All that Adrienne gained was the right to do for her daughter what the Red Cross nurse, or the Nanny, would have done, and even this menial role had to be fought for every day. The Dowager Countess Uzdy watched her every move, hoping to catch her out in some negligence and so use Adrienne's inexperience as an excuse to shut her out again from any contact with her child. The regular taking of the temperature, each medicine or other treatment given, every little change of the symptoms of the girl's illness, had all to be recorded with exact details of the hour and minute – and woe betide anyone who made the smallest omission or error!

That every minute of the day was occupied by this constant preoccupation and worry was, at least in one way, helpful to

Adrienne, indeed beneficial: it kept her occupied. The days and then the weeks went by, and the work made Adrienne put aside the bleakness of her everyday life. One new little joy she had, and it came from the child herself. Little Clemmie had begun to warm towards her mother. During the long convalescence, as Adrienne would sit beside her bed, the little girl would sometimes look up at her mother and smile and often, when the time had come for Adrienne to leave the sickroom and someone had come to relieve her, little Clemmie would try to keep her there, saying, 'Don't go yet. Don't go, please stay with me!' and at the same time putting her little hand in Adrienne's. When she did this she would look slyly up at her grandmother, for it seemed that she only did it when her grandmother was also in the room. When Countess Clémence was not there the child did not say such things . . . or did she? No! Only when the old woman was present. And so it seemed that perhaps she only made up to her mother because she knew it would annoy the old lady, and for no other reason. Adrienne tried hard to put this thought from her for she desperately wanted to believe that her child was genuinely fond of her.

When the little girl was well enough her grandmother took her away, to Meran where they had been so often before. Adrienne came to believe that if little Clemmie had not been whisked away from her so quickly then she might have been able to find her way into the child's heart. But taken away she was, and so the fight for the girl's soul would have to start all over again. And this time it was Adrienne who decided that the battle must be joined . . . and Adrienne who was determined to win.

This is what Adrienne had been thinking about as she stared at the weird shadows on the ceiling of her room.

In the adjoining drawing-room the latch of the French window made an audible click. In the wave of joy at seeing Balint again all these painful memories were wiped from her mind.

'This is no life!' Balint said again. 'This is no life at all!' and he started again to enumerate all the arguments why Adrienne would have to find a way to divorce her husband. They were lying in bed, their bodies clasped tightly together, quite motionless. Their total mutual surrender made every position one of ease and comfort and, just as their souls fused so completely that they had no need of words to understand one another, so their bodies fitted in such harmony that they might have been un-sophisticated wild animals entwined (even if in the cages of a zoo) in the simplicity of uncomplicated sleep. Their faces were very close, so close that their softly murmured words were almost kisses in themselves.

Balint was pleading ever more urgently for Adrienne's divorce. It was necessary, it was inevitable. He used every argument, going over and over the awful circumstances of her life – and his.

It all sounded completely convincing as they lay together, naked flesh to naked flesh, his arms holding her closely, his hands caressing her skin and his lips breathing kisses. Everything spoke to them of freedom, of liberation, of the inevitability of their being forever together. Even so Addy managed somehow to remain calm and matter-of-fact.

She was thinking that perhaps their dream really could be real-ized. Recently Uzdy no longer seemed actively to exercise his old tyranny and indeed while she had been nursing their child he might almost have been avoiding her . . . not that that proved anything for it had happened often before in their life together. Uzdy, she knew well, was nothing if not unpredictable. But there was another question, a serious question, that weighed upon her mind. What was to become of the child? It was unthinkable that she should leave her behind, abandon her! Little Clemmie could not just be sacrificed, as she would be if Adrienne went away and left her to the influence of her husband and mother-in-law. That would be the ruin of the child. Already she was strangely intro-vert and silent, unnaturally reserved for someone of her age. For this Adrienne was sure that her mother-in-law's cold severity was entirely responsible and she felt it was for her to come to the child's rescue. But could she succeed? Even supposing that Uzdy were willing to divorce, one thing was quite clear. He would want his revenge and would stop at nothing to punish her. The old woman would fight to the death to keep her grandchild with her and if Uzdy listened to anyone it was to his mother. There-fore this would be the most dreadful of all obstacles she was bound to encounter. After the last five months' long struggle for control of the child Adrienne felt it would now be humiliating to withdraw.

All this flashed through her mind a brief instant, but she said nothing of it to Balint, only just murmuring to him, 'And the child? What would become of her?'

Balint was taken completely by surprise. Up until now the interests of Adrienne's daughter had never come between them and indeed had almost never been mentioned by her mother except when she had once told him how the child had been taken away; but then Adrienne had always spoken of her as someone who had not been hers for a long time. It had never occurred to Balint that he also had to think about the child's future.

'Why,' he said lightly. 'You will take her with you, of course!' As he spoke it flashed through his mind that this little stranger might now for the first time come between them and help to strengthen her mother's resistance to his pleading.

'I couldn't leave without my child, I couldn't do it, I couldn't', and for the first time she did not look into his eyes as she spoke but gazed past him into the darkness. Balint could not bear to think that now she had gone away from him and that all her thoughts were miles away. His embrace became ever tighter, his mouth wandered all over her face, her neck, her shoulders and his kisses now had an extra purpose – to bring her back to him so dazed by his love that the fire in their souls would be rekindled and that its thousand different forces would all combine to wipe from their minds any thoughts or worries, anxieties, arguments or interests other than the joy of the moment.

What Adrienne had just said started a stream of thought which for some time lay dormant in his subconscious mind, emerging briefly and unformed only from time to time as he lay suddenly aware of his eternal solitude. Now he was lying on his back with his face almost covered by the waves of her long thick hair. From behind the wild thicket of her black curls and without Balint's consciously forming the words, he heard his voice saying, 'From me you will have a son, a beautiful son who will be the fruit of our love. He will inherit your ivory skin and my forehead, your golden eyes and my hair and, and ... he will carry with him always what has been started between us, our thoughts and our beliefs.'

He said it very softly. And each time that his voice faltered, at each break in the phrases, he felt her hands squeeze his shoulders, and every soft nuance of pressure was an acquiescence in what he was saying. It was an answer clearer than any word, an answer of deeply felt agreement. And when he no longer spoke her arms slipped down until she held his body tightly to her and her mouth found his among the tangled locks of hair. A long burning kiss followed that was the seal of an unspoken promise, a vow, a solemn treaty of eternal intent . . .

Just as dawn was breaking Balint stepped out of the French window of Adrienne's sitting-room into the narrow strip of garden between the house and the little wooden gate which opened onto the bridge across the narrow branch of the Szamos river. Here he had to be careful to leave no traces but luckily the snow was so hard in the shadow of the northern side of the house that it was only just when he reached the gate itself that he had to take an extra long stride so as not to sink into the mud beneath the snow. He looked back to make sure that he had left no tracks. There were none.

Once across the rickety little bridge Balint had the choice of walking along the path, now muddy with the first signs of the end of winter, or taking a detour through the park itself. As he was wearing galoshes he decided to brave the park. A light rain was falling but he did not care. It was so beautiful to walk in the growing light of dawn, for his heart was filled with hope – and this hope seemed to be echoed by the sleeping landscape beneath which he could sense the coming of spring.

Even the air seemed laden with promise, as was his own heart.

When they had said goodbye in Adrienne's scented bedroom all she had said was, 'I'll try!' and this was how they had parted. She would try to find an opportunity of raising the question of divorce, and, thought Balint, of course she will succeed, she must succeed. After all Adrienne and her husband hardly lived a real married life and so why should Uzdy want so hard to keep her, as Adrienne seemed to think? Surely it was only Adrienne's absurd fancy that he would not agree to set her free? And anyhow there were laws which covered cases like hers.

Balint strode through the park filling his lungs with the fresh air of the early morning and his heart with renewed hope for the fulfilment of his love for Adrienne. The giant trees around him were like motionless giants of lilac-coloured shadow and at their feet was here and there a patch of still unmelted snow. Little streams were flowing in all directions over the turf, softening the earth and preparing the way for the upsurge of new blades of grass, of flowers and weeds, now lying dormant underfoot. Nature was preparing to renew itself, to rise once again to confront the future, with her eternal strength. In the air of the coming day there floated imperceptibly the scent of renewing life, of fecund spring itself. As Balint strode so confidently towards home his whole being was celebrating not only the coming undisputed possession of the woman he loved but also that thought which had sprung unbidden to his lips only an hour or so ago: Adrienne would bear him a son.

When finally Balint emerged from the avenue of trees he decided to make a further detour before approaching his home. He would take, he thought, a path through the little winding streets of the mediæval part of the town, thus avoiding the main square and any possibility of meeting any acquaintance on their way home from a night of carousing with the gypsies.

Just as he was about to turn the corner into the old Bridge Street a carriage drawn by four horses tore at great speed down the main road. The horses were flecked with sweat and the roof of the carriage had been raised against the cold wind. If there were anyone inside they could not be seen, and anyway Balint was too far away to distinguish anything clearly. As he emerged from the gloom of the narrow little street the carriage was already disappearing round the corner of the market. It had all happened in a flash, and Balint did not pay much attention to the incident, though his mind registered it, just as a fleeting impression, because such a thing was so unusual. No one normally arranged to arrive from the country at such an unholy hour.

Adrienne was sleeping deeply when somewhere a door opened and light streamed into the room. She woke instantly and without moving her head from the pillows opened her eyes. The light was coming from the door to her bathroom which was just opposite the foot of her bed, and in the doorway stood Uzdy in fur coat and hat.

At first Adrienne thought she must be dreaming, so improbable did it seem that Uzdy, who had left for the country only a few hours before, should now actually be there, in her room.

But in a moment his arm shot out, as if he were pointing at her. Something flashed in his hands and there were three sudden explosions that cracked as sharply as a whiplash. Three bullets crashed into the wall above her head and Adrienne realized instantly that her husband was shooting at her. As if jerked by an

invisible spring Adrienne sat up and faced her husband totally
disregarding that there must be two more bullets in the little
Browning. If those two shots were fired she would now be a
direct target.

Adrienne cared nothing for that. She merely stared at her
husband, her chin held high and her wide-open eyes filled with
scorn. She said nothing; she merely looked at him. Between her
full lips her teeth shone white, and the wild black curls of her
hair twisted round her head like the snakes of Medusa. Adrienne
waited; there had to be two more bullets for her. For a few
moments they stared at each other in silence.

Then Uzdy lowered her arm.

'*Alle Ehre!* – congratulations – I call that real courage! Really!
Alle Achtung – all my respects – really!' He pocketed his weapon
and in an instant was back in the doorway, bowing from the waist
with a curious ironic stiffness, his beanpole figure bending so
deeply that he almost gave the impression of being snapped in
two at the waist. Laughing uncontrollably he repeated over and
over, 'That's something! That really is something!'

And Adrienne realized that this demonic laughter resembled
nothing more than that of a naughty child after a successful practical joke.

'Are you mad?' asked Adrienne coldly.

Uzdy did not reply, but merely turned on his heel and left the
room, closing the door behind him. His laughter could still be
heard coming from the room beyond.

Then there was a moment's silence before, from the courtyard,
came the jingle of harness and the clatter of horses' hoofs. Uzdy's
four-horse carriage must be turning towards the gates. For a little
while could be heard the rattle of the wheels on the cobble-
stones, then it grew fainter and finally died away altogether.
Count Uzdy had left as abruptly as he had arrived.

Adrienne remained sitting up in bed for a long time. Only
now, when all danger had passed, did her heartbeats begin to
pound in her throat and the terrible thought came to her that
perhaps Uzdy had now had himself driven to the Abady house
and that there were still two more bullets in his gun.

She jumped quickly out of bed, ran into the freezing drawing-
room next door and hastily scribbled a few lines:

U was here this morning! He is quite mad. He's gone now, but I don't know where! Be very careful! I'll go for a walk this after-noon. If nothing has happened before then you'll find me in the main square.

Then she rang the bell. It was some time before her maid, Jolan, appeared. The old woman's room was far away in the main house and, as it was still very early, she was not yet properly awake. By the time she reached Adrienne's apartments her mistress was once more in her bed.

'Please take this at once to the Abady house in Farkas Street. Tell them to hand it immediately to Count Balint. If he is sleep-ing then they must wake him. I need an answer.'

Three quarters of an hour went by and each minute of waiting was a torture to the woman lying there in her bed. The church clock had already struck eight by the time that Jolan returned, but as, when she entered the room, her expression was unclouded by worry, Adrienne stopped worrying. Clearly nothing untoward had happened and so AB's visiting card, on which he had scribbled 'All right!' in English, was hardly necessary.

Necessary or not Adrienne felt comforted. She barely glanced at the card and in a few moments was asleep.

There was no opportunity for her to tell him anything as they walked together in the town, for young Margit was with them. Later, back at the Uzdy villa, it was the same because several people, including the Laczok girls, Adam Alvinczy and Pityu Kendy, dropped in for tea.

All Adrienne could do, when chatting about the bazaar, was to give special meaning to the phrase 'just like yesterday' by glancing at Balint as she spoke and looking straight into his eyes. In return, to show that he had understood she had some special message for him, he dropped his eyelids for a brief moment and turned his head away. This had become a long-established tech-nique between them when other people were present and there was no chance of talking privately.

Uzdy did not return from the country that day and so Balint was able to come to her room at night. Adrienne showed him the three round bullet-holes in the cream-coloured wallpaper above the bed. Lying there upon the bed they calculated that had Balint been there the previous night the bullets would have passed straight through his chest; and leaning backwards on her elbows Adrienne lay back pretending to lie just where Uzdy would have shot Balint through the heart.

Though today they laughed and joked and made light of it all, for Adrienne their mirth had a darker side to it. Now she could no longer bring herself to believe that Uzdy would ever agree to a divorce. Previously she had only half believed it, but last night's experience had proved to her that, far from being complacent or indifferent, Uzdy had now become even more dangerous. That such a renowned shot had aimed above her – just in fact where he would have hit Balint had he been there an hour before – and that he had stopped shooting the moment she sat up, proved to her that it was not she but her lover who was in danger. Therefore if she were to raise the question of divorce it would be Balint rather than herself who would be in peril. Indifferent as she was to any danger to herself, she dared not do anything that put at risk the life of the man she loved. Though nothing in her manner revealed it Adrienne had spent all day in thinking this out and she had come to the conclusion that she must wait until Balint was not there – perhaps away in Budapest, or better still abroad – before trying to bring up the subject. Even then it would have to be in some devious, roundabout way and until then she must not, under any circumstances, give the smallest indication of what she intended. She would find a way, she had to; but in the meantime she would not even mention to Balint that there was any change in her plans. Accordingly she continued to talk as if she were preparing to discuss the matter with her husband because she knew that if she showed the slightest reluctance then Balint would take matters into his own hands.

And so they continued to talk as if their plans were certain. Though Adrienne was all too aware that she would do anything to avoid immediate action, she found it surprisingly easy to float along on the stream of the previous day's dreams, talking of what would be, and how it would be, and of the child that would be born to them, of how he would look and what he would inherit from each of them.

And so she whispered these things in his ears and interspersed her words with kisses and created in the darkness of her room a fairy-tale world whose shining centre was that real yet unreal being, the unborn son, first as a baby, then as a growing boy and finally as the fully grown heir to Denestornya ... and then again to the fantasy that was once more a tiny infant enchanting them with the wonders of its little pink body.

The child already had a name; it was to be called Adam as if to underline that with him their world was to be reborn and that humanity would take on a new and perfect form, as Goethe had imagined Euphorion in his *Faust*.

Again and again they returned to this theme so that all their nights together would be partly devoted to discussing their as yet unborn son as if he were already the living expression and fulfilment of their love.

CHAPTER FOUR

'COUNT BALINT IS getting up now. He's dressing and will soon be down,' said Mrs Tothy as she entered Countess Roza's big drawing-room where Mrs Baczo, knitting in hand, was sitting alone waiting for her return. It was half-past one, time for luncheon, and this information was meant as much for their mistress, who was at her desk just through the open door sorting out her letters in the little boudoir, as it was for the other housekeeper.

The two women in the big room remained silent for a moment or two before once more beginning to gossip together. They spoke softly, almost in a whisper, and yet loudly enough for everything to be overheard by the countess, should she so wish. And they knew well enough that their mistress would listen avidly to every word they said.

'Well, all I can say is the young master deserves a good lie-in!' said Mrs Tothy. 'He came home very late this morning.'

'Indeed he did!' agreed Mrs Baczo. 'And even then he wasn't left in peace for long. Someone brought him a letter before eight had struck!'

'So they told me,' went on the other. 'From the Monostor road! Cook was just returning from the market and saw the maid who brought it.'

At this point both women sighed deeply as if their hearts would break. Then Mrs Baczo started again, 'And they even insisted on waking poor Count Balint! The woman insisted that it was urgent and she had to carry back a reply.'

'Do you think the young master had been out drinking with the gypsies?' suggested Mrs Tothy cunningly.

'Hardly that!' the other laughed scornfully. 'He hasn't been out doing that for many a year. Oh, no! He went somewhere quite different, I'll be bound . . . and not where he was expected either or they wouldn't have sent a messenger after him so early.'

'Well, at least that's something to be thankful for, if he's going somewhere else for a change!'

The two women laughed together maliciously, but they did not pursue the subject for at this moment Balint came in fresh from his bath. It did not matter for they had already said quite enough.

Roza received her son's morning hand-kiss more warmly than she had for some time. During lunch she listened to all that Balint had to tell her about the bazaar in high good humour, for she had been delighted to have, as she believed, overheard quite by chance that her son had returned home very late that morning and that apparently he had not, for once, been with that accursed woman! Maybe he had even broken with her, for why else would they have sent looking for him from the Uzdy villa if he had been there only an hour before? Countess Roza gloated over the thought of how humiliating it must have been for that Adrienne if she had expected Balint and then he had not come but gone to some other woman. The old lady did not care who that other woman might be for she had always been rather pleased by the idea of her son's success with women, whether at home in Hungary or abroad. It had first come to her notice when Balint had been abroad as a diplomat. Then, when he had been home on leave, and for some time afterwards, letters would arrive from abroad in obviously feminine writing; but Roza would never ask any questions, she would just ponder and smile. It was the same when he used to ride over at night to visit Dinora Malhuysen at neighbouring Maros-Szilvas — which she always heard about from the servants — though again she never asked questions. Countess Roza did not judge such women for she only thought of them as being different, of another race, and would put them all in the same category whether they were professional cocottes or women of her own world who took lovers, or even a single lover, believing such beings to be merely playthings that the good Lord provided for men and who, in any case, would never arouse in them any truly deep feelings.

The first woman she had been afraid of had been Adrienne. She saw how much she meant to her son and she saw, too, how much he suffered when, a year and a half before, he had come back from Venice where they had been together. Recently Countess Roza had not failed to notice how her son seemed to arrange all his movements, and his work, according as to whether he would be able to see Adrienne; and she hated the younger woman for it.

Adrienne was the only person in the world that Countess Roza had ever hated, and her feelings were all the stronger, all the more unforgiving, all the fiercer and more unmerciful because she believed every word of the malicious gossip her housekeepers made sure she overheard. There was no one in the world that Countess Roza held in more contempt than that wicked heartless Adrienne; and it was for this reason that it was with a feeling of joy and triumph that she allowed herself to believe that Balint had now abandoned and so humiliated her.

It was as a result of the bazaar that something else came to pass.

Crookface Kendy had been there when old Daniel Kendy and Laszlo Gyeroffy had to be carried helplessly drunk from the hall. He had become quite used, from many years' experience, to the fact that his second cousin, Daniel, got drunk whenever he could. He dismissed him with the two short words 'old swine'. Daniel was past saving.

But the sight of Laszlo Gyeroffy bothered him. Whenever he turned round there was Laszlo, unsteady on his feet, wobbling uncertainly as he tried to move, being propped up beside the door because his legs would not carry him. All this happened quite close to where Crookface had been sitting. At the moment when they had propped him up Laszlo's face was turned towards him, though because he was surrounded by other people only the upper part of it could be seen, his forehead and those eyebrows that met so strangely in the middle. It was almost as if the young man were looking at him and his angry, somewhat glassy stare, filled old Kendy with recollections of things past, so much so that it seemed to be the glance of someone else and as if that other person were looking at him mutely crying out for help. Of course such fantasies were nonsense; the boy was dead-drunk and well on the way to passing out completely. Besides he knew nothing of all that, he had had nothing to do with it! But that glance, that glance that was so much the same . . .

Two days later Crookface sent his man to Laszlo Gyeroffy with a message to come and see him at his house on Belszen Street, and to be there at twelve noon that same day.

When the two men sat down facing each other they both remained silent for some minutes. Then Crookface said, 'You utter fool!' and then stopped.

Although the insult was so unexpected the younger man did not take offence. He looked up wonderingly at the old man but said nothing. Then Crookface really started. He recounted everything he had heard about how Laszlo was living, about his fecklessness, reckless prodigality, about his debts and about his drinking. He spoke harshly and, as was his way, used coarse and vulgar epithets.

Still the young man listened without saying a word. There was so much force and deep feeling in everything this deep-chested, eagle-beaked, twisted-mouthed old man had to say – and, behind his words, such concern and good will – that Laszlo listened patiently, almost humbly. Everything that Crookface was now saying so harshly was exactly what Laszlo, if ever he happened to wake up sober, had become accustomed to thinking of himself. Crookface's accusations were no different from the self-accusing thoughts with which Laszlo would torture himself and which would only make him despise himself all the more. And when he had said all that to himself he would once again take refuge from this self-inflicted judgement – and from further accusations of which Crookface knew nothing – by reaching for the brandy bottle. As the old man talked on so Laszlo came to feel that it was not another being who was adding up his faults and frivolity, his waywardness and total lack of any sense of responsibility, but that he was merely looking in a mirror and seeing his *alter ego* repeating what was always and forever in his own soul. No one would be as severe as he himself and it might have been to himself that he was listening.

Crookface went on for a long time until Laszlo found himself desperately looking round to see if there was any liquor to hand. There was none, but Laszlo was by now so used to nipping whenever he felt the need that the present deprivation made his whole body scream out for its regular dose of alcohol. He could not ask; it was against all etiquette!

Crookface now started to say what he thought should be done and, as was his manner, his advice took the form of an order. 'You will file a petition in the Chancery court asking to be made a Ward of Court and asking for an official guardian to be appointed since you are incapable of managing your own affairs. I will accept the office of guardian; and I'll keep you on the straight and narrow path no matter what! I won't allow you to destroy yourself in this way!'

Laszlo's face changed. Again those words 'destroy yourself' which Balint had used to him not long before. Now someone else was saying the same thing; another person was trying to save him, to order him around, maybe even offer to pay for him as once did Fanny Beredy and more recently Dodo. Laszlo felt himself swelling with anger and resentment and rebellion at this constant meddling in his own life by other people. It was the bitter rebellion of the weak against the strong.

'If I want to destroy myself I will! It's none of your business!' he shouted angrily and stood up. Now the words poured from him. 'All my life, ever since I was a child, I've had people telling me what to do, pulling me in this direction or in that, my guardian, my aunts, everybody. Everything's always been arranged for me; everyone's told me what to do. Well! Now's the time to say No! No! No! I've had enough! Enough, I say! Now I'm going to do as I please and live as I want . . .' and he went on saying the same thing, time and again, building up his courage by shouting and making as much noise as possible; and repeating over and over again, 'It's my life and nobody else's!' and 'I'm not going to take anything from anyone else ever again, from nobody, nobody, I tell you!' until, gesticulating wildly, he screamed out once more, 'If I want to destroy myself I will! Everyone has the right to do as he wishes with his own life!'

Old Crookface sat quite still. He said nothing but just listened and as he did so he was watching Laszlo carefully. Those eyebrows that met in the middle, those unusual little movements of the arms as if he was first reaching back and then throwing his words forward . . . and even those last words 'everyone has the right to do as he pleases with his own life!', how they reminded him of the past! And what a throw-back Laszlo was! Julie Ladossa all over again! Memories of the past flooded back: Julie Ladossa had talked in just the same way and said just the same sort of thing. She too had rebelled against everything; and she too had destroyed herself, knowing what she did and doing it of her own free will. He had loved her since she had been a girl – and out

of spite she had married someone else. Out of spite too she had
bolted from her husband, not with Crookface but because of
him. It had been a clash between two rigid, difficult characters
and when she had said the things that her son had just unwittingly
repeated so many years later, she had thrust her arms forward in
the same way and looked at him with the same expression in her
eyes, the very same eyes . . .

The old man stood up. Putting his hand on his young companion's shoulder he said, 'Don't be angry with me, son. Don't be
angry! There's no need, you know, and . . . and I ask your forgiveness.' Crookface had never said this to anyone before,
neither had he ever spoken so gently. He went on, quite softly,
'There isn't enough love in the world for anyone to throw it carelessly away. I know you feel you've had less than your share, and
I understand how you feel. No doubt what I said sounded wrong
and interfering, and perhaps I ought to have spoken differently.
You've had no father and no mother, and many things . . . things
that people have had . . . have been lacking in your life. This is
what you resent so much and what is so hard to bear. But I would
like, if it's possible and if you feel you can do it in your own way,
that you should . . . Well, you should pull yourself together; and
I . . . I'd try to help, if you would accept it?'

As Crookface spoke, faltering as he did so, a remarkable
change came over Laszlo's face. First his mouth opened and his
chin dropped and then his eyes opened wide in wonder before
filling with tears. All the rigidity of his body, so recently tense
with anger, melted away until he was like a puppet whose strings
are broken. He fell into a chair and started to weep, with deep
racking sobs.

Old Kendy remained standing where he was.

'Well! Well! Come on, now! Mustn't do that, you know!' he
said in a deep, rumbling voice and then, most unexpectedly and
with clumsy awkwardness, he started to stroke the young man's
hair just as if he had been his own son. 'Don't . . . don't do that!'
he repeated, his gruff voice deeper than ever.

Laszlo cried for a long time as he crouched ever deeper in the
large armchair. At last something had been set free inside him,
something hitherto imprisoned had been liberated. Soon he was
crying quietly, crying for himself and his wasted life, for the hurt
he carried within himself for so many years, and for the talent
that he had abandoned so frivolously, for his dissipated life and

for the chances he had missed. Now all was clear to him. It was a long time before he looked up at the old man who had waited so patiently, wiped his eyes and his face and said, 'Forgive me, sir! I am deeply ashamed. I don't usually . . . Please, forgive me!'

The old man looked down, and then, his old self again, merely grunted some brief four-letter obscenity and said, 'Nothing to be ashamed about! It happens, you know. Does you good, like enough!'

'But what can I do?' asked Gyeroffy humbly.

Crookface pulled up a chair and sat down. Briefly he drew up a plan. Laszlo should go home at once and make a list of all his debts – and if necessary get someone to help him. Also he should list all his possessions, forestlands, houses and farms, even if he had disposed of them in some way. When this was done he should bring them to him and together they would discuss what should be done. Matters could not be completely hopeless and anyhow one had to make a start somewhere.

Laszlo agreed to do what Crookface had suggested and the two men shook hands. As they did so Kendy just added, 'And try not to drink so damn much!'

It was many years since Laszlo had felt so at peace with himself and so light-hearted. When he left Crookface's house he saw a café-bar across the street. For a moment he hesitated. Then he went in and the need that habit had instilled in him triumphed over his will. In a few moments he had downed three large measures of brandy.

That evening he left for the country.

The day of the bazaar led also to an important event which astonished everybody: young Margit's betrothal to Adam Alvinczy. How very unexpected, they all said, for everyone had known for ages that Adam was desperately in love with Adrienne. And now he's marrying her sister!

In fact no one was more surprised than Adam himself, who hardly knew what had happened nor how it was that he found himself betrothed, and betrothed to Margit of all people. And the strangest thing of all was that it didn't feel strange at all: on the contrary it all seemed the most natural thing in the world.

Since the bazaar, when as usual he went to the Uzdy villa at tea-time with the rest of their little band of friends, he no longer tried to sit near to Adrienne or even find a place where he could gaze longingly at her, but started to seek out Margit who – quite by chance of course – always seemed to be found alone in the corner of the drawing-room farthest away from the others. He would join her at once, justifying this move by saying to himself that there was no point in approaching Adrienne who disdained his great love. The other guests, Kadacsay, Pityu Kendy, the other three Alvinczy brothers and the Laczok girls, soon began to take it for granted that Adam and Margit would only whisper things to each other so, as soon as the two of them sat down some way apart, they would be left strictly alone. As a result they could discuss their favourite subject to their hearts' content.

And that subject, now, was the amazing difference between Adrienne's heartlessness and Margit's understanding.

They milled over this fact and examined it in every detail every time they met. And so it came to pass that one afternoon they were to be found together in their favourite place in the corner. Baron Gazsi, far away in the centre of all the others, was telling some extremely droll tale of an adventure he had had with a horse and a wild boar sow – in which he had, as always, come off the worst – for Gazsi, unlike most people who tell stories about themselves, told only those stories in which he could represent himself as an unwitting clown. This manner was well suited to his woodpecker nose and plaintive eyes, while his way of rolling his 'r's so heavily made his sad self-deprecating stories all the more hilarious. Where Gazsi was, near the fireplace, everyone was in a constant roar of laughter.

'How merry they all are over there!' said Adam sadly to little Margit. 'What fun they are all having! But you're so good to me, sitting always with me and listening when you could be happy and laughing with the others. Dear Margit, aren't you bored by all my complaints?'

'Oh, no! I'd rather be here,' she answered. 'I'm like a nurse, you know. I like being of use. It's a great joy to me if I can help to ease pain, especially yours – though I know it's hopeless. I could listen to you for ever.'

'I've never known anyone as good as you are, Margit! Do you know, I'm almost happy when I'm with you! If only you could stay with me always. You're such a comfort, a real kindred spirit!'

Adam spoke very softly, which was only natural as they were sitting so close together on the sofa where, as it happened, there was plenty of space so to sit quite so close was not really necessary.

Nevertheless they did sit so closely as to be almost touching and this, no doubt, was because in this way they could talk quietly without being disturbed by the loud chatter of the others. Their heartfelt words seemed all the more intimate when they were whispered into each other's ears, and it was also easier to explain their inner feelings in this way and Margit, for once, could never have uttered her next words if they had had to be said out loud.

'Of course! That would be the best! You marry me and I'll always be with you. I'll be your best friend and I'll take care of you and we'll talk about Adrienne all the time, just as we do now.'

'My darling!' he whispered, enchanted. 'You would accept that? Knowing that my heart . . . ?'

'This one?' she said quickly, touching his chest with her little hand and leaving it there for a moment. 'This one's broken, I know. And you're not in love with me, I know that too . . . and never could be.'

'That's true, of course,' said the young man sadly, still believing this to be the truth, 'though I'm sure that if I had never met Adrienne I could have fallen in love with you!'

So they went on talking of what could never be and appearing to share their sad yet honey-sweet thoughts until they noticed that everyone was preparing to leave. When all the others had said goodbye and had already left the room, Margit put her hand on Adam's sleeve. 'Wait a moment!' she said, and her words were no less than a command. 'We'll tell Addy now!'

This was an awkward moment for Adam, for how, after singing so many hymns of love to Adrienne, could he possibly tell her that he intended to marry her sister? However he need not have worried; young Margit handled it all with the greatest tact. She took his big hand in her small one, led him over to Adrienne, and said, 'See, Addy, poor Adam is so unhappy that we have decided he will marry me! Don't you see, this will be the best!'

Adrienne did not laugh, nor was she angry or even surprised. She looked at them both with total seriousness and understanding and then she put up both her hands and pulled down Adam's head and kissed him on the forehead as a sign that he had her blessing. He had never achieved anything like that during his long courtship of her.

Adam blushed deeply and tried to think of some beautiful and romantic words with which to thank her; but nothing came because just then little Margit squeezed his hand with more force than he could ever have imagined she possessed.

This strong grip, though Adam never knew it either then or afterwards, was to be symbolic of their future together.

The next day the news was all over town. Old Rattle was summoned by telegram. He was delighted by his new role as Father of the Bride, embracing everyone he met, even total strangers, and shouting, every five minutes, despite floods of tears, 'Oh, my poor wife Judith! Why couldn't she have lived to know such joy?' while the tears flowed down his cheeks even when his sorrow had turned to guffaws of delighted laughter.

Count Akos at once started a round of visits, mainly to the houses of old ladies of his acquaintance where such scenes were repeated several times a day, and to the Casino. He would even stop people in the street to laugh and cry and tell them of his great happiness and, of course, of his great sorrow.

PART FOUR

CHAPTER ONE

THE COUNCIL OF war was held in front of Balint's tent. Balint
himself sat on his shooting stick, 'Honey' Andras Zutor, the head
forest guard, sat on the ground in front of him while Geza
Winckler, the young and fully qualified forest superintendent
who had been engaged by Balint to replace Nyiresy, sat close by
on a tree-trunk.

Below them the meadow on the Prislop sloped gently down
towards Feherviz – the White Water. With small groups of trees
the meadow almost looked like a park consciously laid out by
garden experts. To the right of the little group of men were the
steep slopes of the Munchel Mare, planted with a mixture of
beech and pine trees, while to the left and behind them the forest
was formed solely by dense plantations of pine trees. In front the
view was closed by the peaks of the Humpleu range, which at
this time in the late afternoon, with the sun behind it, was in
deep shadow. High above was the crater-shaped rocky summit
of the Vurtop whose chalky whiteness gleamed softly behind the
inky shadows of the tree-capped mountains in front.

Balint loved this place and had always camped here since he
had started coming to the mountains. Recently he had had a
shelter for the horses built in the corner of the meadow, together
with a long log cabin for the men who came with him. Nearby
was a spring of fresh water; Balint's own tent was always pitched
some sixty yards away, a little higher up, partly because he liked
to be alone and partly because he felt in some way mentally
refreshed by contemplating that wild stretch of mountain and
forest. From where he would sit, in front of his tent, Balint was
conscious that the stream from the spring in the meadow below
ran its course, unseen, through the great valley that was concealed from him by the trees until eventually it flowed into the
main stream of the Szamos. Here all was peace and quiet, and
the silence, in that landscape of sombre trees and jutting rocks,
was that silence only to be found in the mountain forests.

Now it was the end of July, when the grass and the leaves on the trees were at their most lush and at their greenest.

At this moment the three men were listening to a report by a fourth, the forest guard Juanye Vomului, who stood before them at a respectful distance.

The *gornyik* Juanye was a stocky man, powerfully built and broad in the shoulder. He held his eagle's beak of a nose high and he stood there proudly as befitted a man who was no tied peasant bound to his master but a freeholder, well-to-do and independent, who served the Abady family of his own free will. Everything in his demeanour and dress drew attention to his pride and importance, and even the broad belt studded with copper nails was as imposing as any on the mountain. His cotton shirt and trousers were clean and new and his huge fur hat was large enough to make a waistcoat. This last he had politely placed on the ground beside him and he stood there bare-headed, his shoulder-length black hair so heavily greased that it was barely ruffled by the strong wind. During the previous year Vomului had taken over responsibility for guarding the parcel of land on the Intreapa where control of the felling needed a man with courage and authority.

The *gornyik* explained his problem. Two hundred acres had been felled and by the end of spring all the wood had been carted away. In May the land had been replanted, at considerable cost and trouble. By the middle of June the grass had grown but as soon as it had been high enough the men of the nearby village had driven their cattle there to graze, eating the young trees along with the grass. He, Vomului, was powerless to stop the villagers not only because the 200-acre plot marched with the village common lands but also because each time he tried to confront them he was menaced by axes and, when he protested, threatened with being beaten to death. Not only that but alone he could hardly drive off so many animals and hold them hostage. Now the villagers brought in their cattle when they wished and the whole 200-acre parcel was likely to be destroyed.

Vomului spoke well and in a well-mannered fashion. He stood erect, his weight on one leg, the other stretched out in front of him. When he was asked a question he would first change legs to show that he never spoke without prior thought and reflection. And when he wanted to emphasize a point he would spit sideways as if a gob of spittle would be the seal of his honesty.

The council lasted for some considerable time until they unanimously decided what to do. Firstly all sixteen of the Abady forest guards would be mustered and together they would be strong enough to drive away the invading cattle. To achieve this the new superintendent would go down to the little town of Beles, round up the men and, making a wide detour, come through the Gyero-Monostor forests by night and be on the Intreapa by dawn. Balint himself, with four men and Honey Zutor, would start off early, and at daybreak rendezvous with the others on the boundaries of the village lands. In this way the villagers would not be forewarned of their arrival and would have no time to drive their cattle away from their illegal grazing.

By five o'clock the sun, though still high in the sky, had begun to disappear behind the high mountains to the west. The valley in front was in deep shadow, while, to the north, the bare peaks of the Munchel Mare shone golden with the late afternoon light. A light breeze rose from the valley as invigorating as sparkling wine.

Balint took his sporting rifle, though he had no intention of shooting anything, slung his bag over one shoulder and started off into the forest, intent only on watching whatever wild life he might encounter. At first he followed an old cart-track, now carefully seeded with grass since some order had been restored to the Abady forestlands. He did not have far to go before arriving at the hide he had had constructed high in the trunk of a giant fir. The tree stood at the edge of a precipitous drop, below which there was an immense clearing in the form of a semi-circular sea-shell, which reached as far as the slope up to the ridge opposite. Through the clearing ran countless little rivulets of water that united only by some rocks where they combined to form the start of a stream that would eventually find its way into the White Water far below. From Balint's hide could just be heard the splash of the water as it fell into a cleft beyond the rocks.

Balint climbed the rough ladder and sat down on the floor of the hide. Taking out his binoculars he carefully inspected the landscape in front of him, pausing at every clump of trees or shrubs for the tell-tale signs of the presence of deer, usually only just the tops of their heads for that was all that there was to be seen when they were resting in the tall grass. They were always hard to see, however carefully one looked. Balint could see no sign at present and realized that he had arrived in time.

In the crystal-clear air a solitary eagle floated high above his head, describing wide circles with outspread wings seemingly motionless. Nothing else moved. It was a moment of Nature's infinite calm. Alone in his eyrie Balint felt happy and for once at ease with the world.

The last few months had been quiet and devoid of incident. When Margit had announced her engagement Adrienne had decided that she must wait until after her sister's marriage in the autumn before mentioning the subject of divorce to her husband. She felt that for the moment she must do all she could to replace their dead mother, supervising the preparation of Margit's trousseau and her bridal chest of linen and doing all the work that normally fell to the bride's mother. She felt, too, that she would never be able to do this properly if she was harassed by thoughts of the confusion in her own life, and indeed confusion amounting to havoc was sure to be the result of the awful disputes that would inevitably follow her telling Pal Uzdy that she wanted a divorce. As it was these summer months passed tranquilly enough. Adrienne and Margit went together to Budapest to go shopping and order everything that was necessary – and there it was easy for Balint and Adrienne to meet, and to make love, just as it was at Kolozsvar and when Balint went to stay at Mezo-Varjas. During those months life for them seemed perfect. They could meet often and be together with no fear of disturbance and, while they went about their daily lives, each occupied with their own duties and responsibilities, they would both weave dreams of their future life together when their union would be perfect and indissoluble. And during this time they managed somehow to put on one side all thoughts of the problems and resistance they would be bound to meet later.

Political life in the capital was also going through an unusually calm period. The agricultural minister, almost unnoticed, put through some essential reforms concerning the husbandry of livestock; Parliament passed the budget, held long debates on modernizing the House Rules; and the government, though not aided by a revolt of their own party members, succeeded in raising army officers' pay. There was still unrest in Croatia where insurgents had insulted the Ban – the appointed Governor – but everywhere it was common knowledge that talks had begun between the Croatians and the Hungarian government which seemed likely to end in agreement.

The 'little war' that Slawata had hinted at the previous autumn never materialized and relations with Italy remained as amicable as ever. All the same, King Edward of England went ahead with his plans to visit the Tsar at Reval and did so in such a flamboyant manner that no one could have mistaken the visit for anything but a public flaunting of the Anglo-Russian alliance. The only real cloud on the political horizon had been the revolutionary movements in Turkey, which had begun with army revolts in Monastir and Salonika and ended with the Sultan Abdul Hamid granting a constitution, lifting the censorship and declaring a general amnesty. It was obvious to everyone that he had not done this of his own free will and so people began to speak of a new historical movement in Istanbul that could well come to preoccupy both Russia and England, whose interests in the Bosphorus were diametrically opposed. All sorts of modifications might be made here and there to the map of Europe without much disturbing the balance of power, but he who could wield the most influence over the dying Ottoman Empire held a trump card in the councils of the great powers of the West. Maybe, thought Balint, it will all be to our advantage. Perhaps, as it was in England's prime interest to keep the Russian fleet bottled up in the Black Sea, King Edward might look with a more kindly eye upon Austria-Hungary?

It was thoughts of this kind which preoccupied Balint as he sat in his hide halfway up the great tree and scanned the scene in front of him for any signs of life. Now the late afternoon shade softened all the outlines so that changes of scale or vegetation were marked only by their colours, the bright shining green of the young beech shoots, the blue of the pines, the angry green of the grass on the edge of the little streams and its fading yellow by the clay banks. Two fallen tree-trunks gleamed white against the soft grass, cutting a hard line as if etched with a sharp knife, and everywhere there was slight movement as a soft almost imperceptible breeze kept the grass in shimmering motion which concealed the solid earth beneath.

From somewhere near the river could be heard the cry of a kingfisher. No other sound was to be heard until suddenly there was a very soft crackling, so soft that it would never have been noticed if everywhere around there had not been such total silence. It came from the edge of the forest to the right, and Balint swiftly looked in that direction.

A doe raced out of the undergrowth, ran in a wide curve to the bottom of the valley and then turned and ran back to a little hillock where she stood waiting. In an instant she was followed by a buck. The chase must already have lasted some time since the buck showed flecks of foam round his mouth. The buck stopped almost as soon as he saw the doe some fifty feet away on her little hillock. As if totally unconcerned she made as if to graze for a moment. Then she raised her head, looked straight at the buck and gave the mating call, a low whistle. At once he ran towards her. She, ever coquettish, waited motionless until he was less than two paces away and then made a great jump and ran off.

The two deer ran almost together towards the foot of the cliff below Balint's hide. Here the buck nearly caught up with his quarry but she found a new way to tease him, racing round and round a little grove of hazel bushes with him in hot pursuit until the buck abruptly stopped, so out of breath that Balint could hear him panting. For a few instants they remained still and if Balint had dropped something it would have fallen between them. Suddenly the doe whistled again and was off, the buck close behind her, zigzagging across the valley, leaping over the fallen trees and bushes, stopping and starting as the doe seemed to order, and then finally disappearing over the ridge and out of sight. Balint wondered how many more clearings they would find for the chase before the female finally decided to end the game. He had been enthralled by this glimpse of love-making in the wild.

Now dusk began to fall and the golden light faded from the peaks of the Munchel. Lilac shadows spread over the valley and the scent of wildflowers and fallen leaves became overpoweringly strong.

Abady was just getting ready to go back to his camp when another movement at the base of the clearing caught his eye. Something brown was moving at the edge of the fir tree plantation.

A giant mother bear, followed by two cubs, ambled slowly out into the clearing with that strange swaying walk, the head apparently wobbling from side to side almost as if the animal were shaking its head in puzzled consideration of a new idea. After a moment the mother bear paused to allow her two cubs, tiny beside the huge bulk of their mother, to join her. Then all three moved slowly and deliberately towards that part of the meadow which was the most boggy and where the wild clover grew and all the fresh buds were at their most succulent. Seen through the binoculars it seemed to Balint as if the trio were as close as if they were at his feet. He could even see the sparkle in the cubs' eyes as they nibbled at the feast to which they had been brought. The mother, on the other hand, grabbed at whole clumps of grass, gnawing them to the root and leaving round bare patches where she had eaten. When one of the cubs strayed too far the mother would bark out a gruff command and the cub, for all the world like any well-brought-up youngster, would return at once to his place to be greeted with a light cuff over the ear, for family discipline was not the prerogative of humans.

After feeding for some considerable time the family moved slowly away in the direction of the waterfall. Balint started to climb down, taking care that his gun did not clatter against the rungs of the ladder. As quietly as possible he started to walk back to the camp along the grass-covered path. It was not yet completely dark and as he came to a turn in the path he heard a very faint little *tap-tap-tap* on the ground coming from the young trees that bordered the pathway. Standing quite still, Balint looked in the direction of the noise which continued, though hesitantly, as if whatever creature was making it did not know his way.

Then Balint heard the plaintive call of a young roe-deer – a much higher and softer note than the mating call of the adult female – and all at once a very young roe-deer jumped onto the path and nearly bumped into Abady himself. Hardly noticing the presence of a human the little animal looked this way and that, uttering repeated little pipings and flapping its large ears in one direction after another. It was clearly in distress, its ears turning in every direction in the most comical manner until Balint imagined that the little animal was saying to itself that suddenly it understood nothing, that its mother, always until then so protective and so omnipresent, had run away and left her all alone in the dark frightening forest, and that nothing like that had ever happened in the world before! There was no way, reflected Balint, that the young fawn could have understood what happened in the forest when the mating season began, and that later, when her mother had played out the game of flight and refusal and eventual surrender, she would come back and look after her offspring. In the meantime the fawn stood there,

its tiny patent-leather-like snout sniffing in all directions trying
to pick up its mother's scent. Balint held his breath and for
several minutes the man and the little deer stood there within a
few yards of each other. Finally it was the animal that moved.
It lifted its head, piped twice, turned its ears in the direction of
the clearing below and trotted off.

Balint was so diverted that he broke into silent laughter, happy
that the forest had now returned to its former calm and primæval
silence.

He thought of the villagers and their invasion of the new
plantations and was at once strengthened in his determination to
put a stop to the illegal grazing.

The next day Balint was already in the valley of the Szamos
by noon. He was on horseback, the *gornyiks* on foot. They all
carried guns and some of the men also had hatchets. Although
one pack-horse would have been quite enough for their needs
they had brought a second with them, telling the three casually
employed extra men, who had been told nothing of the real
purpose of the expedition, that they were going right up the
valley as far as the Puspokseg district where the country markets
held untold riches! This plan had been concocted in the greatest
detail for the benefit of the men of the mountains who were
curious, clever and shrewd, as otherwise Balint's plan to surprise
the Gyurkuca peasants would soon have been discovered and at
once known to the whole district. And, if this happened, of
course not a trace of the villagers' cattle would be found on the
forbidden land and everyone would have had a good laugh at
the noble lord's expense.

It took some time for the little party to traverse the village for
the houses were strung some two kilometres along the bank of
the river. Fortunately it was a Sunday and so none of the villagers
were working away from the village. No one, therefore, saw the
little band turn away from the river left towards Ponor and suddenly disappear swiftly into the darkness of the pine forest.

They travelled in silence, led by Juanye Vomului as they had
now reached that part of the Abady forestlands which was his
responsibility. Just as night was falling they reached a small
meadow where the horses were watered and fed and from which
a steep path would lead them at dawn to the mountain ridge
which formed the near side of the newly planted clearing.

Because the hammering would be sure to be heard and give away their presence they did not construct the usual shelter but rolled themselves in their blankets and slept on the ground. A tiny fire they did make, but this was so insignificant, and anyhow so soon doused, that it could not have been seen from a distance.

It was still dark when they took to the road. Blindly they struggled upwards in the darkness hardly able to see the path. When they reached the summit dawn was beginning to break, and though the smaller stars had already become invisible in the slowly brightening sky a few of the brighter ones still shone high above them. Thick fog covered the valley of the Intreapa but the ridge opposite could be clearly seen as a hard purple shadow silhouetted against the blushing eastern sky. To the right of where they stood lay the two-hundred-acre plot but as it was still in shadow it was impossible to see if there were any cattle grazing there. On the side where the Abady property marched with the village common lands the boundary was marked by a short straight opening on a steep slope which needed only four men to control it effectively. At the bottom of the valley was the stream which led down to the Szamos. Abady's plan was to corral all the cattle into one group and then drive them away beside the bed of the stream.

Balint picked his way slowly downhill. Now it was getting lighter and he could see, on the other side of the valley, Winckler marshalling his men into place so that they would be ready as soon as the morning mists cleared away. The two men met briefly at the stream and then Winckler returned uphill so as to direct his men when the drive began.

Then the early morning breeze got up, caused by the sun warming the air in the lower valley of the Szamos, which then rose to the upper valleys disturbing there the cold night air and provoking chilly gusts of wind which lasted until the sun could penetrate the depths of the upper valleys. Suddenly, as if touched by a magic wand, the fog disappeared, and the whole valley was clearly to be seen. There, in front of the waiting band, was the Abady clearing, on both sides of the valley, filled with cattle, the cattle of the Gyurkuca villagers. There must have been at least two hundred of them, calves, oxen, heifers, little spots of white clearly defined against the green grass and the cut tree-stumps.

One of the *gornyiks* started the drive with a soft whistle. Abady's men moved slowly forward but after a few minutes, before they had time even to reach the edge of the plantation, a strange thing happened.

From one of the ridges above them came the deep bellowing sound of a mountain horn, wild and startling and somehow almost melodious as well, a sound something between a hunting horn and an organ; it was the three-yard-long *tulnyik*, the calling horn of the mountain people, and now there was not only one, but another, on the other side of the valley, and then a third from right in the centre where the ridges on both sides of the valley came together to form a miniature pass. It was a long-drawn-out sound, full of terror and menace and so powerful that the very air seemed to tremble.

At the first wave of sound the cattle seemed to go mad, running helter-skelter in the direction of the village, pregnant cows, elderly oxen, young calves and yearling heifers alike, racing towards the beaters, jumping over fallen logs, barging into carefully constructed woodpiles, rushing homewards with all the impulsion of the Gadarene swine; they had been called by the clashing sound of the great horns resounding from the hilltops around them. In an instant twenty or thirty of the beasts had already reached the stream below, running with all the force of a cavalry charge. The horns continued their deafening sound, and now it was mingled with the frightened lowing of the cattle and the shouts of Abady's beaters. It was an inferno of sound in the previously tranquil valley.

Such was the force of the stampede that it would have been impossible to 'arrest' a single animal. In a few moments the horns ceased and the cattle had all disappeared. The two-hundred-acre plantation was empty.

Abady's men were all in a rage of frustration and when Juanye Vomului reached Abady's side he threw his sheepskin cap on the ground and cursed as he had never cursed before, spluttering with anger, though nothing could stem the flow of his expletives. The other *gornyiks* did their best to outdo him, just to show how keen they were, but none succeeded.

Clearly there was nothing to be done. The trap had failed.

Honey Zutor suggested he should take a party up to the ridge above and try to catch the shepherds who had given the signal, but they all realized it would have been to no purpose. Everyone concerned would have been long gone. And so, while Winckler turned back to take the path to Beles, Balint took the easier route to the foot of the Ponor where Zutor and Juanye would rejoin him with his horse.

It was already noon before Balint reached the banks of the Szamos river, and there, so as not to have to ride through the village, shamefaced after his fruitless expedition, he forded the river to take a different path, one that lay through the woods and emerged at the sawmill of Toszerat whence the road led either up to the mountains or down to the main valley. When they reached the mill Balint found there Gaszton Simo, the arrogant and pretentious district notary who had in some way become aware of Abady's movements and was obviously waiting for him. As soon as Abady came into sight he galloped up on his handsome dapple-grey gelding.

'And what brings you this way, my Lord?' he asked slyly, little shoe-button eyes glistening with mockery. There was no doubt, thought Balint, that Simo already knew where he had been and what had happened. When Balint did not reply at once, he went on ironically, 'Working again, I suppose, ever diligent on behalf of these benighted peasants? I must say I admire your persever-ance almost as much as your all-merciful heart!'

'Why pretend you don't know?' said Abady roughly, extremely cross that such a mountebank should dare to mock him.

Simo was not in the least abashed. He gave a light laugh and then said, 'Well, Mr Deputy, now you can see what a wicked, dishonest depraved lot they are, these men you are so anxious to protect!'

'Of course I protect them and want justice for them. I won't tolerate their being subject to extortion and blackmail; but neither will I tolerate their doing damage to my property. And what's more I can understand that they know no better when for years the example set by their so-called betters has been just as bad! Grab, grab, grab, that's all they know!'

The notary cleared his throat. He knew only too well that this last remark was directed at him but, determined not to show it, he now adopted an attitude of the utmost good will and co-operation.

'This is a matter you can safely leave to me, my Lord,' he said. 'I will send a few gendarmes to reinforce your *gornyiks*. They'll patrol the high valleys at night and they'll arrest the men with the horns. Then your Lordship's forest-manager and his men will be able to drive away the cattle with neither let nor hindrance. Always at your service. Naturally!'

'I'll think about it,' answered Balint shortly, for though the idea was nothing if not logical he still did not want to have any dealings with Gaszton Simo. Also he was determined to be under no obligations to such a two-faced character of whose honesty he already had the gravest doubts.

'As you wish,' said Simo with a slight bow. The notary then lit a cigar. When the two men reached the road, Abady lifted his hat and said, 'Good-day to you, Mr Notary!' and turned his horse towards the mountain road.

'I am taking the same road,' said Simo. 'I'm going up to Retyicel on business.'

'I hope you didn't take this long detour just to see me,' said Balint. 'Wouldn't it have been much quicker for you through the Gyalu Botin?'

The notary laughed softly. 'Maybe for that too,' but he did not say more.

For a while they rode side by side without speaking. Then the notary said, 'What's the news from the great world of politics? My uncle the Chamberlain – you know who I mean – just returned from Budapest and he says there's an alliance between the Constitution and Independence Parties, and that's why Ferenc Kossuth has got the Grand Cross of the Leopold Order. Is it possible? Or did he have it already?'

'It was awarded for arranging the commercial treaties,' said Balint drily.

'Well, well, well!' Simo seemed to be pondering what he had just heard. 'Fancy that! The son of the great Hungarian patriot sports a Habsburg decoration! It's hardly credible. In Banffy-Hunyad they are all saying that he's sold his soul for a peck of gold, but I defended him, of course,' he added hurriedly. 'After all, he is my chief!' This last statement hardly rang true as Simo then went on to add a few critical remarks of his own. Still, as he still wished to seem loyal in front of such an influential person as Count Abady, he soon fell silent again. A little later, as Balint still rode on without saying anything, the notary returned to his original question. 'This alliance,' he said. 'Do you think it'll ever come about?'

There was little that Abady could say. Of course there had been discussions. The Independence Party members were using this project as their price for accepting the proposed reform of the voting qualifications; and indeed, such an alliance would have been of infinite value to the country since it would automatically bring to an end the constant secret struggle between the various parties forming the Coalition, that struggle which continued effectively to paralyse the government's freedom of action. At present nothing could be decided without much bargaining and concessions by both sides. No serious advances were possible and the only measures to find an easy path through Parliament were those which enshrined the vote-hunting slogans that had been aired at the election booths. Even the great project for introducing universal suffrage was delayed by the jealousies and petty arguments of the party leaders.

'I really have no idea,' replied Abady after a long pause. 'As I am not a member of any of the parties concerned, I know very little about it!'

The truth was that he did not want to discuss the matter at all, at least not until something definite had been decided. Personally he longed for the projected fusion of the two great parties to become a reality as he was sure that one immediate effect would be to remove all those loud-mouthed demagogues whose trumpeting of parochial nationalist slogans diverted any attention from the increasingly menacing turn of events in the great world outside Budapest and the boundaries of Hungary. This was a time when the nation desperately needed a strong and undivided government, especially now that a liberal constitution had been established in Turkey and the increasing power of revolutionary elements there might lead to serious disturbances in the neighbouring Balkan states. Simo, as if he had read Balint's thoughts, himself suddenly switched to the Turkish question, though it was possible, thought Abady, that he only did this to show off the range of his political thinking.

'Well, then, what do you think about the news from Turkey? What an extraordinary thing, eh? Perhaps now that they've got a constitution they'll give us a hand against Austria, what? After all the Turks and the Magyars are brothers, or ought to be. Time was when we marched shoulder to shoulder against Vienna. Everyone was talking about it in the club at Banffy-Hunyad. There they were saying . . .' and he drifted off into a lengthy discourse,

quoting what Bocskay and Gabor Bethlen had written, and saying how the best solution to all their problems would be a great
union between Turks and Hungarians which would soon bring
the hated Austrians to their knees. It was a marvellous mixture
of rhetoric and muddled thinking and Balint found himself
growing more and more irritated by the folly and stupidity of it
all. He could hardly wait to rid himself of the notary's tiresome
presence and so, seeing a barely passable path leading into the
forest and thence through dangerously rocky places to the Prislop, he turned abruptly into it, thinking anything was better than
having to listen to any more of this nonsense.

'I turn off here! Goodbye to you!' Balint said suddenly just as
Simo was in mid-sentence, and plunged into the thicket, his men
striding behind him.

Damned stuck-up aristocrat! said the Gyurkuca notary to
himself as he rode on. In about fifteen minutes the road entered
the dark forest. Here for a moment Simo stopped, looked around
him carefully, undid the leather clasp of the holster that was
strapped round his waist, and making sure that there was nothing
to hinder him reaching for his gun, rode slowly into the shadow
of the forest.

The path that Balint had chosen was not really suited to anyone
on horseback. The little mountain ponies themselves could pass
anywhere but the branches of the surrounding trees were so low
that Balint found himself repeatedly lying flat in the saddle while
even the horses had to duck their heads. Soon Balint decided to
dismount and continue on foot.

As his pace was faster than that of the *gornyiks'* ponies he soon
found that he had left them far behind and was walking alone in
the great forest.

There were several tracks on the mountainside, all leading to
the meadow on the Prislop, and soon Balint found that he had
to choose between two of them, one above, one below the other.
He chose the higher. Soon he emerged from the dense thicket
of young pine saplings into a more open part of the timber forest
where, among the more recently planted trees there were some
older ones whose growth had become stunted in the rocky soil
and whose branches were covered in moss. Here the sloping
ground was dotted with burr-covered burdock while the young
summer bramble shoots, now bright green but soon to be laden

with blackberries, grew as thickly as if they had been planted
by hand.

So unexpected was the dramatic contrast between the brilliant
green of the brambles on the ground with the soft lilac-coloured
shade of the tree-trunks above that Balint stopped in wonder at
the beauty of it. In the branches above hung silver-grey tassels
of moss seemingly woven into veils of net. Everywhere there
were only these three colours, silver, grey, and vivid green: and
the more that Balint gazed around him the more improbable and
ethereal did the forest seem until it was only those strands near
at hand, which moved gently in the soft breeze, that seemed real
while everything further off, the pale lilac shading into violet,
was like clouds of vapour in slight perpetual movement as if
swaying to the rhythm of some unheard music. And everywhere
around, at ground level, was this green carpet, also stirred by
almost imperceptible movement, from the valley below to
the edges of the lilac-shaded forest above, so that Balint had the
impression of a magical seascape. This was enhanced, here and
there, by rigid blocks of projecting rock, grey-black slate which
shone in the sunshine as if covered by invisible spray. Indeed the
rocks really were wet, wet with the humidity of the mountain
forest, so wet indeed that tiny droplets were constantly falling
from the sharp edges of the rocks onto the damp sponge-like
earth beneath. Even the thick soil of the path was damp and
resilient underfoot.

Balint moved slowly on. He felt strangely trance-like, as if
some hitherto unrevealed secret would suddenly be unfolded
before him, as if a golden stranger would step out from the lilac
strands of moss to welcome him to Paradise. And, as always when
suddenly aware of unexpected beauty, he thought of Adrienne
as if anything in the world that gave him pleasure must stem from
her pale skin, her full lips and golden onyx eyes. He could almost
see her coming towards him through the lilac and silver threads,
her familiar long steps and individual tread gliding over the
glittering ocean of green.

At once he decided that as soon as they were married they
must come here together, at the same time of year, at the same
hour . . . and wander, hand in hand, in the silence of this magical
forest.

From his dream Balint was awakened by the faint flutter of
wing-beats. Before him there rose a little bird, smaller than a

quail, with a strange swooping flight. It rose in the air and then dropped again, and Balint saw that it was a young snipe, barely more than a fledgling, and still very awkward. The beak seemed disproportionately long for the body and even so it seemed as if its wings were not yet strong enough to support the little bird in anything but awkward stumbling interrupted flight. For a moment Balint watched the little bird's efforts as twice more it flew up and then came to earth again, cowering in the grass as if too tired to try again. The man then walked swiftly on so as not to frighten, or tire further, the little snipe in its first efforts to learn to fly.

Another quarter of an hour's walk brought Balint to the edge of a steep cliff. It was an almost perpendicular rock, some six or seven metres high, partly covered by stunted pine and young Balkan maple trees which hung down from the summit, their gnarled trunks seeming to search for light and air above the open space of the meadow below. Here, Balint saw, the little band of forest guards had already arrived and had made there a stop on the way where there was water and the grass was green and so made it a good place to rest and feed the horses before tackling the last stretch of their way to the Prislop.

Andras Zutor and his companions were sitting in the shade at the foot of the rock. They were talking excitedly among themselves and it had been the sound of their voices which had brought Balint to the edge of the cliff above them. He was just about to call out that he was there when he heard a phrase which made him stand still and hold his breath: '. . . and that's why the notary is so frightened, and why he came this way round.'

They spoke, of course, in Romanian, but Balint could now well understand everything that was said, and he was curious to know what all this was about. The voice came from young Kula, the boy from Pejkoja who had been enlisted to look after the horses on Balint's trip to the mountain.

'Of course he's frightened!' answered old Zsukuczo, who lived on the Gyalu Botin, near the road from Beles to Retyicel. 'Didn't they shoot at him not far from where I live? Of course he's frightened, wouldn't you be?' he said, and laughed as he did so.

'Is that really so?' asked Vomului, as if he were astonished by the news which he knew perfectly well already.

'Where did this happen?' asked Zutor.

'I told you. Close to where I live. It was there on the hillside where the road follows the boundary line above the Korbului creek.'

'On our side?'

'No! No! The shot came from the village common land. I was standing in front of my house and heard it all quite clearly. And I can tell you I didn't move for a few minutes either!'

The old man laughed again, snapping a twig between his fingers before throwing it aside. Then he went on, 'I don't care what happens outside our land. Besides it's better not to know too much. Still I looked into it a bit later, just to be sure.' And he went on to give all the details, speaking slowly, as country folk do, especially in the mountains where people rarely finish a sentence.

It seems that he saw the hated notary ride by his house. Then there was the sound of a shot. Half an hour later he went to see what he could find. There was no one about and it was clear that whoever had fired had missed his target. As an ex-poacher who could read any sign or trace left it was easy for old Zsukuczo to reconstruct what had happened. There, in the mud of the path, he could see how Simo had suddenly and sharply reined back his horse – so sharply indeed that the animal had almost fallen backwards on its rump. 'Next I looked to see if they wanted to give him a good scare, or whether...' Soon he found what he was looking for, a rifle bullet, lodged in a tree-trunk just beside the skid-marks. The shot had come from somewhere on the steep hillside above the path, from the cover of a group of young beech trees. Whoever the marksman had been, he was good shot, that was clear enough even if he had not actually hit the target. The old man again laughed and then, as if to show his appreciation of a good joke, spat in a wide arc.

'So ever since that day Mr Simo always makes a sort of detour so that no one can guess where he's going, yes?' said young Kula.

'And ever since that day he also carries a revolver!' said Krisan, and they all laughed in quiet mockery.

'Hasn't he made any official enquiry then?' asked Honey.

Todor Paven, the tall man from the Humpleu, replied, 'Heavens no! Even he knows such things can never be cleared up properly. People say he's never even mentioned it.'

'Wouldn't have been no loss!' muttered young Kula.

Then Honey, whose part in the conversation had until now been merely to ask questions while quietly sucking on his pipe, spoke up harshly. 'No more of that in front of me, my lad! Time we moved on. Get up, all of you!' and himself rose to his feet and started to walk away.

Meekly the other men gathered their things together, brought up the horses, and moved off in the wake of their leader.

Balint stayed where he was for quite some time as he would not have liked any of them to know that he had been listening to them. Only when they were already some distance away did he too start to follow. As it happened this precaution was quite unnecessary for his path turned sharply up the mountainside and rejoined the other only at the ridge just before they all arrived back at the camp.

When Balint had finished his supper he called Andras Zutor into his tent, told him that by chance he had overheard the conversation in the meadow and asked him what it was all about and what had happened to lead up to such a situation. Zutor now knew his master better than he had two years before at the time the money-lender Rusz Pantyilimon had been murdered one dark snowbound night and when red-hot pincers would not have drawn any answers from him. Now he answered quite freely. It seemed that the extortionate money-lending had not been stopped by Rusz's death. Now there was not one but two such loan-sharks operating in the mountain villages, one at Meregyo and another at Rogosel. Both worked in the same way as had Rusz. The Romanian *popa* Timbus, the priest from Gyurkuca, was still the local representative of the Union Bank, and it was still he who arranged the loans for those in need. The notary Simo continued to prepare the contracts and the written contracts continued to contain clauses which had not been explained to the borrowers, most of whom could neither read nor write. Everything Simo did was for the benefit only of the lenders.

Abady then interrupted, 'Surely that's impossible to prove. No one will bear witness against the village priest, we saw that two years ago. Has Simo himself done anything illegal, anything we can prove?'

'Plenty! There's not a contract written he doesn't benefit from. That's why he never asked for an enquiry into the shooting. He'd have had to tell the county sheriff, who's a good friend of his, and he couldn't do that and be sure the enquiry didn't find out something of what was going on.'

Balint thought deeply; the instinct to help others, which was so strongly embedded in him, was aroused once again. He must do something to get that thieving notary off the people's backs. However he realized that he would now have to work out some approach more shrewdly and subtly than he had at the time of the outcry against Rusz Pantyilimon and the *popa* Timbus when the men of Pejkoja had come to him for help but turned to secret violence when the priest had threatened them.

'Listen, friend Zutor,' said Balint quietly. 'Could you find me some documents on these transactions, very discreetly, of course, so that no one notices?'

'I could try, my Lord,' said Zutor, somewhat on his dignity.

'But don't tell my manager Winckler, or anyone else!'

Zutor's eyes sparkled. 'You can be sure of that, my Lord. No one but your Lordship!'

'Make some notes for me, and when I next come up we'll go through them together and see what we can use.'

'It shall be done, my Lord!' said Zutor quietly.

Balint got up and the forester clicked his heels as if about to take his leave. Abady, however, gestured to him to stay for a moment. 'One other thing! This afternoon Mr Simo suggested that when we decided to have another drive against the cattle he should provide some gendarmes who would go on ahead and confiscate the horns which warned the cattle. It seems a good idea and so I may tell Mr Winckler to co-operate with him. This does not affect what I've just asked you to do.'

'I understand, my Lord!'

Zutor saluted his master and left the tent. Balint watched as his powerful stocky figure stumped off in the moonlight. Honey was barrel-chested and he walked proudly on his short legs, marching away as befitted a former non-commissioned officer who had reached the rank of Master-at-Arms during his service with the Hussars.

Two weeks later Winckler's report reached Abady at Denes-tornya:

Mr Notary Simo, as agreed by your Lordship, sent up a detachment of gendarmes on Thursday. Two went through the Ponor to the

south ridge and two to the north from Vale Boului. I myself left
Beles after dark and by Friday morning the foot of the Intreapa was
closed by our party of sixteen gornyiks and gendarmes. When the
fog lifted I searched the valley with my binoculars and to my great
surprise there wasn't a head of cattle to be seen. Nevertheless we
beat the whole valley hoping that there might be some stray beasts
still hidden in those parcels of undergrowth not yet cleared. Our
search was vain; there was nothing at all to be found on your Lord-
ship's land, even though everywhere we saw fresh tracks and drop-
pings so that anyone could tell the whole herd had been there and
been driven away only late the previous evening.

The damage was appalling: seventy-eight per cent of the young
trees have been destroyed. Though the law says that the estate must
replant immediately I cannot advise this until the culprits have been
seized and punished and until we can be sure it won't happen
again. The enormous expense would otherwise be wasted. It seems
that the gendarmes returned there on Saturday but once again they
found nothing there.

It is clear that the villagers were warned, again at the last minute,
but I have no idea who could have betrayed our intentions. Surely
not one of our own men? Anyhow even they did not know our plans
until the last minute, and then I took them immediately up into
the forests so that not one of them had a chance to speak to anyone
else. I do not suspect the gendarmes who are known to be reliable.

By the same post came a letter from Honey Andras Zutor. He
wrote without punctuation, but his meaning was utterly clear.
He told the same story, but with certain additions:

I don't think it right or normal if it please your Lordship the notary
had two gendarmes with him when he went up the river and on
the way went into popa Timbus's house afterwards coming out and
following the gendarmes on horseback until they arrived at the foot
of the Ponor where he dismissed them and came back towards
Toserat but not the way he come the popa sent his servant for Nyik
Vasilika who is rich and lives some way off and he too went some-
where but I don't know where but it must have been some way as
Grunspan the innkeeper at Gyurkuca told me he must have gone
a long way as it was already eleven when he returned and went in
for a slug of brandy and his boots were covered in mud though it
didn't rain anywhere there except in the mountains and on the

Boului we had no rain at all and not in the village either, that
the notary visited the popa and the rest was told by one of the
gendarmes quite by chance when I asked him why the notary
needed an escort and he said it wasn't an escort because he only left
them at their posts and when he went in to see the popa which seems
true because I too saw from the Humpleu on the other side of the
river that Nyik Vasilika went with the servant to Timbus because
I came that way from Skrind hoping to see something as your Lord-
ship told me to keep my eyes open but it was too late to see the
notary visit the priest but I saw what I said and it was then seven
o'clock and getting dark and as Forest Manager Winckler waited
for me at Beles when it got darker I wouldn't see any more . . .

Balint was not at all sorry. As it turned out it was a lucky chance
that the operation had still proved fruitless even after he had
accepted the notary's offer of help. Although they were quite
within the law to ask for the gendarmes the fact that Simo had
himself offered them showed that the notary found himself under
an obligation to someone, and by playing this double game and
making sure that the trick did not come off he was clearly repay-
ing a debt and was now free of it. But in doing so it was he himself
who broke the thin thread of any confidence Abady might still
have had in him.

I wonder why he did it, mused Balint. Why should he betray
the plan he himself had suggested?

There were several possibilities. The offer of help might have
been made simply to curry favour with the powerful landowner;
Simo was quite adept at this as Balint had seen when he was
setting up the co-operative in the mountains. But any display of
good will coming from him was sure to be false; he hated Abady's
strict management of the forests where the new order had put an
end to the illicit deer shoots that he had had with the old and
now retired manager Nyiresy. When that old rogue had still been
the Abady forest manager they had lived like lords themselves,
organizing wild festivities, getting free wood for themselves and
others, while ignoring all restraints of law and order. Now Abady
had put an end to his life as a little tin god in the mountains and
he couldn't forgive him. Of course there were probably other
reasons too, more serious ones that he hardly dared speak of. No
doubt, after the shooting and other incidents he was frightened
that the mountain people would try to take their revenge on him

for helping the money-lenders and the foreclosures. Perhaps, as the whole village was involved in the matter of the illegal grazing, he had felt it wiser to prove he wasn't totally against them and perhaps felt he would breathe more easily as he went about his business if he did them a good turn for once.

This at least was Abady's train of thought. Still, he realized that he had not yet found the answer to the cattle problem. Something else would have to be tried. Perhaps he could go straight to the Prefect of the district and get gendarmes from somewhere not under Simo's jurisdiction. Maybe that would be the answer . . .

CHAPTER TWO

THE CHURCH BELLS had already started their second peel when Countess Roza and her son walked out from the shade of the north-west tower of the castle of Denestornya and started the short descent which led to the village church. As long as Balint could remember the bells that signalled the time for going to church had always sounded the same. It was that same sound that pealed forth when he had been a child, a schoolboy home from the holidays from the Theresianum, or a young man on leave from his diplomatic posts abroad.

This weekly attendance at church had become something of a pilgrimage for Countess Roza. She too remembered the familiar sound of the bells from her own childhood when, the spoilt princess of an enchanted domain, she had demurely walked down the same path firstly with her parents, later with her husband, and then for so many widowed years, alone or just with a servant in attendance. And it had been just the same for generations of Abadys before her. The path was paved with ancient pebbles. Every now and then there was a short flight of stone steps, and these were now deeply worn even though it was only folk from the castle who used the path which led to the small door of the cemetery. This was always kept locked, and only they had the key.

The family never drove to church, no matter how bad the weather. This would have meant a long detour from the castle courtyard, through the home farm and back through the village until eventually they reached the rococo gateway where stood three graceful statues of angels, one holding the Ten Commandments, the second the Abady coat of arms, and the third leaning elegantly on a long trumpet patiently awaiting the order to sound the Last Trump.

Anyhow, whatever the reason, Countess Abady, who was determined that all the members of her household should also attend church on Sunday, never ordered the carriage on this day.

Abady stopped for a moment on the edge of the narrow path. He loved to look out from there. Though the gentle hillside was covered with a thick plantation of young pine trees, from this place there was a gap through which one could look out over the rich Keresztes plains towards the distant Torda mountains. Even further off could just be seen the hazy blue outlines of the high ridges of the Jara, while close at hand the sunlight picked out the stone façade of the old church. Just behind it, half hidden by groups of lime trees and elms, Balint could see the red roofs of the old mansion where his grandfather, Count Peter, had lived; and it was the memories that were brought back by this glimpse that had such an effect today on Balint's imagination.

As a boy Balint had often escaped from his tutors and stolen over to visit his grandfather. At that time the pines had still been quite small and Balint would pick his way through their thickly enlaced branches pretending that he was Cooper's 'Leather Jerkin'. When he climbed the cemetery wall he would imagine it to be the palisades of a great fort. By the time he had also scaled the wall of his grandfather's mansion he was often in a thoroughly bedraggled state with torn trousers and filthy stockings. Thinking about it today he could still see the old gentleman, himself the soul of neatness, with a smile on his carefully shaven face and his small pointed moustaches waxed to a fine point, turning in welcome as Balint climbed wearily up to the porticoed terrace.

After Count Peter's death Balint's mother had allowed her agent Azbej to instal himself in a few of the rooms and Balint managed to avoid going there as he did not wish to be angered by whatever horrors the common little lawyer might have perpetrated. Perhaps he had even repainted some of the eighteenth-century rooms in garish colours, and Balint did not want to be pained by the sacrilege to his grandfather's memory.

Recollecting himself he hurried after his mother who was now some way ahead.

* * *

The church gave the impression of being completely white, both inside and out. The interior walls had been lime-washed and even the ancient benches were as white as constant scrubbing for several centuries could achieve. The floor was covered with great slabs of white limestone. The organ was painted pale grey with its elaborate decorations picked out in faded gilt and the balda-chino and the pulpit were of pale carved stone. The ceiling too was painted, each square panel with a different pattern of either flowers or heraldic emblems. These, however, were all so faded that the general impression was one of radiant whiteness, so much so that one hardly noticed that on the ceiling there were tulips and carnations and that here a white hart was drinking from a colourless mountain stream and there an oddly-shaped pelican was feeding its young with its own blood.

In the congregation many of the men seemed to be dressed in white too, so snowy were their best linen shirts. Contrasted with them were the principal men of the village – the estate manager, the local sheriff and leading tradespeople and the treasurer of Balint's new co-operative society. These people, all in dark clothes, sat in the front rows. Black predominated also in the women's pews for though some of the young women and girls wore multi-coloured head-scarves the older ones who sat in front of them were swathed in black from head to foot. High on the wall behind the choir rail was the tablet showing the numbers of the hymns and psalms to be sung, and this too was painted black. However the most sombre of them all was the priest himself whose voluminous robes were of the darkest hue imaginable, and the old priest himself, as he leaned forward – with his long beak of a nose – over the edge of the pulpit, resembled nothing as much as an old crow in a tree.

Directly beneath him was the place reserved for the Abady family. Here the benches were also of scrubbed white pine but the book-rest was covered in the same light-green velvet as were the cushions of the pulpit. A Book of Psalms and a Bible were always placed on this rest. Directly behind it sat Balint and his mother. Here the benches formed, with the altar-table, an almost perfect square, the men in front and the girls at one side. The altar was covered with an embroidered cloth, as it always was for the Sunday services, but today, as it was the Feast of the New Bread and there was going to be Holy Communion, it carried also the silver vessels of the Denestornya church plate bearing the bread and wine, and these in their turn were covered by an ancient altar cloth of faded brocade, though the shape of the objects beneath could clearly be distinguished.

The first psalm had come to an end and the organ was playing softly. The girls, who until now had clustered together at the entrance to the church, tiptoed forward in single file, hurrying and jostling each other until they had found their places and could kneel for a few moments in prayer. Then they sat up, silently sniffing at the fine lawn handkerchiefs or bunches of rosemary they held in their hands. This was exactly as it always happened for it was an unwritten law that the men of the village should take their places first, followed by the important trades-people and the village elders. Then came the women and boys who went to their seats in the choir beneath the organ and only when all the others were in their places could the unmarried girls take their places too.

Now the organ boomed out a hymn-tune. The priest intoned and then the whole congregation rose and sang together. Balint at once noticed how rough some of the voices seemed, even to the point of singing wildly out of tune – but there was no mis-taking the deep faith and the eagerness and the sincerity with which they sang. It must have been like this with the early Chris-tians when the Message was still new.

After the prayers the vicar read the passage from the Bible that was to be the text on which he based his sermon.

He was an old man with an old man's quavering voice and he lingered long over the first syllable of each word. Everything he said Balint had heard before, and the rest of the congregation many times more than he; but it was all for the best, for the simple folk of the village understood it better than if they were hearing something new and so took it more to heart. And the text too was familiar because it was always the same. It was the Parable of the Sower and the Seed, and the sermon itself dealt with the seed which fell on good ground and brought forth fruit an hundredfold.

The sun's rays lit up the interior of the church, catching here some small particles of dust which seemed to dance lightly in the still air, and there the bright colours in a girl's head-scarf, the silver in the greying hair of one elderly villager or the flaming copper-coloured cheek-bones of another. The sparkle in the air was almost vaporous, so much so that the fine white of the church walls might have been covered with a layer of fine cream.

In some places, where the annual whitewashing – that ritual to ensure that the church interior was always immaculate – had been repeated for several hundred years, the lime wash was sometimes nearly three fingers deep and smoothed and softened every hard edge or angle of the vaulting, the groins and the projecting capitals of the columns.

To Balint the old church had never seemed so beautiful.

He looked around, as he had so many times before. On one side the three arches which began where the organ had been placed high up on a stone balcony were supported firmly by columns of Byzantine solidity. On the other, high above the girls' benches, the last arch was joined to the stone balustrade which guarded the door of the Tabernacle and the *Porta Trium-phalis*. Opening behind the pulpit these doors dated from the time when the church, then of course the home of Catholic rites, had been built in the twelfth century. Naturally no papers still existed to prove the age of the building, but its origins were nonetheless unmistakable.

This was one of the early churches constructed with two rather than three aisles. One, the most important, was the nave in the style typical of the times of Bela III and unique to Hungary. Here, in the apse and the transept, the columns and arches all dated from the original construction. The rest of the church had seen many changes. A good part had been burnt at the time of the Tartar invasions when much of the building had been destroyed – except for the dressed stone exterior walls – and had had to be rebuilt; and this was why the old main entrance on the west side was walled up while another door had been opened beside it. The pew door was surrounded with gothic arches similar to those in the rebuilt nave.

Later came the Reformation when, because the sermon was the most important part of the Reformed service of prayers, the pulpit became the principal feature of the church interior. So as not to obscure the altar this was placed at the side, just where the transept began. Its elaborate carved stone decoration was in High Renaissance style.

Soon taste changed again and so the new baldachino and the organ casing were carved in flamboyant rococo.

So the little church, like the great castle on which it was dependent, grew and changed, and was transformed from its simple beginnings into a model of eclectic development whose diverse features, though organic parts of the whole, reflected the needs and desires and tastes of successive centuries.

Here too everything tended to extol the glory of the Abady family. What came first to view was the inscription round the pulpit: *Erected to the glorious memory of the most noble and powerful lord Gyorgy Abady Statuum Praes, anno 1690*. On the baldachino and again on the sounding board above the pulpit the Abady arms were prominently emblazoned, with the date 1740; while the monogram of that Count Denes Abady who became Chancellor of Transylvania and Master of the Horse to the sovereign was carved in high relief surrounded by garlands of leaves and flowers. Along the walls, all in similar narrow gilt frames, were all the printed announcements of the births, deaths and marriages of Abadys down the centuries, those of the women crowned with a double coat of arms – their own and their husbands' – while those of male Abadys carried only the heraldic device of their own family, a golden gryphon with spread wings on a red ground, that device which in mediæval times had been borne by the Abadys' first ancestors, the Tomai chieftains. Under each announcement were written their titles and the distinguished posts they had occupied.

Just in front of the family bench were hung, one above the other, the notices of Balint's father and grandfather.

Once again, as he always did each time he was there, he read the fading print and was carried back in memory to the days of his childhood.

The first memories, those which included both his father and mother as well as his grandfather, Count Peter, were hazy enough for he had been barely eight years old when his father had died so suddenly. The image of Count Peter, on the other hand, was much more vivid. He could remember the old man sitting beside him, in the place of honour where his mother now sat so placidly, her little chubby hand resting on the Book of Psalms in front of her. Count Abady's fine profile and always closely shaven face, his wavy silver hair, even that scent of tobacco and lavender soap that seemed his special attribute and which the child had always associated with his grandfather's presence, still seemed so real to Balint that he imagined that if he turned his head, the old man would still be there.

The fact that the framed announcement of Count Peter's decease on November 3rd 1892 hung before his eyes meant nothing to Balint. For him his much-loved grandfather was still and always would be alive and well, and all that he had taught the child was as fresh in his memory as if it had been said the day before.

One remark, made by the old man when Balint had been about fifteen, came back to him today. The three of them, Balint, his mother and grandfather, had just left the church and started on the short path which led to his grandfather's house where they always lunched on Sundays. Balint, thoughtlessly, had said something to the effect that it was marvellous to think that everything around him had been created by his own ancestors.

Count Peter had stopped at once, and for a moment had looked sharply at the boy. He must have thought that his grandchild had unwittingly imbibed some of the pride of race and family conceit of Countess Roza who, as an only and thoroughly spoilt child, had imagined herself queen of all she surveyed; for very seriously he now addressed himself only to his grandson.

Though the kindly smile never left his face there was no mistaking the rebuke his words implied.

'There is nothing at all marvellous or wonderful about it, my boy, and especially there is nothing to boast about. What has happened has been entirely natural. Long ago, when the country folk were all serfs, everything belonged to the landowner, the so-called noble who himself held it from the King. It was therefore nothing less than his bounden duty to take care of everything, to build what was needed and to repair what needed repairing. That our family have done this only shows that they have always done their duty, nothing else. Let this be a lesson to you!'

The old man was silent for a moment. Then they all left the cemetery.

On both sides of the path were planted standard roses. Count Peter stopped on his way, took a knife from his pocket, cut a few blooms and, after deftly removing the thorns, offered them to his daughter-in-law. Then he went on, 'That members of our family often obtained great positions in the state was no accident and no particular merit to them. Such places were naturally offered to people of high rank, nobles whose fortunes and family connections were necessary if they were to do a useful job. We can be proud that our forebears honestly carried out what was expected of them, that is all. Family conceit because of such things is not only ridiculous but also dangerous to the character of those who come to believe in it. I have often thought about this and have come to understand what such feelings can lead to, especially when they are not used to guide our behaviour but rather to puff up a sense of inbred superiority. If a man knows himself he will neither believe himself all of a sudden to be more of a man because of the job he has been called upon to under-take, nor indeed less when the time comes to relinquish it. If others come to you for help or advice you must not come to believe it is because you are in any way better than they are. It is no more than that for historical reasons the state has come to rely upon people with your traditions and breeding. This is why for centuries the structure of Hungarian society has been based on using aristocrats to fill the high offices of the kingdom. When we accept, or refuse, office this is something we must always remember. And it will be easier for us to do what we must if our conscience is clear and we know that our decisions are taken for the right reasons and not merely adopted out of pride. This is the real meaning of *noblesse oblige*!'

If Countess Roza also spoke up on this occasion Balint had no memory of it. All he remembered were his grandfather's words and they remained always with him.

When he had finished the old man had been silent for a little while. It had been as if he too had at that time been recalling something that happened in his past, something of which he now never spoke. This was indeed so.

In October of the year 1860 the Emperor Franz-Josef, without telling him in advance, had nominated Count Peter as a member of the Dual Monarchy's Imperial State Council and the official letter of appointment was sent to him from Vienna without any warning. Count Peter had not been prepared, in the uneasy climate of the day, to accept this dubious honour and had accord-ingly sent his refusal in writing to the monarch. Copies of both documents had been kept in the archives of Denestornya; and this is where Balint had found them many years later. At the time the monarch had been angry and resentful, so much so that Count Peter Abady had been proscribed as a dangerous opponent of Habsburg rule and was not forgiven until the Compromise was signed a few years later. Only then had Balint's grandfather been received back into favour and his integrity all the more appreciated.

After another few moments of silence the old man had given a light laugh and put his hand on the boy's shoulder. They had just reached the balustrade which surrounded the mansion's stone-pillared portico.

'And so, my boy, if by any chance it should turn out that you were born proud, which would not entirely surprise me,' and he gave a swift and fleetingly mocking smile as he glanced at his daughter-in-law, 'then take pride only in making yourself more industrious, more useful, and more steadfast, both in body and soul, in trying to do your duty so that in this way and in this way only can people look up to you as a man worthy of admiration and respect. And if you really believe that your ability to serve others and to work harder than most people is due to your family's ancient origins and traditions, then maybe this will be true for you; for faith, no matter from what it draws its strength, is the most powerful incentive there is.'

These were the things that Count Peter had said and which had been inspired by the old church which stood as a monument, formed of stone, woodwork and ancient writings, to the noble past of the Abady family. Those words had been the essence of his teaching, and Balint planned to pass them on to his son, the son that Adrienne was to bear. Perhaps, he thought, in five or six years' time they would be able to sit there together. It was a dream that now came to him so vividly that he could almost believe that the boy was there beside him. Next to the pulpit would sit his mother, as today. Next to her would be Adrienne; and there, between them, the child Adam, that child they longed for so much and who would be the fruit of their dreams and hopes, the crown of their love, and of whom, when they were together, they spoke so much and of whom, when they were apart, they would write at length as if he had already been born. They took this fantasy to ever more deceptive lengths, building for themselves an edifice of folly about the black wavy hair the child had inherited from his mother, about the birthmark on his shoulder that was the image of Balint's own, how young Adam would toss his head when asked a question and what his face looked like when he thought that no one was looking at him . . . they thought so much, and talked so much, and all about that boy who was to be the most wonderful boy in the world.

The priest brought his sermon to an end 'in the name of the Father, the Son and the Holy Ghost, Amen.' The congregation rose for the next prayers.

Up above Balint and his mother all that could now be seen of the priest were his hands joined in prayer and higher up his huge moustaches and stubble-covered double chin. The old man had raised his eyes to Heaven and was now intoning the last prayer of all. Though he drew out the first syllable of each word and though his voice was cracked and feeble, what he said was beautiful, warm and said from the heart, and of course the words were those beautiful words of the ancient Prayer Book: '. . . lead us, oh Lord, on this earth to sow mercy, goodness, love and justice so that in our turn we may reap the same in this life and later our souls be brought to eternal bliss, through your Son Jesus Christ in Heaven'.

Hearing these words Balint awoke from his dreams and started to pray with great fervour; and in his prayers, though not expressed in words, were still inextricably woven those dreams of his successor, that heir the certainty of whose coming was more to him than Hope itself.

The priest now moved up to the altar-table and stood there, his raven-black gown contrasting richly with the radiant whiteness all around him. Carefully folding back the brocade cloth he revealed the ancient vessels of the Communion Service – two chalices, a huge cup and the small dishes for the bread, all of them of massive silver-gilt and all placed upon silken mats lavishly embroidered with gold and silver thread. A ray from the sun fell on the altar from one of the high windows, picking up a gleam of silver from the chased and engraved chalices or a sudden flash of gold or scarlet from the embroidery on the altar cloths. The sunlight transformed those ancient works of man's artifice into a festive, almost transcendental display of pious splendour.

In the white simplicity of the church the Communion vessels, which dated mostly from the seventeenth and eighteenth centuries, glowed with the promise of another world. One of the chalices was of the old mediæval pattern with a nodular design on its stem, while the rest of the decoration was in High Renaissance style; and this mixture of ideas stemmed from the fact that in Transylvania the goldsmiths still used gothic patterns long after they had been discarded elsewhere. The other chalice had been formed in the image of a lily, the segmented petals radiating from an elaborately perforated stem. This, too, was at least two hundred years old as were the silken mats on which they stood. All these things had been the gifts of successive generations of Abadys who had felt a spiritual need to furnish their church's altar with the richest and most beautiful artefacts of their day. In this they were by no means exceptional, for in Transylvania there was hardly a village church, great or small, that could not boast that the vessels they used so reverently every Sabbath were worthy of display in some great museum.

Balint recognized each vessel with renewed pleasure.

His joy, however, was short-lived for the dismal thought then came to him that maybe, by the rules of the church, he should not attempt to partake of the Bread and Wine. Did not adultery joyfully persisted in without repentance burden his soul and prevent his being in a state of grace?

This was something he had never before thought about. His wide reading of natural history, and even of theology – reading that he had faithfully maintained especially when he had been writing his treatise on 'Beauty in Action' – may have widened his general outlook but it had also nearly obliterated any faith he may once have had in dogma and the teachings of his Church. He had come to believe that all such things were the creation of man and that they were but reflections of the feelings of the days in which they had been formulated. He believed in the spirit of the Reformation, when such men as Luther, Calvin and John Knox challenged the *ex cathedra* infallibility of the Pope and when traditional dogma had been scrutinized anew and not a little discarded. The strong Protestant conviction that the traditions of the Church and the decisions of the great Church Councils had been in conflict with the simple truth enshrined in the Gospels had been so strongly imbued in his youth that for many years he had always gone out before the Communion.

Had he been alone now in the family pew he would have left as did several other members of the congregation; indeed the singing of the choir was always prolonged at this point so as to make it possible for those who wished to go without disturbing those who wished to stay. Even the priest was waiting for the

departure of those who, for whatever reason, felt themselves
unworthy to remain, before he began to expound the nature of
the Sacrament and emphasize that acceptance of the Bread and
Wine should only follow a strict examination of their own souls
by those who remained to take Communion. The priest, he
explained, was merely the medium by which the Sacrament was
passed to the faithful. He himself was unable either to absolve or
to punish, he was empowered only to recall to the faithful their
bounden duty and to remind each and every one of them that by
the Calvinist creed each man stood alone before his Maker . . . and
that every man too must search for the truth in his own heart, and
must himself be judge both of his virtues and of his shortcomings.

Countess Roza remained firmly in her place. With no sign of
doubt she sat there completely motionless. If Balint had risen to
go at this point it would have caused a scandal. He paused, not
knowing what to do.

The priest was reading out the awe-inspiring text that defined
so clearly every individual's own responsibility: '. . . therefore if
any of you be a blasphemer of God, an adulterer, or be in envy
or malice, come not to that holy Table; lest after the taking of
the holy Sacrament, the Devil enter into you and bring you to
destruction of body and soul.'

He listened to the ancient words, standing completely still;
and, as he did so, he searched his own soul as he never had before,
candidly, clearly and in total humility. He thought about his
whole life; and that he was guilty in his actions there could be no
doubt. But in his thoughts? Ah, that was different. With every
nerve, every act of will, every thought he had sought the way to
find the right, decent solution to his relationship with Adrienne.
Their intentions had never been sinful or base; and never, in their
new-found love for each other, had they ceased to seek a solution
to their problems which would conform with the law. Both of
them fervently desired that their offspring should be worthy
successors of their race and creed. As Balint was so ruthlessly
examining his own actions and intentions, he had the strongest
feeling that his failings would be understood and pardoned by
Him who sat down to eat with publicans and sinners and who
saved the woman taken in adultery.

Now came his turn to be handed the chalice, and, bending
over it, he made a secret vow. With all his strength and all the
will-power he could muster, though he knew he would never be

strong enough to deny his love, he would strive to overcome every obstacle that stood between him and marriage with Adrienne. The priest's words seemed to be an unexpected reply to his prayers to be sent a son and heir.

'Ask, and it shall be given unto you ...'

CHAPTER THREE

THAT AFTERNOON BALINT went into the tower that stood at the south-east corner of the castle of Denestornya. This was the oldest part of the great house. It had been there before the Tartar invasions, and from it came the name that had lasted for so many later generations. Once it had stood alone, guarding the slopes below and, unlike the later parts of the castle, it was constructed largely from undressed stone. Its walls, too, were exceptionally thick – more than three metres at their base – and there were neither arrow-slits nor windows on the ground floor. On the first floor of this tower had been placed the castle archives, collected in chests of bleached pine that were placed in alcoves formed by the stone arches which encircled the interior walls. Every chest was labelled alphabetically and in these had been placed all the documents. In the centre of the room was a vast oak-topped table, on which there was a map of the castle domains, and under it were drawers containing the old plans of the building itself, including all the elaborate alterations of the seventeenth and eighteenth centuries.

It was amongst these plans that Balint made his search. He wanted to find out how the rooms in the west wing had originally been arranged. They had been altered many years ago for one of his great-great-uncles and had not been used since his death. It was here, he thought, that he would live after his marriage; but he guessed that many changes would have to be made, including, of course, installing those modern comforts that had formerly been unknown.

After poring over the plans Balint was just about to go himself to look once more at these rooms when he heard the sound of a car horn which seemed to come from the horseshoe-shaped entrance court. He looked out through the deep embrasure of one of the few windows.

A car entered the court at speed and stopped in front of the

main doorway. It was obviously brand-new, and was bright red
in colour. To Balint's considerable surprise Dinora Malhuysen
and Dr Zsigmond Boros descended and started to mount the
steps to the door. Dinora, thought Balint; what could Dinora be
doing here? Since the great scandal two years before Dinora had
gone nowhere since, through no fault of her own, no one would
now receive her. All she had done had been to sign, without
realizing the implications of what she was doing, bank drafts for
the benefit of her lover, the Austrian lieutenant of hussars, Egon
von Wickwitz. When his frauds had been discovered – and he
had fled the country rather than kill himself as his colonel had
suggested – the publicity that the scandal aroused had left
Dinora's husband, Tihamer Abonyi, no choice but to divorce
her. Since then all doors had been barred to her, and she had been
treated everywhere as a pariah. She also found herself greatly in
debt. It was rumoured that she was rarely to be seen on her estate
in neighbouring Maros-Szilvas, and apparently spent most of her
time in Budapest or elsewhere.

And now she had come to call on Countess Roza, stepping up
to the castle entrance with all the assurance of someone whose
arrival was expected!

Whatever it may have been for Balint, Dinora's visit came as
no surprise to his mother, who had written to the young woman
who was shunned by everyone else, and asked her to call, saying
how she would welcome such a visit. Countess Abady always
followed her own instincts and had never been swayed by the
opinion of others. And her own instincts were always highly
individual and owed nothing to convention. A woman who had
been widowed when still young and who had ever afterwards
remained faithful to the memory of her beloved husband, Countess Roza had never been even interested in another man. If she
ever thought at all about what other women might do she dismissed those who had lovers merely as different, almost as if they
belonged to a third sex. She did not judge them as she would have
judged herself. She did not condemn them either. They were
different, that was all. And with this lofty, indeed almost regal
disdain for the opinions of the vulgar, it never occurred to her to
follow the lead of those who now decided to cold-shoulder the
poor little Countess Abonyi.

This alone, however, would not have been enough to justify
suddenly inviting her to come to Denestornya.

Countess Roza had her own plans and her own reasons. Since that day in March when Balint had received Adrienne's letter, she believed her son had finally broken with the only woman that Countess Roza had ever hated or wanted her son to avoid. Recently, however, there had arrived three letters in quick succession, and Countess Roza, to whom the mail was always brought first and who knew well what Adrienne's handwriting looked like, realized that all was not as she had hoped; and the thought gave her a good scare. Of course, she thought, that wicked woman is so full of evil that she will somehow worm her way back into Balint's heart; and she wondered what she could do to stop it. It was then that the idea of sending for Dinora came to her, for Dinora's property was not too far away and it seemed that she had recently come back to live at home. In the past Balint, when still a student at Kolozsvar University, used – secretly, as he thought – to ride over to see the little Countess Abonyi, always going at night and taking the short-cut by the ford over the Aranyos river. It had been a nice distraction for him then; and it could be again. After all, her son needed amusement and surely, like most other men, the best amusement for him would be a pretty woman. Countess Roza never marshalled her thoughts with such cynical precision. They merely hovered uncertainly over what seemed a likely possibility. Nevertheless she had an unusually sly smile on her plump face when on the previous day she had sent a groom riding over to Maros-Szilvas with a letter of invitation.

Balint found the guests on the lower terrace where his mother liked to have tea in the summer. From there a magnificent vista stretched out over more than a mile of well-mown parkland flanked by tall stands of poplar.

His mother was already there and the butler was just laying the table.

'I do hope you'll forgive me,' Dinora was saying, 'for bringing Zsigmond Boros with me. I haven't kept a carriage since Tihamer and I separated. We had such beautiful Russian trotters, do you remember? But Zsiga – Dr Boros – said that it was a luxury I couldn't afford. And indeed what need have I of a carriage now? And then he had just come to pay me a visit, and he has a car, so I thought, I hope indeed, that you wouldn't mind.'

Just a trifle coldly Countess Roza replied, 'On the contrary, I am very pleased.'

Then Balint came up and as soon as she saw him Dinora
jumped up, saying, 'AB! How marvellous! I *am* glad to see you.
Of course you know Zsiga Boros; isn't he your colleague in
Parliament? When did you get here? How are you?'

When everyone had finished greeting each other they sat down
to tea. As was the custom in Transylvania this was an enormous
meal of cold meats, hot scones and cakes brought out in relays by
the two old housekeepers, butter, honey, fresh strawberries, tea,
and iced coffee served with mountains of whipped cream.

Boros swiftly brought into play his beautiful baritone voice
and in carefully modulated tones started to praise the layout of
the park and its trees, the splendour of the view from the terrace,
the grandeur of the horseshoe-shaped entrance court and of the
great hall through which they had just passed. In this way he
managed, bit by bit, to melt Countess Roza's stony little heart.

At first she had been extremely suspicious of him. She found
his clothes too well-cut for a country lawyer who was, when all
was said and done, barely a gentleman. His spade-shaped beard
was obviously no stranger to the curling tongs; there were too
many rings on his fingers, and he reeked of scent. The old lady
felt instinctively that there was something not quite right about
this exaggeratedly elegant appearance. However, when Boros
roundly declared that Denestornya reminded him of no less a
place than Chambord, the French royal castle on the Loire,
Countess Roza finally gave in and allowed herself to thaw. This
was because, apart from her son, the only thing in the world that
she truly loved was the huge beautiful house in which she had
lived all her life.

When tea was over she herself suggested that Dr Boros might
like her to show him the state rooms. Balint and Dinora could
go for a walk!

A little later, when they reached the lime tree avenue, Balint said,
'And how is sweet little Dinora? I've often thought of coming
over to see you, but they said you were away.'

'That was a nice thought, AB. But you know it isn't all that
fun to be alone in the country. Besides, nasty little writs kept on
being served and they tried to effect a seizure; so I thought it
better not to be there so that they couldn't find me. It's all right
now, of course. Everything has changed since Zsiga – Dr Boros,
I mean . . .'

'You can call him Zsiga to me, you know,' said Balint re-assuringly.

Dinora smiled and gave a little shrug of the shoulders. 'Well,' and she paused before going on, 'and after all why not? He's a most agreeable companion. And do you know,' she said, putting her hand on Balint's arm, 'he's taught me no end of things, things I never dreamed of . . . He's quite a surprise, I can tell you!'

'Legal things, of course!' said Balint with a laugh.

'Don't be silly,' said Dinora with a sensuous little giggle. Then she stopped speaking for a moment as if she were pondering over some secret. 'Perhaps he learned it all from some famous *cocotte*, for it seems he goes every year to Trouville or Ostend.'

'Is he as rich as all that?' Abady asked, somewhat taken by surprise. 'That sort of trip costs a lot of money!'

'Oh, yes, plenty! And now he's got even more, quite a large sum, I believe. He's taken a very nice flat for me in Budapest. It's not in my name, of course, so no one will bother me with those tiresome writs!'

'But they can always put Maros-Szilvas up to auction if you don't settle your debts!'

Dinora laughed gaily. 'Oh no, they can't! We've put the prop-erty in Zsiga's name! On paper I don't own anything . . . so they can't catch me!'

Balint was dismayed at her folly. 'But my darling Dinora, do you mean everything you own is now in his name? This is madness! You've put yourself entirely in his hands.'

'Oh, he's really a complete gentleman and . . . well, he's crazy about me!'

'But he can't marry you. He's got a wife and children already!'

'I don't care! I wouldn't marry him anyway! What on earth for? Oh, for heaven's sake, let's talk about something else. Life is so beautiful, and I am glad to see you again, Little Boy! Do you remember? That's what I used to call you . . . Little Boy!' And she brushed against him just as cats do. Then she went on, with great charm and warmth: 'Do you remember how awkward you used to be? But you were very sweet . . . and you could talk, how you could talk! I said then that one day you would become a great man.'

And she brought back the past to him so vividly he could not return to more serious subjects. Anyway, he reflected, she wouldn't have listened and anything he said would have been wasted. Sweet little bird-brained creatures like Dinora must just be allowed to go on chirruping.

Balint waited for a few days before telling his mother about his plans. That she had gone so far as to receive the ostracized Dinora seemed to augur well for her relenting towards Adrienne. In the end it was Countess Roza herself who gave him the opportunity to raise the subject. Mrs Tothy and Mrs Baczo, ever vigilant and used to telling everything they saw or heard to their mistress, told her that Master Balint had taken to repeatedly visiting the unused rooms in the castle's west wing. They had even discovered that he had made careful measurements and noted down everything that he had done.

'Are you planning to do something with Uncle Pali's rooms?' asked Countess Roza one day after dinner.

Mother and son were together in her small sitting-room. Here the countess's sofa was placed in the corner rather than in the centre of the room as it was in the house in Kolozsvar. Otherwise everything was arranged in just the same manner. The countess sat in the middle of the sofa, Balint in an armchair on her right; while the two housekeepers had their places opposite her, sitting busily crocheting at the table placed in front of the sofa.

'Possibly. I do have something in mind and I wanted to speak to you about it, but...' Balint, looking at Mrs Baczo and Mrs Tothy, let his voice die away without finishing the sentence.

Without even waiting for the dismissive wave of the hand that Countess Roza always used to send them out of the room, the old housekeepers gathered up their work and bustled away.

'I was thinking,' he said, 'that if I were to get married I might think of living there, if it would be all right with you, Mama. Those rooms would really be everything we needed. The west wing is quite separate from the rest of the house and hasn't been used for ages. It only needs very little alteration, and it wouldn't affect any other part of the house.'

'You are thinking of getting married?' cried Countess Roza. 'Now what would be the greatest joy I have ever known. Oh, tell me, tell me! I've waited so long for this, but didn't dare to worry you about it, to try and push you...' She stared hard at him with her slightly protuberant eyes and grabbed at his hand with her chubby little fingers.

'Yes, I am,' he said. 'I've thought about it for a long time.

I can't go on like this ... and for many years I have loved a woman...'

'A woman!' cried Countess Roza, startled, and withdrew her hand from Balint's as abruptly as if she had just touched fire.

'Yes! You've probably already guessed. It's Adrienne Miloth; we've been in love for years.'

Countess Roza, for a moment, was speechless. Her joy was so suddenly turned to grief that she could hardly find words adequate to express her fury.

'That – that – that *person*! No! No! Never!' and she went on repeating the same words: 'No! No! Never!', spluttering them out as if she were choking from suffocation.

'But, Mama, darling Mama, I love her! I love her deeply and I've never loved anyone else. I never could love anyone else, not ever, I swear it. And she loves me!'

The old lady drew herself up and said scornfully, 'Loves *you*? That's absurd – wicked. And she's made you believe it? How can you be so blind, so stupid? What a donkey you are, my son!' she said, as all the lies and slanders about Adrienne that had been repeated to her by Aunt Lizinka and the housekeepers rushed through her mind, and she thought of all the tales about affairs with Uncle Ambrus, with Adam Alvinczy and Pityu and a dozen others which those pitiless ladies had fed her for so long.

Balint felt the blood rushing to his head. With a great effort he tried to control himself and speak calmly. But when he spoke the anger within him could not be entirely suppressed.

'I alone can know what she feels for me. It is after all my business and no one else's!'

For a moment mother and son confronted each other without speaking.

Then Balint, speaking very slowly and with unmistakable emphasis, said, 'I have decided to marry her as soon as she can obtain a divorce!'

Countess Roza then did something she had never done before: she lost her temper. Jumping up suddenly, she beat the table with clenched fists.

'I will never agree! Never! Never! Never!'

Then, as if ashamed of this extraordinary outburst, she went over to the window and sat down at her desk staring blindly in front of her. She did not speak but her eyes glistened with rage.

Balint tried to reason with her. Again he repeated what he had said before, trying always to speak in a quiet, restrained, almost humble, manner, for he well knew his mother's tyrannical nature.

Because Countess Roza had such a respect for tradition he started by bringing up the case of his grandfather on his father's side, who had also married a divorced woman. This had been generally accepted, and there was no stigma attached, since they were both Protestants. Then he returned to Adrienne and again told his mother that she was the only woman for him and that he could never settle down with anyone else. There never would be another, there never could be. Though he started calmly his mother's stubborn refusal to answer him, even to speak at all, soon began to pierce his hard-won restraint.

Slowly the soft persuasive manner he had tried to adopt hardened into something much more natural to him.

'After all,' he said, 'it is not as if I were still a child. I am of age and I have every right . . .'

'So that's how it is, is it? So it has come to that?' interrupted his mother, drawing herself up to her full height, tiny though it was, and looking coldly at her son. 'So now you dare to tell *me* the things you have a right to. All right. So be it! Do whatever you please. But I tell you this: never, never, as long as I live, shall that woman enter this house. Do you understand me? Never! And now go. I have nothing more to say to you!'

Once again Balint tried a more conciliatory approach. 'My dearest Mama, don't say things like that!'

'No? Now leave me, enough has been said. Go now. At once!'

Balint realized that he had no alternative but to do as he was told. He tried respectfully to kiss her hand but she would have none of it, merely waving him to the door with an angry little gesture.

Countess Roza remained in exactly the same position, with her arm stretched out in command, until the door-latch clicked into place behind her son. Then, as if all the strength in her body had suddenly left her, she collapsed and sat sobbing at her desk. She sat there for a long time, racked with tears, her head shrouded by the sleeves of her dress as if she never wanted to see or hear anything ever again. It had not been like this since, so many years ago, she had wept for her young husband dying of an incurable disease in the next room.

The old lady cried so hard that she never noticed that one of the housekeepers looked in but retired swiftly, not daring to trespass on such grief. After a long time, during which Countess Roza was so absorbed by this devastating sorrow that she did not notice anything that happened near her, she suddenly sat up and pulled herself together. She wiped her eyes and smoothed back her ruffled hair. Then, getting up, she stepped briskly out of the small sitting-room, crossed the great hall on the first floor of the house and, carefully speaking as if nothing had upset her, told one of the waiting footmen to turn down the lamps.

No one who had not witnessed the scene between mother and son, and who now saw her walk calmly towards the door of her apartments, could possibly have guessed the turmoil she had just endured.

The next day mother and son did not meet until lunch-time. Balint greeted his mother as he always did by kissing her hand in the old formal manner; but he waited until they were alone before again referring to his marriage plans. He had spent half the night preparing what he was going to say, but it was all in vain for he had hardly begun before his mother interrupted him, saying in a calm but merciless manner, 'I don't wish to hear anything more about it. Nothing will change what I have already said. I will only add this: the day that you marry the person you have mentioned we will become strangers to one another. In the meantime, until that dreadful day comes, everything will go on just as it has before, until the very last minute. What is mine is also yours, but our life together will become impossible if ever you speak of this again. I say this so that you are forewarned.'

And then, so quickly that he could have no time even to think of a reply, she added lightly, 'I'm going to walk down to see the mares. Hollo's foal has been stung by a wasp, it seems. On the nose, poor little thing. There must be a nest somewhere about. If we could only find it we could have it removed.'

And so everything appeared to remain just as it always had been. Balint and his mother walked together around the property, planning flower-beds and ornamental shrubs, discussing a wooden bridge that was rotting away and must be repaired, and deciding which horses should be got ready for the autumn hunting season. They talked about fallow-deer, about hares and about pheasants. But it was all for appearances' sake only, a sort of formal game that was played to disguise the fact that there was only one subject in both their minds: Balint's plan to marry Adrienne.

Their words were carefully chosen, but as artificial as a drawing-room comedy; and their air of being without a care in the world was only a pretence.

Four days went by, heavy, painful days for them both. It was agony for Balint to see how his mother was suffering, and so he decided it would be better to absent himself for a while. It would be better for both of them if he were not there; and perhaps in time they could forget that dreadful scene in the little sitting-room, which was the first time in both their lives that they had had a real clash.

When Balint told his mother that he would soon be leaving again she did not ask, as she always had before, either where he was going or when he would be leaving. Instead she merely nodded her agreement and said, 'All right!' – nothing more. It was obvious that she imagined that her son was going to the side of the woman she hated; and she clung to this conviction even though Balint declared that he was going straight to Budapest for the next session of Parliament as there were to be important debates on electoral reform, the Turkish Question and on Balint's own project – the foundation of the country co-operatives – all of which urgently called for his presence in the capital. Whenever the subject was broached she always avoided discussing the matter, repeating the words 'All right! All right!' as if she wanted somehow to make it unnecessary for Balint to go on lying to her.

However, everything that Balint had said was true; and for the moment he had no plans to see Adrienne again. But nothing would persuade Countess Roza to believe him; and so, for the moment, all confidence between them was shattered and it looked as if no words could heal the breach.

Balint went away sadly. When his carriage turned to pass under the great gateway of the horseshoe court, he looked back, as he always did, to wave to his mother who never failed at that point to come out onto the balcony above the front door of the castle. Today there was no one there to wave him goodbye. Perhaps, thought Balint, she had returned once again to the little sitting-room. Perhaps she was there hiding her tears from the world . . . and perhaps that was the reason she did not come out to watch him go.

Balint's heart constricted with pain . . .

CHAPTER FOUR

THE BIG COUNTY fair of Szamos-Ujvar was always held on a Tuesday in September. Of all the Ujvar Fairs this was the biggest and most important, both because of the pig-fattening and because it was the time when the distilleries did their buying. Herds of cattle were sent to this market by the farmers, and all the tradesmen and wholesalers were there. It was now that pig prices were at their highest, indeed it was the best moment to sell off any unwanted stock, even horses now that they were in good condition after being at grass most of the summer. It was at this time, too, that anyone with foresight bought their winter clothes – boots, woollen underwear and overcoats and warm blankets – as well as ploughs for the autumn sowing, harness for the beasts of burden, and a myriad other necessities for the farmer. And many people came, too, just for the fun of it, for a big county fair was as good as a carnival. Men and women streamed into the little town from all around: from Mezoseg, from Erdohat and the valley of the Szamos, even from as far away as the district of Kovar. Even if they had no need for serious buying and selling they came to enjoy themselves, for at the fair you could hear the latest news and drink brandy sweetened with honey. People came for all sorts of reasons, just to be there; and they would come in from twenty kilometres away merely for a swig of brandy, a new stem to their pipe, or for a single box of matches.

The first day was devoted to the livestock sales and the second to all other merchandise. For this reason the livestock to be offered for sale started pouring into the market site long before dawn, for it was important to secure a good stand and also to have time to put out some feelers about this year's prices . . . for bargaining was no affair of a minute!

The handsome Mrs Sara Bogdan Lazar had left her property at Dezmer while it was still dark. In front of her carriage were driven some thirty oxen of various types – animals she had bought in the spring, fattened up on her rich prairie-lands, and would sell at a substantial profit in the autumn – and also some newly-weaned calves. The cattle were driven in front of her so that from her half-closed carriage, which was driven slowly so as not to exceed the pace of her stock, she could keep a careful eye on her cattle-hands, make sure they didn't dawdle on the way joking with the girls from the farms they passed, and above all that they didn't harry the beasts and make them go lame before they were offered for sale.

It may have looked odd that this elegant carriage driven by a coachman in livery should have four large bales of hay strapped onto the box, but Sara Lazar was never one to trouble herself about such things, for she was far too interested in the management of her farms to be bothered about the trivia of appearances. She was her own manager, and there was hardly a man in her district who understood the business half as well as she did.

So there she was, on the ground as early as anyone; and she always stayed until the very end. Although there was much interest in her stock from the moment that the market opened, she never lowered her prices so as to make sure of a sale. A man she knew – a buyer for the important Papp Brothers' enterprise – had given her a tip that prices would be higher than usual this year. He had given her the slightest of winks from a distance, but this was enough for Sara. The Papp brothers always knew what to expect for they were the biggest cattle-dealers in the district, shipped their goods to Vienna and other places abroad, and kept their ears firmly to the ground. So Mrs Bogdan Lazar remained cool and held out for high prices herself. She ate her lunch from a hamper, right next to the animals she had brought for sale, and she was proved right. At the very end of the day she sold all she had brought at the very highest prices, for as the demand was greater than the supply, the prices went up as soon as there were fewer beasts left on offer.

When everything had been settled Sara sent her men home and then had herself driven to the centre of the town as she wanted to find the friendly fellow who had tipped her the wink about the day's prices. He had well earned the few hundred crowns she would give him, and such gestures were much appreciated and ensured he would go on helping her in the future. She knew just where to find him: in the garden of the Green Tree Inn which, if not very elegant, was roomy and hospitable and had been chosen by the cattle-dealers as their favourite hostelry.

It was not easy to get through the town for by now it was evening and the roads were full of drunken men and herds of animals being driven away by their new owners. The most difficult to pass were the pigs, for even three strong men found it difficult to make them move, especially as they were kept captive by a string tied to one of their hind legs. Nothing daunted, Sara managed to find a way through the crowd of people, animals, stalls and tents, and finally reached the Green Tree. Boldly she walked straight in. The courtyard and garden were both crowded and the gypsies were playing their hardest so as to be heard over the din of good-humoured talk. Everyone was in a good mood for it had been a profitable day; and so the music played and the drink flowed. The waiters were kept busy carrying trays of food, tankards of beer and huge carafes of wine.

Mrs Lazar looked around her and soon found the man she sought. He was sitting with a lot of other men, leaning on his elbows at a large table near to where the gypsies were playing. She hesitated for a moment wondering if it might not be better to send him her tip by post. However she soon decided that it was better to do it straight away and so she started to brave the crowd of drunks so as to get closer to him. It did not take long, for drunk though most of them were, nearly everyone at the inn knew and respected and had done business with this handsome sensible woman, and so they made way for her with courtesy and a good grace.

The Papp Brothers' representative soon saw her too, leapt up and went over to meet her. They exchanged a few words, standing there face to face, and then the envelope with his commission somehow found its way from her handbag into the inside pocket of his coat. In spite of the noise they managed to talk for a moment.

'Why were the prices so good today?' asked Sara. 'Surely this was something of a surprise?'

'They say,' said her friend, 'that the army is buying. This would explain why the Remount officer was here and why he bought so many horses. I don't know much about it, but they say it's because of the troubles in Turkey.'

'The revolution in Istanbul? Is it possible?'

'That's what they say.'

A roar of laughter interrupted them. It came from the direction of the band. Sara looked over in that direction.

Where the band-leader normally stood there was a slim young man of medium height, and he was playing the violin. His clothes were shabby, both frayed and wrinkled, but they had once been of excellent cut. On his head he wore a copper saucepan that someone had placed there instead of a hat. He was very drunk, but still he played with wonderful skill even though now he was acting the clown and making such fun of everything that the crowd was in fits of laughter. He was full of tricks, crouching, dancing, rolling about like a clown in the circus, walking on tiptoe and reeling from side to side. But, drunk though he was, he still played faultlessly. Now he started the thumping rhythms of the old comic song 'Mistress Csicso had three daughters...' and while he played he shouted out the words, not, however, those which most people knew, but an obscene version full of rude words and vulgar innuendo. And to underline the ribaldry he made the violin itself seem to cry out, hiccup and burp its way through the verses.

It was Laszlo Gyeroffy.

This was a popular music-hall song he had often played in the old days, now rendered obscene. Once he had played it at evening parties in fashionable and elegant drawing-rooms, and had sung gently its original comic text, not the appallingly vulgar words he now spat out with such zest. But here in the garden of the Green Tree, surrounded by drunken country folk, this was what was required by those for whom he played and who would also pay for his drink.

When Laszlo was drunk enough the crowd could do anything they liked with him. Today he had not noticed that someone had put a copper pan on his head and another fixed a napkin to his coat so that it fluttered behind him like a monkey's tail.

It was by no means the first time that he had made such an exhibition of himself. During the summer he had come several times either to the Green Tree Inn or to one of the other hostelries in the town, and after he had spent the little money he had brought with him he would play wherever there was someone ready with the price of a drink. If he was not quite drunk enough, and if the jokes they played on him were too coarse and humiliating, he would rebel; and then, though still unsteady on his feet, he would suddenly become haughty and rude. However, as the need for the drink grew on him, so he became accustomed to the fact that they were laughing at him. He accepted it and even went out of his way to seek it, finding a bitter twisted joy in the fact that he had fallen so low. Long ago, when he had got drunk with people of his own kind, he had sometimes drawn himself up with unexpected pride and stalked off wrapped in his own ridiculous vanity.

Nowadays there was still an element of this to be seen in him, but it was modified by the coarseness of his new companions. Laszlo, somewhere deep down, still thought of himself as a Fairy Prince under a spell, who had become a slave of his own will and who revelled in the mud to which he had condemned himself. He mocked himself and also those who mocked him; but this self-deceptive euphoria did not long survive the onslaught of brandy after brandy. Nowadays he could no longer carry his wine as he had before ... and in no time he would become sodden with drink.

As Sara was watching one of the revellers in the crowd got up holding his braces in his hand. He stepped over to Gyeroffy, and winking to his friends as it were to show what a good idea he had had, he said, 'Could his noble Lordship dance as well if I tied his knees together?' and he laughed maliciously. A roar of laughter greeted the suggestion. Someone shouted, 'This'll be worth watching!' while another offered Laszlo a litre of wine if he could dance without stumbling. Laszlo stopped for a moment and gazed around him as if he took nothing in. Then he laughed stupidly and mumbled, 'All right. Of course. I can do it any way you like ... any way ...'

Something stirred deep inside the handsome Mrs Lazar. Whatever it was, pity or a sense that mercy should be shown, something moved her deeply as the men crowded forward and started to bind Laszlo's knees together. At this point Gyeroffy was staring straight at her and, though no one could have told if he could really see her or not, Sara read this look as a cry for help. The gleam of moisture at the corners of his eyes may have been nothing more than the inadvertent tears of the very drunk, but to Sara they seemed like the mute plea of an animal led to sacrifice. Of course she already knew Laszlo by sight, for he had sat for a long time at the liquor stall just in front of her stand at the charity bazaar, and he had been drunk then too. At that time she had found the sight mildly disgusting and had not thought of him since. Now, however, some latent maternal tenderness took over and she was ashamed of the unthinking cruelty of men who mocked the weak and helpless.

Without stopping to think and guided entirely by instinct, she stepped quickly over until she was by Gyeroffy's side.

'Take that off at once!' she said in a commanding voice to the man who was kneeling at her feet and strapping Laszlo's knees together. 'Take it off! At once, I tell you. You ought to be ashamed!'

Everyone was stunned into silence. Sara's voice was so full of command, her whole demeanour so severe and her large plum-shaped eyes so full of anger and disdain, that no one dared utter a sound. And when she took Gyeroffy by the hand and led him away people jumped up from their seats and made room for her to pass.

All Sara said, as they walked towards the door, was, 'You come with me now!' and he followed her meekly without saying anything.

And so it was that they walked out together through the two lines of now silent revellers, out from the courtyard of the inn, the tall stately woman who walked like a queen and, led by the hand like a little child, Laszlo Gyeroffy.

Once outside she had to push him into the carriage. Then she had the roof raised so that she would not be seen driving away with a young man sodden with drink at her side.

Laszlo fell asleep almost at once.

Soon it began to get dark, for it had been a cloudy day and now rain was beginning to fall.

The horses trotted slowly. Laszlo was still asleep, lying back awkwardly on the cushions. How tormented he looks now that he is sleeping, she thought. In her hand Sara held Laszlo's hat which had fallen over his face when he went to sleep. She looked at him for a long time, thinking how pale he was and noticing how his eyebrows met in the middle and how there they were slightly raised as if he were still silently and unconsciously complaining of the sad life that was his lot.

He was like a lost child who no longer even looked for the way home.

At first Sara did not think far ahead. All she had wanted to do was to rescue him from that terrible place where everyone made fun of him. When they passed through Kozard – where she knew he lived – she thought she would wake him and drop him off. There would surely be someone at his house who would be able to look after him. But the rain fell ever more strongly and they were well past the village before she noticed it. And then she realized that she did not care. It would really have been most awkward to stop and throw this drunken young man out of the carriage, to explain and give orders. She did not even know where the Gyeroffy manor house was, apart from the fact that it was somewhere near the village; and by now it was getting late. Sara remembered that she had to get home, for today was already Tuesday and on Wednesday she must appear at the County Court; and, what's more, she still had a long way to get back to Dezmer. Sara found no end of arguments to justify her going straight home, as one always does when instinct takes over from logical thought.

The strongest argument for Sara was that Gyeroffy would only have begun to sleep off his drunkenness by the time that they got back to Dezmer; but there at least he would be able to get out of the carriage with some semblance of normality. He could then sleep in the ground-floor guest-room; and the following day he could go home by train.

It was, perhaps, just as well that she had recently sent off her young son to learn German at the college at Szeben. It would not have been easy to explain to him why she had picked up a drunken young aristocrat at the market. Of course she could explain it – and after all there was nothing much to explain. Two years before it had been easier, and of course quite different, when Wickwitz used to visit her. Although he had been her lover, he was also well known to her son who admired the good-looking young soldier-sportsman and thought of him as a friend. That he was far more than a casual visitor the boy had had no idea. Sara was far too careful – though of course now there was no question of anything like that. After all, what she was doing for young Gyeroffy she did out of pure pity. Still it was better, she thought, that that large growing boy who was now almost a man would not be at home. Better! Far better!

This had all happened on Tuesday. When Laszlo awoke on Thursday morning, the sun was high in the sky and shone in golden lines between the wooden laths of the shutters. The room itself seemed if anything darker than it was because of the brightness of those strips of light. Some tiny autumn flies made a faint buzzing and it was this that Laszlo first noticed.

He sat up in bed and looked around. He had no idea where he was and when he tried to remember there was only the faintest recollection of being drunk and playing in the inn at the Tuesday Fair at Ujvar, but no memory at all of what had happened and how he had got to wherever he was. He could just remember playing something that was funny, though he could not recall what. There had been many people around him, people who were laughing, people with big, big heads and wide-open mouths that laughed, and laughed and laughed ... He had some memory, he thought, of a tall dark-haired woman who had suddenly stepped between him and the laughing heads. Huge coal-black eyes had looked hard at him and then someone — had it been the same woman? — had said something. And afterwards, then what? Nothing. Nothing at all until he had awoken with a jolt and seemed somehow to be in front of a house he did not know. At least he thought he did not know it, but it had been dark and as he was still very drunk he had not been able to see it properly.

All this seemed to have happened a very long time ago.

Laszlo slept for the rest of that day. At dusk he woke up again and heard the sound of someone bustling about in the room; it was a little maidservant he did not know, and a room he had never seen before. 'Your bath is ready, sir,' she said. 'I can add some hot water if you wish.'

It was with an almost erotic pleasure that Laszlo lay in the steaming hot bath. He stayed there a long time, and all around him everything was clean and sweet-smelling, the soap, the towels, the brushes and sponges. When he got back to his room he found that the lamps had been lit and a clean shirt had been laid out on the bed. On a chair nearby were his newly-ironed clothes and on the floor beside them were his newly-shined shoes.

Laszlo's first impression was that it was marvellous to feel so clean, and this impression stayed with him for a long time.

And what happened later was equally surprising.

He was called down to dinner, and though at first he felt deeply ashamed his hostess soon put him at his ease. 'I do hope the razor was properly sharpened,' she said, laughing. 'It belonged to my late husband and hasn't been used for years. I tried to strop it myself, but I'm not sure I really know how. The shirt belongs to my enormous son, but he isn't at home now.'

Laszlo at once felt that there was something charmingly simple about this woman, a natural, elemental goodness. And, too, she was beautiful and emanated a marvellous scent which in some way was the scent of naturally healthy creatures.

They had dined alone, and later he played the piano. This also seemed so natural that it was as if they could have spent the evening in no other way. Just as it was with what happened afterwards.

Now he wondered about it.

Laszlo had played for a long time. The room was lit with only one lamp, and suddenly this had started to smoke. They both noticed it at the same moment, jumped up and moved towards it, she because it was natural to her in her own house and he either by pure instinct or because he felt he should help. They had lowered the flame and the room, for a moment, became even darker than before, until they could hardly see each other even though they were standing side by side and very close. Of course he had put his arm around her and pulled her closely to him; and they had kissed. It could not have been otherwise.

For a long time they had stood there in each other's arms, just kissing. Sara had not resisted, not at first, but when he had held her even more closely and started to pull her away with his strong arms, there was a moment when she said weakly, 'No! Don't! No! No!' but though she repeatedly said 'No!' her voice changed and her statuesque body started to tremble and it was clear she didn't mean it. Long afterwards, whenever he thought about it, Laszlo could remember the feel of that voluptuous body trembling in his arms.

Later, as he covered her face with kisses, he had found that it was already wet, wet with the tears that rolled slowly down her cheeks.

Now he wondered why she had been crying and why she trembled so. Laszlo never normally pondered on such things but, as he lay once again gazing into the strips of light that were filtered through the louvred shutters, the question just presented itself to his mind. Even so he did not seek an answer. Vaguely he heard the sound of water running and realized that someone must be preparing his bath. He leaned back against the pillows feeling how good everything was, how good and how clean. Even the bed itself was fresh and scented and for a long time – not since life had torn him away from the luxury of the houses where lived his grand Kollonich and Szent-Gyorgyi relations – he had not known the sensuous pleasure of being so clean and well looked after. Stretching out in sheer content he closed his eyes and went to sleep again.

The door opened and Sara came in, a long silk wrapper

emphasizing rather than concealing the curves of her statuesque figure. Now her hair was confined in a net and the narrowing effect on her head made her shoulders seem even wider than they were. She brought in Laszlo's breakfast, a delicious selection of hot scones, cold meats and yeast cakes, with a pot of steaming coffee, all on a huge tray. Pulling up a chair to put the tray on she sat herself down on the edge of the bed.

'You're up early!' said Laszlo, wondering at such energy.

She laughed, her white teeth shining. Just above her red lips there was a faint line of down as dark as her hair, and her long lashes might have been brushed in with charcoal. Her eyebrows too were long and finely etched like those of the ancient Egyptians. Her skin was a clear brown, glowing pink over the cheekbones and shining with the golden colour of richly whipped cream. It vanished into the V-shaped opening of her wrapper only to be seen again where her arms emerged from the silken sleeves. Only now did Gyeroffy fully appreciate what a beauty she was.

'Oh!' she said. 'I've been up for a long time. Every day I walk round the place at dawn. Then I come in, bathe and generally clean up. I always get up before the servants do. Well, then, did you sleep well?' she asked, with a mischievous smile. Then she said, 'Shall I pour you some coffee?'

For a while they chatted gaily together. There was no longer any sign of that strange fear that had seemed to come over her when she first gave in to Laszlo's embrace. Then she had felt that she was being swept away by some sad tragic force she did not understand. Since the death of her elderly husband she had had affairs only with two men, one of them a distant relation who just happened to come unexpectedly into her life, and the other with the Austrian lieutenant of hussars, Egon von Wickwitz. Both of these affairs had been quite different from what was happening now. Both those men had pursued her for some time, and both had only been accepted after she had thought the matter over carefully. And both had been accepted for clinical reasons of health and peace of mind. This was something quite, quite different. This was a storm, a sudden, unexpected, roaring tempest which, like an elemental force, swept everything before it. This was something she had never felt before and it frightened her. Her deep-rooted sense of self-preservation recoiled from the thought that if she did not resist from the first then she might unwittingly find herself the helpless slave of a fate she had never sought. And so she did resist . . . but it was a vain effort and she had not felt like this since those days so long ago when she was an inexperienced girl. Her attempt to deny him was doomed to fail, for, despite herself, and her fear, she was being driven mad by desire.

This morning, from dawn until breakfast-time, while she supervised the milking and watched the animals' fodder being measured out, and while she thought out and gave directions to her men for the day's work, she never stopped wondering about what had happened the night before. And she asked herself how it was possible that this had happened to her now.

Sara was a contented, thoughtful and carefully composed sort of woman. She liked everything to be cut and dried, and she liked to be able to look at her own life – and at other people – with the certainty that she was in control.

When she had rescued Gyeroffy so abruptly from that horrible scene in the inn, she had acted out of pure pity. She found it disgusting that he should be made fun of in that way and she had acted swiftly and without reflection to put a stop to it. During the journey back to Dezmer she was conscious only of having been sorry for him, nothing else; for her inner motives and compulsions had remained latent and unrecognized. Indeed, when they had arrived at the portico of her house she had felt only disgust at the sight of the dirty and dishevelled young man who was so far gone in drink that they had practically to carry him up the steps. After that she had not seen him for a while. They told her the next day that he was still sleeping. Though she went to look in on him, and saw to it that he was being looked after, it had only been out of natural goodness, maternally caring for him as she would for anyone else who came to her house. And she did nothing to hasten his being roused for, deep down inside her, she had been reluctant to be faced again with someone whose dirty and unkempt appearance had already so revolted her.

That was how she remembered him, and how she had thought of him as she waited for him to join her for dinner the previous evening. And that was why she was taken by surprise to see, not the degraded drunkard she had expected, but rather a well-groomed and handsome, indeed very handsome, young man. Now that his well-cut clothes had been cleaned, repaired and ironed, she could see at once that he came from a good family and she was impressed with the gentlemanly manner with which, though he was clearly embarrassed, he begged her pardon for his previous behaviour. Everything about him now breathed the air of a man of the world accustomed to elegance, and his manners were those of a *grand seigneur*. He was quite different from anyone she had ever met and it was at this moment that she began to feel an unfamiliar magic creeping over her and overwhelming her judgement and her carefully nurtured prudence. As this handsome, gentle and well-mannered young man began to speak, as he picked up his knife and fork to eat, as he touched the corner of his mouth with his table-napkin, and as he sat down at the piano to play out his gratitude in music rather than words, she found him everything that was modest, well-bred, calm and composed, and indeed almost childishly charming. And as he played the expression of his face changed; it was as if from somewhere deep in his soul there was emerging a radiant Fairy Prince whose joys and triumphs had been in the remote past.

She had never before heard music such as he now played, music that was by turns plaintive and cruel. Though her piano had not been tuned for some years and the songs that he played sounded most unusual, Sara began to feel that all her life she had known this pale young man whose eyebrows met in the middle and who, from time to time, would look over towards her and explain the music that he was now creating just for her and for her alone . . .

It was of these things that Sara was thinking when she went out so early to her farms. She tried to analyse her emotions, feeling that her fears and reactions the night before had been silly and morbid, if not absurd. Perhaps she had, for some unknown reason, been unusually nervous; but anyway, she reflected, what did it matter if she had only just met him and yet fallen straight into his arms? Was she not her own master? Did she have to account for her actions to anyone or to anything except her own conscience? At last, in full control of herself, and knowing how beautiful and desirable she would appear in that silken wrapper, she brought his breakfast to his room and sat down on the side of the bed. And as she did so she was not unconscious of the fact that the edge of the wrapper had opened more widely around her neck.

'Do you like it black or white?' she asked as she started to pour it out for him.

There was no answer . . . but the coffee grew cold in the cup.

* * *

Laszlo's life now began a new phase. Soon he was spending all his time with her, moving to Dezmer as if it were his home. At first he would spend a little time at his own house at Kozard, but he was so dismayed by the disorder and squalor of it that he soon returned. It was only now that he began to see how bleak he had allowed his own place to become.

The single room in which he lived was now almost bare both of furniture and objects. For the last year he had gradually been selling all his belongings, and not only the most valuable, though these he disposed of in Kolozsvar through the agency of the Jewish shopkeeper, Bischitz. Now all the old Gyeroffy family pieces, *objets d'art*, rosewood tables and cabinets, and the French bronzes his parents had bought together on their honeymoon in Paris, were to be found in plump little Frau Bruckner's show-room in the provincial capital. Laszlo had got into the habit of taking the lesser things himself into Szamos-Ujvar, selling them for almost nothing, and then swiftly drinking the proceeds. He had even got rid of one of his English shotguns.

For the last year or so any money that Laszlo had been able to lay his hands on had either been gambled away in some tavern or else spent on drink.

Six months before, when old Crookface Kendy had spoken to him with such kindness and understanding, Laszlo had tried to pull himself together. He had written to Azbej asking for a list of his debts but though he had had a reply Azbej had written that the statement was not complete and that there were still some modifications that he would forward as soon as they came to hand. Put off in this way, Laszlo had soon lost interest and only remembered about the matter if he happened to catch sight of Crookface somewhere in Kolozsvar. On these occasions he would give the old man a most reverential bow, but all the same he kept his distance.

This was all that Kendy's well-meant intervention had managed to achieve.

Now, after the experience of Sara's well-run, spotless manor house, Laszlo felt unequal to facing life at Kozard. He continued to return home from time to time, but for ever shorter visits. Indeed he only went so as not to have to admit to himself that he was now living on the charity of a woman.

Sara, who was no fool, herself made things easier for Laszlo to accept. She arranged matters so as to make it appear as if she needed him to help run her property. Sometimes, though carefully concealing the fact that the proposal was only half serious, she would ask him to oversee the ploughing or the cutting of the clover. She well knew that Laszlo was completely ignorant in such matters, but she wanted him to believe that he was being of use to her.

More importantly she induced Laszlo to take up his music again. Each evening she would make him play and when he had tried out for her some of the unfinished compositions he had brought over from Kozard, she made him get down to finishing them.

Laszlo had never been so quietly contented as he was in the first six weeks of their liaison.

CHAPTER FIVE

WHEN THE NEW coalition government came to power a new idea emerged in Hungarian politics; and it was enshrined in the phrase 'the Corridor'. There was great excitement 'in the Corridor' that day, they said. The Corridor is unmoved by the latest developments; the Corridor has not yet formed its opinion; the Corridor is quite indifferent. Leading articles in the newspapers discussed at length the mood, wishes and opinions of the Corridor, which were known to be desperately uncertain, incalculable and capricious.

The Corridor was spoken about with all the awe once accorded to fabulous oracles.

That the Corridor should achieve such spurious importance was, in the circumstances, inevitable. At the time of the Coalition there was no opposition to speak of, and what there was consisted only of some twenty or so members from the ethnic minorities and a few socialists who had no influence and who were in any case generally thought of as dangerous enemies of the state. The three parties to the Coalition only ruled at all as a result of continual discussion between themselves. Everything that was finally presented to, and passed by, the House, had been the subject of previous and secret meetings between cabinet ministers, by the co-ordinating central committee, and also at smaller party meetings, so that every resolution had already been accepted by, and was therefore binding upon, each constituent party in the government. Every measure was presented in finished form, cut and dried and accepted by all parties. There was no longer any possibility of change since to suggest modifications at this stage would have been tantamount to rebellion against the party leadership. Whether it was a question of ideology or merely a matter of form, such suggestions were taken as irresponsible and unnecessarily captious.

And so no one bothered to try.

And what is more, there now seemed to be no life left in the parties themselves. Each party leader, chairman, or working party, acted alone and mostly behind closed doors. This was what had been brought about by the fact of coalition.

The Coalition itself was in an uneasy state of nervous tension. On one side there were the Independents and Liberals who looked back to the uprisings of 1848; while on the other were those who supported the 1867 Compromise – and these, of course, included the Conservative and Clerical Parties. Such an alliance of opposites could only endure – like an ill-assorted marriage – by careful avoidance of all subjects which might, indeed certainly would, lead to quarrels and disagreement. Such subjects were legion and included almost every important issue of the day as well as the fraught questions of the demands for independence from Vienna of the banking and customs systems.

These last had once been part of the programme of the Independence Party alone. Now, however, such matters had had to be included in the election platforms of all parties officially subscribing to the Coalition, and this posed a severe problem for the supporters of the Compromise as to how to square such revolutionary ideas with their own conservative consciences. The real but concealed problem of these people was to prevent the realization of ideas foreign to their own without at the same time bringing about the demise of the Coalition itself.

If this was no easy task for the two conservative parties it was even more difficult for the radical 1848 men and especially for Ferenc Kossuth, their leader, for it was still the primary aim of them all to maintain the formula for co-operation which had brought about the much longed for parliamentary peace.

One of the reasons for this was that now that the Coalition had come to power it had become simple for party leaders to explain that the reason why various long-standing aspects of party policy had not been realized was that as all the parties were partners with each other, indeed fighting side by side, no one could now do anything to alienate their former opponents, not if they wished to remain in power. Everything that could be conceded must be conceded – and the public accepted the argument. And, not only that, but should the Coalition break up in confusion and disagreement, the majority Independence Party would inevitably be called upon to form a government and then it would find itself, in turn, obliged to return to all those hotly disputed policies that had for years been the basis of its party manifestos, but which had never had a chance of being realized while the party remained in opposition. To put forward such policies now would inevitably lead to a new election and this would have to be fought on the basis of a party programme in which even its leaders no longer had any belief.

All the same, the difficulties and considerations which prevented the achievement of any major reforms still left plenty of less controversial things to be decided. There were, for example, such parochial matters as trade permits, and the appointments of Prefects and District Commissioners which had somehow both to take into consideration the candidates' professional qualifications and also be distributed fairly between the various parties of the Coalition. Apart from such less vital matters there was one great issue which could not be avoided; this was the matter of universal suffrage which had been promised by the Crown and which, once made law, would no doubt have an incisive effect on future elections. It was matters such as these which those ministers who were also party leaders had continually to discuss, still behind closed doors, balancing concessions with concessions, so that the needs of all three groups should be satisfied. All this took time and a great deal of trouble and thought, as well as endless precautions lest any details of these consultations should leak out before each matter was finally agreed. And, as every agreement left behind it a trail of hard-won concessions, it was hardly surprising that, as the party leaders were obliged to keep many of their activities a secret from the rank and file, the life of the political parties was in a state of stagnation. And the party leaders had no choice in the matter for if anything had been known of what was about to be conceded – even though it was, of course, merely a matter of party expediency – then such a storm would have broken over their heads that the Coalition would have been endangered.

Furthermore, it was not as if the individual parties were so very united themselves.

The Independence Party was split into two camps – one right of centre, one left – and these in their turn were divided into innumerable little splinter groups, each of which had its own leader. Three well-known politicians – all favourites of the public – Ferenc Kossuth, Albert Apponyi and Gyula Justh, became leaders at one time or another. Like determined punters on the racecourse who would select and bet on their own favourites, so these men juggled with their professional futures by guessing which political party would come out on top and to which therefore they should nail their colours.

There were so many groups that among them were now to be found some that were permanently in disagreement with the government – universal coalition though it was made out to be – and these were grouped round those demagogues whose loud-mouthed public utterances were most to their taste. In this way such radicals as Ugron, Barra, Hollo and Polonyi all had their day of glory; but in their cases it would last only briefly, for their followers were a fickle lot and by no means as sincerely loyal as were those, for example, of Kossuth or Apponyi. Their numbers varied too, according to the political weather-vane, so that the existence of only a few groups heralded calm weather while, like seagulls waiting on a beach, a plethora of little parties preceded a storm. A catchy slogan, a resounding speech or cunning little manoeuvre would have an immediate effect on the loyalties of many party members – and the mood of the Corridor would undergo a subtle sea-change. And it was these moods that ruled the country.

Parliament now seemed to be composed entirely of shifting political groups . . . and the Corridor.

The real corridor ran right round the Chamber itself. It was wide and grandiose and in it large sofas were placed about every ten paces. At the corners – for it ran straight along each of the four sides of the Chamber – there were plenty of little nooks and corners, especially near the entrance to the Press Gallery and where the great staircase began. In these discreet little corners it was possible to form little groups that sat at the feet of some party

chieftain or other listening either to his teaching or maybe just
to his doubts, sorrows and feelings of insecurity. On one side
there was the drawing-room and this was even better arranged
for secret plotting than was the corridor itself. Here, half hidden
by the dark pillars, news could be whispered and messages
received; and, when there were even darker secrets to be discussed, where better than the deserted Cupola Hall where the
sofas all had such high backs that no one could see who was sitting
in them? And everywhere the curtains that covered the doors
were so thick that every sound was muffled. In such conditions
it was no wonder that there were sown the seeds of great tem-
pests, and since no one knew who were the sowers, these were
the hardest to subdue.

The corridor had now become the only place where political
life was at all active. To those accustomed to the usual cut and
thrust of debate in the House itself, this new informal,
unofficial, private method of bringing about legislation was
both bewildering and disturbing. Now it seemed that all sense
of responsibility had vanished to be replaced by the sort of
irresponsibility normally only to be expected from the demagogues. Nearly everyone seemed infected by the insidious
attraction of backroom intrigue and that spurious sense of
power that made people join secret societies. Members of
Parliament now only entered the House when some already
decided measure had to be voted onto the Statute Book. Everyone met and talked in the corridor, for there one could indulge
freely the dubious pleasure of saying whatever one liked about
the great and important of the day. Indeed anyone could say
anything about anything . . . or anybody . . .

And in fact it must be admitted that to stroll down the corridor
when Parliament reassembled in September of the year 1908 was
a real pleasure, a pleasure rarely to be found by attendance at the
official debates. In the House itself business seemed largely to be
confined to the reading by notaries of endless legal papers that
were best condemned to eternal oblivion, and to the formalities
of the opening session. Outside, on the other hand, one was free
to choose and discuss whatever subjects one found most exciting.

And there was plenty to discuss: for example, the banking
system. A week before Balint arrived Istvan Tisza had made a
speech at Bihar roundly condemning the idea of a separate
national banking system, reinforcing his argument with a forceful

parade of economic fact and theory and a careful *exposé* of the inevitable effect of such an innovation upon the value of the national currency and the stability of interest rates. It was a good speech and Tisza backed his views with sound professional reasoning.

The public, always watchful where its own pocket was concerned, for once became interested, and took the matter seriously, as did some of the more thoughtful members of the Independence Party who, as a result of Tisza's remarks, now began to question this aspect of their own party's official policy. For these people it was perhaps an unexpected blessing that a counterbalance now presented itself in the form of a banker who was, there could be no doubt of it, a far greater expert on banking questions than the ex-Minister-President. This man, of course, was not a politician – he was no less than a real banker. And while Tisza had only been a mere ex-Minister-President – and an enemy of the Coalition to boot – the Corridor's favourite new oracle was not only a professional banker but without doubt, they said, a far more patriotic Hungarian than Tisza himself.

The banker's articles had a great effect on the Corridor and, as they were firmly in favour of an independent banking system, were warmly received by all who wanted to be seen as true patriots. Everywhere people praised the skill of his arguments and there were some who even announced with the air of those with inner knowledge that he was intimate with the Rothschilds and that, if one read between the lines, it was clear that he himself would be able to achieve what he wrote was so desirable and that he was offering his services to do just that for his country. What a wonderful fellow, said the Corridor, while whispering that, miracle of miracles, he also knew how to find the money to pay for such an innovation. Of course he had said that an independent national bank would have to raise interest rates but that would be no obstacle, oh, no! There were even some, Hollo's unimportant little group principally, who went so far as to declare that if interest rates rose then the level of national borrowing would be reduced and soon vanish altogether. Naturally, for if interest rose then money would be cheaper! Why? Because all the middlemen would be destroyed. It was as simple as that!

This was a marvellous theory, which might not perhaps have held up if anyone had paused to ask who were the middlemen in the Austrian banking world, or even in that of Budapest. No one was prepared to hear a word against these comforting predictions, nor was the Corridor prepared to consider for a moment the suggestion put forward by the Andrassy Party and the People's Party – who had always been opponents of an independent banking system – that it was the Rothschilds who were behind these articles because they realized that it was to their great financial empire that Hungary would have to turn to finance the establishment of a national bank, and so they would be able to grab for themselves the immense business such a development would entail. The Corridor's view was that one should never listen to such unlikely rumours and anyhow what was wrong with making the Devil your partner if the country benefited?

The other great subject of discussion was the proposal for introducing general suffrage and everywhere it was rumoured that Andrassy was pushing the idea of a plural vote which meant that university graduates and other learned men would have two, or even three, votes each.

Rumour also had it that Andrassy, who was now considered by many people to be the Nigger in the Woodpile, was now busy redrawing the constituency boundaries so as to ensure that in districts where the ethnic minorities were in the majority, their vote would predominate just as the Hungarian vote would carry the day where Hungarians were in the majority. Who ever heard of such a thing, cried the chauvinists? Give a say to Romanians, Serbs and Slovaks in a Hungarian province? Make sure that in districts largely inhabited by such people a non-ethnic Hungarian would be able to win a seat? Merely to think such rubbish was unpatriotic! Of course there was always a simple way out – to reduce the numbers of members that represented the areas of mixed race and double those to be elected in such purely Hungarian districts as the Alfold – the Great Hungarian Plain – and the Dunantul. This was an especially attractive idea to the rank and file of the Independence Party since it was precisely where the Independence Party had its most loyal support. Such an arrangement, they whispered, would also ensure that whatever else happened their own party majority would be ensured for ever and ever.

Such an arrangement would also have the virtue, they cried, of rendering quite unnecessary the idea of the plural vote if Andrassy had planned this in the nation's best interests; while if he had really intended it only as a privilege for university graduates then the idea should be thrown out at once as being a sinister attack on the Equality of Man!

This was what the Corridor, though in hushed tones, was saying about the proposals for reform of the voting laws and the introduction of universal suffrage; and the only significance of it was that people felt free to discuss the matter with such freedom.

However, it happened there was at this time another issue of such importance that even the reform of voting rights took second place; this was the proposal to fuse the largest political parties – the Independence and Constitution Parties – with, per-haps, the inclusion also of the People's Party. If this came about then only one effective party would exist and all political struggle would be for the benefit of that single party. And then it would be that single party which would enjoy the popularity of bringing in the reform of the voting rights. In this case, of course, plurality might not be such a bad idea after all, and neither would be the redrawing of the constituencies. Great Heavens! they were say-ing, better not close the door on such ideas; perhaps after all it would be better to keep their options open?

Then an awful doubt would strike – supposing, just supposing, that universal suffrage was brought in by a different party? Then it would be that party which earned the public's acclaim. If it were not the Independence Party but some other that was responsible for introducing universal suffrage? Then it would be that party which would pocket all the popularity and not they but Andrassy, perhaps, who would benefit. Oh, no! they cried, we're not going to be that sort of fool!

And so the talk went on, rumour tempering rumour, and all that was certain was that somewhere, secretly, discussions about a marriage of the great parties were taking place. Even the views of the party leaders were not known for sure. Some said that Kossuth was in favour while Justh was not. No one was quite sure what Ugron's view was; but nearly everyone was in agreement that Polonyi was hedging his bets by talking to all sides at once ... even though this might bring him into disrepute with the government. Still, politics were politics ...

These subjects were, after all, purely internal problems for the members of the Coalition. There were others, however – exter-nal problems that united rather than divided the Coalitionists. The most important of these was the sinister import of Count Tisza's political activities. The former Minister-President was suspected of every wickedness; it was he, they said, who was behind every obstacle that might hinder the achievement of the Coalition's programme. Tisza was the only man who was feared by everyone, and hatred of him formed such a bond between the diverse members of the Coalition that it at least had the effect of keeping the alliance in being. If once we are divided, they said, then the dreaded Tisza would get in again – and that would be worse than anything! This fear had kept them together from the start.

More recently there had arisen another subject for speculation and rumour. This was not quite as exciting as getting worked up about the wicked Count Tisza, but it still served to keep people's tongues wagging. This was the mysterious goings-on of Kristoffy.

Everyone remembered that in the spring Kristoffy had started to canvass the idea of founding a Radical Party. Since then little had been heard of the project. Now, however, in September, the joyful news came that the idea had been abandoned, the party premises had been given up, and the party itself dissolved. The Corridor did not rejoice for long, for as soon as the new session had been opened it was revealed that what had really happened was that Kristoffy was now addressing himself to the vast numbers of agricultural workers rather than to the more limited ranks of those members of the middle class who had a liking for radical ideas. Now, in association with a number of petty leaders from Pest, he had started to advertise meetings under such new names as the Peasants' Party and the National Agricultural Workers' Party. No one had ever heard of anything so absurd as to start organizing political parties formed of those people who owned nothing, and who talked irresponsibly of the redistribution of landed wealth and even of emigration.

No one in the independent camp had been worried by the radicals in the middle classes. That was only a minor irritation and in any case was confined to the towns and to a limited number of ineffective intellectuals. Neither were they worried by the apparent rise of trade union influence. Neither of those two issues was truly Hungarian, after all – one was merely play-acting, and of course the other was just a matter of Jewish trouble-making! Neither mattered at all. But to start stirring up the village people – that was quite another thing. That meant trouble. Just as people were beginning to get worried about Kristoffy the news came in that something similar was going on at Somogy.

There some country bumpkin from Nagyatad, one Istvan Szabo, was making a real nuisance of himself. That, they said, really must be stopped – and quickly, for did not the Hungarian peasantry form their very own faithful band of loyal supporters? No one must be allowed to monkey about with them!

At once there was an outcry and the Corridor rang with calls for immediate and drastic, if not draconian, action. Andrassy must, they demanded, send out cohorts of gendarmes and put a stop to all this nonsense. Such gatherings as were now advertised must be strictly forbidden, on pain of God knows what, as it was clearly unpatriotic to distract the attention of simple electors from such vital matters as independent national banking and customs systems with subversive talk about minimum wage scales, the law of master and servant, and emigration. It was ridiculous to bring up these issues now. Why, had Daranyi not just introduced new legislation to deal with such matters, even though it had not yet come into force; and was there not a new commissioner to control all emigration matters and a new contract with the Cunard Line, not to speak of the magnificent newly-constructed clearing house for emigrants at Fiume? You only had to go and look; it was truly beautiful!

What irresponsible demagoguery it was to spread gossip about the Coalition not caring about the needs of ordinary people! How dared people say such things! It ought to be put a stop to!

If Andrassy wished, from the lordly height of his social position, to appear impartial, and therefore to make it clear that he respected the right of all people to gather together and express their political opinions, saying that *they* had the same rights of assembly as *us*, then someone should make it clear to him that *our* meetings are right and proper, because *we* are true patriots, whereas *they* are nothing but a band of lackeys and play-actors! Someone must tell him! And as for this new party: well, it just shouldn't be allowed, it was as simple as that! In fact it was everybody's patriotic duty to see that it was suppressed. If Andrassy failed to do his duty then someone should point out to him that in any case the 1848 Party still had a majority in the House and could therefore outvote anything anyone else might propose.

It was this sort of thing that was being said by those whose interests lay in the Great Hungarian Plain. Those whose interests were not so tied up with the country's largest agricultural province merely shrugged their shoulders and asked themselves, and everyone else who would listen, whether there was any point in worrying about such things now when the next elections were still three years away.

The newly assembled Members of Parliament met each other in the corridor of the House and argued out these matters, some shouting their views for all to hear, others whispering in dark corners or plotting their next moves in the shadow of the drawing-room's lofty pillars. No one, however, bothered to discuss what might be going on in other parts of the Dual Monarchy, let alone on the world's great stage. It was true that at this time there were no world-shattering events to discuss – though what was happening outside the boundaries of Hungary proper was, for anyone with eyes to see, symptomatic of some very important trends.

For instance, there was the great 'Sokolist' meeting held at Susak, the sister-town of Fiume, at which the Czechs and Slovenes and Croats all fell on each other's necks and embraced warmly. Shortly after this there were bloody riots in Kraijna when Slovenes and ethnic Germans fought a bloody battle – but as all this happened on Austrian territory no one in Budapest was much interested.

Nor was there much interest in the fact that the Ban of Croatia – Hungary's own appointed viceroy – and his deputy were publicly insulted in Zagreb and now could not move about without a special escort of bodyguards. No one had much to say either about the long-drawn-out business of appointing the new Serbian Patriarch of Karloca, even though the first two candidates proposed by the Serbs were rejected by the monarch and a third had to be found who was considered acceptable to the state.

All these things were, of course, almost parochial since they were events within the boundaries of the Dual Monarchy. As to news from other parts of Europe, this was looked upon merely as a moving picture to be gazed at with amused detachment. No one really believed that what they now read in the foreign pages of the newspapers could possibly be of much significance. Apparently the British fleet had visited Reval! Oh, really? You realize it's a most sinister display of Anglo-Russian friendship? Is it, indeed? Well, I never! The Bulgarian army has taken over control of the State Railways! Why on earth would they do that? Won't it provoke the Turks? What rubbish! Prince Ferdinand would hardly be jaunting about all over Europe if he were planning to declare war. Isn't he expected here tomorrow?

Leading articles in the London newspapers were now obsessed with the rumours that Austria was about to annex Bosnia-Herzegovina. What nonsense! cried the Hungarians. Don't those stupid English journalists know that Austria alone cannot make decisions that affect the Austro-Hungarian Empire? And if they don't even know that, what do they think they are scribbling about? In any case no one would think of such a thing! Would you? No, of course not, any more than I would ... or anyone else for that matter. Anyway we live in peaceful times, which is why the Austrian Aehrenthal and the Russian Izvolsky have just had such a happy meeting at Buchlau. You've read all about that, haven't you? Most reassuring! Really, what are those hysterical English writers worrying about?

Anyone arriving in the House on the morning of September 22nd 1908 could make his own choice of which of these themes he himself wished to discuss. He could also decide, in that famous corridor, how he would do it – with gay unconcern or serious disapproval, loudly or quietly in a discreet alcove, it was as he pleased. Only one rule had to be obeyed, if he were to find a sympathetic band of listeners, and that was that he must remain strictly within the mood of the Corridor and to do this he would have to express one or other of the views we have just described.

This, it must be understood, was because though every Hungarian politician prided himself on the independence of his thinking, he was never quite so pleased when someone else seemed to be thinking independently too.

Towards noon the news spread rapidly that Andrassy had arrived and was busy explaining to leaders of his party the views of its president concerning the proposed reform of the voting laws. Suddenly nothing else mattered and every other subject was dropped while all who could hurried to where Andrassy was so as to hear what was going on. Even those who did not manage to get within listening distance were happy because everyone felt that the Corridor was being honoured by being the first to hear the leader's hitherto secret thoughts. It was tantamount to showing the world that the Corridor itself was a political force to be reckoned with!

It was, of course, politically astute of Andrassy to make his views known in this way, casual though it might seem to an outsider. The mood of the Corridor was more easily influenced by a seemingly informal and confidential discussion between friends than it was by a formal speech in the House itself. And so now he stood, clearly at ease, facing not only his admirers but also those antagonists who had not ceased to criticize him in their newspaper articles – though not too overtly since until now no one had been sure what views they were criticizing. Now he was able to answer all objections or questions in words that were generally reassuring but which might not look so impressive if printed in the daily Record of Proceedings.

He could have chosen no better way of convincing his opponents, for when Andrassy spoke in this way one could almost feel the honesty and personal conviction behind his words.

Standing at the centre of a milling crowd, he gave the impression that his frail body was held straight only by force of will and the burning conviction that what he proposed was right; and that without such spiritual support it would have instantly crumbled. He might have been a living example of a painting by the Spanish school – El Greco or Zurbaran – an ascetic saint whose Christ-like hands with long and emaciated fingers held a thick Havana cigar rather than a crucifix. Sunk deep in his face, his eyes seemed unnaturally large as they shone with all the intensity of a fanatic.

Andrassy's way of talking matched his appearance. His manner was the opposite of that of any demagogue. His listeners somehow felt that he was almost physically in labour, wrestling with his subject, and that a heavenly solution would be born at any minute. As he spoke he hesitated, almost stammered, as if he searched blindly for the right words, and this technique was so perfected that every really important phrase or proposal was always underlined by a word so brilliant, exact and appropriate, that his listeners were as carried away with the feeling that they, and they alone, had been a part of this troubled birth. The strange thing was that none of this was intentional. As it happened this manner had been forced upon him by the need, in two decades of parliamentary service, to master a physical handicap; and he had done it in such a way that anyone who did not know his story might have assumed that the manner had been subtly and astutely, but consciously, developed.

And so, on this September morning in the corridor, Andrassy made it publicly known that his policy as regards the reform of the suffrage was based firmly on the principle of the plural vote, which for him was a *sine qua non*. The bill was not yet ready as several important aspects remained to be worked out in detail.

But, whatever else might be modified – even to the point of disappearing altogether – 'plurality' was the backbone of his proposals and he would stand or fall by it!

It was this that Andrassy now wanted to make clear. It was a warning to the Corridor, for no one could be in any doubt that if Andrassy went the Coalition went with him, and that this would automatically entail the demise of the Independence Party. It looked as if he had planned this announcement so as to put a stop to the growing campaign in the Press and the whisperings in the ranks of the 1848 men and the group which followed Hollo. And he was not mistaken. Hollo's party backed down and, after a few last little splutters in one or two leading articles, so did the newspapers.

So, for the moment at least, there was peace again in the ranks of the Coalition.

Outside these ranks there was much skirmishing about and growling by those who followed Kristoffy and by the frankly socialist. People there were who knew in advance about Andrassy's plans and who had only waited for him to declare himself. A few days before, the socialist newspaper *Nepszava* – the People's Voice – had somehow obtained a copy of the Plurality Bill (probably purloined from the secret recesses of the Ministry of the Interior) and published it in full, paragraph by paragraph, down to the smallest detail. This had meant that it had been impossible for Andrassy to manoeuvre or bargain; and so he had in reality been forced into declaring himself publicly in an attempt to still the tempest of speculation and rumour that had been created. Rumour might have been stifled, but not unrest. Soon there were stormy demonstrations in the streets of the capital and shots were fired.

It was in this electric atmosphere that the news arrived in Budapest that what the London newspapers had predicted had come to pass.

The Crown announced the annexation of Bosnia-Herzegovina.

It was October 3rd. Budapest had just had a number of royal visitors. A week earlier Prince Ferdinand of Bulgaria had been in the Hungarian capital and only that evening the King of Spain had taken his leave after a three-day visit accompanied by his queen. The royal couple, after paying their respects to the

Emperor Franz-Josef, had everywhere been fêted. Balls and receptions had been given in their honour and, exceptionally enough, even the Archduke Franz-Ferdinand had swallowed his dislike of Hungary and come to pass a few days at Budapest for the sake of his Spanish cousin; though he had somewhat ostentatiously slept in the royal train rather than at the palace. The capital was filled with visitors, many foreigners and a cohort of diplomats from Vienna, who had all come for the Spanish king's visit. At the same time there was a large delegation of elderly Austrians who were attending some convention or other, and many young men with the entrée at court who came at this time because it was also the beginning of the racing season.

Fortunately enough the weather was so good that it might still have been summer. Partly because of this, and also, of course, because of the influx of visitors from abroad, it was to the Park Club that most people now went in the evenings. Here people would dine and entertain their friends; and here too grand balls were given almost every night. Sometimes, as this evening, it was only a small dance – a *tancerli* – so instead of opening up the large ballroom they danced in the inner dining-room on the first floor. In the big dining-room next door some people were still at table though it was quite late.

Abady arrived with two foreign couples, people he had first met when he was still a diplomat. Driving out to the club after the opera Abady had been worried that there might still be signs in the streets of the riots that that afternoon had followed the first socialist demonstration calling for the immediate reform of the voting qualifications. After the mass meeting held in the wide spaces of Arena Street a belligerent group had decided to go on to the Inner Town. Along Andrassy Street they went, but as soon as they had arrived at the corner of the Vorosmarty Street, there was a clash with a police cordon and they were beaten back by the drawn swords of officers on horseback. Abady was afraid that some sordid traces of the ensuing battle might still be there and so, ashamed for his country, he leaned out of the carriage window to look around. To his relief everything had been cleaned up; and if there were any armed guards still about they must have been so discreetly posted that no one would notice their presence.

The orchestra was playing waltzes in the inner room and so it was as a matter of course that they went there to dance after supper. Balint at once took one of his friends' wives onto the floor but it was hardly a success since they were playing a Boston waltz and his visitor was quite unable to 'reverse' – an art, he reflected, that had only really been mastered by the Viennese and the Hungarians.

Balint tried his best for a few turns but soon stopped, feeling slightly dizzy as he had had to use more energy that usual to push his partner in the right direction. For a moment he leaned against a side table wiping his forehead, and as he did so his partner was whisked away by someone else.

He had only been there for a moment when, as softly as a bird alighting on a branch, a girl in a tulle dress stopped beside him and a familiar voice said, 'Hello! Do you remember me?'

It was Lili Illesvary; but how she had changed! There was no sign of the layer of baby fat in which she had been enveloped only a year before. She seemed to have grown both taller and more slender and was no longer the chubby schoolgirl she had been when Balint had seen her at Jablanka. Now she was a girl ready for marriage with a smooth skin, slim neck and shoulders which might have been the model for a Greek statue. She must, too, have known herself how pretty she had become for when she smiled up at Balint her violet-coloured eyes and finely drawn mouth, whose soft outlines tempered the firm chin inherited from her Szent-Gyorgyi ancestors, were full of self-confidence.

'Don't you recognize me?'

'But you must be Countess Lili!' Balint could not conceal both his surprise at the beauty of the girl and also the pleasure it gave him. Lili understood him completely and so smiled all the more.

'We were in Vienna for the spring season,' she said. 'I never thought I could have danced so much. It must be almost a year since you last saw me. I was barely out of the schoolroom then!'

She spoke with such gentleness that Balint was again enchanted by the sweetness of that rather throaty voice which he had particularly noticed at Jablanka. Then she went on, 'I've seen you recently at some of the big balls, perhaps a couple of times, but when you didn't come over to speak to me I thought that maybe you hadn't recognized me. Of course you may not even have seen me as there's always such a crowd at those big "do"s. Anyhow, you don't dance with young girls, do you? Only with married women, perhaps?'

It flashed through Balint's mind that maybe she was referring to Adrienne, but Lili's fine eyes shone with such genuine pleasure and candour that no one could imagine there was a grain of malice in what she said. Then she continued '. . . and then there's always such a crush that all you can do is say hello to each other and dance away . . . like a machine!'

'But you like to dance, don't you?' said Balint.

'Oh yes, of course. But you, er, Count Balint . . .' and he could hear in the hesitation that she was trying to decide if she should use his family name rather than the more familiar 'Balint'. 'You talked to me once or twice at Jablanka; and, you know, those are the memories that stay with you . . . the person with whom one seemed to hit it off.'

'Of course. It was at the big shoot!'

'Yes, then too, but also afterwards, when we were talking about Uncle Antal's horses and you told me that you had a stud too. You said that all the mares had old Hungarian names.'

'How well you remember it all!'

'Of course I do. I could even tell you their names. If you like I'll recite them all! You have no idea,' she said, taking him into her confidence, 'how wonderful it is to be treated as a grown-up when you're still really in the schoolroom.' She said 'schoolroom' with as much disdain as if it had been decades since she had been anywhere near it. 'Anyway, one always takes note of what people tell one.'

They went on chatting for a little time. The music stopped and though most people started to leave the room they went on talking. Then Lili looked around and saw that they were quite alone.

'I'm sure they want to air the room,' she said. 'Would you like to take me to the buffet?'

They walked slowly back through the large dining-room, the drawing-room beside it, and the card-room; and, as they went, Balint looked hard at Lili and thought how amazing it was what effect a single season could have on a young woman. Barely a year before Lili had been still in her teens, awkward, gauche and unformed. Now, in the way she moved, spoke, looked around her, she had all the elegance and quiet dignity of an experienced woman. It would have taken years for a young man to have acquired such poise.

Lili had learned her lessons so well that it was with perfect self-confidence that she made her way through the crowded room,

fan in hand and elbows held closely to her sides. Neither too fast
nor too slow, she moved lightly between the groups of people
gossiping or talking politics, between the couples engaged in
flirting and behind the fat backs of elderly people sitting at cards.
She never seemed to look where she was going but somehow
skirted all obstacles without for a moment deviating from her
course.

'Shall I tell you a secret?' she asked when they were standing beside the buffet table. 'I think you're going to be asked to
Jablanka again this year. You mustn't know anything about it, of
course, but I'm telling you now so that you don't go and accept
any invitations for the first week in December.'

'Thank you, Countess Lili. Did Uncle Antal say something
about it?'

'No! Nothing positive, but...' and she turned away as if
reaching for a cream cake. As she did so Balint just had time to
notice that she was blushing. Blushing? Why should she blush at
saying 'nothing positive'?

There was, of course, a very good reason. Lili had just remembered the cunning she had had to employ to get Abady invited.

She had never herself said anything positive either; but every
time she had been at Jablanka she had lost no opportunity of
somehow inducing others to say something nice and compli-
mentary about Balint Abady. The head *Jäger* – amazingly enough,
for it was quite unjustified – had somehow been led into praising
Balint's skill with a gun; the stud groom had been slyly reminded
how Count Abady had immediately recognized the best among
the innumerable foals; and she herself, having cross-questioned
Pfaffulus about Abady's ancestors, had brought up the subject of
his family tree in front of her uncle, knowing well that Count
Antal set great store by such things and that noble birth and a
long line of distinguished forebears were important elements in
his approval or disapproval of other people.

In this way Balint's name somehow kept on being mentioned
at Jablanka, and often in Antal Szent-Gyorgyi's hearing.

Only recently Lili had decided that the time had come to take
more definite action. One day she talked to her cousin Magda
and told her that she ought to lose no time in seeing that this year
her beloved Peter Kollonich should be invited. Magda swallowed
the bait and so was herself responsible for killing off Peter's
chances. Unwisely, not being a subtle or wise girl, Magda saw fit

to ask her father outright and in this way Lili obtained what she wanted. Count Antal answered his daughter in his most icy manner, 'I'm not asking any of our relations this year, except for Balint Abady!'

It was the memory of this that had made Lili blush, for she knew that she had knowingly prepared the trap for Magda and that, quite shamelessly, she had advised her to do the one thing which would annoy her father and stop any chance of Peter being asked to the shoot. For a moment or two Lili did not turn back to face Balint. Then an arm in formal evening dress stretched out between them and a voice said, 'I beg your pardon!'

Lili and Balint both looked at the speaker. It was Count Slawata, who was just pushing a cream bun towards his mouth.

'Oh, *Servus* – at your service,' he said when he had quickly swallowed his mouthful and, with his short-sighted eyes peered at Abady and recognized him. Then he said, bowing to the girl, 'I kiss your hand, Countess Lili. Please don't think I'm always so greedy . . .' and he reached for another titbit, 'but *Seine Hoheit* – his Highness – has only just left.'

He was referring to the Archduke Franz-Ferdinand, whose confidential adviser he was, and who had ostentatiously left for Vienna the moment the King and Queen of Spain had taken their leave.

'There were masses of telegrams to send and a lot of official reports; so I didn't get any supper.'

'*Schwerer Dienst* – very hard work!' said Abady, with a hint of irony.

'Not really. But interesting, you know, especially now. And especially today when we have got some results for once. Today is the third of October – and success has crowned our efforts!'

Balint realized that Slawata was unusually happy and pleased with himself. His whole body radiated a sort of nervous, tense joyfulness. His round snub-nosed face seemed almost about to split, so tightly was his skin stretched across the chubby cheeks. His eyes flashed behind his thick-lensed glasses.

'What was today's great success?'

The adviser to the Ministry for Foreign Affairs had been waiting for just that question. With a theatrical movement he stepped back and pulled out a watch from his waistcoat pocket with studied slowness. 'Here it is five minutes to midnight. In Paris it will be five to eleven and the leading article in tomorrow's

Le Temps will already be in the press. As soon as the paper is on the streets the whole world will know what has happened – so I am now free to tell you the news: it is that our ambassador in Paris today informed the President of the Republic of our annexation of Bosnia-Herzegovina. At last we have been able to bring this about: it was effective from midday today!'

Something tightened in Balint's throat. He remembered all at once that argument with Slawata a year before, in his bedroom at Jablanka, when the politician had talked about the need for a war. Now, as a thousand fears and questions crowded into Balint's mind, the music started up again and people streamed from the buffet table back into the ballroom. Lili was whisked off to dance again and Balint found himself briefly separated from Slawata.

Standing alone by the buffet table Balint remembered that the Congress of Berlin had indeed given paper approval for the annexation, but no date had even been mentioned by any of the great powers. Furthermore it was implicitly accepted that Bosnia-Herzegovina, though until now still nominally a province of the Ottoman Empire, would never be handed back to Turkey. All Europe would have objected. It was therefore clear that, though it was one of the Congress's official aims to uphold the integrity and sovereignty of the Ottoman Empire, no one thought of this as anything other than a face-saving formula not to be taken literally. Still, Turkish sovereignty had been guaranteed by international decree and could not lightly be discarded unless all the guaranteeing powers agreed. If the Ballplatz had not taken care to obtain such accord by undercover diplomatic negotiations, then Austria's unilateral action might well be considered an unforgivable breach of internationally valid agreements and so, whether the annexation was justified or not, Austria would be vulnerable to attack which might lead to untold complications.

Dismayed by his own thoughts, Balint turned once again to Slawata and said, 'But surely this could lead to trouble? Has the way been properly prepared? Diplomatically, I mean?'

'*I-wo! – sowas ist doch ganz unmöglich* – that is quite impossible!' replied Slawata unconcernedly; but then, seeing how worried his companion looked, he piled his plate high with galantine and foie-gras, and beckoned to Balint to follow him to a nearby sofa, saying, '*Komm, alter Freund, ich werde dir's erklären. So ganz leichtsinnig sind wir eben auch nicht!* – come, old friend, and I will explain it all to you. We are not as irresponsible as all that!'

* * *

Slawata seemed now to take Balint into his confidence, apparently speaking quite openly and giving chapter and verse for each statement he made. On the question of diplomatic consultation he said that there would have been no point in asking the opinion of the subscribing powers in advance. This would only have led to lengthy discussions which at best would have had inconclusive results. Only two countries had any real interest in the matter: Russia, which was bound to oppose any extension of Austrian power; and Turkey, whose new government, unless faced with a *fait accompli*, could hardly be expected to agree to the loss of one of its own provinces.

On the other hand, he went on, if the annexation happened now, it would probably be accepted in Turkey as part of the payment to be made for the removal of the old order and the final elimination of the sins of the Sultan's imperial policies. Since at the same time Austria was to restore to Turkey the control of the Sanjak of Novibazar, this could be advertised by the Porte as a triumph for the new leaders in Istanbul. There only remained the Russians. They had, to a certain extent, been prepared in advance. When the Russian foreign minister Izvolsky had called upon the ambassador Berchtold at Buchlau, his Austrian opposite number, Aehrenthal, had brought up the question of Bosnia-Herzegovina, stating that unless action was taken soon the new rulers of the Ottoman Empire would be bound by their constitution to insist that Bosnia send representatives to the Turkish parliament, which would not only be absurd but also unacceptable to all the signatory powers. Izvolsky had offered no objections to this argument, which could be taken as acquiescence even though no 'protocol' had been signed at the end of the meetings. Of course, no doubt both sides had made notes so that even if the Russian minister was taken by surprise by the timing of the annexation, he could hardly claim that he knew nothing about it! And in these circumstances there was little that England and France could do; after all, they could hardly pretend to be more Balkan than the Russians!

Berlin had not been informed either, for the simple reason that if one of the powers had been told then Italy would have to have been told too – and this was most undesirable as the news would swiftly be passed on to the Entente.

'*Und die guten Italiener hätten ausserdem gleich irgend ein Equivalent verlangt* – and the good Italians will no doubt have an equivalent claim of their own!' said Slawata ironically.

'But the alliance consists of three members and all information ought to be shared. If it's not, then the Italians are no longer in honour bound,' suggested Balint.

'So much the better! So much the better!' cried his companion. 'In spite of Aehrenthal I agree with Conrad. The best thing would be an Austrian attack upon Italy. But, of course, Aehrenthal will do anything to hold the alliance together.'

And then he returned to one of his favourite subjects. If events followed the lines he suggested then the world would soon see which was the stronger: '. . . Franz-Josef – *Der alter Herr, oder wir, Jung Österreich* – the Old Gentleman, or we, Young Austria!'

And so it came about that the international crisis provoked by the Austrian annexation of Bosnia-Herzegovina heralded a new era in European politics. Aehrenthal, quite unwittingly, created a diplomatic precedent by presenting all Europe with a *fait accompli* that was contrary to the Treaty of Berlin and bypassed all international discussion.

On the very same day as the annexation of Bosnia-Herzegovina, Bulgaria declared itself an autonomous kingdom instead of only a semi-independent principality nominally subject to the Sultan in Istanbul; this, of course, was done with the full knowledge and approval of the Ballplatz. Both these events were to prove the models for Italy's occupation of Libya in 1911, without either legal or diplomatic reason and without declaring war on Turkey, and also for the 1912 Balkan war. Together, Austria's annexation of Bosnia-Herzegovina and the unilateral declaration of Bulgarian independence, though only formal provocations and not actual acts of war, served as precedents for more violent and more cynical acts of oppression and effectively killed off that moral force which until then had been accorded to the given word. And at the end of the line came that most dramatic – and least morally justified – of such acts: Germany's 1914 invasion of Belgium. And that started the First World War.

Of course the annexation itself had been inevitable and long foreseen. It is unlikely that any other course could then have been taken by the unwieldy Austro-Hungarian monarchy, to whom Fate had then dealt a hand that was almost unplayable. As in Greek tragedies there had arisen a situation in which every

option open to Vienna conflicted with another of the Monarchy's prime interests. That the empire remained a cohesive
whole depended upon a complicated web of alliances, treaties,
unwritten agreements and historical relationships, and the
recognition of the loyalties and rights that these conferred. To
dishonour any one of these ancient obligations was to undermine
and deny the validity of the whole structure.

It was therefore as a breach of the given word that the international Press interpreted the latest events, and on which was
based the storm of criticism and disapproval that was directed
against Vienna. The campaign started with the publication in the
London newspapers of photographs of the Emperor and his heir,
the Archduke Franz-Ferdinand, labelled succinctly 'Breakers of
their Word'. Such an unspoken and insulting personal attack
seemed extraordinary coming from England where one was
accustomed to more measured tones.

The first obvious effect of this action by the Monarchy was that
from that day Great Britain became one of Austria-Hungary's
most implacable enemies.

In Istanbul the reaction was limited to a boycott of Austrian
goods, for there everyone's eyes were on Bulgaria since her
troops had been massed on the Rumelian frontier; and it was
against this new threat from the north that Turkey responded by
mobilizing her reserves.

The wildest turmoil raged in Belgrade. Volunteer forces were
enrolled, there were street demonstrations almost every day and
the mob attacked Austro-Hungarian shops and looted them.
Montenegro prepared itself for war by dragging cannon onto the
heights of Mount Lovcsen, and Vienna responded by sending
warships down the Danube to Zimony, calling up the reserves of
the south-west provinces and banning the shipment of arms to
the neighbouring states of Bosnia and Herzegovina.

While all this was going on in the Balkans the diplomatic
representatives of those great powers opposed to Austria swung
into action. Izvolsky rushed to Paris to repair the effects of his
first mistake in listening without comment to those conversa-
tions which had implied general acceptance of the forthcoming
annexation. Now he proposed another conference which would
have the declared intention of handing over to its neighbours
the Sanjak of Novibazar, a Turkish province set between
Montenegro and Serbia, thereby giving the latter a corridor to

the Adriatic. After Paris he went to London and there, in the middle of the month, settled the arrangements for the preliminary discussions. At the end of October Prince George, heir to the throne of Serbia, was received by the Tsar on a state visit.

It now seemed to the initiated, as indeed it did several times in the next few months, that war was inevitable.

The Hungarians, of course, seemed totally to ignore the implications of what was happening outside their own frontiers. There was some passing comment in the Press, but no one took it as having any relevance to their own affairs, for, perhaps wisely, the newspapers had adopted a conscious policy of not being alarmist. And at that time there were few who had any feeling for the significance of events abroad. Most people read the foreign news as they would any amusing but transient tale, as two-dimensional and as trivial as a comedy on a movie screen. Neither Franz-Josef's Speech from the Throne, nor Aehrenthal's explanations – nor even the daily telegrams from London, Belgrade and St Petersburg – held the smallest interest for anyone in Budapest. With a yawn most readers turned to the next page where more was to be found about the death of the popular parliamentarian and journalist, Aladar Zboray, than there was about the Bosnian affair. Not that Zboray did not deserve the attention he got, for he was a most affable and loveable man and an opposition speaker whom everyone liked.

It was, of course, possible that the Press purposely honoured their departed colleague at such length as such paragraphs always seemed, at the very least, reassuring.

There were, nevertheless, other matters which merited attention.

On the day of the Speech from the Throne there was another armed demonstration which marched right into the centre of the city as far as Octagon Square. Much was made of this, as it was about the future role of Bosnia-Herzegovina in the Austro-Hungarian Empire. There was no lack of legal experts who harked right back to the time of the Angevin kings, stating that even then Bosnia had been Hungary's vassal, just like Croatia and the long-disputed Dalmatia, without fully grasping that by doing so they were advocating that very Trialism they so hotly condemned elsewhere. In domestic matters the newspapers wrote excitedly about the proposed fusion of the great parties and a rumour spread, emanating apparently from Hollo's supporters, that the real reason for all these public demonstrations was simply that they had been the result of collusion between Andrassy and the Socialists, and that he had gone to these lengths so as to create a climate in which his proposals for a Plural Vote were sure to get accepted!

It was, perhaps, hardly surprising that such petty parochial matters, rather than remote international events, should be the first to awaken general interest. After such a long period of peace there were few people who believed in the possibility of war, and it was, after all, only natural that people should take an interest in what seemed to affect their own lives. People had lived for so long in an atmosphere of party strife, and the need to remain within the bounds of legality, that their first attention was automatically directed at such matters. It is, after all, a generally accepted rule that only some cataclysmic event or terrible danger can wipe away the preoccupation with the joys, sorrows and troubles of everyday life. The news was mulled over when they read the morning newspapers, argued and discussed in the clubs and coffee-houses and possibly even discussed at the family meals but, while it was, everyday life went on as usual and most people only thought seriously about their work, their business interests, property, family and friends, their social activities, about love and sport and maybe a little about local politics and the myriad trifles that are and always have been everyone's daily preoccupation. And how could it have been otherwise?

CHAPTER SIX

THE DAY PROMISED to be fine and bright. Some morning mist veiled the tops of the low hills, making their outlines hazy and uncertain, while below them the meadows seemed to stretch to an infinite distance. The fine weather would certainly last until the afternoon.

It was November 3rd, an important day for the hunting community because on it was celebrated the Feast of St Hubert, the patron saint of huntsmen, and each year on this day there was a special meet of the Transylvanian Hunt which was almost as much a social occasion as it was an important day in the sporting calendar. The hounds would meet at noon and by that time many people, mostly gentlefolk from the nearby towns and their manor houses in the neighbourhood, would have arrived at the chosen place. So that more people would be able to watch the hunt, the St Hubert's Day meet was held in the lowlands of the Szamos river valley.

Even in Hungary the hunting vocabulary was largely composed of English words, such as 'a meet', the 'Master', 'huntsman', 'whip', 'tally-ho', 'run', 'check' and 'casting'. As a result dedicated sportsmen were quite clear as to the meaning of a sentence in mixed Hungarian and English, such as 'At the "check" after the first "run", when the Master "cast back", I was acting as "whipper-in" at the side and didn't hear the "tally-ho" . . .' but to the uninitiated it would mean nothing.

This year the Master had chosen a place for the meet that had room for a vast crowd of people. It was a meadow near Apahida, barely eight miles from Kolozsvar, where the road beside the Szamos turned suddenly northwards and where it was joined by a smaller road that served the city's vineyards. The place was ideally suited to the meet, for broad meadows spread on both sides of the road and there was plenty of space both for the riders and for the multitude of carriages that would bring the spectators. And when the hounds set off up the valley searching for the scent of a hare the carriages would all be able to follow along the highway itself. It was even possible, in the unlikely event that the quarry ran straight, that they would be able to follow the chase until its end; though, as hares were all too apt to run uphill, there was not much chance of that.

At eleven o'clock it was still early and only one rider had already arrived and was walking his two mounts, both covered with splendid saddle-cloths, slowly round the meadow.

Then a four-horse carriage arrived from the direction of the village, raced across the bridge over the river and stopped at the edge of the meadow. It was a large open landau and in it were seated Adrienne and her aunt, the amiable Countess Laczok.

'You see, Aunt Ida,' said Adrienne, smiling, 'we aren't at all late, in spite of your worrying so!'

'You were quite right, my dear, we needn't have hurried!' agreed Countess Laczok, laughing to herself as she remembered the fuss she had made so as to set off in time. 'But I was so excited, you know, for it's a great day when your two big sons go out for the first time; a great day indeed!' And she clasped Adrienne's hand in hers.

They had driven over in the Miloths' carriage, that wide, deep-sprung landau so typical of the plains. It was drawn by four big-boned chestnuts which Adrienne had brought to Kolozsvar from Mezo-Varjas as there would be much coming and going this autumn with Margit's approaching wedding and she had not wanted to make use of the Uzdy horses.

They were followed by two other carriages, one of which was quite ordinary and brought the two Laczok girls, Anna and Ida. This was driven by Pityu Kendy, who had Anna by his side, while Ida sat behind them with a new acquaintance, a young man called Garazda who was studying law at the University of Kolozsvar.

The other vehicle was riding high on its four wheels and was what used to be called an 'American chariot'. It had just two seats in front while behind there was only a narrow bench just large enough for a stable-boy. This was driven by Adam Alvinczy, and beside him sat his fiancée, Margit Miloth.

Adam, as tall men are apt to do, looked very dignified. Now he had even more reason to do so; firstly because he was engaged and soon to be married – so he could almost already be counted among the ranks of the married, and therefore serious, men. He was even beginning to look down on his old drinking friends, most of whom were still bachelors, and indeed often discussed with Margit what a worthless lot they were.

This air of new-found dignity also stemmed from the fact that Adam had practically given up drink himself and now sipped only a bare glassful of wine at mealtimes. This had been his own decision and had needed no urging from Margit, though it is true that before he had made her that promise, she had, without putting any pressure on him, one day let slip how nice it would be if he did so.

Adam's air of assurance came also from the fact that he was now independent. He had given up his share of his mother's inheritance to his brothers in exchange for their settling the substantial debts he had acquired during his wild days as a bachelor. When he did this his father had handed over to him in advance the estate of Tohat. Though it was the least valuable of the Alvinczy holdings, the rest of which would eventually be divided between his brothers, Margit had said it was better to possess it absolutely now and not wait for the future. She had discussed the whole matter with her future father-in-law, had the papers made out under her own supervision, and in no time at all the property was theirs. As a result they no longer need be upset or worried whatever debts the other three young Alvinczys might incur. This is how Adam looked at it – and Margit, of course, agreed with him – and it was perhaps fortunate for the young couple, since Gabor was apparently gambling even more heavily than before while Farkas seemed to be throwing his money around in Budapest. It was fortunate, too, because Margyar-Tohat was not far from Mezo-Varjas and so, as Margit pointed out happily, Adam would be able to help her father with the running of the Mezo-Varjas estate, and that this would be a kindly act as, even though farming was the most fascinating occupation in the world, old Rattle Miloth had never learned the first thing about it. Until this moment Adam had never thought about it either, but naturally everything was now changed since he had become engaged and had somebody with whom to discuss the future.

He was also proud of his beautiful new chariot. This had formerly belonged to Dinora Malhuysen when her complaisant husband, the amiable Tihamer Abonyi, had driven it with his matched pair of Russian trotters. After the scandal and the Abonyis' divorce the trotters had been sold, and one day it had occurred to Margit that maybe the beautiful American chariot might be for sale too. She guessed right, and Adam was able to buy it for a ridiculously cheap price, even though it was still in marvellous condition. All they had to do was to paint over the Abonyi coat of arms on the sides, and it looked as if it had been made for them. Maybe it was not sufficiently sturdy to be driven over any but the best-made roads, but it was so beautiful that that was a small price to pay.

A little self-importance was no doubt justified if one was a mature young man who regulated his life in such a clever and independent fashion! That was how Adam saw himself, and who was to say him nay?

These three carriages, the first to arrive, were driven at a slow walk round the meadow until, about fifteen minutes later, a cloud of dust announced a new arrival. It was the egregious 'Uncle' Ambrus Kendy who sat back against the cushions of his carriage with the youngest Alvinczy, Akos, beside him. Both were smoking large cigars with a lordly air. Next to the driver sat a footman carrying a large basket of flowers which Ambrus had brought for Adrienne. Women like such gestures, he thought, even when

they bring no reward. Nevertheless it looked good for everyone
to see that he courted that 'darling woman' in such a way. There
was the impression, for all to see, that surely these public attentions were not in vain and though this was unfortunately not true,
well, it did no harm to let people think differently.

Ambrus's carriage was followed by two hired fiacres into
which were squeezed Laji Pongracz and half his gypsy band,
while a third contained a table, chairs, cases of champagne and
brandy, and a waiter. Next to the driver was the gypsy musicians'
servant anxiously clasping a giant double bass.

Ambrus swore loudly in his usual fashion, climbed down from
his carriage and, followed by the man carrying the flowers,
walked up to Adrienne's landau.

'Well, God-be-damned, you beautiful ladies get up early!' he
cried as he kissed their hands. 'Here am I, rising before dawn,
trundling along these dusty country roads, trying through thick
and thin to be here to greet you with music and flowers, and what
do I find? To my undying shame you're here before me! Ay-ay-
ay, that's just my blo ... bad luck!' Then, bending double in
mock humility, he turned round, stamped his feet and called out
to the band-leader, 'Get on with it, you dummy! Play that sad
song; can't you see my sorrow?'

'You are a fool – but a very sweet one!' laughed Countess
Laczok who, of course, was Ambrus's cousin and had always
thought him a great charmer.

Adrienne was laughing too, though a trifle coldly and with a
distant air. She knew that this new escapade of Ambrus's was
meant for her – for he claimed, in his fashion, to be in love with
her – and was designed only to compromise her in front of other
people. He wanted them to talk about her in connection with
him, as they had after his exhibition at the charity bazaar, and
that was the reason for this display of flowers and gypsy musicians
who were never normally brought to a meet. Every tongue was
sure to wag, which pleased him immensely and was not, as it
happened, as displeasing to Adrienne as her manner suggested.
The truth was that she rather encouraged these attentions and
the rumours to which they gave rise.

Of course it was all false. The rumours had no foundation but
they served to draw attention away from the truth; and while
people talked about her and Ambrus they were unlikely to gossip
about the fact that the day before Balint had returned from

Budapest, had already called to see her that afternoon, and again later . . . at night!

Adrienne knew that she could only play this dangerous game – which was now her whole life – if everyone's attention was somehow drawn away from her real lover; and so she laughed coolly at Ambrus's antics and stuck a flower from his huge bouquet in her bosom.

By now more and more carriages were arriving from the town and from the surrounding countryside. Some were aged vehicles dating from the time of their grandmothers, others were ramshackle country *tarantas* which were usually found only on the remoter farms. As each new vehicle arrived the men would get down and wander off to greet friends, while the ladies would remain seated and wave to each other from a distance. Ambrus's wine-carriage had an immediate success, as did the gypsy music, even though everyone knew that the choleric old Master would explode with anger at such an unheard-of innovation. All the same, however unsporting it might be to bring gypsies and a running bar to a meet, everyone admitted that it gave a special flavour to the occasion especially as in Transylvania the moment someone started to disapprove everyone else would gang together and teasingly mock the other's discomfiture.

Some riders came on their own, others in groups. Opposite the railway station of Apahida stood the hunt's own headquarters and residence, the Hubertus House. There also were the kennels, the club-rooms and a vast range of stables for the visitors' horses, and from there most of the day's riders now trotted up to join those who were already at the meadow.

Among those who had already arrived were some of the older men like Stanislo Gyeroffy, Laszlo's former guardian, on a large-boned shining black horse; the other Sandor Kendy, who was nicknamed 'Zindi' to distinguish him from Crookface, and, mounted on a powerful light chestnut, Major Bogacsy who, since retiring from the army, had been president of the Chancery Court which looked after the interests of orphans. The younger riders included Farkas Alvinczy, Isti Kamuthy, Pityu Kendy and Balint. Most of these last clustered round Adrienne's carriage; but Balint merely waved to her from afar.

The retired major curvetted around the Miloth carriage. He had been one of Countess Laczok's dancing partners when she had still been the young Ida Kendy, and now for more than twenty years he had always fancied that she would have married him if he had ever asked her. Today, therefore, he smiled at her from beneath his huge tomcat moustaches and flashing monocle, trying hard to suggest the intimacy of a shared past. For once his expression was pacific, indeed almost endearing; normally, as befitted the great if self-appointed expert on all matters affecting duels and the code of honour, he was all too apt to pull hideous and, he hoped, ferocious faces. Today, too, his stocky figure was to be seen at its best under great loops of gold braid for, so as to show everyone what a brave warrior lurked behind the mildness of the civilian, he had once again put on his uniform.

Until now Uncle Ambrus had remained at Adrienne's side, but when all the younger men rode up on their splendid horses he went back to his wine-table and the gypsies, feeling that a man on foot did not cut such a gallant figure as those who, like fat little Isti and Pityu Kendy, paid their court from the lofty dignity of the saddle.

The young men also had the advantage of their smart hunting clothes. Most of them wore green coats with gold buttons, which were the form for hare-hunts; but on that day some there were who wore the hunting pink normally reserved for chasing deer or fox. However, all sorts of things were allowed on St Hubert's Day, especially in Transylvania.

Everyone wore white breeches and capped boots and, with one exception, black velvet hunting caps. This was Isti, who was wearing a top hat and going from carriage to carriage explaining, with his usual lisp, that 'that black velvet cap would not be allowed in England. There, only the Mathter and the Hunthman have the right. It'th quite out of order . . . !'

But no one minded or even took any notice. The riders looked splendid, whatever they wore, and the general picture was beautiful which was all that counted with most people. In the sparkling autumn sunshine the combination of colours, the green and red coats, the sheen of health on all the horses and, all around, the elegant, beautiful and highly painted carriages filled with the blossom-like dresses of the young girls went to make up a picture of rare beauty, like an old English print.

One new automobile there was which somewhat upset the general effect. This belonged to young Dodo and her new German husband, Udo von der Maultasch. It was only six weeks

since he had managed to marry the richest heiress in Transylvania, and his manner was by no means as humble and retiring
as it had been during the days of courtship. This morning he descended from this smart new Mercedes-Benz and walked about
everywhere explaining to anyone whose attention he could
catch that all this was not really the right way to organize a hunt
and that 'bei uns in Pommern – at home in Pomerania' it was all
done quite differently. Those young men on horseback escaped
him easily by merely trotting away, but he soon found a captive
audience in Akos Alvinczy who was seated with Uncle Ambrus
at his wine-table. Ambrus was not having any of this and just
brushed him off with one of his usual expletives.

Poor Dodo remained alone in her great new motor, for no
one came near her, the others saying among themselves, 'That
stinking motor! They only brought it to annoy the horses!'

Young Margit saw this and felt sorry for her, so she got down
from the American chariot and went over to greet her. This was
partly because Margit was by nature good-hearted and partly,
perhaps, because she had remembered that Dodo owned some
property near Tohat, where Margit and Adam would soon be
living, and, if they were good friends, then maybe she and Adam
could lease it from Dodo on favourable terms.

All at once everyone's attention was drawn to a commotion
from two different directions. From the Tarcsa road Joska Kendy
arrived at speed, driving his familiar long farm wagon behind
four raging dapple-grey horses. Cracking his whip like a circus-
trainer he drove like a storm into what until then had been a
peaceful gathering of horses and carriages, many of which had
now to move swiftly out of his way. With a shrill whistle Joska's
war chariot stopped beside Ambrus's little encampment, the
greys rigid as if carved from stone. Once again Joska cracked his
whip, this time just over the horses' heads, but they did not move
knowing that this was just Joska's way and was no signal for them.

Pipe in mouth, Joska spoke up. 'Well, I see you've got a tavern!
Is no one going to offer me a drink?' And he looked around him
with a sharp all-seeing glance from his small slanting eyes. This
glance was directed, not at the girls in the carriages, but at all the
horses gathered there at the meet. Joska was only happy when
buying or selling a horse and he wanted to see at once what horses
were present on which he might do a profitable deal. He had
come alone to the meet, accompanied only by a single groom

who now jumped down from the folding seat at the back and went up to hold the heads of his master's greys.

Simultaneously, and of even more stormy appearance, there pranced forward ten whinnying stallions on the road from the Hubertus House to the north. As if on parade they came, side by side, right across the full width of the road, ridden by ten young infantry officers from the garrison at Szamos-Ujvar, who were no doubt anxious to show what good horsemen they were and so rode to the meet in strict military order. Their steeds were servicing stallions from one of the state stud-farms and every year some thirty of them were lent to the hunt so as to try them out in the field. As a rule only three or four of them came out at once and then just for the whips or some specially chosen hunt member. Then, even if full of go from their diet of oats, they could be placed in front or kept to the sides of the field. But today, ridden straight into the centre of a group of desirable mares, they caused no end of a furore, rearing and screaming and kicking out at each other and any other animal that came near and generally making it quite clear to everyone that they were all too ready and willing to get on with their principal function.

This was far more serious than Joska's four-in-hand, since for him it was only necessary to give way while from the new arrivals one had to get clear without delay. Even so there were some mares who seemed rather too interested, while the stallions could not abide the geldings.

The newcomers did their best to jump about in every direction but their riders remained unperturbed. The band of young officers stayed close together making a perfect circle round the meadow; and, no matter how restive their mounts, carried themselves as uniformly upright as Army Regulations required. The dust had hardly settled and peace been restored after their arrival when the hounds arrived.

They were led in by the Master, old Bela Wesselenyi, who himself had founded the Hunt and who after so many years remained its guiding spirit. He was riding a magnificent thoroughbred, tall, glossy and well-groomed, and his short stirrup leathers made him seem even shorter than he was in reality. His forty-year-old red coat, cut in the short style of the sixties, had faded from scarlet to pink and his face too shone red under the black velvet hunting cap. His snow-white moustaches and square-cut Franz-Josef beard gleamed white in the sunshine. All around the Master milled the hounds. Long-eared and spotted, they kept closely together, pressing up against his horse's legs and sometimes looking up as if to make sure their master was still there. A hound on its own so often seems lost since for countless generations they had been accustomed to live always in a pack and always under human guidance. Hounds are never therefore alone and should one lose its way it can be for ever, so frightened and forlorn do they become when bereft of their master and companions. It is only when actually in full cry in the hunting field that such dogs lose their timidity and dependence.

Close behind the hounds rode Istvan Tisza, the second Master, dressed in a dark green, almost black coat which suited his swarthy complexion.

He had bred his own horse which, though it was over sixteen hands, seemed smaller, for Tisza, unlike the Master, rode with long stirrups in the old style of the Spanish Riding School. And his seat never altered, whether on the flat or clearing the highest fences. Always he sat completely upright and never lost his calm.

A little further back rode the two Whips, Gazsi Kadacsay and the younger Aron Kozma, a grandson of the Kozma who had once been agent to the Abadys at Denestornya. Later he had made a fortune on his own account and this had been increased by his sons who were as intelligent and industrious as himself. They worked in perfect harmony and followed a policy of acquiring land from the former aristocratic owners who, through their own fecklessness, arrogance and disdain for the sources of their worldly position, had fallen on bad times. The Kozma brothers then re-divided the land, rationalized its use and brought it back into useful and profitable production. The third generation were equally industrious and sensible and because they, unlike their fathers, had been brought up with money under their belts, felt themselves free to indulge their inclinations by being active in local affairs and taking part in those sports hitherto only open to the gentry. This younger Aron had been recruited by Balint to help in his co-operative schemes and was now his right-hand man in the Mezoseg district. He planned now to hunt the first of the four days at Zsuk, return to his place some eighty kilometres away to look after urgent business, and drive back on the evening of the third day so as to be in the saddle again for the last meet of the season. He was a slim young man with the Tartar features more common in the Crimea.

Baron Gazsi was riding a thoroughbred mare of impeccable breeding, still in racing condition without an ounce of fat on her. He had bought her two months before straight from the racecourse; and he had bought her cheap as she by no means deserved the gentle name of 'Honeydew'. The mare was so nervous and bad-tempered that in spite of her good points and marvellous turn of speed the trainers had found it impossible to get the best out of her. There were times when she would suddenly stop and throw her rider, or when she would start bucking as in a Wild West show, keeping it up until she had succeeded in getting rid of her jockey. She would even throw herself backwards and had already killed one and crippled two others.

Gazsi had been fascinated with the challenge she presented and was now applying all the psychological horse-sense he knew in an attempt to break her in properly. Today he sat in the saddle as gently as if it were a basket of eggs.

Gazsi's own contact with her mouth was so light that one might almost say that he was not using the bit at all but guiding her by balance alone. The effect was immediate: after throwing her new master twice, she had settled down and slowly allowed herself to be tamed. Kadacsay was extremely pleased with himself and it was not long before he went so far as to take her out with the hounds. Somehow Honeydew had been made to understand that the whip was for the hounds, not her, and though she still sometimes gave a little buck in protest Gazsi merely stood up in his stirrups, as if in courteous salutation, thereby making it even easier for her to buck as much as she wished. And very soon she gave it up altogether, no doubt thinking it hardly worthwhile if her rider did not resist. Nevertheless she never lost the habit of folding her ears back close to her head and woe betide any other mount who came within kicking distance – for then she struck out like lightning.

Even this did not disconcert Gazsi. He just tied a white board on his back with the words 'I KICK!' so that anyone who came up behind him should be warned.

The Master rode a wide circle round the meadow to see who was out that morning, and then stopped to greet the ladies. Without even glancing in Uncle Ambrus's direction he gave the sign to move off and led the way over the road and across the railway tracks. Behind the hounds rode the whips and behind them the stallions with their soldier riders. A little further back rode the two young Laczok boys in the charge of their father's head groom. Countess Laczok, who had made the Master responsible for their safety, stood up in her carriage and waved to them to pass by her; but the two youngsters already had their hands full keeping their mounts from crowding the riders ahead of them and could not have left the field even if they had wanted to. It was enough to keep behind Baron Gazsi and Aron Kozma and nothing could take that joy from them.

Once over the track the field split into two, half the riders going to the left of the pack along the banks of the river, the rest beside the railway line. In front of them the flat meadows of the Szamos valley stretched northwards, and across these meadows rode the hunt, hoping to put up a hare either from the meadows themselves or from the ploughed fields on either side – or even from among the corn stalks in those fields not yet ploughed. And as soon as the riders had gone past, the carriages too moved off, following the hunt from the road which skirted the meadows.

Margit said goodbye to Dodo and got down from the car. She looked around to see where Adam had driven their beautiful carriage.

The carriage was there, a little way off; but where was Adam? There was no sign of him. She looked around again and soon saw that he had joined the group at Uncle Ambrus's. She ran towards him and was about to call out when she saw that her fiancé, who was standing with his back to her, was noisily toasting the others with a beaker of champagne and brandy, while Ambrus, Akos Alvinczy and Joska Kendy cheered him on.

Margit was filled with rage. How could he break his word to her like that! There he was, drinking again as soon as her back was turned! In a flash she decided to punish him. She would show him! And, as all the adventure-loving blood of the Miloths rose in her, she ran across to where Joska's famous four-in-hand was standing nearby, jumped up into the driving seat and called over to that dashing gentleman-driver, 'Joska! Take me after the hunt! Across the fields. I dare you!'

'Of course I dare!' cried Joska, as he ran over, and jumped up beside her. An almighty crack of the whip and away they dashed.

Only then did Adam grasp what was happening. Dimly coming to his senses he stammered, 'M-M-Margit! I only . . . Oh, Margit! Margit!'

But Joska's dappled greys were already far away. They did not remain on the road for long, but bumped across the railway tracks and into the meadows behind the hunt. No other carriage could have been driven like that, but then Joska's wagon was no elegant gentleman's carriage but a strongly-built farm cart, low on the ground and slung on iron chains rather than delicate springs. It could be driven across bumps and ditches without coming to harm.

Hardly had they crossed the rail tracks when from far below by the river bank came the cry 'Tally-ho!'

By the time Adam had recovered his senses, dashed across to his own carriage and galloped some way up the road, the hunt was well away below him and the field streaming off into the distance.

As was only to be expected, the hare did not run straight along the valley to amuse the carriage trade above but soon cut off in a sharp turn up the hillside. The pack of harriers were in full cry behind him and after them the Master, the Whips, the soldiers, the Laczok boys and the rest of the field. The hare ran quickly across the railway line and, about two miles from the meadow where the meet had been held, crossed the road in front of the following carriages and disappeared up the bare hills to the left.

And behind them all came Joska and Margit in the four-in-hand at full tilt. Adam was in a terrible state. For a moment he had a wild hope that they would stop when they reached the road, but that was not the way of Joska. As if he were the Devil himself he set the horse diagonally at the uneven hillside and raced away after the last of the riders. All Adam could do was watch them helplessly as the low-slung wagon careered wildly as it followed old cart-tracks and cattle-crossings, and slithered its way across the dried-out yellow clay hillside. In a few moments they too were at the top where the hunt had just disappeared and then, after galloping briefly along the crest of the hill, they also disappeared from view.

In his distress Adam for one moment even thought of chasing after them, but he quickly reflected that his delicate American chariot would be broken to pieces before he had gone fifty yards up that terrible rough hillside. He looked around for a horse he could borrow but there was none there not harnessed to some carriage or other. And what's more there was no one there capable of holding his high-spirited pair of horses if they decided to bolt, for the little stable lad clinging precariously to the jump-seat could barely hold their heads when he left the carriage. And so he was chained to that elegant carriage, which was as showy as Dodo's new motor and as useless except on the tarred road, forced to sit up there for all to see, unable to lift a finger to help his bride and made to watch whatever might happen with his heart beating hard and his head full of fear and anger and shame.

It might perhaps have been less cruel if after they had disappeared over the crest of the hill he could have imagined a halt in the chase and Joska's horrible juggernaut being peacefully trotted along some country lane. But this was not to be. The hare, as they are apt to do, cut a circle and now reappeared running fast horizontally along the precipitous sides of the hill, with the pack in close pursuit and behind it the Master, the Whips and the entire field – with the soldiers still riding formally in a close-knit row. And there, barely a hundred yards in the rear, raced those four dapple-greys, firstly downhill with Joska's wagon skidding after them, then horizontally over gorse and hawthorn bushes, lurching over stream-beds and goat-paths, tilting first in one direction and then in the other and all the time, with pipe clenched in his mouth, that dreadful Joska, reckless of everything except the chase and the reins in his hands, in full sight of Adam, and beside him young Margit with her hat on her shoulders, her hair loose and flying in the wind, holding hard to the seat with her hands but laughing and happy, happy, happy . . .

But Adam had never been so unhappy in his whole life.

As the hunt streamed across the railway tracks and crossed the road before climbing up the steep hillside on the other side, they passed in front of a half-covered open carriage which was being driven towards Apahida. In it sat Laszlo Gyeroffy who, after a day spent at his home at Kozard, was now returning to Mrs Lazar's house at Dezmer.

Now, seeing riders in their full hunting panoply of pink and dark green, he remembered that it was St Hubert's Day and that, round the next bend in the road, he would surely meet everybody from his own world, that light-hearted, pleasure-seeking, hard-drinking world that he had shunned ever since the day of the spring bazaar. The succeeding months had at first been a time of increasing deprivation and degradation. Then he had met Mrs Lazar, started leading a normal orderly life again, begun to work by helping her to run her substantial estates, and by now was feeling almost happy and at ease. He certainly had no desire to encounter any of those former friends who all knew his story.

Praying that he might pass without being seen he had the little carriage stopped and its rain-hood put fully up. He was just in time, for the ladies' carriages were just around the next bend, hidden only by a few cottages beside the road.

'Drive on,' he called to the driver. 'Quickly, now!' and sat back on the seat pulling up his legs beside him so that anyone looking at the vehicle from the side would think there was no one in it.

This was quite unnecessary as everyone was so busy watching the hunt that Laszlo's carriage passed unnoticed. Laszlo laughed softly to himself at the success of his ruse and sat up in a normal position. He did not stop to have the hood pulled down again as he was in a hurry to get to Apahida in time to meet Sara who had been loading some ewes onto a goods train.

In a few moments he was passing the meadow at Tarcsa.

Ambrus had had the music stopped as soon as the Master led the field out and the ladies' carriages moved off. 'Pack up!' he called out, 'and let's get the hell out of here!' He was in a bad temper because he had had to admit, even to himself, that all the trouble and expense, the gypsy band, the champagne and the flowers, had hardly been a success. Despite all his efforts to be the centre of attention, despite the loud-mouthed talk, the laughter and the chaff, no man with his feet on the ground could compete with the gallant riders in the elegance of their beautifully tailored red and green coats, their sparkling white breeches and, above all, the advantage they had perched up on those gleaming polished steeds! What he would not admit, even to himself, was that, surrounded by all those handsome, athletic young men, he felt old and unwanted; and it was this unacknowledged feeling lurking within him that made him even crosser than he had been before.

'What the hell are you all dawdling about for?' he shouted. 'Get on with it, you louts!'

Shouted at in this angry fashion the musicians and the waiter completely lost their heads, and in their attempt to scramble back into their two carriages the chairs, the double bass and the cymbals somehow got strewn all over the road.

Meanwhile Uncle Ambrus and Akos Alvinczy walked off to

find their own vehicles which had been left a little way off down the road.

At this point Mrs Lazar's carriage drove up at a swift trot. The driver called out a warning and though young Akos jumped out of the way, not Ambrus. He had always been somewhat heavy-limbed and slow of movement – which he justified by saying 'no gentleman ever hurries!' – and so now he stood his ground and with an obscene curse waved his stick in front of the shaft-horse's nose. The driver reined in at once.

'What the Devil do you think you're doing?' shouted Kendy in a rage. 'Are you trying to run me down, you peasant? Who are you? What sort of a dumb fellow are you?'

As he spoke he came nearer to the driver's seat and in so doing saw Gyeroffy inside. He stepped back in amazement.

'So it's you, Laci? Are you trying to knock me over or what?' Laszlo got down.

'Forgive me, sir,' he said politely. 'My driver doesn't know you . . .' and, to soothe him, he added with a smile, 'and anyway no one would ever expect to see *you* standing in the middle of the road!'

'Nor is it my habit, but it's St Hubert's Day and the meet was here. I brought along some gypsies and a little wine. It was a fine sight, my boy! I'd offer you a drink but everything's been packed up by now.'

'Thank you, sir, but I'm in rather a hurry and must get on. Goodbye, sir.'

They shook hands. Laszlo got back into his carriage and they were just moving off when Ambrus suddenly went up and leaned in towards him. 'Wait a minute!' he said, laughing. 'Wait, I say!'

During their brief conversation he had been looking at the carriage and the horses. He had heard a rumour that Laszlo had been seen in Kolozsvar with the attractive Mrs Lazar and that he was now living with her. Ambrus never liked to hear of other men's successes with women and now his own disastrous outing made him want to hit out. With a cruel and mischievous expression in his eyes, he was about to speak when Laszlo remonstrated. 'Really, sir,' he started, but Ambrus cut him short.

'First of all, young fella-me-lad, don't "Sir" me! I'm not that old! And now, what the Devil are you up to, cowering back in the shade in bright sunshine? You're up to no good, I can see. What sort of funny business is it, then? Come on, out with it!

Where are you off to? Whose carriage is this? Any fool can tell
it's not yours. Come on, out with it! I won't let you go until
you come clean.' And he stuck his foot like a spoke up between
Laszlo's seat and the driver's.

Laszlo did not really see any harm in all this and he was living
such a calm natural life with the charming and kindly Sara that
it never occurred to him to be anything but honest, let alone to
protest.

'I'm going to Mrs Bogdan Lazar's place at Dezmer, and this is
her carriage. It's no secret.'

At Sara's name Ambrus yanked out his foot and began an
ironic dance of joy, twisting his body and stamping his feet and
crying out, 'Ay-yi-yi!' while clapping his hands as if in applause.
'That's good, that is! That's rich! Bravo, my boy. Ay-yi-yi! Free
room and board . . . bed *and* breakfast. That's rich, that is!'

And more in the same vein, but Laszlo did not wait to hear.
His face darkened as he said curtly to the coachman, 'Drive on!'

Ambrus shouted more coarse jokes after the rapidly disappearing carriage, but Laszlo heard nothing. He leaned back into the
cushions and it was a few moments before he began to realize the
full import of what Uncle Ambrus had been saying. Of course
he had at once sensed that Ambrus was out to hurt and to offend
but when he began to grasp Ambrus's real meaning it was as if
he had been hit by a sledgehammer.

It was some time before he had fully disentangled the implications of Ambrus's mockery from the coarse way it had been
expressed. For some time now Laszlo had floated through life
without heeding what was happening around him, and so he
needed a few moments to come down to earth. He had still not
fully analysed his new train of thought when the carriage drew
up at the station and Sara got in. They drove off at once.

After a few seconds Sara, after looking hard at Laszlo, said,
'What is it? Something's wrong, I can see. What's happened?'

'It's nothing. Nothing at all, really. Why?' replied Laszlo in
the most casual tone he could muster; and he looked her full
in the face trying hard to smile.

'Are you sure? Do you feel all right? Something is wrong, isn't
it? What's happened?'

'No, no, nothing! Nothing at all!' he answered and they took
each other's hands and looked hard into each other's eyes for a
long time, she with concern and he with a fear he could not

understand. Then suddenly Laszlo's internal brakes failed and he could no longer control himself. He buried his head on her shoulder and wept like a persecuted child. For a long time he cried, feeling without reason that he had somehow lost this sweet loving woman to whom he owed his rescue from the hell of the last few years. At this point he knew only too well that the day would soon come when he would reject and throw her away, just as he had rejected and thrown away everything good that had ever come to him. And so, in the grief this moment of self-knowledge brought him, he clung ever more closely to her, grabbing her arms, her shoulders, her hands, so as to make sure that at least for this moment she was still there beside him. Still there, still there . . .

It was as well that the rain-hood was still up so that they could stay clinging together without anyone seeing them. And nobody did see them.

The hare that was put up down by the river was a real St Hubert's Day hare who clearly knew what was required of him. After showing himself several times on the crest of the hill – where the ladies could get a good glimpse of the hunt – he allowed himself to be caught after only twenty-five minutes of the chase. This, everyone agreed, was most considerate of him since it was time for the luncheon that had been prepared for them all at the Hubertus House.

The kill took place at a bend in the valley just beyond the last crest of the hills; and then, after the 'worry-worry' when the hounds had devoured the dead hare, most of the riders trotted back to the road to rejoin the ladies. Not the Master, however. Knowing the dangers of bringing a pack of hounds among such a crowd of horsemen, he took them off to drink at a spring on the hillside and then led them back to the crest of the hill, whence he could take them quietly back to their kennels.

A small band of riders stayed with him. These were Tisza and the two Whips; Abady, Farkas Alvinczy, Bogacsy, the retired major, and, of course, the two Laczok boys who would rather have died than miss a moment of their first hunt.

They were crossing a meadow at a slow trot and the hounds were widely spread out because it was unlikely that they would find here as they were riding through fields where the horses were always being taken for exercise.

Everyone was surprised, therefore, when a hare suddenly sprang out from behind a diminutive blackthorn bush.

The pack howled its delight and raced in pursuit. However, this was no young animal like the first quarry, but rather a huge meadow hare, strong and experienced, who had been chased by farm guard-dogs for several summers. He was in magnificent shape, well-muscled and gleaming with health; and as he ran it was clear that as yet he was not even in much of a hurry. With his great ears pricking backward and forward as he ran he made a few playful leaps as if to tell his pursuers he knew he could out-distance them all. Disdaining the usual advantage of racing uphill, he turned back to the north and sped away down the valley.

And so started one of the greatest runs of that season or any other.

The riders galloped gently across the soft meadow-grass. In a few moments they were down in the valley and there, clearly visible, was the great hare running smoothly up the hill on the other side.

The most notable feature of the Zsuk hunting grounds was that, though to the north the slopes were gentle and the fields rich and productive, on the southern side were steep cliffs with outcrops of bare rock emerging from the yellowing clay-skids. This was the chosen escape route of the quarry and with his long muscular hind legs he overcame all its difficulties so that he was already disappearing over the crest before the pack of harriers were barely one third of the way up the hillside.

Even so the hounds were naturally faster than the horses who, with the often considerable weight of their riders, needed to be carefully nurtured at this hazardous start to what promised to be a long run. The Master arrived at the summit soon after the pack and there he was joined by the rest of the field, some of whom rode up at a gentle canter while the others, more cautiously, took the hillside at a trot. When the Master arrived it was clear that the first of the hounds, which were the youngest and strongest and also, of course, the least experienced, had lost the scent and were nosing around in all directions and wagging their tails with excite-ment. Then there arrived the old lead-hound Toss-it-up and he, with years of experience behind him, hardly had his nose to the ground when he picked up the scent, let out a howl of delight, and raced off down the opposite side of the hill with the rest of the pack in full cry behind him. Again the hunt raced downhill.

However there were three hounds which did not hear the call as they were still searching some thorn bushes below the summit. From above Gazsi caught sight of them and spurred Honeydew again down the slippery clay slope. This the mare clearly did not like and although she did as she was told she showed her dis-approval by quickly turning a full circle on the twenty-degree slope, as if she were executing a quick waltz, and found time to buck at the same moment. It was one of her party tricks on bad ground. Most other horses would have lost their footing with such a caper and if they had not fallen themselves at least got shot of their rider. But Honeydew was a marvellous creature and Kadacsay an excellent horseman.

Quite unperturbed by Honeydew's eccentric prancing Gazsi had no sooner reached the lost hounds than he was cracking his whip, calling to them and leading them swiftly back up the hill at a fast canter before hurling himself forward to rejoin the rest of the pack.

Now they were all off at a dizzying pace. And this was not only because these Transylvanian-bred harriers, unlike their counter-parts in England who were not known for speed, had become as fast as deer-hounds, but also because the hilly Zsuk country exacted a rather special technique of sparing the horses when going uphill but letting them take the sharp descents at a full gallop. This was the only way that the riders could keep up with the hounds, and both riders and horses had to learn what to do if they wanted to keep up – in old Hungarian hunting parlance to *shincoraz*, which came from the French *chien-courant*.

And so it was for the whole run. Down at full gallop, up gently. Down again, up again. Down, up; down, up; down, up – in a straight line like a Roman road.

The hounds streamed out behind the leader like a bouquet of yellow and white flowers. Only Kadacsay kept close behind the Master, while Tisza and Balint followed at a respectable distance so as not to crowd the pack. Kozma stayed behind them and Akos Alvinczy and Major Bogacsy a hundred yards behind them. Lastly came the Laczok boys whose two stallions, though excel-lent mounts, were somewhat slow and arrived at the crest of each hill just as the rest of the field were already behind the hounds at the bottom of the succeeding dip.

The weather now grew misty and it was difficult to see far ahead. As a result they could only rarely catch a glimpse of the hare. Even so they knew they were on the right track since Toss-it-up was leading the pack in full voice and he had never been known to make a mistake.

'I'm sure the hounds have switched to a fox!' Gazsi called out joyfully to Abady. 'Such a miracle hare can't exist!' and to regain his place as chief Whipper-in he spurred his new thorough-bred up the hillside at the speed of a hurdle-race. Honeydew responded at once, eager and fresh, and quite unperturbed, heedless of the spurs. It was clear that she revelled in these long runs.

After a steep run downhill the bed of the valley and the river became wider. It was a place, called 'Borsa' from the hillside above it, where the banks were made of boggy mud and the water too wide to jump. Balint crossed by an old bridge but Gazsi lost time looking for a shallow fording place.

The Borsa hill was one of the highest in the district. Its sides were deeply eroded and in places very steep indeed. When the first riders arrived at the bottom of the hill they found that even the hounds had had to spread out among the little bushes that were all that grew on that bare earth. Even so they did not have to wait, for the pack soon found the scent again and as the first four horsemen dug their spurs in to take the slope without drawing breath, the hare, who had stopped running for a moment, jumped up just ahead of the lead-hound.

So there, for all to see, was proof that it was no fox but still that mighty hare himself.

Once over the crest he needed all his strength to make one last effort and reach the shelter of a densely-grown thicket in the centre of a wood some five hundred yards ahead on the borders of the neighbouring Doboka County.

The rest had done him no good. The effort was now too much for him. He shot ahead of the hounds before falling back only to try again. And then, quite suddenly, he made a great leap in the air and fell dead in front of them without being touched by the hounds. All around him they milled; but they did not touch him. They too were exhausted and they just gazed up at their master with tongues hanging out and it seemed that they might have been saying, 'Well, we did well, didn't we?'

As the Master dismounted he called back to the three who had kept up with him, 'That run lasted a hundred and three minutes!'

He lifted up the hare; it was as stiff as a board.

When the others had also dismounted, their horses did not

have to be held; even Honeydew was as mild and tame as anyone could have wished.

'What a run! Wonderful! Wonderful! This'll be a day to remember!'

Everyone was repeating the same words and congratulating each other and trying to work out how far it was from the Zsuk meadow to the Doboka boundary, for this is what they had taken at a gallop without a check. It must have been twelve or fourteen kilometres; uphill–downhill all the way! That said something for their horses and for the hounds! They were still talking of nothing else when the rest of the field turned up, first Aron Kozma, then Bogacsy on his sturdy chestnut; a little later came Farkas Alvinczy who was covered with mud from a fall at the Borsa creek and finally, happy and flushed with victory, the two Laczok boys and their groom.

'Well, you boys,' laughed Gazsi as they cantered up, 'you're in luck to have such a run the first time out.' And Balint thought he must write to his mother to let her know instantly how the new mare from Denestornya had stood the pace, how she hadn't hesitated for a moment and was one of the four to be in at the kill – and two of them English thoroughbreds; also what good condition she was in with tendons strong as iron and no sign of a saddle sore. Why, she had hardly been sweating at all, even at the finish. He knew how pleased his mother would be, for she loved her horses as much as if they had been her own children.

After finding some water for the hounds they started for home, riding straight across country, but very slowly as it was obvious that the hounds were now very tired.

The afternoon light was fading and from the west the sun was setting in a blaze of red. From the top of each hill-crest the hills ahead were silhouetted in wavy lines of deep lilac shadow and resembled the huge waves of a petrified ocean.

The Master, the Laczok boys, Farkas Alvinczy and Bogacsy rode ahead of the others. Tisza had stopped to light a cigar and as Balint and Gazsi had waited for him those three were now somewhat behind, riding three abreast with loose reins. For a while no one spoke.

'I'd like to ask you something,' said Gazsi at last, turning to Tisza who nodded to him to go on. It was merely this, went on Gazsi: as a hussar officer on the reserve list he had been given a secret order to keep his regiment informed at all times of his whereabouts. Just that, nothing else: but the more he thought this over the more it seemed to him that the only reason could be a possible mobilization because of the Bosnian affair. And mobilization meant that there was a possibility of war. Could this really be possible, he wondered, and went on to ask why, if that were possible, anyone had even considered the annexation?

Though a political leader and former Minister-President, Tisza was not normally given to talk about such matters, and in any case there were few men with whom he would have discussed affairs of state. But he approved of Abady, who had selflessly undertaken much important work, and who had been sensible enough not to join any of the quarrelsome political parties. He had also been attracted to Kadacsay because of something he had said some while before.

At the time of the 1905 elections there had been an argument in the Casino Club of Kolozsvar with most of those present reviling Tisza, who at that time was still in office. Gazsi had defended him until someone shouted, 'You're no better than a traitor, talking like that! You'd sell your own country next!'

Then Kadacsay inclined his great woodpecker nose and replied, rolling his 'r's, 'Of cour-r-rse I'd sell it. Sell it r-r-right now. But no one would buy it while you lot still lived here!'

There had been a roar of laughter, and then everyone had calmed down for in Transylvania a good joke wiped everything else from people's minds. Nevertheless it had taken courage to reply like that in the overheated atmosphere of those days, and so Tisza was honouring his honesty when he decided for once to say what was in his heart.

Tisza began by saying that no matter what political problems arose nor what international friction resulted, the crisis would eventually be smoothed away without further complications. And this would in no small measure be due to Austria's over-whelming military strength.

He went on in much the same vein, developing his arguments rather as if he were rehearsing for himself a speech he would later make in the Upper House, outlining in hard dry phrases the significance of the nation's current foreign policy and what were the implications for the future.

'Personally,' he said, 'I am convinced that the annexation was necessary; and so I am ready to bear its consequences. There is no point in discussing whether the government took all the necessary diplomatic precautions or exercised the desired-for tact in carrying it out.' He refused even to discuss such aspects of the affair and would advise everyone to refrain from such a profitless activity. It was every patriotic Hungarian's bounden duty to support the actions of the monarch, for internal solidarity was of prime importance to any healthy country faced with opposition or danger from abroad. The uproar created by the other great powers in Europe was quite out of proportion to the real importance of this matter.

'All this consternation,' he said, 'is just an exercise in rabble-rousing directed against the Dual Monarchy.' It was, of course, he explained, led by the English, whose disingenuous action in making out that Austria-Hungary had only done it so as to stab the Turkish constitution in the back was obviously motivated by spite. England was now using the Turks as a pretext for her concern, just as she had the Poles in the sixties and the Danes in the Schleswig-Holstein affair. The only effect of this simulated concern for other people was to arouse their passions and create false hopes about matters which would soon be dropped in midstream. What was certain, however, was that the fifteen-year-old peace in the Balkans was at an end and that Europe was now entering the first, and perhaps most serious, phase of a new East–West confrontation. The Dual Monarchy must now draw its own conclusions from the electric atmosphere in the Balkans, must be even more alert than before for signs of trouble; and, above all, must be ready to make unexpected sacrifices.

'The government was quite right to offer so many concessions in the Commercial Treaty with Serbia. The policy is the right one and must be upheld, especially now when it is so important to bind closely to us all the small states by which we are surrounded. Naturally,' he said, 'whether the Treaty will stand will ultimately depend on the attitude of the Serbs themselves. It is vital for us to maintain our existing policy towards the Balkan peoples, namely safeguarding the peace and doing all we can to secure their economic and cultural development. At the same time we must do all we can to hamstring any movement which might tend to limit their independence by welding them into a powerful aggressive conglomeration that would be part of an all-powerful hegemony in that part of Europe.'

At these last words Balint looked up suddenly and stared at Tisza.

What an interesting man he was, thought Balint. That last sentence! To think that Tisza not only understood so clearly the ambitions of Russia but had also anticipated the plot that Slawata had outlined a year before when he had tried to recruit Abady to the ranks of those whose aim was the aggrandizement of the Austro-Hungarian monarchy and the creation of a chain of minor thrones for the Habsburg family.

The slow rhythm of the horses' hoofs was like the beat of a funeral drum as Tisza went on explaining his innermost fears. As he spoke, his voice seemed to take on a deeper more anxious note. Then followed some prophetic phrases.

'There are many people who hate us, and there are powerful forces in Europe today that may not find this the moment to provoke a general conflagration; but, mark my words, don't ever forget that some day, when they think the time has come, there will be a war and it will be fatal to the Monarchy. Our enemies will see to that!'

Then followed some phrases that would have amazed Tisza's enemies, those who saw him only as the arch-enemy of everything they held sacred. He said, 'Our first military aim must be to create confidence at home and simultaneously to convince both our allies and our opponents of the reality of our power. It is now absolutely vital to find solutions to all the current disputes concerning the army. Both the ruler himself and the political parties must now put aside all partisan slogans and passions and concentrate, now that we are so surrounded by menace, on building up our forces and strengthening our national resolve. We should be ready for any sacrifice!'

Balint was astonished to hear these words from the very man who was publicly vilified as the arch-enemy of a unified Austro-Hungarian army and whose satanic influence was believed to be at the very root of Vienna's distrust of the Hungarians. Tisza now fell silent and they rode without anyone speaking. Balint, deeply impressed by those last words, stared hard at the grim-faced rider beside him.

It was now almost dark. The road narrowed, so that Balint and Gazsi, riding on Tisza's right and left, took a path just below the crest of the hill leaving the highest place to the prophetic politician, who was thus silhouetted black against the faint light still in the sky. His horse was dark too and so was his upright figure, rigid and unrelenting, from the dark saddle to the tall black riding hat. But darkest of all was his face.

He rode on alone, standing out against the darkening sky, always alone, always on the highest part of the hill, forever above the others and forever alone.

His horse carried him forward at a slow even rhythm.

And so they rode on into the gathering night.

PART FIVE

CHAPTER ONE

IN EARLY AUTUMN Balint Abady made a tour of the country co-operatives he had founded. He travelled in a small car that he had recently bought because it would have taken too long to cover the distances involved by train and horse-drawn carriage. His object was to obtain a clear picture of how all the different branches had developed and what they might need so that he could make a full report to the congress that was to be held in the capital at the end of November.

And, of course, Lelbanya was included in the tour.

Here, thanks to the discretion and persistence of the notary Daniel Kovacs, everything that Balint had planned from the time of his first election as Member for Lelbanya had been achieved. The Co-operative Society was flourishing, and the old manor house of the Abady family, which Balint had offered as the local headquarters, had been asked for by the town itself, just as Kovacs had predicted. The farmers' circle had been properly organized and this too had been set up in the same building. The experimental farm had been established on the land surrounding the house, though in a modified form from what Balint had originally suggested. Instead of making a market garden whose produce when sent to market would have seemed to the local people as unfair competition to their own wives' efforts, the greater part of the land had been turned into a nursery for fruit trees where the farmers could obtain grafted apple, walnut and cherry trees. The small part remaining was used for raising vegetables for seed – but the produce was not sent to the local market. The spring that rose beside the house had been cleaned out and channels dug from it to make a proper irrigation system.

Abady was now sitting with Aron Kozma in the large room that ran the whole width of the house. Kozma was with him because he had been persuaded to accept the task of supervising all the co-operatives between the Maros river and the valley of Sarmasag – all, that is, except those in Saxon villages which were run by the Saxons themselves. Lelbanya was one of those in his charge.

It was an agreeable spacious room, sunny and clean, quite different from the dirty squalid workshop it had been when inhabited by the untidy and ill-kempt carpenter who had been the Abadys' former tenant. Now the smell of stale sawdust had disappeared and the walls had been freshly whitewashed and covered by the reading-club's bookshelves. In the middle there was a long table and it was here that meetings were held and where visiting agricultural experts were invited to give lectures.

It was eleven o'clock and the two men had just finished checking the cash-books from the treasurer's little room next door and going through the heavy registers which had been placed on the long table for them. Now the books had been sent back and Balint and Aron stayed on a few minutes to talk things over.

Balint was just about to get up and return to the local inn, which was proudly called the Grand Hotel and where he was sure to find a queue of petitioners waiting to see him, when a young-ish woman came swiftly in through the main door. She seemed to be scared of something and glanced nervously behind her before she closed the door. Then she almost ran to them, gabbling, 'I am Victor Olajos's widow. Mr Kovacs is my uncle but he mustn't know I've come to see you. He told me not to, but I thought ... I thought there'd be so many people at the inn waiting for your Lordship and if I went there someone would tell him.'

She sat down, rather out of breath, and then, somewhat confusedly, told her tale. She was the second wife of Olajos who had had a son from his first wife. The boy had been two years old when they had married three years before. Now the husband had died leaving nothing to her and no provision for the child. It just wasn't possible that he had had no money at all. There had been something, dollars from America she thought, but now there was no sign of it and it just wasn't fair. If it hadn't been for her uncle taking them in both she and the boy would now be on the streets. But Daniel Kovacs couldn't really afford it. He had always been poor himself and now he had a growing family to feed and clothe and send to school. She was ashamed to live on his charity so she thought, maybe, that the Chancery Court, the one that looked after orphans ... or someone ... ? This was what she had come to say. She needed help ... so perhaps, perhaps his Lordship?

'Help me! Please help me!' she said.

Balint was going to ask her for more details but Aron gave him a look to tell him he would explain later and the widow Olajos left quickly, nervously looking around as she went in case anyone had seen her.

'I know about this business,' he said. 'It all happened in our neighbourhood and it's quite hopeless. Victor Olajos was a tricky customer, shrewd and restless, always up to something and probably none too honest. He may once have had some money but you never know with those people what goes on or where the truth really lies. The first wife's brother lived in America and when his sister died in childbirth this brother sent 10,000 dollars to be held by the Orphans' Court and invested for the child's benefit. He must have sensed that Olajos was pretty unreliable and he wanted to be sure of the boy's future. I remember it well because it was such a huge sum and so caused a great stir. Then we learned that Olajos had bought a big piece of land at Kortekapu. It was not good land and there was nothing on it but a run-down sawmill. I know it well as it's quite near our own place. We were all surprised when Olajos died and it came to light that he had somehow induced the Court to pay over to him, as his son's official guardian, the boy's whole capital, which had been worth about 50,000 crowns, and had then somehow persuaded the officials of the Court that it had all been invested in a piece of land worth no more, at best, than 20,000 crowns.

'To make matters worse, Olajos had never kept up payments on the mortgage with which the property had been encumbered when he bought it and so, when he died, the company had foreclosed and the property been sold by auction for a mere song. The widow and child were now penniless, because it seemed that Olajos had nothing of his own. There can be no doubt that the Orphans' Court acted irresponsibly and it was certainly very odd that Olajos, who had a very bad reputation, had been able to persuade it to hand the money over to him at all. I fancy he must have had some crony in the office who had influence with the chairman of the Court, old Bartokfay, who was honest but naïve, a real "Hail, fellow, well-met!" sort of type.'

'So you think there's nothing we can do?'

'Nothing! And we can't even ask old Bartokfay, who's not been at all himself since his stroke in the spring.'

Balint found himself strangely affected by this story, which impressed him all the more since he had such a high regard for the notary Daniel Kovacs. And so it was the memory of the widow Olajos's sad predicament which influenced him when he came to make his speech at the provincial assembly held at Maros-Torda at the end of November.

One of the principal items on the agenda was the resignation of Bartokfay, the acceptance of his dictated letter of resignation and the choice of a successor. The old chairman of the Court had been very popular, especially with all the junior officials who mostly belonged to the radical 1848 Party, as opposed to the senior men who, led by Miklos Absolon, were aggressive supporters of the 1867 Compromise. Here, therefore, was one more example of a confrontation between the two basic political opponents in Hungarian politics – those who wanted complete independence and those who supported the union with Austria.

For some reason Absolon did not appear and so it was left to Beno Peter Balogh, the former Provincial Notary who had lost his job when the Coalition government came to power, to lead the party at the meeting. Though the Independence Party were now in the majority enough of the unionists were present to show that they were still a power to be reckoned with. Successive speakers praised the virtues of the retiring chairman, and even of his uncle who, many years before, had been the local Member of Parliament. Someone proposed a motion to perpetuate the memory of Bartokfay, who, it was said in a sly reference to the upheavals of 1848, had lived through 'stirring times' and whose sterling virtues should never be forgotten. The text barely mentioned his official activities but was principally composed of grandiloquent phrases more suited to heartening troops before a battle than to commemorating an aged politician.

Abady sat on a bench at the side. The proceedings irritated and annoyed him and so he refrained from speaking himself. As delegate after delegate rose and added their praises for the truly exceptional qualities of the departing chairman, so Abady found himself thinking more and more of the story told by the widow Olajos. He was all the more upset because, after hearing of that case at Lelbanya, several others had been brought to his attention, all concerning the property of orphans and all seeming to point, at the best, to culpable negligence.

It was really monstrous, he thought, that today so many people should go out of their way to heap praise on a man who had clearly been so slipshod in carrying out his responsibilities and who probably deserved censure and possibly even disciplinary action rather than these hymns of praise. And, as no one present seemed inclined to tell the truth, he decided that he himself must say something so that at least there would be some record in the minutes. The best moment, he thought, would not be now during all these farewell eulogies but later when it came to the election of Bartokfay's successor. Then he would get up and mention, in general terms, that there had been several short-comings in the past administration of the Orphans' Court and that knowledge of these would be the best lesson for the future. After all, few matters deserved closer scrutiny than the well-being of orphans who could not look after themselves.

At long last, amid prolonged cheers, the Prefect Ordung rose, added his own sycophantic words of praise, and obtained a unanimous vote in favour of the motion beatifying old Bartokfay.

Then he asked the meeting to nominate a new chairman for the Chancery Court.

Now Abady rose and asked if he might say a few words. Speaking calmly and in measured tones, he said that he had no inten-tion of denigrating the departing chairman and certainly not of impugning his honesty or personal integrity. However it should not be allowed to be passed over that recently the administration of the Orphans' Court had left much to be desired.

Murmurs of consternation ran through the hall. Bartokfay's nephew, an emotional man who had succeeded his father as local member and who had been reduced to tears during the sustained eulogies to his uncle, now rose and thundered, 'I won't listen to a word of such rubbish!'

As if it had been a signal other people now leapt to their feet and shouted, 'How do you know that? How can you say such things? Proof? Where's the proof?' while others called out, 'The noble Lord's a Unionist, that's why he talks like that!' These last remarks at once brought supporters of the last government to Abady's side and they too jumped up, calling, 'Hear! Hear!' And so the delegates split into two opposing factions; not, of course, that they thought for a moment about the truth of the matter for now there was a party line to follow.

The angriest faction was composed of those belonging to the

party in power, the strident supporters of separation from Vienna. They it was who called out, 'This is libel! Calumny! Trumped-up charges! Let's have some proof or shut up and apologize!' And these last remarks were like a battle-cry for Abady's supporters who now hoped to hear something to discredit their enemies and so joined in the cries of 'All right! Proof! Let's have the proof! Out with it!'

When the noise had subsided a little, Balint raised his hand. Everyone fell silent, eager to hear the worst.

'If you want proof, I can supply it,' said Abady; and without mentioning the widow's name he told her story hoping that that would be enough to satisfy them. Not at all. Although the ranks of the Independents at first seemed disconcerted they soon rallied when Abady's own supporters reacted with peals of artificial laughter, and then Bela Varju, one of the most fervent of the 1848 Party, let out a roar like a bull bison and scornfully shouted, 'Out with it! Tell us the names! We need real proof; without the names it's obviously pure invention. Calumny, no less!'

And so what had so often happened to Abady before now happened again. He was forced to go much further than had been his original intention. When he had risen to speak he had only wanted to make the point that new rules should be adopted by the Orphans' Court so as to ensure strict surveillance of the Court's administration of the children's assets. Now he had been so deflected from his original purpose that he could not even declare it. His intervention had been taken as a piece of party political aggression and his disinterested proposition turned into a basis for party dissension. Without mentioning a single name he found himself branded as a slanderer.

Abady had no choice but to tell the full tale, leaving nothing out and mentioning all the names. Happily he made no mistakes as, in matter-of-fact tones, he related names, dates, sums of money – the whole sad little tale. This dispassionate approach had a remarkably cooling effect on the Independence Party members, not a few of whom remembered some of the circumstances. But on Abady's own supporters the effect was the opposite. Instead of the artificial laughter with which they had greeted such an insignificant tale they now took it up as a real scandal and, with equally insincere indignation, called out, 'There you are! Didn't we tell you? Monstrous! Outrageous!'

Ordung rang his bell for order. In his powerful voice he called for silence, threatening, if he were not obeyed, to take disciplinary action against those who disturbed the dignity of the meeting. With hatred in his eyes he turned to Abady and asked, 'I would like to ask the speaker if he has anything further to say?'

'I have,' said Abady; and in a few words he outlined his original proposition. Then he sat down.

'As this proposal does not figure on the agenda,' ruled the Prefect, 'it cannot now be discussed. It shall be passed to the committee of the Orphans' Court.'

Abady got up and left the room. He fled, not from the anger of the party whose representative had been attacked, but rather from those who had rallied to his side. This they had done, he was forced to accept, not because they thought he was right or that justice ought to be done, but solely out of party interest, for to them nothing else mattered.

Abady's intervention had unexpected consequences.

Two days later an article appeared in the Independence Party's local newspaper; it was signed by the lawyer Zsigmond Boros. The subject was Abady's words 'the Orphans' Court should inspect more closely the manner in which the orphans' assets have been invested'. Balint had phrased it in those words so as not to impugn Bartokfay's personal integrity. Boros used this phrase to attack Abady.

He wrote that he did not doubt the widow Olajos had believed everything she had recounted to Count Abady. He wished only to elucidate the facts. Five years earlier the mill and the land had indeed been worth 50,000 crowns, as he personally had confirmed when Bartokfay had asked for his professional opinion. This he would declare to the whole world. The problem, as he saw it, was that Olajos had defaulted on his mortgage payments, which had amounted to some 12,000 crowns, and had completely neglected the maintenance of the mill. He, Boros, could hardly be held responsible for that! There followed a few well-turned sentences, designed to touch the hearts of his readers, about how the old chairman was now incapacitated by illness and attacked when he could no longer defend himself. Then followed a number of equally well-turned but poisonous phrases about the thoughtless aristocrat who was rash enough to meddle with things he knew nothing about.

Balint was taken by surprise by this unprovoked attack. He had no idea that such a prominent man as Boros had been in any way connected with procuring that dubious property for the Olajos boy. Reading the article, it was now clear that Boros had come out into the open only because he had assumed that Balint had, for some purpose of his own, withheld the lawyer's name and so, with this counter-attack, he hoped to forestall the criticism that might follow further revelations. After all it was not easy to prove the value of property, especially after the passage of years.

It was a clever article, self-assured, authoritative and calm in tone and its venom was partially concealed by the manner adopted, the patronizing manner of an older and more experienced man telling the facts of life to a blundering youth.

Balint felt unable to ignore this now personal attack, and so he sent a short statement to the newspaper maintaining everything that he had said at the meeting.

From such a trivial and inadvertent incident was started the avalanche that finally brought about the downfall of the mighty Dr Zsigmond Boros.

Countess Roza developed another persistent cold that autumn and again decided to follow her doctor's advice and spend the winter by the Mediterranean. This time she went to Abbazia which had been suggested by Balint who was unhappy about the course of international events and thought it better that she should remain on Austro-Hungarian soil. Though naturally he had said nothing to his mother about the possibilities of war and its inevitable consequences, the old lady had understood.

This time she did not protest or need to be persuaded, as had been the case two years before when she had been to Portofino. Ever since the scene that had occurred when Balint had told her of his plans to marry Adrienne, relations between mother and son had remained cold. Whatever signs of love or trust they sought to display both knew it was mere play-acting; for the truth was that whenever they were together Adrienne's invisible presence was always there too, an adored picture in the son's eyes, a baleful and hated vision in the mother's. And so she left willingly and without demur, knowing that if she were to remain in Kolozsvar she would inevitably hear daily the name of the hated woman she believed to have enticed and seduced her beloved son. To remain therefore might have led to another disagreeable scene between her and Balint and the idea of wintering at

Abbazia came as a welcome solution, an escape that neither could have construed as surrender. Her son accompanied her on the voyage. After a few days in Budapest they took the express train to Fiume, and it was a sign of those troubled times that it was delayed for five hours on the way. The immediate cause was the movement of troops, for the long military transport trains were too much for the small provincial stations where they had to wait. When these had been constructed there had been peace for so long that no one had thought of anything but ordinary civilian traffic. Balint was filled with misgivings when his train stopped and he found himself face to face with crowds of young reservists who had been called back to the colours. He felt only slight re-assurance when he recalled Tisza's words about the possibility of a peaceful solution.

They stayed at a hotel by the sea and Balint remained with his mother until after the New Year. The tension between them was unabated but he had no reason to remain at home that year. Young Margit's wedding had been on December 10th, celebrated with much pomp, with hundreds of guests many of whom, like the bridal couple, had worn traditional Hungarian festive dress. Balint, of course, had been invited but Adrienne had asked him not to come as too many people's eyes would be upon them. As soon as the wedding was over Adrienne wanted to be free to start making plans for her divorce and she felt it would be better to take every precaution to avoid furnishing food for gossip. Also, to make things even more difficult, Adrienne, who had to act as mother of the bride, moved from the Uzdy villa on the Monostor road to the Laczoks' town house from which Margit was to be married. This meant, of course, that they would not be able to spend the nights alone together. Directly after the wedding it was planned that Adrienne should go to her father's place, where they would be joined at Christmas by the young couple and in this strictly family reunion there would be no place for Balint.

When Balint left his mother he went first to Denestornya. There he found a huge pile of letters waiting for him, far more than usual. Most of these came from people unknown to him, from such places as Csik, Gyergyo and Maros-Torda. Some of these letters merely wanted to congratulate him on his stand against injustice, but many of the others contained complaints and accusations and complicated accounts of problems for which his

help was asked. And almost every single letter told him something more about Boros, about some abuse which had resulted
in loss to the writer. One envelope contained merely two newspaper cuttings describing some lawsuit to do with a dispute about
forestlands together with an anonymous accusation that Boros
had dishonestly approved an agreement which was against his
client's interests. Nauseated, Balint threw it away.

It was clear that his speech at the meeting had been the root
cause of all this, and yet no one would have believed that Balint
had taken up the issue almost by accident and would have had
no idea that Boros was in any way implicated if the lawyer himself had not taken up the cudgels and protested his innocence so
publicly. Now all those who had suffered from Boros's dishonest
dealings saw in Balint a messiah who had been sent to smite the
hitherto mighty and untouchable lawyer.

Among the more serious letters there was one from Tamas
Laczok, the renegade younger brother of Count Jeno Laczok of
Var-Siklod, who was now working as an engineer in a Szekler-
owned railway company. His letter was peppered with phrases in
French, for it had been in Paris that he had obtained his professional diploma after many years of thoughtless dissipation and it
had been in the French colonies that he had gained his experience.

It started off *'Très cher ami . . .'* and went on to congratulate
Balint on taking issue with Boros. After a few light-hearted
remarks he turned to facts and figures and his subject was the
same forestry matter that had been reported in the newspaper
cuttings. It seemed that in the Gyergyo district a pine forest had
been bought by the Laczok Timber Company which had been
founded by 'my darling brother Jeno' and the banker Soma
Weissfeld to exploit the Laczok forests. Somehow, they had
arranged matters so that Count Jeno and the banker lived like
kings on their dividends while the younger brother, who held
a one-third share, received almost nothing. The company also
bought timber from a communally-owned forest nearby and this
was brought to the works by train. One day a spark from the
engine set the forest on fire and about three thousand acres were
destroyed. The loss amounted to millions of crowns. The community took the company to court, claiming damages and the
cost of replanting the trees. Zsigmond Boros was appointed
lawyer for the communal owners with power of attorney to settle
in their best interests. Boros had used his powers to obtain a

settlement out of court, even though it was most disadvantageous to the community who had lost so much of their forest. Despite protests at the community's next meeting the settlement had been reluctantly accepted, largely owing to the persuasive oratory of the famous lawyer. The letter went on:

> *J'ai tout de suite flairé une cochonnerie – I smelt a rat at once! Only now, after I read about your interest, did I come to my senses and start to check through the balance sheets of Laczok Timber. And what did I find? Boros got 80,000 crowns from us, discreetly paid through Weissfeld's bank. I have all the details and will send them to you if you wish. It's quite enough to hang the man!*

After a few French jokes Laczok brought his letter to an end with the words:

> *Now I am trying to get the community to have their case against our family firm reopened. Of course if they succeed I will be one of the losers but I wouldn't mind that as long as it brings down my beloved brother. He can drown in it for all I care; and my sister Alice too who has always hated me! I've never worked so hard at anything in all my life!*

Balint threw down the letter with distaste, even though he realized that what it contained was almost certainly true. It fitted in too neatly with Dinora's idle chatter at Denestornya that summer when she had admitted that Boros was daily expecting some large sum of money. But Tamas Laczok's hatred of his brother, which oozed out of every word he wrote, shocked and disgusted him. He would never have believed it of the good-humoured, good-tempered fellow he remembered meeting once at the inn at Vasarhely. Physically Tamas was the exact double of his brother Jeno. Short and thickset, they could have been twins, the only obvious difference being that while Jeno sported only a pair of imposing moustaches, Tamas also wore a beard. Perhaps, thought Balint, it's because they are so alike that they hate each other so much.

Most of these letters Balint just threw into an empty drawer but Tamas's letter he answered. He wrote that he had only spoken out in the public interest and did not intend to start a man-hunt. Then he put the affair out of his mind, thinking that now, as far as he was concerned, the matter was closed.

CHAPTER TWO

IT WAS NOT long before Boros got wind of what Tamas Laczok was up to and so to prevent the matter coming to court he quickly applied to his own professional body, the Vasarhely Law Society, for an enquiry into his conduct. Of course he was soon cleared of unprofessional dealings, for the settlement out of court had been legally accepted by all parties and, since the Law Society had no power to subpoena documents or witnesses, Tamas could produce no tangible evidence to back up his allegations. Boros took good care to see that the newspapers gave wide coverage to his vindication and even persuaded one of them to print in full the beautiful speech he had made in his defence. Then a banquet was held to celebrate his victory, with many toasts and speeches. Here, too, he made a speech and one sentence – in which he spoke of being 'stalked stealthily by evil men, the enemies of all independent thought, who sought to fling dirt at any champion of the people's freedom' – was loudly cheered, being taken as a reference to Abady. And so he stood there at the head of the table, proud and fearless, holding his head high and with his well-trimmed beard the very picture of virile innocence, to everyone present the personification of noble probity.

At about this time there appeared a short notice in the commercial columns of the Budapest papers. It announced that the State Railways had signed a ten-year contract giving the firm of Eisler a monopoly on supplying railway sleepers. Few people took much notice, for there were many far more important matters to think about.

In the New Year the Prime Minister and Kossuth, as leader of the Radical Party, announced an increase in the defence budget and also in the numbers to be called for compulsory military service.

When this became known some of the more extreme members of the Independence Party ran at once to Gyula Justh demanding an official protest from their party. Unexpectedly they received an uncompromising refusal. Justh, it appeared, had already agreed to the increase in conscription, and had not even tried to extort in exchange any concession to the other long-standing party demands such as the introduction of Hungarian as the army's official language of command. Everyone was taken by surprise as such a *volte-face* was the last thing anyone had expected of Justh. They did not then know, of course, that he had already thrown in his lot with the party surrounding the Heir and was secretly, through Kristoffy, conspiring to frustrate the liberalization of the voting franchise.

All this caused great excitement when the House reassembled. Then one of the directors of the National Bank made some indiscreet allusion to banking cartels and at once the followers of Hollo and Barra made such an uproar that no one paid any further attention to such matters as conscription and the army estimates. Never had there been such discord since the Coalition government came to power.

Nevertheless those in the timber business and landowners with forestry holdings were seriously upset by the deal between the State Railways and the firm of Eisler, because it meant inevitably that they would be at the mercy of the Austrian company who could depress the selling prices for sleepers at will since the State Railways company was almost the only buyer for that class of timber. The new arrangement was contrary to all established trading conditions imposed on the administration of public transport. However, as Kossuth had countersigned the monopoly contract, there was not much anyone could say in protest. Some of the timber companies tried to come to terms with the Eisler firm but the forest owners were slower to react. For the moment they said nothing.

Abady himself could think only about the news from abroad.

Almost every day the international situation shifted and changed as dramatically as a kaleidoscope. For the first ten days of January it seemed that war was inevitable. In Vienna the Ballplatz demanded an explanation and an apology for the harsh words uttered by the foreign minister of Serbia. No sooner had this storm subsided than the Montenegrins leapt to their feet proclaiming that they would go to war all on their own, if need be, should the great powers not at once settle their legitimate aspirations. Three days after that everything changed again when the results of the talks between Austria-Hungary and Turkey were made public and as the agreement included the acceptance by the Turks of the annexation of their former province, in return, of course, for an indemnity of some 54 millions, the Serbs found themselves obliged to stop their own protest. For a moment there was a lull ... until, all of a sudden, the news came that the Bulgarian army had been massed on the Turkish frontier and that there was general mobilization in Serbia.

All this was treated by the Press, as much abroad as in Budapest, in somewhat subdued tones; but Balint had learned to read between the lines during his years as a diplomat and it became more and more evident to him what a double role was being played by Russia. It was cleverly done but it seemed to him quite clear that while her foreign minister Izvolsky was presenting himself to the great powers as an international peacemaker, he was simultaneously inciting the Serbs to defy Vienna and doing all he could to subvert Bulgaria, who had been much more friendly before the crisis.

There was a further development when Russia agreed to pay an indemnity as a *quid pro quo* for Turkey's dropping her claims to Bulgaria. This was easy enough, for Turkey had owed this sum – and much more – to Russia for more than forty years and, by writing it off in this way, a debt that would never have been paid was settled by the stroke of a pen, while Prince Ferdinand could henceforth be greeted as King of Bulgaria by the Tsar at St Petersburg. Nevertheless things were not quite what they seemed, for when Izvolsky told the Russian Duma of the Berlin agreement, which gave Austria-Hungary a free hand in her dealings with Serbia, he also declared Russian support for the southern Slavs, thus heralding the subsequent formation of the Balkan Federation which, three years later, was to attack Turkey and make a mockery of Vienna's cherished Eastern policies.

As always, these things were hardly noticed by the Hungarians, and life went on as usual in Budapest. Among the party political leaders only Andrassy saw clearly where these events were leading; but he was powerless to act for it was now the great banking issue which occupied everyone's minds. The alliance between Kossuth and Justh was beginning to wear extremely thin, with one of them supporting the idea of an independent national bank and the other carrying the banner of the traditional links with Vienna. The leaders of the Independence Party could not make up their minds and cheered on alternatively one side or the other. Still it was becoming clear that while Kossuth's position was progressively weakened so Justh became more and more the choice of the majority.

* * *

All this time Abady felt like a sleepwalker. He moved about automatically and had never before felt himself to be a stranger in his own country. His thoughts were only for the sinister developments abroad and for all those otherwise insignificant pointers to what was now going on in those circles close to the monarch and his heir. At Jablanka, where he went for three days' shooting, they spoke of little else. It was most elegantly done, as was natural in that house, and few words were wasted, for Antal Szent-Gyorgyi did not relish vulgar enthusiasm or indeed any form of exaggeration. But for those with ears to hear the message was clear enough. This time Slawata was not there . . . but the faithful Pfaffulus, as always, was exceptionally well informed.

The foreign minister Aehrenthal, it seemed, was anxious to settle everything peacefully. As a career diplomat he naturally favoured making agreements without resorting to force, for if the guns were once fired then any subsequent arrangement would be due to the military and not to the diplomatists. For him the true art of foreign politics lay in sitting around a baize-covered table until war was definitely avoided. Opposing this view the war minister, Conrad, strongly urged a sudden attack to eliminate the Serbian opposition, draw Bulgaria back into the Austrian fold and restore the Monarchy's dwindling prestige in the Balkans. In this he may have been right. It was certainly the last moment when such a move would have been possible, for most of the other great powers had let Austria know that she had a free hand in the matter while Russia was not yet ready to intervene. However the Emperor wanted peace and so, for once, did Franz-Ferdinand, for though he detested Aehrenthal because of his support for Hungarian national aspirations, he hated Conrad even more. In Vienna, therefore, there was a triangular battle behind the scenes in which personal animosity carried more weight than political acumen.

During these winter months it was only possible for Balint and Adrienne to see each other sporadically. Adrienne was busy arranging to spend more and more time away from her husband so as to accustom him to her absence. Had she come to Kolozsvar they could have often been together now that Margit had flown the nest and so, knowing that she would not have been able to resist the temptation, she went to her father's house for weeks on end on the pretext that old Count Akos was not well and that Judith's condition had taken a turn for the worse. In this way she could prepare the ground for her divorce, for as yet she did not dare either raise the subject or do anything to bring it about. Her little daughter was still at Meran with her husband's mother and she was convinced that Countess Clémence would never let the child go back to her mother if she caught the slightest whiff of Adrienne's plans for divorce. And under no circumstances did she wish to risk the little girl being left with the half-mad Pali Uzdy. So she had to be careful.

It would only, she told herself and Balint, be for a few more months, but until then they had both to be very circumspect and meet only occasionally and for brief encounters, lest anything should happen to destroy their chances.

Now their aim was not only to be always together, possessing each other and wanting nothing more as in the first days of their love. Their longing for a child had become their deepest desire and the phantom boy who held their minds in thrall became more and more real to them as each day passed. In their letters they wrote of little else.

In Adrienne it was symptomatic of the deepest of all female instincts, the urge to give birth and be a mother. It was the strongest expression of a woman's love that she could give what to them both would be the most precious gift, the richest in shared joy and rejoicing. And the greatest gift any woman can give a man is the child of their love, borne in joyfully accepted pain and in danger of her life.

This is what Adrienne felt during those months and it was with growing joy that she read in Balint's letters how he shared her yearning. It was a double joy for she knew that the desire to be a father was not natural to all men but rather an acquired social instinct, unknown to primitive peoples and only fostered by the growth of civilization. Even so the urge was strong in some men and Adrienne was all the more grateful that it was so strong in Balint.

Sometimes in Balint's letters he referred to the themes he had taken up in his unfinished treatise 'Beauty in Action', when he tried to show that all the beauty in the world stemmed from a law of nature. Then he had been under the influence of the first mutual declaration of their love for each other. Now, that Beauty was to be the beauty of their future lives together when they could declare their love to the world and live freely and frankly without lies or pretence. And the culmination of this freedom would be the birth of an heir, who would carry on his race and all that his parents held sacred. This heir would love everything they loved, their honour, traditions and the family home where these had been nurtured. He in turn would pass it all on to the next generation, and the next, and the next, for an infinity of human tradition in which Balint saw himself merely as a link in that never-ending chain which tied the past to the future. In this way his love for Adrienne, which had begun as desire to possess the woman he loved, was gradually transformed, by the idea of this longed-for birth of a son, into the adoration for the most beautiful and graceful of mothers.

After his return to Budapest Balint went once or twice to visit his mother at Abbazia, but he never stayed more than a few days lest the joy of seeing each other again should wear thin and the suppressed enmity between them be allowed to surface again.

One day at the end of February when he entered his hotel on returning from Abbazia, the hall porter told him that a Mr Frankel, the managing director of a timber firm that handled the produce of the Abady forests, had come twice to see him. Balint assumed that he wanted to discuss some matter relating to his own affairs and, as he was rather pressed to complete writing the speech in which he would support a new bill in Parliament concerning the co-operative societies, he decided for the moment to delay telling Frankel of his return.

He was sitting at his desk, surrounded by charts and tables and other statistics, when at about noon the door was quietly opened and Dinora Malhuysen slipped into the room.

'What are you doing, Little Boy?' she asked from the door. 'Working hard, I suppose. My! How important we've become!' She laughed as she came towards him. Then she lightly tapped his cheek and sank down into an armchair, opening as she did so the soft chinchilla collar round her throat. She leaned back.

'Dear Dinora, what an unexpected pleasure!'

'Unexpected? Naturally! Anyway, you can talk! You never once came to see me! It wasn't at all nice of you. You've never even seen my lovely new flat in Szemelynok Street. You can't spend all your time at that boring Parliament. Couldn't you spare a moment to come and see me ... or don't you want to?'

Balint smiled. 'Of course I do. I love seeing you!'

'Well then? But, seriously, I've always thought of you as my best friend, perhaps the only one. That's why I came ... I have something important to ask you. Will you do it, Little Boy? Do you remember "Little Boy"?' and Dinora's sensuous lips framed the little phrase with special significance because it had been her special nickname for him when they had been lovers. Even so her eyes revealed how anxious she was.

'If you tell me what it is, and if I can, then I will, of course.'

'I knew you would! Well, it's like this, Zsig ... Zsigmond Boros, you know who I mean, well, he's been very good to me, and I want to ask you – please don't do anything to harm him. You won't, will you? Please don't! It'd be such a little thing to you, but to me it's very important. And he's not a bad man, not really. You won't do anything, will you? For my sake?'

Balint frowned. He realized that it must have been Boros himself who had sent his mistress to plead for him, that darling foolish scatter-brained little Dinora; but as he had no intention of pursuing Boros anyway he promised to desist quite easily.

'Don't worry, darling Dinora, I won't hurt him. You can rely on that.'

She jumped up and pressed her lips to his and kissed him repeatedly, saying each time, 'Thank you, thank you, thank you!'

When he was finally able to disentangle himself Balint said, 'You know I never said anything about Boros at that meeting at Vasarhely. I didn't even know that he was in any way involved in ... in that sort of thing.'

'Oh, you are good! Good and kind! I'm so relieved, so glad,' and she started to twirl about the room in a little light-hearted dance of joy. Then she stopped and looked coquettishly back at Balint. 'You know ... if ever you're bored I'm always ... well, I wouldn't hold you to anything...' and her eyes made it clear that this was the only way she knew to express her gratitude.

'Thank you, my sweet Dinora, but at present I am not bored,' he said with a smile, though the truth was that indeed he was, bored and unhappy; but to share her with someone like Boros? It would be better, he decided, to avoid her for a little while.

'That's quite all right. I only said it so that you'd know and ... Well, goodbye now, goodbye.' And she went out as swiftly as she had come in.

That same afternoon the porter rang up to say that Mr Frankel had called. Balint, who was tired from all the work he had been doing, was only too pleased to be interrupted and so asked for him to be sent up.

Frankel had not come to discuss the affairs of the Abady forest holdings. He came for something quite different, and he brought with him a whole stack of official-looking papers. These proved to be copies of documents and correspondence between the Ministry of Trade and the State Railways concerning the monopoly contract signed by the Minister with the Eisler Timber Company. There was also one other paper; it was a photograph of a receipt for 100,000 crowns given to Dr Boros by Eisler and Company.

'I am aware,' said Frankel, 'that your Lordship has already referred publicly to Dr Boros's activities. That is why I have made so bold as to bring these documents for your perusal. Should your Lordship feel disposed to take up this matter, which is of the greatest possible interest both to forest owners and to the timber trade, both of which feel that a most unfair irregularity has been committed and that the contract would be sure to be cancelled if the whole truth were known.'

For a moment Balint did not answer. He looked through the documents that Frankel had brought, and as he did so he realized why it was that Dinora had so hurriedly come to see him that morning. It could only have been that Boros had somehow heard that the timber merchants had got something on him and were about to appeal to Abady for help, and that he had sent Dinora hotfoot to forestall them.

The papers that Frankel had brought were irrefutable proof of the irregularity and dishonesty of the official proceedings and Boros's signed receipt spelt professional death at that time when to be found out was the ultimate sin.

'Why,' asked Abady as he handed back the dossier, 'do you come to me? There are many other Members who speak more frequently than I do and whose words carry more weight. Any one of them would handle this matter far better than I would. I ... I ... am really not the best man for it.'

Frankel shook his head.

'Only your Lordship could do this properly. Dr Boros has a high position in the Independence Party and the deal was signed by Kossuth. No one in the party would handle it and there is no one who has left the party who would be taken seriously. Almost no one would be likely to come forward from the Constitution or People's Parties because the only person capable of achieving their policies as regards the general franchise or the banking question would be Kossuth, and he is clearly as much out of the running as Justh. What we need is someone who is truly independent, who has no party ties and who cannot be suspected of any motive of personal gain. Your Lordship owns forests, it is true, but they do not produce timber suitable for railway sleepers. Everyone would know that Count Abady spoke only in the public interest.'

'All the same I will not do it,' said Abady drily. 'Kossuth is an honourable man who certainly signed in good faith. The only thing you can accuse him of is ignorance or gullibility; and in so doing you cast a slur on him he does not deserve. No! I will not do it.'

'Pity,' said Frankel as he got up and replaced the dossier in his briefcase. Then he added, 'If your Lordship should at any time change your mind and need these papers they will always be at your disposal.' Then he said goodbye and left the room.

Balint smiled as the door closed behind his departing visitor. He knew that he would never have agreed to do as Frankel wished, but it pleased him all the same that he had been able so soon to keep his promise to Dinora.

The new tax proposals were bitterly attacked in Parliament, and in particular the concessions to the co-operatives. At that time so much importance was given to the principle of private enterprise that people even saw injustice if the state reduced the burden on organizations designed to help the under-privileged.

Most of the members looked askance at the whole co-operative movement, partly because its principal supporters were Sandor Karolyi, Gyorgy Banffy, Zselinsky and Aurel Dessewffy, all of them aristocrats. Istvan Bernath and Rubinak were country-bred members of the Agrarian Party which favoured giving voting rights to agricultural workers and in any case kept well away from everyday political issues while avoiding allegiance to any party. Others objected on obscure theoretical grounds of their own.

The principle of free enterprise, unhampered by any control of prices, was held sacrosanct, as were the traditional notions of astronomy. In 1908 people were not to know that even these last were soon to be challenged by Einstein's theory of relativity! In the popular view anything that deviated from what was held to be the accepted order of matters economic, anything that gave added value to state enterprises or indeed any other concern, however altruistic, was held to be a sin against received truth – for such was the usual view of the principle of free enterprise.

And so the new tax proposals, especially as regards the co-operatives, which, though presented by the Minister-President Wekerle had been worked out by Daranyi, the Minister for Agriculture, were hotly contested. No one seemed to notice that by so doing they were not only giving support to those owners of village stores and innkeepers who lent money at exorbitant interest, but also penalizing the peasants who actually worked the land.

There were also those who supported the Bill, and among them was Abady.

This time he spoke better than he had two years before, so much so that he was listened to with interest, especially by Daranyi, who once or twice nodded his approval. Even so it was clear to him that the majority did not take the co-operatives all that seriously. Doubtless they thought some other matters more pressing, especially as at that very moment the banking questions were being discussed in committee in another room.

Every now and then members would rush into the chamber with news of how matters were going at the committee session and how the atmosphere there was getting hotter and hotter. Finally it was heard that the government had managed to get the discussion adjourned before it had been taken to a vote.

Balint gathered up his papers and stepped out into the corridor where he found a large group of other Members all discussing the day's affairs. On the far side stood Boros who, when he saw Abady, made a movement as if he would walk over to congratulate him. As it happened he only started to make such a movement as Balint quickened his pace and passed by swiftly. This happened so rapidly that no one noticed – but Boros knew instinctively that Abady had hurried away on purpose, and in this he was perfectly right, for Balint really had felt disinclined to shake hands with the lawyer in front of so many people. To do so would have been tantamount to telling the world that they were friends.

For a brief moment Boros watched Abady walk away. He frowned, then he turned once again to the group who were still deep in discussion of the banking question.

At once he dominated the argument, giving his opinion precisely and in the most lucid language. He defended Kossuth's view
even though it was opposed by the committee, and explained
why the link with Austrian banking was so important. He found
some touching phrases to describe the ailing party leader and
indeed he served his master well for, at least as long as he was
speaking, even Justh's followers found themselves in agreement.
And, as always, he spoke beautifully, tear-wringing phrases fell
from his mouth expressed in sonorous tones as rich as any cathe-
dral organ. He was a master of oratory, ready, no matter how
hard-pressed by worries, to express the most beautiful sentiments, using his voice like a well-tuned instrument from which
he could obtain whatever effects he desired.

At this time he really did have a great deal on his mind. Since
the meeting at Vasarhely quite a number of his clients seemed to
have lost faith in him. For many years he had had the management of a number of private fortunes. Most of the landowners
in the Maros valley lived entirely by the advice he gave and even
left their money and their valuables in his care. Nobody had ever
questioned his accounts or enquired how their money had been
invested. Now everything had changed. Boros was besieged
with letters every day, some making polite enquiries, but others
there were who demanded immediate and detailed statements
of account. Some made sinister references to the law and legal
obligations.

Boros's first action was to do what he had always done: he
robbed Peter to pay Paul, using one client's money to satisfy
another. This he had done for many years, optimistically assuming that he would never be unable to replace whatever was necessary out of the huge professional fees he earned. Hitherto this
system had served him well, but now everybody seemed to want
satisfaction at the same time. This spelt trouble.

And trouble it certainly was, for Boros had no reserves of any
kind. What he earned he spent, at once, and usually considerably
more. His home and family cost a lot, for his wife liked to cut a
dash at Vasarhely; but the real expense had been his annual
visits abroad to such fashionable watering-places as Deauville or
Biarritz where he lived the life of a bachelor whose hobby was
keeping beautiful women. Beautiful they were, of course, but
always very expensive. And recently there had been Dinora. He
had bought her a flat and furniture and many splendid presents.

He made out to her that it all came from the income of her property at Maros-Szilvas, but whatever he told her was never questioned by Dinora who merely enjoyed the life they led together. This life cost Boros a staggering sum, and the 100,000 crowns he had recently received were soon spent, as much of it had to be paid out to stop the clamouring mouths of suspicious clients. Even so it was not enough, for there were legions of them and as soon as one was satisfied his place was taken by others . . . more, and more, and more. Some he was able to send away with a draft without heeding that it might never be honoured.

Having calmed his parliamentary colleagues with his eloquence he left the building and went straight to Dinora's flat where he usually lunched even though he still lived in his own old apartment across the river in Buda. This arrangement was in any case soon to be ended for he had recently been able to acquire the top-floor flat above Dinora's and had planned to move there as soon as he had time to do so.

From the Parliament building to Dinora's was only a matter of a few hundred yards. By the time he arrived Boros had come to a decision.

Abady had neatly avoided him and this could not be accepted. He absolutely had to catch him and force him to shake hands where everyone could see. If he could do this all would be well, for it would be the equivalent of giving satisfaction, almost of an acknowledgement that Boros was blameless. If he did not shake hands then he must be challenged to a duel. That would perhaps be best, for a duel on such a serious matter would solve everything. When the legal year closed there was always calm for a few weeks. So it would be if he managed to shoot Abady, for people were such cowards that no one would blame him. And if the opposite occurred . . . well, that too would be a solution.

He rang for the lift attendant and as he went up he counted the floors, each marked by a faint clanking sound as he passed . . . two, three, four, five. His own flat was on the sixth floor, right at the top. When the lift gates were opened he looked first up and then down through the mesh of the lift shaft. They had come up in seconds – and yet it was a long way down.

Balint went to Transylvania for ten days, three of which he spent at Denestornya, two in the mountains, and the rest of the time at Kolozsvar so as to see Adrienne who had to pass through the town and stopped there just so that they could have a few hours together.

He returned to Budapest by the morning express and at the station found two of his acquaintances who were travelling by the same train. They were Count Adam Alvinczy, father of the four Alvinczy boys, and Tamas Laczok. Alvinczy seemed worried, as indeed he was for his son Farkas who was now in Parliament and had got himself so into debt that his father was going to Budapest to see what could be done to settle the problem.

Laczok was in radiant good humour.

'*Salut!*' cried Laczok as soon as he saw Balint approaching, and then explained that he too was on his way to the capital to deal with '*une énorme affaire*' which he would explain as soon as they were settled in the train.

'I found out,' he began, 'that the Minister of Agriculture is the final authority on all that concerns the affairs of community properties in the country districts' and so he was now on his way to the Ministry. Even though Abady – '*mon jeune ami*' – seemed disinclined to have any part in exposing the scandal of the settlement of the lawsuit against the Laczok Timber Company he, Tamas Laczok, was not the man to give up so easily. All right, it was possible that Boros had won the first round, had managed to have himself cleared of any underhand dealings by the Law Society's investigation and had even brought a suit for slander against the newspaper that had published the allegations against him; so he would now have to be tackled in a different way. This time Laczok would go direct to the Minister and demand that he send inspectors to the community concerned and take over its administration. If this happened then someone would be sure to talk. 'Here,' shouted Laczok, 'here are all the details they need. *Tous les documents, mon cher! Tous les documents!*'

Balint gazed at the squat little man with wry amusement. He was a bizarre figure, sitting there in the railway carriage, bolt upright like a Chinese statuette with long pointed beard and bald head. His slanting eyes glistened with eagerness and expectation and from time to time he slapped at his briefcase with his short fat arms and cried, '*Mon frère Jeno, il va en crever* – my brother Jeno will do a bust!'

My brother will do a bust! This was the only thing that really mattered to him: My brother will do a bust!

* * *

Once again the capital was bombarded with disquieting news from abroad. Troops were sent to the southern border; and, even more seriously, the government declared the imposition of censorship.

In Russia the foreign minister Izvolsky told the Austro-Hungarian ambassador that though his masters were at one with the other great powers they still wanted an international conference to discuss the Bosnian annexation. Hope flared in Belgrade where everyone clamoured for war.

The Ballplatz replied by leaking the fact that Serbia would soon be issued with an ultimatum; but the Serbs went on mobilizing just the same.

The Monarchy found itself on the threshold of war.

While the storm clouds gathered both the Austrian and the Hungarian Parliaments found themselves beset with other problems. In Vienna the recent concessions to Budapest concerning the administration of the joint armies were violently attacked, and this despite the fact that both the foreign minister Aehrenthal and the war minister agreed that they were a good basis for the modernizing of the army. Behind these attacks stood the sinister figure of the Heir to the throne. Franz-Ferdinand did nothing himself; but it was his intimate friends who provoked all these attacks, and they did it on his orders.

In Budapest parliamentary business was in a turmoil with everything turned upside-down. The committee considering the banking question threw out all the proposals put before it and this was taken as a triumph by the men surrounding Justh, who did not even try to conceal their joy.

Those radical followers of Hollo and Barra stamped about the corridors of the House like generals after a great victory and if their footsteps did not resound it was only because the carpets were so thick. The government was powerless and only remained in office because of the foreign situation.

This was the atmosphere that Abady found in the corridors of the House. Here he found the scent of triumph too strong to be supported, and so he retired to the almost deserted drawing-room.

For almost half an hour he allowed himself to be bored to distraction by Isti Kamuthy who mouthed endless political platitudes at him – all, of course, from what Isti believed to be the soundest of English sources – until he suddenly noticed that Zsigmond Boros had just entered the room by a door on the opposite side. Out of the corner of his eye Balint saw the lawyer look around and at once realized that he was probably looking for him. Indeed he started to walk towards him in a most decided manner.

Balint took out his watch, glanced at it and turned quickly to Isti. 'I must run! *Servus!*' he said quickly and turning away left the room abruptly. Little Isti was much put out as he was right in the middle of what he considered to be a very clever sentence indeed.

CHAPTER THREE

THAT AFTERNOON TWO Members of Parliament came to call upon Abady. They were well-known seconds who were always employed when any matters of honour were concerned and had acted at the duel when old Keglevitch had been killed by a thrust to the heart.

'On behalf of our friend Zsigmond Boros,' said the elder of the two, 'we have come to demand satisfaction. Our friend could not help noticing that your Lordship intentionally and most offensively rose and turned away when our friend was about to greet him this morning. According to our friend this was not the first time that such a thing has occurred but until this morning our friend could not be sure that your Lordship's apparent attitude was intentional. Today, however, it was so obvious as to leave no room for doubt.'

Balint answered icily, 'I am free to come and go as I please, am I not?'

'Of course, but our friend is entitled to feel himself insulted if someone leaves the room because of him.'

Now the other second spoke up. 'Our friend will only be satisfied if your Lordship declares most solemnly that he did not intentionally avoid Dr Zsigmond Boros and, on the contrary, that he holds him in high esteem. Furthermore our friend demands that your Lordship beg his pardon verbally in front of witnesses as well as in writing!'

At this Balint started to laugh. 'I really see no reason to beg anyone's pardon, let alone Dr Boros's. However,' he went on seriously, 'I suppose you had better be in touch with my seconds. Please inform me where they can find you tomorrow morning. I am not sure that I can be in touch with them any earlier.'

'From ten o'clock ... at the House.'

They bowed stiffly and left the room.

What an absurd performance, thought Balint – stupid, stupid, stupid! Perhaps it had been rather conspicuous, the way he had got up and left the room so suddenly. Of course it had been clumsily done, but what had been the alternative? However the fact that Boros would not be satisfied by a simple straightforward explanation but was pressing for what amounted to a Certificate of Good Conduct made it clear that the lawyer wanted something beyond a normal settlement. What it was Balint did not then grasp, but in the meantime he would have to find seconds himself. He had no idea who to ask; certainly no one in politics or this would become a political affair.

Then he realized it might be best to get someone from Transylvania, someone serious who was unlikely to do or say anything foolish and who was respected by everyone. Far better go to one of his own countrymen. Keep it in the family!

His recent travelling companion, the older Adam Alvinczy, occurred to him. It was the ideal solution, for Count Adam had acted in a number of such affairs of honour and always with restraint and good sense, though he was no genius when it came to brains. Although his son Farkas was a Member of Parliament he sat as an independent, so that no one could say there was any political reason for Balint having chosen his father.

He asked the hall porter of his hotel to telephone round and find out where Alvinczy was staying. He soon had the answer: it was the Pannonia Hotel and Count Alvinczy was at home at that moment.

Balint had himself driven there at once, and the old gentleman agreed with alacrity, asking only who should be asked to act with him.

'I leave that to you,' replied Balint. 'I should prefer whoever it is also to be from Transylvania, but it doesn't really matter. I don't think anyone too young would be really suitable,' he added, so as to make sure that he did not ask Kamuthy.

'All right, my boy. I'll have a look round at once.'

Later that evening Balint, who was then at the Casino Club, was called to the telephone.

'I just wanted to let you know that I've found the ideal man, someone who fits your needs perfectly. I have asked him without waiting to consult you. It's Miklos Absolon, who is staying at Rudas having treatment for his bad leg.'

'Oh!' said Balint. 'Oh! Absolon!' and there was no mistaking the disappointment in his voice. The old man noticed at once and said, 'Don't you like him? I thought you'd be pleased!'

'Well, yes, of course he's an excellent choice; but he's hotly opposed to the Independence Party at home in Maros-Torda, while Boros is their champion there ... so people might think there was something political in all this.'

'I hadn't thought of that!' said the older man. 'But you did authorize me to act and as he's already accepted it would be difficult to go back on it now.'

'Oh, no, for Heaven's sake! Not now! Anyway I'm very grateful and you're the man in charge. You've far more experience than I have in these affairs, so I trust your judgement.'

'You can rely on me,' Alvinczy assured him, 'to see that no irrelevant side issues are brought into this. But thank you for warning me all the same.'

The next day Balint was visited by Alvinczy and Absolon who had already spoken to Boros's seconds.

'What they want is quite absurd. It's sufficiently unusual to ask for an apology,' said Alvinczy, after telling Abady that they had insisted on exactly what they had demanded the day before, 'but to ask you to humble yourself publicly is really going too far. I will not agree!' He then added that they now said that if their demands were not accepted they would insist upon the most punitive conditions allowed by the duelling code.

As yet Miklos Absolon had held his peace. Now he placed his short crutch on a nearby table and his bad leg on the chair opposite him. Balint noticed with renewed amazement how much he looked like his nephew Pali Uzdy, despite not being tall and having such broad shoulders. He must once have been a powerful man, reflected Balint and, looking at his typically Tartar face with its wide cheekbones, it was easy to believe that, when he travelled Tibet in disguise, people really took him for a Kirgiz nomad.

He took out a very black cigar and in one movement bit off

the end with his snow-white teeth, spat it out, and said, 'As I see it the essence of the matter is this: did you avoid shaking hands with Boros on purpose or not? If it was sheer chance, then you shake hands now and that will be an end of it. If on the other hand – and this I'd find quite natural – you avoided him deliberately, then the matter is quite different.' His slanting eyes glistened as he looked hard at Balint. 'So answer that, my boy!'

'I knew exactly what I was doing. I did it on purpose.'

'May I ask why?'

Abady hesitated. Then he said, 'That I would prefer not to say!'

'So,' said the old explorer mockingly. 'You don't want to say. Well, well!' He took his leg off the chair in front of him, stamped it on the ground and then looked up seriously at the younger man. 'I must tell you that if you will not explain yourself because you have given your word of honour not to, or if a woman is involved, you need not answer. In all other cases you are obliged to do so. We are your seconds and we have a right to know.'

'I don't agree,' said Alvinczy mildly, because he did not care for Absolon's hectoring tone and had been fidgeting in his chair since he had begun his interruption. 'If Abady doesn't want to say . . . well, that's his affair and does not concern us.'

'But it does!' shouted Absolon, curling back his lips in a snarl. 'If our young friend has good reasons to refuse to shake hands with Boros then we have to know what they are. Would you allow him to engage in what might be a mortal contest with an unworthy opponent, someone who may not even have the right to fight a duel? Just think of it: Balint might be killed and the truth only come to light when it was too late. It would be unthinkably negligent on our part to let such a thing happen. It *does* concern us and it is our responsibility!'

At the word 'responsibility' Alvinczy caved in.

'I'm sorry! You are right, of course, absolutely right.' From then on the discussion was conducted entirely by Absolon. Balint realized that he had to answer their question. So he explained, as briefly as possible, that since the Vasarhely meeting he had been sent a pile of documents all accusing Boros of dishonesty and corrupt pleading. Some of the tales may have been exaggerated but many were obviously true enough. That was why he did not wish to shake hands with the man and, since he had not consciously intended to offend Boros, he regretted that the lawyer had noticed it. 'But I would rather fight with him,' he said, 'than publish all that dirt. I don't want to destroy him, it's not in my nature, but neither do I want anyone to think that I raked all this up just to save my own skin.'

'So you'd rather shoot it out with a rogue like him. That's what he is and we both know it!'

'Yes,' said Balint drily. 'And that's why I'm asking you not to make any use whatever of what I've just told you!'

'Indeed! I see.'

There was silence for a moment while Balint and Absolon looked hard at each other. Then the old traveller started to laugh, 'All right then, we agree . . . but I'll keep it in mind all the same.'

Now it was Alvinczy's turn to object. He burst out, saying, 'Excuse me, my friends, but I cannot and will not agree. It is contrary to all the rules,' and he started to explain that it was quite wrong to allow the man they represented to face a possible death just because he refused to reveal his reasons. 'No! No! No!'

Absolon reacted only with a superior smile. He got up, took his crutch in one hand and with the other patted old Alvinczy on the shoulder.

'I'll explain it to you later,' he said. Then he turned to Balint. 'You can rely on me. I'll arrange everything just as you wish. May I therefore just say that you had no intention to offend?'

'By all means.'

'All right. Leave the rest to me.'

When Balint was alone he found that he was extremely put out. He regretted that he had not followed his original instinct, which had been to protest at the way Absolon had now somehow manoeuvred the whole affair in a quite different direction from that he himself had intended. Absolon had somehow managed to make this trivial dispute with Boros part of the ancient party feud that had existed for so long in the districts along the valley of the Maros. And with his sharp mind he was well on the way to arranging that where he led Alvinczy was bound to follow. And there was nothing that Balint could do about it. And yet . . . and yet . . . ? Well, there was one thing he could do: he could keep the documents from being used. If Absolon were to ask for them he would merely say that he had thrown them away and, as it happened, this was almost true. He had given back the dossier that Frankel had brought and he had thrown Tamas

Laczok's original letter in the fire. All the rest had been shovelled into some drawer or other in his study at Denestornya; and anyway most of it had been worthless. This last thought comforted him.

Abady's and Boros's seconds met that night in one of the Casino's private rooms.

Alvinczy and Absolon started off by declaring that their friend had had no intention to offend. This they were quite prepared to have recorded in the club's minute-book. In their opinion nothing more was needed and the affair could therefore be considered as closed. Boros's seconds hesitated for a moment. Then, with none too good a grace, they agreed to consult their friend and let him decide if this satisfied him. They did not, of course, have even the faintest idea that Boros might have secret reasons of his own for wishing the duel to take place.

The following morning the four seconds met again and now it was the turn of those representing Boros to open the discussion. Boros, it seemed, insisted on all his original demands and would only be satisfied if Count Abady were to declare publicly and in writing that he had not avoided him on purpose, that he held the lawyer in high esteem, and that he deeply regretted it if he had, even involuntarily, given Boros reason to feel offended.

When Boros's seconds finally finished what they had to say, old Absolon burst into mocking laughter. The others reacted with shock and one of them asked, in a slightly menacing tone, 'May I ask you why you find this so amusing?'

'That you will find out soon enough!' answered the old man with a malicious smile. Then, more seriously, he went on, 'I must tell you that our instructions are that what we have just proposed is as far as we will concede. Count Abady declares that he did not intend to give offence. Further than that we will not go.'

'And that we will not accept.'

Absolon's smile now held no hint of humour or good will. Though his lips were drawn back to show a glint of white teeth, his expression was one of frightening malice. Speaking very slowly, he said, 'All the same I would advise you to accept. I advise it very strongly. Mr Boros should be thankful to get off so lightly.'

Boros's seconds were taken by surprise. Puzzled they asked, 'What? What do you mean?'

Absolon leaned back in his chair. He laughed again, and now his voice held even more menace as he said, 'I mean that we agreed to make you this offer only because of the quixotic and irrational good will of Count Abady, who has insisted that we do so. And now, speaking no longer as a second but as Miklos Absolon, I tell you that Mr Boros is no better than a common thief. This is the message I send to him. Kindly deliver it!'

Boros's seconds both jumped to their feet and challenged Absolon on the spot.

'That I do accept!' replied the old man, and lit a fresh cigar.

Now the quarrel between Abady and Boros was relegated to history. Brief announcements were penned by both sides and duly appeared in the press in obscure little paragraphs that no one read.

On the other hand the Absolon–Boros affair was the only matter anyone bothered to talk about. Agitated little groups gathered in the great corridor of the Parliament building, for everyone knew that Absolon was the long-standing leader of Tisza's Party in Maros-Torda. As a result this new affair was at once made into a political issue.

Dr Boros's popularity had previously suffered a severe setback when he sided with Kossuth against all those clamouring for an independent banking system. Despite this Justh's supporters had always remained loyal, and to a man had stood to cheer him whenever he entered the House. Now many Members came over to make a point of shaking his hand and soon he became even more a favourite than before. Then newspapers of the Independence Party devoted prominent paragraphs to him, all portraying him as the nation's great hero who had drawn his sword against the demons of evil and darkness. They wrote nothing about the offence of which Absolon had accused him, only of course because they did not know what it was. All they could say was that the insult was unforgivable. In no time at all there appeared a daily column giving an appreciation of Boros's great qualities and reporting news about the forthcoming duel.

The column appeared daily because Absolon's seconds had demanded a Court of Honour and this meant the appointment of a suitable president, which itself entailed much wrangling and delay. When the court finally assembled old Absolon repeated his message to Boros. He was ordered to provide proof of his allegation. At once Absolon's seconds, Count Alvinczy and Major Bogacsy – who had been hurriedly summoned to the capital – asked for an adjournment for eight days so as to have time to collect their evidence and bring the necessary documents from Transylvania.

Balint found himself increasingly perturbed and distressed by the turn of events, all the more so since he had heard from Alvinczy that Absolon had lost his temper at the first hearing of the Court of Honour and declared that he himself did not have any documents. Balint's dilemma now was that he could not decide whether or not he should ask Frankel for the dossier concerning the Eisler contract which the director of the timber company had said would always be available to him. He had no desire to get involved in this hornets' nest which the original challenge from Boros had provoked. Besides which he was reluctant to be responsible for Boros's downfall when he had promised Dinora to do him no harm.

Would it not be better, he asked himself, to let the affair take its course without any interference by him? After all, he rationalized, Absolon had brought all this upon himself. He, Balint, had wanted none of it and indeed had really nothing to do with it!

On the other hand, could he really stand aside and keep silent about what he knew to be true? Had he not already said before two witnesses why he would not himself shake hands with the lawyer? Even if he had not mentioned any names, neither Frankel's nor anyone else's, was it not true that he entirely agreed with what Absolon had said of Boros? Surely the old man had the right to feel that he could count on Balint not to let him down when he was risking his life because of what Balint had told him? And fight old Absolon would certainly have to do – probably under the most dangerous conditions – unless he could prove the truth of his accusations. And this he obviously would not be able to do without Balint's help. He was hardly the type to start checking facts and figures. It was unthinkable, thought Balint, that by his silence he should allow the honourable old gentleman to get himself killed when right was on his side.

After many hours of painful brooding Balint finally made up his mind: only if the worst came to the worst would he ask for Frankel's dossier. This was because he did not want to cause any harm to Kossuth. With any luck that dossier would not be needed; and, maybe, some of all those papers now peacefully at rest in that study drawer at Denestornya would provide what was necessary. They could never have served as evidence in a court of law but there was sure to be enough to satisfy a Court of Honour. He resolved to go home at once and see what he could find.

Before leaving he went to see Alvinczy, and afterwards Absolon, to tell them what he intended to do.

The old Tartar was in a merry mood.

'Well, my boy, it's nice of you to take this matter to heart, though I don't think there's really any need for proof. It's only that old ass Alvinczy who invented all this stupidity. Of course they'll all believe me. When I say someone is a swine, then he is one! And if they won't believe me then we'll fight it out instead: it won't be the first time I've put a shot in someone's belly!' Whereupon, with great relish, he embarked on a tale about how, some twenty years before, on the shore of the Tsertsen Lake, he had shot three robbers with a small revolver. 'All three fell like rabbits, like rabbits, my boy. And these were real tough customers, not like your legal lick-spittle! This is nothing, my boy, nothing at all!'

Balint left quickly.

Although he had intended to spend only three days in Transylvania – one in Kolozsvar to see Adrienne, and two at home at Denestornya to collect the evidence he wanted – things turned out differently. Although it was already the end of March when Balint left to catch the night train to Budapest, the snow was falling as heavily as if it were January. In the darkness the carriage-driver hit a road-stone, one of the wheels was broken, and Balint missed the train.

This was particularly provoking because he had promised Absolon's seconds to be back on the fourth day. As yet it was not serious for the Court of Honour would not meet until three days later. So as to minimize the chance of any further mishaps on the road he travelled to Kolozsvar by the slow afternoon train the next day, and waited there for the Budapest express. He was now worried because, in the train from Denestornya, he had had time to look through the papers he had come for. None of them, on its own, amounted to much. It was only after reading the lot that a general picture began to emerge, and that picture amounted to a most serious indictment of the lawyer's honesty. He decided to show everything he had got to Alvinczy and Bogacsy and if they didn't think they amounted to proof then, as a last resort, he could always turn to Frankel. His documents really were proof, decisive proof; but Balint decided he would only ask for them as a last resort.

Then, if the Court of Honour declared against Boros without making public Balint's and Absolon's reasons, that would be for the best. Balint consoled himself with this thought, for then there would be no more political consequences.

Dinora was happy. Boros had told her that he wouldn't wait any longer for his furniture to arrive from Transylvania but would move immediately into his new flat, high up on the top floor above her; so he would always be close at hand.

'This is wonderful,' she cried, 'but what about all your things?'

'I'm fed up with waiting for them. I'm just going to bring over some of the nicer pieces from the Buda flat. I made the appointment with the movers this morning.'

'I can help,' she said. 'I'll do it very well. You'll see! Oh, it will be fun!'

Boros's expression clouded over.

'No, no! Not yet. It'll all be heavy work now, and anyhow I know exactly how I want it. So I'm going to do it all myself . . . and I'm going to do it alone.'

'What a perfectionist you are!' laughed Dinora. 'I never realized it before.'

'When everything is finished you can come and see for yourself. And then you can give it a few finishing touches.'

He put his arms round her and kissed her on the neck.

This conversation took place on the day when the Court of Honour agreed to the eight days' adjournment. The next morning the lift was continually rumbling up and down. Under the cage for the passengers was a compartment designed to carry goods. Most of what Boros brought came up in this lower compartment: only what would not fit in was brought up by hand.

Half the workmen stayed down below, the other half worked at the top; and the work took all day. The first pieces to arrive were the largest. Boros devoted the whole day to the move. He had his bed placed exactly where he wanted it, then the wardrobes and chests of drawers. He fussed over his writing-table to make sure it was in a good light, then drove everyone mad by shifting the bookcases another inch to the right. The sofa he placed just so, and then he supervised the work of the carpenter who had been summoned to repair any little damage the movers might have caused.

When something really heavy had to be manhandled up then Boros himself would help the workmen, pulling his weight just like the rest of them.

On the second day the carpets arrived, also two large gilt mirrors which he had recently bought and which required great care and skill in hanging. Also many smaller objects like lamps and vases and *objets d'art*. Finally only the chests and trunks were left. There were about ten of them; some filled with linen and clothes and three packed with documents. These needed fewer men, even though the document chests were heavy enough. Once at the top, however, he only needed the porter to help him unpack, so he paid off all the other workmen except two whom he instructed to remain at the bottom and come up only when the last trunk had been sent up, not before.

It started getting dark and so the lights were switched on at each floor; only the staircase well remained dark. Boros looked down the lift shaft and realized that it was enough to make any-one feel giddy. All one could see were rows of banisters, one after the other, six floors of them seeming to get smaller the further down they were. The ground floor could hardly be seen from where he stood.

Now the first load started to come up. It was the document chests, as Boros had ordered. The lift stopped with the passenger cage practically at the ceiling and the freight compartment on a level with the floor. Boros and the porter started to unload the chests, first the smallest, then the next and finally the largest, which was so heavy that they could hardly get it out of the lift. In the end they succeeded but only so far that the lift itself could descend but the shaft gates could not be closed. The porter wanted to pull it further away but Boros told him to leave it for the moment. He himself, he said, would try and in the meantime the porter could take the smallest chest into the back room of the flat. 'Can you manage it on your own?' he asked. 'It must be about fifty kilos, I imagine!'

'Of course I can. Leave it to me,' said the man eagerly, grab-bing the handles and, leaning backwards to keep his balance, he staggered into the flat.

Boros rang the bell and the lift started slowly to descend, making clicking noises as it passed each floor.

The lawyer straightened up, his pale handsome face apparently as imperturbable as ever, the silvery electric light reflected on his smooth bald head.

He took a small flask from his pocket, swallowed its contents and threw it away. Then he bent down, down towards the lift shaft, and, grabbing the trunk with all his force he pushed it over the yawning chasm before him and fell with it.

Brave and manly, he had planned the 'accident' down to the last detail; and so died Dr Zsigmond Boros, lawyer and Member of Parliament.

Balint only learned about Boros's death on his return to the capital, and read the account of the funeral. First of all the Speaker announced the death in solemn and moving words. Then came the funeral itself. There was an enormous crowd in the procession to the cemetery. Everyone of any importance in the Coalition government was present – everyone, that is, except those ministers who were in Vienna bravely discussing the army concessions and the banking problems; and Kossuth, who was ill in bed.

There was no lack of speeches made by members of the Independence Party, representatives of Boros's constituency and even the Minister of Finance himself because Boros had once, very briefly, been an under-secretary there. Then the procession started which was to end at a special Tomb of Honour donated by the city fathers. Behind the coffin walked the widow and his two sons, the elder of whom had just started his legal studies.

After the family came his political colleagues, including those who had opposed him on the banking question, for it was an unwritten law on such occasions that, particularly in view of the tragic manner of his death, everyone had to bend over backwards to bear witness to the solidarity of the party and to acknowledge its authority and power even in the wake of the funeral cata-falque. These sentiments had been the principal theme of the pre-funeral speeches; and they were repeated again by the grave-side to such effect that here was born the legend of Zsigmond Boros, heroic defender of the people's liberties. Now he was compared to the ancient Hungarian champions of civil rights and even to the martyrs of Arad. That this noble man should so sud-denly have been taken from them was accounted a catastrophe for the nation, and the tale that he met his death by an accidental fall down a lift shaft was believed by everyone who had no reason to think otherwise.

Even so there were those who tried to make out that the impending duel was somehow symbolic of a wicked intrigue against this noble man – as if some evil plot had taken him unawares and somehow contrived his death before he could rise and smite those who traduced him. What a fate . . . and how unfair it was!

All the speeches were so moving that there was hardly a dry eye among those present; and when the gypsy band started to play his favourite tune – '*Once I too would drive the coaches of lovely women* . . .' there were loud sobs from the crowd, despite the fact that some of those women who knew all about his womanizing thought this reference verged on the indelicate. Few people noticed, but at this moment his widow seemed somehow to draw her skirts back from the graveside.

The Coalition papers all printed fulsome accounts of the obsequies and obituary notices resounding with such words as 'dauntless warrior in the cause of right', 'hero', 'champion', and many other fine-sounding phrases.

In the face of such competition an important speech made by the German chancellor von Bülow, which told the world of Germany's solidarity with Austria over the Bosnian question, was practically ignored by the Hungarian papers. Nevertheless these days saw the death-throes of the annexation crisis, for the Serbian Prince George, who had headed the war-with-Austria party, gave up his right of succession to the crown of Serbia and, as a result, the government in Belgrade promised to be good boys and stay faithful friends of the Austro-Hungarian monarchy; and so Aehrenthal's policy proved to have been right all the time.

Abady was happy enough when he read the news from abroad; but he was still concerned about some of the more exaggerated aspects of Boros's funeral and all the eulogies that had been spoken and written about him. It made him wonder if he should not still protest and yet, on more careful analysis, it seemed nothing had been said of any real importance – it was all pompous froth. All the same he decided to consult Alvinczy and be guided by what he thought Balint should do.

From outside the door of Alvinczy's room he could hear the

noise of a heated argument. Inside he found four men – Alvinczy himself, Bogacsy, Absolon ... and Tamas Laczok.

Laczok had come to persuade Absolon and his seconds to make public a set of documents which he had just brought with him from Transylvania and which, having only now realized there would be no Court of Honour, he felt the others should see. He was furious because of all the rubbish he had read about Boros in the newspapers.

'*C'était un infâme coquin, tout comme mon cher frère* – he was an infamous rascal, just like my dear brother,' he shouted. 'Why should we put up with all this ridiculous praise? We ought to show them all what nonsense it is.'

The little room echoed with the sound of his anger. His long beard waved in the air as he jumped about in his wrath – but, of course, he was not really outraged by what had been written about Boros; he was angry because his death meant that he could no longer discredit his brother by telling the Court of Honour the truth about the lawyer!

'It's up to us to show the world what that fellow really was, and that he deliberately killed himself. I hear that the word's going around here now and I know that they were on his tracks back at home. A writ of seizure has been issued. That's why he did it, the coward!'

Bogacsy and Alvinczy demurred politely but Absolon only found the angry little man a source of amusement.

'I for one don't think he was a coward,' he said, principally to annoy Laczok. 'He certainly did it in style. I'm really quite sorry about it.'

'Sorry? You?' shouted Laczok.

'Of course,' the other answered. 'Only once in my life have I seen a more beautiful act of self-destruction, in Japan – a *hara-kiri*. Now I know that he was worthy of having my bullet in his gut!'

'You can't mean it? Fight with a bandit like him? *C'est absurde!*'

'Don't be unkind about bandits! In China it's a highly respected profession and qualifies its members for decapitation by the sword – a noble and beautiful death!'

At this point Balint intervened. 'Have they really started proceedings against him?' he asked, because he remembered that Dinora had had Maros-Szilvas and her new flat put in Boros's name.

'Certainly!' Laczok was delighted that at last he had a chance of showing what he brought with him. '*Voilà!* Here it is! I brought the telegram to show you. It happened five days ago.'

The next day, quite early, Balint walked slowly to Szemelynok Street, wondering as he went what he could do for poor Dinora and feeling rather guilty that he had only now realized how much she might be suffering because of all this. He was afraid too that Dinora might believe that he had broken his word to her even though he had really meant to act as she wished. Needless to say it was fairly clear now that what had driven Boros to suicide was the knowledge that proceedings were starting in Transylvania: this, and the establishment of the Court of Honour.

In the entrance-hall there was no sign that anything untoward had happened there; everything was in perfect order. All Balint could see was that there had been a recent repair to the top part of the wire mesh surrounding the lift shaft. He supposed that this had been where the heavy trunk had torn a hole.

He rang for the hall porter.

'Take me up to Countess Malhuysen, if you please,' said Balint. 'I believe it's the fifth floor?'

'The Countess left three days ago,' the man said; so Balint explained who he was and, hoping to induce the porter to talk, slipped a crown into his hand. Eagerly the man told the whole story to Balint, every detail of the 'sad accident', everything which he himself had thought and done (which didn't interest Balint in the least), and then what had happened since, which was what Balint had come to find out. The day after Boros's death his family arrived, first the widow and the two sons and then later they were joined by another gentleman. After an hour in the lawyer's flat the widow and sons went to the cemetery while the other gentleman stayed behind. When they had gone, he went down to call on Countess Malhuysen. What happened in her flat he did not know. Only that late that night they had to bring down her luggage and the Countess left, accompanied only by her elderly maid.

'Did her Ladyship leave a forwarding address?'

'No, your Lordship, she didn't leave anything.'

Balint found all this very upsetting. He imagined that the un-known man had presented himself because of the writ against

Boros and wanted to make sure of what Boros owned in the capital. Obviously he had scared little Dinora so that she left in a hurry. Now it would surely turn out that the property she had put in his name would be seized with any other assets he might possess and then be sold to pay his innumerable creditors. And so it turned out. Nothing remained either for Dinora or for his family; everything had to go to pay Boros's debts and his family was left in poverty.

But what had happened to Dinora? For a long time Balint was haunted by the thought of her fate and he pitied her from his heart. How could such a bird-brained, helpless little creature survive in this hard, hard world? For weeks she was often in his thoughts.

One day something happened to cheer him up.

He had gone to Vienna to attend an international congress and in the evening joined a party of friends at Ronacher's Variety Theatre. He saw her at once, sitting in a box on the other side of the theatre with a rich young Viennese banker. She seemed happy and gay ... and ablaze with diamonds so huge that their sparkle could be seen right across the theatre.

CHAPTER FOUR

AT THE TIME of Boros's suicide another tragedy was following its appointed course, that of Laszlo Gyeroffy.

The causes could be traced back several months, to St Hubert's Day when that poisonous innuendo 'free bed ... *and* breakfast!' was so maliciously thrown at him by Uncle Ambrus.

The words were like a poison slowly eroding his emotional balance. Outwardly he seemed to go on as before. In the evening he would play the piano or violin for Sara and in the daytime he would perform whatever little tasks she gave him.

Perhaps it was no longer with the same enthusiasm as before, but at least he still did whatever she asked. Perhaps he was quieter, less talkative, but then he never had had much to say. If there was a change it was nothing you could put your finger on — yet Sara's female intuition told her that something was worrying him, and so she tried to swaddle him with even more kindness and protection.

It was for Laszlo's sake that she made a sacrifice which cost her dearly. Christmas was approaching and she made careful arrangements to be sure that her schoolboy son should not come home this year but stay on with the family of the schoolteacher with whom he lived. It was a great treat for the boy, who had written some weeks before asking permission to go on a skiing tour with some friends in the Hetbirak forests. He did not know, of course, that his mother had planned this herself, writing to the teacher who had charge of him and suggesting this arrangement as she knew how fond the boy was of all sports. All the same his absence was a great sadness for Sara, especially as her conscience was troubling her.

It could hardly have been otherwise, unless she had sent Laszlo away instead, for it was unthinkable that she should have celebrated Christmas as one of a threesome consisting of herself, her son and her lover. And she could not bear the thought of Laszlo, who had no one, being forced to go home alone.

Even so their Christmas Eve festivities were sad enough and Sara sat by her little tree in the darkened sitting-room, silently thinking of her son. She had long realized that Christmas would not be the same when he had grown up and gone his own way – but this time she had chased him away herself.

Laszlo too was thinking of all those past Christmases spent with the families of his aunts, where giant trees reached the ceiling even in those palatial houses, with presents heaped round them on the floor, and with the merry laughter of his cousins, especially with Klara ... Klara, who was so good to him, who always took his side, and who had been his friend, his pal, his love ... Klara, whom he had lost through his own folly.

So this Christmas he reached even more often than usual for the brandy bottle, and Sara did not even try to stop him as she had in the past weeks. Before that it had not been necessary, and for two happy months Laszlo had kept off the bottle. Recently, however, it seemed that he could not get enough brandy inside him, so much so that Sara had had to lock up all the liquor in the house.

Then Laszlo started going more and more often to his dilapidated property at Kozard, and when he returned he always smelled of brandy. Sara did not say anything, she didn't dare. Instinctively she realized that he was labouring under some stress, some emotion, which she could not recognize but which threatened their life together. The more convinced of this she became the more she relaxed her precautions.

At the same time she tried hard to keep him occupied. She asked the neighbours to invite him to shoot, and she bought a horse as she hoped it would be a distraction if he could ride around the countryside. Then, each day, she would suggest he canter over to check on whether the wood-cutters or some other labourers were doing what they should.

Sara soon saw that her remedy seemed to be working. At the very least it was an occupation for him and Laszlo himself was nothing if not co-operative. He was always in a good mood and eager to oblige; for he had enough to do and it made him feel he was of some use.

That his services were practically worthless Sara kept to herself. Further, seeing that it made Laszlo happy, she entrusted him with more and more things to do for her. Instead of going to the Kolozsvar market herself, she would ask him to go for her; and though she never failed to send with him the farm overseer or some other experienced employee, who had his own detailed orders from her, she would tell Gyeroffy that he alone was the one she trusted to take money for the livestock they sold and to decide what was an acceptable price.

Despite these precautions Mrs Lazar sometimes found herself faced by the fact that he had foolishly sold something at a loss. Then she swallowed her disappointment and said nothing, hoping that sooner or later he would learn, and not wanting, at this stage, to undermine his self-confidence.

However, things did not turn out as she hoped. One day in January Laszlo did not come home until the morning after the market-day. A little later he went to Kolozsvar by way of his own home at Kozard, taking with him a small overnight bag for he had left no clothes there. It was three days before he came back by carriage, with an unusually cold and hard expression in his eyes, and it was several days later before he seemed completely sober. Sara could not imagine where he had got hold of anything to drink.

This time Sara was frightened. She had given her heart to the young man and she clung to the illusion that she had rescued him from depravity. At first she did not say anything and pretended that she had noticed nothing. But when it happened more than once, she searched his room.

There she found three bottles of brandy, two empty and one with some dregs still in it; obviously he had smuggled them in.

This was too much to pass unremarked. Very gently Sara spoke to Laszlo, full of kindness and understanding and forgiveness. Shamefaced he admitted everything, humbly begged her pardon, swore it would never, never happen again; and for ten days he was on his best behaviour. Then, quite suddenly, on some transparently untrue excuse, he went again to Kozard and from there on to Kolozsvar. This time he stayed away for four days.

When he finally returned she managed to search through his travelling valise, but she found nothing. Why, she asked herself, did he look so guilty? Was it only that he had been drinking? Surely there must be something more because he had always done that while away and until now had never worn that humble, apologetic, hang-dog expression. Was it because he felt guilty about breaking his promise? She was touched to think that that might be the reason, and a great warmth flowed towards him from her loving woman's heart. So, for her own solace and to show him that she forgave him, directly after luncheon, which they had eaten in silence, she leaned towards him and offered her mouth in a kiss of peace.

For a moment he hesitated and then he put his arms round her and bent down until his lips brushed her cheek.

Only for a brief moment − for Sara stepped back abruptly, looking up into his face with wide-open eyes: from Laszlo's collar, clothes and hair there came a strange unpleasant smell − the reek of cheap scent.

And as soon as she caught the first whiffs, she knew what it meant: he had betrayed her with some common whore. For a few seconds she looked the traitor full in the eyes. Then he dropped his gaze, turned away and slowly left the room.

Sara cried for a long time that afternoon. Laszlo was not to know this, any more than that for the last four days her eyes had been full of tears. All the same, when evening came she forgave him.

The next few weeks were painful for both of them. Every time that Laszlo went into the town her heart was torn with the thought that he would get drunk and find himself in bed with a prostitute. Still she sent him more often than before, realizing that this was the price of their reconciliation. If she had not done so it might appear that she was nursing a grudge and keeping him at home as a punishment; and that would have been dangerous too. This she had found out one day when, in Laszlo's presence, she had given her orders directly to the farm overseer and sent him to market on his own. Gyeroffy's eyes had hardened and he had sulked at once, not speaking to her for the whole day. In fact he had such a sinister expression that Sara had become quite frightened, thinking that he was planning to leave her. She never tried it again; far better, she reasoned, to suffer a hell of anxiety than lose him altogether. Not that, she prayed, not that!

Now she left the liquor decanters out, for if he really needed a drink it was best that he should find it at home. When he got drunk she pretended not to notice; and she did all she could to conceal it from the servants. This system too had its bad side, for when Laszlo drank more than a certain quantity he developed that strange arrogance which in the past had made his friends laugh at him. He became overbearingly conceited and rude to anyone who came near him. This stage, however, never lasted long. All of a sudden he would become deflated and beg her forgiveness in floods of tears and self-abasing confessions of guilt and remorse.

After such scenes they would make love passionately as if that would wipe out all that had happened.

Those were stormy days for them both ... and stormy nights.

At the end of March Gyeroffy went again to Kolozsvar. Sara had sent him in to collect an unusually large sum of money, some 16,000 crowns that she was owed by the pork butcher to whom she had sold her fattened pigs.

That evening he did not return home, nor the next. Three days went by and still he had not come.

Sara became very anxious. It occurred to her that it was always possible that Laszlo had spent the money or lost it, but she swiftly dismissed the idea which indeed would have been a small matter compared with the thought that he might have left her. When he had still not reappeared by noon of the fourth day, Sara ordered the horses to be put to her carriage and drove into town. She went straight to the Central Hotel as she knew he always stayed there when he did not return.

Her instinct had been right and, said the porter when she enquired, he was in his room. She went up and opened the door suddenly thinking that maybe he had a woman with him. Gyeroffy was alone, walking up and down, as he had been for some hours. He had not shaved for four days and in his dirty crumpled shirt he looked a wreck. The brandy bottles on the table were empty.

When the door opened and Sara came in he looked at her with undisguised hostility.

'Well? What do *you* want?' His tone was disagreeable and the expression on his face harder and more stubborn than she had ever seen it. Then he said again, 'Well? What do *you* want?'

'Me? Why?' said Sara in the lightest tone she could muster, for she was determined to appear unconcerned. 'I came in to do some shopping and as I was here I thought you might like a lift home. Do you want to come in the carriage with me, because . . . ?'

Laszlo interrupted her, 'You're lying, I know it! Why? What for? Do you think I don't know you're always spying on me? That's what you came for, isn't it? I suppose you're worried about your money? Well, you needn't be, it's all here . . . and more, much more! Do you want it? Do you want me to settle the account? Good, because that's what I want too.'

Sara's large eyes filled with tears. She did not answer, but turned away, so that he should not see how hurt she was, and tried hard to get control of herself. Then, as calmly as she could, she said, 'Please, Laszlo, don't talk like that. Not here, not in the hotel,' she added imploringly.

He came downstairs with her and they got into the carriage and started for home. Outside the town they met a strong north-west wind, cold and gusty with rain and snow. They had the hood put up and well-anchored onto the mudguards, and huddled together as far back as possible.

Sara was reminded of that other ride home on St Hubert's Day, when they had sat back clinging to each other, though not then so estranged and hostile. Nevertheless it was from that day that Laszlo had started to change and Sara's road to Calvary had begun.

For the woman it was a dreadful ordeal to sit there together in hostility and silence. Finally she could stand it no longer and made a great effort to speak, fighting all the time against breaking down in tears. 'Why are you so horrid to me? I haven't done anything to harm you!' she said sadly, neither angry nor offended.

She spoke only in sorrow from the depths of her rejected maternal love.

Gyeroffy hardly seemed to notice her and answered coldly and unconcernedly, 'Oh, shut up! I'll tell you later, when we're back at the house,' and his voice trailed off as he stared ahead of him, seeing nothing but going over and over in his mind what he had been thinking about for the last three days.

After collecting Sara's pig money from the pork butcher in the Hidelven district he was walking back into town along Bridge Street when he had seen old Crookface Kendy coming towards him. In the last few months, if Gyeroffy had caught sight of anyone he knew, he would take avoiding action by turning into a side street or going into a shop, anything not to have to greet somebody. He did this instinctively without even giving himself a reason, for always lurking somewhere near the surface of his mind was the disagreeable memory of that unfortunate meeting with Uncle Ambrus on St Hubert's Day when the older man had laughed at him with insulting innuendo with the words 'Free room and board, eh? Bed ... *and* breakfast!' He didn't want to repeat that experience.

He never consciously thought about that cruel jibe and whenever the words swam into his mind he chased them away by thinking of other things. Still, they were never far away and he was tortured by the thought that they might be true. To himself he explained this urge to avoid old friends merely as a desire to break entirely with his former life. Of course it was a lie and deep down he knew it, though he did all he could to delude himself.

Earlier he had been pressed by the pork butcher to drink a toast and very soon he had had another and then another until before long he had drunk at least five good measures of strong brandy. Then the time came to return to the hotel where the carriage was waiting. One the way he stopped at a bar and downed a few more, for once he had started it never seemed possible for him to stop. Tipsy, and swaying from side to side, he left the bar to walk to the hotel; and by now his first humble, obliging, indeed almost obsequious manner had been submerged by swagger and arrogance.

He had been in that state when he saw Crookface coming towards him not fifty steps away. As it was now lunch-time there was no one else on the street.

If Laszlo had not been drunk he would have turned into the nearest shop or, if there had been no possible way of escape, he would have greeted the older man with humble respect and hurried away. This is what he had done each time he had seen Kendy since that day a year before when he had spoken to him so kindly. But now he was drunk, and not only drunk but also proud and grateful; and it suddenly occurred to him that he must, at once, do something to express that gratitude. So he stopped in his tracks and standing sharply to attention swept off his hat with the same grandiloquent gesture with which actors playing Spanish grandees salute their king.

Laszlo was just starting this majestic formal greeting, when old Crookface made a half-turn and crossed to the other side of the street. He was only about thirty paces away. Then he disappeared into a shop.

Had he recognized the young man coming towards him, and had he deliberately turned away because he had seen that Laszlo was drunk, or perhaps because he had heard that he was now being kept by a woman? Was it pure chance, and did he really have some business in that shop? Laszlo was never to know; but the mere fact that it had happened at all had a terrible effect on him.

Laszlo found himself left standing there, with his arm extended in an incomplete and meaningless gesture. He was filled with consternation, and his face contorted with horror. In the few moments that it had taken old Sandor Kendy to cross the street, Laszlo had sobered up completely from the shock at what had just happened.

Then he put on his hat and walked slowly back to his hotel.

As soon as he reached Mrs Lazar's carriage he told the coachman to go home and himself entered the hotel and booked a room. An hour later he rang and, when the servant came, told him to send someone at once to the Abady house, find out where the lawyer was, and ask him to call on Count Gyeroffy at the hotel. A quarter of an hour later they reported that Mr Azbej was out of town, at Denestornya. Laszlo sent off a telegram: 'PLEASE COME AT ONCE!'

Laszlo stayed alone in the hotel. He did not go out because he might have met someone he knew and that he did not want, indeed he was afraid of it. No one should see him! No one! Surely they would all act like Crookface who had refused to accept his salute, and turn away at his coming. He asked himself over and over again: how could that kind old man have done it, he who had been like a father to him, who had tried to set his life in order and who had offered his help with so much friendliness and warmth? If Count Sandor Kendy cut him then he must have been right to do so, completely right: for did they not both know that Laszlo was a man without honour!

It had not been at all the same when, three years before, he had been thrown out of the Casino Club in Budapest because he could not pay his gambling debts. Then he had been let off lightly and allowed quietly to resign. Even though a public scandal had been avoided it was still a black mark against him, an invisible mark of shame; and yet he had not himself felt it as such. Even if no one but he knew it, he himself was proudly aware that he had obeyed an even higher rule of honour. Then he could have paid up and, in the eyes of the world, remained a gentleman, one who settled his card debts. He had preferred then to incur the obloquy of everyone who knew him rather than default on redeeming Countess Beredy's pearls, which she had pawned to save him the last time he had lost more than he could afford to pay. That would have been a private dishonour, a burden he was not prepared to carry, and so he had chosen, cold-bloodedly, to commit social suicide, an act of self-destruction in which the suicide himself lived on to experience damnation in this world rather than in the next. For Laszlo this had always been a heroic decision, a grandiose act which, though it did little to compensate for the social ostracism it entailed, at least left his self-esteem untouched. It was different now; whichever way he turned, he could not avoid knowing that his dishonour was real and could not be argued away.

He could not deny that now he was being kept by a woman and that Uncle Ambrus's cruel jibe was all too justified. The words rang in his ears – 'Free room and board! Bed . . . and breakfast!' – and they were true. Did she not cook him delicious meals, and have his linen washed and ironed, and sleep with him and buy him horses to ride? He knew that she had only bought the animal for his sake and then had invented errands in town to keep him occupied. He had long known that he was not really useful and that she only did it to obscure the real truth, which was, quite simply, that she was keeping him just as streetwalkers supported their pimps. Why, it was a miracle that she hadn't offered him money; but then this was probably only so that he shouldn't spend it on other women. But if he'd asked, then to be sure she would have given him even that. It was a mercy that somehow he hadn't yet fallen so low! But if it went on, wouldn't it soon come to that too?

What little cash Laszlo had needed on his drinking bouts in town had been found by selling pieces of furniture and little knick-knacks found in drawers and cupboards in his own home. These he had either disposed of to the shopkeeper at Kozard or else brought in his little travelling-bag to Kolozsvar. The house was now almost bare; the household linen had all gone and so had the copper pans from the kitchen. There was nothing left to sell, nothing from which he could raise a *sou*. All that was left to him now was to get money from Sara, and at this he balked. It would be an abomination – he'd rather die!

Even that, however, was denied him for he was not so far gone that he could bear the idea of killing himself while he thought himself indebted to his mistress. Every last *sou* must somehow be paid back – so that no one could say he'd died owing such a dishonourable debt. And so he sent for Azbej.

As he hardly expected the little man to get to him before the next day he spent the evening trying to quench with brandy the self-reproaches which so tortured him.

Azbej appeared about ten o'clock the next morning. He appeared to find nothing unusual in the fact that Laszlo was still in bed, and did not even enquire if he was unwell. Instead he pulled up a chair beside the bed and sat down on its edge, as he always did, either as a mark of respect or else because he had no choice since his legs were so short. When he was comfortably settled he turned his face to Laszlo, that face which, with its bristly short-cut beard, so resembled a hedgehog when curled up in a ball.

'Here I am,' he said, pursing his little red lips. 'How can I serve your Lordship?'

His voice was humble and his manner so servile. All the same his bulging prune-like eyes gave the lie to this impression. They had observed Laszlo keenly, noted that he had no luggage and had slept in his shirt, and seen that there was an empty brandy-bottle on the bedside table, along with a dirty collar and a used glass. There was a glint of triumph in his eyes as if he knew now that what he had worked for for years was at last within his grasp.

Gyeroffy sat up. He crossed his arms on his drawn-up knees and for a moment stared straight ahead without saying anything. Then, in a stern voice, he said, 'I need money. Quite a large sum. Immediately! At least 15,000 crowns.'

Azbej spread out his arms in a gesture of helpless dismay.

'But, your Lordship, where from? We've already sold the forestlands, as your Lordship knows, and we got our price even though the timber was still standing. All that we had to pay out at once so as to prevent Samos-Kozard being auctioned over your head. The interest on your Lordship's loans was very high – usury would be a better word – but it all had to be paid since your Lordship acknowledged the debt. And then there were the legal charges. The farm implements have been my property, I mean my wife's, for many years; and your Lordship will remember that I paid ten years' rent in advance, not to mention that supplementary payment which I gave your Lordship from pure goodness of heart. And what's more I've written off that enormous sum out of my own money, as I have already reported to your Lordship, and shown you the receipts. Your Lordship found everything in order, I know; and now I have no more money, not a penny!'

Laszlo looked sombrely at the fat little man and a deep furrow appeared between his eyebrows. 'All the same I need this money, no matter how! I must have it, do you understand?'

The lawyer said nothing. A slight gesture indicated that he was powerless.

For a few moments both remained stubbornly silent. Finally Gyeroffy leaned forwards and said, 'You take Kozard, everything included. I'll hand it over . . . but I must have the money. Do you understand? I must!' and then seeing that Azbej was pretending to be surprised, he shouted, 'Don't look so astonished! Isn't that what you've been planning all these years? You can cut the play-acting!'

This clear-sightedness was something new for Laszlo, but then he had been settling accounts with himself ever since the previous afternoon. He had reviewed all his actions and stupidities and coldly assessed everything that he had neglected and left undone. He had judged himself severely and as he did so he had judged others too, looking hard at everything he had done and allowed to be done; and now it was quite clear to him how doggedly the little lawyer had led him into this final trap.

'If your Lordship pleases, I have only tried to be of use to your Lordship. Nothing else, ever! It never occurred to . . .' protested Azbej, but Laszlo cut him short, shouting, 'Stop play-acting! Answer me!'

Azbej was far too intelligent to take offence. After all, the moment had arrived when that beautiful little country house, with its valuable land, would at last be his. This was not to be missed and had better be quickly grabbed before Gyeroffy thought better of what he was doing and started looking elsewhere, perhaps to his relations and maybe even to Balint Abady, who was one of the few people the lawyer feared. Therefore he quickly denied himself the luxury of being offended, and restricting any expression of resentment to the simplest of gestures, he replied, 'I must work out some figures. Of course I'll agree if that is what your Lordship desires.' He got up and backed towards the door, bowing obsequiously as he went. Then he promised to return in the afternoon with a definite answer, and left the room.

Soon after lunch he was back, carrying a huge stack of papers, and at once proceeded to quote facts and figures and statistics. At long length he explained that the Kozard property was saddled with ancient debts and with all those advances that he, Azbej, had been from time to time obliged to pay. Even if one valued everything at the very highest figure – and one must not forget that the roof was leaking, the cellars flooded and the stable-roof in a state of collapse – it still did not amount to anything like what Count Laszlo now owed to Mr Azbej. And what's more there was no security for that debt which was never likely to be repaid. Azbej went into all this in great detail, showing as he did so all kinds of confusing documents, statements of account and receipts, all of which proved categorically that nothing remained of the smallest value, nothing. In fact less than nothing!

While this was going on Laszlo walked up and down the room, stopping from time to time to pour himself a glass of brandy or perhaps to glance at his own signature when Azbej held it up as proof of what he was saying. He was so angry that he could not keep still, for he detested the charade which the lawyer was now acting, mainly so as not to abandon the role he had played for so long. When Azbej finally came to an end and fell silent, Laszlo stopped in front of him and said, 'Well?' Nothing else.

'If your Lordship pleases I can offer him 15,000 crowns. Of course it'll mean a loss to me, but I'll give it all the same . . .' the lawyer answered quickly, not daring any longer to prolong the matter. Then he rapidly turned down-to-earth and businesslike, saying that he would have the contract drawn up and send for the notary to legalize the papers when they were ready for signing.

'Would your Lordship wish to go to his office or should the notary come here?'

'Here!' said Laszlo. Then he thought for a moment and went on, 'One other thing! That empty estate cottage by the village shop, the one at the corner of the main road! That's not included in the bargain, I want to give it to our old agent Marton Balogh. The old man worked for us in my father's time and I don't want him to be homeless.'

'As your Lordship wishes!' said Azbej, and backed out hurriedly before Laszlo could think of anything else he wanted to keep for himself.

Sara's carriage rumbled across the level crossing beside the station at Apahida, drove up the hill on the right and stopped in front of her house. Now the sleet had turned to snow and the storm was so gusty that they were almost swept off the steps that led to the front door; it was the same storm that had prevented Abady catching the night express.

Still in their overcoats Sara and Laszlo ran straight into the dining-room beyond the hall. Here they took them off, Gyeroffy still by the door, Sara just the other side of the big table. Then, although it was only five o'clock, she lit the hanging lamp, for it was already dark and the windows covered with snow.

When she had finished she looked at Laszlo.

He stood near the table where the lamp cast a harsh glow on his face. His chin was covered with stubble and there was an unusually deep vertical furrow on his brow. To Sara this seemed inexpressibly sinister. Laszlo's hair fell in a dishevelled mass over his forehead and with his dirty collar and wrinkled suit he looked far more depraved than he had seven months before when she had rescued him from the inn at Szamos-Ujvar and brought him home.

Then he had been drunk; now he was sober, menacingly sober, and standing stiffly upright as if hewn out of granite.

An icy hand seemed to clutch at Sara's heart, for in his face she saw a cruel determination. His eyes were shining with hatred. She could hardly believe it, but hatred it certainly was, hatred which Laszlo had conjured up for himself. He had now convinced himself that it was this woman who was the root cause of his moral degradation. It was she who had picked him up, who knowingly had kept him by her, lulling his conscience with the dark beauty of her body and confusing his judgement by loving, lascivious kisses and his soul by enchanting draughts from her soft mouth, so that she could keep him by her in shameful servitude just as Circe had kept Ulysses's crew in a pigsty, so drugged that they did not notice their degradation. And so it was with him. Everything she had done, she had done so that he too should remain unaware of the baseness of his life, the life of a parasite kept by her as drones are kept by worker bees. How could she have done it? How could she have taken advantage of his weakness, his poverty and his restless, homeless life and then have surrounded him with such luxury that he should not notice what she had made of him? How could she have done it?

For some moments they stood looking at each other across the table, she hurt and frightened and he with unrelenting malice. Sara wanted to say something, but though her lips moved no sound came from them.

Gyeroffy reached into the inside pocket of his jacket and took out two envelopes. He threw one to her.

'Here! Take it! It's the money for your beloved pigs, 16,000 crowns of it. You were afraid I'd steal it, weren't you? Well, you were wrong. It's all there, to the last penny. Count it!'

'Laszlo!' the poor woman cried. 'What do you mean? The idea . . . !' She felt she was living a nightmare.

'Count it! Now, in front of me! I don't ever want it said that I took your money. Go on, count it!'

Sara was so upset and frightened that she did not dare disobey. As quickly as she could she went through the motions of counting and then replaced the notes in the envelope. Now Gyeroffy spoke again, and this time his voice was even colder than before and had an ironic ring to it.

'We might as well settle all our accounts at the same time. Here is what I owe you! Count it!' he repeated and he threw the other envelope on the table in front of her. A few thousand-crown notes fell out as it hit the table in front of Sara. Totally bewildered she asked, 'What's this? What's it for? I don't understand.'

'It's 15,000 crowns. I have stayed here since September. That's 210 days at fifty crowns a day. Fifty crowns for bed and board – quite generous, don't you think, but then I wanted to pay for everything – everything, do you understand? – every single thing you have done for me.'

At first Sara did not grasp what he meant but when the full implications became clear to her she drew herself up and in her anger herself became a figure of menace, tall, with broad shoulders, her black eyes burning with anger between those thick lashes and her mouth curved back like one of the Furies. For an instant she remained quite still. Then her arm shot out and she pointed to the door.

'Out! Get out! At once! Out! Out!'

Laszlo crumpled as if some spring inside him had suddenly broken. He turned away and ran to the door not even noticing that the money was thrown after him. He grabbed his coat and ran out into the snow.

Behind him the door was slammed by the wind.

Laszlo stumbled down the hill. The storm was in his face but he felt nothing, not even those myriad ice-needles which seemed to press into his skin. He ran down the valley, ran like a hunted animal keeping to a familiar path, oblivious of where he was going or what was happening to him, ran until he could run no longer. Then, though almost at the end of his strength, he still tried to run, for he sensed that the demon of arrogance and evil that had possessed him had now done its work and would soon vanish; and he was afraid that when that happened he would break down and weep.

He ran too to escape from the fact that this attitude from which he had somehow expected to find some moral satisfaction had turned into a morass of shame, shame for his lack of gratitude, for his intolerable rudeness and brutality.

When he reached the main road he saw in front of him the squalid little inn beside the station. He burst through the door.

The room was filled with smoke and the few railway workers who were sitting there with their brandy took no notice of the newcomer and indeed did not even notice how wet, muddy and dishevelled he was.

'Brandy! Brandy! A half-bottle of brandy!' he muttered.

'Which sort, aniseed or sweet?' enquired the innkeeper curtly.

'Either. It doesn't matter,' replied Laszlo. 'But make sure it's strong, very strong.'

Laszlo drank it all down almost as soon as it was on the table. Then he had another, and another. Now he was already fuddled with drink and it occurred to him that Sara was sure to have sent someone out to look for him and that they had better not find him there, anything but that. So he flung a couple of crowns on the table and rushed out once again into the storm.

He ran on like a man pursued. On the road there were large patches of snow and between them puddles of black water. Laszlo ran straight ahead no matter what lay in his way and hardly even noticing whether he stepped in mud, water or snow. On the edge of the village there was another inn. There he stopped again and drank more measures of brandy; and the more he drank the more he became convinced that someone was following him and that sooner or later he would be caught and taken back. But who it was and where he would be taken he no longer knew; only the fear stayed with him, the fear that someone was after him and that therefore he had to keep on running, running, running, even though his legs could hardly carry him.

He managed to stagger through the village, though the snow was piling up in drifts beside the road and it was snowing so hard that no one, sober or drunk, could have told where they were. Somehow he pushed himself onward.

Now the road turned towards the bridge over the river. Laszlo did not notice as mindlessly he put one tired foot in front of the other, his head bent under some intolerable and unknown weight. Every conscious thought had been wiped from his mind by exhaustion and alcohol; but still, like a hunted animal, he somehow managed to go on.

Then, quite suddenly, there was no ground beneath his feet, and he fell into nothingness, into what was, in fact, a deep ditch half-filled with snow and slush. In this he lay with the upper part of his body spread-eagled face downwards on the sloping bank.

And so he remained, unconscious of the snow which fell ever more thickly on his back.

CHAPTER FIVE

MIKLOS ABSOLON SAT at his ease between two columns
on the veranda of Borbathjo, his elegant baroque manor house
in the largely Szekler district of north-eastern Maros-Torda. His
bald head was covered by a tiny velvet skullcap embroidered with
pearls that he had brought from Bokhara and the collar of his soft
silk shirt was open round his thick bull-like neck.

It was May and the sun was shining. Absolon had nothing
whatever to do and he was just sitting there, barely even allowing
himself to think. His attitude was that of an inscrutable oriental
sage, content merely to contemplate. After all, it was warm and
the sun was bright. The view from where he sat was not particularly interesting but stretched into the far distance, right across
the Kukullo river, which here was only a meandering stream,
surrounded by water-meadows bright with the yellow of buttercups and the lime-green of young grass, up to the valley where
the hillsides were covered with forests of beech, pine and hornbeam, all now in bud, and, still further to the south, to the peaks
of the eastern Carpathians.

The view was so familiar to him that now he barely noticed
it. He had known it from his childhood before the days when his
restless urge to travel had carried him to the farthest and most
unknown parts of Asia. Of course he had come home from time
to time, until that day when he returned with a crippled leg and
could roam no more.

If Absolon was thinking of anything at all it was to reflect that,
after all, everything, everywhere, was much the same. What
essential difference was there between squatting on a rock at
Kuen-Lun disguised as a pilgrim and apparently watching the
goats outside a Tibetan monastery, or lying at ease in the shade
of a Kirgiz tent in the Taklamakan desert, and sitting here at
Borbathjo, in the heart of the Szekler country, on the veranda of
the house in which he was born?

Life could be beautiful, thought the old traveller, wherever
you were – provided that, if there was no reason to travel, one
was content to sit still and enjoy it, unlike those city folk who
always seemed so fretful and nervous. This was his philosophy,
though he rarely thought about it in such simple terms and never
discussed such things with other people.

After sitting there serenely for a good hour and a half, during which time he only moved to throw away the butt of one cigar and light another, he noticed a carriage driven by four horses coming towards him from the road to the west. This was most unusual, for even in the height of summer few people used the lonely road which ran from the little country town of Szasz-Regen to the natural mineral springs at Szovata. In spring it was nearly always deserted but for the odd Szekler peasant's cart or the light gig of some neighbouring landowner. What he saw now was an open travelling carriage.

With the sharp eyes of a hunter he could make out that the carriage was drawn by four excellent chestnut horses and that the leader had a white blaze. Inside the carriage there sat a lone woman.

Absolon wondered who it could possibly be, as he knew everyone who lived in the district and most of them at one time or another used the road which ran directly below his grounds. All the same his appraisal was not based on any real curiosity – for what did it signify what one looked at? – but rather on that mild interest aroused by the unusual. It happened, so he watched: that was all.

The carriage came nearer and nearer winding through the three sickle-shaped curves that skirted the base of the hills to the right, until at last it was coming straight towards the high bank which marked the boundary of the Borbathjo park.

Now Absolon could see the driver more clearly, an old man with imposing moustaches and elaborate braiding on his long Hungarian driver's coat. The driver's high seat partially concealed the woman behind him, and all that could be seen from where Absolon sat was the white parasol which blossomed above her like a giant mushroom.

Quite suddenly, it seemed, the carriage was close at hand and now disappeared behind the ivy-covered wall which surrounded Absolon's property. It could still be heard for a few moments and, to the old man's surprise, then came the sound of wheels and hoof-beats on the wooden bridge beyond the vegetable garden which had to be crossed by anyone coming to the manor house. Then he could hear the horses panting as they trotted laboriously up the slope to the house. It was the most unexpected thing – someone was coming to see him, and it was a woman, alone.

A large hand-bell had been placed on the veranda balustrade. Absolon rang it vigorously and almost at once a plump middle-aged woman with a pretty face stepped out of the house. She walked swiftly towards the old man who was still gazing outwards, stopped just behind him and put her hand on his shoulder. 'At your service, my Lord,' she said.

It was Marisko, Absolon's housekeeper and mistress of many years' standing. It was she of whom Aunt Lizinka had spread so many malicious tales, saying that she was nothing more than a 'crack-heeled servant, no better than she should be, the slut!'

Like all such calumnies there had once been a grain of truth in what the old gossip had said. It was true, for example, that Marisko had started as a kitchen-maid at Borbathjo at the time when Absolon had returned from his wanderings. She was from the next village, sixteen years old, had never worked anywhere else and had never been known to be flighty with the young men. It was quite untrue to say, as Aunt Lizinka often had, that she was 'a bad one!'

Absolon, though crippled, had still been a man in his prime and had no sooner seen the girl than he had lusted after her; so he did as the Tartars did, took her to bed and the following day sent generous presents to her father. In the East it had been the custom and so he had done the same. That very morning he had sent over four magnificent oxen which had at once been accepted, not as the price of shame, which would have been the case with money, but as a generous gift from one free man to another. Four oxen! That was indeed a worthy gesture.

Marisko had stayed at Borbathjo ever since, for it was not in her nature to betray her master with anyone else. By nature she was utterly faithful and upright, with a straightforward, open expression in her velvet-dark eyes and a ready smile. And whenever she looked at her lover and master, as now, her eyes caressed him with loving kindness.

'A visitor has arrived,' said Absolon. 'The carriage has just turned into the drive. Someone must go down to greet them. And you,' he went on, 'must make some tea.'

'Of course,' she said. 'At once!'

The powerful old man heaved himself up and stood still for a moment. Then, with his cigar clenched between his teeth, he pressed his short crutch to his bad leg and with surprising speed hurried so fast through the house that he was already standing in the portico of the entrance when the four-in-hand entered the courtyard.

This portico was unique to Borbathjo. It was a kind of open hall with a roof supported on wooden pillars, and it joined the main house to the rest of the manor's buildings. It was simply paved with ordinary brick and the pillars were roughly hewn. It was furnished only with two long wooden benches, but on the walls were hung the old explorer's hunting trophies. Heads, horns, claws and fangs of all the fauna of Asia looked down on Absolon as he stood there, leaning on his stick and waiting for his guest to arrive. A servant stood at the foot of the steps below him.

The carriage drew up, and Adrienne got out.

For some time she had been planning to visit her husband's uncle, ever since, in fact, the time of Margit's wedding when he had been the best man. It was then that they had become friends, for Adrienne had sensed at once that old Absolon understood her, shared her views and her outlook on life and appreciated her in a way that no other member of her husband's family had ever done. When the wedding itself was over he had driven out especially to see her and had stayed for a long time.

This was most unusual for Absolon who was known rarely to seek the company of women; and so for him to ask permission to call, and to stay for a long time, were quite exceptional marks of respect and sympathy. Then too Adrienne had sensed a certain compassion in his voice as if he had seen and understood the awful problems of her married life. It was after this visit that Adrienne, after much self-searching, had decided to come to Borbathjo and try to enlist on her side the one member of her husband's family who would be sympathetic when she sued for divorce, someone to whom Uzdy and his mother would listen, someone who could support her plea to be freed from the slavery of the past few years. Absolon had the guts to speak the truth to Pali Uzdy; he was intelligent and fearless and would know how to plead her right to have custody of her daughter, and he would even be strong enough to prevent Uzdy from harming Balint, should it come to that.

Adrienne had gone over it in her mind time and time again. She had not come before but waited until now because she had just had a letter from her mother-in-law saying that she would return home with her grandchild at the end of May. This would mean that Adrienne would then be able to start her divorce proceedings since she would no longer be held back by the fact that little Clemmie was out of her care.

Making her now familiar excuse, she left her husband's house at Almasko and took the train to stay with her father at Mezo-Varjas. On the following day she ordered the carriage and had herself driven to Borbathjo. In this way no one at Almasko would know about it, for she was the mistress in her father's house.

It was a long way – fifty kilometres to Regen, where she lunched, and then thirty more to Borbathjo – but the Miloth chestnuts were sturdy animals and were so used to long journeys that they arrived as fresh as when they left.

'My dear niece, how nice of you to come to visit me!' said Absolon as he kissed her hand with old-fashioned ceremony. He would kiss the hands of any young woman, of older ones never.

Adrienne looked around her with interest. Borbathjo was a most unusual house. It was set above the side of the hill and appeared from the smooth paving of the courtyard to have been built on one floor only. But from where the portico with its wooden pillars joined the two parts of the building together the garden fell away in such a steep slope that the main part of the manor house had in fact been built in two storeys, so that the long veranda was high above the flower-beds. Here there was a group of wicker chairs in which Absolon and his guest sat down, and it was here that Adrienne told him why she had come.

Adrienne told her story simply and sincerely. She held nothing back, not even the brutality and unpredictable behaviour of her husband, nor the difficulties with her mother-in-law, even though she was Absolon's sister. And without realizing it she even let him know, though not in so many words, that she loved someone else with whom she wanted to start a new life once she was divorced from Uzdy.

It all came out so easily, far more so than she had ever imagined it would. So much sympathy and understanding radiated from the simple, sincere old man who sat opposite her that it was just like talking about some long-understood problem which never needed explanation because it was already so familiar to them both. It was not like trying to make a stranger understand some subject to which he was a stranger. Absolon's family likeness to her husband did not bother her, though he had the same Tartar face with prominent cheekbones and slanting eyes, wide mouth with fleshy lips, and his skin held the same oriental pallor. The difference, though Adrienne hardly realized it at the time, lay in the fact that while Absolon was absolutely natural and devoid of artifice, Pali Uzdy was all contrivance and took pains to present an air of undisguised evil; it was as if he wanted to be taken for Lucifer himself with an exaggeratedly long pointed beard and moustaches that curled away from his lips.

Besides this there was, and perhaps it was more important, a totally different expression on their faces. Whereas Uzdy adopted an air of sardonic mockery, his uncle, at this moment at any rate, seemed the personification of concerned good will; though he was capable of malice if provoked.

It took some time for Adrienne to tell her tale, and when she finished the old explorer picked up the crutch which lay beside his chair and struck the floorboards heavily. He always did this when about to say something important. With one of his eye-brows lifted high on his forehead he looked sharply at her and, speaking each phrase deliberately and carefully as if it were the result of deep thought, said, 'All right, I will help you, but it won't be easy. You'll bear a heavy responsibility, you know, but I'll do it all the same. There will be no problem with my sister Clémence. I'll deal with her when the time comes; but my nephew Pali will not be so easy.'

Adrienne looked up at him anxiously, enquiringly.

'I just mean to say that my late brother-in-law was mad and we had better not forget that when dealing with his son. It is that fact that makes it so easy for me to accept everything you've told me, and, perhaps, some of the things you haven't; and it is that we have to guard against. We must remember what might happen – though of course it might not; but we must make sure that you . . . and maybe someone else . . . are properly protected.'

For a moment Adrienne was startled, for it was clear that he was referring to some other love and yet she had said nothing except that she wanted to make a new life for herself as soon as she was free. She realized that here was a man of clear-sight whose instinct could be trusted, a man for whom all human frailty was natural. Then, seeing the effect of his last words, he added light-heartedly, 'Tea-time! I can't think why it isn't already on the table.'

He heaved himself up, and even though the bell was within reach and he only had to ring it when he wanted something, he stumped off into the house.

Adrienne remained alone, leaning on the balustrade and gazing into the distance. How sympathetic the old fellow was, she thought. How ready to help, to be kind and useful. How tactfully he had let her know that he had understood what could not be said, how he had himself introduced the one subject that must not be mentioned, her love for Balint.

Was it possible that he had heard something of it? Could he possibly have known that she was in love and that the man she loved was Balint? It seemed hardly possible, for even though she never discouraged the old ladies from gossiping about her she had seen to it that it had always been that group of young men like Adam Alvinczy and Pityu, and the egregious Uncle Ambrus, who had given rise to their talk; Balint, she was sure, had never been mentioned.

No, no! It couldn't be. Old Absolon could not have known anything definite; and his words must have sprung simply from his deep knowledge of life, from the wisdom of the truly tolerant.

She was absorbed in these thoughts as she looked down over the spring flowers in the beds below her.

The sloping garden had been made in horizontal terraced beds each about five paces wide. In each there was now a mass of tulips and narcissus in full flower and at the sides there were standard roses, as tall as small trees, which were just coming into bud. The garden was symmetrical and was bounded on three sides by clumps of lilac and on the fourth by the house. The garden was like those in French chateaux of the eighteenth century and had presumably been laid out when the old fortified slope had been terraced and the baroque manor house, with its high double roof and stuccoed ceilings, erected in a style so much more sophisticated than the rough-hewn portico and the simple outbuildings the other side of the courtyard.

It was a sheltered garden, peaceful and smiling, and it seemed to reflect the tranquil personality of its very singular owner. And yet it could hardly be he who lavished all that care upon it, though it was obvious that someone did, for it was laid out with skill and a most individual taste.

How gardens could betray their creators, reflected Adrienne as she thought back to the one at Almasko where Uzdy would not allow a single flower, and where the lawns were so carefully cut and weeded that not even a daisy dared open its petals!

'Excuse me, my Lady. Tea is on the table,' said a voice behind her.

It was Marisko, who gestured to the table where the meal had been laid. It was a feast, with a splendid *Kuglhopf* cake, biscuits and hot scones in covered silver dishes, and several kinds of cold meats. Next to the teapot was a large jug of coffee, with some buffalo milk; for though Absolon himself drank only china tea Marisko had thought that perhaps this unknown lady might prefer coffee. She offered Adrienne a chair. 'Please to sit, my Lady.'

Adrienne sat down but did not eat. 'I'll wait for my uncle,' she said.

'Don't do that, my Lady,' said the housekeeper. 'You see the Master is telephoning to someone and it may take some time. He would be very angry with me if I didn't make you start without him,' she added with an indulgent maternal smile. She pronounced the word 'Master' as if it were written in capital letters.

Adrienne, when she heard that Absolon drank tea, chose coffee, for she realized that it had been made specially for her and would otherwise be wasted. Marisko stood at a slight distance, leaning silently against the door-post. Her rounded peasant's body was well-formed and was set off by the simple grey bodice and skirt worn by the prosperous countrywomen of the district. She looked kind and sympathetic. Adrienne liked her at once and, as she knew that Marisko had been her uncle's mistress for many, many years, she wished to be friendly and so started to chat with her. At first she just praised the cakes and then the wonderful display of spring flowers beneath the terrace. Marisko had answered all Adrienne's questions briefly and with a correct smile, but it was clearly only out of politeness.

'And who looks after the garden?' asked Adrienne. 'I've rarely seen anything so pretty, and so well laid-out.'

'Ah, my Lady, that's one of *my* jobs,' and Adrienne's obvious appreciation softened her hitherto somewhat reserved manner and she became quite talkative.

She had learned about gardening, she said, from an old man of eighty who had worked all his life as gardener at Borbathjo but who had been retired for years when she first arrived. She loved the work, especially as the Master, though he'd never say so, was very fond of flowers. She'd found the gardens, oh, very neglected, almost abandoned, but she'd soon put a stop to that, she couldn't stand such neglect and laziness . . . and then suddenly she fell silent, alarmed at the thought that she might be stepping out of her place. Silence, she thought, was more appropriate for housekeepers.

'Why don't you sit down?' suggested Adrienne. 'It would be much less, less awkward . . . for us both.'

'Oh, no! Not for the world! I really could not, my Lady. I'm not used . . . I could never get used to that!'

Marisko spoke nothing but the truth. She never sat when meals were served, not even when alone with her master. She would bring in the tea, serve it and leave the room. At lunch-time or dinner she would stand by the sideboard like a butler of the old school and keep an eye on the footmen who served the meal. She herself never ate with Absolon but retired to the kitchen when he had finished. When everything had been washed up and put in its proper place by the cook and the maids, then and only then, and also if there were no visitors, would she rejoin her master and sit with him quietly and diligently getting on with some embroidery, crochet-work, knitting or even just doing the mending. This was how the countrywomen behaved, as she remembered from her childhood in her father's house.

If Absolon was in the mood and felt like talking she would answer most eagerly; and she loved to listen, time and again, to all his traveller's tales. Even so she would never start a conversation, not even about how the estate was run, though it had been she who organized everything so efficiently and who gave the farm manager his instructions. All this she did with care and intelligence, which was just as well as old Absolon knew nothing of such matters and never bothered his head about them. Perhaps he imagined that there was not much to be done as the Borbathjo property was comparatively small – only a few hundred acres – and because his fortune all came from the husbanding of the Absolon forests, which was done by a quali-fied manager.

Marisko disappeared as soon as Absolon came back.

The sun began to set, sinking behind the distant mountain peaks. A golden glow spread over the landscape and the light fleecy clouds were tinged with pink in the pale-green sky. The shadows on the nearby hillside glowed yellow as if lit by some hidden fire and even the whitewashed walls of the veranda turned deep orange.

A cold breeze got up, as it always did here at the foot of the Gorgeny mountains when the sun went down, and the spring evenings were surprisingly cool.

'We'd better go in now,' said Absolon. 'It isn't good to stay too long out of doors!' He said this only out of concern for his niece. With his iron constitution he could have stayed there until midnight without coming to any harm.

Inside the house the rooms were ablaze with light, for Absolon had ordered that all the gas-lamps and chandeliers should always be lit at dusk. In this way he resembled those nomadic chieftains who would live for months in the desert in the greatest simplicity but when they came to Samarkand, or Peking, or Isfahan, and settled there, had to be surrounded by every luxury the age provided.

Absolon's house too showed the same oriental taste. The walls were whitewashed and the age-old wide floorboards scoured until the knots stood out. But they were covered with the rarest of Eastern carpets, some of them made of silk and interwoven with golden threads. Divans were strewn with silken fabrics from Bokhara and cushions covered with Chinese embroidery, each one a miracle of skill and beauty. Absolon rarely sat on them himself, though he did occasionally lie down and take a brief nap there on sultry afternoons in summer.

His favourite seat was an ordinary bentwood Thonet armchair whose air of practical simplicity seemed quite out of place among all that sophisticated luxury; but then Absolon was concerned only with comfort and not with impressing visitors with the purity of his taste.

The walls of the large drawing-room, under the baroque plaster scrolls on the ceiling, were hung with more hunting trophies. These were the best in his collection, unlike the massed legion out on the entrance portico. What hung here were real treasures and some were so rare or so exceptionally large that their equal was nowhere else to be found, though Absolon had never bothered to advertise the fact; these were his private solace, not symbols of achievement to dazzle the world.

There were the heads of three gigantic mountain-goats from Kuen-Lun, a mountain ram from the high Pamir plateau, some

weirdly-shaped yaks' horns, and the stuffed neck and head of a
wild camel which was already slightly moth-eaten. These bizarre
trophies were placed sparsely on the white walls of the great
room. Two other objects stood out, perhaps because they were
not also the harvest of far-flung hunting forays.

One was a small and now faded photograph. 'This,' said
Absolon, 'was Przewalski, the famous Asian explorer, and standing next to him in Tartar dress, that's me. A Russian officer took
us together in Kotan. It's one of my most treasured souvenirs.'

The other object was more spectacular. It was an exceptionally
long sword, beautifully wrought and decorated. It was hung
horizontally above a sofa in the middle of the wall. Adrienne had
exclaimed with astonishment when she first saw it.

'Yes, it is a good one,' said Absolon modestly. Then he laughed
and said, 'I don't know of another like it, even in the East. Wait
a moment, I'll take it down.'

He unhooked it from the wall and handed it to his guest.

The sword was purely ornamental and was more than four feet
long and completely straight. The hilt and the mounts of the
scabbard were of enamelled gold studded with precious stones
and between the metalled parts the rest was covered with cherry-
coloured velvet, so vivid that if there had not been some slight
signs of wear anyone would have taken it for new.

'How beautiful!' cried Adrienne and then repeated the word
'beautiful' several times.

The old man beamed with pleasure. His Tartar-like face was
again creased with laughter as he said, 'You've seen nothing yet!
Look at the blade! There's nothing in the world like it!'

He leaned forward and took the sword from Adrienne and,
balancing it on his arm, drew out the blade.

What the old man had said was indeed true: the blade was
even more beautiful than its case. Near the hilt the steel had been
inlaid with a lattice-pattern in gold and its whole length was
decorated with an inscription, also in gold, and the letters were
interspersed with inset rubies so placed that they looked for all
the world like drops of blood.

When they had both looked at it for some time Absolon put
it back on the wall and then started to tell its tale.

'Legend has it,' he said, 'that it once belonged to Tamberlane.
This might be true, but the old paper I was able to see said
nothing about it. Of course the man from whom I had it had

himself acquired it in no very straightforward fashion, for it seems that his father had somehow extracted it from Timur's tomb.

'How did I get it? That's another story. It's true that I did not buy it, indeed I never have had the money to spend on such a treasure. Anyway the Kirgiz nomads would never sell such a valuable possession. Camels, women, horses, yes; but not weapons ever, they are heirlooms. No, I got this from Alp-Arslan Beg who had been my friend for some years. It's quite a story. His tribe lived on the northern slopes of the Pamirs and in one of his frequent wars with his neighbours he was wounded and three of his sons had been killed. Only one boy remained alive, a three-year-old child. Prince Arslan fled to the mountains with him and his women, and there they were again attacked, this time by Kashmiri bandits. Arslan was wounded again, and the boy, and his mother, with the other women and all their remaining possessions, were carried off. I came upon him the next day – it was just after I had shot that big ram over there – and found his camp almost totally destroyed.

'As it was clear that the bandits had gone off to the south, and as there was only one track, even for bandits, through the eternal snows of the road to Kashmir, it wasn't difficult to follow them and surround them with my three faithful Tartars. The bandits had their women with them, and were also driving some stolen herds of sheep, and these had slowed them down. With my hunting rifle it was quite easy to pick them off – the wild ram was much more trouble! So I came back to Arslan with the woman, and with his son and all his other possessions. Among them was this sword. Alp-Arslan was overjoyed to get the boy back but he wouldn't touch the sword. In fact it was quite a problem to get him to accept the sheep. The sword, he said, was mine, the rightful spoils of war. And that is how I got it.' Absolon laughed again. 'Paid for in blood, eh? Other people's blood, of course! But then that was how our own wild ancestors acquired their land, was it not?'

He continued to fascinate Adrienne with the stories of his extraordinary adventures until well after dinner. Then Adrienne told her host that she must go to bed because she would have to leave for home very early the next morning.

'I won't keep you up,' he said. 'I know you have a long way to go. It was brave of you to have come all this way to take me into your confidence and I feel most honoured by your visit and

by your trust in me. As you have to go in the morning perhaps
you would be so kind as to take me as far as Regen? I have a little
business there and I would so enjoy your company on the trip.'

'Why, of course,' cried Adrienne. 'I would love it.'

Absolon himself showed her to one of the principal guest-
rooms. Marisko was there waiting and she explained how to turn
out the lamps and showed her that there were candles, matches
and water on a table by the bed. Then she turned to go but
stopped at the door and said, 'Kiss your hand, my Lady!' and went
swiftly out.

Adrienne lay back on the lavender-scented pillows and thought
about what had happened that day and what was to come in the
future. She was pleased about how the day had turned out and,
as she recalled how well she had been received by her husband's
uncle and how kind he had been in promising to help her, something he had said when asking if he could drive with her to
Regen kept recurring to her mind. Those words 'I have a little
business there' seemed to have no particular significance and
might indeed have referred to a hundred different little errands,
and yet, and yet? Surely there must have been some reason for
her to remember just that phrase so clearly?

Had it been that, as he spoke, he had raised one eyebrow in
just the same way as he had when he had been so careful in choosing his words about the arrangements for her divorce, about her
special responsibility, about Pali Uzdy? She was sure it had been
that, it must have been that.

As the thought came to her she drifted off to sleep.

The sturdy Miloth chestnuts trotted so eagerly in the morning
air that it seemed that they had hardly set off when they were
already approaching the town of Regen. Absolon had been unusually quiet on the way for he had been doing some hard thinking and felt he had to prepare himself for something unexpected.
He had noticed something wrong at the time of Margit's wedding. Although it seemed to most people that though he might
be calm and wise he was also perhaps rather remote and unconcerned, it was rarely noticed what a sharp observer he was.
It was the constant awareness of the hunter, still as much a part
of him as it had been in those years in the wild where for more
than a third of his life he had trained himself to notice everything,

the faintest sounds, the slightest movement, the least sign of something out of the ordinary; for it was on such things that a hunter depended, sometimes even for his life.

Pal Uzdy had naturally been at the wedding; and his uncle, who had not seen him for some time, had been disturbed by some decidedly odd mannerisms he seemed to have developed. Old Absolon noticed, for example, how often Uzdy would adopt unusual, even awkward, poses. He could see him now, standing in a group of people, but remaining oddly still with his right hand held in front of his face with the forefinger pointed back towards his nose just as if he were inspecting something caught under his nail. The stance was utterly contrived and, apparently, meaningless. When he moved he put one foot in front of the other with concentrated deliberation as if it were only by so doing that he prevented them from running away with him. When he spoke to anyone he affected a proud, disdainful manner which suggested that he despised them all. None of this was completely new to him for his manner had always been individual and usually ungracious; but his oddnesses had never before been so pronounced. Absolon was uncomfortably reminded of his brother-in-law shortly before he went off his head. Pal Uzdy's father had then shown much the same peculiarities as his son did now.

He had been thinking of this ever since that moment the day before when he had told Adrienne he sympathized with her wanting a divorce.

It was because of this that he had at once put through a telephone call to Regen. It had been to the principal of the hospital and it had been to warn him to expect him the following day. Now he was trying to decide how best to reveal to Adrienne that he thought it best, before giving her any further help and advice, to consult this particular doctor and indeed to take her to meet him. Dr Wolf Herman Kisch was a most distinguished practitioner and before accepting the post of running the Regen hospital he had been a consultant specialist in nervous diseases. He had worked with the internationally renowned Kraepelin in Berlin and also spent a year with Charcot. Absolon felt that they would be better qualified to deal with this delicate problem if first they had the benefit of Dr Kisch's advice. It was even possible that he would agree to help.

He lit another cigar and then turned to his niece. Carefully choosing his words so as not to alarm her, he said, 'Among other things, my dear niece, it occurred to me that since we are here we might take the opportunity of calling on an old friend of mine, Dr Kisch. He might give us some good advice on how best to tackle your problem.'

'Tell a country doctor about our private affairs? In Regen?' said Adrienne, astonished by such an out-of-the-way suggestion.

'Oh, he isn't at all what you think of as a country doctor. He's a most exceptional man and there are very few like him, not only here but in all Europe.' Without pausing long enough for Adrienne to veto the idea he proceeded to tell her Dr Kisch's story. He had been born, related Absolon, in the large German-speaking village of Dedrad nearby. He had been outstanding at school and after graduating at the Saxon University he had been offered a grant which would cover all his expenses to study medicine abroad if, in return, he would undertake to come back and take up any position for which they might want him. Kisch accepted. He qualified as a doctor and soon specialized in the new science of psychiatry. In this he undertook some highly important research and as a result the University of Jena offered him a professorship; but he could not then accept the offer. Just at that time, five years before, he had been called home as his sponsors wanted him to take up the direction of the brand-new little hospital at Regen. It had thirty beds and every modern improvement known to science. If he accepted it would mean giving up all idea of international fame, of time to pursue his researches, of everything for which he had seemed so uniquely qualified. Dr Kisch had stood by his word: he came back.

'You see, this really is a man to whom we could tell the truth about my nephew. There can be no doubt that if Pali Uzdy is not actually mad he is certainly not normal, so it would be a wise precaution to have him looked at by a specialist in mental cases. It would have to be done very discreetly, of course; and someone like Dr Kisch might advise some cure or other, some way to make him relax and take things more calmly. It might be a help in ensuring that ... that things went smoothly, that there weren't any unexpected ... er ... unpleasant consequences.'

Absolon's words were uttered with the same special inflection he had used the previous day when he had said, 'I will do as you ask and try to help. You ... and anyone else ... must be protected.'

'But aren't there excellent specialists at Kolozsvar?'

'My nephew probably knows them, if only by sight. He cannot possibly know anything about Dr Kisch. We might introduce him as some eminent fellow on a walking tour. As it happens, he really is an avid collector of butterflies, so it would seem quite natural if he suddenly turned up at Almasko.'

Adrienne did not answer, she was too upset by what she sensed lay behind the old man's words, by the possibility that Uzdy might need treatment for some nervous disorder. Though for years she had thought him remarkably odd and eccentric, it had never before occurred to her that he needed psychiatric treatment or that he might be heading for real madness; and the idea filled her with horror, for if that happened there could be no divorce and she would be bound to him until one of them died.

Absolon, perhaps sensing her thoughts, said reassuringly, 'Perhaps I'm being over-cautious, but it seemed like a good idea which might be a help in getting everything settled quickly. I'm sure it would help me to do what you ask.'

'All right!' said Adrienne. 'I trust you. I'll do whatever you think best.'

As they were driving into the town they caught up with Absolon's carriage which had left Borbathjo at dawn. It was drawn by four well-groomed ponies, sturdy and sleek with shiny coats and very long manes and tails. Absolon did not use a normal travelling carriage but preferred a long low country wagon such as the peasants used to go to market. The driver and groom were dressed to match, in the classic peasant's trousers and jerkins, just like all those who worked at Borbathjo both inside the house and out, for Absolon did not care for livery, thinking it somewhat pretentious.

When Adrienne's carriage drew abreast Absolon called out, 'Go straight to the White Lamb, unhitch the horses and wait there!'

As he spoke they were rumbling across the old bridge over the Maros and were soon jolting through the town on what were well-known to be the worst cobble-stones in the district. Right through the town they went and out on the other side, where the new hospital stood upon a hill.

It was a handsome building and on its façade, in huge letters, was written STÄDTLICHES KRANKENHAUS – Town Hospital. Inside, all the notices and signs were also written in German. The porter, who had already been warned of their arrival, showed them straight into the *Warteraum* from which opened another door labelled ORDINATIONS-ZIMMER DES OBERARZTES – Interview Room of the Doctor-in-Charge.

Almost at once a young doctor came in to conduct Absolon to his superior. Adrienne was left alone and was at once filled with unreasoning anxiety, which she did not understand for she had become accustomed to hospitals during the long years of her mother's illness and when her sister Judith had spent some time in various sanatoriums after her breakdown. At all those times she had been quite unaffected by the coldness and sterility of her surroundings and had paid no attention to it, accepting the frigid unwelcoming atmosphere as being appropriate to a building that had to be as functional as a machine-tool.

Today, however, she felt that there was something malevolent about those white walls, something that menaced her personally. The feeling came to her most strongly that she had arrived at some new and frightening crisis in her life and that her divorce was no longer just a matter of escaping from a hated husband or protecting the well-being of her lover but had somehow become the impersonal material of a medical case-history.

She was far too agitated to sit quietly waiting so she got up and walked over to the window. But once there she hardly noticed the ravishing view over the roofs of the old town, nor the ever-widening valley of the Maros which seemed to melt into the infinity of the misty blue sky above. She saw nothing of the radiance of the spring sunshine, nor the young green shoots on all the trees, nor the budding horse-chestnuts. She felt surrounded by impenetrable darkness, blinded by misery and with her whole soul torn by the agonizing question – what could it be that Absolon and Dr Kisch were taking so long to discuss?

Of course it was not really a long time and very soon the door opened and a pleasant voice said, '*Darf ich Sie bitten, Gnädige Frau* – perhaps we could talk now, my Lady?'

It was Wolf Herman Kisch. Absolon, who had come in with him, now left them alone.

Dr Kisch was a large big-boned man, almost as tall as Pal Uzdy. Though he could hardly have been more than forty he was completely bald. He had very pale blue eyes and wore enormous glasses and on his long-jawed face his mouth was a thin line with the lips normally kept so tightly closed that deep furrows had appeared on each side. And yet his manner was so endearing and sympathetic, his smile and the way he spoke so full of understanding, that it was as if some inner magic had ironed away those deeply etched lines of bitterness and disappointment.

As soon as she saw him Adrienne's depression lifted, her anxiety fled and she almost felt at ease as she sat there in front of him. What he now said was also reassuring.

Dr Kisch said that even though he thought it was hardly necessary for him to come to Almasko, of course he would do so because he had been asked by his dear friend Absolon with whom he often stayed in the country. Perhaps, too, it would be a wise thing to do as maybe he would be able to put his finger on something that was troubling Count Uzdy; and, if he knew what it was, perhaps too he could help in alleviating the stress it had caused. He hardly even mentioned the matter of divorce except to say that with people like her husband it was always better to act with care and circumspection. All this was wonderfully soothing to hear, not perhaps the sense of what he was saying but the sound of his voice, which was so caressing and sympathetic that Adrienne's fears were soon allayed.

Dr Kisch's technique was so accomplished that very soon they were talking about Adrienne's problems with as much ease as if it were mere drawing-room chat. She felt no shyness at all and they talked for a long time, until finally the doctor rose and straightened out his long body, which was made to look even taller than it was by his narrow white coat, and escorted her back to the waiting-room where Absolon sat placidly smoking a cigar. Then they discussed what they would do.

Dr Kisch said that he would not be able to get to Almasko before the middle of June when he would be taking some leave. He would definitely not arrive in a carriage as if paying a call but would come on foot, walking through the mountains and showing up as if by chance. He often went on walking tours, he said, and there wasn't a corner of the surrounding ranges that he didn't know well. '*Es wird mir eine Erholung sein* – it will be a holiday for me,' he said as if it were they who would be doing him a favour. '*Psychopatische Probleme haben mich immer sehr interessiert* – psychopathic cases have always interested me,' he said, and this was the only thing he did say which might have been taken as an allusion to all the sacrifices he had made when he had decided to come back home. For a moment his lips were again tightly pressed together as if in silent resignation; and then he went straight on in his natural friendly tones, '*Ich komme sobald ich kann . . . ich gebe Ihnen Bescheid* – I'll come as soon as I can. I'll let you know.'

He went down with them to the carriage and there he said some more encouraging things to them both before he walked slowly back to the tiny little hospital which must sometimes have seemed to him, who should have been something great in the world, like the tomb of all his desires.

But *Mannestreue*, that old German tradition that a man must be as good as his word, did not apply only to the glamour and chivalry of mediæval knights: heroism and self-sacrifice could be just as noble in the grey obscurity of ordinary people in a little country town.

Now the Miloth chestnuts were trotting briskly towards home. The lead-horse tossed his mane with eagerness and his companion lifted his muzzle as they climbed each slope as if scenting ever more familiar air. The shaft-horses leaned dutifully forward into their harness and the four of them somehow always managed to keep an even speed whether they were going up or down in that mountainous country. The sun glinted on their shining coats and they were not even beginning to sweat despite the distance they had travelled that day.

With so many of her fears allayed by the skilful Dr Kisch, Adrienne could once again appreciate the beauty of the spring landscape. Now they were already driving through the well-known and well-beloved hills of the Mezoseg country where she had been born. Each time they rode a crest in the hills a fantastic panorama was spread before them. Range after range of mountain peaks lay to the south and the west and here and there was a rocky summit towering above the others, all of which were now tinted gold by the setting sun with deep lilac shadows in the valleys between. Once, as they rounded a bend in the road, Adrienne caught a glimpse to the north of the high peaks of the Kelemen and Negoj ranges which sparkled with snow and ice all the year round. A few fleecy clouds floated high in the pale blue sky, and from time to time a glimpse could be caught of small lakes in the valleys, their shores bordered by reeds and their surfaces dotted with moorhen and wild duck. Sometimes too there could be heard the faint chorus of frogs croaking their love to potential mates.

At one turn the carriage had to stop to let by some hay-carts and here it was that Adrienne heard the song of a nightingale that must have been hidden in some thicket near the road. And at the sound every last hint of anxiety fled away from her as quickly as it had come. She no longer felt cowed and oppressed and she kept on hearing in her mind the last few words of that kind and sympathetic doctor, who had said, '*Seien Sie guten Mutes, Gnädige Frau, seien Sie guten Mutes* – be of good heart!' And though perhaps his words had been just what he always said to his patients, Adrienne did not think of them as such. To her they were a promise, a pledge, a hope . . .

She felt as if she had passed the first stop on her way to freedom.

PART SIX

CHAPTER ONE

IT WAS HALF-PAST ONE. Hundreds of news-vendors streamed out into Rakoczi Street carrying great stacks of newspapers, some in baskets or canvas bags, some under their arms. They were very different sorts of people, men with one leg, bent old crones and blind men led by children, though for the most part they were made up of growing lads, fleet-footed boys in their teens who raced each other towards the fashionable and crowded Karolyi and Museum Boulevards and the streets of the inner town, all shouting the news at the tops of their voices, knowing that he who shouted loudest would sell the most copies. They skidded and slithered in front of cars and trams, defying death by their daring, and ran on regardless, some on the pavements, dodging between the passers-by, and some in the middle of the streets in front of carriages and cart-horses, bicyclists and the wheels of angry motorists who responded with a chorus of klaxon horns. And no matter where they were, running among a thousand perils, they never stopped shouting the names of their news-papers and, to entice the passers-by, the day's sensational head-line: 'LASZLO LUKACS, HOMO REGIUS, LASZLO LUKACS...'

It was not often that the newsboys had such a good day. In a few moments they were surrounded by people and every paper sold. As it happened, business had been exceptionally good ever since April when the Wekerle government had resigned for the first time. Since then there had been several important royal audiences, and 'official sources' declared first that there would be an independent Hungarian State Bank and then that there wouldn't; there were rumours of secret intrigues with Vienna; and then, by the influence of the left-wing Independence Party, Parliament had been adjourned — it was all splendid fodder for the hungry newspapers! Then came revolution in Turkey and sensational developments, the army revolt in Istanbul (one minis-ter dead, two wounded!), street fights with troops brought in from across the Bosphorus and general mobilization in Salonika.

Pera rang with detailed rumours of the massacres in Armenia (women raped, children impaled!). Always there was some new sensation. One day the papers declared that troops from Salonika had marched on the capital and were camped round the walls; then they had marched in, besieged the Jildiz Palace and captured the Sultan Abdul Hamid. Sultan murdered! Sultan not murdered! Abdul Hamid escapes! He didn't escape but was torn from his throne and cast into prison! Then there was a new sultan, Mehmet V, who was brought out of obscure captivity and thrust onto the throne – and then there was a dictator, the Pasha Mehmet Sefket, who commanded the army at Salonika.

In May there were more juicy items to follow: a real Japanese prince visited Budapest. That sold a few more papers; then the Austrian Minister-President Bienerth attacked Burian openly in the Vienna Parliament, which completely put in the shade the pan-Slav conference in St Petersburg at which the Czech, Croatian, Serb and Slovak delegates were hailed as suffering brothers in a speech by the Tsar himself.

Then came June and still the news did not dry up. More audiences were held in Vienna as government crisis followed government crisis. Then a new development. Sensation! For the first time ever the Hungarian leaders Wekerle and Andrassy were received by the Heir, the Archduke Franz-Ferdinand, who was well known to hate Hungary. Although the leader-writers dared to produce only a watered-down version of what they knew about this historic encounter, it was clear to anyone who read between the lines that Franz-Ferdinand had received the men from Budapest with arrogant frigidity. At home there were more demonstrations calling for an independent banking system and noisy meetings were held in the great courtyard of the Town Hall and also in the country. Kossuth and Justh had a vitriolic argument at an important meeting of the Independence Party and it took, or so it was made to appear, three days of backroom negotiations before the two leaders could be induced at least to go through the motions of being friends again.

It was all very exciting; and it was very good for sales.

Now came the real bombshell. Laszlo Lukacs, once finance minister in the Tisza government, was rumoured to be bringing a royal decree from Vienna. Ignoring both the Minister-President Wekerle and the Independence Party leader Kossuth, he had consulted only Gyula Justh. Not until his appointment as *Homo*

Regius – the King's personal representative charged with forming
a new government and standing apart from all party loyalty – had
been publicly announced did he visit Kossuth; and even then he
held aloof from all the other Coalition leaders.

This was the greatest sensation of them all.

In front of the National Casino the news-vendors were doing a
roaring trade. Balint bought some papers and started to read them
as he walked towards the staircase. Then, bored with their exaggerated tone, he threw them away and went calmly up to the
first floor.

There he found a mass of angry politicians, mostly from the
Coalition and People's Parties, and with them some of the
followers of Apponyi. From inside the Coalition it seemed as if
the arch-enemy was Gyula Justh and he it was who everywhere
was being attacked by these noisy groups in which it seemed that
everyone was explaining everything to everyone else, and
that they were all doing it simultaneously. It was the same in the
great glazed-in terrace of the dining-room where Abady went
next. At every table he heard the same complaints.

Loudest of all was Lubiansky, whose patent of nobility had
been on the point of being gazetted; and now, because of the
change of government, all those years of planning and plotting had gone for nothing! Poor Lubiansky had been so eager
to have his daughters transformed into *Comtessen*, which would
have been a help in finding them husbands, and his sons given
just that extra fillip in their search for willing heiresses, but now
he would still have to endure being addressed as 'your Lordship'
merely out of courtesy and not because he had a right to it.

But even angrier than Lubiansky was Fredi Wuelffenstein
who, as usual, was laying down the law on constitutional precedent in terms of what was and what was not gentlemanly behaviour. This, for him, was the only criterion of proper conduct.

'No gentleman would have done what this Lukacs has!' he
roared. 'By-passing the Coalition leaders! Going behind the
back of the government to consult that awful busybody, that
demagogue Justh! You just don't do that sort of thing! Of course
I know what it's all about; they want to sabotage the new suffrage
laws and undermine our legitimate demands for the army, just as
in Kristoffy's time. All that creature Justh wants is to chuck away
our national aspirations! Into the dustbin with Hungarian sword

tassels and our thousand-year-old national language. My Hungarian blood boils at the thought of it!' he shouted, and wiped his forehead which was covered with beads of sweat brought out by his self-induced passion.

Antal Szent-Gyorgyi, who was sitting with icy calm at the next table, now said to Fredi, with disdainful irony, 'These demands – were they in the Constitution Party's programme too? I hadn't realized.'

Wuelffenstein swallowed the bait, not noticing that Szent-Gyorgyi was making fun of him.

'Oh no! We only accepted them at the time of the elections so as to keep those '48-ers quiet!'

He answered with extra politeness in the hope that the owner of Jablanka would again invite him to one of those much envied shooting parties. He went on, 'And so it would not be at all the right thing to do not to support those demands wholeheartedly, even though Kossuth and Independence members, and even more so Justh himself, seem to have dropped the matter and now only talk about the banking question, so naturally we have to go on with it. After all a gentleman's word is his bond, ain't it?'

And so it turned out that this *volte-face* on the part of the Constitution Party provoked yet another government crisis. While the men of 1848, for whom the army demands had been a banner and a rallying cry, now dropped the matter, the leaders of the Constitution Party, Wekerle and Andrassy, who had only accepted this distasteful policy so as to cement the Coalition, now found themselves its only supporters. There were those who declared, from the height of their political acumen, that the change was due merely to the Constitution Party's desire to hinder the establishment of an independent banking system, which they thought would harm the economy, and that the best way to achieve this would be cynically to offer the chauvinists an unimportant tit-bit in its place. This at least had a certain logic. Nevertheless the switch in policies did seem rather strange and independent observers watched with astonishment as both leading parties ignored their own traditional programmes and worked hard to promote those of their opponents! As it happened, though the crisis lasted many months and the fight was most bitterly fought, it all came to nothing for in the end the King refused both demands.

And so it turned out that all the energy and emotion put into this prolonged struggle, which paralysed the government of the country and ended only with the final demise of the Coalition, resulted only in further diminishing the prestige of the Monarchy.

Now some latecomers brought more news: details of Lukacs's proposed solution.

Farkas Alvinczy, who hitherto had always been a somewhat dim figure at the Casino, now had his brief hour of glory – barely more than fifteen minutes, as it turned out – for he had been with Kossuth and was able to give an authentic account of what was being planned.

Lukacs's proposal, it seems, was that a new government should be formed consisting only of members of the Independence Party, whose sole task should be the immediate establishment of universal suffrage. Apart from the Independents, certain posts – those of President of the House, Minister of the Interior and Chancellor of the Exchequer – were to be filled from the ranks of those former supporters of the links with Vienna as set out in the 1867 Compromise but who no longer owed allegiance to any party. This opened the doors to the free-thinkers and those who were tainted by memories of the Bodyguard government, as it had been called when the King had appointed General Fejervary to be Minister-President.

'Justh accepted the proposal,' cried Alvinczy, 'but Kossuth turned it down this morning. I had it directly from him!'

Alvinczy was visibly proud and pleased to be playing such an important role as the bearer of the news everyone was waiting to hear. He was all the more pleased with himself, for though he had been a Member for three years, and was a tall, handsome, elegant young man, who had even been known at the gaming-tables – without ever playing as recklessly as had Laszlo Gyeroffy a few years before – until now he had hardly been noticed. So he told his tale over and over again, to anyone who would listen; and each time he did it in exactly the same words, as honest men with a limited vocabulary are apt to do.

The news created great excitement. Only two of those present listened calmly and without enthusiasm. One of them was Antal Szent-Gyorgyi, who had almost certainly known in advance because of his close connections with the imperial court, and who in any case would automatically approve anything the Monarch might decide; and Balint Abady.

Abady's aloofness sprang only from the fact that his whole

mind was now filled with the question of Adrienne's divorce. A few weeks before he had had a letter from her announcing that her daughter was now back with her. Then another letter had come telling all about the visit to Absolon and the consultation with Dr Kisch. Balint had not understood why the doctor had had to be dragged into it all and, though still remaining resigned to the need for patience, was beginning to fret at the idea of further delays. And so, whatever daily sensations shook the world of politics, Balint's mind was occupied solely with thoughts of Adrienne, now far away at Almasko where their fate would soon be decided.

It was with indifference, therefore, that he listened to Alvinczy's great and important news; and he took equally calmly Szent-Gyorgyi's invitation, which was in itself a most exceptional distinction, to go with him by car to Alag where the great annual steeplechase was to be run that afternoon and in which one of Count Antal's horses was the favourite. 'All right!' he said when asked, and that was all, for was it not the same where he went and what he did or said or heard, when the only thing that mattered was when Adrienne would be free of her husband? Beside that, no one, and nothing, was of the smallest importance to him, and he barely noticed that in the car waiting for them below there were already two exceptionally pretty girls, his cousin Magda Szent-Gyorgyi and Lili Illesvary.

He had talked a lot to Lili when they had both been at Jablanka for the previous December's shooting party. Later, during the carnival season, he had seen her at the few grand balls he had attended and it had turned out – by chance, of course – that they had often found themselves next to each other in the ballroom or buffet. Occasionally they had danced a waltz together and once he had found himself, during the spring season, asking her for a cotillion for she admitted, as if it were a shameful secret only to be whispered about, that she didn't have a partner. All this had happened so naturally that it had appeared to Balint, who had been so taken up by the thoughts of his love for Adrienne that he had hardly noticed the existence of any other woman, that if he had spent more time with Lili than with any other girl, it had all been purely by chance. Of course he had enjoyed being with her for she talked well and her conversation had been both piquant and soothing like a draught of fresh orangeade.

It was the same now. Apart from some of those whose life was spent with horses and whom Balint barely knew, there were few women at the races, and so he passed the whole afternoon with Magda and Lili.

On their way back they asked him to dine with them that evening and one of them – it might have been Lili – said that they would be going to the Park Club.

When he arrived there were only a few people on the long terrace, just some young men staying at the club and the Lubiansky girls with their father; and, at a table some way off, Laszlo Lukacs and his beautiful wife. Sitting with them was another man whom Balint recognized even though his back was turned to them. It was Count Slawata, the confidential adviser to the Heir. Balint wondered if it was Slawata's presence that had made Lukacs choose a table so far off and well away from the bright lights of the chandeliers. Was there perhaps some connection between Lukacs and those plotters in the Belvedere Palace? Could it be that the *Homo Regius* – the King's Man – was now also in direct touch with the next ruler?

Balint did not want to have to meet Slawata at this time; and furthermore he was in no mood for prolonged political discussions; and so, when they had finished dinner and the girls had first talked of dancing to the gramophone and then decided that it was too hot and that they would rather play some parlour-game, Balint at once agreed to join in. It was still partly that he did not really care what he did, but also he now felt quite unable to listen to any more of old Lubiansky's endless complaints about the way the country was being governed, and also wanted to get as far away from Slawata as possible.

They went indoors and settled in one of the cool drawing-rooms. Lili suggested they play the old parlour-game of 'Up Jenkins' which meant that they had to separate into two equal groups who sat on opposite sides of a table with the leaders of each group facing each other in the centre. One of them selected some small object, such as a coin or a ring, to be the 'Jenkins' and, on the command 'Up Jenkins!', he showed it to the opposing team. When the command came, 'Down Jenkins!', he put his hands under the table and, concealed by the cloth, passed it to another member of his team. Now came 'Jenkins on the table!' and all the team who were hiding Jenkins had to put their hands on the table.

Who had Jenkins? This was the game and there was much laughter and mockery as they all made guesses. In the end the leader had to decide and could point to only one of the hands on the table. If he was wrong there was much triumph on the side with Jenkins and gloom on that of the seekers, and the game went on until Jenkins had been found. Then Jenkins crossed the table and it all started again.

Magda offered a ring to be Jenkins, and the two leaders were Lili and Balint.

They were sitting facing each other across the table. Lili was wearing a light summer dress with rather short but wide sleeves of *broderie anglaise* and through the many little embroidered holes in the material could be caught glimpses of the pink skin of her arms and shoulders. The dress was suitable only for a young girl and was almost childish in its virginal whiteness – but was far more arousing than any sophisticated *décolletée*.

At first Balint hardly noticed. Slowly, however, indeed every time that Lili lifted her hands in some gesture to show everyone the ring and the wide sleeves slid back on her bare arms, he found himself flooded by a strange magic. It was as if she sat there before him clad only in a wedding shift, her flesh barely covered by fine gossamer, smiling expectantly and looking at him with some unspoken question in her eyes. Even Balint knew that this was no game, no meaningless attempt at flirtation but was rather the eternal urge of the female to attract and to lure. Everything about her told him the same story. Her petal-like skin with its elusive scent, the slightly parted lips, the dress falling in soft folds around the infinitely desirable curves of her firm breasts: this was no trivial, shallow game but rather the subconscious display of the finest weapons in a woman's armoury of attraction.

Balint felt a twinge of guilt at having sensed it, and guilty too at finding himself aroused by desire and yet being unable, in spite of the laughter and simplicity of the childish nursery game, to free himself of it.

This was the only time when, for a brief moment, he was made to forget the agony of waiting which otherwise totally engrossed him. He could think of nothing but when he would get news from home and discover what had happened at Almasko.

Balint heard with indifference what was happening in the great world around him. Whereas a month or two before, during the long winter months, worry about the possibility of war and the fate of his beloved country could make him forget his private worries, this was no longer true. The deepening political crisis at home – Wekerle's resignation, Lukacs's embarrassed handing-in of the royal commission, the King's insistence on a new coalition, new rifts between Kossuth and Justh – and alarming news from abroad with Sir Edward Grey's depressing analysis of the international dissensions, the menacing build-up of the British Fleet, the Eulenburg scandal and the sudden resignation of the Chancellor Bülow, now all seemed so trivial to Balint that he barely took any of it in.

On the other hand not a day passed without him becoming more and more anxious about Adrienne.

In her last letter she had said that soon the doctor from Regen would turn up with old Absolon and so at any moment the great decision should be made. Balint now felt he must return so as to be within reach when their fate was decided. In this way he would get the news more quickly and would be on the spot if she needed help. He could get over to Almasko in no time in his new car, and could whisk her away to safety if she felt in any danger from her husband. Balint felt he must be ready for anything, and for that he had to be at home.

On July 9th he made up his mind to go as soon as possible. It was late afternoon and too late to send a telegram to Denestornya, because it could hardly get delivered before he would be there himself. It did not really matter, for he was sure to find some little horse-drawn gig or fiacre at the station at Aranyos-Gyeres. At eight in the morning he got down from his sleeper and was surprised to notice that the express did not leave again at once but remained stationary at a side platform. In front of the booking office the station-master was standing, white-gloved and in full formal uniform. With him was his assistant, similarly dressed, and both looked nervous and unhappy. Uniformed railway staff were running about in all directions, checking the points, and two constables were marching officiously up and down and ordering everyone to keep off the platform.

'What's going on?' Balint asked as he shook hands with the old station-master. As he did so one of the constables was unceremoniously pushing Balint's porter out of the way. 'What's all this about then?'

'The Heir's private train is due to pass through in a few minutes. It has already signalled and we have strict orders to clear the station of everyone but the railway staff. Please forgive me . . .' and he trailed off clearly embarrassed at having to treat Count Abady in this fashion, for he had known the family all his life as it was the station for Denestornya. Then he accompanied Balint to the exit; even for the noble Count himself he could not disobey orders from so high a source.

A few moments later Balint had got into a small one-horse cart, and was nearly clear of the village, when from the bridge over the river came the rumbling sound of an approaching train. From the engine came a discreet whistle, then there was the scream of brakes and the train started to slow down. At the platform it stopped, but only for an instant, and then, quickly gathering speed, trundled off in the direction of the mountains.

Balint did not pause to wonder why Franz-Ferdinand's train had stopped, if only for an instant, at such an obscure wayside station. Neither did any of the other passengers who had been herded like cattle into the waiting-room. But if someone had noticed and had thought fit to alert one of the more chauvinist of the Budapest papers, there would have been screaming headlines and a big political row. The reason was that the person for whom the train had been halted, and who had hurried discreetly out of the station-master's office and through the already opened door of one of the saloon-cars, was none other than Aurel Timisan, the champion of the rights of the large Romanian minority in Hungarian Transylvania.

The *Werkstadt* – the Archduke's private office in the Belvedere Palace – had been in secret contact with Timisan, as it was with many of the other minority leaders, for many months. It was someone from there that had given Timisan orders to join the train at Aranyos-Gyeres, sent him his travel papers and ensured that the station should be cleared so that no one should see him climb aboard. A few stations later the process was reversed and he left the train still unnoticed. He had just had time to hand over the lists of names that the Heir's principal private secretary had demanded.

The next day, in the Romanian town of Sinaia, the Archduke Franz-Ferdinand received a group of political exiles. They were the leaders of most of the ethnic minorities of the far-flung Habsburg empire, that empire over which he expected soon to rule.

While he was assuring these good men of his good will and future patronage, a band of students tore through the elaborately decorated streets of the little spa, tore down all the Hungarian flags, those symbols of the independence of the Monarchy's sister country, and trampled them in the mud.

CHAPTER TWO

BALINT READ ABOUT the riot at Sinaia at tea-time at Denestornya, when the Budapest morning papers arrived. At the same time the midday edition of the Kolozsvar paper arrived carrying an official denial on its front page. This declared that absolutely nothing had happened; the Archduke had received no one and no insults had been offered to the Hungarian flag. The previous day's report was based on a most regrettable mistake – or so announced the official spokesman of the Palace.

Whether anyone believed this was another question; Balint certainly did not. Everything he knew about the personality and views of the Heir to the throne, and everything that Slawata had told him in confidence several years before, affirmed the truth of the reports. Nevertheless he tried hard not to think about the matter and meekly to accept the official denial, for in this way he was able to turn aside from what in other times would have filled him with alarm because of its dire implications for the country's future. To have worried now about the Heir's complicated plots would have torn him away from that one personal problem that needed his whole attention.

The time had come when he would have to tell his mother that he would soon be married. The problem was how and when to do it.

That it would be painful for them both was certain. He need not do anything until the news came from Almasko, but then he would have to act at once, for afterwards he knew that he would not be able to remain more than an hour in the same house with his mother. He knew her so well; and what she once said with such firmness she never went back on. When she heard that the marriage with Adrienne was not only certain but imminent she would act as if her son had died and this she would maintain, if not forever, certainly for a very, very long time. Only if the longed-for grandchild was born, and then, if it were a boy, an heir to her name and to Denestornya – only then, might she begin to relent and possibly forgive.

Balint realized that it was now, during these few days at home, that he had to make all his preparations.

First of all it was clear that he could not be with Adrienne either here or at Kolozsvar, for they could not live together in the same town as Countess Roza. The only answer was Budapest, where things would not be so obvious and the irregularity of their situation, even if only temporary, would not be so painful for either of them. He would therefore have to take a flat there.

Next it was clear that he would no longer receive the allowance that his mother had made him since he first joined the diplomatic service. It was only too probable that Countess Roza would stop it at once. His salary as a Member of Parliament was negligible, not that he was really in need of it for he was entitled to receive that part of the Abady inheritance that came from his grandfather, Count Peter, his father's father. Until now this had never been administered separately, for the entire estate income had been paid directly to his mother and Balint had had no reason to want anything different. The twin properties of Denestornya had been thought of as one ever since they had been reunited by his parents' marriage, while the forestlands in the mountains, of which Balint had inherited a quarter share from his father, had never been divided either.

Even if it did not amount to a great deal, he still had an income on which he would be able to live. Since Balint had reorganized the husbandry of the forests some years before, at which time he had made some profitable contracts with an Austrian timber merchant from Vienna, they had begun to bring in more money, and Balint knew that he could count on some 20,000 crowns annually.

It was possible that there might be something else too, for he remembered that his grandfather had also possessed some property in the lower Jara valley. This was now let, but as it belonged legally only to him he would be able to claim the annual rental, whatever it was.

Then there was the question of his grandfather's furniture, which had all been stored in some unused rooms at Denestornya, ever since Countess Roza had allowed Azbej to move into the old manor house where his grandfather had lived. He remembered well the huge desk made of root-wood, but of the rest he only had the haziest memories. Of course lists had been made before the house had been emptied for Azbej, and his mother had often referred to an inventory having been taken; but where was it?

Balint searched the library and when he did not find it he realized that it must be in Azbej's office in the old manor house below the church. He would have to go there and ask him for it.

These thoughts were occupying Balint's mind as he sat on the covered veranda drinking tea with his mother. He tried hard to give her the impression that he was absorbed only by the newspapers, from which he kept reading aloud passages he thought might interest her; but in reality he was thinking only of his own problems.

Countess Roza, too, nodded approval or surprise at whatever her son read out, but she wasn't paying any attention either. All she noticed was the remote, closed expression on her son's face; and the more she saw how worried he looked, the more she was convinced that the day of that accursed wedding was approaching and that soon she would lose the only and the last person she loved.

Balint unhooked the key of the cemetery from the nail on which it hung at the bottom of the staircase, and hurried down the path on the west side of the hill on which the castle had been built. He passed swiftly the now sizeable fir trees that grew beside the worn stone steps on the path until he arrived at the gate below. As he went he recalled that day a year before when he had gone with his mother to Communion on the Day of the New Bread. Then he had been buoyed up with hope and confident that he would be able to arrange amicably the matter of his marriage.

It was then that he had vowed to bring order into his life.

The disappointment when he discovered his mother's determined opposition now overwhelmed him again and almost dispelled the distaste with which he revisited the house where his beloved grandfather had lived.

He had not been there since the old man's death. By the time that Balint, then a fifteen-year-old schoolboy at the Theresianum, had got home from Vienna, Count Peter was already lying on his bier in the main aisle of the little family church. After that his rooms had been locked and when, years later, Countess Roza had emptied them to make room for Azbej, Balint had always managed to avoid going to see the garden, the wide porticoed veranda and the rooms where, in his imagination, the old man lived still.

Today, however, he had to go there; he had no choice.

The door out of the cemetery opened with difficulty and the rusted lock screeched. Inside the manor house garden the once immaculate path was almost submerged with weeds. This was the way he had come with his mother, every Sunday after church, to lunch with Count Peter. The lilac bushes on each side were now so neglected and overgrown that there was hardly room to pass between them. Balint began to hate it all; and it was worse when he reached the garden itself. All his grandfather's once lovingly-tended roses had disappeared and only here and there was to be seen a fallen stem surrounded by suckers. On the house itself only one undernourished climbing rose was still there, the rest obviously having died.

Balint's worst disappointment was the sight of the house itself. The four Greek columns of the portico, which had once been bright with clean whitewash, had been gaudily covered in shiny green paint to resemble marble. On the ceiling had been daubed some crude butterflies, birds and clouds, and on both sides of the main door were coarse murals, one of Fiume and the other of Naples with Vesuvius belching smoke.

In front of this motley background, lying on a straw bed covered with fireman's-red coloured cushions, was a fat slatternly little woman wearing a half-open dressing gown covered in velvet peonies. With her were two children asleep, one at the breast and the other lying on her knees, while a third was sitting on the floor trying to eat a pear from a basket that had been left there.

For a moment all was peaceful. Then a storm broke out. The child with the pear let out a fearful scream when it saw Abady, the woman woke up and struggled to her feet, dropping the other two; and then they all ran howling indoors, the heels of the woman's slippers going slap-slap on the wooden floor, and the children howling as if they had seen a Bogey-man. And then, just as suddenly, there was silence again as they vanished into the house.

Despite his distaste, Balint could not help noticing how absurd the scene was, particularly as the woman and the children had been so exactly like Azbej himself, brown and hairy and so round that they seemed to roll rather than run. Alone with the spilt basket of pears, Balint realized that it must be Azbej's wife and that now, no doubt, she was calling her husband.

He turned back towards the garden, all appreciation of the comicality of the scene having vanished as he looked in growing horror at the sight of that once so elegant snow-white veranda disfigured and desecrated; for it was here that he had best remembered his grandfather sitting in a tall wicker chair, meerschaum pipe in mouth, with wavy silver hair and a smile of infinite kindness and wisdom. Balint preferred to look at the garden, for though it was neglected and allowed to run riot, at least the deterioration was the work of nature and not inflicted by the barbaric taste of man.

He did not have to wait long. In a few moments the fat little lawyer came out at a run, bowing as he did so. 'What an honour! I am indeed fortunate,' said Azbej, and he repeated the words several times, always bowing again as he did so. 'I am always at your Lordship's command . . . your Lordship should have sent for me . . . I am always at your Lordship's command.'

'I need some information,' replied Abady. 'Perhaps we should go up to the office in the castle.' And when Azbej enquired what he needed, he explained that he wanted to look at the inventory of his grandfather's furniture and belongings.

'But that is here in my study, if your Lordship pleases. I keep all the old documents here. I beg your Lordship to come in.'

And so, though he was loath to do it, Balint found himself obliged to enter the house.

The first room they went through was the former dining-room, once painted pale green and hung with family portraits. Now it was used as a sitting-room and was furnished with red-plush sofas and a lot of little occasional tables in some sort of oriental style, hung with tassels made of tiny little wooden balls stuck together. The walls also were red, painted to resemble brocade up to the height of the doors, and from then up the frieze and ceiling had been done in imitation wood-panelling.

Next they went into Count Peter's study. This had not suffered the same transformation. Where the Empire bookcases had stood there were now open wooden shelves in the American manner, and Azbej's modern desk stood in just the same place as had

Count Peter's. But at least there were no such horrors as Balint had seen elsewhere; probably, he thought, because Azbej perhaps only perpetrated his 'improvements' to please his wife.

However it was clear that the estate papers were kept in good order and that Azbej knew where everything was to be found. In a few moments he was able to hand the inventory to the younger man.

Balint looked at it carefully, and as he did so Countess Roza's trusted agent stood beside him, a questioning glint in his prune-shaped eyes.

Balint read through the papers and said, 'I am finding it rather expensive staying in a hotel whenever I'm in Budapest; so I'm thinking of taking a flat. Also it is tiresome always having to lug my files and other papers about with me; and I really don't know what to do with all my books. So I think I'll start making use of some of these pieces again. Please be so good as to have the inventory copied. I don't yet know what I want but when I do I'll mark it and let you have it back.'

Azbej's cherry-red little mouth, which seemed so gentle and small in that forest of bristly black beard, now formed itself into a deferential smile.

'This is the file concerning all the properties of his late Excellency Count Peter,' he said, as if he knew exactly what Balint had in mind in coming to see him. 'Perhaps your Lordship might like to look over that too since I am so honoured to have your Lordship here today,' and he handed him the papers. 'I have waited a long time to have an opportunity to account for my stewardship.'

Balint leafed through the papers, among which he soon found the title-deeds to the Jara valley property. 'Is this let? How much does it bring in?' he asked, as if it were a casual enquiry made by chance.

The fat little lawyer was not deceived, though his face gave nothing away. 'Four thousand five hundred crowns a year, your Lordship,' he said, still speaking with great deference. 'However the lease falls in very soon, at Michaelmas, and if your Lordship wishes it, the rent could then be considerably increased. Oh yes, considerably increased!'

As Abady got up to go, it was clear that the lawyer still wanted to say something. Somewhat hesitantly Azbej suggested that Balint might like to take away the file of his grandfather's estate, adding that he did not need the originals as there were copies of everything in the office. 'All this is your Lordship's own property,' he said, and repeated, 'your Lordship's personal property,' with just perceptible emphasis.

Balint took the file, put it under his arm and turned towards the door. Azbej accompanied him as far as the door into the cemetery and stood there bowing, three times in all, until the lock clicked behind his visitor. Then he straightened up and rubbed his little hands together, his eyes glinting with malicious joy as he thought of the use to which he could put Balint's visit.

As Azbej walked slowly back to the frog-green columns of the former Abady manor house, he was turning over in his mind how best he could let the Countess Roza know that her son was planning to reclaim what he had inherited from his grandfather.

The first move was made the very next day, when, as usual, he told his two allies, the housekeepers Mrs Tothy and Mrs Baczo.

They, in their turn and in their usual way, gossiped away in front of their mistress about the wickedness of the world in general and, in particular, though in veiled terms, about what was going on under their very noses; and when one of them had said 'Master Balint had actually demanded and then taken away the documents', just that, no more, Countess Roza had been given a good idea of what they had wanted her to know.

The old lady at once sent for Azbej who confirmed the news she had heard, and added that it appeared that the young master was planning to go to live in Budapest. He went on to say, more than once, how surprised he had been by Count Balint's manner, how he had given his orders in unusually forceful terms and how he had given the agent no opportunity of asking his mistress for instructions. He told his tale with much skill and as always with great deference and never failing to be careful of what he said, for he knew that Countess Abady would never allow anyone to criticize her son in her presence, no matter how angry she might be.

For the poor old lady the news was like a knife-thrust. That her beloved son should start gathering up family papers without a word to her – papers that he was, no doubt, going to use against her – was enough to make her fancy that her whole world was crumbling around her.

She said nothing to him, for there was nothing she could say and nothing she wanted to say. But she hardened her heart, preparing herself for the awful battle she knew was soon to be waged between them.

And so the relations between mother and son became even colder and more distant as the days went by.

A few days later a letter from Adrienne arrived at Denestornya. It gave a brief account of the Saxon doctor's visit to Almasko and merely said that nothing could be decided at once and that they would still have to wait some weeks, perhaps a month, and then, maybe then, she would be able to tell her husband of her intention to sue for divorce. At present it was still impossible and so they would still have to wait. Wait!

Though she did not say so in so many words, it was clear that Adrienne was deeply depressed. She did not go into any details beyond saying that Dr Kisch had made a good impression at Almasko.

Dr Kisch had planned his arrival carefully and he had furthermore been helped by what appeared to be a happy chance, though it is true that some clever people seem to be able to create their own chances.

One day Pal Uzdy was practising target and clay pigeon shooting on the hollowed-out hillside near the edge of the Almasko park that he had had specially laid out for that purpose. The stands were at the foot of the hill and there stood the rifle-racks and a telescope on a tripod with which to check the accuracy of the shooting. In front was a small meadow and at its farther end a trench had been dug from which the lad who had been trained for the purpose fed the five mechanical disc-throwers. On the other side, in front of the hillside, rows of targets had been set up at exactly 50, 100, 200 and 250 metres' distance from the rifle stand. The whole area was fenced in by a thick wire mesh above and on both sides of the target. At the right-hand side of the range were the first trees of the surrounding forest.

At one time Uzdy had practised every day, but recently, since he had become interested in his new theory of numbers, he had come less often. Lack of practice, however, had not affected his skill as a marksman and, no matter what calibre of bullet he used, he rarely missed the centre of the target.

On that morning he had been down at the range for some

time, firstly shooting at the clay discs and, when they ran out, at the 250-metre target.

This was placed near the top of the hillside. Beside Uzdy, the girl Clemmie's English nanny watched the target through the telescope and announced the results. This had been her job since the girl had been given a French governess. Uzdy, though he never spoke to her and had never seemed to notice her existence, had suddenly developed a liking for the elderly spinster and now always gave her this task.

At one moment the butler Maier came to ask if his master wanted to come back to the house for tea or if he wished it brought down to the range. Though normally he sent a footman on this errand, on this day he came down himself. When his master gave no answer but went on shooting, Maier just stood patiently waiting. As he did so he kept his eyes on the hillside.

Although it was quite late in the afternoon the sun was still shining brightly and where the blackthorn and beech seedlings had been planted on the steep hillside every branch was clearly etched against the yellow clay soil. Here and there some outcrops of chalk rock gleamed white and the grass seemed even greener than usual, even through the mesh of the wire fence.

A figure came out of the forest above the range, a tall man wearing a plus-four suit of green linen and hobnailed boots. He was wearing thick glasses, carried a butterfly net in one hand, with a rucksack on his back and a tin box slung over one shoulder. He was walking along a rarely used path which, before this hillside had been fenced in, had formerly been a cattle-track that came through the woods and then diagonally down the hill where the shooting range now stood.

The stranger moved forward with slow deliberate steps until one foot hit the wire mesh. Then he stooped and, being obviously very short-sighted, bent down to see what it was that stood in his way. Then, having exceptionally long legs, he stepped over the fence and calmly continued on his way . . . in the direction of the targets.

The old English nanny saw him first. So, perhaps, did Maier, but he did not say anything.

'Look out! There's a man up there!' called out the nanny in English and then everyone, Uzdy, Maier, the nanny and even the boy in the ditch, all shouted to the traveller who, heedless of the uproar, walked straight on into the path of the bullets. He took no notice of the noise, presumably not thinking he might be the cause of it, but merely walked calmly onwards.

At this Uzdy lost his temper. In quick succession he fired three bullets which hit the rocks a few inches in front of the stranger's feet. Pakk! Pakk! Pakk! Three sharp metallic clangs. Little fragments of rock shot about.

Only now did it seem that the traveller realized he had perhaps strayed into a dangerous spot. He turned in the direction from which the bullets had come and then, still quite slowly, descended the steep slope of the hill.

Pal Uzdy was chuckling triumphantly.

'Please forgive me for trespassing on private land,' said the stranger when he had jumped the ditch and reached the rifle stands. He then lifted his hat and introduced himself. 'Wolf Hermann Kisch, from Szasz-Regen.'

He said nothing else, and nothing at all to indicate that he was a doctor by profession. He spoke fluent Hungarian with hardly a trace of a German accent, and he explained that he was a keen collector of butterflies and had wandered rather further than he had planned. That was how he had happened to come so far, roaming wherever the chase took him. Uzdy was now roaring with laughter, but the doctor took it all in good part. Looking around he saw the elderly Englishwoman and said, 'Your wife, I presume! I kiss your hand, my Lady.' He didn't seem to notice Maier, though it had been with him that he had planned his arrival that morning when the old butler had walked over to the inn at Korosfo. Maier had started life as a trained nurse.

That was how Dr Kisch had introduced himself to Almasko, and Uzdy had at once asked him to stay, considering the doctor as his special acquisition, almost as his prey. It was as if he were proud of him. Countess Clémence, just as obviously, disliked him. She too did not know his profession.

For some time now Uzdy had no longer listened to anything his mother had to say. There was even a hostile glint in his eyes when he looked at her. This had started when the old lady had got back from Meran, and was most unexpected in Uzdy who had always been scrupulously polite and attentive to her. Now he would answer her with unconcealed irritation and sometimes he even queried her household arrangements even though that had always been her undisputed domain. Then too he would tease and persecute the new governess, and he would do it in such a way that it was clear to everyone that he only did it to annoy his mother.

However he took an immediate liking to Dr Kisch and on the first morning of his stay took him into his confidence and revealed to him all the details of that tremendous secret by which he would reform the whole world's science of figures. All through Dr Kisch's stay they would be closeted together for hours on end, go for long walks together, and spend half the night in talk in Uzdy's study. Though it was forbidden to everyone else the doctor was told to enter that holy of holies whenever he wished, whether invited or not.

Seeing this Adrienne began to realize what an accomplished man he was.

Altogether he spent five days at Almasko. On the sixth day he left at dawn. The night before, when he said his goodbyes, his host made him promise to return at the end of the summer.

'I'll come then because the most interesting butterflies are to be found at the beginning of the autumn,' Dr Kisch replied, playing his part as a specialist in such matters.

Though offered the carriage he left on foot as he had come, taking the path to the crest of the hills where it joined the road to Banffy-Hunyad. It was barely dawn when he left.

A few hours later Adrienne went for a walk, not on the same path but in the same direction. They had agreed this in advance for it had been quite impossible for them to talk privately while the doctor was staying in the house. The matter had been fixed by Maier, the butler, who was the only person at Almasko whom Adrienne could trust with the knowledge of the doctor's real identity and the purpose of his visit. They had worked it all out when she returned from seeing Dr Kisch at Regen.

Adrienne had always been an early riser and often in the mornings would go for long walks in the forest, so there was nothing unusual about her doing the same that morning.

Filled with anxiety she hurried through the young trees. Her heart was beating furiously for she realized that her fate would shortly be decided and that she would soon know whether it would be possible to bring up the question of divorce. She had no presentiments, either good or bad, for she had been able to read nothing in the doctor's face, even though she had been watching closely for five long days.

As she emerged from the woods Adrienne saw that Dr Kisch was waiting for her just beyond where the last trees had been felled. He was sitting, exactly as planned, on one of the posts that marked the boundary of the Uzdy properties.

As it would not be wise for them to be seen together, for no one gossiped more than country people and many of them used this little road on their way to market, Adrienne at once suggested that they left the path and walked back into the trees.

There was only one direction in which they could go. Only there, into the Abady lands at that ancient beech tree surrounded by young shoots, to the same spot where she and Balint had renewed their love the year before, could she be sure of not being seen. For months before that, during their long separation, she had often come there alone, hoping subconsciously for that longed-for reunion, for that unplanned meeting which one day had become a reality. Why had she chosen that spot? Because it was there that she used to meet Balint at the very beginning of their love for each other, and because it was their own secret meeting-place.

Adrienne had come to look on the giant old tree as her friend and protector, for it had been the only witness of their mutual fulfilment and so to her was symbolic of their passion for each other.

Now, when Adrienne had led the doctor to this secret place, she leaned back against the great trunk. He stood before her and told her what she had to know.

He spoke carefully, choosing his words with his usual circumspection. He started by going over the known facts: Uzdy's parents had both been mentally afflicted, the father clinically mad and Countess Clémence seemed to him to be far from normal. This in itself did not mean very much, for hardly anybody would be considered normal if all their oddnesses and quirks of behaviour were to be known.

Adrienne nodded her understanding but did not interrupt, only her large topaz-coloured eyes widened in anxious expectation.

The doctor went on, his soothing voice blunting the effect of the harsh facts he had to convey. His meaning, however, was utterly clear. He believed that Uzdy was at present in a state of high nervous tension. This might, indeed probably would, diminish in time, especially if he took regularly the calming medicine he had recommended.

'I didn't give him an official prescription as a doctor would,' he said smiling. 'He believes me to be some sort of amateur quack. I had to make it appear that way if he was going to take me seriously! He thinks it's something to stimulate the brain for the unusual but interesting work on which he is engaged. Nothing else can be done for the present. We have got to wait until this degree of over-excitement had died down.'

Then he explained that people like her husband suffered alternating periods of excitement and unnatural calm, and that these periods could be longer or shorter and could even disappear altogether. There was always the possibility of cure. Now followed the doctor's considered diagnosis for which Adrienne had been waiting with agony in her heart. Dr Kisch's voice became lower as he pronounced the fatal words: '*Bei dieser heute latenten Erregung könnte jede seelische Erschütterung irgend einer Art eine heftige Krise zum Ausbruch bringen, die nicht ohne ernste Folgen bliebe* – in this state of latent excitement any spiritual shock might bring on a crisis which could have dangerous secondary effects.' This obviously meant her divorce, for that would be a severe 'spiritual shock' – it was, in fact, the exact opposite of everything that she had been hoping for these last long years.

When they finally said goodbye Dr Kisch added some phrases so as not to sound too discouraging, words that could be taken as hopeful but which, in the pain and disappointment of knowing that they still had to wait, Adrienne only remembered long afterwards.

For some time she remained there at the foot of the tree. She gazed ahead of her across the familiar clearing, in front of which she had so often paused before taking the path which led to the log-cabin that Balint had had built so that they should have a place to make love. It was here that a sudden wind had once torn down the young undergrowth, and now it seemed to the young woman standing there with such unnatural stillness that great swirls of mist were rising all around her and that the whole world grew darker and darker until she was alone in a sea of blackness. Then her knees buckled and she slid unconscious down the trunk of the great tree and lay in a faint between its entwining roots.

It was a long time before Adrienne came to, and by then the noonday sun was shining on her face. She had been lying on the same soft bed of moss on which she and Balint had fallen into each other's arms that evening in May a year before.

CHAPTER THREE

ADRIENNE'S FIRST LETTER found Balint at Denestornya, the next at Budapest. In between he received a brief note which 'Honey' Andras Zutor, the forest guard, delivered to Abady at Banffy-Hunyad. All this said was:

We can't see each other, not for a long time. I'll write to Budapest.

Adrienne had had to send it there because Balint, when he had received her first breathless message at Denestornya, had at once written back that he would come to the cabin in the forest so that they could meet.

Though the fact that this new turn in events meant that the inevitable break with his mother was now delayed was some slight consolation, the despair he sensed from Adrienne's brief letter was a deep source of worry. It was because of this that he had decided to go to the Kalotaszeg so that they would be able to talk matters out face to face. Life at home was becoming more and more intolerable as the relations between mother and son grew ever colder and more tense. Everything they said to each other had an artificial ring, so much so that they might have been two sleepwalkers speaking at each other. Mother and son would still have their meals together, walk down to see the horses, stroll in the park and round the gardens, but it was all a sham; to both of them everything they did was no more than a charade designed to fill in the ever-diminishing time they had together before the storm broke.

On the surface they both maintained the fiction that nothing had changed between them.

One day Balint read out to his mother a report that had been sent to him by their forest manager Winckler. It said that this summer red deer had appeared on the mountain, and that he supposed that they must have come from the Gyalu range or from Dobrin, the Andrassys' place, where quite a number had been set free ten years before. Two groups of hinds had been sighted, with some youngish stags in attendance, and there were reports of great bulls with magnificent sets of antlers though it was not clear if they referred to one bull or to several different ones.

Balint showed the report to his mother, explaining as he did so how marvellous it would be if the red deer could be induced to stay. He thought he should go there at once and order larger feeding troughs and salt-licks to be provided to attract the deer in the coming winter. Roza Abady listened stony-faced; she didn't believe a word of it. All she knew was that a letter had arrived from Almasko, and she was sure that her son had received a summons. Accordingly she hardly glanced at the papers her son passed over to her, but said icily, 'Yes, of course. All right. Go if you must!'

Her protruding eyes might have been made of glass.

Balint only spent a few days on the mountain. He heard what the *gornyiks*, who had seen the deer, had to tell him about their tracks, and in turn had given his instructions about food troughs and the provision of rock-salt. And with the manager he discussed all those seemingly endless subjects that crop up in any substantial forestry holding; but his heart was not in it, for all he could think about was Adrienne's divorce.

Everything he did, he did automatically, like a robot, and, most unusual for him, he did not even notice any of the beauties of nature. Indeed he could hardly wait to get away.

The letter he found waiting in Budapest was longer than the first, but still far from clear. Adrienne related what the doctor had said, but in hesitant, imprecise terms; and she also told him of those few more encouraging words he had said before they parted. There was something else which made Balint wonder where all this was leading to. When Adrienne wrote about how Dr Kisch had said that in Uzdy's present state of mind any sudden shock might provoke a dangerous reaction, she had added two phrases about her daughter Clemmie: '*We also have to consider her future. The child's stability must be protected too!*'

Adrienne had added these two little phrases only so that Balint should not begin to worry about his personal safety. She had known that he would never accept this as a valid reason for delay, but she had written honestly and truthfully because she was not only devoted to the child but also worried about her, since it was

clear that old Countess Clémence did more and more to alienate
the child from its mother. As it happened Adrienne's anxiety was
not entirely justified because Clemmie lived in a separate wing
of the house at Almasko, along with her French governess and
the old English nanny, and it was easy to keep from her anything
that happened in other parts of that large house.

Balint knew this and so Adrienne's innocent remarks first
startled him and then sparked off a new and disconcerting train
of thought.

It occurred to him that Adrienne had become so obsessed with
that long-standing war with her mother-in-law over who should
have most influence over the child that she might now be tending
to subordinate all her feelings about the divorce to the single
matter of whether or not she would be able to keep custody of
the child. Though natural enough in itself this, to Balint at least,
was a minor issue when their future together was at stake: and
above all minor to Adrienne since the child had been effectively
removed from her care ever since its birth and so, in many ways,
had never really been hers. Until now this was how Adrienne
had seen it and indeed she had often said so.

The little girl, with her closed expression and somewhat brus-
que movements like a robot, seemed to have nothing youthful,
and certainly nothing childlike, about her. She was essentially the
product of Almasko and of Uzdy's own kind, and Balint could
see in her no sign of that marvellous creature who happened to
be her mother. He would willingly have accepted her if Adrienne
brought the child with her, but he could see no reason to sacrifice
their happiness if the others wanted to keep her.

As these thoughts passed through his mind the image of their
own much longed-for son rose within him, as it did each time
that Adrienne spoke of bringing little Clemmie with her.

Oh yes! thought Balint, it's high time the idea of our son were
replaced by the real thing. What Adrienne needs is the fact of
motherhood, not just the desire for it.

There was something else that Adrienne would have to face.
She too must burn her boats if she was going to come with him.
Just as he was prepared to become a stranger to his mother, to
sacrifice his home and exile himself from his beloved Denestornya, indeed to give up everything that was dear to him for her
sake, so she too must make her choice: was she prepared to leave
everything for his sake, or would she give up their chance of

happiness together for the sake of clinging on to that strange girl she hardly knew?

Everything depended on that, and on nothing else.

He decided not to do anything until the end of August because that was when Dr Kisch had promised to go again to Almasko. In the meantime he would go to Budapest and wait there for news. If Adrienne still wanted to put off any decisive action then he would have to act himself; but not until then.

In the meantime there was something more important that he had to do. He had to find a place for them to live, for quarterly leases started on the first of August.

After only a few days' search he found the ideal thing, a third-floor apartment whose entrance was in Dobrenty Street at the foot of the Castle hill in Buda, but whose windows looked out over the Danube at the quietest part of the long quays. It was a modern house with three superb rooms overlooking the great river. When he was first looking over the apartment he leaned out of one of the windows. From there one could see for miles, up and down the river, past the bridges and, over the multitudinous roofs of the outer parts of the city, far into the distance, to the east, towards Transylvania.

It would be wonderful to live there, even if he were an exile, far from his native land, from his home, from Denestornya, where until now he had always imagined their life together. However much it hurt to be an exile it would still be wonderful as long as Adrienne were with him.

For a few moments he imagined her presence so vividly that it was almost as if he could feel her curls brushing his face.

Parliament was in recess and nothing of any great importance seemed to be happening abroad, excepting perhaps certain signs that the Entente was likely to become a reality.

King Edward of England was once again taking the waters at Marienbad, though this time he did not go to see Franz-Josef but merely sent him polite greetings by telegram. And this year there were no visits by diplomats, and events showed that presumably these were no longer necessary as the contours of an Anglo-Russian understanding were there for all to see. For instance, Russian troops occupied a part of Persian territory – which, only a year or two before, would have meant war – and

Great Britain said nothing; obviously it had been done with her full knowledge and consent.

Despite the growing evidence that the central European powers were gradually being encircled, at home in Budapest no one thought of anything but their own internal affairs. Justh made more speeches at Independence Party meetings up and down the country, but these, as might be expected, were principally concerned with domestic politics and the vexing question of an independent banking system. There was a high treason trial in Zagreb, with more than fifty accused, but it made more stir in the Paris papers than at home. At Schwechat near Vienna the harvest festival was spoilt by an orgy of bloodletting when Czechs and Germans decided that a riot was the way to settle their differences.

When Balint read all this it only enhanced his general feeling of bitterness without raising any feeling in him; he was totally engrossed in the agony of waiting.

He tried to do some work, so as to alleviate his self-enforced idleness. He drafted a report to the co-operatives' central authority demonstrating that, as now formed, those co-operatives that incorporated the people in the mountains were not as effective as they should be, for the simple reason that the farmers seemed reluctant to make proper use of the new cheap credits that were available to them. Balint, of course, realized that even though the notary Simo might make a show of trying to recruit the men of the mountain into the co-operative, they, no doubt intimidated by other influences, kept away. The apparent failure of his efforts to help these people added to Balint's growing frustration and bitterness.

As each successive August day crept by he wrote three letters to Adrienne telling her of his yearning, his love and his desire, nothing else. He said nothing to her, not a word, not a hint, of his plan to break with his mother whatever the doctor might say. He had decided to tell her only after it had already been done.

August drew to a close. It was already September and a week passed before there was any news. Then, after the long tedious days of waiting, a letter from Adrienne at last arrived, even more laconic than before, her words tinged with a new sadness – Uzdy's condition had perhaps improved somewhat, Dr Kisch had stated, but not enough for him to be exposed to any emotional excitement. They would have to wait! Always wait! Wait!

The next day Balint went home to Transylvania. The time had come for him to act.

Early in the afternoon Roza Abady was sitting at her desk in the yellow drawing-room at Denestornya. For once she was alone. The bright sunlight outside was reflected in a myriad little points of light on the gilt bronze decorations of the furniture and lit up bright carmine spots on the red carpet.

The door opened and her son came in. He was paler than usual.

Countess Roza looked up, sitting very still. Then she too turned pale because she saw in his face that the moment she had dreaded for the past few weeks had now come. Her clear eyes looked at her son with cold determination.

For a moment neither of them spoke. Then, still standing, his voice hoarse from emotion, Balint said, 'I have to tell you, Mother, that I have decided to go ahead with the marriage I have already spoken to you about. This is why I have come ... to tell you. I cannot go on like this, I have no choice.'

Roza Abady hardly moved except almost imperceptibly to stiffen the backbone in that small plump body. Sitting rigidly in her throne-like chair, she was like an old monarch dispensing justice, calm but unforgiving.

'I have told you my view,' she said. 'You have made your choice, so there is nothing more to say.'

Her lips parted as if she would have liked to add something more; but she was unable to say another word. Then she lifted her arm, one finger pointing implacably towards the door.

Balint too would have liked to have said something, but he was too moved to speak. He bowed deeply and then walked slowly out of the room.

Gently he closed the door behind him and started to descend the stairs until he felt so giddy that he had to stop for a moment and steady himself on the baroque stone balusters. He was relieved that there was no one there to see him as he made his way to his room on the ground floor of one of the round towers. There he picked up his travelling bag, which he had packed just before going to see his mother, and took a last look round that beloved room, gazing for a brief moment through the window to that wonderful view over the park. How many times he had stood there never once realizing that the day would come when he would have to say goodbye! Then he turned away abruptly, crossed the hall and went down the shallow steps to the main entrance.

He got swiftly into his car which was already waiting and told the driver to drive to Kolozsvar. As they rumbled out across the great horseshoe court, Balint looked back just once, as they passed under the arch above which the stone Atlas bore the weight of the world upon his shoulders.

It was five days since Balint had come home to Denestornya and he had passed them in bidding a sad farewell to his beloved home. He went all over the castle, looking into all the rooms except his mother's own suite.

In the big drawing-room on the first floor he caressed the four lead statues by Raphael Donner which graced the mirrored console tables and gazed at the pair of Chinese lacquer commodes which stood on each side of the doorway. Lightly he touched the elaborate rococo frame of the portrait of that Count Abady who had been Master of the Horse to the King, and let his eyes range over the tiers of old leather-bound volumes in the library. In the smoking-room he looked intently at the faces of all those painted ancestors and in the old nursery he started the wall clock which once had made him laugh so much each time the cord was pulled and two tin frogs jumped out and started a battle which never seemed to come to an end.

Wherever he went there was not a room, not a sudden twist on a stair, not a piece of furniture that did not have for him a wealth of secret childhood memories.

He had walked down to the avenue of lime trees where he had learned to ride, and felt the now ancient bark of the tree-trunk at which his first pony had so often shied and thrown him. He walked through the pine woods in the upper part of the park and wandered all over the Nagyberek – the Big Wood – that island where all alone during the summer holidays from his school in Vienna he had come to play Cowboys and Indians (he, of course, was always an Indian), Leather Jerkin and the Mohicans, and sometimes even dashing Hungarian hussars bent on some daredevil adventure.

In the paddocks he had fed sugar to the mares and patted their wide-eyed offspring that followed so closely behind. One by one he caressed his own horses and said to them a silent farewell. He tried to leave nothing out, for who knew that it might not be the last time that he would ever set eyes on everything that had always been most dear to him – until he had met Adrienne.

Who could tell if his mother would ever relent and forgive? And if she did not, might she not decide to leave Denestornya away from the family, thereby disinheriting him for ever? Balint remembered well the instructions that his dying father had written to guide his young widow in running the place after his death. In that thick copy-book in which Tamas Abady had also inscribed exactly how he had wanted his son brought up, there was a sinister paragraph in which the dying man had specified that if the eight-year-old boy did not survive, and if the widow did not remarry, she was not to will the lands and the Abady fortune to distant relatives but rather give it to some worthy foundation such as the University of Nagyenyed, in some fashion which would preserve the name of Abady.

He had been told this several times by his mother. He did not really believe that this was what she would now do, but it was by no means impossible, for he knew how implacable she could be once her mind was made up. Now that she had been deeply hurt, her anger might lead her to interpret her late husband's instructions in just such an unforgiving fashion. It was for this reason that he had said his goodbyes before he told his mother that he was going ahead with his plans to marry Adrienne.

Now that he was leaving the sense of loss and the pain of farewell were doubly poignant. The car was moving swiftly to the east along the crest above the village. Below him he could see the church and the square block of his grandfather's old manor house. Beside them the giant trees of the park stretched out towards the plain. There too was the winding course of the Aranyos river, the great wheatfields to the west and the gallops where they had trained the young horses. Then, all of a sudden, they had turned a corner and everything was lost to sight. A few moments later they had descended towards the Keresztes meadows and from there the car sped onwards to the north.

Then, briefly, the great castle could be seen again, immutable and ageless on its slight elevation above the plain-lands, the long western wing golden in the afternoon sunlight, the copper roofs of the sturdy corner towers glinting green against the blue sky. He could even see the veranda where he used to breakfast with his mother. Balint had hardly taken it all in when the vision

disappeared once again, shrouded from his view by the intervening trees. For a while longer the roofs and the towers could still
be seen etched solid above the sea of green leaves but soon they
grew ever more distant, further and further away, until at last for
ever unattainable.

Even so Balint still looked back. With death in his heart it was
like gazing into some deeply loved face he would never see again.

Now they were driving through the street of little houses
which was the village of Gyeres. Denestornya might have been a
thousand miles away.

CHAPTER FOUR

THE RAIN FELL steadily, sometimes more and sometimes less, but
it never stopped.

Abady had come up to the mountains three days before.

When he had so painfully torn himself away from home he
had had only one idea: to see Adrienne. Accordingly, after packing up all his things at the Abady house in Kolozsvar, he had
driven to the forests near Hunyad. He had left the car at the top
of the ridge and come down alone and on foot; and there it was
that they met, in the little cabin that Balint had built, and had
spent just a brief hour or two together, for Adrienne could never
get away for longer, and there they had sheltered together against
the insistent rain and against the whole world.

When Adrienne had gone back to Almasko Balint had not
known what to do nor where to go. After all the storms of the
last few days he longed for peace and solitude. He needed time
and quiet to concentrate all his thoughts and decide what he
would do next; so he had come up to the high mountains where
he could be alone, and there, too, he would be close enough to
get news quickly from Adrienne if she too came to a decision.

'Honey' Andras Zutor had soon found horses and a baggage wagon, the saddle-ponies were already at Skrind with the
gornyiks, and Balint's tent was brought up the next day from Beles.

They went straight up to Balint's favourite camping site on the
highest slopes of the Prislop.

There was something essentially soothing in the quietly
drizzling rain which seemed like a silken veil whose function was
to soften the harsh outlines of reality. Through its barely visible

threads one could only just make out the saffron leaves of the maple trees or the green of the other deciduous trees whose colour had not yet started to turn. Here and there was a group of hawthorns or a wild plum which had already acquired a faint blush-like tint, and the low-hanging branches of the nearby pines were shining brightly as if lacquered.

Everywhere there was silence apart from the soft murmur of the raindrops on the canvas roof of the tent. No birds sang, neither the kingfishers' tiny piping, nor the songs of blackbirds or mountain jays; the birds of prey no longer called hoarsely to each other and at night even the owls were keeping their own counsel. Everywhere there was silence, as of infinity or death.

Balint barely moved from his tent. He who was usually so passionately interested in everything that lived or grew or moved on the mountain now lay passively on his trestle bed doing nothing and seeing nothing. Even when Honey brought in his reports, Balint hardly seemed to notice his presence. Not even the news that the dishonest notary Simo had now gone too far in his oppression and abuse of the people of the mountain brought any definite reaction from Balint. The information that Honey brought was enough, if brought out into the open, to have Simo dismissed – which would automatically have freed the peasants from his tyranny and acquisitive ways. It was a complicated matter of a tax-fraud; but fraud there had been and if Balint had stood by the oppressed and demanded a full-scale investigation from the county magistrates, the problem of Simo would have been settled once and for all. At any other time Balint would have been fired with zeal to put matters to rights and he would have rushed to the aid of those poor mountain people, at once planning a line of attack and the best way of doing good for others. Now he just read the report and then put it away in his knapsack, deciding nothing except perhaps that he would look at it some other time.

Some of the day he would sit at the door of the tent, gazing out in front of him but seeing nothing but the images of Denestornya . . . and of Adrienne . . . and thinking of nothing but them.

How wide her eyes had opened when he told her that he had broken with his mother! And how scared she had looked! 'You really did that?' she had said. 'You did that terrible thing?' And he realized that Adrienne had been frightened because she knew at once what a great burden this placed on her, she for whom the sacrifice had been made. And Balint had not spared her when he told the tale. He had underlined everything, cruelly repeating his mother's words, and his own, consciously doing it (though hating himself for it), so that she would feel obliged, at last, to break with her husband.

With her mouth she had given him her kisses and she had held him tightly in her arms as she had given her body to him for consolation, but she had known then that this was not enough and that she could no longer repay him with caresses but only with her whole life; and diamond tears had glistened on her long, dark lashes.

Later, when it was already long after noon, the clouds lifted slightly and the rain slackened.

On the old hornbeam tree opposite Balint's tent, two bluetits started to chatter, chirping merrily as they flew from branch to branch. Somewhere a siskin could be heard and below the little camp the rushing of the stream was now louder than the rain, though before there had seemed to be a universal silence. From the bed of the valley little streams of vapour started to rise and float lightly on the hill-slopes. Very slowly the weather cleared.

The man in the tent saw little of this. His thoughts were still in the recent past and his heart was bitter.

Always he had assumed that it was certain what would happen when he told Adrienne of what he had done for her. He had known that naturally then she really would make up her mind, accept what he had done for her and publicly tell everyone that she was suing for divorce. But it had not happened like that at all, and perhaps it never would happen. What had she said? 'I can't do it yet!' she had cried. 'It's impossible! It's horrible, but I still can't do it! I can't!' And she had gone on repeating, over and over, 'I can't! I can't!' There was despair in her voice, but that was what she had said. And she had told him again how the doctor had said that any sudden shock would have a terrible effect on her husband. If she demanded a divorce now it could provoke no one knew what awful reaction. It was a terrible responsibility and she alone must carry it. It was she who was responsible, responsible for everyone. Then she had added those words she had not known would hurt him the most: 'And then there's my daughter.'

And so they had parted once again, agreeing to wait, as they had before. The parting was agony for both of them, for even though it was not a final goodbye, neither knew when or how they might meet again, if ever, nor whether there was still any hope for a future life together. All was uncertain. A promise lay between them; but could it ever be fulfilled?

'I'll write, as soon as I can. I'll think of a way . . . I'll do everything in my power,' she promised.

And again her long dark lashes were wet with tears and there was despair in her eyes as she walked away.

Now the mists were fast disappearing, leaving only a few wisps to hide the tops of the very tallest trees. A light breeze stirred in the valley, so light that though the leaves began to rustle the men in the meadow could hardly feel it.

Balint was still wrapped in his dismal thoughts. Why, he asked himself, was it so impossible for Adrienne to broach the subject of divorce? He knew that she was not afraid for her own life or safety, nor especially for his, for had they not courted disaster night after night spent in each other's arms in Uzdy's house where Uzdy himself might at any hour suddenly and unexpectedly return from the country? Then they had played with death with no thoughts for their safety. What, therefore, could be this dreadful obstacle today?

No matter how hard he fretted he could not find any better answer than that Adrienne must be determined to have her daughter with her, which would be impossible if Uzdy disputed the divorce. It was those words 'And then there's my daughter.' Didn't they prove what was in her mind? Subconsciously he felt that this explanation was wrong, and yet he could find nothing better to replace it. There couldn't be any other reason . . . There wasn't any other reason . . .

Dusk began to fall and with it the sunset began to cast a faint rosy glow on the mist covering the distant mountains.

Balint, still wrapped in his own dismal thoughts, did not notice it, but the calm of the forest evening was suddenly broken by a deep booming sound. Immediately, from the log cabin where the foresters lodged, two men came out and made their way down to Abady's tent. They were Honey Andras Zutor and old Zsukuczo, who guarded the forests on the slope of the Gyalu Botin and who, though now the head game-warden of the district, had once been a famous poacher.

Together they hurried towards the younger man.

'A stag is calling,' said Honey. The old man said the same thing in Romanian: '*Striga taur.*' And they both pointed to the right where the summit of the Munchel Mare would have been visible but for the mist which covered it.

Balint jumped up. Motionless, the three men listened. For a few minutes there was nothing to be heard. Then again the deep organ-like call boomed out, as powerful as a lion's roar.

'Raincoat! Telescope! A hat!' said Abady, as he picked up his Mannlicher sporting rifle, not that he had any particular desire to shoot anything, but in those days no one walked the mountains without a gun on his shoulder. When all was ready they walked swiftly and noiselessly; the ground was so sodden that neither leaves nor fallen branches snapped beneath their feet. They followed the track that led to the high watershed of the range and there they stopped briefly until the stag called again. This time he called twice, bravely and boldly, and the sound seemed to come from the right of where they stood.

'He's going towards the Burnt Rock,' whispered the old poacher who may have had poor sight and red-rimmed eyes from too high a consumption of brandy but whose hearing was as sharp as a lynx's. 'That's where he's going, for sure,' and the stag, as if to confirm what he said, called again exactly from the direction the old man had indicated.

The little band moved off in that direction as quickly as they could. As in all forests that were well-maintained and well-guarded, the grass grew high on the tracks and the men were soon soaked to the waist. They pressed on, hoping to hear the call again, and, as the forest was now in almost total darkness they could run freely with no risk of startling the quarry and making him bolt. In half an hour they had arrived by the Burnt Rock and even in the dark they knew well where they were from the skeletal stunted trees and the gravel underfoot.

They stopped, and from the pine trees came a few lazy drops of rain. Far below they could hear the noise of a mountain stream now swollen from the persistent rain of the last few days. For some time they heard nothing else. At last, quite close, there came a loud call, abruptly rapped out like a word of command. It was imperious, but at the same time it held something of yearning in its timbre. It was the voice of the King of the Forest.

For some time the men stood there without moving . . . but they heard no more. Slowly, and walking carefully, they started to pick their way back to the campsite.

When they arrived Balint said, 'We must be back before day-break. Maybe he'll stay until morning.' Then he gave his orders: 'Wake me at three!'

Everywhere there was thick fog and the little band could never have found their way if they hadn't taken a powerful lamp. With it they advanced confidently, though with more care than they had needed the previous evening. When they were halfway there Honey stayed behind in the little meadow near the rushing stream that led into the Retyicel valley, because from there he would have a wide view of the surrounding country. Balint and the old gamekeeper picked their way carefully to the spot they had reached the day before. Thence they could command all three valleys that ran down from the mountain, the Retyicel, the Vale Arszna and the little one below that turned into the Vurvuras.

By now it was half-past four, but it was still night and they had to wait patiently, without moving, for dawn, for the stag might be anywhere amongst the trailing pine branches. It was possible that he had moved on in the night, but it was equally pos-sible that he was standing there only a few paces away.

Zsukuczo squatted down on his heels and started murmuring something that might have been prayers but which was more likely to have been a jumble of by now meaningless words which, a thousand years before, had been some invocation to the forest gods.

They had to wait a long time before the dawn made it possible to see their surroundings. And it was not one of those sharp sparkling dawns when a triumphant nature set the world ablaze with a myriad soft tints of colour. Rather was it hesitant, almost apologetic, with the mountain forests swathed in an ambiguous foggy light such as lamps will throw when the shades are made of some milky sanded glass.

For most of this long wait Balint completely forgot where he was and why he had come, for his thoughts had turned once more to the bitter disillusion of the last few days. Then, out of the lightening forest came that deep booming call, deeper far than any human bass voice could achieve. It was the voice of the stag.

It seemed to come from further up, close perhaps to the summit, and a few moments later it came again.

'He's up there!' whispered the old *gornyik* excitedly. 'There! Up there! Follow me, *Mariassa* – my Lord!' and, as nimbly as any youth, the old man jumped up and made for the dense undergrowth, not in the direction of the sound but diagonally across it, for he knew instinctively how a true hunter could cut off his quarry. His old hob-nailed boots made no sound either on stones or heather; and he went swiftly forward, crouching under low branches, sliding on wet pine needles, stepping over fallen logs, always avoiding any open spaces and never ever making a sound as he went.

Balint was hard put to keep up with him.

They arrived at a small clearing beside a rock that resembled a saddle carved out of stone. Here Zsukuczo did not go out into the open but crouched down at the edge of the undergrowth. The fog was denser here in the open and they could barely see twenty paces ahead of them. The pine trees on the other side of the clearing were only vague shadows, barely darker than the fog, and the rocks above seemed as insubstantial as painted canvas.

But somewhere, not far away, there was a faint rustling and then the sound of wood being struck as if the trees were being hit by a stick. Then the undergrowth to their left parted and the stag appeared, walking with long confident strides out into the open. He was enormous and powerful, the size of a horse. He carried his head high, as proudly as any monarch, and his antlers were formed of so many branches that, although he was so close to the men that they could have hit him with a lightly lobbed stone, they could not count them.

Then the stag stopped and threw up his head so that the two thick fore-antlers – each as formidable as a Turkish sword – pointed straight up to heaven, and his huge voice boomed again with so much power, and so deep a sound, that no instrument yet invented could have reproduced it. It was the strength of the primæval call and his hot breath, as if to match the strength of his need, billowed forth like a cloud in the cold morning air.

Then he called again, and with head still raised high went slowly and majestically back into the forest. There was no thorn, thicket, pine-branch or treacherous ground that could for an instant hinder his path, no obstacle that would not be brushed carelessly aside as he went on his proud way. Fallen branches, broken by the cutting spread of his antlers, cracked beneath his feet for here he was the master, the antlered sovereign who would never deign to pick his way through that wilderness that was his realm. For a long time the three men could hear the great animal as he went on his way through the forest towards the Munchel, where, the night before, he must have left the hinds.

Balint felt a sense of great joy to have been able to see the stag so close in all his indifferent nobility and for the first time in days had forgotten his own sorrows. The old poacher turned game-warden, who was now accustomed to this strange lord's perverse delight in merely looking at game when any normal man would have shot it at once, was compensated for his disappointment with a handsome tip, though he never understood why the master's gloom had lifted as if by magic.

Later, when they met up again with Zutor, Balint sent old Zsukuczo on ahead while he and the head game-warden sat down on a fallen tree and discussed all the information that Zutor had collected about the notary Simo. Balint was now eager to pursue the matter, and they discussed how they could arrange matters so that Balint could meet those who had been oppressed without alerting the oppressor to what he was doing.

By now Balint had decided that he would stay up in the mountains for longer than he had originally planned. The calm, and the freedom from having to greet acquaintances and make small talk, would help him come to terms with his unhappiness and, perhaps even more important, if Adrienne by any chance should come to some sort of decision, it would be easy for her to send him a message if he remained so close to Almasko. Up here in the cold clear mountain air his tautly stretched nerves would relax and he decided that every day he would walk for miles hoping to tire himself out so that, after months of hopeless insomnia, perhaps he would also learn to sleep normally again.

On the way back to the little camp Balint and Zutor often stopped to listen, but they heard no more calls, maybe because the stag had changed his course, or perhaps the wind had changed and the murmur of the forest blanketed all sounds.

It was still barely nine o'clock when Balint got back to his tent.

He was just eating the bacon he had roasted over the little fire in front of his tent and reliving the happiness that the morning's excursion had given him, when he heard the sound of a horseman arriving at the foresters' cabin. A few moments later Winckler, the new forest manager, came down to see him.

He was not expected as Balint had understood he was out on the Beles part of the Abady forest holdings and had therefore made no attempt to contact him and arrange a meeting. His arrival here, thought Balint, must be just a happy chance, but when he looked up at his face he at once realized that Winckler had come up on purpose and that something very serious was the matter. The young engineer had a wounded and offended air about him and so Balint, after their formal greetings, at once said, 'Something's the matter! What has happened? What's wrong?'

Winckler took off his pince-nez and rubbed each side of the bridge of his nose – which was a habit of his when angry or upset – and replied in a cold and haughty tone, 'Wrong? Why? Nothing's wrong! Nothing at all! A little unexpected, surprising perhaps. To me at least, for I can hardly suppose that your Lordship doesn't know about it as I understand that it is he who gives the orders in these parts!'

He broke off, and then remained silent as if he were at a loss as to how to continue.

'I don't understand,' said Balint. 'What is all this? What are you talking about?'

Winckler drew a grey envelope from his inner pocket and handed it to Abady with an angry gesture.

'I think you'd better read this,' he muttered and turned away.

It was a letter signed by Azbej, and though it started merely by saying that Countess Roza had decided to cancel Winckler's appointment as supervisor to the Abady forests, the next sentence had a second, and to Balint, sinister double meaning. Azbej wrote that from now until Winckler's contract expired at the end of the year his reports should be sent directly to the countess's estate office and it was from there that he would receive all further instructions. This was to be strictly carried out.

It was as if the world had suddenly grown dark.

So it was not only the engineer who had been dismissed but he himself as well. Though it had been he who had found and engaged Winckler, and though it was his efforts and devoted labour that had now put their forests in order and made them pay, he too was now forbidden those beloved mountains, just as he had been exiled from Denestornya. The engineer, a decent

man who was doing a magnificent job, had to suffer so as to reinforce Balint's own punishment; and the unscrupulous lawyer
had stoked the flames of the old lady's anger to still further discredit the influence of the son, whose zeal might one day expose
Azbej's own speculations.

For some time Balint could not utter a word. Then he gave
the letter back.

'Didn't you read the last sentence?' he said. 'You surely don't
think this was my work? Don't you see what it means?'

Winckler re-read the letter. Then, realizing its implications,
he said, 'I'm sorry! I was so angered by what it meant for me that
I didn't take it in. It was stupid of me. Please accept my apologies.
This is quite different – not at all what I thought!' The anger
faded from his face, for though choleric by nature he was at heart
a kind and understanding man. Then, in a rush, he went on,
'I was hurt, you see, and especially as I assumed that it came from
your Lordship who I had always thought appreciated my work.
It was only that! Now I don't mind so much. I can always find
something else, though . . . I was hoping to get married, but that
can wait a bit . . . that can wait, I suppose.'

Winckler, though he had little experience of the vagaries of
human nature, had understood at once that the letter from
Countess Abady's agent was itself only a symptom of a greater
and more dramatic upheaval. Since he could in no way question
or comfort his former employer, he wanted somehow to show
his sympathy, and the only way he knew was to cover his confusion with a flow of somewhat incoherent words. And again it was
typical of him that he took off his pince-nez and started to polish
them with his handkerchief.

That evening Balint left the mountains. Disgraced, and with his
authority taken from him, he felt it impossible to remain.

What was his position? It was not even that of a tied estate-
worker. How could he stay on where, until now, he had been the
master on whom everything depended, where everything had
been done by his orders, when he did not even know whether
Azbej might not go so far as to forbid the estate foresters to supply
him with pack-animals or to do anything else he might wish?
There was also another reason why he should go away as quickly
as possible. Soon it would become public knowledge that he no
longer counted for anything in the mountains and he did not want

his former dependants to start feeling sorry for him, especially as he knew how Gaszton Simo and his angry band of followers would gloat when they heard of Count Abady's disgrace.

He struck camp at once and rode straight to Mereggyo where Winckler left him. Here they parted without anything further being said but with a warm handshake to express their mutual sympathy. Then he rumbled down to Banffy-Hunyad in a hired farm cart. It had been a lucky chance that he had left his car there and so could continue his journey by road, because he did not want to risk meeting anyone he knew at the station.

Night fell as he drove away from all those places he had loved so much. Now he could not see anything of that country to which he was bidding farewell, and as he drove swiftly through the dark all his attention was on the road illuminated by his head-lights. The cold air was in his face and he told himself, ironically, that he was like a chicken hypnotized by the glare; and it was also with a certain tart irony that he was now able to look back on what the day had brought: at dawn, the royal stag in all his sover-eignty; in the morning the arrival of the irate Winckler; and now it was he who was running as if pursued by the Fates.

Also, he thought, what luck that rascal Simo had! Just when Abady had acquired the power to ruin him and make him pay for his oppression of the mountain people and for his arrogant swagger, chance had intervened and saved him.

What luck that man has! he thought. And what a crazy world!

The next few weeks were dull enough for Abady, though the political scene was lively.

While he had been away in Transylvania the Coalition had been on the verge of collapse, and the atmosphere in Budapest ever more tense.

All over the country the campaign for the establishment of the independent banking system had been stoked up, but at the same time that section of the Independence Party that was led by Justh did all it could to fight against the policies of Ferenc Kossuth, still their nominal leader, proclaiming that in this matter they would accept no compromise. They even went so far as to demand that Wekerle's government should at once vote the fantastic sum of 500 million crowns for defence.

That the army desperately needed the money at a time when all Europe was arming and Russia seemed to be preparing for a general war was true enough, especially as Austria-Hungary's military equipment was so antiquated. It was perfectly true that the Dual Monarchy would be useless, whether as enemy or ally, unless its army could swiftly be modernized, but it was still fruitless to raise this demand at a time when the government was powerless to act. Again there was raised the spectre of the cold hand of the Heir, who was thought to be plotting to bring to power his own nominee, Laszlo Lukacs.

Once again the government resigned and Wekerle went so far as to announce in Parliament that the Coalition had been dissolved. But the Monarch said: '*Weiterdienen!* – go back to work!' and refused to accept the resignations.

This was the situation that Abady found when he returned to Budapest, so he was on the spot for all that followed. The government crisis was so drawn-out that it seemed like eternity. It was complicated by a kaleidoscopic change of allegiances. At one moment there was a short-lived cabinet headed by Wlassits; just before that one led by Kossuth, and just after it another with Andrassy; but all were so brief that they passed almost unnoticed, appearing and as swiftly vanishing on that fantasy stage of politics, insubstantial as some mad nirvana. Each one had his own unreasonable reasons to excuse his failure: Wlassits had no majority; Kossuth would only remain if he could go on carrying simultaneously the banners of the independent banking system and the separation of the Austro-Hungarian Customs; and Andrassy insisted that Vienna should yield on the questions of appointing Hungarians to army commands and using the Hungarian language in army orders. He was adamant on these principles and the Crown was equally adamant in refusing, even though Andrassy had proposed a face-saving formula by which the Hungarian army demands were accepted in theory but not put into practice. None of these contradictory moves did anything to alleviate the general malaise nor stop the decay of the Coalition.

It was not long before the general public wearied of all the artificial excitement, and the more they were bombarded by leading articles in the Press, each party lambasting the policies of its opponents, the more the man in the street became disillusioned with the lot of them. People no longer believed a word of what they read in the Press, until all the different political elements in the Coalition had lost credit with the general public. The fundamental flaw that brought the Coalition down was that when it had first come to power its leaders had pretended that they had now won everything for which they had fought while in opposition; while the truth was that they had capitulated on almost all points. All that nationalistic nonsense that had been used to win votes before they achieved power proved to be nothing but a bag of campaign tricks once they were in office. That famous *Pactum*, whose very existence had been so hotly denied until the fiction could no longer be maintained – since it had become clear to everyone that it had been the price paid for getting office – and the fact that after three and a half years nothing had been done to realize the promised universal suffrage, had brought the whole political structure into disrepute with the ordinary citizen.

The leaders of the different parties forming the Coalition fought against each other in a sort of vacuum, though they themselves still thought the battles were real and significant. They proclaimed the same slogans, for which they had once been worshipped as demigods, but now the effect was not the same. Those ideas which had once raised cheers of enthusiasm and support – the old questions of banking, customs, Hungarian sword-tassels for army officers etc. etc. etc. – now raised no more than disillusioned yawns. And the politicians were so wrapped up in their own importance that they never even noticed.

Sadly enough, this disdain for internal politics was reflected by an equal disregard for the signs of more sinister developments abroad. It should have been a warning to Hungary that when all the defendants in the Zagreb treason trial were given heavy sentences of imprisonment, the French Press hailed it as a welcome sign of Balkan disintegration. What, it should then have been asked, was the true significance of the meeting at Racconigi between the Tsar of Russia and the King of Italy? No one knew, no one cared, and no one bothered to ask. True, there were cheerful gossipy items in the Press about the meeting of the two rulers, one of them the ally of the Anglo-French *Entente Cordiale* and the other of Austria and Germany, but it was complacently assumed that nothing would shake Italy's loyalty to the central European powers. The newspapers wrote, 'There is no question of Italy quitting the Triple Alliance.' No one thought to look further, and nothing was said to reassure those who might have been surprised that the Tsar, who had never been a peripatetic monarch like King Edward of England, should have gone to Italy at all. And yet, as was learned much later, it had been during this visit that plans were laid that led later to Italy's change of heart during the Great War.

Even Abady, who had formerly followed all such developments with growing concern, kept himself aloof, wrapped up as he was by his personal sadness and his worry over Adrienne. He only attended the sessions in Parliament once, and that was because he had been summoned by the Speaker who had sent a message that more members were needed to make a quorum so that the business of the House could continue. When he got there he discovered that the unfinished business was simply that the House could not legally rise until the date of the next session had been fixed and that there were not enough members present for any decision to be legal. In the past no one had minded or bothered to count: now it was different.

It had started when a Slovak member had been absent and one of his friends had tried to vote for him. A count was taken and there were too few members in the Chamber. Justh adjourned the session while everyone telephoned everyone else to come quickly. At the next count there were still only fifty-nine when there should have been at least a hundred.

Pandemonium! Old hands grumbled, but the House Rules were the House Rules and had to be obeyed. Bells rang throughout the House, footmen were sent searching every corner for stray members ... and all was in vain, for now only fifty-seven could be rounded up.

Despite every effort by five o'clock only sixty-seven supporters had been gathered in. Only sixty-seven: no one else could be found.

This is when they thought of Abady, who hurried in a little after eight. As he passed along the corridor he found he had to pass a laughing group of People's Party members who were merrily puffing at their cigars and gloating over the impotent rage of Justh and the more vociferous anger of Hollo. And the more they discussed it all, the more it was obvious that for them it was all the most enormous joke.

'Don't hurry!' one of them called to Abady. 'There never was such a lark! Come with us to the bar and drink some champagne. Nothing's going to be settled until noon tomorrow at least. And why rush to the aid of those separate-bank cranks?'

In the Chamber they were counting heads, but even with

Abady there were still only ninety-eight. Meanwhile the clerks kept rushing in with more news of absent members and whether they would come in or not. Then, all at once, the number jumped to one hundred and four, and the Speaker dashed out calling: 'Stay where you are, everybody! Please stay just a moment!' Jubilation! Then the Speaker returned with Justh and the session was legally brought to an end with no surrender on either side.

Balint walked slowly home. He was filled with sadness, for what had rejoiced the fractious People's Party and deeply angered the Independents had merely induced in him a sense of gloom and depression. So this is what they had come to, all those politicians who not so long ago had taken office with such enthusiasm and such patriotic fervour! To think that Parliament itself, for so long the pride, indeed the glory, of the Hungarian people, could be desecrated by such a miserable, pathetic performance!

There were those who thought of it as nothing but a huge joke, and there were those who saw nothing but a clever manipulation of those tiresome Rules. There was also, and this was perhaps the most depressing thought of all, that large majority who didn't even bother to attend the House as the debates had become little more than word-chopping and argument. The Upper House no longer even met and all law-making had long since ceased. Indeed, thought Balint, there was no longer a government, no one party had a majority and the whole machinery of governing the country had ground to a halt. It was all meaningless, empty, like the dried carcass of a dead insect from which all life had long since departed. There were plenty of good men there, honest fellows from the country, and there were honest and experienced leaders too, men like Andrassy and Wekerle, full of good will and selfless devotion; but they were powerless in the morass of the present malaise. It was as if a curse had fallen on Hungary.

After this brief interlude came more days and weeks of empty monotony. The public and political indifference weighed on Balint's spirits like a leaden cloak. He felt alive only when he sat down to write to Adrienne.

At first he wrote only occasionally, but as time went by his letters became ever more frequent until by the end of October he was writing every two or three days. He no longer cared if anyone noticed at Almasko. He did not even care if his letters stirred up trouble, indeed he would have welcomed trouble which would at least have rescued him from that hell of ashes in which he was living. So he poured out his soul into more and more letters, pleading, demanding, hotly exacting a decision; and since he wrote with passion and thought, weighing every word and every argument, the letters were good ones. He searched his mind for words of reproach which he knew would strike home, for he wanted her to be so hurt that she might be forced into action. He wrote about the spiritual misery of his life of exile, how he spent night after night alone in his dark little hotel room, how he dreamed every night of Denestornya, of that beloved home he had thrown aside for her sake. And then there would be letters in which he wrote only that he could not write because he had nothing in the world to write about.

Sometimes he would include something more trivial. One day, for example, he had run across little Lili Illesvary. It had been a chance meeting just as she was passing through Budapest with the Szent-Gyorgyis, and he had dined with them that night. During the evening he had again been invited to Jablanka and Lili had smiled at him saying, 'I will be there too!' Afterwards it had occurred to Balint that he might be able to use this to make Adrienne jealous and so in his next letter he had told her of that occasion in the summer when they had played 'Up Jenkins' at the Park Club and he had found himself physically excited by her. He had gone on to praise the girl, saying how sweet and pretty and desirable she was and quoting her words which had seemed then like a caress. It was cruel of him, he knew, but perhaps it would bring some reaction.

Mostly, however, he wrote about that son for whom he longed so much, until his letters spoke of almost nothing but that. Over and over again he wrote how vital it was to him that this boy, his and hers, should be born to them, and how he could think of nothing else but his need for an heir who would be the ultimate bond between them. In his later letters even his desire for Adrienne became merged with his yearning for their boy until the image of this unborn child melted into that of Adrienne herself. It was her body, her beautiful, desirable body, that now became the instrument forged only to bring forth the ultimate object of their love.

Adrienne's replies, on the other hand, gradually became shorter and shorter. At first she tried to convince him by argument, and, though by no means sure of herself, to explain herself, to convince him that at present it was impossible to come to a decision, to make a definite break. She wrote that she had a great responsibility but that . . . well, one day . . . And though her letters became ever more brief and incoherent, through her faltering words there throbbed a passion as affecting as a heartbeat. Finally all she could say was '*I think of you all the time . . . Don't torture me . . . You can't possibly know, you can't know . . .*' and nothing more. For some time she had not mentioned her daughter, and Balint instinctively felt he had chosen the right course and went on writing those cruel letters, though his heart bled for her each time he did it.

On November 10th the post brought him a letter; and this time it was a long one.

'*I can't stand it any more!*' she wrote. '*I can't stand it!*' Then, with almost businesslike dryness she said that she had made up her mind to ask for a divorce at once, no matter what happened as a result. She had written to Absolon to come to Almasko and she would give him a letter to hand to her husband announcing that she was going home to her father's house at Mezo-Varjas whence she would start proceedings. She could trust no one else and old Absolon was only to give Uzdy the letter after she had left the house. Balint was to stay in Budapest and on no account to move from where he was, nor write her a single line, not even of thanks, because she wouldn't be able to stand it. '*It is because what I do now – this reckless chance I must take – must be done for myself alone and not also for you. If a catastrophe follows it must be I alone who am responsible!*' Only in this way, she wrote, could it be possible, and only in this way was there a chance of success. '*I will let you know at once if there are any developments, important developments. Don't be impatient because it will be at least ten or twelve days before I'll be able to tell you anything.*'

At the end of the letter there was a short postscript. '*Uzdy seems quieter now.*' And then there was a single word, twice underlined: '*Maybe??*'

CHAPTER FIVE

'MAYBE??' THESE FIVE letters and the double question-mark encapsulated the anxiety and spiritual turmoil that had been

Adrienne's lot ever since Dr Kisch had made his first visit to Almasko. It was only now, three months later, and especially since the doctor's second visit at the beginning of September, that Adrienne had begun to understand the full meaning of those careful deliberate words with which Dr Kisch had given his opinion. He had repeated much the same thing when he came again in September, and it was now clear to Adrienne that what the doctor had been saying implied that her husband, if not already mad, was certainly on the verge of madness.

They had been married for nearly ten years and she had often thought of him as eccentric and cranky. To herself she used the word 'crazy' but not in this sense, not pathologically. She had never thought of him as incipiently clinically mad. The thought had never occurred to her. Now she had to face reality, to face the fact that he was menaced by that monster insanity, which could wreck her whole future – for if he really did go off his head she would never be able to divorce him, such was the law.

Adrienne was careful to keep this appalling thought to herself. She did not even mention it in her letters to Balint, telling herself that she did not want to worry him further. Subconsciously she was bowing to the superstition that if the thing was put into words then it would become so, as if the words themselves could conjure up the fact. She hardly even admitted it to herself, though now she watched anxiously every word and movement her husband made. Of course she had always watched him, but now it was different. In their first years of marriage she had had to be on the alert whenever they were together, but this was to protect herself from his violence and unpredictability; later, when she had learnt from Balint what love really was, she feared for her lover's safety. Now her vigil was more clinical and she watched over Uzdy more as his nurse, dispassionately, without ill-feeling.

It was from this time that she found her hatred for him diminishing, for it was no longer her husband who was the enemy, but rather that dreaded sickness which if allowed to strike would utterly destroy everything she lived for. She found that she could even think of the onslaught of madness as something alien, some malignant superhuman force that came from God knows where.

Everything that Uzdy now said or did was for her merely a symptom to be studied, analysed and interpreted – but it was all so contradictory, so confusing, that the more she watched the more confused she became herself. One day she would be filled with hope, the next with despair.

On the surface nothing had changed. Uzdy lived as he always had and behaved as he always had, one day arrogant and ironic, another disdainfully polite; and yet there was always that latent ferocity lurking behind the façade of normality. He continued to work at those wondrous tables of figures that he believed would one day transform the world, indeed more devotedly than ever since Dr Kisch had praised his endeavours. He barely seemed to notice Adrienne's presence and mercifully never came to her room at night, though this might have been due to exhaustion after long hours of work in his study or even to those soothing medicines the Saxon doctor had prescribed. Superficially everything was normal until something happened which seemed to disturb him. There should have been nothing in it, and its effect was only gradually noticeable.

It was after Countess Clémence came home from Meran that Adrienne began to notice that her husband seemed, though without any obvious reason, to be annoyed with his mother. He would pick on her, taking any occasion to reprimand her, sometimes with an insolent rudeness that had never before been the old lady's lot. Adrienne did not remember his ever doing this before, though she admitted to herself that she might not have noticed in the summer and only did so now because she was watching him so carefully.

And, as soon as she did notice, she saw that the habit was growing. The first obvious clash came when the new young French governess arrived and Countess Clémence made her senior to the old English nanny. In those protocol-ridden days this was quite correct since the governess was an educated woman with an official diploma. Uzdy did not protest but lost no opportunity of humiliating the girl, all the while gazing maliciously at his mother. Then there was a host of unusual little incidents, all essentially trivial. Uzdy would suddenly start cross-questioning his mother as to why she had sent the carriage somewhere, or he would demand a detailed explanation for the replacement of one of the under-gardeners; he even expostulated with her for sending a basket of plums to the priest from Nagy-Almas who came each Sunday to say mass at Almasko. He, who had never bothered his head with anything to do with the daily running of the house, now took his mother up about all sorts of little everyday details of housekeeping. And when he did so one could tell from his tone of voice that, though he was making an effort to control himself, he now used with her that ironic insulting manner which would end in angry shouts when he lost control.

When this happened Adrienne felt herself go rigid with anxiety. What, she asked herself, could be the reason for this suddenly revealed resentment? What was the cause of this latent hostility which seemed as if he were demanding expiation for some secret offence? What could it be that had made Uzdy change so much towards his mother when for so many years he had always taken her part against her daughter-in-law? Why did he now turn against and ill-treat the one person he had always seemed to love and revere?

And why did the old lady take it all without a murmur?

Countess Clémence, faced with this inexplicable change in her son, would reply to him, giving the shortest possible answers in a calm but ice-cold manner. As always her expression showed no emotion and was as stiff as ever; her face might have been made of marble and her eyes of glass. She did not look at her son, but at something far, far away in space . . . or perhaps in time?

There was no regular pattern, no continuity. Sometimes ten days or a fortnight would pass without incident, and then suddenly a stormy scene would interrupt their calm. In the middle of October one such scene disturbed Adrienne greatly.

They were sitting in the big oval drawing-room after lunch. Adrienne was doing some needlework and her mother-in-law sat, as she always did, stiffly upright on the sofa with a table in front of her. Uzdy was pacing about the room from the stove to the windows and back again. It was the same as any other day and, like any other day, no one spoke. The habitual silence was broken only by the sound of his footsteps on the wooden floor.

Adrienne did not look up from her work but she was still able to see that every time her husband passed in front of them he darted a piercing look at his mother. This went on for a long, long time, until Adrienne became convinced that something strange and terrible was about to happen. It was as if the air under that high coved ceiling might suddenly transform itself into a menacing cloud above their heads. If the old lady felt it too she gave no sign. Her face was in shadow and her high-piled hair was edged with silver from the light behind her.

When Uzdy returned from what seemed like the hundredth time he had paced the room he stopped behind his wife's chair, grasping it with both hands which Adrienne could sense were trembling uncontrollably.

'I should like to ask,' he said to his mother, 'why you are spying on me?'

'I have no idea what you mean!' she replied.

Uzdy laughed, with menace in his voice. 'You? You have no idea? All right, I'll tell you! For some time now I have seen dark figures skulking under my windows. They march to and fro, stopping, spying and sneaking away. Then they come back again . . . What about that?'

'It must be the night-watchman,' said Countess Clémence icily. 'As far as I am aware, that is what he is supposed to do.'

'So that's it, is it? The night-watchman? Well! Well! Well!' Uzdy leant forwards so that his chest brushed against Adrienne's hair. 'The night-watchman, eh?' Then, suddenly, he shouted, 'It's a lie, a lie, a lie!'

Countess Clémence did not answer, but just shrugged her shoulders. Then her son spoke again and this time his tone was more controlled. 'I went out myself last night, just to be sure. I walked round the garden, and I saw . . . do you hear me? I saw! All right, you'll say "the night-watchman" . . . They were everywhere. Lots of them. Behind every tree . . . everywhere, whispering together. Of course they were hiding, but I saw them and I know!'

He paced up and down the room several times more, quickly and excitedly, so much so that the soles of his shoes slid perilously on the parquet. While he moved he said nothing but then he came back to the table and started again. 'I know, I tell you! I know only too well. You sent them to spy on me. Well, just watch out! Just watch out! And I know some more too; they put things in my wine . . . and in my food. You see, I know. Don't deny it! I know!'

The old lady answered drily, 'How could anyone do that? We all eat and drink the same things.'

'Will you shut up!' shouted Uzdy, banging his long arm down on the table. 'Shut up! I tell you. Shut up and listen! I know you, and I say,' his voice rising, 'just watch out!' Then he straightened up his long thin body, waving his arms in the air, his fists

clenched. 'Just you watch out! Watch out! Watch out!' he cried
in a high thin scream like an animal in pain.

Then he spun round, like a spring just released, and slid over
to the main door, wrenched it open and stormed out slamming
the door behind him.

The two women sat for an instant as if turned to stone. Then
Countess Clémence rose and, calm and erect, with head held
high, her cold glance directed ever straight ahead of her, stalked
out of the room. Adrienne was left alone.

The first thing Adrienne thought about, as soon as the first
shock had passed away, was how deeply painful all this must
have been for that proud spirit; and for the first time in her life
she almost felt sorry for the old lady. She had known her for an
enemy since she first announced her engagement to Pal Uzdy
and only now, in their common anxiety, common to both
perhaps but not shared, did Adrienne begin to feel compassion
rise in her. And, as her instinct was always at once transmuted
into action, act she did. She jumped up from her chair and
thinking only that somehow she must express what she felt, she
made her way to Countess Clémence's room which she had not
entered more than twice or three times since she had come to
Almasko.

The room was dark, with a little light filtered through the slats
in the shutters and for a moment Adrienne was startled to find
that it also appeared to be empty. She looked around. To the right
was that picture of Christ with its face turned to the wall. The
tiny hanging light before it was not lit, and the prie-dieu was
pushed away in a corner. Adrienne recalled that the old lady had
decided not to be on speaking terms with God since he had taken
her husband away from her, and was just about to withdraw when
a voice quite close spoke from somewhere at her left. 'Well, what
do you want?'

Adrienne could now make out that her mother-in-law was
lying stretched out on a sofa covered in black velvet and, as she
was always dressed in black herself, she could hardly be seen
except as an insubstantial black shadow, especially as her head
was turned away towards the window and her tall white coiffure
covered by a widow's cap. She lay on her stomach with her
elbows on the sofa and her head held up by tightly clenched fists,
and Adrienne suddenly felt that there was something infinitely

touching in her position, so like someone lying on a coffin and protecting it with her body.

'I came,' she started, 'just to say how dreadful it was. We must *do* something . . .' and then she stopped. She had thought she would reveal what until then she had kept to herself, namely that Dr Kisch's visit had been no chance accident but that she had asked him to come; and she was now going to propose that they send for him at once. However she was so put off by the old lady's abrupt manner, and also, though she hardly knew why, embarrassed, that the words would not be spoken.

Countess Clémence appeared not even to have heard what Adrienne had started to say and interrupted her curtly. 'This is my business, mine alone! Whatever I decide to do I shall certainly not tell you! Tell *you*!' and her tone was one of barely contained hatred.

To Adrienne it was as if she had been struck in the face. All feeling of compassion for the old lady fled and was instantly replaced by deep resentment and dislike for the old tyrant. However, before she could reply, she was met with a torrent of words. 'Tell *you*, who have brought all this upon us!? You, who have brought a curse upon the house and who have poisoned my son against me, who have seduced him with your girlish white skin. Yes, you! I knew it from the first moment. Go away! Get out of this room at once! Get out!'

She said all this without moving, hissing the words from her thin lips while her eyes glistened like those of a madwoman.

There was nothing more that Adrienne could say: the mother seemed as mad as her son. Her anger evaporating, Adrienne went out into the clean daylight of the corridor and from there straight into the great entrance court and stood, with her back to the house, gazing into the distance.

The tree-covered mountainside beyond the lawns was dark, so much so that the forest seemed almost to be moving towards the castle and blanketing out the sky. Adrienne felt that the trees were blocking out the whole world and that she would be kept for ever in that dreadful prison.

That same evening everything was back to normal. Until dinnertime Adrienne had seen no one, then she went into the big drawing-room, where the family always assembled, and was sitting there in silence with her implacable mother-in-law when the door opened and Uzdy came in, apparently in high good humour.

'Well,' he said to his mother, laughing merrily, 'I gave you a good scare, what? And didn't I do it well? You thought I'd gone mad, eh? What a joke! I could have been a wonderful actor, as good as Talma ... Yes, Talma, the real thing,' and, gently caressing her arm, he led his mother into the dining-room where he continued to chat merrily and lightly, like a child, just as he used to before he had become so gloomy.

For some days he remained the same, as if he were making a special effort so that the others would forgive that appalling scene. No matter how hard Adrienne studied him she could see no signs of anything unusual. Every alarming symptom had disappeared, and only very seldom did she catch a momentary glimpse of a dangerous flash from his eyes. She wondered if that sudden loss of control had now spent itself and whether, perhaps, his outburst of temper had dissipated whatever crisis had threatened him. Had not Dr Kisch said something about 'agitated phases alternating with periods of calm'?

And because she wanted to believe it, she did.

All the while she was tormented by Balint's letters. With that leaden burden of anxiety weighing on her mind, she read and re-read them with hopeless pain in her heart. Even so they were her only hope of eventual freedom. The letters kept arriving, long, long letters full of desire and love; and each of them seemed to burn her fingers as she held it. And they were doubly tormenting because even if he did not spell it out, every word flamed with reproach, with the accusation that she had done nothing while he had sacrificed everything for her.

That was when Adrienne finally made up her mind. It was not easy, and, even as she did so she still wondered if her departure might not set off another terrible attack. She was terrified that her actions might provoke an irreversible relapse and that, of course, would render all her efforts in vain and chain her to Uzdy for as long as he lived. She wondered if she should not call in Dr Kisch once more and let him decide. At least then she would be sure.

And yet she did not dare. Balint was waiting for her and their future together, and the son that was to be born to them. She had to go, to be with everything that she held dear.

All the same she had to act sensibly, and that was when she

thought of Absolon. The old explorer had always come once or twice a year to visit his sister and so there would be nothing unusual if he should suddenly arrive now. He was well-disposed to Adrienne and if anyone was esteemed by her husband it was he. He was the only person who could help her if the bombshell should explode; and so she wrote to him on the same day that she sent her long letter to Balint. She told him all the details of what she was going to do and what she wanted him to do for her. Five days later his answer came: he agreed to do just as she asked but told her he could not come immediately as his crippled leg was giving him much pain and he had to go first to Szasz-Regen where Dr Kisch would give him some treatment. This would only take a few days: then he would come at once. He would send a telegram to his sister to announce his arrival. It was the best she could hope for.

The following days passed slowly for Adrienne who was in an agony of anxiety fearing that Uzdy would take another sudden turn for the worse. But nothing happened. It seemed that his recovery was complete and that he had completely regained his equanimity. Adrienne noted with relief that her husband was once again taking an interest in estate matters, which had been totally neglected since he had started working on that strange theory of numbers. He even ordered that the daily postbag should be brought to him every day before being sent off to the post office in Nagy-Almas so that he could send off at once his replies to the reports from the agents resident on his extensive properties far from Almasko. That was what he had always been accustomed to do in the past. Every detail of the management of his estates had invariably been controlled by Uzdy himself through a voluminous daily correspondence, and the fact that he had taken all this up again seemed to Adrienne to be an encouraging sign. Adrienne therefore saw nothing odd in the fact that Uzdy often now not only held back the mail, sometimes for an hour or more behind the locked doors of his study, but also, as he always rose late, that he had the bag brought to him last. This seemed quite sensible as his room was on the ground floor which had to be passed by the courier on his way out.

It was lucky, thought Adrienne, that Uzdy had only adopted this system after her correspondence with Balint had stopped.

Only one alarming symptom remained. From time to time

Adrienne thought she detected a covert glance of hatred directed at his mother; but it was so slight she managed to convince herself that this was merely a faint echo of something from the past.

November came to an end in a blaze of gorgeous weather, as it so often did in Transylvania around St Catherine's Day. They called it the Old Wives' Summer – and it always came to a sudden end with the first snows.

One day Adrienne went out early for her usual walk. From a path high above the castle she saw one of the Almasko carriages being driven swiftly along the road to Nagy-Almas. It was empty and a young groom sat beside the coachman. This meant that it was going to the railway station and the groom's presence also meant that a guest was expected and that he would be needed to help with the luggage.

Her heart throbbed at the thought that it must be Absolon and that very soon now she would be free. At once she thought of everything that had happened in the past few weeks, and all seemed set fair. Nothing had occurred to make her fear a further delay and so it was now, at last, that her long hoped-for flight would become a reality. For a long time Uzdy had seemed calm, and as normal as he ever had been. Now at last all her efforts to arrange a divorce would be crowned with success. She must succeed . . . she would succeed!

The carriage must have gone to meet the 9.30 train, and Uzdy's American trotters were so fast that Absolon could be at the house within the hour. Adrienne did not want to be there when he came in case anyone should guess that she knew he was coming, so she decided to come in herself a little later.

She went for a long walk in the woods and when she next looked at her watch it was already after eleven. The guest must have arrived about three-quarters of an hour before, so it was now safe to return.

Adrienne had hardly started down the winding path from the woods when she was startled by something utterly unexpected. Uzdy jumped out from behind a tree, not with his usual stilted gait but hurriedly, almost running towards her. It was as if he had been hiding from something and had been waiting only for her.

And so it was.

'I've been waiting for you, dear Adrienne,' he said, 'and I'm thankful I've found you!' He sighed deeply, and then, somewhat awkwardly, tried to laugh. 'It's strange, isn't it? But it doesn't matter; strange things happen in life, very strange,' and he hesitated for a moment before going on. Then, very seriously, as if begging for her help, he said, 'I want you to stay near me today, all the time. Please stay with me! Don't leave me today! Will you do it? Will you?'

'Of course. Gladly. But what's happened?'

Uzdy bent his tall figure until he could speak directly into Adrienne's ear. She saw fear in his eyes.

'My mother,' he said. 'My mother has had a doctor sent out from Kolozsvar. It's a plot ... against me! She says he's coming to see our daughter, but I know she's lying. That's why I came out to find you, so that they wouldn't find me alone – not alone, not for a minute alone!'

He put his hands on her shoulders and they were shaking with terror. Then, barely audibly, he whispered, 'The old witch wants to put me in the madhouse, just like my father! You mustn't let that happen! Please don't let it happen! If you are with me they won't dare!'

'Surely not?' said Adrienne. 'You must be imagining it. Why on earth should she?'

'But she does, I tell you. She does.' Uzdy was now howling like a frightened animal. 'I've suspected it for a long time, and now I know. I opened her letters and read them ... That's why she's got him here; I know. But let's go now! Come on!' and he grabbed his wife's hand and walked off so fast with his long legs that Adrienne could hardly keep up with him.

In the centre of that round lawn that was bordered by the carriage drive he slowed down, put his hands in his pockets and strolled casually towards the house as if nothing was the matter. The change was so abrupt that Adrienne would almost have believed that she had dreamed what had just occurred between them had he not turned briefly towards her and hissed, 'Stay with me. Stay always with me.'

In front of the house Countess Clémence was talking to a man Adrienne had never seen before. When her son and daughter-in-law came up she introduced the man as Dr Palkowitz, a professor from Kolozsvar, and said she had called him in to see her grandchild, explaining rather breathlessly and at length that the little girl had become very nervous, was not sleeping well, suffered from nightmares and often woke up frightened in the night; and therefore she had thought it best, just to be sure, to consult a specialist, though it was nothing, of course, just a precaution. It was always better with children, wasn't it, to have them looked at from time to time.

She said far more than was necessary, and far more than her usual taciturn manner allowed her. She spoke, too, in an affected way, as people who are not used to deception are often apt to do. Finally she added, 'I might as well have him look at me too, while he is about it!' and laughed self-consciously as if it were all rather trivial.

The doctor, a small, chubby, merry-looking man, carried on the fiction himself, saying, 'Of course, why not? When a doctor visits a country village he expects to have to look at everybody. I'm quite used to that. It often happens.'

Then Uzdy spoke up, with a submissiveness Adrienne had never seen before. Stooping slightly, he shifted his weight from one foot to the other and looked first at the doctor and then at his mother. He was like some huge, skinny wolfhound who senses trouble and tries to avoid the inevitable beating by cringing subdued at his master's feet. When he spoke his manner was strangely sweet and obsequious. 'Perhaps the doctor ought to have a look at me too? All right, why not? Let's do it now, right away. That would be best, wouldn't it, Mama?' Then he turned directly to Dr Palkowitz and said, 'Come along then, down to my room if that suits you. And Adrienne too, of course, if she'll come. Yes, she too, of course.'

With somewhat exaggerated waving of his arms he gestured them towards the front door and into the house, making the doctor go in first. In the corridor he kept Adrienne beside him, holding her hand as tightly as if in a vice. The smile never left his face.

Old Maier was waiting for them. To him Uzdy said, 'Tell them to harness up the other pair of horses in half an hour.' Then he turned to the doctor and explained, 'That way you'll be home by early afternoon. That'd be best, wouldn't it? We don't want to take up too much of your valuable time, do we?'

At the angle of the corridor they turned right towards the stair that led to the ground floor. Adrienne would have preferred to turn back there for she hated those stairs which her husband had used every time he came to his wife's room. The treads creaked and it was a sound to which she never became accustomed however often she heard it. And every time she heard it, she shuddered. She herself never used that stairway. But now, as she had given her promise to Uzdy, and as the doctor was with them, she could hardly turn back. Uzdy led them to his room where all the windows were heavily barred, like all the others in that wing of the house because it was there that Uzdy's mad father had lived out the last years of his life. It was small and unpretentious, furnished only with the bare necessities. A narrow iron bed was set against one wall. Uzdy made the doctor sit down on a chair while he himself sat on the bed, drawing his wife to sit beside him. He was all politeness and humility, and made little bows as he spoke.

'Here we are! Please sit down! Now, ask your questions – in your own time, of course.'

The doctor gave an embarrassed little cough, and then began nervously, 'Er-er-well, in her ladyship's presence. Well, it's a little unusual.'

He was unable to say more because Uzdy at once interrupted him, at the same time clinging tightly onto his wife's arm, saying, 'We have no secrets from each other, do we, Addy? We are absolutely one, one! Isn't that so, Addy? Please start your examination, doctor.'

The usual questions followed, about sleep, capacity for work, and even some more intimate matters. Uzdy answered everything calmly and apparently quite satisfactorily. He spoke slowly, seeming to weigh each word carefully, but Adrienne sensed that he had rehearsed it all and wondered if the doctor, who was now meeting Uzdy for the first time, had noticed it too. Next came the testing of the reflexes – knees, eyes, walking about with closed eyes – followed by listening to the heart and lungs with a stethoscope. Uzdy went through it all patiently, and only Adrienne noticed how fiercely he looked at the doctor's hands whenever he touched his head or put the stethoscope to his heart.

The examination was a long one. Finally Dr Palkowitz drew himself up and declared, 'I congratulate your Lordship. You are in perfect health, a trifle nervous perhaps, but that is quite usual for all intellectual people. I'll just prescribe a light sedative which you might take for a while. I can't think of anything else!'

He took out his fountain-pen and swiftly wrote some words on a paper. There was no time for Adrienne, but as the doctor knew he had been called in only to examine her husband, he did not press the matter.

'The carriage will be ready and waiting,' said Uzdy. 'You'd better leave at once so as to catch the train!' and he led them straight out through the service door, through a store filled with stacks of wood, and into the stables. The carriage was standing ready at the stable doors and the doctor climbed in and sat down. All the time Uzdy kept up a stream of obsequious thanks, saying, 'I really am most flattered by your visit, honoured indeed! Thank you! Thank you!'

When the carriage had disappeared through the gates of the stable yard, then Uzdy straightened himself up to his full height.

Slowly he and Adrienne walked back to the house.

When they were halfway there Uzdy stopped. His face shone with triumph as he looked down at her and said, 'I'm most grateful, Addy, I really am. Now you'd better go in . . . go to your own room.'

Adrienne turned and went swiftly into the house. She felt far more at ease and had been reassured by the doctor's opinion. She was glad to be alone now, for that hour and a half in her husband's room had been an ordeal; and as soon as she had sensed that terrible suppressed excitement rising again in him she had been terrified he might suddenly lose control of himself. It had been a great relief when all had passed off so well. Perhaps there really wasn't anything seriously wrong after all? But if this were so why, as she was about to enter the house, did he call out after her, 'Remain in your own room! Don't move from there, do you understand!' in almost menacing tones? And why was his face so distorted, with swollen veins, and dark red in colour? Suddenly her composure was shattered by the thought that nothing had changed and that his controlled manner during the doctor's visit was nothing but a charade. And why should he order her to stay in her room?

Though she did not understand she still did what she was told, though once there she found no peace. She was haunted by that strange transformation she had seen in her husband in the course of a mere hour and a half. What did it mean, that humbleness towards the doctor, for humbleness was utterly alien to his character? Also the memory of his terror when he came to seek her out in the wood filled her with pity and anguish. No matter how hard she tried to remain calm, her agitation increased and she felt

that some unknown horror was creeping up to take her unawares. Without knowing why, she started to listen for some
unusual sound. It was instinctive and lasted perhaps a few minutes
only, perhaps a bare quarter of an hour. And, as she listened, her
heart beat ever louder and louder.

Then, as if in answer to her waiting, there came a long drawn-
out howl from some distant part of the house.

Adrienne ran swiftly out into the corridor. There was nobody
there, nor anywhere else, it seemed. The castle might have been
deserted with no one outside in the courtyard and no one in the
halls either. The door to the drawing-room was open and she ran
quickly in.

There on the floor, most unexpectedly, she saw her husband
lying with old Maier kneeling beside him, trying to loosen his collar. An armchair was overturned and beside it was lying a long bare
oak-log. Adrienne at once wondered how it had got there from
the woodpile in the storeroom. Standing behind the sofa was old
Countess Clémence and her face seemed paler even than the ash-
grey colour of the wall against which she was leaning. Adrienne
took all this in at once, and also that the old butler was saying to
her, '*Bitte einen Diener rufen, bitte schnell! Der Herr ist ohnmächtig* –
Please call for a servant, quickly please! The Master has fainted!'

That old Maier had unconsciously reverted to German meant
that he was deeply worried. Adrienne ran out and called the
footman. Then she ran to the pantry and fetched a glass of water.
When she got back to the drawing-room Maier had lifted Uzdy's
head and shoulders onto his lap and the footman had put his arms
under Uzdy's knees. Together they raised him from the floor and
started to carry him out.

'Here's some water,' cried Adrienne. 'Put some on his forehead!' but Maier merely said, 'Not now. When we get the Master
to his room!'

As they carried him out Uzdy's arms and legs hung down like
a broken puppet. Adrienne now saw that his temple was covered
in blood.

'What's happened? For God's sake tell me what's happened?'
she cried, turning to her mother-in-law.

The old woman had remained motionless with closed eyes
until Adrienne spoke. Then she slowly opened them, wider and
wider as if she were seeing some terrible vision. Then she put

back her shoulders and walked stiffly out of the room, closing the door behind her with determined quietness.

It was only later that Maier told her what had happened. He had been cleaning the silver when Count Uzdy came back into the house, on tiptoe, with that oak-log in his hand. Maier had immediately sensed trouble and had tried to intercept his master, but Uzdy had been too quick for him. Countess Clémence had been in the drawing-room waiting for the doctor to make his report to her and sitting at her usual place on the sofa. Her son had rushed at his mother, raising high the oak-log to strike her. Luckily the table had been between them and so Maier had been able to grab his master, catching his wrist in that vice-like grasp taught to male nurses, and tripped him so that he fell to the floor. Maier had learned the technique while working in the lunatic asylum at Graz where he had also been taught that it was almost impossible to subdue a violent patient in the grip of madness and that it was far better not to try to wrestle with them but rather to pin them down when dazed by a fall. All went as he had planned except that Uzdy had hit his head on the heavy wooden back of an armchair, split his temple open and passed out from the resulting concussion. Maier at once thought it best not to attempt to bring him round where he was but to get him quickly back to his own room. If he came to in different surroundings the memory of what had happened would probably fade all the more quickly. Now, as Maier told all this to Adrienne, her husband was lying quietly in his own bed with a cold compress on his temple. He was not likely to want to move for the time being; but later it would be different. Count Uzdy would have to be under constant surveillance.

That afternoon Absolon arrived at Almasko and Adrienne at once told him the whole story. Then they held a family council and agreed that someone must always be by the sick man's bedside. Only four people could be relied upon to undertake this vigil, Adrienne, Absolon, Maier and the English nanny. His mother must be kept away from him, for when Maier had told him that Countess Clémence had been enquiring after her son, Uzdy had clenched his fists and such hatred glinted in his look that Maier had had quickly to change the subject. No doubt the sight of his mother would provoke another fit of rage.

Although Countess Clémence had sat with Adrienne and her

brother while they discussed what course to take, the decisions were taken by them alone. The old lady sat there without even opening her mouth. Her face seemed as if turned to stone and they were not sure she even heard what they said. Then they decided to send for Dr Kisch and let him advise them what to do next.

Then followed three dreadful days.

Dr Kisch had arrived but he did not visit the sick man so as not to excite him. He said that he would see him soon enough when the time came to take him away; for, after hearing all the details, Kisch had realized that Uzdy would have to be closely confined. It had been immediately obvious to him that Uzdy was too far gone to be left alone in the freedom of his own home: it was too dangerous for him, and for everyone else.

On the fourth day Adrienne was on duty. It was the hour of dawn, but it was still dark. A small night-light flickered on the window-sill and Uzdy, propped up on several pillows, was apparently asleep. His wife was sitting in a chair at the foot of the bed, and not a sound was to be heard, except for the ticking of the clock.

The hours crept slowly by, terribly slowly, because she was haunted by the thought that at eight o'clock that morning Dr Kisch would come to Uzdy's room to take him away. The Red Cross ambulance wagon had been there since the previous day, hidden in the stable court. Two nurses had come with it, and they were going to take the patient to the clinic for nervous diseases in Kolozsvar – which was always referred to as 'The House with the Green Roof' – and there he would be kept in close confinement.

For Adrienne it was the end of everything for which she had yearned, waited, and struggled for so many years. It was the end of her dream of freedom, just when it had seemed so very close. It was the end of any chance of happiness, of anything which for her would make life worth living. It was the end of that dream for which Balint had given up his home and it tolled the death-knell of any chance of a free honest life, of having another child, and especially of that longed-for, oh, so-often-imagined boy who had never been born and who never now would be born! She felt as if, when in half an hour they would take her husband away as hopelessly mad, her love for Balint would die or at least be subtly transformed into unending frustrated pain. Now she would have to remain in that hateful house for ever, chained to an absent husband she had always loathed, living in hell with an estranged daughter and a half-crazed mother-in-law.

She had thought of nothing else during the past few days, but it had never assailed her with such force as it did that morning just as she was waiting for the final stroke of fate which would throw her life into havoc. Right up until this last minute she had felt that there might be some hope, that something, anything, would happen ... some miracle that would cure him. She had been like a drowning man clutching at imaginary straws.

So she sat there, her head hanging low and her face covered by her hands. She could feel the pulse throbbing in her throat, and she looked back dismally at the seemingly endless sorrows of her life. She had been really happy only once, during those four short weeks she had spent with Balint in Venice; and even then, though dazed by the happiness of passing her nights in his arms, she had been menaced by the thought of that self-destruction she had thought to be a price worth paying for the fulfilment of their love. Now she thought she should have killed herself then. At least she would have been saved this present suffering.

Tears rose in her eyes and suddenly she was racked with sobs. No matter how hard she tried she could not control them. Leaning forward as if mourning the dead she cried ... and cried ... and cried ... her tears falling through her fingers onto her blouse and into her lap.

Then a voice said, 'Are you crying, Adrienne?'

Uzdy was looking up at her from his pillows. She had no idea how long he had been awake. Now he was staring at her with surprise in those strange slanting eyes. She looked back at him, unable to reply. His expression was amazingly peaceful. She had never seen him look like that before.

Uzdy did not move his head, and his long hair lay on the pillow like a dark wedge reaching up on each side of his face in strange peaks, his eyebrows and sharply pointed beard making him more than ever like everyone's idea of Mephistopheles. Only now there was nothing satanic about him and on his lips was a slight, apologetic smile.

'Why do you cry?' he asked gently. 'Surely not for me? Why should you cry for me?' He spoke slowly as if he were really only talking to himself. 'I know you were never happy with me,' he went on, 'so why should you cry for me now?'

He paused, and then went on, 'Perhaps I oughtn't to have ...

I know I should have behaved differently, quite differently . . . but I didn't know how. It was a mistake, a terrible mistake. My own mistake, of course, but then I didn't know . . .'

Adrienne was again racked by sobs, so much so that she pressed her fists into her temples and put her head between her knees. Now she was crying silently, her blouse quivering as her back shook with her sobs. When she was at last able to look up she saw that he was looking intently at her, probably waiting to say something more. When he did speak it was very quietly, like a voice from another world, 'No matter what happened, no matter why, or how . . . I must tell you I loved you very much!' he said, and closed his eyes as if infinitely weary.

He did not open them again, not even when daylight flooded the room and the clock chimed the hour of eight, nor when the door opened and Maier came in. His eyes were still closed and he seemed to be asleep when Adrienne rose and brushed her husband's locks with her long, cool fingers.

In the corridor outside, behind the Saxon doctor, two dark figures moved forward carrying an iron stretcher.

Adrienne slipped quietly to the stairs, thinking she would flee to her own room so as not to see anything of the terrible scene that would be enacted below when those fateful figures bore down upon poor Uzdy. Try as she would she could not go more than a few steps. Her legs seemed as if made of lead and she found herself forced to remain, leaning against the wooden walls of the stairway. From downstairs she could hear the sound of a door opening and footsteps. Then her husband's voice, full of surprise, called out, 'No! No! No!' quite strongly. And then nothing. Nothing!

The silence frightened her. Then there were more steps, and this time they had something of a military ring. The glazed door leading to the garden opened and she could just hear some sort of command. They must have gone out, thought Adrienne, and rushed down the stairs. In the bright sunlight before her she saw a little group of men carrying a stretcher and on it lay Pal Uzdy, his body covered by a white sheet like a shroud. She supposed they must have given him some quick-acting injection. His face looked as pale as if sculpted in wax.

Adrienne's knees buckled and she tried to support herself on the bars of the window by which she stood. And once again she wept, but this time it was not for herself. They were the tears of pity.

CHAPTER SIX

ADRIENNE WROTE TO Balint, not from Almasko but from Kolozsvar where she had gone the day after they took Uzdy away. There were so many things that had to be done.

On the first three pages she related the bare facts, as drily as possible, recounting what had happened day by day, like a historical chronicle. She wrote in short sentences, each like the hammer-blows of Fate, and the last one read: '... *and the day before yesterday they brought the poor man to Kolozsvar.*' After that her writing became more confused, with broken sentences and words scratched out and replaced by others.

With this everything is over! I can never get a divorce and so you can't marry me, never, do you understand? Never! Not while he's alive ... and he may live for years. He could even outlive me. We can't count on Uzdy's dying, even though that would give us our freedom. We can't! And even less on his getting better. So you see everything we've planned is impossible.

All sorts of other things must be over between us too. The life we used to lead is impossible now. Don't deny it, you've said it yourself many times. I've all your letters here in front of me. Remember when you wrote 'What sort of a life do we lead, always pretending, lying, hiding like thieves – and that of course is what we are because we steal our meagre ration of happiness, sometimes for a few hours, rarely for a whole night together, always taking precautions, watching to see we are not discovered, like convicts on the run'? Every word you wrote is true, utterly, absolutely true. In another letter you said '... so don't you see how degrading, how humiliating our life is now? We are forced to treat as a shameful secret what we should blazon to the whole wide world.' You then went on to say 'This can't go on!'

I never answered those words before, or I would have said you were right. Perhaps I thought it wasn't necessary, but I've always known it – I sensed it in Venice, remember? That's why I wanted everything to end, to die rather than come back to this slavery. It's just as true for me as for you. We can't go on ... I couldn't stand it again!

There's a lot more too, things you didn't write about, but which I felt all the more, perhaps. Our child? To be afraid of having a child when it's what I long for above everything. Always to be afraid, knowing the disaster it would be if we weren't ready, when it should be our greatest joy. That has always been with us, but think what it would be like now! Is this what we've got to look forward to, for ever and ever? Even if I wanted to I couldn't do it, not now. Supposing it happened? Could we destroy it before it was born or bring it into the world and then hide it . . . our son? Even if I could accept that, for his sake how could we burden him with the shame? Once again I have to quote your own words, words you have written to me in your letters: 'I want a successor who bears my name. Not a day passes when I don't long for it more than ever. I am now thirty-two years old and I suppose this yearning is true for all men at that age. It is at the root of all religions, in ancient days as much as in our own. It has been true for Christians, Jews and Chinese, all these have wanted descendants who will remember and revere their forebears. The curse of Jehovah lay on those who had no sons: and I am the last of my line. Without an heir my family dies with me. I am now the last link in the chain . . . and if that chain is broken?' All this you wrote to me yourself. You also said 'I want to pass on to him our traditions so that, with faith and decency, he will accept the responsibilities so gladly shouldered by my father and grandfather'. And then you went on 'It is the only hope of immortality in this world, and I cannot renounce it!'

Why do I write all this? It is because I want you to marry. I command you to do so in the name of our love. Don't argue with me. This is what you must do. If we ourselves do not erect barriers between us, we will never be able to keep away from each other – and then we'll just be in the same intolerable situation as before. Do this now, at once! When I finally made the decision to leave Uzdy and get a divorce I knew that I was taking the awful risk that it would send him mad and that I would be responsible. That's why I hesitated so long. You can have no idea how hard I tried to decide before; and when I did decide it was with full knowledge of what I was doing. Also all of this that I am now saying to you today – and that I now expect of you.

Who should you marry? I have thought of that too. Lili Illes-vary. She is in love with you, and you like her. The family desires it or they wouldn't have invited you so often. She is pretty and healthy and worthy to bear the son I cannot give you.

It would also be some slight consolation to me. It has been bad enough to shoulder the responsibility for Uzdy, but I could not live

*knowing that it was I who had denied you an heir. If that were so
there would be only one course for me, the one I had intended in
Venice. That would set you free, of course, but I don't think you'd
want it, you couldn't! Neither can we go on . . . as we have till now.
Oh no! We came too close to Paradise. We stood on the threshold
and caught a glimpse through the door . . . it was a dream, radiant
and full of promise. But the door was slammed in our faces. Now
we can never go back to that misery, stripped of everything like
beggars . . . No! Not that! Never ever that!*

A little further down on the page was a single phrase:

I don't want to see you until you've done what I say!

* * *

The letter had arrived at midday; it was now early evening and
the sky was dark. Balint had sat down in an armchair in the
window of his hotel room to read what Adrienne had to say; and
he had been lying there ever since. He was like a man felled with
a sledgehammer.

The light from the street lamps on the Danube quays was
reflected in a long rectangle on the ceiling with the glazing bars
of the window casting a black cross in the centre. To Balint it was
like looking up at his tombstone from the depths of the grave.
The letter had fallen to the floor beside him.

The door opened and a small woman ran to his side. It was
Roza Abady, but he noticed nothing until she pulled up a chair
beside him, sat down and put her hand on his arm.

'It's only me,' she said with a gentle smile. 'I got here at noon
and heard you were at home. So I came to see you.'

She spoke as naturally as if she had last seen him the day before
and as if nothing had ever been the matter between them. She
looked deeply into his face, her eyes filled with anxiety and compassion though she was trying hard not to make it look as if she
had come to him at once when she had heard what had happened
to Uzdy. Of course the news of his being incarcerated in the
House with the Green Roof had spread like wildfire and Countess Roza had at once grasped what this would mean for her son.

Though she was filled with joy that his hated marriage was
now forever impossible, she knew what a terrible blow this
would be to him and the thought of what he would be suffering
soon overcame her own immense relief. Her only thought was

to go to him at once, surround him with her own love and do what she could to alleviate his sorrow. There would, she realized, be nothing that she could say to him, but at least she could forgive him and take him back and restore to him everything she had so cruelly taken away. Those months of searing loneliness, when she thought that she had lost him forever, had long before cleansed her of that overweening pride that had brought it upon her; and so she had been happy to seize the first opportunity of making her peace with him without humiliation.

'I am going again to Abbazia for the winter,' she said. 'I liked it very much last year and, as it's so close, perhaps I'll see you from time to time? You will visit me occasionally, won't you? I shall not need you to take me there this time as I can travel quite well alone now. You see I'm not as helpless as I used to be,' and she babbled on, talking about quite trivial unimportant things that had no relation to the drama that had thrown him into turmoil. She told him that she was going to stay in Budapest for a few days and, so as not to let drop any hint that she was there only to be near him, said she had decided to have a medical check-up.

She did not switch on the light, sensing that she would never be able to get so close to him if the room were brilliantly lit. In the dark she could sit beside him, tenderly stroking his hair ... and in the dark he would not have to mask his sorrow.

They stayed together for a long time until the evening shadows darkened into night as the old lady did all she could to talk away her son's unhappiness.

The next few days they were constantly together, spending the mornings either at museums or in the doctors' waiting-rooms. In the afternoons and evenings they went to concerts or to the cinema, but not to the theatre as Countess Roza, who had always loved plays, did not now want to go lest it should upset Balint.*

In the middle of the month she left for Abbazia. Balint took her to the station and settled her in her compartment, staying with her until the train left.

'I'll be with you for Christmas,' he said, and then, after a short

* *Translator's note*: This last phrase seems to be a Freudian slip on the author's part for though it hardly makes sense in relation to Balint and Adrienne, it may possibly be an unconscious echo of an important moment in Miklós Bánffy's own life when he found himself obliged to renounce his love for the well-known actress, Aranka Varady. Some years later, after his father's death, they married and Katalin Bánffy-Jelen is their daughter.

pause, he added with special emphasis, 'The day after tomorrow I'm going to shoot at the Szent-Gyorgyis'.'

Countess Roza looked up sharply. She had understood at once that something important lay behind his words. As if merely to follow his lead she then asked, 'Who's going to be there? The same party as last year?'

'I don't know about the guns, or even the women guests, except for my aunt and Magda . . . and Lili Illesvary. I know she'll be there.'

The old lady's face lit up, but she didn't say anything. Then she took his face between her chubby little hands and kissed him on the forehead.

'Go now, my boy,' she said softly, 'and may God bless you!'

The express train to Zsolna was getting up steam under the sooty glass roof of the Budapest-West station.

Balint bought several newspapers and then mounted the train, put his luggage on the rack, settled down in his seat and was soon immersed in the news. For days it had been rumoured that a solution had been found to the impasse that had rendered impotent the Coalition. The rumour had been lent credence by the fact that the Minister-President, Wekerle, had managed to bypass all those who had obstructed the government by tabling an 'indemnity' motion which meant that the Budget voted in the previous year could be renewed for a further year without a vote. This had had, albeit briefly, the happy effect of re-animating the moribund Coalition; but it had unfortunately also led to several other less desirable results. November had seen the Independence Party split into two groups, one led by Justh and all those who stood for an independent banking system for Hungary, and the other by Ferenc Kossuth. A venomous internecine battle then began which was made the most of in the Budapest press, and soon Justh was made to resign his post as Speaker of the House because Kossuth and his followers had thrown in their lot with the party that supported the 1867 Compromise with Vienna, and had thrown him out. War-cries sounded on all sides urging the Hungarians to the fray; and more hate-filled slogans were hurled at the government even than in the times of Tisza or Fejervary. Then the ex-Speaker managed to block the 'indemnity' with a technical objection, and followed this up with legal demands for closed sessions and calling for a vote on any trivial matter that happened to be under discussion. Kossuth was now wrecking the Coalition by applying the same obstructive tactics which tradition had reserved for dealing with governments whose party could command a majority.

And so the circle was closed. The Coalition had been brought into being by using those very same obstructive tactics that had destroyed one government after another. It had come in on a wave of patriotic fervour, brandishing a multitude of popular slogans and promising every chauvinistic project imaginable. That is how the Coalition came to power, dishonestly keeping quiet about the capitulations that had had to be made on the way. And then it had to face the eternal reality of office, that the state's interests could not be ignored. And here the Coalition had come unstuck: it could not even bring in the universal suffrage law that had been its principal battle-cry.

During its entire term of office the Coalition had achieved nothing. From the very first all those separate parties, though still claiming that they were allies, indeed friends, had done nothing but fight each other. The public good was forgotten, submerged in a sea of party rivalry, and so the only result was to damage the dignity and prestige of that historic Parliament they had all once sworn to preserve.

All this was in Balint's mind as the train carried him to Jablanka. The first paper told him of the efforts of Aladar Zichy, Andrassy, and even Wekerle, and predicted that one of them would find a solution despite the obstructions offered by the bankers. Another reported that Khuen-Hedervary had been received in audience by the Monarch and appointed to be the next Minister-President with instructions to dissolve Parliament and hold new elections, presumably thereby giving the country the opportunity of voting back the very politicians they had turned against four years before!

And so ended an era in which nothing whatever had been achieved. The balance sheet consisted only of omissions, the worst of which had been the defence of the nation. Four years had been lost; and Hungary was now less prepared even than Italy or insignificant little Serbia.

The express had long since left the Danube. Evening came and Balint found himself still staring through the darkening light onto a sad, sooty, seemingly endless plain. The first snows had melted and it had then frozen again. The train rushed northwards across ice-covered fields. The smoke from the engine swirled overhead and from time to time, whenever the stoker opened the furnace door, bright red glowing sparks were reflected on the frozen earth outside.

In half an hour he would arrive, get out, seat himself in the carriage which had been sent for him; and in another half-hour he would be at the Szent-Gyorgyis' country place where he would do what he had promised in the telegram he had that morning sent to Adrienne.

It had been his only reply to her letter, and read:

'AT NOON TODAY I AM LEAVING FOR JABLANKA AS YOU HAVE ORDERED ME TO DO.'

BOOK THREE

THEY WERE
DIVIDED

'And the fingers went on writing in letters of fire upon the plaster of the Wall of the King's palace. And the third word was UPHARSIN – thy kingdom shall be divided.

'But none could read the writing so drunk were they with much drinking of wine, and they wasted the Lord's vessels of gold and silver which their ancestors had laid up in the house of the Lord, and they argued with each other praising their false gods made of gold and silver, of brass, of iron, of wood and of clay until there was no strength left in them.

'And the armies of the Medes and Persians stood ready before the walls of the city and in the same night everyone within it was slain.'

PART ONE

CHAPTER ONE

BALINT ABADY STEPPED quietly into the family box at the theatre at Kolozsvar. Even though he knew it well, for the Abadys like all the other old families in the district rented the same box every year, he still had to grope his way in the darkness to hang up his coat. Still somewhat blinded by the light from the stage he sat down in the best seat facing the stage, for his mother had stayed at home at Denestornya. Balint himself had driven up from the country, just for one night, because he wanted to see the gala performance of *Madam Butterfly* that was being given that evening, and especially the Butterfly herself, the famous Yvonne de Tréville, who often came from the Opéra Comique to sing in Kolozsvar.

He was late and the great love duet that closes the first act was just beginning. The music throbbed with passion, with love and desire; the sweet tones of the violins carried Puccini's soaring melodies and above it all was the pure smooth voice of the French diva.

Balint was on the point of surrendering to the music when he felt himself overcome by a strange feeling of agitation, as if he were in the presence of an overpowering force, a force even more potent than the storm of emotion that was being enacted before him on the stage. It was like an electric shock to his nervous system and something, he knew not what, made him turn round.

Adrienne Miloth was sitting in the next box, almost directly behind him.

He was startled to see her there because he had heard that she had gone to Switzerland with her daughter and he had not thought she would have returned so soon. This evening he saw that she and her sister Margit were guests in the kindly old Countess Gyalakuthy's box. There she sat; and though she was so close she seemed as insubstantial as a phantom.

Her face was lit only by the moonlight from the stage which

cast the faintest glow on her delicately aquiline nose, her cheeks and her generous mouth. Balint could just see the pale sheen of her skin where the neck and shoulders merged into the deep décolleté of her silver dress. Everything else was hidden in the darkness of the theatre.

She was looking straight ahead, quite motionless, as still as a marble statue. In the reflection of the cunningly contrived moonlight on the stage Adrienne's eyes shone emerald green; and she sat there rigidly, without moving a muscle, though he could hardly believe that she had not seen him come in because he had sat down just in front of her. They were so close that with only the slightest movement their arms would have touched.

Balint felt that he could not stay there another moment. It would be impossible for him, for them both, to sit next to each other and behave as if they were strangers. How could they listen together to that passionate music which spoke so eloquently of desire and love and desperate yearning? No! No! No! He must not stay! He could not stay!

The memories of their love so overwhelmed him that he found himself trembling. He got up silently and slipped out of the box, reeling slightly like a man who has been struck a heavy blow.

Though he could not sit next to her he still could not leave the theatre in which she sat; so he descended the great stair, crossed to the other side of the auditorium and, with his coat on, stepped through one of the doors and stood at the side of the stalls in the shadow of the balcony. No one would be able to see him there, he thought, so he would remain until the act came to an end and then slip out before the lights went up. From there, too, he could gaze at Adrienne whom he had not seen for more than a year: and even then it had been a mere glance from afar.

She did not seem changed. Maybe her face was a little thinner, perhaps there was a trace of bitterness about the lines of her mouth, but she was still supremely beautiful, every aspect of her as lovely as when she had been his love, his friend, his companion in body and spirit, in those days when they had planned to become husband and wife. But an implacable fate had separated them.

In his imagination he saw her stripped of that shining metallic gown, bright as a suit of armour, standing naked before him as she first had five long years before in Venice, then so often afterwards in their little hut in the forest, or at the Uzdy villa, or at

her father's house at Mezo-Varjas, or in Budapest, indeed anywhere their homeless love could find refuge. Balint's heart contracted with bitterness when he thought once again of how he
had been forced to abandon her and how she had ordered him
to marry Lili Illesvary whom she herself had picked out for him.

Adrienne had then made her conditions: their affair must
cease, and she would not even meet him socially unless he got
married and so erected a barrier between them. He had found
he could not comply and so they had not seen each other again.

The love duet continued, growing ever more intense, more
impassioned. For a moment its message of love and desire was
overshadowed by two brief echoes deep in the orchestral texture
of the music with which the Shinto priest had cursed the lovers'
happiness; and when he heard it Balint felt most poignantly that
it symbolized the story of their own doomed love. However this
sad reflection did not last long, for that song of yearning flowed
out from the stage, stronger than ever, irresistible and triumphant. It was as if the whole wide world was composed of spring
and moonlight, blossom and sublime melody. As the music
mounted to its stormy climax Balint felt as moved and shattered
as by the climax of love. It was the music of their past, now forever denied them.

The curtain fell to a tornado of applause, and Balint slipped
quietly out.

The October night air was already cold. The sky was clear and
the pavements glistened from the light rain that had fallen that
afternoon. Without thinking where he was going Balint started
to walk towards the centre of the town. He walked at random,
with no object except to be alone, alone with the torment of
all those thoughts by which he had been assailed that evening.
Glancing at his watch he saw that it was just a quarter past nine.
This gave him nearly three hours of freedom, for at midnight he
was expected to go to supper at the house of the Prefect, who,
as general director of the Kolozsvar theatres, was giving a party
after the performance in honour of the French diva. For three
hours, then, he could try to walk off his chagrin, to master that
surge of bitterness that had been stirred up by the sight of
Adrienne sitting so close to him.

As he wandered aimlessly along the dark streets he was assailed
so fiercely by a torrent of haphazard memories that he felt like a
man pursued by the Fates from whom it was impossible to hide.

And yet hide he must! It had been the same the previous summer, on the only other occasion that he had seen Adrienne since their parting.

Then he had just been leaving the hospital, after bringing in one of the stable lads from Denestornya, when he caught sight of Adrienne through the bars of a tall iron fence. He had shrunk back into the shade of the doorway so that he shouldn't be seen; but from there he followed her with his eyes as, with head held high and looking straight ahead of her without a glance to left or right, she strode determinedly up the path which led to the lunatic asylum or, as most people euphemistically called it, the House with the Green Roof.

Off to see that mad husband, Balint had thought bitterly, he whom she had never loved and who had never loved her.

His heart had swelled, like that of an exile who catches a glimpse of his forbidden home from far away.

As he had hidden then, so he felt impelled to run now, to escape from the theatre and wander anonymously through the town. Without realizing where he had been heading Balint found himself in the main square, and here he was almost overcome by a strange lassitude. It was as if that impulse which had hurled him out of the theatre had sapped all his reserves of energy.

He walked on, without taking note of where he was going, until, at the corner of the market-place, he almost knocked over the charcoal grill of an old woman roasting chestnuts. Ashamed of himself, he stopped and in an attempt to pull himself together, and to make amends for his clumsiness, he bought a paper cone of nuts that the woman held out to him. As he started absent-mindedly to peel them he remembered that he had been invited out to supper and had better not arrive with stained fingers. Abruptly he shoved the warm paper cone deep into one of his coat pockets, deciding to give it to the first child he might meet; but although he passed several hanging about near the iron bridge or in front of the cinema, by then the chestnuts had been forgotten.

Of course, he reflected, he ought to have married Lili Illesvary. Everything would then have been different. He could have met Adrienne and, with no constraint between them, talked of their by now shadowy past in a way that could provoke no comment if overheard. They could have met as old friends, if nothing more. At least it would have meant that he would have seen her from time to time and touched her hand as he kissed her fingers. Also he would have had a home of his own, and a family to return to, instead of wandering aimlessly with nowhere he wanted to go. That was what he ought to have done, yet he had carelessly thrown away even the half-happiness such a marriage would have brought him. Now he had nothing; no love, no family, nothing!

It had been entirely his own fault. The opportunity had been there, at Jablanka in the middle of December, and if he had failed to take the opportunity offered he had no one but himself to blame. But he had done nothing.

His host, Antal Szent-Gyorgyi, and his sons had welcomed him as warmly as ever, without being over-demonstrative which in that house was thought to be not very good form. His cousin Magda's greeting was a shade more enthusiastic, for she gave him a teasing smile and pressed his hand a little harder than was usual. His aunt Elise, Countess Szent-Gyorgyi, received him with maternal warmth and tenderness and somehow, though without ever alluding to the matter, contrived to let him know how much she approved of, and would encourage, his marrying Lili. It was clear to Balint that they all knew that that was why he had come to Jablanka, and that everyone was in favour. Canon Czibulka, or Pfaffulus as he was nicknamed in that house, an old and intimate friend of the Szent-Gyorgyis, also discreetly showed that he approved the match by giving a special antenna-like movement of his bushy eyebrows when he first shook Balint by the hand. Pfaffulus had already been at Jablanka for several days as the shoot had been held unusually late and, as Advent had already begun, he came over daily from Nagy-Szombat to say mass in the castle chapel. The priest's tacit approval warmed Balint's heart for it made him feel that in that house everyone knew about and looked kindly on his plans to ask Lili to marry him.

All the same he did not see her until all the guests assembled in the lofty stucco-decorated drawing-room which had been the monks' refectory before the former monastery became the Szent-Gyorgyis' country home. She came in from the library, which was at the opposite end of the room from where Balint was standing, seeming almost to glide weightlessly across the highly polished wooden floor. She was dressed in a flowing white tulle gown and she moved with that quiet assurance natural to girls

brought up in the highest society. As she crossed the room she
nodded to those other guests she had already seen and went up
to greet two new arrivals, the guests of honour who had just
come from Vienna. Once again Abady smiled as he admired the
impeccable way in which she moved, reflecting how perfectly
she fitted into those grand surroundings and what a perfect background was formed for her by the great white hall-like room, the
crimson and gold furniture and the huge family portraits in their
elaborate frames. For all the apparent frailty of the girl, as she
moved slowly round that luxurious room in her diaphanous
creamy white dress, her step as light as that of any butterfly, one
could still sense that inner core of steel that was the mark of
her race.

So this, thought Balint, is the girl who is going to be my wife!
Infinitely well-bred, the scion of countless generations whose
sons and daughters, being always rich and independent, had
never needed to marry some ugly duckling for her dowry or
accept anyone second-rate for his money. Now she had nearly
come up to where he stood. She did not increase her speed nor
for a moment change her demeanour; and yet there was something special in the movement she made in putting out her hand
to him, in the yielding softness with which she took his, and in
the joyful flash of her cornflower-blue eyes.

Balint sensed it all at once and knew exactly what it meant.

During the three days of shooting Lili was often to be found
beside him and remained with him for the whole of the most
important beat on the third day when once again Balint found
himself allotted the place of honour at the extreme right-hand
end of the line of guns. They somehow seemed to spend hours
together, and even on those long afternoon walks on which, of
course, they were never alone but always accompanied by several
other young people, the two of them often seemed to be left to
walk some twenty or thirty paces behind the others. And then
Lili, who otherwise was lively and talkative, would remain silent,
leaving it to him to decide what they would talk about. She was
hoping he would propose: and that is when he ought to have
done so, either in the long hornbeam avenue or else when coming back from visiting the thoroughbred mares.

Recalling that moment Balint conjured up in his mind the thin
layer of powdery snow that covered the frozen ground and which
had crackled under their feet. The others had lingered by the

fences of the paddocks and that is when he should have spoken. It was there that he ought to have uttered those few banal words that were the classic form of suggesting marriage. And yet for some reason he had held back and said nothing. Stupidly he had said nothing. Had he felt that in that wintry landscape his voice would sound too matter-of-fact, too cold and businesslike, too unspontaneous? But of course he knew then, just as he knew now, that it would not have mattered how he had said it, for the girl had only been waiting for him to speak.

Balint stopped at the bridge over the mill-stream. For a moment he thought of going on into the park, which at that hour would be completely deserted, and he walked on a few steps before reflecting how silly it would be to get his patent leather evening shoes all muddied just before he went to the Prefect's evening party. Far better to go where he could stay on the sidewalk, where the slight humidity from that afternoon's rain would have left few traces. So he continued along the road which led to the railway station.

As he wandered so aimlessly in the night Balint thought back to that time a year before when he had spent so many autumn evenings just wandering about the streets as aimlessly as he was now doing. Anything, he had thought, to keep on the move and quiet his growing anxiety as he waited for Adrienne's letter, that letter which would at long last announce that she had started the business of her divorce. Until then every little note she had sent him had just been one more excuse for delay: '. . . it is impossible now', or 'Not yet, we have to wait, wait, wait!' That was what she had written, and then he had not understood the dreadful dilemma in which she had been placed, fearing to make any move that might push her sick husband into insanity, that insanity that had come all the same and forever destroyed their hopes.

He wondered if Adrienne was still sitting in Countess Gyalakuthy's box at the opera or whether she too had left the theatre devastated, as he had been, by the cruel chance that had brought them physically so close after so long apart. Had she too been shattered by that cruel game the Fates seemed to be playing with them?

Somehow, he thought, he must arrange that this should never happen again. He would leave Kolozsvar the next day; indeed if it had not been for that stupid supper party, he would have gone that very night.

In the morning he would go back to Denestornya, to his mother and to that old home which was the only place in the world where he could find peace. My home, he thought, with its age-old beauty and magic, where, though always enveloped in a veil of sadness, there were only the two of them to wander in that enormous house: he and his old mother. And now there always would only be the two of them. There was no one else, there never would be anyone else. There was no future and no young life to follow.

Had he proposed to Lili at Jablanka then at least he might have had that hope. What madness had prevented him?

It had been quite clear that the Szent-Gyorgyis, in their typically unobtrusive way, had made sure that there would have been no obstacles in the path of such a marriage. They had even thought about the difference of religion and, with a tactfulness that amounted almost to an art, had taken pains to let him know that his being a Protestant would create no difficulties.

The memory came back to him with sudden clarity, perhaps because it had all been so surprising.

On the afternoon of the second day of the shooting party Balint had just changed and was on his way to join the others in the drawing-room when he met Pfaffulus in the passage. He had the impression that the priest had been waiting for him.

'I was just on my way to the chapel,' said Canon Czibulka in his slight Slovakian accent. 'If you've never seen it perhaps you'd like to come with me? It's really very fine, well worth seeing.'

They walked together to that part of the former monastery that formed the rear part of the cloister-court and faced the main entrance over which was the refectory now transformed into the main drawing-room. In the centre of the first-floor gallery which encircled the court was a massive stone doorway, whose carved and ornamented architraves framed the door-posts which bordered a pair of huge doors inlaid with many different kinds of precious woods in the full opulence of ecclesiastical baroque.

Pfaffulus pushed open the doors, which swung back noiselessly. They went in.

The chapel was the size of a church and the semi-circle of

windows behind the altar must, Balint had realized, have projected out towards the mountainside. Although darkness had nearly fallen there was enough evening light to cast a soft mystical radiance in front of which the lines of the baldaquin over the altar stood out as if etched in black on grey. Then Pfaffulus had switched on the electric chandeliers and the chapel blazed with light. It was indeed beautiful.

Along each side wall stood the carved wooden stalls where the monks had sat for worship, the panelling divided by columns which supported a carved rococo veil that seemed to swirl with an almost musical rhythm towards the altar. All along its border were placed winged angels' heads and surmounting all this splendour was the monastic order's symbolic bird, a raven carrying bread in its beak, huge and gilded, like an emphatic exclamation mark floating above the mellow brown woodwork of the canopy itself. Over the tabernacle the baldaquin, fringed with golden tassels and supported by twisted columns, supported a picture of the Virgin surrounded by a golden sun-burst. On each side angels dressed identically in blue and gold, with gilded wings, knelt in the exaggerated attitudes so beloved in the baroque era.

A thick floral carpet covered the stone flags on the floor.

'It is beautiful, isn't it?' Pfaffulus had said; and he took Balint round showing him the carvings on the stalls and explaining the reliefs, all of which commemorated some miracle or incident in the life of the holy Saint Paul the Hermit, founder of the order.

Then he crossed in front of the altar, genuflecting swiftly as he did so, to show Balint the Abbot's stall and a series of holy pictures by well-known artists. They had almost returned to the chapel doors when the priest stopped and sat down, a thoughtful look on his fine expressive face. It was as if he had just remembered something.

After nodding appreciation at Balint's words of thanks he looked up at the younger man and, seemingly unable to keep to himself what had come so strongly to his mind, grasped Balint's arm and pulled him down to sit beside him. As he did so he said:

'Do you know what this chapel means to me? I love it as if it were a living human being, not only because of its beauty but also because of so many things that have happened to me within its walls.'

He explained that it was at Jablanka that he had started his professional career, as tutor to Count Antal Szent-Gyorgyi. Later, after several years spent in Rome, he had returned as the castle's resident priest; though he had never accepted any parish of his own even though the Count was patron of several rich livings and pressed him to take the best of them. He told Balint that he had preferred to remain quietly where he was and continue his studies in canon law.

Then he gave an especially sweet smile and went on:

'I have another very dear memory. It was in this church that I officiated at the wedding of Count Antal's other sister, the Countess Charlotte who married a Swede, Count Olaf Loewen-stierna.' As he said these words Pfaffulus's thin pointed nose seemed to grow even longer and he raised his eyebrows expres-sively. 'It was very bold on my part, as the bridegroom, of course, was a Protestant and I should not really have performed the cere-mony without the promise that the children should be brought up as Catholics. But what could I do? The old Count gave his orders and said that one could not ask such a thing of a Loewen-stierna, who was descended from one of Gustavus Adolphus's generals; and anyway he would despise the young man if he abandoned his family traditions. If he, as a good Catholic father, did not demand it, then I should not either. Naturally I did as he wished.'

Here the round little priest had leaned forward and spoken confidentially into Balint's ear.

'Of course I had committed a fault; even perhaps a sin, yes, a sin. And yet it was my sin, and mine alone, because in such circumstances only the priest can be at fault. I went straight after-wards to see the Prince-Cardinal. It was then Monsignor Simor. To him I confessed my fault, my crime. I knelt before him and he gave me a thorough scolding and some pretty harsh penances with which to atone for my lapse. Then he invited me to eat with him. Afterwards he had said: "You were wise, my son, not to ask for guidance because no permission would ever have been given. Yes, you did the wise, the clever thing. The family of Szent-Gyorgyi have done much for our church for several centuries and so they fall into a very special category. I am sure that this is how the Roman Curia would regard the matter too."'

Czibulka had then fallen silent, gazing ahead as if conscious only of his own memories. Then he had got up and looked at Abady as if excusing himself for having burdened the young man with such personal reminiscences.

'You must forgive my idle chatter,' he said. 'I seem to have gone on at length about things which only concern myself. But this chapel, you see, means so much to me.'

Then he had made another quick genuflection towards the altar, switched out the lights, and escorted Balint out of the chapel. They walked back together to the drawing-room where everyone was gathering for tea.

They had thought of every way to encourage and reassure him, and so everything had depended on him and on him alone. And then he had let the moment pass and so thrown away his chances, if not of love then at least of a kind and loving wife, of a family, and of a nest to come home to.

It had been on the last evening of his stay that he had let the final opportunity escape him.

He had dressed for dinner early and when he had entered the drawing-room he had found it deserted. Then, through the open doors to the library, he had seen Lili, who for some reason of her own had also dressed before the others. She had been kneeling on a chair drawn up to a long table in the centre of the room, leaning forward with her bare elbows reflected on the polished wooden table top as she turned the pages of a large album of engravings. She had seemed totally engrossed in the pictures before her.

At that moment he had instinctively known that she had come down early to the library with a single purpose, and that that had been, if possible, to give him one final occasion on which to make his proposal, final because it had been the last night of that gathering at Jablanka to which he had been invited just for that purpose.

'Do you know this collection?' Lili had asked when Balint had come up to her and leaned beside her on the table. 'It is very rare. It's the record of a journey to Egypt by a Hungarian, a Count Forray. Aren't these coloured engravings lovely? Do look! Look at this one! Isn't it beautiful?' and as she had looked up at him the question in her wide open violet-blue eyes had had nothing to do with the pictures on the table.

Together they had turned the pages slowly; and as they did so sometimes their arms or their fingers had touched and sometimes they had exchanged a word or two: 'This must be Malta!', 'Do look at the camel-driver!', 'The Khedive's palace . . .', words without any real meaning whose purpose had only been to break the silence.

Several times Balint had thought that the moment had come to speak the words for which she was waiting. He had only to take her hand and murmur a few short sentences and with that simple action he would have wiped out the past and started a new era in his life. Adrienne had wanted it that way and had expected it of him; but somehow the right words had never come, only those banal phrases about the engravings in the album on the table before them. And yet, as he was saying something obvious about the temple at Karnak and how large its stones were, he had been wondering if he ought then to have said 'I love you', which would have been a lie, or whether all that would have been needed was 'Will you be my wife?' until the moment had passed and they had been obliged to get up and go into the drawing-room where the other guests had started to gather.

Lili had then got down from the chair on which she had been kneeling and slowly straightened up. Balint remembered that he had wondered then if she thought he might have been embarrassed to speak under the bright glare of the electric chandelier above them, especially as she had walked straight over to one of the deep window embrasures, where the thickness of the old walls would have made them invisible to the guests in the other room. She had gone right up to the window and then, with her face close to the glass, and clearly to find another reason for the move, she had murmured 'Do look at the frost. It is like flowers made of ice!' and then she had turned and glanced back at him.

But Balint, who had followed her only as far as the beginning of the deep window embrasure, had just stood there still looking at the vast library.

The walls were lined with wooden bookcases almost to the ceiling, all curved and convoluted with elaborate carved and gilded decorations and divided by twisted columns of different precious woods. Above the elaborate cornice were metal conch shells and gilded *putti* brandishing highly-coloured heraldic shields, all in the most sophisticated manner of the Viennese baroque. The atmosphere of abounding opulence was over-whelming, and when Balint had watched the slim girlish figure of Lili stepping so elegantly across the inlaid parquet floor he had suddenly felt that all this was her proper background, where she

truly belonged. This somewhat foreign luxury, itself so truly
Austrian, was her birthright; and yet it was alien and strange to
anyone with his downright Transylvanian background. How
could he uproot her and carry her off to his own so different
home? Even if she were in love with him, he had thought, would
she not feel herself transplanted into an alien, possibly hostile,
soil. For all its size and grandeur, Denestornya in its simple Hungarian way could not compare with this sophisticated splendour,
just as the way of life in Transylvania could hardly be compared
with what Lili was used to. All this had flashed through Balint's
mind as he had stood there looking at her, and it was like a sudden
draught of cold air in his face. More, it had been just one more
inhibition to be added to the others.

   'It must be icy outside.'

   'It was six below zero at dusk.'

   'How bright the moonlight is!'

   'That's why it's so cold. The sky is quite clear now.'

   With these and other meaningless, inane phrases they had
filled in the gaps between pauses that seemed endless to them
both. At length Lili had turned away from the window. For an
instant she had looked straight into Balint's face and then, seeming to glide across the floor, she had returned to the drawing-
room without saying another word.

   Knowing now that he had finally lost her, Balint had followed
her slowly, his heart filled with sadness: and yet it had been a
mild sadness and on his face had been the slight ironic smile of
someone who had had to forgo a pleasure he had never really
expected to be his.

What madness it had been to throw all that away!

   Thinking back to the past Balint stamped his feet in momentary anger and quickened his pace. In a few moments he found
himself in the square in front of the station, which was full of
bustle and noise for the express from Budapest had just arrived.
Several luggage-laden motors passed him on their way to the city
centre and this sudden rush of activity brought Balint to a halt.
For a moment he hesitated, trying to choose between continuing
on the muddy pavement in front of some warehouses, or crossing
the road which was even muddier. Neither seemed sensible.

   As he stood there motionless for a moment newsboys ran
forward offering the capital's midday papers. Thinking that

anything might be a distraction from his self-torment, Balint stopped one, took a paper at random, pressed a coin into the lad's hand, stuffed the paper into one of his greatcoat pockets and, without waiting for the change, turned away and started to walk back to the city centre. I'll go to a café and pass the rest of the time reading, he said to himself, but he had only gone a few steps before he had already forgotten what he had just decided.

At dinner on the last night of his stay at Jablanka they had discussed the problem of Croatia. The Friedjung trial had been brought before the Viennese courts at the beginning of the month, December, and the Austrian newspapers had arrived at the castle that afternoon. They had all written about the case, and almost everything that had been printed had been disagreeable and critical.

It had all started when Professor Friedjung had written a most controversial article, which had been published in the *Neue Freie Presse* at the end of March 1909. The subject had been the annexation of Bosnia-Herzegovina, and in it the Professor had named some fifty Croatian politicians whom he had accused of belonging to a irredentist organization supported by the government of Serbia. It had been fairly obvious from the start that Friedjung's revelations had been inspired by the Austrian Foreign Office, for the material for the article could only have been provided by the Ballplatz. That these accusations should have been broadcast to the world's press in this way had shown the whole affair to have been part of a plot by which the Dual Monarchy was to be forced into sending an ultimatum, with impossible terms, to Belgrade and then, when Serbia inevitably refused to comply, declaring war.

Some trouble had been gone to in order to prepare the world diplomatically for these developments. Germany had already confirmed her solidarity with Vienna; Russia, though reluctantly and with a bad grace, would not intervene, and various other European powers had made it clear to Belgrade that Serbia would receive no support from abroad.

The article in the *Neue Freie Presse* had appeared on March 25th, which had also been the date planned for the ultimatum, though this had never materialized because on the same day the Crown Prince of Serbia, George Karageorgevitch, had resigned his post as head of the pro-war party. A few days later Serbia showed herself willing to accept any terms offered her. Nevertheless the incendiary article had appeared and events later showed that, no matter what had transpired in Belgrade, the Friedjung article was part of a far-reaching plan hatched in Vienna and would have been published anyhow. A month later the monarchy's Prosecutor-General arraigned another group of fifty-four Croatians, all accused of treason. This had been brought about by Baron Rauch, the Coalition-nominated Ban of Croatia, who was as anxious to see irredentism wiped out in Zagreb as were the Austrian politicians to stop Serbian irredentist activities in Vienna. The Zagreb trial had lasted five months and had ended that October with thirty-one of the defendants found guilty. Appeals had been launched, and it had been fairly obvious that they were likely to succeed since the whole prosecution had been based on the weakest of cases. The Zagreb trial had provoked a most disagreeable anti-Austrian feeling abroad and the French press had written about the 'Death of Justice' in Vienna. The strong reaction abroad and the indecisive results of the Zagreb trial now gave new heart to those who had been pilloried by the Friedjung article and so they had accused him of slander.

This trial had opened at the beginning of December and Professor Friedjung had at once declared that he could prove the truth of everything that he had alleged; and he presented documents to support his accusations. These, of course, had been provided by the Ballplatz and sent secretly to the famous and respectable historian. Then, as the trial entered its second week, things began to go wrong; some of the documents had been shown to be forgeries.

It was this that had been the principal subject of conversation that last night at Jablanka. It had been the considered opinion that the professor had been right in principle and that those he had accused, especially Supino, the author of the Fiume Resolution, had certainly been Serbian agents, but that the Austrian Foreign Ministry had carelessly failed to verify all the material produced by their own spies. It had been clear that, unfortunately, there had been more than mere muddle or justifiable human error. What had emerged was no less than intentional falsification. It had been generally accepted that this was always to be expected when recourse had to be made to common or garden spies, who were often paid by both sides, and especially in this case where some of the secret agents had been Serbs who, no doubt, had received the false documents from Belgrade with the full knowledge of the Serbian government!

Naturally this had been discussed frequently during the three days' shooting at Jablanka and whenever the scandal had been mentioned it had always been in that bland, well-informed, unexaggerated, half-spoken, half-insinuated manner which was the well-bred style adopted by the Szent-Gyorgyi circle. On the last evening it had seemed to Balint that they could talk about nothing else and though, the year before, he had been fascinated by the political discussions in his cousins' house, now his own inner turmoil prevented him from taking any interest in what they were saying. On that last evening he felt he could no longer stay talking politics with the group round the drawing-room fire; and so, as soon as everyone had drunk their coffee, he left the room and went to see his aunt. It was, of course, right that he should do so as he would be leaving at dawn to catch the Budapest express and would have no other opportunity of taking his leave. But his hurried flight to Elise Szent-Gyorgyi's own sitting-room was really because he could not bear to remain in the same room as little Lili whom he had just hurt so much. To reach his aunt's rooms he had to pass once again through the library, and there, on the table, still lay the album of Forray's travels, slightly askew, just as it had been left when Lili had pushed it aside and gone to the window. The big red and gold leather-bound volume glittered under the savage glare of the chandelier overhead and had seemed to him the *corpus delicti* – the proof of the crime he had just committed against both himself and her. His heart had constricted when he saw the book lying there in front of him.

His aunt Elise had been sitting in her usual chair which was protected from any draught by a glass screen. In front of her were two women guests from Vienna. Before he had come in they had talked only of unimportant Viennese society gossip but this had stopped when Balint entered the room. Then she had grabbed his hand in her own and forced him to sit down on a sofa beside her chair. For a moment neither aunt nor nephew had spoken. The two Austrian visitors had grasped at once that their hostess wanted a few words alone with Count Abady and so, after a few desultory sentences, uttered only so as not to make it look as if it were his arrival that had caused their departure, which would not have been polite, they took their leave saying that they hoped the Countess would forgive them but that they were expected at the bridge tables and had then disappeared from the room.

'It is nice of you to come to me so early,' said Balint's aunt, who had been born a Gyeroffy in far-off Transylvania, and she looked closely up at him with her large brown eyes. 'I love to talk to you. When you're here I don't feel quite so far from home!'

She had smiled and put her hand on Balint's arm. He lifted it at once and put it to his lips. For a few moments neither had spoken and then Elise Szent-Gyorgyi had started enquiring after all her old friends and relations, starting with Balint's mother. She asked after people she had not seen for more than twenty years and told her nephew little anecdotes about them, things that had happened during her girlhood, tales of country balls and May Day festivals and picnic outings to the forests of Radna. She asked after the father of the four Alvinczy boys because he had once been her favourite dancing partner – very handsome he had been, she said, and admitted having something of a crush on him while she was still in the schoolroom; and also after old Uncle Daniel Kendy, even then too fond of the brandy, who had been so much admired by all the young girls because he had been so good-looking and elegant and they had heard that he had cut a dash at the court of the Empress Eugénie and so was the first *homme du monde* any of them had ever met.

And so she had gone on reminiscing about her youth and her own home and letting Balint tell her everything he could recall that had happened to her old acquaintances. From time to time she had paused for a moment and imperceptibly the little pauses had grown longer. Balint had had the impression that behind her very real interest in everything he could tell her had lain something else, something that she had been turning over in her mind, uncertain, perhaps, how she could bring up the subject.

Balint had thought that she would probably ask about her other nephew, Laszlo Gyeroffy; but this time her mind had been on something else . . .

After a little time Countess Elise had fallen silent and had then seemed lost in her own thoughts. Then suddenly she had said, 'You can have no idea how good it is to hear all this!' and turning again to her nephew she took his hand and kept it in hers. She seemed to be looking into the far distance.

'Do you know,' she had gone on softly as if confiding in him some carefully guarded secret. 'Do you know that after all these

years I still feel that Transylvania is my real home, not here in
Northern Hungary. I feel at home there; not here! The people
there are my own kind, but here they are somehow like foreigners, like Austrians, like Viennese. Don't misunderstand me,
I am very happy here and my life with Antal beside me has always
been a happy one. But that is because I have always loved him so
much. We married for love, and I would have married him, and
no one else, no matter how poor he might have been or what
sort of life he led.' Then she had paused for a moment before
going on: '. . . but all this . . .' and she made a wide circular gesture
with her hand which somehow embraced, as clearly as if she had
spelt it all out, the castle at Jablanka, the vast estates, their assured
position in society, 'all this . . . this is still not really me. It has
always been strange. This world is not my world and has never
really become so. Now that I look back on my life I can see that
it has been our great love, and only that, which has made our
marriage so happy. Not only my love, but his also. It is that which
has made everything right and harmonious for both of us. It's
true. It is love, true love, which is the only thing which makes it
possible to endure everything and which absolves everything.
If we had not had it ours would have been a life of disagreements
and bitterness for both of us.'

Then, as abruptly as she had begun, she fell silent again. After
a moment or two she had given a light laugh and said, 'Oh dear,
how I do run on! Prattling away like anything . . . and such nonsense too. All that chatting about the past has made your old aunt
think of . . . well . . . so many things.'

So this was what she had wanted to tell him, and for which she
had had to prepare herself. She had spoken only so as to be of
some help and consolation to him, so as to reassure him that
although she had seen at once that he had failed to ask Lili to
marry him and that he felt guilty about it, she at least sympathized
and did not blame him. Somehow she had made it clear to him
that she had understood his reasons perhaps even more clearly
than he himself, and that somehow she knew not only that he
was still in love with someone else but also that he instinctively
thought of the charming Lili as an alien creature from another
world. Balint had been deeply touched by his aunt's delicacy and
finesse and even more by the obvious love and goodness that had
made her speak of such things. It had been a bitter hour for him
and he had needed help and affection: he had been all the more

grateful because he had sensed that for him, and him alone, Countess Szent-Gyorgyi had revealed something so intimate of her life and feelings that she would never had admitted to anyone else; and she had done it only because she knew that he had needed help.

Aunt and nephew stayed together for a long time in the cosy intimate little sitting-room, all cushions and soft upholstery, that Countess Elise had made for herself. The carpets were deep and soft, and the furniture comfortable and unpretentious. The walls were covered in some dark material. It was in complete contrast to the grandeur of the rest of the castle where the huge white and gold rooms were filled with elaborate baroque furniture much of which had been gilded. Everything at Jablanka was perfect of its kind, as well as being very grand ... but it was also, perhaps, a trifle cold. In the little private sitting-room where the mistress of the house had made her nest, everything, whether large or small, was a souvenir of her Transylvanian girlhood. Most of the quantity of pictures came from her old home at Szamos-Kozard and she even had two little oils of the old manor house before her brother had rebuilt it. There were watercolour portraits of her Gyeroffy parents, grandparents, aunts and uncles; and in-numerable little pictures of children, mostly relations, were scattered all round the room, on tables, window-sills, and on hanging shelves, along with countless small objects, photographs and miniatures, all of which held for her some memory of times long past and cousins long since departed. All of this had spoken unequivocally to Balint of his aunt's deep and ineradicable love for her homeland ... and also of the spiritual barrier she had never really vanquished that stood between her real self and this grandiose westernized world in which she had lived so many years. That evening, for the first time, Balint had understood the little room's almost symbolic meaning.

A year had gone by since that last evening at Jablanka and yet, as he wandered along the dark streets in the drizzling rain, he could now see it all in his mind and relive everything that had then happened to him. Once again he saw the two of them sitting in that slightly over-heated room which was so different from everything else in the house. It was like a tiny island, he thought suddenly, which Fate had one day wrenched away from its parent Transylvania and deposited there so far from home.

* * *

Reliving those bitter memories during those hours of aimless wandering did nothing to alleviate Balint's deep-rooted bitterness, so much so that he now felt he could not face a happy social gathering in his present mood. For a moment he wondered if he could make some excuse so as to get out of going altogether, perhaps sending word that he had developed a bad headache, or some such lie, but then, he thought, how could he do it? He could hardly go up to the Prefect's front door and say that he wasn't well enough to come, for the doorman would be certain to tell his master that it was Count Abady himself who had delivered the message! And if he sent a waiter from one of the cafés that were still open it would soon be known that he had been seen there. Better, perhaps, to go home and send round his valet with a visiting-card and a little note? He looked at his watch and saw that it was already half past eleven and all the servants at the Abady house would be in bed asleep. He would have to wake someone, who would then have to dress, and it would all take far too long. He was already late for the party, and the other guests, and the famous French singer, were no doubt at that very moment waiting for him. No doubt, as he spoke good French, he was expected to be the diva's supper partner, and if he waited any longer it was more than likely that everyone would have gone in to eat and that his place, beside the guest of honour, would remain empty. It would be a gross lack of politeness to stay away a minute longer than it would take him to reach the house.

All this was going through his mind as he walked, now more swiftly than before, towards his host's house. He knew that the opera had ended some time before because a number of carriages bringing other guests from the theatre had already passed him in the street, which was now again silent and deserted. Everyone must have already arrived at the house. Balint quickened his pace, almost breaking into a run, because he realized that whether he wanted to or not he would have to go to the party.

The Prefect's house blazed with light, but the street outside was deserted except for a one-horse carriage which was waiting to one side of the front door.

Abady was just stepping hurriedly past it when the tall figure of Adam Alvinczy, Margit's husband, jumped out and grabbed his arm.

'I've been waiting for you,' he said excitedly. 'Margit sent me to catch you here!'

Somehow Balint was not surprised, as he had sensed that the chance encounter with Adrienne was bound to provoke something no one could foresee.

'Well?' he said. 'What is it?'

'We knew you'd be here. Margit says you're to come at once ... there's some trouble at home; that's why she sent me. Come on then! Quickly!'

As they got into the carriage Adam called out to the coachman to drive at once back to the Uzdy villa.

Balint felt his throat constrict so that he could hardly speak. Somehow he managed to ask what had happened.

'I don't know,' said Adam. 'All I can tell you is that when we got home from the opera Adrienne rushed straight to her room and locked herself in. Margit has stayed near her, in the bathroom next door, as she doesn't dare to leave her entirely alone. She is very worried.'

They did not speak again. As they drove out of town towards the Uzdy villa on the Monostor road all that could be heard was the clatter of the horses' hooves on the paving-stones; and to both men the five minutes' journey seemed far longer. As they drove along Balint could think only of one thing, the small Browning revolver, that deadly little weapon which Adrienne had once asked him to buy for her, though she had carefully concealed from him that even then she had thought of killing herself with it. Since that day, and especially when a little later they had parted, perhaps for ever, after the month they had spent together in Venice, the thought of that revolver had haunted him, for he knew how uncompromising she was and also how haunted she was by the spectre of that ultimate solution to her troubles.

And now the spectre walked again, and perhaps what he had always feared had finally been accomplished. He was in agony lest they should arrive too late to prevent what he knew instinctively to be uppermost in her mind ...

The carriage stopped in front of the wrought-iron screen which divided the villa's garden from the road. Adam opened the little-used side gate with his own key and called to the coachman to wait where he was. Then he and Balint hurried in, past the long dark single-storeyed wing of the house which reached almost to the banks of the Szamos and which contained Adrienne's own apartments, and entered the building through the glazed veranda that ran along one side of the main entrance court. Adam at once turned not to the right, to the door to Adrienne's sitting-room, but to another door at the left which led to her bathroom.

They went in as quietly as possible. Inside they found Margit crouched at the end of a narrow bench with her ear pressed to the keyhole of the door which opened into the bedroom. Hunched up like that she might have been taken for a young girl if her advanced state of pregnancy had not shown her to be a grown woman. As soon as they entered the room she turned towards them and got up. Then she drew Balint to her side and, speaking very softly but with great determination, said:

'Thank goodness you've come! Now you must stay right here. It's all right, I know you're expected at that supper party but Adam will go in your place and will explain that you're not feeling at all well. It won't look at all strange as everyone will have noticed that you left the theatre early, and they'll think it most considerate to have sent someone in your place. No one will be at all put out.' She turned to her husband, saying: 'You did keep the carriage, didn't you? You'd better hurry now. I'm sure you'll carry it all off excellently ... Oh, and you'd better send back the carriage as we may need it. Tell the man to wait and give him the key to the small gate.'

Margit had obviously worked everything out in advance and, being cool-headed no matter how anxious she might be, gave her orders clearly and simply.

As soon as Adam had gone she turned to Balint and, in a whisper that could not have been heard from the next room, told him exactly what had happened that day. In the morning Adrienne had got back from Lausanne where she had gone to place her daughter in a boarding school. Countess Gyalakuthy had heard of her return and asked her to join the others in her box that evening. She said that somehow she didn't much like the idea, that opera was not really for her, '... but as we thought you were at Denestornya ...'

'I only came up for this evening.'

'Yes, but we didn't know that then. Anyhow it's beside the point. I was sitting beside her in the box and I could see her face. It was terrible, because I know her so well ... but nobody else noticed anything. I was very scared for her, but there was nothing I could do. It was impossible to leave, and anyway I don't think she wanted to move. At last the opera came to an end and we could go. We brought her home in our carriage and she never uttered a word. We came in with her, though she clearly didn't want us to; in fact she did all she could to make us go away at once. Adam waited outside but I refused to leave her. She looked terrible, terrible. I've only seen her look like that twice before . . . but never so intensely, so determined. I was really afraid for her; her eyes were without expression, glassy . . . and her hands were shaking. I managed to stay with her until she had undressed, but then she suddenly pushed me out of the room and locked the door. That's when I sent Adam to find you because there wasn't, there isn't, any more that I can do. I don't know what she's up to in there. Once or twice I heard her groping about and then it seemed as if some small objects fell on to the floor. Since then I've heard nothing . . . for quite a long time. I've knocked repeatedly, but she doesn't answer though I know she's awake . . . she's certainly awake. Only you can help now!' She stopped, and then, after a pause, went on:

'If it isn't too late: I know she's got some veronal.'

Balint got up and stepped towards Adrienne's bedroom. Then with tightly clenched fist he knocked twice on her door and in a loud voice said, 'It's me, AB. Please let me in!'

They waited. It was only about twenty seconds, but to those in the bathroom it seemed like an eternity. They heard nothing, no words, no footsteps, nothing. Then the key turned twice in the lock. Abady at once grasped the handle: the door opened before him. He stepped quickly into the room and closed the door behind him. Inside the room was in complete darkness, but Balint knew it too well to need any light. He knew everything in it, even the warm scent which might have been that of carnations or other flower-petals but which came from no manufacturer's bottle and was like no perfume from a shop but which rather was the slightest, yet intoxicating aroma, as of a subtle secret poison . . . it was the intimate scent of his love. Only two steps and he was at the side of her bed. He sat down quietly.

'Is it really you?' asked a muffled voice from deep among the pillows.

'Yes.'

His hands sought her shoulder and started to caress the hair that curled loosely about her. Then he spoke again, thickly as if he could hardly get the words out:

'This has no sense, no sense at all.'

For a few moments there was no reply. Then she clutched at him with both arms holding him in an embrace so tight she might have been a drowning swimmer clinging to her saviour. Their lips met in a long, hungry kiss.

Between them the stiffly starched shirt of his evening dress crackled softly.

Balint wanted to switch on the light but Adrienne was still too upset to let him do so.

'Margit is waiting outside. I must tell her you're all right,' said Balint. 'Besides, I must see my hair isn't ruffled ... and put my tie straight ... I'll need the light to do that.'

'No, no! Not yet! You don't need the light just for that ... and anyway it doesn't matter!'

'But Margit may want to come in. It'll be better with the light on.'

'No, she mustn't come! Not now! Tell her she can go home and come back later ... but I'm not having any light, not now!'

There was nothing he could do to persuade her, so he smoothed his hair with his hands and did what he could to straighten his collar and tie. Then he went back into the bathroom.

Margit was lying at full length on the narrow bench beside the wall. She was fast asleep, with her head cushioned on her soft arm, like a faithful guardian at rest as soon as danger was past. She seemed to be sleeping so deeply that Balint felt it was cruel to wake her.

'Is it all right ... ?' she muttered before she was fully awake.

There was no need for Balint to say anything because Margit saw from his face that all was well and at once said, 'I'll be going home now,' and her little mouth stretched wide as she yawned deeply. Then she slipped into her evening fur coat and with hardly another word bade Abady farewell and disappeared. How Abady was to leave the house if she locked the gate behind her and took away the key, she didn't say, though whether this was because she was still so sleepy or whether she may have other reasons no one could have told, for little Margit never explained and never said anything that was not strictly necessary.

Balint turned off the bathroom light and returned to the dark bedroom.

* * *

The clock in the neighbouring monastery struck three. Its sound reverberated in the darkness almost as if it chimed in the room itself.

The sound woke them. They had fallen asleep entwined in each other's arms, the curves of their bodies fitting closely together with the ease of long-standing habit, just as a pair of great cats such as pumas or panthers sleep coiled together in luxurious repose. Adrienne had found her accustomed place with her head tucked into Balint's shoulder and her strong richly curling hair partly covering his lips and nose; but he slept all the deeper for, far from disturbing him, these wild locks of hers were like links in a magic chain that had bound them together for so many years. These lovers needed no one else, for both found everything that was needed in the other, every gesture and movement of their lovemaking, whether new or familiar, was accepted with trust and serenity, even their unity in the climax of love; and on this day it was just as it had always been whenever they had been able to come together to lose their own selves in each other.

'It's already three, I ought to get dressed,' he murmured into the thick tangle of her curls.

'Are you cold?' she asked, but she did not move.

'No! But I can't stay for ever . . . and I really must put on the light.'

'If you must; but promise me not to look around! Promise!'

'I promise.'

Balint switched on one of the little bedside lamps and Adrienne picked out one of her wraps for him.

Although Balint had meant to keep his promise, as soon as he started to put on Adrienne's silken kimono he could not help seeing that the little Browning revolver was lying on the table beside the bed and that on the floor nearby were a number of tiny unused cartridges, little copper bullets and the yellow cardboard box from which they had come. He realized that she must have tried to load the revolver but that she had dropped the box in her agitation and that it must have been only this chance that had saved her life. Adrienne noticed that his face had clouded over and took his head in her hands, turned it back towards her and started kissing his eyes with her wide generous mouth. She did not let go but pulled him down again as if he were her prisoner among the soft pillows and cushions on the bed. Later, when they could again look each other straight in the eyes, her

expression was gently apologetic and there was something
shamefaced in the little smile with which she looked up at him.
They did not speak about what they both knew he had seen
there.

They talked about all sorts of things and then, prosaically
enough, about the fact that they were both hungry.

'And there's nothing in the house because we were all going to
eat at Margit's. This is awful,' Adrienne wailed in mock dismay.

Then Balint remembered the chestnuts which, though he had
hardly known what he was doing, he had bought on that long
lonely bitter walk the evening before. Finding his coat among
the clothes he had strewn on the floor by Adrienne's bed, he
searched in the pockets and found them and also the paper he had
bought a little later.

'I've got this bag of chestnuts, but they're stone cold. Perhaps
we could warm them up?'

'That'd take far too long, the fire's been out for ages,' said
Adrienne, laughing. 'I'm so hungry! Let's have them as they are!
They'll taste every bit as good.'

So as not to soil Adrienne's sheets with the chestnut peelings
they used the newspaper as a table-cloth in the centre of the bed
and leaning over from each side they tackled the long-cold nuts
with gusto. As they did so Balint told how he had nearly knocked
over the old woman who was roasting the chestnuts and how,
automatically, he had bought the paper from the news-vendor in
the station square; and he related both tales as if they were unreal
amusing anecdotes from a remote past which now hardly concerned them, indeed as if they had never really happened.

It was the same with all the suffering they had both endured
during the past year and a half. The pain and bitterness and the
torment they had both gone through all those months when
Uzdy's incipient madness was slowly growing to its climax; the
ultimate catastrophe of his complete breakdown; Adrienne's
renunciation of their love and her decree that they must not see
each other; and the seemingly endless days and nights of sorrow
and self-recrimination that they had both suffered; all these
things now vanished from their minds like the mists of early
morning. Not only did they not think about it but they barely
even wondered if there had ever really been any reason for the
torture they had endured. They did not remember it because it
no longer existed, because they were together again and at home

in each other's arms, because they belonged to each other, a real couple, male and female of the same species, and because anything which did not concern them now was as unreal as a mere phantom.

So, together on the wide bed, he in her silken wrap and she with her night-dress slightly torn and slipping down over one shoulder, they fell on the sooty chestnuts with hungry delight.

'Wasn't it lucky you bought them!' said Addy.

CHAPTER TWO

WHEN KAROLY KHUEN-HEDERVARY formed a new government in January, 1910, few people, and especially those who had been immersed in the fantasy world of Coalition politics, believed it would achieve any more than had its predecessors. Everywhere it was said that the new government would soon suffer the same fate as that of General Fejervary five years before for it was still believed that a government made up of people not in Parliament had no solid base and therefore would not stand the pace. Indeed so frosty was the lack of welcome with which it was received that when Khuen-Hedervary announced that Parliament was to be adjourned he was met with an immediate motion of 'No Confidence'.

But things had changed and the political climate in 1910 was not at all what it had been five years before. The public had become disillusioned and now there were not many who bothered themselves with anything so trivial as a change of government.

In 1905 such had been the general optimism that people had really believed that Hungary stood on the threshold of a new golden age. The resounding promises of reform and improvement which had been brandished as the election slogans of the parties forming the Coalition – as, for example, the separation of the army commands and the establishment of an independent Customs service – had everywhere been taken as if these goals had already been achieved or, if not exactly achieved, at the very least only temporarily delayed by the unpatriotic plots of their political opponents, that wicked *camarilla* whose sinister influence would be swept away as soon as the Coalition came to power. Few people had then paused to reflect that the trade-unionists would never really co-operate with any other group and had only joined in the call to overthrow the existing government because they themselves had never expected to be called upon to face the realities of political power; nor that there were forces in the running of a great nation far greater and more complicated than were admitted in the seductive paragraphs of the radical press. It never occurred to the majority that the real national interest lay in the sound administration of agriculture, industry and commerce, in the defence of the realm and the maintenance of law and order; and in fair treatment of the ethnic minorities and the under-privileged. It was on how such matters were handled that the prestige of the Dual Monarchy and its position as a great power rested; and it was on Austria-Hungary's position as a great power that the continued prosperity of the individual depended. And yet, simple and logical as this proposition might have appeared, it still seemed beyond the grasp of the general public.

During the period of Fejervary's government the leaders of the Coalition began to grasp that their fight was hopeless because they had argued themselves into a totally false position. It was this that led to the famous *Pactum* between the radical coalitionists and the Emperor.

And now they made their first great irremediable mistake: they declared publicly that the compromise was a triumph. This barefaced lie, like the principle of original sin, bedevilled the five years of their reign until, totally divided, quarrelling over every issue, accusing each other of ineptitude and incapacity, the Coalition ended in total fiasco. The general public, for once, grasped what had happened and withdrew its support, turning away with bored contempt. Khuen-Hedervary quickly grasped what was happening and cleverly turned the situation to his own advantage.

The new government's initial programme was intentionally, and wisely, colourless and confined itself to generalities. The only exception was a declaration of support for the idea of introducing universal suffrage, expressed only in the vaguest terms. Indeed the whole document was so imprecise that everyone, conservative or radical, could read into it support for anything they themselves desired.

The first real action taken was to correct some of the most glaring of the Coalition's mistakes. Rauch, the Ban of Croatia,

whose rule had been so disastrous, was dismissed and the judg-
ments in the Zagreb treason trial set aside. All prosecutions for
sedition that were pending against representatives of the ethnic
minorities were immediately abandoned.

The country started to breathe more easily as the consequences of the rash measures of the recent past were gently swept
aside. It was all somewhat grey and colourless, but it was obvious
that matters were being handled with simple common sense and
so everyone began eagerly to prepare themselves for the inevitable general election. Such was the mood when Parliament was
adjourned.

Everyone was content except for some members of the
Independence Party who had brought forward a bizarre theory
that as they had been elected to office and as the Budget had not
yet been voted, there could be no new elections. When Khuen-
Hedervary rose to move the adjournment they made such a noise
that no one could hear a word he said.

Khuen remained standing at his desk and waited until the
uproar died down, but as soon as he opened his mouth again
the commotion raged once more. At last seeing no other solution, as this was likely to go on indefinitely, he decided to move
closer to the stenographers so that they at least would be able to
hear and take down a record of his words. Hardly had he stepped
down from his place when some rebellious members sitting on
the extreme left jumped up and started bombarding him with
anything they could lay their hands on such as books, inkpots
and paperknives. A heavy inkpot struck him on the forehead and
blood poured down his face. Despite it all, and throughout this
unexpected tempest, Khuen-Hedervary maintained his usual
good-humoured calm.

This appalling scene scandalized the public, and even the party
leaders of those who had behaved so badly condemned what
had happened. The unruly members' excuse, which was published on the following day – namely that they had thought the
Minister-President was moving from his rostrum to insult them
personally – was believed by no one. It was indeed absurd to
imagine that one frail elderly man was about to tackle physically
a group of several hundred able-bodied members sitting together
on the benches at the extreme left-hand side of the Chamber.
When, on December 13th, 1904, the same group, more or less,
had attacked the security guards in the Chamber, the public had

believed their tale not knowing, though the members had, that the guards had been expressly ordered not to retaliate if provoked. Now no one credited this kind of fantasy. Everyone thought that, rather than try to excuse themselves, it would have been better and more dignified if they had admitted the fault and merely explained that they had been carried away in the passion of the moment. That at least would have been honest, or could have been taken as such, and might have suggested extenuating circumstances. As it was, all that happened was that the riotous members and their parties lost all respect; and the incident was not forgotten when the time came for the elections and the voters started to weigh up the Coalition's record.

The result was soon seen: barely a hundred candidates from the three main parties of the Coalition were elected to the new Parliament. On the other hand Khuen-Hedervary's supporters got a huge majority, and it was generally thought that now some constructive work could be begun.

Begun? Yes; but whether he would be able to achieve anything was another matter.

Obstruction, that cancer at the heart of all attempts to put through progressive measures in the Hungarian Parliament, which had paralysed successive administrations for the previous ten years and which had now become the habitual weapon used by the insubordinate left wing even against its own leadership, might well be used again to frustrate the new government. It could rise at any time, brandishing no matter what popular slogan, and it would always find support in that section of the press whose only allegiance seemed to be to the trouble-makers. There were also other sources of possible weakness, less obvious, less familiar, but these lay hidden for the present from both the government's supporters and their political opponents.

The government announced that its first aim would be electoral reform. As this was only mentioned in outline everyone could declare their support, whether they wanted only minor changes or radical reform of the suffrage qualifications. Thus a substantial majority declared its support for the cabinet without anyone knowing which standpoint was the stronger even inside the government party. The Independence Party, as it had been for some time, was split in two. Kossuth and his followers took up a moderate stance while Justh led his splinter group so far to the left that a few months later they joined up with the socialists.

It was this later move which led to that surprising situation when Tisza and Kossuth stood together on the same platform while the other wing of the government party, led by Laszlo Lukacs, made approaches to Justh and the left-wingers.

All this proved the old adage that where elections were concerned it was best to leave such important issues in as much uncertainty as possible.

It was also clear to some observers that one reason for Khuen not making any more precise declaration of his policy was that he had no wish to antagonize Tisza, for without him and his liberal party followers' support he would be bound to fail to obtain any reform at all. Khuen's over-riding purpose was to re-establish harmony between the King and the Parliament, the twin pillars of the Constitution, and to this end he subordinated any other consideration and welcomed to his side anyone who would serve his purpose, even if he was not otherwise an ally or supporter. And so was formed the 1910 Parliament which was the first one in many years not to be composed entirely of blinkered politicians blinded by their own unthinking allegiance either to the 1867 Compromise or to the independence principles of the Men of 1848; and which consequently was also the first Parliament to take notice of what was going on outside the Kingdom.

As the traditional party slogans had become anathema to many people a surprisingly large number of districts – thirty-one in all – voted for candidates free of any party commitments. This had never happened before. Another side effect was that many of the new members, though they belonged officially to one party or another, by no means always followed slavishly that party's official line. This was clear for all to see when it came to dealing with the project for electoral reform. It began at a conference of conservatives held in the Vigado building where Istvan Tisza and the extreme Independent Mihaly Karolyi were shown to hold the same opinions. On the same day the former Minister-President and Protestant leader, Dezso Banffy, met at the town hall with two pillars of the conservative party, Pal Sandor and Gyula Lanczy, and also with the Christian Democrat Giesswein and the democrats Vazsonyi and Jaszi, to agree their joint programme for a radical revision of the right to vote.

There was at this time another issue which transcended traditional party lines: this was the Transylvanian Movement.

This had come into being as a result of a widespread feeling in

Transylvania that its individual traditions and history, as well as its own very special spirit, had become less and less recognized, let alone respected, by the central government in Budapest, who were all too apt to think of Transylvania as just one of a string of otherwise insignificant provinces. Nothing of its riches, either of historical achievement or individual culture, nor of its real problems, was accorded any real importance in the capital. The Transylvanian spirit was slowly being drained away in the maw of Hungarian self-sufficiency and at best was ignored. So delicate, so subtle were Transylvania's real problems that it needed much knowledge and experience to know how to handle them. When the central government did interfere it did so with brutal indifference, usually doing more harm than good.

Balint Abady had seen this with growing concern and so was one of the founders of the movement whose aim was to encourage a better understanding and a more just treatment of his beloved homeland. He first drafted a programme and then in March started canvassing his ideas and whipping up support from his fellow Transylvanians, starting with Tisza himself in Budapest. Through the lawyer Timisan he tried to interest the Romanian minorities. In all this he deluded himself that he was only doing his duty, but the reality was, of course, that this plunging into work on behalf of Transylvania and immersing himself once more in the development of the Co-operative movements, was really for him little more than a narcotic taken to relieve the pain of his sorrow and self-torment.

Tisza, though sympathetic to Balint's ideas, still ordered his followers to hold aloof from the movement because it smacked too much of particularism. Tisza listened politely with his habitual quiet, somewhat derisive smile. He told Balint it was all very interesting . . . but he didn't offer any support.

Balint, bitterly disappointed, had gone on with his self-chosen task, but without joy or hope, despite the fact that the first public meeting was not inauspicious.

The banner of the Transylvanian Movement was unfurled on March 12th at one of the principal hotels in Vasarhely.

Also present with Balint were the other original founders of the movement, Istvan Bethlen, Miklos Banffy, Zoltan Desy and Gyozo Issekutz as well as many others who attended without knowing in advance anything of what they were about to hear.

Among them were many who were not native Transylvanians
but who had come to represent districts in the province as a result
of the peculiarly feverish atmosphere of the elections at the time
of the Coalition.

Abady brought with him his detailed proposals for the movement's programme and in his speech he concentrated on three
points: the forthcoming electoral reform, Transylvania's special
commercial interests, and the many problems posed by the existence of the minorities.

The first two subjects met with little comment or opposition,
but the third at once aroused all sorts of conflicting reactions.
Balint wished to obtain support for a new law governing the
rights of the minorities. At this point the representatives of
the Szekler people started to demur, mostly those who were not
of indigenous Szekler origin but who had come into Transylvanian politics from Budapest or the Great Plain, and who had been
invited only because of their official positions. At once an acri-
monious discussion started which threatened to get worse as
Abady stood firmly by his proposition. Then Istvan Bethlen,
who was presiding, decided to adjourn the meeting for a short
while so as to give himself a chance to talk it over with Abady in
private. Bethlen well understood the implications of what Balint
had proposed and agreed with everything he had said. Nevertheless, seeing the mood of those who disagreed, he advised Balint
to drop any specific details concerning the actual proposed law
lest further discussion should bring about the disruption of the
meeting and thus bring the movement to a halt before it had even
got under way. He proposed that Abady's text should be allowed
to stand as it was, in general terms, but that discussion of the
details of the proposed minority law should be left until later, it
being understood that when the movement was firmly established the matter could then be brought up again and the introduction of the law openly demanded.

Abady was reluctant to agree, but could see no alternative. As a
result his amended speech was read at the general session of
the conference which was held at the county headquarters the
following day. His proposals were accepted unanimously by
the thirty-odd delegates, who included Under-Secretaries of
State, Prefects, MPs and other elected officials in the presence
of an exceptionally large audience. Everything of real importance
was contained in the section of the speech entitled 'To all the

Peoples of Transylvania'. After a short introduction, during which he referred to the forthcoming elections, he said:

'Now is the time when we should all stand together, regardless of party, in all matters which affect our native land and which affect our peaceful existence now and in the future. It is time to put an end to that harmful situation where decisions affecting us are taken without our being consulted. That is all wrong. We no longer ask, we demand, that our special conditions should be taken into account in all law-making that concerns us. Finally we must have our say in all affairs that concern the well-being of our own homeland.

'This demand is justified historically. When Transylvania was made an integral part of the kingdom we surrendered unselfishly the autonomy we had known for centuries and refrained from imposing any conditions in return. We did not stop to worry about the possible loss of material or personal advantages which had been part and parcel of our inherited independence. But . . . but this patriotic selflessness merits the *quid pro quo* that the central government should show as much special understanding, love and consideration for intrinsically Transylvanian matters as we would have shown ourselves. This is their moral obligation, but today there is no sign of it . . . unfortunately.

'It is unfortunate, too, that with very few exceptions we have found ourselves treated as unwanted step-children so often are, disregarded, ignored, not worth bothering about! And if they do for once take a casual glance at the many complicated issues of which our society is composed, and the problems these entail, no one tries to understand what it is all about.

'We suffer deeply from this indifference and ignorance. In particular we are forced to witness the degradation of our ethnic minorities, the destruction of our middle class and the continual recession in our industry and commerce.

'A national policy that is as uncaring as it is ignorant as regards our minority problems is now increasingly provoking dangerously irredentist and seditious tendencies, tendencies which can be justified as provoked by unfair treatment. We must say outright that for centuries in Transylvania people have lived happily together regardless of race or creed or language and that to do this we need more than manufactured opinions and slogans borrowed from other lands and other peoples. These merely inject poison into our system.

'With full knowledge of our own national circumstances, and in the interests of all Hungary, it is clear that we must eliminate those walls of mistrust which otherwise divide us. We must tear down those artificial barriers which separate our peoples; we must disregard all difference of language and religion, and above all we must strive to ensure that there is trust, mutual trust, between the ruler and the ruled. Everybody who is or wishes to be at home in this country must be welcomed and made to feel at home with confidence that nowhere will he find any form of discrimination, for that will never bring peace and ease and prosperity to our land. No administration can achieve anything without consultation and mutual trust.

'In making these considerations the basis for our demands we offer a friendly hand to anyone who, regardless of race or language or religion, desires to work for the peaceful evolution of our land.'

This ended what Balint had to say about the question of the minorities. Then he tackled the subject of economics:

'We demand that the central government fulfils its moral obligations towards us and that firstly this is shown by a just investment in Transylvania's cultural and material welfare. At present everything goes to Budapest and nothing comes back.

'Almost nothing is initiated nationally to encourage our commerce, though in the last ten years commissions dealing with Szekler and forestry matters have been notable exceptions. However, the artificial separation of our economy from that of the rest of the country has resulted in stagnation and idleness. All the profit of our rich mineral deposits, our mines, forests, power-stations – as well as the accumulated receipts from high taxation – in no way returns home to benefit our own land or its inhabitants.

'It is time, therefore, to call an end to fruitless begging and dreary complaint. We must make it clear that only by acceding to our demands can the country safeguard the future of the average landowner and ensure that a prosperous middle class can be firmly established. For the prosperity of all we must encourage the building up of small and medium-sized agricultural estates, regardless of the creed and nationality of the landowner. It is on this that the advancement of our social and cultural order depends and, above all, it is upon this that the life and dignity of our agricultural population depends. Our peoples must have the liberty and the right not only to work and earn their daily bread but also to own land and gain respect and prosperity as equal citizens of the same country.

'We must have our fair share of the implements of commerce and industry, and so we demand from the national railways, which until now have only served our country in a derisively feeble fashion, that services are introduced that are worthy of the real importance of our land. And we insist that central authority should back fully the development of our industrial potential.

'It is our duty to point out to all Transylvanians that it is in their interest, again regardless of race, language, creed or party, to join this movement. It is their duty, too, to do this now when we stand on the threshold of elections that can influence our entire future.'

Finally he spoke about electoral reform.

'At the forefront of all political activity stands the question of introducing a just system of voting rights for everyone.

'Admitting the rightness in principle of a system of universal suffrage and in no way wishing, even if we could, to hold up the process of emancipation, we must be careful to do nothing that could hinder the introduction of a law designed to broaden the basis on which we elect those whose function is to make our laws. At the same time we must raise our voices in protest if the chosen route seems to us to be wrong. To the whole nation we must then say that there is no progress if it is not done right, and if we disregard those dangers which would be inherent in any ill-considered legislation. Remember that once this reform has become a reality, it will be here to stay and will not easily be changed or modified. We must be on our guard to make no false steps.

'We cannot accept as a qualification for the right to vote any such simplistic formula as being able to read or write or speak Hungarian properly. This would be no valid criterion of either patriotism or the capacity to vote intelligently. Our conviction is that the coming law must first of all avoid any withdrawal of existing rights, which would only foster resentment and encourage old hatreds, and that secondly it must be based on a realistic approach to the rights of the individual, allowing him in all cases to be able to select those whose integrity, decency and patriotic spirit, and their political maturity, qualify them for a seat among the law-makers.

'We must raise our voices in the cause of sanity and balance, and if we do object to any proposals we think ill thought-out or immature, it must be that we do so only because our aim is peace and harmony in everything that affects the well-being of all and that we set our face against any legislation which appears to favour only a limited section of our society. In defending Hungarian sovereignty we are also defending the security of property and culture.'

Before coming to a close he listed the movement's aims and demands and then ended with a few resounding phrases:

'As individuals, scattered over the land, we will achieve nothing. Let us therefore unite, regardless of party loyalties and political conviction, to serve our country as best we may. Let the voters shake hands and stand together to serve those whom we elect to make our laws. And never forget, no matter under what banner you fight, that we are all successors to those worthy forebears whose role, whether eminent or obscure, played such a vital part, century after century, in keeping alive the honour and prestige of Transylvania!'*

CHAPTER THREE

THESE WERE THE things that Balint was thinking about when, early in the afternoon, he started on his way back to Denestornya.

He was encouraged by the fact that so many had rallied behind his call for support for his proposed Transylvanian Movement. Of course it had only been a beginning, but it had been full of promise, and if every motion in Parliament that concerned Transylvania sparked off another meeting, another discussion, and another agreement, it would not be long before the movement became a force that no one would be able to ignore. And this itself would have further and more widespread effects. Sitting upright behind the steering wheel Balint felt himself once more young and strong and full of hope. The car, as if catching some

* Translators' Note: The body of this speech encapsulates much of Miklós Bánffy's own first speech to Parliament made after the summer election of 1910 when he presented himself to the electorate as a candidate independent of all party ties. All his life, whether as a Member of Parliament, minister for foreign affairs, or as a private citizen, Bánffy fought hard for the principles of honesty, decency, tolerance and co-operation between people of all creeds and classes, and above all justice and fair treatment for his beloved Transylvania. P.T. & K.B.-J.

of its owner's happy mood, seemed to purr with joy and power as it started up the slope of the Felek.

As he drove Balint thought back to that time, more than a year before, when in the same car he had driven away from Denestornya after breaking off all relations with his mother because she would not accept his decision to marry Adrienne as soon as she could become free. Although he had been back several times since — for Countess Roza had forgiven her son as soon as she learned that Adrienne's divorce had become impossible since her husband had gone mad almost immediately after Balint's visit to his cousins at Jablanka, then again in spring and in summer, and lastly a few days before when he had come from there to attend that *Madam Butterfly* at the Kolozsvar Opera, this was the first time that he had felt he was really returning home. Previously there had been no joy in his visits and they had left no mark on him. He had gone back merely out of duty and habit, and he had never been able to throw off the leaden depression that stemmed from those agonized hours of sorrow and self-reproach.

Until this day everything he had done he had done automatically, but now he felt alive again, thinking with pleasure and eagerness of all the work that lay ahead for him. Now he made plans, fantastic plans, involving ever more work and more responsibility. Such was the effect of his rediscovery and repossession of Adrienne.

Work, more work! He felt he could tackle anything.

The previous spring he had been asked to accept the chairmanship of the Consumers' Council. Then he had hesitated and the question had been left in suspense. Now he decided to accept, but only for Transylvania, and his mind was soon busy thinking out the innovations he would propose and how he would try to improve the range and quality of the goods offered at country markets. He remembered seeing wide-bladed scythes in Holland, similar, he thought, to those in use in Tyrol. Perhaps these could be imported through the Co-operatives? He would introduce new and improved seeds, such as peas . . . and maybe soya beans. This would all have to be discussed with the agricultural experts so as to be sure of suggesting what would be most likely to succeed and which would prove the most beneficial: he would have to ask Aron Kozma who understood so well the needs and tricky moods of the village folk.

Where, he wondered, would he find Kozma now? And then

he remembered the hunting at Zsuk which had just started and decided he would go himself, which he had not been able to do for the last year because if he had gone to Kolozsvar there had always been the risk of meeting Adrienne. Of course he could then have stayed at the Hunt Club residence at Zsuk, but he had not been in the mood even though his mother had offered him the best horses in the Denestornya stables. While he had been in that black depression nothing had seemed worth doing, but now everything was changed. He could go where he liked. Everything was wonderful and full of beauty and the promise of joy and pleasure. Life was once again full of delights. Why, he would ride every day and every evening he would go back to town . . . and every night . . .

Already he started to choose which horses he would take with him – Handsome, of course, and Ivy – and which other? Menyet was promising enough, but at only four she was still rather young. Perhaps Csalma, who was sound and rather slow-moving, but all the same reliable. He would have to think it all out and discuss it later.

So ideas tumbled over themselves in his brain and he was filled with hope and new ideas and expectations. By now he was almost over the last pass of the Felek, which the carters had nicknamed the Horse-killer, and started descending a slope bordered by a few scattered houses.

Then, unexpectedly, he had to brake and bring the car to a stop.

A huge flock of sheep blocked the entire road. There were so many that Balint thought there must be between five hundred and a thousand, and this meant that he would have to wait for some time before he could go on. He knew well that sheep would never get out of the way but would just crowd together behind the leading ram, and that the leading ram would not move unless the shepherd was walking ahead. Also there was nowhere else for them to go, for the road through the village was bordered by solid fences, in addition to which it was a steep downhill slope, and the shepherd boys, knowing that anything that frightened the flock would probably make them panic and that some might get trampled to death if there was a stampede, called hurriedly to Balint, '*Stey, Domnule! Stey!* – Stop, Master, stop!'

Balint did as he was asked and switched off the engine because he realized at once that it would take some time before the sheep could be got through the village and out into some meadow. It was not unknown for it to take nearly a day for a really large flock to cover only a mile or so, which, reflected Balint, just showed that they were not altogether stupid if instinct prevented them from damaging their hooves. And yet it was not always so for those mountain-bred animals were tough and resilient and could be made to move more swiftly when they were on their way to market. Now that they were being taken from one grazing ground to another the leading ram swayed gently from one foot to another almost as if he were performing some slow dance movement while the rest of the flock munched unhurriedly as they went. Some owners used to take advantage of this by renting summer and winter grazing grounds some two or three hundred kilometres apart and for the two or three weeks that it took to go from one to the other the flock fed gratis at the side of the road.

And so Balint was forced to wait; and on this occasion he did not even feel mildly put out or impatient but called back at once: 'Don't hurry! Take it slowly! Slowly!', for his heart was filled with love for everyone including the dirt-covered shepherds who never changed their clothing for weeks on end, the evil-smelling, greasy sheep flowing like a slow river before him, the dogs filling in the rear and the old donkey, heavily laden with the milking cans and the shepherds' few belongings. All this is part of our birthright, he said to himself, it belongs to us and to us alone, for strange though it may be, it is one of the peculiarities of our land and is different from any other.

When the road was finally clear Balint stepped on the pedal and went on his way past woods and forests bright with the golden, copper and saffron colours of autumn and water-meadows still vividly green. Everything seemed beautiful to him, even the occasional bare clay hillside which shone brightly in the late afternoon sunlight. Deeply he inhaled the air that blew so strongly in his face as the car raced homewards.

Just before he reached the village of Also-Bukkos he noticed a man on a horse just turning on to the main road from a track that led from a nearby valley. It was Gazsi Kadacsay whose own property was not far away. Balint was astonished to see him for Gazsi had never been known to miss a day's hunting and the season at Zsuk had already begun. He braked and called out:

'*Servus*, Gazsi – greetings! What are you doing at home at this time? Surely the hunt can't do without you?'

Gazsi cantered up to the car, and when he spoke it was with unusual seriousness, quite different from his habitual joking manner.

'That's just a lot of nonsense, my fr-r-riend. They can do very well without me.'

Then he went on hurriedly as if wanting to change the subject.

'Are you on your way to Denestornya? If you are going to be there a little while I'll r-r-ride over to see you. There's something I'd like to talk over with you.'

'Come whenever you like, my mother is always pleased to see you . . . and me too, I want your advice on which horses to take to Zsuk this year.'

'Hor-r-rses! Of course, always hor-r-rses!' Gazsi spoke bitterly, and smiled in a strange manner bending his head sideways so that his long nose once more resembled the beak of some disconsolate bird of prey. 'But I can't come right away as I must go to my sister's at Szilagy for some family business. Can I come in four or five days? It won't be too far ahead?'

'Of course not, I'll expect you.'

They exchanged a few more words and then Kadacsay, calling out '*Servus!*', turned his old saddle-horse away and moved slowly off.

Balint drove on wondering at the change in his old friend and fancying that maybe he had some money troubles which would explain why he had seemed so gloomy. A few moments later he had forgotten all about it for he himself was so filled with joy and happiness that the possible troubles of other people could not touch him.

Roza Abady sat on a little bench in the great horseshoe-shaped court in front of the stables at Denestornya. Five colts had been selected as the best of that year's products and it was now, in autumn, that she always decided which should be paired off to go into harness and which would be reserved for riding. All the horses would soon go into winter quarters but whereas the saddle-horses would wait until the spring before their training began, Countess Abady believed in starting to teach the future carriage-horses as early as possible when they would be at their most responsive. She knew that no harm would come to them if their first lessons were sufficiently light and steady and no weight was put on their backs. On the other hand it was important to build up the tendons and leg muscles by carefully controlled road work.

At her right stood Simon Jäger, the chief stable lad. He was a short man of about fifty who stood very straight as if he were sitting a horse, his bowed legs slightly apart. He had served in the hussars some thirty years before and he still wore a short pointed waxed moustache. His cheeks were smooth and red and, though he came of peasant stock, his feet were unusually small. He was the owner of his own land, an estate of some twenty acres, but he still took pride in working for Countess Roza at Denestornya – 'at Court' as the local people would say among themselves – not only because it gave him much prestige in the village but also because he loved doing it. His father and grandfather had done the same before him, and his great-grandfather had been Head Keeper to that Abady who had been Governor of Transylvania. And that is how he had acquired his name, as *Jäger* was the German word for a sporting estate's professional keeper. And so it had been passed from father to son at a time when many peasant families did not use surnames.

On the left of the countess was Gergely Szakacs (whose name meant 'cook') who had been chief stable lad before Simon, who was twenty years his junior. He too came from the same district and though he was now pensioned off Countess Roza always liked to have him at her side on these occasions for she much appreciated his knowledge and judgement. He came willingly (even though his pension had been paid somewhat haphazardly when the lawyer Azbej had managed the Abady estate office) for he loved his old mistress whom he knew to be good-hearted, and had been too proud to complain. Also he did not really need the pension money because in the course of a lifetime's hard work he too had put some capital aside and owned a good house of his own. All the Szakacs had been tall and good-looking and this one had been no exception. Now he was somewhat bent and walked with a stick, but he was still a distinguished figure, with short-cut hair and well-trimmed beard, and had an air of authority which suited his position as one of the pillars of the Protestant church.

Despite the fact that she herself was as expert as any of them, Countess Roza always liked to have these two with her when these important decisions had to be made. Jäger and Szakacs could voice opinions without being asked, but Feri Rigo, the head coachman who was also always present, could only speak up when appealed to. At present he was standing some ten paces away and passing on his employer's instructions to the other lads who were walking and trotting the young horses.

The selection took a long time and finally there were just three colts from which the pair had to be chosen. Countess Roza asked for two of them to be walked up until they were side by side facing where she was sitting, as that was how they would appear when in harness as a pair.

Roza Abady looked at them for a few moments in silence. Then she rose and walked all round them with her two companions close behind. The young horses stood quite still, not moving until she got close to their heads when both stretched out their necks expecting to be given lumps of sugar; but as today was one of decision and not of cosseting, none was forthcoming. Back went their ears in disappointment. At last she spoke:

'They are very much alike, but I fancy this one is just a trifle shorter. Young Simon, please bring me the measuring stick!' She still called him 'Young Simon' – though as Chief Lad he was addressed as 'Sir' by everyone else – just as she had thirty-five years ago when he had been a little stable-boy and she had been almost grown up. Apart from this she had never used the familiar form of address after he had been promoted.

'I have measured him already, my Lady ... when he was brought in. He is two centimetres shorter, but he comes from a line that has always developed slowly and I'm sure that in a year or two's time he will have caught up and then they'll be just the same.'

'We should still try him beside the Merges filly,' suggested old Szakacs, waving to the lads to bring up the third choice whose name was 'Mandula'! Taking the halter he said, '*Komelo*' – a strange word that for most people held no meaning.

Many years before Szakacs had gone to England with Countess Roza's father who had wanted to find a thoroughbred stallion to improve the breed in Transylvania. There he had learned many things including the English way of strapping the horses with only one hand – though putting the whole body's weight behind it – the use of flannel bandages, how to make a bran mash and what was meant by 'blistering'. He also learned a few stable commands in English, though they became somewhat tangled when he tried to use them himself. But the stable lads, and the horses, soon understood what was expected of them; and now Mandula stepped smartly forward as if she already knew that *Komelo* meant 'Come along!'.

Again they looked for a long time at the three possible choices and, as in all long-established studs where the breeding followed a set pattern, there was really very little to choose between them, and any one would have been a splendid match with either of the others. Finally Countess Roza turned to the coachman, Feri, and asked what he thought.

'If your Ladyship pleases, I would be happy with any of them; still I rather think that Csujtar's trot is the longer and that he would therefore be better for carriage-work.'

Simon Jäger's eyes shone: 'Mandula would look well with our other hunters,' he said. And in so speaking of the horses as 'ours' he was doing what everyone employed at Denestornya always had. Everything about the great castle and the estate was known, even to the youngest and humblest stable lads, as 'ours', in the first person plural, in *pluralis majesteticus* – the royal 'we'.

They would say: this is 'our' lucerne, 'our' oats, 'our' meadows, mares and stallions, 'our' cattle, oxen and donkeys. Everyone used this majestic 'we' and 'our', from the great heights of the butler and the Chief Stud Groom, through the footmen, barn and storekeepers, huntsmen, gardeners, cooks, estate mechanics and smiths, down to the humblest scullery-maid or stable-boy. 'Our' carriages, 'our' farm-carts, 'our' pots and 'our' pans. It was even used of the Denestornya wildlife – 'our' deer, 'our' hares, 'our' pheasants – exactly as if it belonged to them, which in a very real sense it did, for they were intensely proud of Denestornya and everything about it as if they were in reality the owners of an estate which had no rival in the entire world.

This spirit had crystallized through many, many generations, for there was hardly a single family in the village some of whose members had not, at one time or another, done their stint 'at Court'; and none who had not been the better for it, not only because everything was 'found' for those who were in the Abady employ and so those who had any money of their own could save it. Likewise if any of them thought to build, for example, a house on their own land (for nearly all the peasant families owned some land) they were freely given all the wood or quarried stone they needed. If a pig died it was replaced from the estate farms, and no one worried about sickness or old age, either for themselves or their families, because the 'masters' would take care to see that everything was provided. Not that anyone had, or needed, a contract, for all these things were taken for granted. A man had only to ask, and he was given as soon as he had spoken to the 'master' and explained his problem. The deep feeling of unity in the little village near the castle, the community spirit and the general feeling of good will and fellowship, sprang directly from these ancient traditions. As a result hardly any so-called 'foreigner' – which meant anyone from any other district, however close it might be – ever stayed long in the castle service. The only exceptions at that time were Countess Roza's two housekeepers, who had come to her in her lonely widowhood, and who had then so ingratiated themselves with their mistress. As it was, both Mrs Baczo and Mrs Tothy were loathed and feared by the other servants, who resented the fact that the two women would always tell her whatever they might wish her to believe.

The decision had almost been taken to return Mandula to the stud to be trained later as a saddle-horse, while the other two would be paired off for carriage-work, when Countess Roza decided to take one more close look at them all. She rose and started to walk round them again when a loud blast from a car-horn was heard from outside the horseshoe court and, almost before the countess had time to look up, her son's car came rushing through the great gates.

At the sight of the little group and the three young horses Balint slammed on the brakes, stopped the car and jumped out so quickly that it almost seemed as if he was rushing towards her before the car had stopped.

At once Countess Roza understood that something extraordinary had happened to her son, for it was a long time since he had seemed so young and happy and active. Here was a complete contrast to the sad and listless figure he had been for so long and, though she could not know what it was, she was sure that there was something and was determined to find out the reason. She peered at him with slightly screwed-up eyes, as she did when carefully examining her young horses, though by the time he reached her side she gave no sign that she had noticed any change in him. At once she started to tell him what she had just been doing and to ask his opinion, not that she really needed anything but his approval of the decisions she had already made. Nevertheless she went through the motions of asking a number of unnecessary questions and appearing to weigh up, once more, the arguments and reasoning which had led to her deciding to make a saddle-horse of the Merges filly and send the other two for carriage-training. Then mother and son walked back together to the castle door . . . and all the while she was keeping the talk going as long as she could so as to give her more time to look into his eyes and study his expression. There certainly was a difference, but what had caused the change she could only wonder.

Tea had been laid on the covered veranda outside the big first-floor drawing-room in the west wing.

For the countess only coffee and buffalo milk was served, but as Balint had just arrived the housekeepers quickly put out a full spread of cold meats, hot bread, sweet and savoury cakes, freshly churned butter so rich that it was practically melting on its silver dish, honey in the comb, quince jelly and three different sorts of jam. As if this were not more than enough Mrs Tothy and Mrs Baczo reappeared every few minutes carrying in more covered dishes of hot cakes and doughnuts straight from the oven, fritters, muffins and scones; and then they stood silently to one side with huge smiles on their fat little faces as the son of the house fell on the unexpected repast with the appetite of a wolf.

Countess Roza watched it all with a secret smile that could hardly have been detected by anyone else, casting covert glances at her son's expression as he devoured dish after dish. Not that she asked anything about what she most wanted to know, for she knew better than that. Instead she kept up a flow of small talk, recounting what had happened at home during the five days since her son had gone to the opera in Kolozsvar. Holes had been dug in the orchard where they had planned to put in some seedling fruit trees; that morning there had been some early frost, but only on the lower meadows near the river; the young footman Sandor had announced that he would soon be getting married; and that very same morning they had heard a fallow buck calling from some way off in the park. And with every little tale that she told Countess Roza was wondering: what has happened? What could have happened to put him in such a good humour all of a sudden? And what could she do to find out?

By now the sun was beginning to set. The peaks of the Jara mountains turned slowly to purple and the sky above was streaked with orange and deep carmine. Here and there thin vaporous clouds were to be seen, and through them the rays from the sinking sun soared high above etching great lines of fire on the brilliant green and pale blue of the darkening heavens. The edges of the few clouds were ringed with a rosy fire and it seemed as if the whole world were bathed in a golden light that reached all around them, penetrating even the dark entrance to the Torda gorge, casting a soft glow over the distant grasslands of the Keresztes plain and on the nearby river banks, and even into the deepest recesses of the wide glazed veranda.

Blinking slightly at all this brightness Countess Roza at last tried a more direct approach. Brightly, but still carefully, she said:

'But you haven't told me about the opera! How was the *Madam Butterfly*? Was it well done? Was it as beautiful as everyone expected?'

Balint gave a few banal replies saying that, oh yes, it had been lovely, very grand, very beautiful.

'And the French singer?'

'Excellent. Really beautiful! Superb!'

All these answers, despite their superlatives, he gave somewhat hurriedly without offering a single phrase to explain what he meant or justify his praise. It seemed that for some reason of his own he did not want to be forced into giving details and, as this was so unlike her son, who never had any difficulty in expressing himself with ease and fluency and whose descriptions of what he had heard or seen were usually vivid and to the point, Countess Roza realized at once that she was on the right track and that if something had happened at the opera she would have to feel her way with caution if she were to find out what it was.

'They tell me it's a most dramatic piece. What part did you find the most exciting, the most touching? How was the entr'acte before the last act?' Having read the newspaper articles – which Balint had missed – it was soon obvious to her that she knew more about the tragic love of Cio-Cio-San for Lieutenant Pinkerton than did her son, who did not seem at all familiar with anything except the long first act love duet, for it was to that that he always returned whatever she might ask him about the rest of the work. And then he started to peel an apple and seemed so absorbed in so doing that it seemed to her better to let the subject drop.

Knowing her son so well Countess Roza thought it would be better not to insist any more. One more question, however, she did ask. She wanted to know if he had seen any of their friends at the theatre, and so learned that Margit Miloth and her husband had been in the Gyalakuthy box next to the Abadys' and, though Balint said nothing about Adrienne, his manner was suddenly so awkward and constrained that his mother quickly decided to change the subject, not bringing the matter up again, and then only with great circumspection, until they were seated at dinner that evening.

She reached the subject in the most roundabout manner, as was her way. First of all she talked about the hunting at Zsuk. Then she asked which families had brought out debutante girls that season, and asked if the autumn social life in Kolozsvar was as lively and amusing as it usually was when the hunt season began. She wanted to know who had opened their town houses and who was going to give balls and dinners; and in this way she eventually arrived at her destination, which was to ask about the Prefect's supper party. Now she discovered her first important fact: Balint had had a headache and had not attended. He had been sorry to miss the occasion for he would have liked to have met the diva and seen so many of their friends, but it had been a rotten sort of migraine and he hadn't felt up to it, admitting for the first time that he hadn't even stayed until the end of the performance. Perhaps, he said, thinking no doubt that it was quite an adequate excuse, he had been rather vague about it when they had discussed his doings over tea that afternoon.

In fact the inadequacy of the excuse was just what Countess Roza wanted to hear, for it immediately gave her a clue as to what had really happened. It was clear to her now that her son had met someone at the theatre, and it was for this person's sake that he had left early and for whom he had failed to go to the party. It could only have been Adrienne; and Countess Roza knew it as surely as if he had spelled it out.

For a moment her old anger flared up once again. That woman! That accursed woman! But then her wrath dissolved again almost as quickly as it had appeared.

For twelve long, miserable months after she had forbidden Balint to come home to Denestornya, Countess Abady had sat alone in her great house; and even after her son had been allowed back he had been so gloomy, so distracted, so totally uninterested in everything in which he had formerly taken such pleasure and so listless, that it had been like living with a ghost. Every time that she had looked at her son's weary face her heart had constricted and, though she never for a moment thought that she had acted in anything but his best interests – and, of course, to preserve the family's prestige and honour – it had been a daily sorrow to see him so heartbroken. Only now, this very day, had he been his old self again, young and cheerful and filled with hope and the joy of being alive. She hadn't seen him like that for so long, oh, so long; and her joy and thankfulness for his being restored to his old self prevented her from analysing the reasons too carefully lest they should be too difficult to accept. Nor for a moment did she question the rightness of her royal decree – however arrogant and tyrannical it might have been – but she now realized that since he could never marry that woman, since he could never bring her to enjoy the Abady house and inheritance, what did it matter if by seeing her he could be made happy once more? Of course it would mean that a proper acceptable marriage for him would now be put off for a few more years, but she could accept that as the price for once more seeing peace and happiness in his face.

It only took her a moment to think this out and accept the situation for what it was and so she quickly stopped asking any more awkward questions. Without appearing to have noticed her son's hesitation and embarrassment she switched smoothly to less controversial subjects.

'Tell me about those two daughters of Laszlo Gyeroffy's old guardian, Stanislo. Do they have red-blonde hair like their father's famous wig? And the second Kamuthy girl – I suppose those are the new ones this year – is she as roly-poly as her brother or is she like her elder sister?' Balint, now alive and unconstrained again, did his best to imitate those moonfaced, simple-minded girls and was so successful that Countess Roza roared with laughter and even called upon the two fat housekeepers who sat in silence at the end of the table to do the same and agree with her delighted applause.

'Yes, indeed!' said one, and the other echoed, 'Indeed, yes!'

Recently these two had tried their best to ingratiate themselves with Balint. Their old ally and supporter, the rascally lawyer Azbej who for so long had managed Countess Abady's affairs, was no longer there since he had not long before resigned from acting as her agent. The little lawyer was no fool and, as soon as Countess Roza had made peace with her son, he realized that if he were not very careful the young master would soon find out many things Azbej would rather remained hidden; and that he would then be called to account without mercy. It was better, he thought, to go before this could happen and so, during the previous winter, he had made the journey to Abbazia where the mistress was spending the cold season and told her that family matters of his own obliged him to leave her service. The explanation he gave was that, with the principal motive of doing a service to the Countess's noble family, he had bought Laszlo Gyeroffy's estate of Szamos-Kozard (which, of course, no one else would have bought) and to do so he had used his wife's money. Now he would have to give up everything else in order to be free to run the place. Of course it had all been done only to serve the interests of the Gracious Countess's most illustrious family. He took with him a sheaf of impressive-looking accounts and a carefully worded dispensation which only required the Gracious Countess's signature. This obtained he went on his way and the Gracious Countess herself had said how sorry she was to see him go.

With Azbej's departure Mrs Baczo and Mrs Tothy at once lost that precious ally with whose protection they had been enabled to lord it over Countess Roza's household. They knew that the other servants detested them both, knowing what advantages they had gained from their privileged position and how much they had been able to profit by it. Now they needed a new protector, and both thought they could do no better than to get the young master on their side. Only he would be able to protect them if their mistress, or even he himself, somehow got wind of what they had been up to for so long; and so they worked it out that, if they paid their court well and pleased him and somehow earned his approval, then he would be less inclined to start looking into how they had run the kitchens and stillrooms and asking why the bills for butcher's meat, sugar, coffee and cooking fat had been so high.

It was true that since his return the young master had shown no sign of being interested in anything, let alone such awkward matters as household expenses. When Azbej had first left and Balint had come home nearly everyone employed at Denestornya had one great fear. The estate foremen, the farming

tenants and many others had all been guilty of persistent falsification of their accounts which Azbej had overlooked because,
if he protected them, they in turn would say nothing about his
own even more profitable thieving: now they were all scared to
death that Count Balint would at once put his nose into everything. But it hadn't happened: Count Balint did nothing. It was
the same with the administration of the forest holdings in which
he had formerly taken such a deep personal interest. He came,
he went. He had looked around and dealt without joy with whatever was put in front of him. He had made a few enquiries, but
had initiated nothing new and indeed treated everything with
the same listless indifference.

While at home at Denestornya Balint, as he never had before,
went to bed late and got up late. For days on end he would hardly
leave the house, not even to go out riding, but would sit for hours
reading some book or other.

But from the day he returned to find his mother with her
beloved horses in the horseshoe court, all was different. At dawn
the next morning he rode out with Simon Jäger and jumped all
the fences in the paddock. At midday it was with happiness in his
voice that he told his mother that for the first time that year he
himself had heard the fallow deer calling in that thicket in the
park they called Magyaros; and then he told her that he wanted
to go to Zsuk for the hunting and wondered if she would let him
have three of their good hunters.

'But of course I will,' she cried, delighted. 'You don't have to
ask! Do whatever you like! Take whichever you like! They're all
yours, you know!'

This was no more than Balint had expected. He had known
exactly what his mother would say, almost word for word, yet he
knew she would have been offended if he had omitted to ask. To
play the fairy godmother, to give presents, hand over precious
possessions, particularly to her son, was for the Countess Roza
one of the great pleasures in life. It was a part she liked to play,
and yet it was not really a part as in the theatre but a genuine side
of her character. That is how she felt; and the fact of being asked
was as important to her as the giving. Had she not been asked, it
would have been taken as an affront to her natural goodness and
as an unjustified liberty; for no one must ever forget that everything was hers and that everything depended on her wishes.

Balint went on to mention that Baron Gazsi would shortly be

paying them a visit and also that he would like to invite over the young Aron Kozma as he wanted to discuss Co-operative matters with him.

Countess Roza looked up at her son with interest.

'Which Kozma is that?' she asked. 'Does he come from the prairie lands?' and, when Balint confirmed that that was so, she went on: 'What sort of age is he? What was his father's name?'

'He is the eldest son of Boldizsar, and he has his own land near Teke,' said Balint, who went on to explain what advanced and successful landowners the Kozmas had become and how both generations, the father's and sons', had all turned out to be serious and hard-working and progressive.

The old lady appeared to be paying attention to everything Balint told her, but when she spoke it was obvious that she was really only interested in the first thing he had said.

'So this one is Boldizsar's eldest boy, is he? Boldizsar was the middle one of five brothers and they all grew up here, at Denestornya. Their father was our agent when I was a child, and I knew them all well and used to play with the younger ones. Well! Well! Well! Invite him, do!' She paused for a moment and then went on, with a little smile at her own private memories, saying, 'Invite him, but tell him to wire and say when he is coming. I'll need to have the heating put on in the guest-rooms in plenty of time.'

'It isn't cold yet, Mama.'

'It doesn't signify. The weather might change any day and . . . it is better to know in advance.'

It did not occur to Balint that his mother had had no such qualms when told of Gazsi's visit.

CHAPTER FOUR

FIVE DAYS LATER Gazsi arrived, riding his thoroughbred mare Honeydew, who was now so changed that it was hard to believe that it was the same animal who, a couple of years before, had been the terror of all the jockeys on the track. Now she seemed as quiet as the old spotted farm donkey, though it was true that she allowed no one but Gazsi on her back.

'I had to r-r-ride over,' said Gazsi apologetically, 'because

Honeydew needed the work. Actually I would far rather have dr-r-riven and then I could have brought a suitcase with me. But no one else can even walk this beast and only the other day, when I went to my sister's, she kicked the young stable-boy in the belly. It's r-r-real slavery, looking after this one,' he said as he dismounted in the horseshoe court, and he bent his head sideways and looked plaintively at Balint as he always did when making a tragi-comedy of whatever he was doing. This time, however, Balint sensed that he was not joking for he seemed unusually serious and went on to say something quite out of the usual for him: he spoke of his clothes.

'I know I oughtn't to pr-r-resent myself to Aunt Roza looking like this,' he said, 'so scr-r-ruffy and unkempt, but I have brought something to change into in my saddle-bag. But you can't get much in, I'm afraid.'

'Really, Gazsi,' said Balint, 'that doesn't matter for you! Why, my mother's quite used to receiving you booted and spurred.'

'Of course, of course! Who would expect anything else from a peasant like me?' and he sounded so bitter that Balint instantly regretted speaking as he had.

As it happened the saddle-bag produced a sort of dinner-jacket which had been made by a tailor in Torda. Though his shirt was wrinkled and his collar worn, when he presented himself at the dinner table, Gazsi looked tolerably presentable, indeed almost European. He had obviously made an effort to look civilized, hopeless though his case might be, and he wore an unusually serious air.

Later that evening, when the two young men had drunk tea and eaten some stewed apples with Countess Roza in her little first-floor drawing-room, Balint escorted his guest back through the huge empty dining-hall and down the stairs to the ground floor. They did not speak, for Balint had already noticed how unusually silent and preoccupied his guest had been, both at dinner and afterwards. It is true that he had told a number of amusing tales, in his usual wry, self-mocking humorous way; how he fell into the water while chasing an otter and how the beast just sat on the shore laughing at him; about the guard-dog at a vineyard who was tethered by a long wire and how he had stood still while the dog ran circles around him until it was he who was tethered – and then the dog had bitten him; and several others of the same sort, all clownishly acted out for the amusement of his hosts. Even so Abady sensed that he was going through the motions of being his normal self while his heart was not really in it. He had noticed that each time Gazsi paused for a moment a slight frown appeared on his forehead, suggesting that the same dark thought had once more taken possession of him. Balint wondered what on earth could be the matter and became increasingly worried, waiting for his guest to tell him what it was. At last he did. When they reached the foot of the stairs, Gazsi turned aside and said, 'I'd like to talk something over with you. Can we...?' and stopped.

'Better come to me,' said Balint. 'The servants will soon be round to take away the lamps as my mother doesn't like to keep them up late. I'll give you a candle to get back to your room.' They turned and crossed the entrance hall, and as they did so they could see the lights on the floor above going out, one after the other, until finally one solitary glimmer could be seen moving slowly along until it too disappeared behind an arch and was seen no more.

Soon the two young men were seated facing each other at the table in Balint's circular ground-floor room in the castle's north-west tower. A small reading lamp cast a glow between them, but the rest of the room was in darkness.

Kadacsay hesitated for a moment before starting to speak. Looking now more than ever like a raven with his beak tilted slightly to one side, he seemed to be looking hard at the armrest of his chair as if he would get inspiration from it. Then, speaking slowly with long pauses between each phrase as if to underline that he was choosing his words with extra care, he said, 'I have just made my will ... Yes, my will. It seemed the r-r-right thing to do ... now ... and that is why I came to see you, to ask ... to ask you to agr-r-ree to be my executor-r-r ...'

Balint found this sinister and upsetting. The fate of his own father flashed through his mind, for Count Tamas Abady had developed cancer when he was hardly older than Gazsi was today, and had died within a few months. Had this happened to his friend? Was this why he had seemed so sad and preoccupied? So, trying to hide his concern, he interrupted Gazsi, saying, 'You're not ill, Gazsi? If anything is worrying you I hope you've seen a doctor?'

'No, no! I'm all r-r-right ... as good as ever-r-r, I just thought it seemed sensible to ... to be pr-r-repared, to be r-r-ready just in case ... in plenty of time ...'

Then he went on to tell Balint exactly how all his affairs stood and that he had settled everything with his sister when he had been over to see her a few days before. He explained all about what his property brought in, with detailed facts and figures, and told Balint that he had settled all those small debts he had incurred when still in the hussars so that all that now remained was the disposal of his family inheritance.

'For Heaven's sake, what makes you think of death when you're still so young and healthy?' broke in Balint again, now somewhat irritated by such gloomy thoughts when he himself felt so happy.

'Does everything have to have a reason?' asked the other, and smiled quizzically. 'Perhaps one day my darling Honeydew will go a little cr-r-razy again, throw me and then r-r-roll all over me? Who knows, she killed a jockey like that once! R-r-rather a suitable death for me, don't you think? After all, everyone knows I only know about horses. Anyhow, why be frightened of death? Didn't Schopenhauer say something about it being only our will to live which makes us scared of death and that it was a purely animal reaction? Or perhaps I've got it wr-r-rong...?' and he waved his hand in a gesture of mock dejection before laughing briefly. Then, far more seriously, he went on to tell Balint that he had decided to leave everything he could to his sister's two sons on one condition. That was that each of them, before he came into his inheritance, must spend at least two years at some university abroad, in England or in France, and that it would be Balint's responsibility to choose where. If they didn't agree they were to get nothing. 'I'm determined,' he said, 'that they shan't turn out to be useless fools like me!'

Touched by what he was hearing, Balint listened hard to everything that Gazsi had to say; and all the time he was thinking how tormented his old friend must have been, and how for years he must have lived with this inner turmoil and so now was doing the only thing he could to provide for his nephews what he had yearned for in vain for himself. Later he would remember one or two especially poignant things that Gazsi had said about himself, about his unfulfilled hunger for knowledge and self-understanding, and how this hunger had led him to grab eagerly at any book he could lay his hands on, especially those on history and the modern school of German philosophy. In this way, it seemed, he had tried hard to compensate for years spent only in the saddle and in playing the fool.

'Of course I'll do what you ask,' said Balint. 'I'm flattered that you should have that sort of faith in me. All the same it's not very likely that I'll have to put my oar in. You'll probably live for years and send the boys to England yourself ... and any others who are not yet born!'

Gazsi got up, laughing as he said, 'Even Habakkuk got a r-r-rude answer when he asked the Lord about the future!' and, so as to cover his deep emotion at Balint's ready acceptance, he laughed loudly at his own irreverence. Then he took Balint's hand, wrung it warmly, holding it in his for a little longer than usual, in the way that one does when saying goodbye.

At eight o'clock the following morning they went out riding; not before, because at that time of year the dawn was invariably followed by a thick fog on the flat land beside the Aranyos which was where Balint wanted to go to try out the young horses. Since Gazsi had brought Honeydew, who had been ridden in several first-class flat races, they were only going to try short distances so that the novices from the Denestornya stable could keep up with the experienced thoroughbred mare.

Five horses had been saddled and were waiting for them in the horseshoe court. Apart from Honeydew, there were Csinos and Ivy with Balint's own saddles, and Menyet and Csalma with the stable lads. All four were very much alike, tall bay mares, about sixteen hands, with long elegant necks, wide shoulders and 'a lot of ground under them'. The only difference between them was that one was a shade darker and one a shade lighter than the others, and if Honeydew with her fine bones and pulled-up belly like a greyhound had not been in sight – she was being held slightly apart from the others in case she should take it into her head to start kicking out – they too might have been taken for English thoroughbreds with those unmistakable lines of the true racehorse.

The little band of riders walked slowly out through the great gates of the courtyard, Balint and Gazsi side by side in the lead – though Gazsi prudently held Honeydew a pace or two behind because the mare was already beginning to put her ears back and he needed to be careful to control her uncertain temper – while Simon Jäger and two stable lads followed a couple of lengths behind them. The hoofbeats echoed loudly as they rode under the wide arch.

After crossing the bridge that spanned the former moat they turned left towards the river. Below them most of the wide valley was still covered in wave after wave of thin mist, so diaphanous that it might have been made from the torn remnants of some giant shawl of soft cotton. It spread over the whole plain far beyond the junction with the Maros and, wherever the sun's rays had been strongest, glimpses could be caught of the trees and meadows beneath. In some places, where the plantations were thickest, the park could clearly be seen, but in others thin wisps of early mist still clung to the tips of the tallest poplars until the tiny patches of autumn leaves looked like golden coins suspended in the air. The little band rode down through the bright contrasting colours of the separate groups of birch, pine and maple until, after describing a wide arc, they found themselves where the lingering morning mist reduced all colours to pastel. Although by now one could see some distance ahead it was like looking through milky glass, as in a dream landscape where everything appeared to be at an infinite distance.

They rode over a little bridge, beneath which the river seemed to be giving off wisps of steamy vapour. A kingfisher darted past them with a startled cry, its sapphire-blue plumage drawing a sharp line just above the surface of the water for an instant before it vanished into the deep vegetation beside the river.

'It'll soon be winter if that one has arrived,' remarked Kadacsay in a whisper: and then again they did not speak.

The horses' hooves made hardly a sound on the soft turf. The landscape before them seemed more and more unreal with tall groups of Austrian pines looking like black islands in a white sea. When they were quite close to the woods in which they would soon be engulfed those orange-coloured rays of the sun that had succeeded in penetrating the mist above cast a pale dove-grey haze over the silver foliage of the poplars and gave a rosy tint to the dense leaves of the undergrowth. It was as if Nature were blushing as she was undressed by the sun.

From the depths of the mysterious woods suddenly came a deep rumbling roar not unlike the roll of some giant drum, or empty wooden barrel, though it clearly came from some living source and not from any dead piece of wood. It was an angry sound, filled with demand and desire, a mating call or a battle cry.

They all stopped and the horses pricked up their ears.

'It must be a fallow stag,' whispered Balint. 'He can't be far away!' and he turned his horse and trotted swiftly along a narrow grassy path which led through the wild tangle of willow trees and elders, beneath arches of giant topolya, until they reached the ford. The reeds by the riverbank were tall now and stood like a wall in front of them. A narrow path had been cut through that led down to the flat pebbles below the bank. At that season there was not much water in the sluggish little stream, indeed it barely came up to the horses' hocks because most of it had been diverted a mile further upstream to drive the mill. The Aranyos was always like this in autumn and it was hard to believe that the mighty torrent to be seen in spring was the same river. Of course the proof was there to see on the further bank, which was a small perpendicular cliff two or three metres high, cut clean like some geological illustration with clear-cut layers of pebbles, dark humus, alternating strands of clay and stones, until finally reaching down to a base level of bluish-coloured slate which had once been the bed of some prehistoric sea.

They followed the path through the reeds and crossed the ford, and now, for the first time, they could look out over the Keresztes plain, the largest in Transylvania, towards the bald slopes of the Mezoseg, broken only by canyons of yellowish clay, with here and there little square patches of vineyard; over to the right to the hills of the Maros and to the left, far, far away, to the vertical line of the Torda cleft. Still further in the distance, almost melting into the clouds, were the soft grey outlines of the Jara range. The plain was bathed in sunshine and in front of them were the great fields of now harvested oats at the sides of which enough ground had been left unploughed for three horses to gallop side by side. These were the autumn training grounds, for here the going was not so hard as it became inside the park itself. Along one side posts marked a six-hundred-metre stretch.

They rode the horses twice round the perimeter of the field, as a preliminary workout, and then tried out the speed of the five-year-old Csalma and the novice Menyet against that of the experienced Honeydew.

Balint, Simon Jäger and one of the stable lads watched from

the side. The first try-out went smoothly enough and Csalma kept up with Honeydew without difficulty, even though the mare went full out.

'She'll do us proud, my Lord,' said Simon, and then, almost under his breath, 'I wouldn't give any of our horses for that spindly goat! At five thousand metres she'd be well behind!'

Gazsi now trotted over to Balint, said a few words of praise for the Denestornya mare and then, signalling to the lad to bring up the young colt that was to be tried out next, cantered back to the starting post. Then something quite unexpected happened.

Young Pisti, the lad, said '*Komelo*' sharply and dug his heels into the colt's sides to bring him up in line with Gazsi's thorough-bred and the latter, perhaps believing that the command was for her, or because she was suddenly reminded of those days on the racecourse at Alag which she had so hated, and resented being shouted at once more, put her head between her forelegs, arched her back in a crescent and, turning a full circle, bolted in every direction in the wide open field. Gazsi was taken by surprise and thrown almost at once; but being the horseman he was he landed on his feet without further mishap.

Not so young Pisti! The colt snorted, flung up his tail in a trumpet shape – just like Honeydew – and leapt into the air so that the lad was thrown up like a shooting star and fell to the ground head first.

Both these things happened so quickly that it was like a volcano erupting and the others roared with uncontrollable laughter. Though his mount too tried some tricks of her own Balint managed to canter fairly calmly over towards Gazsi. At the same time Simon Jäger galloped at full speed after the colt, who was heading for home in a panic. It was one of Simon's great passions to catch bolting horses at full gallop. The last time he had done it had been two years before when Balint had been hunting at Zsuk and Simon had brought up his reserve mount. Whenever he was out riding he always kept a sharp eye out for a fall and then he was off, racing after the riderless mount uphill and downhill, standing upright in his stirrups, not bent forward like jockeys in a race but with his ramrod back as straight as the Hungarian hussars of old. In a second the riderless colt and his pursuer had crossed the river and vanished into the trees beyond.

'What a bitch!' cried Gazsi when he had caught Honeydew

and remounted. 'Didn't she just thr-r-row me again, the horr-r-rible mare!' But he wasn't angry; it was all a joke to him, and Balint, looking at the mare with her flattened ears, her mouth drawn back and, in her eyes a wicked-looking twinkle, fancied that it was the same for Honeydew.

The second trial never took place as one of the chef partici-pants had bolted, and so Gazsi and Balint started for home. They turned into the park towards the island of trees called Nagyberek – the Big Wood, and Balint said, 'Let's follow the trail through the woods and maybe we'll get close to the deer. Those fallow stags are completely reckless when in rut, far more so than the red deer. They're restless as anything and stay out of covert for far longer.' Then they sent the remaining lad home and the two of them turned into the thick undergrowth.

Now there was hardly a trace left of the morning mists. The sun shone brightly through the tangled mesh of hops and other wild vines, picking up the autumn yellow of the summer's hem-lock stalks and making the dark web of the bishop's cap creepers look as if it were a grille that protected passers-by from the flames that seemed to shine from the dry grass behind. Here the filtered sunlight picked up the strange contorted bark of a centuries-old tree and the red glow of another, and everywhere there were bright patches interspersed by dark blue strips of shadow. Where there was light it was blinding, and nothing seemed solid and three-dimensional, for the crowns of the giant trees around them cast their shadow at random until even the outlines of the bushes that formed the undergrowth were blurred and insubstantial.

It was still a dream forest, though quite different from what it had been in the thick mist of early morning. Here and there berries gleamed bright red against orange-coloured leaves, the lemon yellow of the maples was mingled with the bronze of the native oaks and everywhere were clutches of tiny berries that shone like black diamonds. There were so many that they might have been floating freely in the air. Sometimes the two riders found themselves crossing small clearings, now vividly green, before plunging once more into the lush jungle-like thickets.

From time to time they reined in the horses and stopped to listen. All around them they could sense an unrest that seemed almost to vibrate. It was a feeling rather than anything they could hear. Sometimes there was a faint sound as of a dry twig being snapped underfoot, though they might have imagined it. And sometimes they heard again that deep rumbling call, though they could not tell from which direction it came. Was it in front of them – or behind – or was that too only in their imagination?

The horses too were fully alert, their nostrils flaring wide and their ears pointing now in one direction and now in another, as if they were also aware that they were close to something wonderful and mysterious.

After a little while they found themselves on the bank of a former riverbed. Kadacsay was a little behind and stopped while Balint went slowly ahead. The riverbed itself was filled with reeds and tall grass and sharp smacking noises seemed to come from its muddy bed. Hardly had Gazsi turned his mare's head towards the noise and started to lean forward in the saddle to peer at whatever was there than a full-grown fallow buck jumped out of the thick reeds and for an instant stood there without moving, only some ten paces away from horse and rider. His widespread shovel-shaped antlers sprung proudly from between the eye-horns on his forehead and his red-brown coat had a line of clear white spots. He was not a big animal – only the size of a yearling colt – but his defiant stance made him formidable enough. Honeydew gave a start and backed a pace or two and the two animals gazed at each other, each as surprised and impressed as the other. No doubt the stag was as startled by the sight of this strange golden-yellow animal as the mare was by him. He pushed forward his muzzle that shone like patent leather and hesitantly made one or two steps forward. Then, no doubt catching the scent of a human somewhere near, he quickly recoiled and vanished back among the reeds.

Gazsi trotted forward until he had caught up with Balint.

'My dear-r-r fellow! Something mar-r-rvellous! A stag comes out in fr-r-ront of us, and Honeydew is fr-r-rightened. Honeydew! For the fir-r-rst time in her life the beast has had a shock! I could feel it thr-r-rough my leg muscles. Her hear-r-rt was r-r-racing! I never thought I'd live to see something impr-r-ress her!'

Later they saw some does and their young, but only from a distance, and a few minutes later they heard some loud clashing sounds which were almost certainly caused by two stags fighting. Then Balint and Gazsi turned their horses and rode slowly home.

Throughout the morning's ride Gazsi had seemed his usual cheerful self but Balint soon realized that this had probably only been because he had been cheered up by their adventures. When he asked when Gazsi would be going to Zsuk all the answer he got was, 'Oh, I don't know. I don't think I'll go ... it's too bor-r-ring. Nothing but hor-r-rses, hor-r-rses, hor-r-rses! Always hor-r-rses! What for, I ask you? I've had quite enough. They bor-r-re me ...' and that tight little frown had appeared again on his forehead.

'But the hunt is unthinkable without you!'

'Then they'll have to get used to it, won't they?' replied Gazsi gloomily.

They returned to find Countess Roza cutting flowers in front of the house. She wore thick buckskin gloves and had already cut a large quantity from the beds that lined the inner court and were thus protected from the early frosts. She walked gaily towards the two young men, giving the impression that she was preparing for some very special occasion. As well as this exceptionally festive manner they noticed that she wore the smart bonnet she normally put on only when she went to church. The wide satin bow was tied coquettishly under her chin and she had put on some new clothes that were noticeably smarter than those she usually wore, even to the extent of sporting a new white lace collar and frills at her wrists. She seemed years younger than when they had last seen her.

'Take these flowers,' she said to one of the footmen who was just passing, 'and tell them to put them in the guest-rooms.' With a spring in her step she came towards her son and Gazsi.

'Now tell me all about it,' she said. 'What did you see on your ride? Let's sit here in front of the house; I love it here when the autumn sun is out.'

She led them to a stone bench from where one could see into the horseshoe court and listened with glee to Gazsi's story – which he made the most of – about how idiotic he'd been allowing the mare to throw him, and about the meeting with the stag and how he had felt Honeydew's racing heartbeats when it was her turn to be frightened. And of course he praised the young horses raised at Denestornya until Countess Roza's eyes gleamed with pleasure. And all the time she was listening she kept on turning her eyes towards the great entrance gates beyond the outer court.

At one moment she said, apropos of nothing, that Aron Kozma

was arriving that morning on the eleven-thirty train, and then turned back to listen to Gazsi once more.

Later on, when they went in to lunch, she made the visitor sit at the place of honour on her right, for even though he was not of their class he was a visitor and a stranger while Gazsi, as a distant cousin, was treated as family. She talked mainly to Kozma, asking after all his family, his father and uncles, but especially after his father, of whom she spoke with great warmth and much sympathy.

No one could have told from her manner to the son how angry she had been, year after year, with the father. It had only been once a year and why this was no one knew but she. The truth was that, starting on her fiftieth birthday, Aron Kozma's father, Boldizsar, had sent her birthday greetings on a postcard and that every year he had mentioned her age for all to see. Before her fiftieth birthday he had never even written a letter of congratulation – nothing until the open postcards when she was fifty – and even she had no idea why he did it. She supposed that it must be revenge for some – by her – forgotten childhood slight but remembered by him for forty-odd years. She had only been thirteen years old when Aron's grandfather had stopped being the Abadys' estate superintendent and had moved away from Denestornya. Since then she had never again met Boldizsar or any of his brothers, all her former childhood playmates, and however hard she tried she could not recall any possible occasion when she might have offended one of them. On the contrary she had loved them all, particularly Boldizsar, who was the same age as she and who was her very special friend. It was very annoying not to know the reason why he should so obviously set out to provoke her and yet he did, year after year, and each time it happened it spoilt her day and made her angry. But now there was no sign of all this: today Countess Roza was all smiles.

It was her form of revenge. If the father was malicious she was determined to charm the son so that when he returned home he would recount how charming and gracious she had been, how affectionately she had spoken of his father, and how gay and happy she seemed to be. She had carefully planned her reception of the son so as to show the father how ineffectual his malice had been. When Boldizsar got to hear of how sprightly and youthful she was, despite her age which he never failed to mention so gratuitously, she would have had her revenge; for she was sure it would be a real punishment for him to believe that she hadn't even noticed his impertinence.

For Countess Roza the game was an easy one, for she was kindly by nature and now she had many happy childhood memories to recall and relate. And while she did so she often looked covertly at the young man's face, as if searching in his dark-featured Tartar looks for a resemblance to her old playmate.

When they had finished their coffee after lunch the hostess suggested that they should all go down to the lower part of the park to look at the horses which, after the hay had been gathered in the meadows in the mountains, were always brought back to graze at Denestornya.

'We should start at once,' she said, and asked Balint to order the horses to be put to an open carriage so that they could do the rounds before it got dark.

'My dear Mama, it's only five minutes' walk. They're all quite close to the house, just the other side of the millstream.'

'Never mind that, I'd rather drive. Will you come with me?' she said to Aron. 'They could drive us round the park so as to give you some idea of the place as it's your first visit.'

This offer was also intended as an honour for the visitor, an honour which Countess Roza always enjoyed bestowing because she, like her father and grandfather before her, had spent much of her life in planning and beautifying the castle's surroundings. She loved it all and she was proud that she had been able to carry on the family tradition of planning not only what she herself would enjoy but also for the future, for her successors. She and her forebears had always known and understood that this sort of landscape, whose noblest feature was the plantations of trees, was only achieved through the devotion of several generations. To see the effect that was then planned one had to wait at least half a century, and so Countess Roza's pride in what had been so unselfishly achieved was only natural.

While his mother and their guest strolled down to the horse-shoe court where the carriage was waiting for them Balint took Gazsi straight to the rose gardens which had been laid out on the terrace in front of the north side of the castle. From there they only had to descend a double flight of stone steps to find themselves on a wide path leading through the park which was bordered on each side by plantations of native oak trees whose tall straight trunks and pointed crowns always reminded visitors of cypresses. Here they waited for a minute or two while the carriage was driven in a wide semi-circle to cross the first bridge over the river. A few hundred paces in front of them was the millstream, and in the meadows beyond they could see mares and their off-spring through the mostly bare branches of the intervening trees.

For a few moments they walked on slowly without speaking. Finally Balint said: 'I've been thinking a lot about everything you told me yesterday. I'm sure that your trouble is that you're too much alone at Bukkos. You think too much, and then you start brooding! You ought to get married . . .'

'The Devil I should!' exclaimed Gazsi with an angry wave of his hand.

'I mean it!' said Balint. 'If you got married you'd see every-thing in quite a different light . . . and you'd have little Kadacsays you could bring up in whatever way you wanted.'

'Devil take it,' repeated Gazsi and paused. Then, a little later, he said, 'I could never cope with a girl of our class, you know, I'm . . . well . . . I'm, I'm too much of a peasant myself. Some little maidservant, perhaps, from time to time, that's my style, if you like . . . but some over-r-r-refined young *comtesse*; no thank you! Anyhow I'm such a clod that there's no one of that sort who'd ever want to marry *me*!'

'Oh yes, there is; plenty of them. What about Ida Laczok? She's been pining for you for years. She'd marry you tomorrow if you asked her,' said Balint and then went on to say what a nice, clever and simple girl she was and, just as an added bait, how everyone knew she had always been in love with him.

'The Devil she is!' said Gazsi once more, but with less disbelief than before.

'It's true! Ever since the ball at Var-Siklod – don't you remem-ber? She'd be just right for you. Pretty, healthy, very competent in the house too. You know her mother relies on her, not on the others. She's the right age and what's more she's no one's fool.'

This time Gazsi made no answer at once but looked unusually thoughtful. Then he said, 'Perhaps you're right . . . but . . . Bah! Who knows?'

Then they talked of other things.

Countess Roza's visit to the brood-mares lasted for some time because she took the opportunity to tell her guest everything there was to know about each and every one of the twenty-four mares and their pedigrees and offspring. Her discourse was long and detailed, and, to anyone interested in breeding horses, extremely informative, because she knew what she was talking about and had had many years' experience.

One of her most interesting theories was about the transmission, not only of build but also of character and temperament, and how to ensure its continuity in a breeding programme. After a while she drove off with Kozma to show him more of the estate while Balint and Gazsi walked up to the pine woods that covered the highest part of the parkland.

By the time they got to the top of the hill the afternoon light was already beginning to fade to a uniform greyness. They had arrived just where one of Balint's ancestors had had built a little classical pavilion or summer-house which consisted of little more than a domed roof supported by stone columns. It was surrounded by some of the oldest pine trees in the park and before it stretched a wide clearing bordered by plantations of different specimens of rare trees. At the bottom of the hill there wound the path they had ridden along that morning and beyond it could be seen the castle's walls with, above them, the conical roofs which capped the corner towers. The old stonework was etched in deep violet against the pale evening sky and the patina on the copper casing on the roofs no longer shone green but seemed black against the saffron-yellow of the sunset.

They sat down, even though it was starting to get cold.

'What a wonderful place this is,' said Gazsi. 'I've never been here before.'

They sat in silence for a little while. Then, though without knowing what train of thought led him to the subject, unless it was the contrast between the beauty and richness of Denestornya and the squalor and unhappiness he had recently witnessed, he said suddenly, 'I saw Laci the other day, poor fellow!'

'Really? Where? When?' asked Balint eagerly.

'Just the other day . . . when I was coming back from Szilagy.'

For a moment Gazsi said no more. Then he related how he had been passing through Kozard and that, in front of a largish peasant's house on the right-hand side of the road, he had seen Laszlo Gyeroffy sitting on a broken-down garden chair. It was only just as he was driving past that he had realized who it was and, as it had taken a moment or two to make the coachman understand what he wanted, he had already been driven well past the house before he had been able to stop and get out. Then he had had to walk back, past some empty land, to reach the place where he had seen Laszlo. As he had nearly got close enough to call out a greeting Laszlo had got up, turned away from him and slipped quickly into the house.

'I didn't know what to do. Should I go in after him ... or just go away again? I'm such an ass in this sort of thing. Well, I just tur-r-rned on my heel and left. What else was there to do? He saw me coming, so I r-r-reckoned that if he went in it must be because he didn't want to see me.'

'How did he look? How was he?'

'I think he looked thinner, but I can't be sure. There was a fence between us, and a little fr-r-ront gar-r-rden ... you know what those houses are like. I just looked up the path, but all I could see was a bottle and a glass beside the chair. He must have been sitting there dr-r-rinking. When he went in I saw him clutching the door-r-rpost and thought that per-r-rhaps he was ashamed for me to see him dr-r-runk. That's why I didn't go in ... per-r-rhaps it was stupid of me. I'm sor-r-ry now I didn't follow him.'

'I haven't had any news for ages,' said Balint. 'I wrote a couple of times last summer, but I never got any reply.'

Then he told Gazsi all that he did know, which was simply that he had heard that Laszlo had sold his property, but that he still lived there in an old servant's house he had kept. On his mother's behalf Balint had written to Laszlo offering him a home at Denestornya, either in a separate suite on the first floor or else in his grandfather's old manor house close by; but they had never had any answer. No doubt this was the way Laszlo wanted it for perhaps he had thought that he wouldn't be free to drink as he pleased.

'You remember Azbej, my mother's old estate manager? It was he that bought Kozard from Laszlo. He says he gives Laci some sort of annuity, but I don't know how much. I am not in touch with Azbej any more,' he added dryly.

For a few more moments they sat there together, not speaking but both of them thinking about Laszlo's sad life. Then Abady got up.

'Come along,' he said. 'My mother will be waiting for us for tea.'

Together they walked silently down the hill. When they had almost reached the castle Kadacsay looked at Balint and said, 'You know I really do feel sorry for poor Laci ... but at least he's lucky to have something to care for, even if it is only the dr-r-rink!'

Before dinner Balint carried Aron Kozma off to discuss with him various matters to do with the Co-operatives. Aron himself had some ideas for which he wanted Balint's approval; and there were certain proposals that Balint put forward which he did not think were feasible. Aron had a logical mind and was full of common sense, and from that short discussion there emerged some straightforward practical measures from all the somewhat nebulous ideas that had been spinning round in Balint's head since his reunion with Adrienne.

As both guests were going to leave Denestornya early the next morning good-byes were said that night.

'Please,' said Countess Roza as she offered her hand to be kissed, 'greet your father from me, tell him everything that you've seen here and tell him too that although the years go by I am still quite sprightly and do not at all feel my great age!'

She had prepared this parting sentence early that morning and intended it as a poisoned arrow for her childhood playmate. She was determined to let him know that his uncalled-for mockery had had no effect upon her, and that his efforts to vex her with his peculiar form of birthday greetings had had no effect whatever.

As she spoke she was sure that it would now be Boldizsar's turn to be annoyed and this pleased her so much that she smiled with renewed benevolence at his son.

PART TWO

CHAPTER ONE

LASZLO GYEROFFY LIVED in the house in the village that he had kept when he had sold his Kozard estate a year and a half before. He had kept it for the sake of his old servant, Marton Balogh, principally because he wanted to be sure that the old man had somewhere to live and would not be thrown out on the street, which he was sure Azbej would have no qualms about doing when he took possession of the manor house. He had originally thought of giving the place to Balogh outright, because it had never occurred to him that he might need it himself.

Not long after Laszlo had flung out of Sara Bogdan's house in a snowstorm and fallen dead drunk into a ditch near Apahida, a small one-horse cart had been driven along the main road. In it had been Bischitz, the Jewish storekeeper from Kozard who was driving home after a day in Kolozsvar. With him had been his daughter, Regina, who was the eldest of his children and the only one bright enough to feed the horse and look after the cart while Bischitz went about his business.

The storm had caught them when they were halfway home and their worn-out nag of a horse could hardly make any head-way against the driving snow. By the time they had reached the iron bridge near Apahida they were hardly moving and it was because of this that they had seen Laszlo by the feeble light of the cart's paraffin storm-lamp.

He had been lying face downwards at the edge of the ditch and he had been almost completely covered by snow. It was Regina who had first seen that there was someone there, and they had known who it was because of the familiar check of the coat he was wearing.

At once they had stopped the cart, pulled him out of the snow, and found that although he was by now almost sober again, he could hardly move but, though frozen stiff, was at least still alive. Together they had lifted him into the back of the cart, laid him down gently and driven him back to Kozard. Bischitz had thought he would leave him at the manor house, but it had been so late when they arrived, and the horse had been far too tired to manage the climb up to the house, so the shopkeeper's wife had made up a bed for him in the only good room in their little house.

Laszlo spent one night there.

In the morning he woke with a high fever. The doctor was sent for, as was Azbej, and when the doctor pronounced that Laszlo would certainly develop pneumonia and would have to stay in bed for weeks, Azbej flatly refused to take him in at the manor house declaring that it was quite unthinkable to look after him there because he was about to start repairing the house and had that very day brought out the masons to start work. There could be no question, he declared, of having Laszlo looked after in his old home. And so it came about that the solution was found of carrying him to the house he still owned on the outskirts of the village and moving in Marton Balogh to look after him. The old servant nursed him and Regina came in often to help, which she did eagerly and efficiently. He was ill for several months, and though by the end of the summer he had got over the pneumonia, he was left with a nasty persistent cough; but his life had been saved.

At first Azbej paid whatever was necessary, largely because he thought this would be a good mark in his favour if ever the Abady family started to look into his dealings with their cousin Gyeroffy. This only came to an end when months had passed and Laszlo was still not fully recovered. One day Azbej told the shopkeeper that he would pay no more, and for a few days no one knew what to do or what would become of the invalid. Then a Dr Simay, an elderly lawyer from Szamos-Ujvar, arrived unheralded at the store. Bischitz had met him some twenty years before and indeed it was to him that the shopkeeper had sold the portrait of Laszlo's errant mother, Julie Ladossa, after the distraught Mihaly Gyeroffy had slashed it almost in half and thrown it out of the window. Dr Simay had arrived just as unexpectedly then as he did now. This time he asked to speak to Bischitz alone. From that day on it was Bischitz who had provided whatever money was needed for Laszlo's illness, and afterwards, though by no means lavishly, who had supplied whatever Laszlo needed to live on. For this he was given just forty crowns a week, no more, no less, and on that meagre allowance he managed to keep Laszlo alive. He was forbidden to lend him any money and was not allowed to give him credit at the store. He had also had to swear not to reveal where the money came from.

As it happened Laszlo never even asked. Sometimes he would get angry with Bischitz if he wanted better or more brandy, for only this seemed to hold any interest for him. He never complained about the food – and anyhow never seemed to want very much. Old Balogh dug the garden behind the house and grew what potatoes and other vegetables they needed and, as he and Laszlo ate very little else, most of the allowance was spent on drink. The accounts were sent, by order, not to Laszlo but to the old lawyer, Dr Simay.

In this way a year had passed, during which Laszlo had really been too weak to go further than the chair outside the front door. Sometimes he did not get as far even as that but sat indoors doing nothing. Occasionally he would get hold of a newspaper – always several days old – and then he would glance over it without much interest. He never read anything else. Every now and again he would find his way into the store and exchange a few words with whoever came in. Usually, however, he talked only to Bischitz and his wife or, if they were busy elsewhere, to young Regina, for even though the child was still not quite thirteen, she was intelligent, knew where everything was kept and what its price was, and so was often entrusted with keeping the shop.

A strange relationship started to grow between the sick man and the child. It had always been one of Laszlo's oddest characteristics that as soon as he had a certain amount of drink under his belt he shed his usual silent and morose air and became instead talkative and boastful. When this happened he would suddenly show himself immensely proud of his once grand position in Budapest society, when as *elotancos* – the official organizer of all the great balls and social occasions – he had been one of the most popular young men in the capital. Later, when he had come back to Transylvania disgraced and ruined because of his inability to pay his gambling debts, his old friends would tease him relentlessly whenever he began to talk about his grand past. Now, though he only had little Regina to listen to him, the same thing would happen whenever he was full of brandy, of which he now needed far less than before to make him drunk and loquacious. After only a tot or two he would begin to tell the girl all about the luxuries and grandeurs he had once known. He only had to get started and words poured from him, tales about the reception for the King of Spain and grand balls at the Palace or other great houses, banquets and dinners and dances and scintillating evening *soirées*. Bischitz and his wife were no good as an audience for Laszlo since they believed it was all untrue and it bored them.

But not little Regina.

She never gave a thought as to whether it was true or not. She did not care. For her it was all as magical and as real as fairyland: the great golden rooms, the velvet-covered furniture, the mountains of flowers, the lovely elegant women in silk and satin who floated in the arms of slim-waisted men in traditional Hungarian costume or officers in full-dress uniform, kings, queens, princesses and princes. It was all far more beautiful than any other tales she had read or been told. And for her, Laszlo, sitting before her, thin and wan, often unshaved and unkempt, his once elegant clothes and expensive shoes now worn and mended, was a prince of legend, doomed by some horrid spell to a life of squalor and misery, but nevertheless still the true ruler of all that splendour of which he had formerly been the central figure.

Whenever he came into the store she would lean on the counter drinking in every word he uttered. Her Titian-red hair surrounded her beautiful but still girlish face like an aureole of flame. Her doe-like brown eyes, fringed by long curving lashes, opened ever more widely as she listened and her mouth, with lips startlingly red against her pale skin, was slightly open as she feasted on all he had to tell. For Regina it all had the effect of some wondrous magic potion, and when Laszlo stopped, as he occasionally did, she would at once refill his glass with brandy and push it towards him, for she knew that he could only go on as long as he was properly supplied with his own brand of magic potion.

From time to time she would ask him some question, as if she hadn't understood something he had said; and then he would tell her even more fabulous details of footmen in gold-braided liveries, carriages lined with silk, tables covered in gleaming plate and porcelain all laden with extraordinary food, and finally of the jewels, giant pearls and rubies, diadems and tiaras sparkling with diamonds of the finest water.

She never wanted to hear tell of anything else and, as Gyeroffy never wanted to talk of anything else, for Regina the great world consisted only of this fabulous luxury and pomp.

Several years before, when she had still been quite a small

child, some inborn curiosity had drawn her to 'The Count', as he was called by everyone in the village. It had been enough simply to catch a glimpse of him from where she stood half-hidden inside the shop doorway, or from across the street or over the fence of the manor house demesne. More recently it had been a great joy for her to be able to help nurse him when he was sick, but none of this had counted for anything compared with the ecstasy of being alone in the shop, with The Count sitting before her and telling his tales only to her. This was a joy so magical and so mysteriously exciting that her young spirit was completely conquered. All the grandeur and glitter of which he spoke was to her little more than the natural background to the fairy prince who sat there with her. For her the only reality was the young man himself, and everything that she heard from him was like some metaphysical halo with which he was crowned but of whose existence only she, Regina, was privileged to know, and which only she could see. It seemed to her, too, that this dream prince sought her out, waiting to come to the shop when he would be sure of finding her alone. He would keep watch until her father left the shop on some lengthy errand such as going in to Szamos-Ujvar or visiting his little parcel of thirty acres of land which was farmed for him by some luckless debtor, and then in no time at all he would come in. It only happened occasionally, perhaps once every two or three weeks; but when it did it was certain that Laszlo would appear, and because the shopkeeper's wife also had several smaller children to mind and the household chores to attend to, it was equally certain that the young man and the girl would be left alone together.

Regina believed that he came only to see her and whenever she thought of this her heart seemed to throb high in her throat.

And, of course, in one sense she was right: Laszlo did look for the moments when he would be sure of finding her alone, but it was not her young beauty that drew him to seek her out, indeed he had never even noticed it. He had not even seen that the child was swiftly turning into a desirable young woman. For Laszlo there were two reasons why he chose those moments to go into the shop, and these two reasons were quite enough for him. The first was simply that Regina, unlike her father, poured generous measures of brandy and often of the best without Laszlo having to ask for it; and the second, which for the young man was probably the most important, was that it meant he could talk about

himself and about that magical past when he had had the world
at his feet and which had been so cruelly snatched from him.
He could talk about the Casino Club, and the Park Club, about
dinners and dances in great private houses where he, as *elotancos*,
would lead the dance. He could talk about the perfections of
Countess Beredy and of her exquisite little palace overlooking
the ramparts of old Buda, and of the great white country castle of
the Szent-Gyorgyis. He could describe the grandeurs of princely
parties at the Kollonich palace near Lake Balaton, recounting
over and over again how the state-rooms were decorated and
how they all led out of one another, how the sunlight gleamed
on the myriad gilt bindings of the books in the library, how the
park was laid out like an English garden and how the shooting
parties were organized with precision and stately attention to
precedence. Above all he could talk to his heart's content about
everything that related to his love for Klara. He could describe
her little room where once, and only once, they had kissed; he
could tell of the dresses she wore and of those little bouquets of
saffron-yellow carnations that she always carried as a symbol of
their love. He could tell Regina everything, even if that everything was now long lost to him, and through no one's fault but
his own. In fact he did not tell everything to Regina. He never
told her Klara's name or anything about her except those things
by which she was surrounded, her dresses, scents, flowers, the
rooms through which she moved and the little capes she would
put round her shoulders when going out of doors. Her name and
her person were too sacred to be mentioned or described, in
much the same way as certain primitive peoples hold it taboo to
say the name of their god. For Laszlo the brandy washed away
any hint of self-recrimination and left him only with the euphoria
evoked by his memories of gaiety and beauty and grandeur.

During the previous winter old Marton had occasionally fed his
master on roast hare. He never spoke about how he had obtained
it, indeed he never spoke about it at all but merely put it on the
table. Laszlo was too listless and filled with his own sad thoughts
to notice and at that time merely ate automatically whatever was
put before him. But when the first snows of Laszlo's second
autumn in the cottage began to fall and old Marton served up
roast hare again, his master looked up and said, 'Hare? Where did
you get that?'

He was not particularly interested, and had asked the question only for the sake of something to say.

'It came.'

'What do you mean, it came? Did somebody send it?'

Marton did not reply but gathered up the dishes and, with much clattering of plates and knives and forks, put everything on a tray and carried it out of the room.

Laszlo had often been irritated by the old man's taciturn manner and called after him angrily, 'Will you answer me! Where did that hare come from?'

Marton paused on the threshold of the kitchen and looked back at his master. For an instant a light seemed to glitter in the old man's eyes. Then he muttered, 'It came!' and went out slamming the door behind him.

For years Marton had been a persistent and adroit poacher, and it had been the passion of his life. He had been a widower for many years and he had no friends. Throughout Laszlo's long minority he had lived alone in the unfinished manor house and there had been little change when Laszlo came of age, for he was hardly ever there. The old man was a tied servant who received a living wage from the estate manager and who was able to fatten a couple of yearling pigs annually for himself. He did not need to poach for his dinner but he was drawn to it by some inner yearning for adventure and so that he could feel himself superior to the other folk in the village; for he knew only too well that many of them despised him and thought him mentally deficient. He did not mind, but whenever he trapped a hare he would skin it at once and roast it and as he ate it he would smile to himself not only because he was enjoying a good meal but also because he felt that somehow he had scored over all those who despised him, the villagers, the gamekeepers, and even the estate manager himself.

Old Marton never tired of telling himself that one had to be a pretty clever fellow to be a good poacher. One had to know what wire or thread was right for each kind of trap or snare and he even knew that the best, though hard to come by, were violin strings. While he still lived in the manor house he had found a packet in one of the drawers and, as Laszlo had long before sold his violin, old Marton quickly slipped it into his own pocket. Of course one had to know, too, exactly how to set the snare so that no passer-by should see it and steal it before the game had been caught. Neither was it an easy matter to go round checking the snares, either at dawn or any other time, without being seen by some curious eye. Furthermore one had to have the Devil's own cunning, and a lot of knowledge and experience, before one could succeed in getting one's prey home undetected.

He had been at it for years, but he had only occasionally been able to bring something home for the pot as in those years small game was scarce in that part of Transylvania, especially on such a run-down estate as Kozard.

While he had been lodged in the servants' quarters of the manor house he would set his snares near the boundary of the park. This had been comparatively easy and it had not been necessary to take many precautions against being seen for no one lived nearby; but since he had moved down into the house in the village things had become more complicated. Azbej had the park fences repaired and so old Marton had no excuse if he were discovered wandering about inside. The only hunting ground left was the forest, down by the riverbed and up the hillside beyond. It was more difficult, but also more exciting.

The old poacher laid his plans carefully and, so as not to make himself conspicuous, went out only occasionally, and when it seemed most likely he would catch something, for example when it looked as if it would snow the following day. He knew that hares were particularly sensitive to the weather and at such times always made for the thickest parts of the woods. At such times old Marton would go off to gather kindling: at least that was what he would tell one of the estate game-keepers if they happened to meet and if, and only if, the other man was bold enough to ask what he was doing. This hardly ever occurred for he was known to be surly, a man of few words who usually gave a rude answer if spoken to. The following day at dawn he would visit his traps and snares, and if anything had been caught in the night he would bring it home concealed under his jacket, while he carried a heavy bunch of dry twigs so that anyone could see why he had been in the forest. At such times he would walk with his back bent as if tired out from his heavy labours and heaving great sighs as he staggered past the outlying cottages. And all the time he would exult inwardly, his soul pouring out a paean of triumph and joy, for he knew that he was cleverer than them all, for was he not carrying home the fruits of his illegal poaching under their very noses while they knew nothing, nothing at all?

Of course the whole village knew and had always known, but they would never have told it either to Azbej, whom they hated as a quarrelsome martinet – and a stranger to boot – or to old Marton himself, for if they had let the old man know that everyone knew what he was up to, there would have been no more fun to be got out of it. As it was they watched everything he did. They saw when he sauntered out to the forest pretending to search for kindling, and how he staggered back under huge loads in the morning before stealing off to the next village to sell the skins. They watched the whole comedy and laughed their heads off when he was out of earshot. Even the children would enter into the spirit of the game, sometimes calling out: 'What are you carrying, Uncle Marton?' and when the old man merely growled back 'Can't you see? Wood, of course!' or 'Mind your own business, you little bugger!' they would pull faces behind his back and laugh about it all the following week.

Laszlo knew nothing of all this.

But on that one day it happened that he was stone cold sober and in a foul mood because his weekly allowance had all been spent and at the shop they wouldn't give him any more to drink. Little Regina would have given him something, but it was Friday afternoon and because of the Sabbath Bischitz would not be leaving the shop and so Laszlo would have no opportunity of getting the girl on her own. He got more and more desperate. Money had to be found somehow or he felt he would go mad. At that moment he happened to glance at the worn chest-of-drawers – a worthless piece of furniture from one of the old servants' rooms that Azbej had generously allowed him to take from the manor house. On its top lay a long smooth leather case with triangular little canvas covers on the corners to prevent it from scuffing and a tiny elegant snap-lock. It was an English-made case for a pair of guns, though now it held only one. It had been sent after him from Desmer when Sara Bogdan Lazar had sent back everything that had belonged to him. The feeble lamp cast only a faint glow and yet the smooth hard leather and the brass of the lock and clasps on its leather straps still shone brightly. Laszlo gazed at the case as if hypnotized.

Laszlo had entirely forgotten that he still had it. He got up and looked at it more closely. There, stamped in the leather top, was his name, engraved with a slight spelling mistake – Count Ladislas

Gieroffy – just as it had always been from the time, so long ago, when the pair of guns had been a Christmas present from his two aunts in Western Hungary. He stroked the letters lightly, thinking back to that Christmas in the Kollonichs' great country house when he had been just eighteen. Christmas at Simonvasar! In the library there had been a Christmas tree that reached to the ceiling. The room had been lit by thousands and thousands of candles. Everything had been so bright and Klara had been there . . . in a white dress . . . still very slim and girlish . . . and he could remember her eyes, ocean-grey, and wide open with joy and happiness . . .

For an instant he stood still, lost in his memories. Then he shook himself and pressed back the catch almost with loathing and lifted the lid of the case until it rested against the wall. There lay the gun, its stock and barrel in separate compartments, and there lay too the place for its pair which had been sold long before. He wondered why he had kept this one, he who had no money for brandy, let alone for cartridges.

Of course he must sell it at once, and he wondered why it had not previously occurred to him to do so.

He took out the gun and put it together. It was so perfectly made, as neat as any chronometer, that it opened noiselessly and the stock and barrel fitted together with a barely perceptible click. Slight though this was the sound made Laszlo shudder, for it reminded him of the countless times he had heard the same sound, without then even noticing it, at the great annual shoots at the Szent-Gyorgyis' or the Kollonichs'; and now it was like a great chime of bells from some infinite distance, from a past which was no more. Quickly Laszlo took the gun apart again and put it hurriedly back in its case. He knew he had to get rid of it as quickly as possible.

Grabbing his hat and jacket he ran out of the house like a man pursued.

For a little while Laszlo followed the road through the village, and then he turned off down a track that led to the old fuller's mill on the banks of the Szamos where there lived a man called Fabian. He was known only by his first name for being of Czech or Moravian origin his family name was Szprnad and no one at Kozard could pronounce it properly. He was obviously rich and so had been known as 'The Millionaire' ever since he had arrived in the village a year before. As well as the mill he had bought up a wool-combing business and had also built himself an oil press. He seemed to be half peasant and half townsman and had come from Borgo where, people said, his father had kept an inn. It was soon obvious that he was an astute businessman: he was also a great drinker and sometimes would carouse so long with his friends that the entire supply of beer in the village was consumed and more had to be sent for in a hurry.

Laszlo had first met him in Bischitz's shop and the newcomer had at once bought him so many tots of brandy that Laszlo had passed out and had to be carried home. Fabian had knocked back just as much, but it had not seemed to have any effect on him and indeed he hardly blinked even after more than a dozen gills of the strongest brand. Since that day the two men had formed a sort of drinking friendship – it had no other basis – and from time to time Fabian would carry Laszlo off to Szamos-Ujvar for an orgy of drink and gypsy music and sex with the town whores which would last well into the next day. The local tarts were what one might expect in such a small provincial backwater and as for the gypsies they came mostly from the poorest of their kind whose families scratched a living digging clay. This is what Fabian enjoyed for he could only relax in the sort of company where the music was unbelievably noisy, where he could tear off all his clothes and where the women were fat.

Laszlo went down the little path that had been trodden in the snow until he could see a faint glimmer of light from the fuller's window. The throb of the oil press was like a giant's heartbeat, and Laszlo, knowing that Fabian was often away travelling, prayed that this time he would find him at home.

He was just in time, for round the corner came Fabian driving his sturdy little cart. The fuller was of medium height and broad of shoulder. A white sheepskin hat covered his shaven head and he wore a beard that was trimmed round the corners of his mouth as far back as the ears so as to show off his wide black moustaches of which he was very proud. His thick fleshy exceptionally red lips were full of life and vigour and all the hair on his face seemed to be brushed horizontally sideways. He stopped the cart and greeted Laszlo boisterously.

'What's this, Count? Coming to pay a visit? That's wonderful!' he shouted in a voice of thunder and, although he spoke Hungarian fluently, one could tell from the long-drawn-out vowels that it was not his mother tongue. 'I'll drive you home,' he went

on, 'but I can't stop as I've been asked to supper at Iklod.' And
he shoved out a giant fist and pulled Gyeroffy up beside him as
if he had weighed no more than a feather. They drove on slowly
for the road was all soft snow and mud.

Laszlo said he wanted to sell his gun, a valuable one, made in
England.

'How much?'

'Whatever you say,' answered Laszlo.

'Count, you're mad!' said the fuller laughing, and he gave the
young man a playful push with his massive shoulder. Then he
added, 'I can give you some money if you're short.'

'Certainly not! If you want the gun then buy it ... but no
hand-outs. That I won't accept!'

'Let's have a look at it then.'

They got down at Laszlo's little house and went in. Fabian
bought the weapon at once but refused to take the case even
though Laszlo pressed it on him. What did he need with the case,
said Fabian. It would only get in the way and anyhow it had
Laszlo's name on it. He went out, threw the gun under the seat
in the cart and paid for it at once, two hundred crowns in cash,
which was an absurdly low price for such a splendid double-
barrelled Purdey. Of course Fabian had no idea what a treasure
he was getting and even fancied he was being over-generous.
Then he drove off.

Laszlo remained alone in the darkening room. Two bank notes
lay upon the table before him and so he had enough money to
drink himself into oblivion. With money he could drink, and
with drink he could forget ... and now especially he needed
something to wash away that sentimental heart-ache he had
momentarily felt when Fabian had seized the Purdey with his
great coarse hands and practically run out of the door with it.
Why, he wondered, had that action given him such a sudden stab
of pain? Why now, suddenly, when so long ago he had decided
that anything that reminded him of his lost past was hateful. Oh,
well, it was good that he had seen the last of it!

Laszlo was still barefooted since he had taken off his sodden
boots and socks on coming into the room. He decided he would
have to send old Marton out for brandy so he picked up one of
the notes and stepped out on to the hallway that separated the
part of the house where he lived from Marton's own lodging.
This was a widish room with a fireplace, behind which was the

kitchen that had been used by all the inhabitants of the house
when it had lodged two tenant families. He opened the door
opposite and there was the old servant crouching down on the
floor with a candle beside him: he was stretching the hare-skin
on a plank of wood. Caught in the act he stared up at his master
too dumbfounded to speak. Laszlo burst out laughing.

'You old rogue! Now I've caught you! Out with it, where did
that hare come from?'

'I caught it.'

'How? Not while it was on the run, I'll be bound.'

'With a snare.'

'Bravo indeed! I like that. Very clever. Where, may I ask?'

Balogh did not want to answer that. Still, he said, 'In the
forest.'

'I see! In the forest! Well, if Azbej can steal my forest I suppose
I can steal his hares! Why not? Now go over to Bischitz's and
bring me half a litre of brandy, the best he has. We'll talk about
all this later . . .'

And so Laszlo became a poacher, and his life was changed. In a
few days he had learned the essentials from old Marton, how the
snares were prepared and where were the most likely places to set
them. After a while they would go in turns to the forest, Laszlo in
the evening to set eight or ten snares in places they had already
planned together, and Marton at dawn to collect the game. They
caught two good hares in the first week.

This was the first thing in many years to give Laszlo any pleasure.
His fingers, trained to the intricacies of the violin and keyboard,
soon adapted to tying the most delicate of snares; and these he
hung with such skill and art where his prey had trodden a path
at the foot of a thornbush thicket, or along a branch, that neither
man nor beast could have said they were there.

There was only one snag: he soon found that hares rarely went
deep into the forests when the weather was fine nor even when
the sky was merely overcast. Then they stayed out in the meadows
and ploughed fields. They went to the woods only when it was
exceptionally windy or when there was snow in the air. Then, and
only then, was it worth the effort of setting the traps and snares.

This was not enough for Laszlo, for he had become so fond of
this new game that he wanted to play it every day.

* * *

Between the house where Laszlo lived and the road was some wooden-plank fencing but only on each side, running from the road to the little stream that ran at the bottom of the slope behind the house. On the left there was only a hedge between, a piece of vacant land between Laszlo's little house and Bischitz's shop; while on the right, between it and the grounds of Laszlo's old manor house, Azbej had added a fence of dry sticks near the bank of the stream. There, as the place was sandy and close to water, he had also placed his new hen-run. Azbej had started to raise Orpingtons whose brown eggs were so popular that he hoped to export them even to England. A long hen-house had been built with a flat sandy yard between it and the stream. At the far end, just under the slope of the hill on the top of which had been built the manor house itself, the new owner had built a house for the farm overseer. It was all neat and clean and new – a model chicken-farm – and the yard was filled with big golden hens who scratched disconsolately at its sterile surface where no insects, or worms, or other favourite morsels were to be found. Their eyes darted from left to right as they searched in vain. Their only excitement came, twice a day, when their feed would be brought in . . . and that was all. They were bored. Every so often one would approach the dry-wood fence and peck its way along searching for some way of escape to the Paradise Garden beyond.

Late one afternoon Laszlo strolled down to the bank of the stream near to where old Marton was cutting up a fallen alder tree. The first snows had come and gone and it had been dry freezing weather ever since. That day it had clouded over and Laszlo went down to ask the old man if the snow was coming again, because if so it would be a good moment to set the traps in the woods and he would have time to do it before it got dark.

Marton stopped his work, leaned on his axe and threw back his head. He wiped the sweat from his face and from his long moustaches, and sniffed the air.

'No snow today!' he said laconically.

Laszlo stood there for some time watching the old man as he worked. He felt thoroughly out of temper because he had set his mind on going to the woods that evening. Finally he turned and started slowly to walk back to the house.

The branches of the fallen tree had blocked the garden path so Laszlo was forced to make a detour along the hedge beyond which Azbej had erected his fence. Until that moment Laszlo had been thinking of nothing but his annoyance that the weather was so contrary but now, seeing before him the new wooden fence, the neat poultry-yard, the farm beyond it and, high on the hill behind, the white manor house itself, with its new pink roof shining through the bare winter trees, a fresh thought struck him. For a moment his face darkened with anger as he looked at everything that had once been his and then slowly a wicked smile appeared on his face. Between the laths of the poultry-yard paling he could see a few hens peering at him and all too clearly searching for an opening through which they could reach the tempting worked soil with its wealth of fallen seeds that was waiting for them on the other side.

Laszlo looked around. There was no one in sight, and even old Marton had his back to him.

It was obvious that he would only need one snare, and that the hedge would hide him as he set it.

He hurried back to the house, collected a snare, and a steel screwdriver from the gun-case, and in a moment or two was back by the fence. He bent down and with a swift turn of the screwdriver forced one of the wooden palings out of its lower socket. Then he grasped a live twig from the hedge in front of the opening he had just made, bent its end back in an arc and attached his snare to it. All this was done so swiftly that in a couple of minutes he was back beside the house apparently just idly looking up at the sky. For a while he stood there, every nerve taut. He listened hard. Dusk was falling and this was the moment when all the birds usually found their way back to the hen-house. In less than half an hour they would all be inside again and so there was not much time left for one of them to discover the trap that had been set for it. Laszlo then began to wonder if a trapped bird would make such a noise when the noose tightened that the farm people would be alerted and discover what he had been up to ... and then the shame of being found out. The shame!

For what seemed like an eternity he heard nothing. Then there was a sudden brief fluttering of wings, and then again nothing. The trap had been sprung.

It was almost more than he could do not to run down excitedly. Nevertheless he managed a lazy stroll and, sure enough, from the branch he had so cunningly bent so as to be sprung by the snare, a fine fat Orpington hen was hanging, as dead as anyone could wish. Laszlo unhooked it swiftly, hid it under his coat, and then he did run, as swiftly as possible, back into the house. He felt no remorse at all for having caught one of Azbej's birds, and that what he had done was nothing less than common theft never even passed through his mind. If he thought of it as anything at all it was as a simple act of revenge and as such it gave him the satisfaction of paying back in his own coin someone who had robbed him. The moment that this occurred to him Laszlo's heart took a great leap of joy and triumph; and if he had somehow regained all his lost inheritance it would have made him no happier than he was at that moment.

From that day on Laszlo set his hen-trap every eight or ten days. He always did this on his own for it was obvious that old Marton wanted nothing to do with it. He never spoke his mind, or indeed said anything at all on the subject, but Laszlo sensed that in his book wild game was God's gift to whosoever might catch it but that poultry belonged to the man who raised and fed it. Accordingly, though he would cook any bird that Laszlo took, he would not eat it. He was even reluctant to pluck and draw such birds, so Laszlo found that he had to call upon young Regina to get this done. She came eagerly. All Laszlo had to do was to give the girl a little private nod when he was drinking his tot of brandy in the shop, or a discreet wave from over the hedge, and she would somehow contrive to come at once, no matter what she was supposed to be doing. Though no one could have noticed that she was doing it, Regina somehow managed to keep a permanent watch on Laszlo's house and on him if he were out of doors. For her any reason was enough if she could be near him.

Sometimes when she disappeared from the store her father and mother would start calling for her, and then she would sneak home, making sure that she always appeared to be coming from somewhere quite other than where she had really been. When she went to Laszlo's she would cross the piece of empty land between the houses through the gate that her father had put in the hedge when he had rented it some years before; but she would never come back the same way, for if she had she knew her parents would guess where she had been. A moment or two after they started calling she would reappear as if coming from the stream, or from the roadway, or even from the house opposite; and even though she sometimes got a slap on the face she never let on where she had been.

Her love for Gyeroffy was like that of a faithful hound.

Of course she was still a child and the deep love she felt for the young man was utterly innocent, though she experienced all the ecstasy and suffering of a grown woman. If Laszlo spoke to her she was happy, and she suffered and felt excluded when he talked to other people.

She loathed Fabian. On those occasions when Laszlo and Fabian went into Ujvar together and did not come back until the next morning, she knew instinctively that they had been enjoying themselves with other women – horrible, coarse creatures, no doubt – and she was consumed by jealousy and hurt rage and cried all night. The following day she would try her best to be angry and not keep glancing at Laszlo's house; and she would decide not to go if he should call out for her. But a single word or a casual glance from him was enough to make her forget all her resentment, and then she would once again be his faithful doglike slave. And yet, behind this unthinking bondage, there was something else – a young girl's perennial curiosity about what the act of love was really like. On the days after his trips to the town Regina did all she could to get close enough to him, either in his own house or else in her father's shop, to be able to look closely at him, to study his face and hands and how he moved; and she would lift her delicate straight little nose and sniff the air around him: and when she thought that she had seen or sensed some legacy of that night spent away from home, a strange scent or a bite-mark on his skin, she would become strangely upset and her throat would constrict. It was unspeakably painful . . . and yet mysterious and attractive too.

Just after the New Year a covered carriage drew up outside Laszlo's house. It was nine o'clock at night, and Fabian had come to celebrate his Saint's Day. With him he had brought a huge cold turkey, some savoury biscuits and sweet cakes and a large hamper of brandy and cheap champagne. He also brought two women. The village gypsy musician was sent for at once and he played standing in the kitchen doorway as there was no place for him in Laszlo's room where the four of them dined and danced and sang. Fabian himself always needed plenty of space, for he loved to jump up and hurl himself about, sometimes dancing with both women at once, throwing himself about with wide-flung arms and all the time yodelling at the top of his voice.

News of the party spread quickly through the village and

soon there was a group of neighbours gathered near the house to
listen to the music and find out what was going on. They were
mostly women, and they cross-questioned the driver about the
loose women he had brought and were deliciously scandalized
by what he had to tell. Some of the younger boys and girls started
dancing on the frozen snow-covered ground; but it was bitterly
cold and soon they all went home.

After dinner was over the Bischitz family always sat in the large
room behind the shop in which the family lived and ate. Here the
shopkeeper kept his account books and also any special delicacies
such as sugar and spices and dried figs which might have absorbed
the smells of dried fish or pipe tobacco if these had been kept in
the store-room next door. On this evening old Bischitz sat reading a newspaper while his fat wife dozed in an armchair, worn-
out from the heavy labour of the daily chores. Regina had already
put her younger brothers and sisters to bed and was folding away
the table-cloth and napkins when their servant Juliska rushed in
and disturbed this peaceful domestic scene with the scandalous
news of what was happening over at The Count's house. Neither
of the old people were in the least impressed, and indeed the
shopkeeper himself, angered at the thought that the drinks had
not been bought from him, bawled out the servant for having
left the washing-up to go sight-seeing, promised her a good slap,
chased her back to the kitchen and then turned to his wife and
said: 'Come on, bedtime!'

Regina stood by the cupboard rigid with shock. She was very
pale and her parents had to call her twice before she heard them.

Regina lay quite still next to her sleeping six-year-old sister, but
she could not sleep. One o'clock went by, and two o'clock, and
still she lay there, her ears straining for the faint sound of the
violin music. At length that stopped and for a long time she could
hear nothing, not even the sound of her parents' breathing.

What was happening over there? What could be happening?

At length Regina could stand it no more. She slipped out of
bed, very carefully so as not to wake her sister, felt for her clothes
and somehow managed to get into them in the dark. Then she
felt for her mother's shawl which was always hung on a hook
behind the door, wrapped it round her and stole to the front door.

It was a dark night with no moon and all that could be seen
was a faint bluish glow on the snow. So as not to wake anyone in

the house with the sound of her steps on the wooden floor, she put on her shoes only when she was already outside and on the last rung of the veranda steps. The shoes she wore were a pair of once fashionable high-heeled but sadly worn ladies' button boots which would have reached up to mid-calf if most of the buttons had not been missing. They had previously been worn by her mother until it had not seemed worth mending them any more.

Regina moved slowly across the frozen yard, her feet skidding on the hard-trodden surface of the snow. She reached the corner of the woodshed and, from the gate in the fence, looked across the empty field towards Laszlo's house. There was a light in the window, a sinister reddish light; and to the girl it seemed as if the wicked flames of hell were beckoning to her and calling for her to come and look.

Clutching the heavy shawl around her she stumbled across the field in which her father had been growing potatoes. Where these had been lifted the earth had been left in uneven little mounds and ridges and holes so that, as the young girl headed straight for the light in the window, she stumbled and slipped and fell frequently to her knees, as her thin, dark figure made its tortured way across. If anyone had been watching it would have looked as if she were battling against a hurricane, staggering to left and to right as she struggled on through the dark night.

Finally she got there. There was not a sound to be heard and only the light that filtered out through the flower-like hoarfrost on the window-panes showed that anyone was still awake inside.

Regina crept up and pressed her face against the lowest pane, despite the fact that it was almost opaque from the ice-crystals that had formed an incrustation of dense arabesques on the glass. Obsessed by the need to know what was happening inside she would have broken the glass itself if that had been the only way. She had to know, she had to! That was why she had come. She started to breathe on the window-pane and then to rub it with a corner of the shawl. Several times she had to repeat the process until at last a small patch at the centre began to come clear as she managed to melt a square no larger than her own little hand.

With searching eyes she looked round the room, her body rigid with emotion and excitement, her hand tightly grasping the window-ledge. She stretched up her neck with the folds of the shawl falling like mourning bands on each side of her face.

She was very pale, except for her blood-red lips, and it was some time before she was able to see clearly what was happening in the room. It was even longer before she realized what it was, and longer still before she really understood.

For a long time she stood where she was, as if turned to stone. Then, overcome by deep disgust, she started shuddering and at length was able to force herself to turn away. Then she reeled from the window and started to run for home, heedless of how she fell and stumbled and tripped in mindless panic. She ran with eyes wide open as if by so doing she could run far away from what she had seen. She ran as a deer pursued by hounds ...

In Regina's head was nothing but the thought of escape. She clattered up the wooden steps of her father's house, fell against the door and then, though somehow she succeeded in opening it, fell senseless across the threshold.

Regina was ill for days and during all this time, though her parents looked after her with loving care, they never discovered where she had been that night. As it happened they never even asked her for they assumed that it was all the result of a fright she had had for, either as a result of being over-excited, or from the effects of her fall, that night she stopped being a child and became a woman.

As for Laszlo he hardly noticed Regina's absence. For some days after that evening's drinking he had lazed about, tired and listless. Fabian had left behind three bottles of brandy, perhaps on purpose, perhaps merely from forgetfulness; and so Laszlo had enough to drink without going to the shop. For some weeks he did not think about setting his traps and so had no need of Regina.

Now he started to cough rather more than before.

When Regina got better their relationship was unchanged. Once again she was ready to do anything he asked but she was, if anything, quieter than before. She was also very pale, and her large brown eyes seemed framed in some bluish dew.

CHAPTER TWO

THE GENERAL PEACE that Europe had known since 1878 finally came to an end in the summer of 1911. The year began without any apparent change but then gradually a few hardly noticeable signs appeared whose significance was only understood much later and then only by those whose business it was to search out the truth of what had occurred. Though these little signposts were so scattered and apparently trivial, for the few who understood such things they showed only too clearly that the general air of calm throughout Europe was at best only an illusion. They were like the faint grey mist on the horizon at sunset or the soft mysterious murmur that precedes an earthquake.

Nothing that happened early that year seemed to suggest that the general confidence in a perpetual peace was not entirely justified. When Prince Nikita celebrated the fiftieth anniversary of his reign by declaring Montenegro to be a kingdom, and the monarchs of Italy, Bulgaria and Serbia all attended the festivities, it seemed to be no more than a family get-together . . . and there was nothing to foretell the coming alliance. A few months later there was another outbreak of unrest in Albania – but no one thought there might be any connection with what had transpired in Montenegro, for was there not always unrest in Albania? When, from the other end of Europe, the news came that the Dutch, that most peaceable of nations, were fortifying Vlissingen, there was a universal outcry, with the English press seeing the sinister hand of the Emperor Wilhelm, who no doubt envisaged a new base for his growing fleet that was only an hour or so from the coast of Great Britain and the English Channel. And when, some months later, the Dutch government countermanded their orders, it was everywhere said that this was forced on them by strong protests from England and France. Accordingly when this little tempest blew itself out, just as had the much bigger one provoked by the annexation of Bosnia-Herzegovina a year or so before, it seemed that all such affairs were but storms in teacups which were bound, sooner or later, to be settled amicably by all concerned. A few discussions over a green baize table, an exchange of diplomatic letters, and all was as it always had been. Even most of the diplomatists thought of international affairs in this way and so it was natural for the general public to follow their example. When it was announced in Vienna that the army was to be increased and the navy given a grand new ship-building programme, most people read the news with indifference, believing it all to be little more than just one more manifestation of *folie de grandeur* on the part of the Emperor Franz-Josef.

In the Budapest Parliament all went smoothly enough, and even the prolongation until 1917 of the Austro-Hungarian banking law passed off with little more than the expected public bickering between Justh and the People's Party on one side and the Economic Minister Lukacs and Ferenc Kossuth on the other. However, as this all seemed merely part of the aftermath of the Coalition period, nobody showed any interest. That these old rifts in the former Coalition were now seeing the light of day for the first time, and were shown to be little more than the private disputes of professional politicians, once again only proved to most people that what the former leaders of the Coalition said and what they did were quite different matters.

It was typical of that long period of international calm that one of the French princes, Gaston d'Orléans, Comte d'Eu, should choose that moment to launch an anti-duelling league! To round up support he travelled all over Europe, stopping in every provincial capital where he thought a branch should be founded. Anyone who joined had to pledge themselves to take any affair of honour to some predetermined court and to abstain from having recourse to sabres or pistols.

The idea was sensible and the prince's motives commendably lofty.

Gaston d'Orléans himself was an eminent and distinguished personage whose wife would have become Empress of Brazil if her father, Pedro II, had not been overthrown by the ungrateful Brazilians. He was received everywhere with the courtesy and ceremony to which his rank entitled him; and wherever he went a branch of his anti-duelling league was founded at once with its full complement of president, general secretary, statutes and plans for regular meetings. It was of course most flattering to be able to refer to this royal prince, the grandson of King Louis-Philippe no less, as one's colleague and chief, and it was nice to be known to share the opinions of such an eminent person. The Comte d'Eu lived in Paris and no doubt, if under his wing, one would soon find oneself received in the most select houses in the Faubourg St Germain.

In Budapest the League was headed by some impressive names and, through the Countess Beredy's influence, her brother, Fredi Wuelffenstein, was made the general secretary. From Hungary the prince was going on to Bucharest and so it was arranged that he should stop on the way at Kolozsvar so as to found the Transylvanian branch of the Anti-Duelling League.

There too he was received with honour and on the evening of his arrival a 'brilliant reception' (as the newspapers called it) was given for him at the Casino. It was followed by a banquet. Everyone with any pretensions to social prominence in Transylvania took care to be there.

An enormous U-shaped table had been set up in the hall. In the centre of the top table sat the prince flanked on one side by Sandor Kendy (Crookface) wearing the Cross of St Istvan, and on the other by Stanislo Gyeroffy (Carrots) who, when he had briefly been a member of Szapary's cabinet, had managed to be awarded the Grand Cross of Alexander for having participated in the negotiations which had led to the signing of a trading agreement with Bulgaria. In addition to the cross itself Gyeroffy was swathed in the wide red, green and white ribbon of the order. By right of these impressive decorations, which entitled their possessors to be addressed as 'Excellency', Crookface and old Gyeroffy had the places of honour on each side of the royal guest and they, in turn, were flanked by all the other local notabilities placed according to the strictest rules of precedence. Among them were the Prefect and his immediate predecessor, the Sheriff, the Mayor, the Rector of the University and various prominent churchmen, as well as most of the provincial titled folk. They made a fine display and as background to the top table had been hung a magnificent Gobelins tapestry.

Facing the guest of honour were the other Sandor Kendy (known as 'Wiggles'), the elder Adam Alvinczy and Major Bogacsy, now retired from the army and acting as chairman of the orphans' Court of Chancery. These were the official hosts.

Now that Bogacsy was no longer a serving officer he was dressed in civilian evening dress and the only thing left to remind one of his belligerent past was an enormous pair of moustaches which resembled nothing so much as a large black pudding suspended over his mouth. He wore the insignia of the Order of Maria-Theresa, which had been awarded him for some deed of bravery in the Bosnian war though what that had been no one knew, for he never alluded to it himself. When Bogacsy did talk about his past he only referred to his prowess at innumerable duels where he had always been much in demand as a second.

Bogacsy was very angry. No one had told him why Transyl-vania was being honoured by the visit of this foreign prince and until he had arrived in the hall all he knew was the name of the guest in whose honour the town was giving a banquet. As a director of the Casino he had naturally taken his place at the head of the stairs to welcome the distinguished visitor and then, as they were waiting for the dinner to be announced, stood for a while chatting with him in the smoking-room. The Comte d'Eu was at his most affable as he talked to the three official hosts and then, in tolerably good German, he started talking about the League for which he was seeking support:

'*Es ist eine verachtenswürdige Sache, dass man in unserem aufgek-lärtem Jahrhundert noch immer duelliert. Das Duell ist pure Barbarei – nicht wahr? Und ausserdem auch ein schrecklicher Blödsinn! Das ist wohl auch ihre Meinung?* – it is a disgraceful thing that in this enlight-ened age men still go in for duelling. The duel is pure barbarism, is it not? Apart from being frightfully stupid! I'm sure you agree, don't you?'

This was said directly to Bogacsy, and the prince then went on to explain how utterly idiotic duelling was: the winner was naturally the man who was a better shot or who knew best how to wield a sword, and what had this to do with who was in the right? It was stupid and unworthy of sensible men and a shameful legacy of the past!

Bogacsy was outraged and almost apoplectic with rage. It was not for him to start contradicting such an eminent guest and yet he knew that everyone within earshot was watching his reactions and with their true Transylvanian sense of the absurd were inwardly laughing at his predicament. Despite the restraint that was imposed by good manners Bogacsy was so angry at the thought of all that silent mockery that surrounded him that he would have exploded in protest if dinner had not then been announced. A difficult moment was somehow avoided; but the duelling major was still so upset that he could hardly touch any of the delicious dishes put before him, even though he had had to fork out twenty-five crowns for his dinner, which even then was by no means cheap.

At the end of one of the wings of the great U-shaped table was seated old Daniel Kendy. Remembering that he spoke French fluently as a result of having once been an attaché in the Austro-Hungarian Embassy in Paris in the last years of the Third Empire, the organizers had decided that he ought to be invited so that when dinner was over they could introduce him to the prince who would therefore be able to talk to someone who knew Paris well. As the old man had no money his nephew Crookface Kendy paid for his ticket, but as a broken-down old fellow of no importance he was seated some away from the guest of honour. It was important to see that old Uncle Dani did not, as he usually did, drink too much. On this occasion the old man swore that he would not, and indeed was full of good intentions, so happy was he at the thought of coming again into his own and being made much of as the old social lion who had once been a favourite at the court of the Empress Eugénie and well known as a man-about-town in Paris in the years that followed. He decided that this night he must do all in his power to be at his best.

He had shaved and dressed with great care, and indeed the effect was impressive. Count Daniel Kendy for the first time in years looked truly distinguished and many eyes were upon him. His slightly thinning silver-white hair was parted in the middle and set off his jet-black eyebrows and aristocratically aquiline nose. His moustaches had been curled for the occasion and beneath his lower lip was an elegant little goatee. The whiskers on each side of his face were long but neatly trimmed, and with the low folded collar, wide lapels and broad starched white shirt and old-fashioned evening suit, he seemed the perfect evocation of the dandified *boulevardier* of a half a century before. His appearance was so striking that the prince immediately asked who he was; and when told his name and history by Crookface, at once declared that he remembered him well from the days when the French royal family had first returned from exile abroad. 'Of course!' he cried. 'Le Comte Candi!' (which is what all the susceptible ladies in those Parisian drawing-rooms had called him). The name still seemed to have a dreamy, erotic ring to it.

Uncle Daniel also recognized the prince, but he could not remember if he had seen him at the Rochechouarts' or at the Princesse de la Moskowa's. At that time Daniel Kendy was a young man with great expectations for whom everybody predicted a brilliant future. If he had not wasted his fortune on drink he too would have been addressed as 'Your Excellency' today. He would have been seated at the right hand of the royal guest, covered in orders and ribbons and distinctions, and not where he now found himself, in an insignificant place amid a noisy rabble of ill-behaved young men. Looking up at the notabilities in the place of honour, all resplendent in their decorations with the noble Gobelins tapestry behind them, Uncle Dani's heart was filled with sorrow and remorse.

As the dinner progressed he became sadder and sadder and sadder.

And what does one do when one's heart is filled with sorrow? One drinks: there is nothing else. And so the old man drank and, once started, he did not stop and the inevitable happened. When the time came for that meeting to which he had so much looked forward and they called to him to come up and be presented, the old man was already so drunk that he could hardly put one foot in front of the other. Then, once again, the sad thought of what he had once been and what, through no one's fault but his own, he had thrown away, once more pierced his poor fuddled brain and all that he was able to do was to stagger towards the prince, weaving from right to left and bending double at every step in a humble parody of a bow, waving his arms, and stammer out sorrowfully in Hungarian, 'K-K-Kendy! . . . n-n-nothing more . . . K-K-Kendy . . . n-n-nothing more . . .'

He was incapable of uttering another word. As the Comte d'Eu turned away, two young men grabbed Uncle Dani by the arms and carried him out; for everyone knew what was likely to happen when he started bowing so obsequiously.

At one of the side wings of the table sat Balint with Gazsi Kadacsay. Because he was a Member of Parliament and also an imperial Court Chamberlain the organizers had wanted to place him with the other important guests, but he had refused, preferring to remain with his own close friends to being put on parade at the boredom of the top table. Furthermore when they had met that evening Gazsi had said that he wanted to have a talk with him.

They had not seen each other for some time. At the beginning of the Carnival season Gazsi had been in Kolozsvar for a week or two, and then he had disappeared and been seen no more. At that time everyone had decided that he would shortly announce his engagement to Ida Laczok, for he had dined there three times, danced with her often, and called daily at the Laczok house at the hour when they drank coffee topped with whipped cream.

He had even serenaded the girl twice in a week, and so everyone had said that the engagement was imminent. Then he had suddenly returned to the country and was seen no more.

At the beginning of the dinner the conversation where Balint and Gazsi were sitting was all about the royal prince's tour to promote his famous Anti-Duelling League. As they were all young and high-spirited, as well as being from Transylvania, their talk was full of mockery. Among them only Isti Kamuthy and Fredi Wuelffenstein, who were sitting just opposite Balint, took the matter at all seriously; Fredi, not only because he was the league's general-secretary in Hungary but also because he always liked to know better than anyone else; and Isti, because he had recently become even more anglophile than ever. 'There are no duelth in England,' lisped Isti, and for him this settled the question and therefore there could be no further argument about it. Fredi was in perfect agreement, but he was out of temper because he had also thought of the same argument but had not been able to get it out first.

The general conversation was not able to continue for long, for almost at once Laji Pongracz and his musicians entered the hall and started to play and from then on it was only possible to talk to one's neighbour.

It was Kadacsay who started.

'I think I owe you something of an explanation,' he said to Balint. 'I only came this evening because I knew you'd be here.'

'Why?' said Balint, surprised. 'What about?'

'About Ida. I know there's been a lot of talk, and that it's not been all that flattering as far as I'm concerned. I don't mind what other people think, but I'd hate you to think badly of me too.'

Balint protested that he had no reason to think badly about Gazsi, but the latter went on, saying that when he had returned home from his visit to Denestornya he had thought a lot about Abady's suggestion that he should get married and that this would be a solution to many of his problems and perplexities. Finally he decided to try out the idea. He had already decided that young Ida was the only girl who might suit him and who, as a woman, he felt he could bring himself to love. Accordingly he had come to Kolozsvar in the middle of January and at first everything had gone swimmingly. The old Laczoks seemed pleased at the idea of having Gazsi as their son-in-law, so much so that Gazsi admitted to have been quite taken by surprise. 'To think that of an ass like me . . .' he had said to Balint in a self-deprecating manner. But though everything went exceptionally well, they never seemed to get further than just dancing together and exchanging jokes. The girl was pretty enough, but somehow this had not seemed quite enough to Gazsi. Surely, he had thought, there must be something more if one was to spend a lifetime together. One would have to know what she thought about things, what interested her, and what her opinions were.

'Well,' he said. 'That was really the problem. The poor girl is very, very stupid!'

He had tried her on all sorts of subjects, some of them quite serious; but when he had started like this, all the silly thing could do was either to stare at him stupidly or start to giggle. She had seemed to think that he was trying to make fun of her and so replied 'What an odd question!' and changed the subject to cooking, or poultry, or even horses as if she knew that that was all the poor boy really understood. When he had asked what she was then reading, she would answer 'Nothing! Nothing at all! After all what's the use? A good housekeeper doesn't have time for that sort of thing!'

'It was terrible,' said Gazsi, and went on to tell Balint how he had finally revolted and dropped his pursuit of the girl. 'Could I take someone like that into my home? Could I really live my life with such a goose . . . and go on breeding brats even more useless than me . . . ?'

He said he had decided he could not bear the thought of someone who just could not understand what he would want for his children. She would destroy everything for which he had struggled; and this was what he had felt he must explain to Balint, lest his friend should think he had behaved badly in making people think he had pursued the girl and then abandoned her.

'I shouldn't think badly of you,' said Balint. 'Who am I to judge other people? Nobody has that right, nobody! And I least of all!'

As he said this Balint's own face clouded over for he was reminded of the time when he had made that sweet little Lili Illesvary think that he was about to propose to her and had then let the opportunity go by without saying what had been expected of him. Suddenly he remembered how she looked in the library at Jablanka and how she had gazed expectantly at him with her forget-me-not blue eyes . . .

After that Gazsi and Balint did not speak for some time, so engrossed were they in their own private thoughts.

All at once Gazsi made a gesture with his hand as if he were brushing away some depressing thought. Then he drained his champagne glass, cleared his throat and turned back to Balint with the cryptic phrase, 'I've had Honeydew serviced!'

'Good God, why? She's your best hunter, isn't she?' Balint was taken by surprise at this statement until he reflected that this was not the first time that Gazsi recently had no longer seemed so keen on what everyone had thought to be his only interest. Perhaps this was just one further example of his new-found disillusionment with horses and sport? Whatever it signified it seemed to Balint that somehow Gazsi's pronouncement was connected with that unexpectedly deep strain of bitterness he had shown each time the two friends had met during the last year.

'Yes, last week. I sent her to "Gallifar" who is standing at stud at Kolozs. He's got a good line – by Gunnersbury out of Gaillarde – quite worthy of my good Honeydew.'

Then he went on, speaking in a low voice as if confiding deadly secrets, to give his reasons in a most unnecessarily complicated way, with much repetition and circumlocution. He said that Honeydew was already seven years old which meant it was high time she foaled, and the right age to produce something good and healthy. She was anyhow no use as a saddle-horse for anyone except himself as she would tolerate no one else on her back. It had recently, he said, become an intolerable slavery for him as he had always to be there to exercise her, for he couldn't entrust her to anyone else and it was no life for a horse just to be lunged for a couple of hours a day. This was much the best solution, for she'd calm down as soon as she was in foal. Then her temperament was sure to change and she'd no longer be so dependent on him.

'What on earth would become of her if I wasn't there ... I mean, if ... if I were to go off on some tr-r-rip. As a r-r-riding horse she'd just die ... At least in this way she'll be of some use.'

Balint found these words disquieting, for he seemed to see in them some connection with their talk at Denestornya when Kadacsay had talked about making his will and about his attitude to death. So as to lighten the mood he answered as if he had taken literally what Gazsi had said about going off on some trip.

'If you're thinking of being away some time, which I think

would be a thoroughly good idea, then I'd suggest Italy. It's already spring there, especially down in the South, at Naples and in Sicily. You could have Honeydew sent over to Denestornya while you're away and we'll give her a paddock all of her own so that she could run free all day long. We often do this with new mares who don't know the other horses.'

'Could I really? Do you mean it?' cried Gazsi joyfully. 'Are you really sure? Do you know I was just working up to asking you if it might be possible . . . not now, of course . . . not yet. But, but, later . . . if the situation arises . . . well, it would be wonderful.' And then, seeing the concern in his friend's expression, he started to talk about all sorts of technical matters concerned with the treatment of mares in foal. He told Balint that he really didn't have anyone at his own home who was properly qualified and experienced, not like the stud groom at Denestornya, and all the others who had worked for Countess Roza for so many years. A first foaling was always a bit tricky, of course, and quite a delicate matter, especially with such a highly-strung animal as Honeydew. Then he started to praise all his mare's good points and went out of his way to say that problems only arose when one put a saddle on her or tried to ride her; then she would grow wild, but at all other times she was as tame and docile as anyone could wish. If she didn't have a saddle on her back then she would never kick out, not at man or beast, never!

He talked on for some time, having apparently entirely recovered his good humour. Then he reached for his glass, filled it to the brim and lifted it to Balint, saying: '*Servus* – greetings! My appreciation and thanks . . . in Honeydew's name.'

While Balint and Gazsi had been talking about the problem mare, on the other side of the table Isti and Fredi had been ever more heatedly discussing their favourite topic – England. They both worshipped England and all things English, the country itself, English gentlemen, English horses, English sports, English clothes and footwear, English girls, English bandages for horses' tendons, English guns and cartridges, English razors, English gardens and English dances. All these things they praised, sometimes in unison and sometimes antiphonally, and for a long time all went smoothly. Gradually, however, this harmony somehow produced discord and by the time coffee was served a real quarrel had started. It all began because Fredi, though he spoke English well and knew many English people, had never set foot in the country and so had had to adore his beloved one from afar, and content himself with what he heard second-hand. Isti Kamuthy, on the other hand, spoke English deplorably and had not only been in London the previous year but had also managed to be made a temporary visiting member of that eminent gentlemen's club, the St James's.

It had come about in the following way. Isti had been extremely active in helping the government candidate at a by-election at Szilagy towards the end of the Coalition. The man had been elected, and when they were all back in Budapest Isti had been singled out for praise by the then Minister for Internal Affairs. Isti, seeing his advantage, had at once stammered out, 'I h-h-have a r-r-request!' and, when encouraged by Andrassy to blurt it out, said that he would shortly be going to London and would be most grateful for an introduction to the Austro-Hungarian ambassador. Of course he had got his letter and had presented it to the ambassador, Count Mensdorf, as soon as he arrived. Mensdorf asked Isti how he could be of service and it turned out that Isti had only one request and that was somehow to be invited to join the St James's Club.

The request had verged on the absurd for, in the view of most foreigners and especially of the diplomatic corps, the St James's was then thought to be the most exclusive club in England to which very few Englishmen aspired even if they possessed the most exalted social background. To be admitted one had to fulfil the most stringent, even if unwritten, conditions; and these applied as much to foreign diplomatists as they did to native Englishmen. A few diplomats had been accepted, but so few that it had been taken as a special mark of distinction. Mensdorf did his best to explain all this to Isti, adding that, according to English etiquette, new members must not speak to any existing member until the other had first introduced himself. This meant that even if Isti did get in it might still be several years before he managed to make any friends and so, the ambassador suggested, it would really be more sensible if Count Kamuthy dropped the idea altogether. He proposed a wealth of other, most tempting, ideas – invitations to spend the weekend at the houses of well-known peers, shooting parties in Scotland, a car-trip through some of England's most beautiful countryside, house-parties for the famed Cowes Regatta. Isti was unimpressed. He wanted only one thing, to be elected to the St James's, and this was his only request. Nothing else. Absolutely nothing else!

It happened that Mensdorf was closely related to King Edward and so he had considerable influence in social affairs. He bestirred himself and the miracle happened: Kamuthy was accepted.

So, for the two weeks that Isti was in England he was to be seen, day after day, from morning till evening, sitting at one of the first-floor windows of the St James's Club gazing proudly out into Piccadilly. No one spoke to him and even the club servants hardly tried to conceal their contempt. Isti did not care. He could sit there in the window, surrounded by huge mirrors, happy in the knowledge that the thousands of people who passed along the street in front of him could look up and envy him and that, among all the more than seven million inhabitants of London there was barely one who was so privileged as to have the right to sit there behind the glass and drink his tea in the sight of all. It was a heavenly feeling.

After his two weeks Isti had come home. Though he had studied his Baedeker until he almost knew it by heart, all he had seen of England were the rooms of his club. It is true that he had marched through some of the museums, not because he was interested by anything he saw there but rather so that he had something to talk about when he returned. And talk he did. Even now he was telling Fredi about his experiences; and this was the origin of their quarrel. When Isti said that he had become a member of the St James's, Fredi was so jealous that he turned as yellow as if he were suffering from jaundice. From then on if Isti used an English word, Fredi would correct his pronunciation. 'You don't say "Anglish" but "Inglish", "Waterloo" not "Water-low", "mewseum" not "mooseum".' Fredi became insufferable and Isti couldn't bear it. He spluttered out that 'thomebody who had never been in England shouldn't prethume to correct him', and at this Fredi rejoined that if one didn't speak English it was ridiculous to go there.

The quarrel got noisier and noisier and Laji Pongracz, who was not far away, heard it and promptly switched to an even louder csardas in an attempt to cover up what was happening. Even so some of those sitting nearby were beginning to notice, and Kadacsay called across the table, 'Watch it, you two! People are listening.'

Whereupon the two would-be Englishmen stopped arguing

and sat next to each other in grim silence. Before long Wuelffen-stein could stand it no longer and, so as to have the last word, turned to Isti and said scornfully, 'Anyhow I don't believe you ever set foot in the St James's!'

Kamuthy swelled with rage and, scarlet in the face at being denied his triumph, jumped up and lisped at the top of his voice, 'Thatth nothing but ungentlemanly intholence! Intholent and ungentlemanly!'

'How dare you?' cried Wuelffenstein, also jumping up and at the same time banging the table with his enormous fist so that a coffee-cup was overturned and went clattering on to the floor. It was fortunate that Stanislo Gyeroffy chose the same moment to rise from the table and with considerable presence of mind guide his royal guest away from the scene of battle into the quiet of the smoking-room. Amidst the noise of everyone getting up from table the Comte d'Eu himself was quite unaware that any-thing untoward had happened. Posting himself in front of the fireplace he proceeded to give a long scholarly dissertation on the history and development of duelling to the group of obsequi-ous old gentlemen who had accompanied him out of the hall.

Bogacsy was there too, sitting facing the prince. He did not remain there long because almost as soon as he had sat down Farkas Alvinczy came up to the back of his chair and whispered a few words in his ear. Then he vanished. The retired soldier's eyes glinted but he did not move because at that moment the prince was looking in his direction. Somehow it seemed that his great handlebar moustaches had grown even longer as Bogacsy's mouth widened in a smile of pure joy. As soon as the Comte d'Eu's attention was engaged elsewhere Bogacsy got up and quietly left the room, leaving an empty place in the royal circle.

Kamuthy's seconds were already waiting for him in the so-called Ladies' Dining Room on the other side of the stairway. They were Joska Kendy, who stood there silently sucking on his pipe, and a mild young man called Garazda who came originally from Western Hungary and was now in his third year at the uni-versity in Kolozsvar. The usual stern greetings were exchanged with much formal ceremony but no shaking of hands. Then Fredi's seconds, Bogacsy and Alvinczy, sat down on one side of the table and Isti's on the other.

Then the traditional words were uttered, 'Our client, Count Nandor Wuelffenstein, demands satisfaction.'

All went according to the customary procedure, and in a few moments everything had been settled. There was no question of a reconciliation, nor of a Court of Honour as was recommended by the Anti-Duelling League to all its members. Armed satisfaction then? Of course! Swords? Naturally! Both sides agreed to light cavalry sabres. Up to what point? Disability, of course! When . . . ?

This was a problem, for Fredi, as general-secretary of the League in Hungary, was expected to accompany the prince as far as the Romanian border; and the prince was due to leave at five a.m. It was too late to change any of these arrangements.

'Well then,' said young Garazda, 'what about when he gets back from the border?'

'Certainly not!' said Bogacsy peremptorily. 'The Code Duverger expressly states that if both parties to a duel are present nothing shall prevent the meeting taking place. The duel can take place at once, tonight. It isn't even eleven yet; by midnight the whole affair will be settled.'

'Very well, but where? The Gymnasium is now closed and there is no other suitable hall.'

'But there is!' roared Bogacsy triumphantly. 'Right here! This room is quite big enough if we push the table to one side. The floor isn't too slippery, in fact it's just right. As one of the Casino's directors I hereby give my official permission.'

Then they got down to details. Two medical men would have to be rousted out of their beds and made to attend. Bogacsy had a pair of light cavalry sabres at his apartment and Farkas Alvinczy two more. They would send for them and the two opponents could draw lots as to which pair was used.

Then Farkas said, in a worried tone, 'Where on earth can we find a sabre-sharpener at this hour? Mine are as blunt as anything.'

Here the major interrupted, saying proudly, 'Mine are sharp as razors! And my man can sharpen the others. He's very good at it: I taught him myself!'

To make sure that all went smoothly certain responsibilities had to be allocated. Garazda undertook to rouse Kamuthy's doctor, while Farkas agreed to get the other, and also to collect his two swords. Bogacsy, as a director of the Casino and one of the hosts at the banquet, could not leave the building while the prince was still under its roof, and so he asked Joska to go to his flat and wake his valet who would collect everything necessary and bring it all over, the sabres and the honing instruments. And so it was arranged that everything could be done at once and precisely as it should be.

Bogacsy now returned to the smoking-room and, finding that no one had usurped his chair, sat down again where he had been facing the prince, who was still in full flood. The duelling major listened with joy in his heart.

'. . . and from where, I ask you, does duelling stem? Who started this barbaric habit? I tell you, gentlemen, it is the last survival of the mediæval *auto-da-fé*. In those benighted times people still believed that God would intervene and give victory to the one with right on his side, to the gentle and true in heart, while the sinner would perish miserably. Even then, of course, they were apt only to let the most experienced swordsmen take their chance with God's judgement. But today, gentlemen, today? Who believes that Divine Providence has anything to do with the outcome? Who on earth would be bothered with such nonsense? Nowadays we all know that the victor is he who has had most practice, be it with swords or pistols. Why, the vilest man can kill the most honest! It is terrible, really terrible!'

An approving murmur greeted these words. Even Crookface belched out something, but whether it was in agreement with the royal proposition remained doubtful. Bogacsy, however, nodded his head vigorously at every word.

This was only to be expected for the battling ex-officer had been uncomfortably aware of what a ridiculous figure he had cut before dinner when all the young men, especially those who were now standing about in the background, had been mocking his predicament. Now it was his turn to lead their silent mockery of the philanthropic prince; and the turn of those mocking young brats to admire him, Bogacsy, the perfect second who could listen so impassively to the royal visitor's absurdly inopportune speeches. Nothing showed in his expression, for it was a golden rule where duelling was concerned, that no one spoke of the encounter until after it had happened. So he sat there stiffly, with his legs stretched out and his paunch protruding, the very picture of authority and elegant sangfroid. He knew he was doing it right and that everyone else knew it too.

It seemed that the royal guest would never stop. On and on he talked – for about an hour and a half – in good German and well-turned phrases. Of course his fluency was helped by the fact that he had said all this many times before, in several different languages and many different countries. And of course, too, he was listened to in deferential silence. There were no interruptions and no disturbances; how could there be?

After half an hour had passed young Garazda came quietly up to Bogacsy's chair and whispered something in his ear. Later Farkas Alvinczy did the same thing, and later still it was Joska's turn. There was nothing conspicuous about it, for each message was delivered discreetly and quietly. Bogacsy himself merely nodded acknowledgement of whatever he had been told, and these nods could equally well have been taken as tacit approval of the Prince's plea to end duelling in Europe.

At long last the Comte d'Eu got up, and so did everyone else, straightened his elegant figure, looked with his sad grey eyes at the people near him, thanked them for their hospitality and warm welcome, and said how touched he was to find himself surrounded by so many people in tune with his philanthropic movement. He had hardly, he said, expected to meet with such success, such understanding and such sympathy among the people of a nation so traditionally warlike as the Hungarians and was surprised, as well as delighted, to encounter such support from those whose habit had always been to settle everything with a sword. And yet, here he was and everybody he met seemed to be in perfect agreement with him and to be only too happy to join the league against duelling. He said he felt filled with renewed strength and confidence and was now quite sure that very soon duelling would disappear for ever and be thought of only as one of the errors of the past.

'*Dank, meine Herren. Dank, Dank, Dank* – thank you, gentlemen, thank you, thank you, thank you!'

These words were greeted by well-bred, if slightly muted, applause; and nobody seemed to notice that at the back, from the direction of the card-room, came some hastily suppressed giggles.

Surrounded by the Casino's three directors and, as befitted his exalted rank, preceded by two footmen carrying tall candelabra, the prince was escorted down the stairs. Just as he reached the swing-doors into the street there was a moment's interruption as a little man with a turned-up collar and carrying a small Gladstone bag scurried in. The newcomer quickly effaced himself, flattening himself modestly against the dark wall of the vestibule. No one noticed that he carried a bottle of disinfectant under one arm and that his pockets were stuffed with bandages!

He was one of the doctors that Bogacsy had sent for to attend the duel.

Though he was a trifle late Wuelffenstein managed somehow to get to the train on time. He was wearing what might have been a white turban on his head and his suddenly swollen nose was decorated with a wide Leukoplast dressing.

He was in a thoroughly bad temper for young Kamuthy had not only opened up his scalp but also slashed him on the nose, which was far more humiliating. Stupid ass! thought Fredi. Dwarfish little beast!

It so happened that, on the command to attack, Wuelffenstein, awkward as some tall men sometimes are, swung out his sword-arm in a wide arc, and little Isti, like an enraged hamster, had jumped in, hit him on the nose with his sword-hilt and given him a nasty slash on the forehead which had needed eight stitches to patch up. But that was not the end of it. The worst moment came when Fredi's nose started to bleed and that was when the fight was stopped, though not the nosebleed which continued ignominiously until the flow had been stemmed by two huge wads of cotton-wool which nearly suffocated him. Now he could only breathe through his mouth and he was racked with anxiety as to how he would look the following day with his nose all black and blue. It was a dreadful thought.

It did not help Fredi's good humour that the Comte d'Eu, instead of going at once to his grand sleeping compartment, insisted on waiting on the platform for Fredi to arrive, and when he did plied him with such solicitous enquiries that Fredi was forced to go into endless untrue explanations to excuse the condition he found himself in, for it would hardly have done for the general-secretary of the Anti-Duelling League to admit to having settled an affair of honour with sabres on the very evening that the league had held its first meeting in Kolozsvar. Up in smoke would have gone Fredi's pride in his new royal acquaintance, gone the dreams of success in the exclusive drawing-rooms of the Faubourg St Germain, gone the thought of royal protection. Fredi's snobbish little soul had been seduced by the thought of meeting grand French duchesses in Legitimist salons, and being on nodding terms with rich manufacturers of champagne; and he knew only too well that none of this would ever happen if it were known what he had been up to that night, which it well might if Bogacsy had not insisted on accompanying Fredi to the station.

But Bogacsy was there with him, for it was the belligerent little ex-major's pride that he took his duties as second with deadly seriousness and would never abandon them until the affair was over and done with. This was especially true today when he could add his own flourish of mockery to the whole ridiculous affair. When he found the anti-duelling prince still on the platform at the station, old Bogacsy was overjoyed and his black-pudding moustache fairly bristled with pride. Though his German pronunciation was appalling, he was still able to give the prince an adroit and acceptable explanation for Fredi's appearance, declaring that his good friend Wuelffenstein had tripped on the Casino stairs, fallen against the balustrade, damaged his forehead and broken his nose.

'*Iss grosze Maleur, Hohayt, iss grosze Maleur . . .*' which even the prince managed to grasp meant 'What bad luck, Highness, what bad luck!' Bogacsy repeated this several times, bowing each time so deeply that it was possible no one saw the triumph in his eyes.

Only when the train had rumbled out of sight did he straighten up. Then he gave an extra twirl to his moustaches and marched off the platform as if he were Caesar and had just conquered Gaul.

CHAPTER THREE

ADRIENNE CAME BACK to Kolozsvar at the beginning of November. She arrived on the early morning express from Budapest, but that was only the end of her journey for before that she had been both to Lausanne in Switzerland and to Meran in South Tyrol. Adrienne had gone to Lausanne to visit her daughter Clemmie, who had been sent to the same boarding school that Adrienne herself had attended. She had found to her relief that some of her old teachers were still there and that they seemed to be just as wise and clever and sympathetic as she remembered them. The headmistress was now Madame Laurent, who had just started her career when Adrienne had been a pupil and who had always seemed to Adrienne to be more of a friend than a teacher. It was because Madame Laurent had taken over the school that Adrienne had decided to send Clemmie there, for she had every confidence in the wisdom and understanding of children's needs that Madame Laurent had always possessed. Now that her daughter had been there six months Adrienne had been to see her and also to discuss with her old friend what could be done with a child who had such a strangely withdrawn and unfriendly nature. Madame Laurent had explained the little girl's problems with such clarity that Adrienne, who had been worried and perplexed, now began to understand more clearly what was needed.

She had been thinking about this for most of the journey home. First of all she had reviewed all that had happened to make her take that painful decision to send her daughter to a school that was so far away from her mother. She knew it had been for the best and that there had not really been any other choice.

Until her husband had finally gone mad the child's grandmother had brought her up. Adrienne had been allowed no say whatever in little Clemmie's upbringing. She had even had to fight with her husband and mother-in-law to be allowed to nurse her when she had measles. The girl had been ill for an unusually long time and when some months had passed Adrienne had come to believe that in reality the little girl did love her mother but had been made to hide her affection because of the iron will of old Countess Clémence. She had been mistaken. When Pal Uzdy finally had had to be removed to the madhouse the emotional shock had completely broken the old lady who stayed in her own room, as motionless as a living statue, staring with unseeing eyes straight ahead of her and hardly ever speaking let alone taking any interest in whatever happened around her. She had withdrawn into herself and everyone else had been kept at a distance; not only Adrienne, whom she had always hated, but also her grandchild whom she was thought to have loved. When the child had been brought in to see her, she had just gestured for them to take her out again, and it had then been clear to Adrienne that Clemmie must be removed from Almasko as soon as possible. Two days later the French governess and English nanny had brought her to the Uzdy villa outside Kolozsvar.

Soon afterwards Countess Clémence also left Almasko. With

Maier and her elderly maid she took off for her villa at Meran and had been there ever since. She never wrote and any news that Adrienne had of her came from the servants when they wrote to thank her for the monthly cheque that Adrienne sent them.

For the first time since her birth Adrienne's daughter belonged solely to her mother.

For a little while Clemmie had been her only joy, for their coming together coincided with Adrienne's second separation from Balint, a separation that she then believed was for ever. And so Adrienne lavished on the child all the love of which she was capable, for she felt that now there was no one else. She spent all her time with her, and tried hard to win her love.

She did not succeed.

From the moment that it was clear that the grandmother was no longer there all signs of love for her mother also vanished. Those little shows of affection that had so heartened Adrienne while Clemmie was recovering from measles were seen no more, and it was not long before Adrienne had realized with a pang that what she had taken as a growing love for her mother had been nothing more than the child's desire to vex her grandmother.

Until Countess Clémence had left for Meran the little girl had always lived with her in the main house whenever the family had been in Kolozsvar. As soon as she had gone Adrienne moved her into Pal Uzdy's rooms in the one-storey wing next to her own bedroom. They were large rooms filled with light and air, but though her mother soon fixed them up as a nursery suite filled with expensive dolls and other toys, Clemmie ignored them all and never played with them. The most beautiful, an engaging and tempting clown, had barely been glanced at as it sat under the Christmas tree and when finally it had been picked up and given to her, the child had solemnly offered her polite thanks – as she had with every other toy given to her – picked it up and placed it at once on the nursery shelves along with all the others: and there they had stayed, lined up in exact order. If they were picked up when the room was dusted and not replaced exactly in line as they had been Clemmie would at once pick them up and replace them carefully in their proper place. Otherwise she never touched them. They simply did not interest her.

However she did show interest in reading and so was given all the best children's books that Adrienne could lay her hands on – the volumes of the *Bibliothèque Rose*, *Alice in Wonderland*, and many others. These too she would accept coolly and always thanked her mother with formal politeness, though never with any sign of joy or pleasure. Once a box of coloured pencils had somehow inadvertently got among the other presents and, though she gave no sign of interest at the time, after a few days Adrienne noticed that whenever Clemmie had a spare moment she would get out the pencils and start making strange designs with them. She never made any attempt at figures – the sort of awkward men and animals that other children did – but instead would carefully and deliberately draw exaggerated coloured contour lines around the capital letters of her books, contours that were filled in with backgrounds of blue, red or green and which were sometimes three times as large as the original letters. Sometimes she would add meticulously drawn hatching to give solidity and depth, and here and there would add a huge eye or some horns. A little later she started doing similar drawings in her school copybooks, all just as precise and careful as if they had been part of her school work. However, if someone called her she would put it down at once, as if she had no real interest in it, and if her mother tried to make some light-hearted comment, or enquire why she was doing it and what it meant, the child would merely reply with cold indifference 'I just do it' or 'It doesn't mean anything' or even, with studied politeness, 'I don't know why, I just do it!'

Clemmie never said anything about herself or her feelings. She never confided in anyone and it seemed as if nothing ever stirred her heart. She was never anything but polite and well-mannered; but she was always reserved and distant. The expression on her pretty, slightly Tartar-like features never changed and she always kept her brown eyes half closed, as if she were being careful not to reveal anything of herself. Her hair was very black and straight, just like her father's; and indeed she seemed to be completely Pal Uzdy's daughter not only in physical resemblance but also in character. In her there was nothing of her mother and nothing of that robust joy of life that characterized her mother's family.

For nearly a year Adrienne fought hard to find the way to her daughter's heart. She fought with love and tenderness and she sacrificed every minute of every day to gain her daughter's love and confidence. Eventually Adrienne realized that all these months of emotional struggle and effort had produced no result at all except perhaps to make matters worse between them.

Every thing she had done had been in vain and it seemed as if in some way it was those same efforts, that constant care and constant attention, that had somehow provoked even more withdrawal on her daughter's part. Adrienne could not put her finger on whatever it was that was wrong: she could sense it but she could find no reason.

It was then that she had made the painful decision to separate herself from little Clemmie and send her to school in Lausanne.

Now, coming back from her first visit to her daughter, she knew that it had been a wise decision, and not only because for the first time Clemmie had seemed pleased to see her mother; she had also shown signs of real affection. It had clearly done her good to be among girls of her own age who enjoyed life and played boisterously all around her.

What the headmistress had reported to her had been reassuring, even if not completely so.

Clemmie, she had been told, was an excellent pupil, obedient and industrious. At first, the headmistress said, she had been worried that, although always polite, Clemmie had been exceptionally unfriendly towards the other girls, but this had gradually begun to disappear, especially after she had begun to take part in the school sports. The girl had been taught tennis, rowing and a number of other ball-games and, so as to put her more at her ease, she had been given five companions of her own age and it had been with the same five that all the games were played. These other girls had been specially picked because they were quiet and well-behaved and even-tempered. Clemmie played tennis with them, rowed with them and indeed spent most of her leisure time with the same little band. And, if this companionship had not actually ripened into real friendship, it was still companionship and the girl certainly seemed to get on well with her new little circle. In this she was helped by the fact that she was more intelligent than the others and this, together with her reserved manner, made the others – all naturally affectionate girls – look up to her as their leader and try to win her affection.

'Normally,' said the headmistress, 'I do all I can to prevent the formation of little clans among my pupils, but here, for once, I encouraged it. There seemed to be no other way if your daughter Clémence was not to start shutting herself off completely from the others . . . and that would have been really bad for her . . . most harmful.'

Madame Laurent was silent for a moment or two. Then she added, '*Car naturellement c'est une enfant assez difficile* – of course she is naturally rather a difficult child.'

It was just this sentence that had worried Adrienne, for it had seemed to point to the possibility of an innate, inherited, danger. Then Madame Laurent went on: 'I firmly believe,' she had said with quiet confidence, 'that with constant attention and a lot of patience we will be able to bring her to a state of mind in which she will be able to cope properly with adult life. I am glad that you brought her to us so young.'

For Adrienne these last words had been a real encouragement and even more so because before she had brought Clemmie to Lausanne she had written fully to Madame Laurent telling her the whole story of the Uzdy family, of Pal Uzdy's madness, of Countess Clémence's decline into silence and melancholia and every detail that could in any way be of use to her.

Adrienne had not come straight home. On the way she had changed trains at Innsbruck and gone to Meran.

She had gone with a heavy heart, but she had gone because she considered it her duty to take care of old Countess Uzdy. It did not matter to her that the old woman had hated her from the day she had married her son, nor that she herself had detested her mother-in-law just as heartily during all those years that they had been forced to live in the same house as undeclared but nonetheless implacable enemies. Now that Adrienne was the only stable element left in the wreck of that sad family she knew she must put all her personal feelings and resentments aside and see to it that the old lady was properly looked after and lacked for nothing. Before leaving Transylvania she had written to the Uzdys' old retainer Maier, who had gone with Countess Clémence to Meran, to say that she would be coming, and she had also sent a telegram when she left Lausanne. So, when she arrived at noon, the old man was on the platform to meet her.

Maier had not changed since those traumatic days when she had last seen him. It was as if neither time nor tragedy could touch him. He was still the same powerfully-built, stocky man with a clear complexion, calm expression and intelligent eyes that she had always known. Now he must be over seventy, for his service with the Uzdy family had started when, as a fully qualified nurse, he had come to Almasko to look after Pal Uzdy's poor mad father. After his death he had stayed on until Pal Uzdy himself had been taken away hopelessly insane and now, for the last year and a half, he had looked after the old countess. She was the third member of that unhappy family to be served by him with a devotion and discretion that was almost saintly.

'And how is my mother-in-law?' asked Adrienne, as she shook hands with the powerful old man. 'Can she see people? When would be the best time?'

His answer was slow and ponderous, 'As your Ladyship will see there has been no visible change, but then that is only to be expected in cases of mental illness. I think ...' He hesitated before going on to say, '... perhaps it would be best to do it as soon as your Ladyship arrives at the house.'

It was a wonderful day, and the autumn sun was as hot as if it were already spring. The snow-covered mountain-tops seemed far closer than the row after row of foothills from which they sprang. It was as if they had somehow floated free of the ravines and pine forests below, and the great peaks of the Ortler range hung weightlessly like vaporous clouds in the azure purity of the Italian sky. Adrienne walked slowly up the hill behind the town's old fortress and all around her were orchards and vineyards and groups of dark evergreens like laurels and cedars that were interspersed with jasmine and camellia. Below her path the valley spread out, rich and fertile, and was dotted with small castles, churches and convents crowning each hilltop. A river threaded its leisurely way through velvet meadows. The whole landscape seemed to smile with peace and happiness.

Countess Uzdy's villa stood a little to the right of the road. Its entrance was on the north side but the main façade looked over the valley to the south west. Like so many Italian houses built on a hillside it had been set in the centre of a large square stone terrace like an iced cake upon a tray, and from it steps led downwards to other terraces and gardens below but from the entrance all the visitor could see of this was the tops of the trees planted at a lower level.

It was only as Adrienne passed through the entrance gates that she realized how apprehensive she was. On her way to the house all she had thought was that this was a routine call and that it was her duty. It was her first visit to Meran and as she strolled up from the station she had been thinking only of how beautiful everything was. Now, as she stood on the threshold of her mother-in-law's house, she was suddenly aware how much she dreaded meeting the old woman again. It was not simply that in a few moments she would once again be face to face with the person with whom, despite Countess Uzdy's never concealed hatred of her, she had had to spend so many years in the same house; it was also that this confrontation would entail explaining why she had come and giving her news of Pal Uzdy and of her little grand-daughter. She would once again have to put up with the old woman's icy stare and her probably offensive and unwelcoming remarks. Of course Maier had told her in several letters that nowadays the old woman sometimes did not utter a word for days on end, that she was usually listless and would sit quite still for hours without apparently noticing anything that went on around her; and that they even had to remind her to get up to go and wash, or take her meals, or go to bed. She had become, it seemed, little more than an automaton and had to be urged and encouraged to go through the ordinary motions of everyday life. Though Adrienne did not for a moment disbelieve any of this, she still wondered if it would be the same when they actually met or whether, at the sight of her, the old woman's venomous nature would overcome her depression and bring her back to life.

And this was not the only thing that made Adrienne suddenly afraid: she wondered too if she herself could muster enough self-control to appear natural and friendly and to talk as lightly and calmly as if that old hatred had never existed. She was desperately worried lest all those years of resentment would rise up and betray her into anger.

As these troubling thoughts flashed through her mind, she turned to Maier and said, 'I think it would be best to prepare her, and so, my good Maier, I should be grateful if you would go ahead and see her first. I will just stay here quietly for about a quarter of an hour. Then you can come and take me in. I'll be sitting on that stone bench.'

The old man said nothing, either in agreement or contradiction, but just looked at Adrienne with understanding. Then he nodded and disappeared into the house. The door closed noiselessly behind him.

When Adrienne found herself alone she sat down in the shade on the stone bench by the door and waited deep in thought. However she only stayed there for a moment or two. Perhaps because it was cool in the shade she began to shiver slightly and so got up and walked round to the front of the house which was in full sun. She went very slowly, assailed by old and disturbing memories, memories that went right back to the first days of her engagement to Pal Uzdy when she had met his mother for the first time. She thought, too, of more recent times at Almasko when, after that dreadful moment when Uzdy had rounded on his mother and attacked her viciously, she had, out of pity for Countess Clémence, gone to be with her in her room only to be screamed at and greeted with the awful and wholly unjustified accusation 'It is you that turned my son against me! You poisoned him! You!'

Adrienne was thinking of this as she turned the angle of the house. Then, still very slowly, she started to walk along the broad terrace that stretched the full length of the south front of the house. On this side there were five long windows overlooking the town. The shutters of four of them were closed and the bright sunlight painted lilac blue shadows below each of the louvred wooden slats. One window was open and when Adrienne reached it she found herself face to face with her mother-in-law who was sitting, barely five paces away, just inside the room. The low window-sill barely reached the level of her knees and she sat there, bolt upright, dressed entirely in black, like a statue of mourning. One shrivelled mummy-like hand lay in her lap. That, and the narrow lace collar at her throat, were the only touches of light to relieve the darkness of her figure. Even her thin face seemed almost as dark as her dress despite the sunlight which lit up her uplifted chin and prominent cheekbones. It was like light on dull bronze, and in some frightening way she had an ancient Egyptian look, calm, mysterious and menacing. She could have been an icon carved from granite so black that it absorbed any light that fell on it.

Adrienne stood in front of her as if petrified; but the old woman's Tartar-like eyes never moved and never showed any glint or sign that she even noticed that anyone was there.

Adrienne did not know how long she stood there, but it felt like an eternity during every minute of which she expected to hear a sharp reprimand, evil malignant words that would be followed by the old woman's leaping to her feet uttering a curse. But Countess Uzdy remained as mute and motionless as if carved from stone.

Gradually Adrienne realized that her mother-in-law was not looking at her and probably had not even seen her. Her eyes were fixed on something infinitely far away, beyond the far horizon and, like a stone idol, saw nothing that was in front of her. Even so Adrienne did not move. She stood there mesmerized as if bewitched by those sightless pebble-like eyes.

Someone touched her shoulder. It was Maier; and only then did Adrienne come back to reality. Silently she backed away and only when the old woman was hidden by the window frame could she bring herself to turn round and follow the old servant back round the corner of the house. Then she turned to him and said, 'Let us go inside where we can sit down and talk over what is to be done . . . I must leave again this evening.'

They went indoors to the room which Maier used as an office. Here the old maid came to pay her respects to Adrienne who then went over all the accounts, checking the bills and receipts more as a matter of form than necessity, for Adrienne knew how trustworthy both these old retainers were. It was a welcome relief to have to think about such humdrum matters for, as she did so, all the accumulated tension slowly left her so that she was able to discuss in a matter-of-fact way everything that concerned the future running of the house, the expenses, the sending of the necessary funds, in fact everything that was needed for Countess Clémence's continued residence at Meran. Finally they discussed her medical needs, the nursing, the doctors' visits and how they diagnosed the old woman's condition. Now Adrienne was at last able to ask Maier what the outlook was and whether there was any likelihood of recovery.

Maier, who was sitting on the other side of the table tidying away the papers he had just been showing his mistress, looked up sadly and in a slow ponderous manner explained that the specialist who had been attending the noble Countess had said that when old people developed this sort of melancholia there was rarely any hope of improvement. The patient could live on to an advanced age, for the body needed very little nourishment when it was not called upon to make any effort. With proper nursing the noble Countess would continue in the same state for many years to come. Of course it was always possible that some sort of crisis might occur and then they would have to be very watchful and careful because in such cases patients sometimes became suicidal.

'We are always on our guard,' said Maier, 'though up until now there has never been any sign of anything of the sort. It seems that even if there should be some sort of nervous crisis the patient usually soon reverts to apathy ... so she would once again be as your Ladyship saw her today, to all intents and purposes unconscious of her surroundings. This can last for years until such time ... such time as the body just wears out and starts slowly to ... to ... crumble away.'

Once alone again in the darkened sleeper Adrienne had thought about everything that had happened during the two weeks she had been away from home; about Lausanne and Clemmie and the talks with the headmistress, and, of course, about that sombre visit to Meran. She had been thinking of nothing else since she had got into the train long before night fell.

But, though Adrienne had gone over and over it all in her mind, repetition had not had the effect of making her memory of what had happened any clearer or more vivid. On the contrary, the closer she came to Kolozsvar, to home, so all the depressing events of the whole trip paled into insignificance compared with the sense of joyful expectation she felt arising in her.

When the train emitted a long whistle and for a few minutes all other sounds were drowned by a deep thundering reverberating rumble, Adrienne smiled happily to herself. They were passing through the Sztana tunnel, the last before she reached her destination. Home! Home! In an hour she would be home! In just an hour she would be lying back on her great white carpet covered with red cushions in front of a roaring fire.

There she would wait, gazing into the flames, until about midnight she would hear a little sound from the latch of the French window that gave on to the garden and her lover would come to her. Then, and only then, as she lay in Balint's arms, would she really feel at home. Then she would forget all her cares, her sorrows and worries, and the memories of the cruel days that were now past. Everything would vanish in their triumphant reunion. And this was the only reality ... only this.

CHAPTER FOUR

A FEW DAYS AFTER Adrienne's return to Kolozsvar there took place one of the season's most elegant balls. It was a Bal des Têtes at which all the women were required to wear elaborate head-dresses.

The idea had come from Elemer Garazda, the young man from the district of Tolna in Western Hungary who was in his third year studying law at the university. In Transylvania he was known to everyone as 'the Garazda Boy', or just 'Boy' for short, for one could hardly see his light-blonde moustache on his youthful pink and white face and also because it seemed amusing to address such a tall robust young man as 'Boy'. He had been chosen as leading dancer and organizer (*elotancos*) of all the dances and balls; and this in itself was a tribute to his popularity and efficiency as well as being an unusual compliment to someone who was not born in Transylvania. In recognition of this he had been doing his best to show his gratitude for the honour done to him, and so he had put forward the idea of the Bal des Têtes so as to show that he was full of energy and enterprise and capable of organizing something new and beautiful and amusing. He wanted to justify the confidence they had put in him.

The Garazda Boy had seen similar balls at the exclusive Park Club in Budapest where they had recently been introduced and had become very popular. The Kolozsvar Bal des Têtes was a charity ball given in aid of some Szekler villages that had been devastated by fire. It was the first ball to be organized in the new ballroom of the Central Hotel rather than in the old Redut Room where all the balls had previously been held.

The occasion had been eagerly awaited by all those who would attend; by the men because they would not have to make themselves ridiculous in some idiotic costume, and by their women-folk because they could go in a classic ball-gown and not spend a fortune on some elaborate fancy dress; and also because they would be able to dazzle their friends, and hopefully outdo them, with some amazingly original and magnificent and hitherto undreamed-of ornamental head-dress.

For weeks before there had been to-ing and fro-ing and thought and planning and much pleasurable secrecy as to what all the fashionable ladies would wear. While everyone tried hard to find out what the others had chosen each was determined to keep their own ideas secret lest anyone should try to imitate what they had planned, thus leading to that social disaster when two or more women were dressed alike.

Nevertheless, in spite of, or perhaps because of, all this manic secrecy several women found themselves in just the situation they had most dreaded. There were eight Turkish turbans, five Dutch bonnets, three Andalusian head-dresses complete with high tortoiseshell combs and lace shawls, six country maidens from the Kalotaszeg district, two Cleopatras and four Little Red Riding Hoods. Not a few extremely cross society ladies had to console themselves with the thought that they had been first in the field with their wonderfully original idea and that somehow and with low cunning the others had stolen the idea from them. The one to be blamed was always their closest friend – that two-faced snake in the grass!

At one end of the ballroom there was a platform on which were the chairs reserved for the Lady Patronesses. There they sat in a half circle beneath a bower of potted palms brought in from elsewhere. Here was to be found the wife of Kolozsvar's mayor, the wife of Stanislo Gyeroffy who had been Laszlo's guardian, Countess Kamuthy, Countess Jeno Laczok and the young wife of Dr Korosi who had recently been appointed Rector of the University, a position which conferred a new distinction on his pretty wife so that, whether she liked it or not, she was stuck with this distinguished group of older women. In the middle of them all was Countess Sarmasaghy, who was almost everyone's Aunt Lizinka, and who had been given the place of honour because all the others were terrified of the old woman's evil tongue and mischief-making ways.

All of these wore head-dresses made of old lace, white or black, with the sole exception of Countess Laczok who had brought out a family heirloom, a cap of pearls stitched with other precious stones, which had once belonged to the wife of a former ruling prince of Transylvania, Mihaly Apaffy, and which had passed to the Laczoks by inheritance through the Bornemiszas. It was a unique object and in it Countess Ida, who was liked by everyone, looked like an ancient portrait brought to life.

On the platform with this group were the ball's official

sponsors, a mixed group of local aristocrats and middle-class businessmen such as the mayor himself, two chairmen of local banks,
the ex-doyen of the court pleaders, and some others. Old Carrots
Gyeroffy was there sporting his famous orange wig, as was Crookface Kendy with his eagle's beak nose, the elder Count Adam
Alvinczy and the inevitable Major Bogacsy. There were some
others too, like Uncle Ambrus, who decided that the official
platform was the best place from which to ogle all the pretty
women as they entered the hall and so boldly walked the length of
the room, and mounted with the official party as if he had merely
come to pay his respects to the Patronesses.

Joska Kendy also managed to get himself on the platform, but
he did this not to ogle the women but to get as close as possible
to pretty young Mrs Korosi, find a chair beside her and whisper
sweet nothings into her receptive ear. Mrs Korosi, for her part,
did not mind at all the opportunity to tell Joska her woes, which
principally consisted of feeling neglected by her husband, the
Rector, who in addition to his political activities as leader of the
town's opposition was constantly occupied with attending meetings, making speeches and lecturing and administering to the
point that his poor little wife was left quite disconsolate. All this
she poured out to Joska in a soft voice so that he, moved by her
sorrows, from time to time took his pipe from his pocket, jammed
it between his teeth, then stuffed it angrily away again.

Many people arrived early and so the long-legged Garazda
Boy was fully occupied from the start in showing people to their
places, running constantly from the head of the stairs to the
official platform and back again. He was very conscientious and
felt it important, if he was to make a success of the evening, that
each lady as she arrived should be seen to be escorted the full
length of the hall down the double line of the other assembled
guests. His assistant was the young Dezso Laczok, who was only
in his second year at the university and hero-worshipped his
superior; these two young men hurried alternately up and down
the room anxiously trying to keep order and see that everyone
was in their proper place before darting back again when a new
head-dress swam into view at the head of the stairs. The Boy,
with his long legs, managed it at a run, while Dezso, who was
smaller, practically skated across the polished floor. Then, with
the new arrival in tow, they would bow ceremoniously as they
made the necessary presentation to the Patronesses. All in all they

managed it very well. It was not an easy task to keep order with such a throng, but they carried it off with only one mishap. This was due, not to any female guest, but to Isti Kamuthy.

Plump little Isti, when in London the previous summer, had had made a pink hunting jacket by one of the most fashionable tailors in Savile Row. It was a marvellous coat made out of some material that was as hard and stiff as zinc. He had been anxious to have it generally admired and had thought of wearing it at Zsuk for the St Hubertus Day meet. Then someone had told him that in England pink coats were not worn when hunting with harriers and so, after repeatedly telling this to all his friends, he had had to be content with wearing an old green coat when out with the hounds as he realized he could not himself now break with such a hallowed tradition. It was a painful decision for young Isti, but the marvellous pink coat – which had cost all of eight and a half guineas – had had to stay unused hanging in his wardrobe. Then the opportunity came. He heard of the Bal des Têtes and decided that if he could not wear the coat in the hunting field he would wear it to the ball, regardless of the fact that all the other men would be in classical black evening dress. If challenged he would say he thought it was a costume ball and so, that evening, he pulled on his white breeches, a pair of riding boots, and donned the pink masterpiece. He himself knew that he would outdo everyone by the splendour of his coat and that all the girls would admire him. And he would cut such a dash that one or two of them might even fall in love with him.

When Isti first set foot in the hall everyone's amazement was everything he could have wished. There was a sudden hush, and then a clamour of joy broke out and he found himself surrounded by a bevy of young girls who crowded round him to touch and admire and giggle . . . and make fun of him. Everyone talked at once, all demanding to know why he had thought to come dressed like that. For some moments Isti thought that he had all the success he had hoped for – but not for long. In an instant the great cluster of girls fell back with an expression of disgust; and then his dreadful outspoken little niece, Malvinka, said out loud what everyone else was thinking.

'Isti! You stink of the stables!'

This was something that he had never thought about; but the moment it had been said he knew how true it was. The much-used leather-patched breeches and the boots which had been impregnated with horse-sweat passed without notice in the hunting field; but in the scented ballroom they reeked of horse; and for Isti the effect was awful. Wherever he went everyone fled from him, and it was the same the whole evening. No girl would let him come near her, or dance with her; and most of the men, in true Transylvanian fashion, started to tease and mock him, making elaborate gestures of disgust while muttering 'stink of the stables, stink of the stables, stink of the stables'. For as long as he could bear it poor Isti wandered about alone, chased away from every corner, feeling lonely and persecuted, as indeed he was. Finally, after a long battle with himself, he admitted defeat, renounced all effort at cutting a dash at the ball and took refuge in the card-room where the clouds of cigar-smoke that hung over the gaming-tables obliterated all lesser odours. Here, at last unnoticed and unsmelt, Isti collapsed into a chair, and nobody bothered him any more.

As soon as poor Isti had fled, order returned to the ballroom. More pretty women kept on arriving, their heads covered with odalisques' veils or bullfighters' hats. If they had come escorted by husbands, brothers or fathers these last went to stand with the other men at the side of the room while the lady, all self-congratulatory smiles, paraded the length of the room so as to show off her miraculous and completely original head-dress. Sometimes it would happen, as she glided down the centre of the room, that an ironic whisper, none too discreet, would be heard. 'Do look! That's the third tulip!' or, when a white-powdered wig went bobbing by, 'Just like a poodle!' More rarely there was heard a soft murmur of pleasure and approval. This happened when Dodo entered bearing the towering feather crown of an Indian chief, and when the pretty little Mrs Fischer arrived with a complete circus carousel on her head on which the little wooden horses went round and round whenever she gave them a touch with her fingers. It was the same when Margit appeared. She still looked as girlish as always even though at the end of January she had given birth to a fat healthy boy, the first grandchild for old Count Adam Alvinczy. In her simple white dress covered in tiny embroidered flowers she looked like a girl at her first ball. On her head she wore a plain red kerchief completely covering her hair and tied just as young peasant girls did in the country. It could not have cost more than twenty cents, but it was tied so skilfully, with two corners erect at the back of her head, and it was so well-suited to her calm brown face, lifted chin and proud dignified walk, that when she went up to the Patronesses and sank into a deep curtsy, everyone was captivated by her charm and grace and applauded loudly. Margit herself blushed with pleasure and stepped modestly aside.

When almost everyone was there and the Garazda Boy was standing by the Patronesses, looking at his watch and wondering if he ought to get the first csardas started, there was a stir at the head of the stairs and Adrienne swept into the room.

There was such a mob of people round the entrance that until she arrived in the central aisle she could hardly be seen. Then the dense phalanx of men in their black evening dress parted in the centre and Adrienne stood in full view. For a moment she stood there without moving and then slowly with long strides started to walk down the hall.

Adrienne's dress was black and very long. It was made of some smooth material covered with tiny shiny metallic paillettes which shimmered and rustled with every movement she made. It was as if she were covered from neck to floor with some magic snake's armour. Her head was held high and on it she wore a wide oriental golden crown as seen in pictures of the Manchu empresses. It was made up of branches of golden flowers bent upwards in wide arcs the tips of which had been decorated with hanging fringes of tiny gem stones. The hearts of all the flowers were sewn with rubies which might have been drops of blood upon the shining golden petals.

Her eyebrows and lashes had been darkened and made longer as Chinese women did and indeed Adrienne, with her black hair, ivory skin and pale face which held no trace of colour apart from her vivid red lips, seemed a true evocation of the Far East. She was like the statue of some legendary goddess who had for once stepped out of her pagoda, and her head and shoulders rose triumphantly from the lowest possible décolletage.

Adrienne's skin glowed with a myriad tiny reflections from the bright lighting of the hall, so that her shoulders, neck and breasts gleamed like highly polished marble. In the proud fullness of her beauty there was no sign of the unformed, skinny schoolgirl she had still resembled long after the birth of her child; and no sign either of the prudish virginal air which for so many years she had adopted whenever some man looked at her with desire in his eyes. All this had vanished some six months before when she had become reunited with her lover and in his arms had been able freely to live the life of a truly fulfilled woman. Her beauty was so sublime that when she entered the room she was greeted by a sudden hush of awe which continued as she started to walk down the hall proudly conscious of the effect she was making.

Balint had been waiting for her not far from the top of the stairs and when she appeared he took an unconscious step towards her, but Adrienne checked him with an almost invisible smile behind which he sensed the unspoken words: 'Now you can see what it is that I brought from Vienna and which, despite your demands, I would not tell you about. I kept it secret even from you, so that you should see me like this, suddenly, unexpectedly, my tribute to you,' and she continued her progress between the double line of guests, many of them clad in all the colours of the rainbow. And as she continued her queenly progress down the hall a soft murmur of admiration rose around her which mounted in a crescendo as the spectators caught sight of the cascade of thin golden threads which fell from the back of her imperial crown, some almost to the ground, and all of them ending in a golden flower with a ruby at its heart. As she walked these flowed behind her, each flower reflecting the red-hot desire that could be seen in the eyes of the men who watched her progress.

Finally she arrived at the platform on which the Patronesses of the ball were seated. Then she sank into the deep curtsy of one being presented at Court, her supple body sinking and rising with all the calm and assurance of a panther; and her bearing was so regal that there was a burst of spontaneous applause.

Adrienne's sweet-natured aunt, Countess Laczok, cried out enthusiastically, 'Oh, how beautiful you are, my darling!' and for once even the spiteful old Countess Sarmasaghy, Aunt Lizinka, suppressed her natural malice and found herself saying: 'I must say I've never seen anyone so beautiful!' Uncle Ambrus, dazzled, roared out: 'Damned fine wench!' and in a few moments she was surrounded by a crowd of men, young and old, who would not budge from her side even though the music had just started. Many of them at once asked her to dance. Some she did not seem to hear, but to others she just gently shook her head, for she was waiting for Abady and when he reached her side she took his arm and the others started to melt away.

Recently it had always been like this. Since Uzdy had been taken away hopelessly insane Balint and Adrienne had made no attempt to pretend or hide their love for each other. They made no secret of it and everyone knew; though whether they really were lovers or not remained uncertain. It did not matter for they both held their heads high and everyone knew that they belonged to each other; and so society accepted the situation. Men no longer chased after Adrienne, even though she was now so much more beautiful than before, for they realized that she would never look at anyone but Balint, and to pursue her would be in vain.

Everyone knew that divorce was impossible for her and so her feelings for Balint, which neither of them made any attempt to conceal while at the same time conducting themselves with so much dignity and discretion, always together at every function but never arriving or leaving together, became an accepted fact. Even Aunt Lizinka stopped spreading her evil tales about Adrienne for there were no men chasing after her and no flirtations to gossip about. Uncle Ambrus stopped yearning after her and hinting that they were having an affair. Now everyone knew the truth, even if not all of it; and as the basis for gossip is conjecture and concealment, here there was neither and so nothing to gossip about.

Boldly and together Balint and Adrienne faced the world openly.

Deprived of her favourite object of malice Aunt Lizinka had had to look around to find another target. She soon found it in the person of Count Jeno Laczok's elder brother Tamas. After a riotous youth and several years of adventure abroad, Tamas had qualified as a railway engineer and had found employment with the Hungarian State Railways. His work had brought him back to Kolozsvar, and his predilection for very young gypsy girls soon became well-known. Aunt Lizinka at once pounced on this juicy scandal and decided to become 'worried' about him. Now, sitting on the Patronesses' elevated dais, she plunged into the matter with glee, explaining with zest and false concern, that she was terrified that her nephew Tamas would land in gaol. 'You know, my dear, that little gypsy girl he keeps isn't even thirteen! Think of the scandal! How dreadful this would be for the family! I know for a fact that the police are after him even now.'

Although Aunt Lizinka's high-pitched screech could be heard

in most parts of the hall, Balint and Adrienne, who were strolling past, heard nothing of it. Other people's affairs were no concern of theirs and so they did not bother to listen. They walked together as in a dream, completely wrapped up in each other and in their own happiness. Soon they sat down together on a bench beside the wall and then Adrienne turned smiling to her lover and said, 'Do you like it?'

'Very, very much!'

'Really and truly?'

'Even more than very, very much!' he repeated warmly and then, very softly, in a low whisper that no one could possibly overhear, he muttered into her ear a few words in English, words whose meaning was their own secret symbol of their love.

For a moment Adrienne lowered her eyelids over her big topaz-coloured eyes. She did not speak, for the little movement was her accepted answer; but her full lips opened slightly to show the gleam of her white teeth . . .

Then with joy in her heart she told him how she had devised her imperial head-dress, how she had pored over illustrated books, and how, when she went to Vienna, she had somehow managed to have it made in the workshop of the opera house. Then she told too how she had secretly brought it home and how, because the hanging flowers at the back had tickled her neck, she had lengthened them herself to make that jewelled cascade that everyone had admired so much.

The ball soon got under way, and the opening csardas was followed by a series of waltzes. Just as Laji Pongracz, the popular band-leader, swung his musicians into the new favourite, the 'Luxembourg Waltz', there was a new arrival. A powerfully built man with a black beard entered the room. It was Tamas Laczok, and his appearance was to cause almost as much stir as had that of Isti Kamuthy an hour before, especially among the Lady Patronesses and the other matrons on the platform. This reaction was not entirely unexpected, even by the subject of it himself, for he, as well as all the others, had been fully aware of all the tales that had been circulating about him. As an engineer of the State Railways he had been sent to take charge of some repair works on the line between Kolozsvar and Apahida and had taken up residence some three weeks before in a small peasant's house in the district of Bretfu.

Though he was not far from the centre of Kolozsvar he had not often come into the town, for his was a solitary nature and he liked his privacy.

Even so the news of the ball had somehow come his way, and though this would not normally have attracted him, he had also heard that old Countess Sarmasaghy was to be one of the patrons together with his younger brother Jeno. To cap it all he had been at the station that morning and had seen the arrival of the banker, Baron Weissfeld, and his family, who had come to attend the ball. The presence of these three had made him decide to put in an appearance himself.

In this he was prompted only by the dislike, amounting to hate, which he felt for all three of them. He was convinced that his brother had plotted with the banker to deprive him of his right-ful share of the Laczok forestry holdings and further, that it had been Aunt Lizinka who had played a major part in seeing that he had been disowned by his family at the time he had been sowing his wild oats. The result had been years of exile. It was, of course, true that this experience had made a new man of him, for it was this that had led him first to study in Paris and obtain his engi-neering degrees and then to find a position with an international firm that had first sent him to Durazzo on a construction job and later to work on the building of a railway across the Atlas mountains. He had remained in Algeria for many years and he could have stayed there with a position of great responsibility. But he had decided that he would rather hold some secondary post at home with the Hungarian State Railways, partly because he had come to realize that he only felt really at home back in Transylvania and also because if he were to return he would be able to haunt his much hated brother and perhaps also find the means of revenging himself upon his old enemies.

If this was the main reason why he had decided to attend the ball, he had also got wind of the scandalous tales that his aunt was now spreading about him. He had arrived late because he had not at once been able to find his evening clothes, and when he had found them his gypsy servant had had to iron them and then he had had to come into town, locate a shop that would supply him with a stiff shirt and white tie, and then go back to Bretfu to dress.

All this conspired to make him late. Now that he had finally arrived he looked around, peering above the heads of the dancing

throng, until he saw his aunt and sister-in-law on the official dais
and he realized that if Ida Laczok was there her husband could
not be far away. Then he saw Baroness Weissfeld fanning herself
on a chair near the others. Screened by the multitude of dancing
couples he threaded his way, stooping slightly like a big game
hunter stalking a pride of lions, towards his much disliked relations, carefully keeping out of their sight until he could suddenly
burst before them from among the throng of dancers.

The surprise he caused them was as successful as he had hoped.

A little while before most of the older men had vanished from
the official platform and taken refuge in the hotel's smoking-
room. It was one of the rooms put at the disposal of the Comte
d'Eu during his recent visit. The Patronesses, however, had not
moved from their place of honour. There, right at the front, were
Countess Kamuthy, Baroness Weissfeld, and Tamas's sister-in-
law, Ida Laczok. They were listening open-mouthed to Aunt
Lizinka who, since she had successfully fought, and won, a battle
in the courts to regain her husband's properties during the
repressive régime of Count von Bach after the 1848 uprising sixty
years before, had prided herself on her knowledge of the law.
Aunt Lizinka was now in full flood describing the criminal proceedings which, according to her, now threatened her nephew
Tamas.

At this point she was saying, 'My dears, it is quite clear. The
law says that such persons must not only be locked up but also
condemned to five years' hard labour. I know for a fact that the
police have already put out a search for the little whore's birth
certificate and that her old clay-digging father, who sold the
child to him, is already in custody.'

Countess Ida, who never thought or spoke ill of anyone and
who found herself forced to listen only because she could find
no excuse to move away, now started to close her ears from boredom and looked round the room to find some distraction. And
the first person she saw was her brother-in-law himself, standing
quite close and clearly able to hear everything that was being said.

There he was, the spitting image of her husband Jeno, if perhaps not quite so plump. He had the same Tartar features with a
single tuft of hair on his otherwise bald pate. With his slanting
eyes almost buried in folds of fat, with his wide-spread eyebrows
which gave him the air of perpetual enquiry, he resembled more
than anything one of those soapstone figurines to be found in

oriental bazaars. In this he was even more like than his brother
Jeno, for while the latter sported only a pair of imposing moustaches, Tamas also wore a long thin beard twisted to the shape of
a lyre. He stood there, just in front of Ida, quite straight on his
shortish legs, with his hands in his pockets, smiling up at her.

'Tamas!' she cried out in surprise. 'Where on earth did you
spring from?'

'*Servus* – greetings!' he replied.

Everyone looked round, and Aunt Lizinka choked in mid-
sentence. Then she too stammered out, 'You? You here? You!
How did you get in here?'

'Because, my dear aunt, I am still at liberty to go where
I please! *J'ai voulu vous tranquilliser à ce sujet* – I just wanted to
reassure you about that!' and he mounted the platform, pulled
up a chair and sat down beaming all around him in good-
fellowship and high good humour.

Faced with such a *fait-accompli* there was nothing that the
others could do. Then Tamas turned to Baroness Weissfeld and,
carefully choosing his words, slowly said, 'Not everyone gets to
prison who deserves it, as your good husband must know.' Then
he turned to Ida and went on, 'How is my brother? I heard he
was suffering from a slight Thief's Cold.' After this, with the
others speechless, he addressed himself directly to old Countess
Sarmasaghy.

'My dear aunt, have you heard of my latest troubles? Oh,
nothing to do with that tale about the gypsy girl, nothing whatever. No, it is all because my second foreman has just got himself
sent to gaol for slander. It's really been most annoying for he was
such a good worker and I don't know how I'll manage without
him. The fool said something scandalous about the head foreman and as he said it in front of several of his work-mates, one
of them denounced him and the idiot found himself hauled
before the court. Three witnesses swore that they had heard the
slander and the judge believed them, saying that there was little
he could have done if only one man had spoken but that three
he was bound to believe. What an idiot the fellow was to spread
slander in front of three other people!' and he gestured towards
his sister-in-law, Countess Kamuthy and Baroness Weissfeld.
'They shut him up, my dear aunt, and you can imagine the
trouble that has caused.'

For a moment or two he paused, a wicked look in his eyes as

he looked at each of the ladies in turn. Then he rose and said, 'Well! As I'm here I might as well have a look round. *Ma chère tante, je me prosterne devant votre bienveillante attention* – my dear aunt, I submit myself to your ever-vigilant good will.'

Then he bowed and went on his way.

As soon as he had left all three women rose hurriedly and fled in different directions, and Aunt Lizinka was left to suffocate in her own venom.

Farkas Alvinczy, who had been the previous dance leader, and a Member of Parliament until the year before, stood in a small doorway behind the gypsy musicians. To emphasize the fact that he was not really attending the ball he had come dressed not in evening dress but in ordinary day clothes. This was to show everyone that he had now renounced the frivolous pleasures of the world. It was his pose that a man like him with a brilliant past, who had been the envy of all other men and the favourite of the most beautiful women in Budapest, who had been an eminent servant of the state and a prominent politician, would now choose to withdraw from society rather than take second place in such provincial revels. How could he, who had tasted every pleasure the world had to offer, now be seen courting the attention of a group of dowdy country-women? Naturally he had not said this to anyone, but his air of mysterious superiority just tinged with melancholy spoke only too clearly for him.

And yet it really was nothing but a pose. It was true that he had been a Member of Parliament, but he had had nothing to say. While in Budapest he had had no more social success than many other good-looking young men, and like other good-looking young men he had had neither more nor fewer adventures with women than had the others. But he had tried to lead the life he imagined and he had even begun to believe it himself to the point at which he now suffered as much as if it had been true. Since he had lost his seat at the last elections he had stopped going out in society and had gone out only to gamble the night away. During the daytime he had slept. He no longer went with the others to sing and dance with the gypsies and it had begun to be whispered that he had become a heavy but secret drinker. Looking at his puffy face and watery eyes people had begun to guess that the rumours were only too true. Still, even if he had started to run slightly to fat he was still exceptionally good-looking.

Young Ida Laczok caught sight of him from across the room and at once said to herself that he would do for her. Since Gazsi Kadacsay had so inexplicably faded out of her life, she would have accepted anyone who asked her, for by now both her sisters were married and she was the only one still single.

Stopping her dancing partner as they waltzed by the gypsy band, she bowed to him and went over and stood near Farkas. He in his turn stepped up to her and they shook hands just behind the double-bass.

'What are you doing with yourself these days?' she asked. 'It is nice to see you again,' she went on with a sparkle of encouragement in her eyes. 'You can't imagine how much we miss you.'

Farkas made a somewhat disdainful gesture and said in a bored voice, 'I just wanted to see how the Garazda Boy was making out. I must say he seems to be doing quite well. He's a clever lad so I expect he'll learn.'

'Oh, but it isn't at all the same as when you did it!' said Ida in a flattering tone and went on with several remarks in the same vein.

Shortly afterwards they were joined by Margit.

'Have you seen Adam?' she asked her brother-in-law. 'He disappeared ages ago. Is he in the card-room? Were you there?' and her voice held an unusually stern and demanding note.

'I was there all right, gambling if you want to know,' Farkas replied bitterly, 'but whether Adam was or not I really can't say, and I don't care. I'm not one to spy on others: they can do what they like for all I care!'

This was intended as a gibe at Margit, for all three of Adam's brothers resented the young woman who had captured him. They were also afraid of her for they knew they could not compete with her practical brain and strong will. Even so Farkas would not have dared to speak to her like that if they had been alone.

Margit raised her little beak-like nose and looked up at her tall brother-in-law's face. Then, with the shadow of a smile, she said, quite calmly, 'In that case I'll go and look for him myself.' Then she turned and walked swiftly away.

Margit stepped out into the corridor. There she hesitated for a moment or two not knowing which of the four double-doors led to the card-room. Then a waiter appeared carrying an ice-bucket and opened the third door. Margit followed him for she had heard the booming voice of Uncle Ambrus saying, 'Come on, me lad, shell it out! We don't play for peanuts here, you know. The bank is sixteen hundred. Who wants it?'

Margit looked around her.

The room was one of the hotel's grand sitting-rooms, but the furniture had been pushed to the walls to make way for a large baize-covered table that had been placed directly under the crystal chandelier. It was surrounded by eight cane chairs for the players, but her husband Adam was not among them. She saw Akos, his youngest brother, but it was only later that she remembered how deathly pale he had looked. She was about to leave the room when she caught sight of her husband. He was lying in a gilt armchair just behind where she was standing. His long legs were stretched out in front of him and he was fast asleep. He was sleeping so soundly that his mouth was slightly open like a young child's and on his face was an expression of happiness and content. He was asleep out of sheer exhaustion, for although since his marriage he had never once gone out carousing with his friends, he had spent all the previous night carrying his new-born baby about who was suffering from colic and who started crying again every time Adam put him down. He adored his son and fussed over him like any nanny.

Margit moved silently over to her husband and ever so gently started to caress his forehead. Still half asleep Adam reached for her hand and brushing it across his face started to kiss her arm just as he might have if they were in bed at night. He did not try to open his eyes, imagining that that was just where they were.

It must have been a familiar movement for Margit broke out in soft giggles. Still, she had to see that Adam was properly awake.

'Anna Laczok, Countess Harinay, doesn't have a dinner partner. I told her you'd sent me to ask her for you. But it would be nice if you'd go and ask her yourself, just to be polite, you know. The dinner will be served in half an hour and it wouldn't look right to wait until the last minute.'

Adam jumped up. 'You're right,' he said. 'I'll go at once.'

As they moved away little Margit looked up at the great height of her husband and said, 'I hope you're pleased I got you such a pretty partner. You can't accuse me of being a jealous wife!'

'Why ever should you be?' he answered good-naturedly and they walked hand in hand out of the card-room, their steps matching each other exactly as the steps do of those who have a total understanding of each other. And although there was no one to see them in the deserted corridor the two of them, linked by their intertwined hands, made a picture of perfect happiness.

Tamas Laczok, having had his fun with Aunt Lizinka, went to look for his brother and Weissfeld. After all, he said to himself, he had gone to a lot of trouble and expense – ten crowns, no less! – to get to the ball so now he might as well see that he got his money's worth, and that meant teasing the others as well. He went in search of the smoking-room.

There they both were, sitting with about twenty other men in a wide circle discussing politics, as Hungarian men always do when a group of them gather together. They were mostly the patrons of the ball, or the husbands of the Lady Patronesses, who were now condemned to wait until they had to escort their wives to the supper-room.

Jeno Laczok, with his vast bulk, sat stiff and motionless, a prisoner of his own fat. He was like a statue carved from stone. Beside him sat the banker from Vasarhely who never left his friend's side in Kolozsvar, partly because he always felt the need of his support when among strangers but also because no one here knew what an important person he was in his home town.

The Rector of the University, Dr Korosi (whose wife felt so neglected), was pompously explaining some abstruse point, when Tamas's rumbustious entrance interrupted what he was saying and so spoiled his carefully constructed argument.

'*Servus* Sandor! *Servus* Adam! *Servus* Stanislo! *Servus* everyone! Greetings to you all. What a long time since I saw you!' and he shook hands all round, introducing himself to some of those he did not know, but not all as they did not interest him much, and Tamas had never been a stickler for convention. When he had almost come full circle he came face to face with his brother. With glee he slapped Jeno's protruding stomach and, seizing his shoulders with both hands, gave him a good shake while roaring out, 'Wow! You look pale! Where did you get that yellow colour?' and though his brother started coldly to deny it, he went on: 'Oh yes, you are! You're very, very yellow. Of course *you* don't notice it as you see yourself in the mirror every day.' Then, turning to the others, he appealed to them all for confirmation, 'It's true, isn't it? Don't you see it? Of course you're all far too polite to say it out loud, but you can to me, you know. After all I'm his brother, and it's my duty to tell him the truth!'

Tamas turned back to his brother and without a word to Weissfeld, who had got up, took the latter's seat.

'You really should have yourself looked at, Jeno! It could be very serious, very serious indeed,' and he dropped his voice to a penetrating whisper and went on, 'Just think about it. Father died of cancer, didn't he? And they all say there can be a hereditary disposition ... not that it's absolutely certain.'

'To hell with you!' said Jeno trying to laugh it off, but his laughter sounded somewhat forced. Tamas knew only too well that he had touched upon Jeno's weakest spot and that his attempt to scare him was not in vain. Ever since their youth Jeno had had this one fear and so, when Tamas knew that his drop of poison was working, he became all solicitous, and said kindly, 'Don't you worry, it's probably something quite different, too much acidity, or maybe gallstones. Anyhow I certainly should see a doctor!' Then he turned to the others. 'Do forgive me! I'm afraid I've interrupted a most interesting discussion with this family talk ... you really must excuse me!' and fell silent. The two brothers who hated each other sat side by side, as alike as twins. Apart from one having a beard and the other not they were almost identical, the same tuft of black hair on their otherwise shining skulls, the same enquiring eyebrows and high cheekbones. They even sat in the same way, solid and granite-like, with their hands planted firmly on their knees.

Dr Korosi now went on where he had left off.

He had been talking about the recent announcement that recruiting to the army was to be increased and its equipment modernized. This had happened in January but the details had only just been made public. It seemed that an extra 50,000 men were required and that the annual army budget was to be raised by 20 million crowns, 60,000 of which would be made available immediately. Three weeks before, Lukacs, the Minister of Finance, had given a most reassuring speech declaring that none of these new measures would entail raising taxes, though at the same time he said that more battleships were to be built. Lukacs had spoken with calm assurance and had explained that the Dual Monarchy's fleet was obsolete compared with those of the other great powers, and that they could not now afford to lag behind in the armaments race that was taking place all over Europe. Austria-Hungary's continued status as a great power, and as an equal partner with her allies, depended upon her armed forces being on a plane of equality with those of everyone else. He talked about the annexation of Bosnia-Herzegovina and the international crisis it had provoked, cited the build-up of the German navy, and referred to the importance to the nation of Hungary's commercial shipping interests. Dr Korosi went on to recount how the news of the increase in the army had been received with indifference by most people who had become all too accustomed to being told over the years that it would soon be necessary, just as they all knew that the real enemy was Russia and that the Tsar, aided by French millions, had for a long time been preparing for war. The question of the navy, however, was something new and very different. Why, people were asking, did the navy have to be built up? Who was the enemy?

Dr Korosi made the most of this last point, for he was the leader of the opposition party in Transylvania. Speaking with a broad, rather flat, accent, for he came from Szeged, he asked, 'Whaat therefore is the Naavy to us? Whaat is it for? Against whom should we use it?' and he went on to repeat what everyone present knew already, that Austria-Hungary had no colonies and no overseas interests, that the German navy was already far stronger than the French, and no matter how many ships were built by the Dual Monarchy they would never be able to compete with the enormous British fleet. That left only Italy, whom everyone knew to be Hungary's staunchest ally, and so no re-inforcement would be needed there for it had already been agreed that Italy would participate in the defence of the Adriatic. Now, though Korosi ignored the fact, not everything could be discussed in political terms nor all official announcements be relied upon. It was not generally known that the Austro-Hungarian general staff had for some time been dubious about the strength of the Italian alliance, even to the point of preparing for the possibility that, in the event of war, Italy might quite possibly side with their enemies. Every alliance, they knew, stood up only as long as it was in the interests of both sides to maintain it, and only the strong kept their friends. The man in the street, however, who was always childishly naïve in anything to do with foreign affairs, would never try to understand what might be going on under the surface. As a result people were now searching for concealed, secret and even totally absurd reasons for the modernization of the navy.

This is what most people believed and now they heard it confirmed by what Korosi was saying.

'It is obvious,' said the Rector, 'thaat the Heir simply wishes to indulge his ridiculous desire to be an admiral! Franz-Ferdinand wants only to emulate the Kaiser Wilhelm, and so he needs a squadron! Thaat, and thaat only, is why the government is prepared to squander all those millions. To satisfy the Heir's absurd ambitions they are only too ready to spend Hungarian pennies to build Austrian battleships!'

'Of course, of course, that's it!' said several of his audience.

Stanislo Gyeroffy passed his hand over his carrot-coloured wig, as if to make sure it was still firmly in place, and then added with an air of official authority, 'I'm not sure that is entirely true; but even if it is then surely it could do no harm to humour the Archduke a little? After all one day soon he'll be our King!'

'He'll only be our King if we crown him!' cried someone impetuously.

'He'll be King anyhow,' said another.

'After the Pragmatic Sanction it needs a Parliamentary decision.'

'I say: until it happens, fiddlesticks!'

'No army, no navy!' cried another, though no one quite knew what he meant. Then followed a hot debate about the prerogatives of Parliament and what clauses should be added to what texts and what should be insisted upon and what ignored. Before long they were arguing hotly about the wording to be used as if it were they who would have to decide and as if it had to be settled right where they sat. They argued about the status of Bosnia-Herzegovina and some demanded that Dalmatia too should be annexed without delay. Others hotly disputed this, saying that it would lead to Trialism, only to find themselves contradicted at once. The battle of wits was as contrived and as synthetic as military manoeuvres and though the weapons may have been as impressive as political invective they could no more win the day than could cannons loaded with blanks. All the same tempers flared and eyes flashed as the armchair politicians snarled at each other. Every issue of the day was brought up and dissected – but no one stopped to think of the welfare of the nation.

Above the hubbub could be heard the high-pitched screech of Stanislo Gyeroffy and the deep baritone of Dr Korosi, who were rapidly arriving at the point where personal insults would be hurled at each other. Then the unexpected happened. It started when someone unwisely suggested that the government might be intimidated by the rising power of the newly self-styled King of Montenegro, nicknamed 'Nikita'. This was picked up by Kalman Harinay, Ida Laczok's husband, who cried out arrogantly, 'Well, as for that, we might just as well be afraid of those apes in Albania.'

At this point Tamas jumped up and let out a roar, 'Don't you judge them by yourself, my lad! Those Albanians are tougher than you ever will be! I know them well!'

This was doubly unexpected: firstly because no one had for a moment thought that anyone present would have any first-hand knowledge of Albanians, and secondly because this plump stocky man whom few of them knew, and who hardly ever spoke, should suddenly interrupt so passionately. Furthermore Tamas's scornful attack on Harinay impressed them because Transylvanians like nothing more than a well-justified rebuke. Some of them laughed, but they all looked at the newcomer with dawning respect.

Stanislo Gyeroffy, thankful to find a diversion from his deepening disagreement with Korosi, quickly picked up Tamas's last words, saying, 'Do you know Albania well? Hasn't there recently been some insurrection against the Turks?'

'There certainly has! It's a real war. According to the *Petit Parisien*, which I get regularly, the Malissors overwhelmed Torkut Pasha and were immediately joined by the Miridiots.'

This was greeted by a storm of ironic laughter.

'What kind of idiots?' cried Harinay, while the others shouted out, 'Is that what they are called? Are the Malissors idiots too? Is that really what they call themselves? Ho! Ho! Ho! That's wonderful, that is!'

'The Malissors and the Miridiots are the two fiercest tribes of Albania! And you, fellow-me-lad,' said Tamas coldly to Harinay who was laughing immoderately at his own pun, '*tu ne rigolerai pas comme une baleine* – you wouldn't be laughing like a whale if you found yourself their prisoner. These are true men of the mountains, bandits all of them.' And he turned away because it had just occurred to him that this was a God-given chance to have a go at the banker Weissfeld. Smiling as if merely going on with his explication, 'This lot are far more than your well-born forest thieves, my banker friend. These are not men who polish the seats of their chairs in their nice safe city offices, no sedentary businessmen who plot behind the security of the limited companies that they have founded. No! Not at all! These are real fighting men, warriors who risk their skins every day of their lives!'

Some of his listeners, who knew something of the forestry combine between Tamas's brother and Weissfeld, realized what lay behind these last words and put their heads together chuckling at Tamas's audacity, while some of the others, not understanding but now aware what a sharp tongue the elder Laczok had, fell silent and for a while did not attempt any further interruption. Tamas went on with his tale.

He was standing at the centre of the circle, turning from time to time to one side or the other, and he looked extremely comical. He was dressed in an old tail coat cut in the fashion of many years before, which was now stretched tightly across his bulging stomach; and with his bald head and long wispy beard he was like an actor in a vulgar farce. This impression was heightened by his exaggeratedly upward-slanting eyebrows, by the tuft of black hair on the top of his skull, and by the droll way that he would twist round with tiny steps whenever Stanislo Gyeroffy, Sandor Kendy or Major Bogacsy asked a question. These mostly came from the ex-soldier, for though he was nowadays principally interested in questions of honour, he had once served in Bosnia and knew something of the Balkans.

The audience, mischievous as ever, soon started muttering behind Tamas's back; and one of them whispered, 'Looks like a blackcock calling for his mate!' at which the others barely suppressed their amusement for few of them were at all interested in what he was saying.

Nevertheless what he was saying was of interest. He must have been a keen observer who rarely forgot anything he saw and he could talk about his experiences with logic and clarity. He had not survived in the Atlas mountains for so many years without managing to keep his wits about him, and this was now clear from what he was recounting. The gist of his discourse was that this new rebellion in Albania was quite unlike any that had preceded it. Now, for the first time, several of the tribes that had traditionally been deadly enemies had joined together to fight the suzerainty of Turkey. Christians and Muslims were fighting side by side and what is more, they had somehow managed to obtain a supply of up-to-date guns as well as apparently limitless ammunition. Many people had been speculating where this came from, especially as the rebels had no funds. The money must have been given to them, but by whom? To Tamas the answer was obvious: it could only be Nikita, the King of Montenegro. One amazing fact led only to this conclusion. Since the anti-Turk movement had begun small bands of the insurgents had taken refuge from time to time across the Montenegrin border; and had swiftly come back. This had never happened before. If any Albanian had dared to set so much as a foot across the frontier into the border district of Chernagora, they were immediately slaughtered by the Chernagorians, while the Albanians did the same to anyone coming in the opposite direction. If this ancient tribal hatred had been abruptly changed to friendship, only one man could possibly have managed it, and that was the wily old Nikita. Therefore it must be he who was providing the ammunition and guns. But where did he get it all from? Well, a year before he had told the correspondent of the French newspaper *La Gloire* that Montenegro obtained her armaments not only from Serbia but also from the great international firm of Schneider-Creuzot. The question was, where did Nikita get his money from, for it was well-known that the Montenegrin treasury was empty? Here again the answer was obvious to anyone with eyes to see: it must be Russia. It must be the Tsar who paid for Nikita's guns and therefore also for those of the Albanian rebels. There was something very sinister going on in the Balkans. It was significant that when Nikita, then merely Prince of Montenegro, proclaimed himself King, Russian grand-dukes were present at the celebrations along with the kings of Serbia and Bulgaria. This in itself was strange since a couple of years before the last two were hardly on speaking terms and were known to detest each other.

The final proof of all this was that Torkut Pasha had been doing all he could to close the Montenegrin border! It was this last move which had meant that the only route left open was to the north through the lands of the Miridiots.

'Wouldn't it be better from the South?'

'Perhaps, but one has to pass the Malissor territory above Elbasa . . .'

At this the whole group burst into a storm of laughter for '*elbasa*' in Hungarian means nothing less than 'Fuck off!'

From time to time one of his listeners, bolder than the others, had ventured some mocking pun if only to make fun of the new-comer. The general restraint did not last long. Each time Tamas used some outlandish foreign name they did not know, someone would seize upon it, mispronounce it, and turn it into an obscene joke. And after the last remark they were almost falling out of their chairs with laughter, the same men who, a few moments earlier, had been making abstruse political arguments with such deadly seriousness that they were ready to fight one another to prove a point. The sad truth was that all of them found anything that did not concern their own country fit only for mockery and laughter. To them such matters were as remote from reality as if they had been happening on Mars; and therefore fit only for schoolboy puns and witty riposte.

Laczok looked round angrily and was about to castigate his audience when the door opened and a waiter came in.

'Dinner is served, gentlemen. The ladies are already on their way to the supper-room.'

Everyone started to get up and the discussion was over. Most of those present hurried to the door for they were hungry after all that talk and laughter, and no one wanted to keep his wife waiting. For a brief moment Stanislo Gyeroffy stayed behind and went over to speak to Tamas; but it was not kindness or good manners that prompted the gesture. In a haughty, pompous tone, he said:

'Personally I found what you were saying not without interest. If you'll sit with us at dinner you could perhaps tell us more?' and without waiting for a reply he strode out of the room, his orange wig resembling nothing so much as a banner of reaction.

For his part Tamas muttered an obscene expletive and started angrily to roll himself a cigarette.

It was then that he noticed that he was not alone. From a chair behind him he heard a faint whimpering sound, and turning he saw that old Count Adam Alvinczy was lying sprawled in his chair. It was obvious that he had tried to get up to follow the others when he had been stricken by a heart attack. He had fallen back on to the edge of the chair and only his head and shoulders touched the back-rest. His face was ashen and covered with beads of sweat, and his wide-open eyes held a look of terror.

Quickly Laczok reached his side.

'Here ... here ...' gasped Alvinczy with a rattle in his throat, '... on this side ... my drops ... in waistcoat ...'

Tamas acted swiftly. He snatched the vial from the waistcoat pocket, ran to the washroom for some water and a glass, and while hurrying back poured in the medicine. Then he helped the sick man to swallow it, pulled him up into a sitting position, loosened his collar and shirt-front, and, soaking his handkerchief with more water, pressed it to old Adam's heart. Then he sat down and waited.

He waited in silence, watching old Alvinczy closely.

The medicine acted fast. The old man relaxed as the pain subsided, his contorted face returned to its normal smoothness and he closed his eyes. His breathing was still rapid but he was no longer gasping for breath as he had been when the attack struck him.

Perhaps I needn't call a doctor, thought Tamas, as he took the old man's wrist and searched for his pulse. Then rhythmically he started to stroke the back of Alvinczy's hand.

For some time he sat there without either of them speaking.

Out in the corridor he heard doors being opened and closed and the sound of people walking about and talking. It must be the card-players, thought Tamas; and, no doubt, the other man's two sons, Farkas and Akos, were among them not knowing that in the next room their father lay near to death.

Then again there was silence.

Much later Tamas heard the music being struck up again and realized that the supper must be over. Alvinczy seemed to be asleep and Tamas wondered if now he could go too; but he did not want to leave the other alone. Then, in a weak voice, Alvinczy started to speak. 'I don't know how to thank you ... but I do ... very much. If ... if you hadn't been there I'd probably be dead by now.'

'Nonsense!' replied Tamas, though he too had thought the same thing.

'Perhaps it would have been for the best,' said Alvinczy, pursuing the thought. Then after a long pause he said, 'Oh yes! It would have been better that way.'

'What sort of talk is that?' replied Tamas roughly, though with kindness in his tone.

'You don't know, you can't know,' the old man said several times in a low voice; and then, almost as if he were talking to himself, he went on brokenly, telling of his great sorrow and his disappointment in his sons.

He had been careful all his life, he said, denying himself any indulgence, any little luxury, so that when he died his four sons would inherit enough to keep them in the style to which his family had always been accustomed. They would not have great fortunes, but they would be able to live well if unostentatiously. He had looked carefully over his widely scattered estates and divided them into four units. Then, little by little, he had improved them by constructing new stables and farm buildings, and he had made them profitable. And what had happened? Before his eyes his sons had begun to undo his life's work. They had spent money recklessly, drinking and gambling as if there were no tomorrow. For years now he had lived in dread of what it would all come to, for hardly a month went by without one of them coming to him with debts to be paid – sometimes huge sums, thousands of crowns at a time – and each time he had paid up, though to do so he had to raise mortgages on most of his property. His finances were in confusion and he too was deeply in debt. Now, if there were any more demands on him, he would have to start selling everything that was left . . .

'Perhaps it is my own fault. If I had brought them up better perhaps they wouldn't have turned out like this. I've got four sons, you know, and all of them . . . well, three of them . . . have proved worthless. They are as bad as each other!'

What on earth, he wondered hopelessly, would become of them? The only one he did not worry about was Adam, for he had married a sensible wife and seemed to work hard. He alone was saved.

'But, my God! What will happen to the others? Let me not live to see it! Let me be spared standing by while they destroy themselves!'

This was the only time old Alvinczy had bared his heart to anyone. Now he talked for a long time, but he had never before uttered a word of what was plaguing his heart. And it was strange that when he did so it should be to a man who was almost a stranger, someone he had seen perhaps three times in his life. His sorrow was something he had always kept to himself, holding his head high, alone in his dignity and despair. He had never spoken before because he had felt that to do so might harm his sons; but the iron discipline on which he had prided himself was, just this once, broken down by the pain and fear brought on by the heart attack. Even now, as soon as he had finished, he suddenly regained his confidence, straightened up, turned again to this stocky man he hardly knew, and with every sign of shame, said, 'I beg you, sir, to forget all I've just been saying. I was exaggerating . . . I just blurted it all out.'

Tamas interrupted him. 'The important thing is that you're better now. Come along, I'll go home with you,' and he stood up, helped the old man to his feet, and led him to the door. They walked slowly down the corridor: Count Alvinczy, tall, elegant and distinguished-looking and Count Laczok, stocky and somewhat absurd in his old-fashioned evening coat.

When they reached the foot of the stairs Tamas asked for Alvinczy's cloakroom ticket and went to fetch his coat while the other rested on a sofa by the wall.

'You don't have to come with me,' protested the old man. 'I can quite well get home by myself.' But he seemed quite relieved when Tamas would not hear of it and said, 'Don't talk nonsense!'

When he had paid off the cab, woken Alvinczy's valet and seen that his companion was safely in bed, Tamas set off on foot for his home at Bretfu. After an hour or two in that smoke-filled room in the hotel it felt good to be walking through the cold air of a March night.

He walked in high good humour, pleased with the success of his outing, for had he not been able to torment his old enemies? He imagined that this joyous feeling sprang only from his having been able to annoy and embarrass his aunt, his brother and that rascally banker. As he chuckled to himself he thought how astonished they would all have been if they had seen him in the role of the Good Samaritan, he whom they had only known, especially his brother, in the role of the heartless old reprobate. Looking only at the ironic side of what had happened that evening it had never occurred to him that his feeling of well-being had sprung from the basic goodness which had prompted his care of the man whose life he had saved.

Walking swiftly along the empty streets he went through the Hidelve district and past the railway station, his fur hat pushed back and his short jacket swinging as he went. His thick country boots made a clatter as he stumped along happier than he had been for some time.

And as he went, he sang. It was an old Parisian music-hall song that had been popular in the days of his youth:

> *'Moi j'm'en fou*
> *J'reste tranquillement dans mon trou!*
> *Pourquoi courir ailleurs*
> *Pour ne pas trouver meilleur . . .*
> *Moi j'm'en fou . . .'*

On he went, swinging his arms and singing at the top of his voice just as if he had been on the stage . . . but, as he had forgotten the rest of the once risqué little ballad, all that came out was '*Tara tara, tara tara, tara tara tara . . .*'

The supper had ended long before with everyone in a good mood: everyone, that is, except Pityu Kendy. At supper he had sat next to Margit Alvinczy, with whom he had fancied himself in love just as previously he had swooned after Adrienne.

Then he and his bosom friend Adam had been able to pour out their mutual but hopeless passion for Adrienne, discuss her heartlessness and bewail her cruelty while all the time enumerating her perfections. But since Adam had married Margit, Pityu had transferred his affections to his friend's new wife – for somehow it seemed only natural to imitate him in everything even to pursuing another unattainable woman. And so it was now to Margit's husband that he poured out his woes, complaining of his hopeless love in much the same words as they had both used previously in discussing her elder sister. And Adam just listened, serene in his own happiness, not minding at all that Pityu now sighed forlornly after his own wife. Nothing had changed. They still talked about the sadness of loving someone who scorned the adoring lover: only the object of adoration was not the same. Adam did not know the meaning of jealousy, but Margit's reaction was quite different from that of her sister. Whereas Adrienne had treated Adam and Pityu as if they had been dolls incapable of real feeling and had teased them both with the same remote playfulness that she had treated all the other men who had run after her, and then promptly forgot them, Margit decided to take Pityu in hand and make a man of him. Principally she wanted to wean him from the bad habits of drinking and gambling. In so far as the gambling went, she succeeded; but the drinking was another matter. Here her influence failed.

That had been the source of some trouble during the ball. Pityu drank too much at the supper-table, and by the time they served the ices she had firmly turned her back on him. When the music of a csardas sounded from the ballroom upstairs and everyone started to get up, she turned back to Pityu and issued her orders.

'You're drunk again! Either stay here and stop drinking or go home! I don't want to see you in the ballroom!'

With that she got up, gathering her skirt behind her, and ran up the stairs. In a few moments she had disappeared among the dancers. What could Pityu do? Nothing would induce him to stay alone in the deserted supper-room; so he went sadly to the cloakroom, collected his coat and headed for home.

Strangely enough, though his head was swimming from the quantity of brandy he had consumed, there was no trace of resentment in his muddled thoughts. What a woman she is! What an angel! But, oh, so cruel, so cruel! And he repeated the words to himself until he reached home.

None of the happy throng that went back to dance after supper had noticed that old Count Alvinczy was no longer among them nor had any idea that he had been taken ill.

Balint, who had been supping with Adrienne, escorted her upstairs with the others. When they arrived at the doors of the ballroom she left his arm and for a moment they stood side by side. Balint looked at her questioningly and almost imperceptibly she nodded. Her lips moved, but she said nothing that even he could have heard. Then she moved slowly on alone.

Balint remained at the head of the stairs until the last couple had come up from the supper-room. Then he hurried down, collected his fur coat and left on foot.

CHAPTER FIVE

IT WAS WELL after midday. Through the wooden laths of the shutters the sunlight cast long narrow flame-coloured lines over the carpet, across the polished parquet floor and even vertically some way up the door. The room was filled with a golden radiance.

Balint awoke, rang for his valet and ordered his bath to be run. Then he closed his eyes again and sank into a half-slumber filled with tender recollections.

In his mind he could see again a bright fire burning on the hearth, a fire which had thrown an almost blinding light on the deep-piled white carpet on which he lay but which left most of the rest of the room in mysterious shadow. He had lit the fire while waiting.

All at once the door had opened and Adrienne had stood before him, the shining paillettes on her dress reflecting the bright flames of the fire with a reddish glow which spread up over her shadowy breasts, under her chin and past the dark lines of her brows until it shone like a spotlight on the golden flowers of her oriental diadem. There she had stood, lit as if on a stage . . .

For a moment she had not moved, until as Balint knelt before her and started to kiss the hem of her skirt she had spread her arms wide waiting for his lips to reach hers. Then, bending slightly, she had taken his head in her soft hands and bent down until their lips met. As her mouth, so vividly red and slightly open, met his in a long ecstatic kiss, the jewelled chains of her crown fell in a cascade over his face and ears and shoulders.

When the man returned to tell Balint that his bath was ready he announced also that a letter had just been delivered from Baron Kadacsay. 'A stable-boy brought it, my Lord. I have put it on your Lordship's desk.'

'Very good,' said Balint, his head too full of the memory of his time with Adrienne to take in properly what he had been told. Then he sank into the hot water still thinking only of his mistress.

Around her slender ankles the dress, so like the scales of a snake, had lain in shining coils, from which had risen her alabaster figure, the fire etching every part of it with its roseate glow touched here and there with misty lilac-coloured shadows. To Balint she had seemed like some Hindu goddess, Parvati, Maya, or Brahmanaspati, crowned in gold with a shower of rubies and other stones falling over her breasts. And though she had said nothing she had been smiling in happiness and triumph.

She had been like some sculptor's masterpiece, a statue that somehow exuded joy as he knelt before her raising his hands in supplication and adoration. Later, as she had lain on the rug that

so resembled the skin of a polar-bear, naked but still crowned
with that jewelled head-dress spread in a wide arc around her
jet-black curling hair, she had still seemed in some strange way
statuesque. The fire had exploded with its own ecstasy as the
flames reached the pine-cones within it as if it too were consumed with the passion that enveloped the lovers who lay in front
of it. As each new shower of sparks exploded, faster and faster,
so had the passion of the two lovers as they moved together in a
crescendo of love.

'When was the letter delivered?' asked Balint when he had
dressed and gone into his sitting-room.

'Yesterday, my Lord. Quite late, after ten o'clock. A boy
brought it on horseback.'

A letter from Gazsi? Sent quite late at night ... by a man on
horseback? It had to be something exceptionally urgent, something really serious.

'Why didn't you bring it to me at once? You knew where
I was.'

'The boy just said to hand it to your Lordship. I asked if it was
urgent and if something was wrong, but he just said that Baron
Gazsi had not said anything in particular and had seemed to be
quite well. There was nothing out of the ordinary at home, the
boy said.'

Balint hurried over to this desk. The letter lay there, an ordinary grey envelope with his name scribbled in Gazsi's awkward
writing, and on the back were scrawled a few words that Gazsi
had presumably added as an afterthought '*I stupidly sent this to
Denestornya, believing you would still be there – Gazsi*'.

The letter itself read:

> '*Dear Balint,*
>
> *Before I leave I would like to talk something over with you.
> Could you come over here tomorrow before one o'clock ... to
> Bukkos St Marton, as I shall be leaving then and do not expect
> to be back for a long time. Sorry to inconvenience you – it will be
> the last time, I promise!*
>
> *So long ... Servus!*'

What on earth could all this be about, Balint wondered. Where
was he going? And what a strange little note. He looked at the

time; it was already half past one, so if Gazsi had kept to his plan he would have already gone.

Could he have caught the one-thirty express to Budapest? He hadn't said anything about it; and anyhow if that had been his plan he would probably have ridden over himself instead of asking Balint to come to him. Perhaps he had had some mishap on the road and gone straight to the station.

None of this seemed likely. Gazsi would never have written like that if he were just setting off on some everyday little trip. It had to be something else, something infinitely more serious. Balint thought back to their last conversation at the banquet and it occurred to him now that Gazsi had seemed unusually disillusioned and depressed, that most of his talk about his future plans could have been interpreted in more than one sense, and that everything he had said might perhaps have referred to his imminent death rather than to some imaginary voyage. After all, Balint reflected, had it not been he himself, rather than Gazsi, who had talked about going on his travels and who had even proposed it? Brushing away such morbid thoughts Balint once more convinced himself that obviously Gazsi had wanted to consult him further about possible travel plans. And yet this did not seem like his friend. No! It was far more likely that before going away he wanted to entrust something to Balint, to make some arrangement about the management of his horses or the administration of his property ... that would be it! That was why he had asked for him; and Balint believed in this happy solution because he was so happy himself that this was what he wanted to believe. All the same a little pin-prick of anxiety remained.

Whatever the reason it was obvious that he must answer the summons at once, and ten minutes later his car was speeding along the highway that led up the valley of the Felek.

It was a day of radiant sunshine even though spring had not yet come. The snows had recently melted on the hillsides and now all the south-facing meadows and slopes looked as if they had just been washed. There was not a speck of dust anywhere and it was too early for the weeds to have started springing up. Everything had been sluiced clean by the melting snow, as if the countryside had just been prepared for some joyous feast. On the north-facing slopes the snow still lay, gleaming white in the sun and, as it too was now slowly melting away, everything that might have soiled its surfaces had sunk to the earth and from its edges

tiny rivulets of water were now beginning the seasonal change
that the sun had already achieved on the other side of the valley.

Balint fancied that he could already smell the first scents of
spring.

The car purred effortlessly up the last incline in the road.
Balint knew he would be at St Marton in another fifteen minutes
and that very shortly afterwards he would be at Gazsi's place.

Once again he wondered what on earth it was that Gazsi could
have wanted so urgently as to send for him like that. As he drew
nearer and nearer to his destination all Balint's suppressed anxieties rose up and assailed him once more; and no matter how
much he tried to reassure himself that he was being stupid and
unreasonable he was unable to banish them entirely. Again
and again he found himself thinking of those words in the letter
'*I do not expect to be back for a long time ... Sorry to inconvenience
you. It will be the last time, I promise!*' Had he not also written:
'*I don't know if I'll ever be back.*' What strange words they were!
In themselves they may have seemed banal and without great
significance, but knowing Kadacsay's bitter indictment of himself, Balint felt they must have some other meaning, ominous
even if not obvious. He remembered too that Gazsi had once said
to him that in the life of a man troubles and joys are usually
equally balanced, but when something occurred to so upset
the balance that nothing was left but trouble and misery then the
only answer was to kill oneself. Of course when he had said this
Gazsi had seemed unusually disheartened and miserable.

Balint tried to go over in his mind everything that Gazsi had
ever said to him and as he did so he tried to remember some
words that might have been more reassuring. Try as he would he
could not think of anything. On the contrary, thinking back to
those discussions when Gazsi had asked him to be his executor,
and also when he had arranged that Balint would take in his
beloved mare, Balint now realized there had been a double
meaning in every word that Gazsi had uttered.

For a brief moment Balint half-closed his eyes so as to concentrate better, and as he did so the sunlight through his eyelids
seemed rose-red and all his worries disappeared as he saw in his
mind's eye the image of Adrienne as she had been in the firelight,
with her parted lips and wide open eyes, with her expression of
almost painful anticipation of that moment when all space and
time were wiped away, when there was no past and no future

and when time itself became an eternity. Her beautiful face, framed in those wildly tumbling curls, could have been that of Medusa or the Tragic Muse herself, and for a moment Balint saw only this and felt only the surge of renewed desire . . .

An instant later he was able to banish the thought as he forced himself once more to think about his friend and pray, as he sped towards him through that countryside halfway between winter and spring, that Gazsi had only written to him in that equivocal manner as a result of some passing fancy or fit of depression at being delayed in some ridiculous fashion, and that he was even now at home, laughing at his own stupidity, with his crow's beak of a nose tilted to one side as it always was when he was telling a droll story about himself and when nothing was seriously wrong.

The car turned into the narrow road that led to Gazsi's village. The road curved round one more snow-covered hillside and ahead, a little higher up, could be seen the roofs of the village and on one side, surrounded by tall elm trees, Gazsi's old manor house.

As Balint drove on towards the hedge that bordered Gazsi's property and the gates, which would shortly appear, he found himself passing several little groups of village people all going in the same direction, one ahead of the other as in Indian file. They were walking in silence and with the heavy tread of the Mezoseg people. He sounded his horn and as the men and women drew to one side, some of the men raised their caps in respectful greeting. Balint wondered why they all seemed to be going to the manor house, and why they all looked so sad.

A moment or two later he had arrived in front of the portico with its wooden Grecian pillars that framed the entrance to the house. Three steps led up to it and standing at the top were two men, Gazsi's estate manager and the local Protestant pastor.

'Where is Baron Gazsi?' asked Balint.

'He died, just an hour and a half ago!' said one of them.

Balint felt his legs giving way under him and he staggered to a bench beside the wall.

Then they told him what had happened.

Baron Gazsi had been writing something all morning. When he had finished he had folded up the sheets of paper and sealed them. A little later he had walked down to the stables and looked into every box giving a lump of sugar to each horse as he always had. Just as the clock chimed the hour of midday he sent for the pastor and the estate manager, sat them down in the sitting-room and gave them his orders. To the priest he had given instructions that the church organ, which had been in bad repair for some time, should be put in order and told them that he accepted the estimate of 500 florins and that he wanted it done at once. He had discussed many small details of the work, told them that when it was done they must send for a man to apply the gold leaf and specified that it should be old Kas from Kolozsvar because he was the best. The elaborate decorations above the organ-pipes, which were a disgrace, must be properly restored and he insisted that before that work was started the pastor should arrange a sensible price with the gilder because he did not want money wasted on anything that was not necessary. Then he had asked the estate manager to bring in the accounts, checked them through himself and drew a line across the last page just beneath them. Then he had written '*I have found everything in order up to this point*' and added the date and his signature. Then he had turned to other estate matters, saying that the young calves that had been selected for the market should not be disposed of at once because the current prices were too low. They should wait until the new grass started to sprout in the meadows. On the other hand the buffalo cows should be sold soon before their milk dried up. Up on the Botos, where it was too cold for wheat, they should sow barley and, if the fields of rye which had been sown the previous autumn proved to be full of thistles in the spring, they should be carefully weeded. All these orders he had given in the calmest manner. Occasionally, as he had been speaking, he had glanced at the clock as if he were expecting someone or had shortly been about to leave himself. Just before one o'clock he had said that he had been expecting Balint, but that perhaps he would not be coming. As he said this he had gone to his desk and picked up a small parcel carefully wrapped in newspaper and handed it to the priest, saying that it should be given to Balint if he should turn up later. If he had not arrived by the evening it should be delivered to Balint's home. Then he had gone into his bedroom and rung for his valet.

The priest and the manager, though not understanding what all this was about, had not thought that there was any reason to be disturbed.

A few moments later Kadacsay had come back into the sitting-room, followed by the valet and a footman who carried a mattress which he had told them to lay on the floor. When the servants had been dismissed he started to explain to his astonished audience why all this had been done. He had, he told them, taken a dose of strychnine and because he knew that this sometimes caused uncontrollable cramps, he had had the mattress placed there as it would be better and easier than writhing about on the wooden floor-boards! Then he had started to give further instructions about suckling pigs and the sheep's feed . . .

Shortly afterwards he had looked again at the clock and said, 'Strange! I don't feel anything yet, though I've taken enough to fell an ox!'

Those had been his last words. A moment later he had lain down and, a few seconds later, had died.

'Is he very disfigured?' Balint asked when the pastor and the manager had finished their tale.

'Not at all, my Lord. Please come and look.'

They entered the manor house living-room, which was long and wide and obviously served also as a dining-room. In front of one of the windows was a small writing desk and, pushed against one of the side walls, was a plain pinewood table that had served for Gazsi's meals. In the centre of the room, where this was usually placed, there was a mattress and on this lay the dead man covered with a white sheet.

Balint kneeled down beside him and drew back the sheet from his head. He looked at his friend's face for a long time.

Nothing seemed to have changed and if he had not been as pale as wax Balint would have thought that he was merely playing some trick on them. His mouth held his usual mocking smile, his woodpecker nose was tilted slightly to one side and his eyebrows slanted upwards just as they always had when Gazsi had been telling a joke. One could almost believe that at any moment he would jump up roaring with laughter as he had so often done. And yet there was a difference. Gazsi's face now held an expression of majestic calm, comprised of a dignity quite new to him – and of contempt, but mainly of contempt.

Balint was struck by the strangeness of it all, for this was not the Gazsi he had known in life. The dead man lying there was someone he did not know, someone who had appeared only in death.

He covered him again with the white sheet and got to his feet.

Then he looked around the room and realized that its simplicity and bareness also signified contempt. Though like every provincial manor house in Transylvania it must once have contained some good pieces of furniture, there was now nothing of value in it. It was clear that such things had meant little to Gazsi for he had given all his good things to his sister when they had divided their inheritance – furniture, carpets, porcelain, everything. For himself he had kept only a couple of threadbare armchairs and a worn sofa. But along the walls there were long low bookshelves made of bare polished planks of natural wood, and on them were great quantities of books untidily stacked, much used and obviously much read. Balint went up to examine them and found to his amazement that they were mostly philosophical works by such writers as Hegel, Wundt and Schopenhauer. There were also some historical works by Ranke and Szilagyi, and a copy of Renan missing its cover, and several volumes of some German lexicon. Most of the books were tattered and some torn in half . . . and all were stained and dirty as if they had been covered in candle-wax or thrown about in anger.

Balint started to pick some of them up, but when it was announced that the doctor had arrived, along with the coroner, the Prefect and the village notary, all of whom were needed to make out the death certificate, he went quickly out into the open air.

Outside it was a perfect day. The sky was so clear that it was almost blinding, very pale, white-grey rather than blue, and so savagely bright that it might have been trying to compete with the snow beneath.

So as not to remain surrounded by the crowd of weeping women, or be stared at by the village children who were gathered outside the house, he walked round to the side and took a path that led up the hill. It was already clear of snow and slightly muddy. After he had gone some hundred paces he found a bench under three young birch trees and sat down. Then he undid the sealed package.

Inside there were two envelopes and also a silver cigarette box with an inscription in gold: 'The Ladies Prize, Debrecen, 1905'. He opened it and inside was a little pile of tobacco dust and a note which read '*I leave you this as a personal souvenir. It is the only possession I value*' and underneath, in brackets, '*You may think it ugly, so don't use it if you don't like it! Gazsi.*'

In the larger of the two envelopes there was a long paper headed AMENDMENTS TO MY WILL below which was a precise list of his wishes for gifts to each of his servants, some other special provisions, and the fact that he wanted 1,000 crowns to be allotted for restoring the organ. These details had not been itemized in the Will held by the notary, though a lump sum had been set aside for them. The next paragraph dealt with arrangements for his funeral: he did not wish to be buried anywhere else but to be laid to rest somewhere in the garden near the house – and there was to be no memorial or epitaph. The last section dealt with his horses. Firstly he wrote that the little speckled gelding who was too old to work should be shot so that he would not fall into the hands of the gypsies in his old age. As to the thoroughbred mare Honeydew, Gazsi left her to Balint and asked him to take her away immediately. At the bottom of the page was that day's date, the date of Gazsi's death, and his signature, written in Gazsi's large awkward writing.

The second letter was for Balint alone. Enclosed with it was Honeydew's pedigree wrapped in a single sheet of writing paper, on which there were just a few lines about the mare. '*As you agreed to let Honeydew foal at Denestornya,*' he had written, '*I hope it isn't presuming to ask you to keep her.*' Then followed a few light-hearted, joking phrases ending '*. . . my sister is apt to be somewhat grasping, but I don't feel she'd want this wonderful animal as she wouldn't have much use for her!*' He ended with the words '*Please don't forget your promise about my nephews. I don't want them to turn out like me.*'

Poor Gazsi, thought Balint. In his last moments he had been thinking of his own great unquenched thirst for culture.

Balint's eyes filled with tears. For a long time he stayed where he was, sitting on the little bench and staring at the snow. He thought how marvellous it was as it slowly melted, disintegrating into tiny particles of ice, thousands of minute crystals gleaming like miniature mountain peaks all turned towards the rays of the sun. It was everywhere pitted with deep little crevasses like spear-thrusts from the direction of the south, deep little holes formed by the sun's heat. And as it was slowly being destroyed by that very sun so the snow resembled white foam inexorably drawn to that relentless implacable light, to that radiance it so much desired but which was to be the source of its own destruction. To Balint the process was like an allegory of all existence . . . and he thought again about his dead friend.

On the same day another death occurred, that of old Adam Alvinczy. He was found dead in his bed in the morning, and this news and the social excitement it provoked drew everyone's attention away from Gazsi's suicide.

Since Count Alvinczy had been a prominent man there had to be an important funeral. A long line of carriages and cars followed the cortege to the family vault.

The following day the lawyer read the dead man's will in the presence of his sons, of his daughter-in-law Margit, and of Stanislo Gyeroffy who had been made executor. It proved to be a harsh and comfortless document. The old landowner had carefully recorded all the money he had had to pay out to settle his sons' debts and on the basis of these figures he had drawn up the inheritances of three of them in three separate columns – three because Adam had been given his share two years before when he had got married. It was a shattering experience for those who were left: Farkas was to receive only the house at Magyarokerek, with just eight hundred acres and three small forest holdings; and Zoltan the meadows near Magyar-Tohat and the house in Kolozsvar. All had been heavily mortgaged. The youngest brother, Akos, got nothing because only two months previously his father had settled debts that already exceeded his share of the family property. '*I regret having to do this,*' wrote the old man, '*but I cannot deprive my other sons just because of him.*'

This came as a mortifying shock to the three brothers, and most of all to Akos who, as soon as the lawyer had left the house, stammered out the confession that on the night of the charity ball he had lost sixteen thousand crowns at the gaming-table and the winners had only given him an extra two weeks to pay up because of his father's death. He now had only thirteen days' grace. Thirteen days, that was all. If he couldn't pay then he would be finished!

There followed a terrible argument, long and utterly fruitless. There was no possibility of help. Farkas's and Zoltan's shares were both mortgaged up to the hilt, in addition to which they would somehow have to find money to pay the inheritance tax.

They could do nothing. The only hope was that Adam would pay for the youngest.

This, from the goodness of his heart, he would have been willing to do, but Margit vetoed the idea at once. They had a child to think about, she said, so Adam's own small inheritance could not be squandered in this way. What would be the purpose of such a sacrifice, she asked? It would only be throwing money away, and in fact would not really help Akos, who would still have nothing and who could not live on thin air! He himself would not want to live for ever on his brothers' charity, an eternal guest! It would be far more sensible, she went on, if he were to go away somewhere and start a new life. The family could, at some sacrifice, manage to raise just enough to pay for his ticket; but to cough up money just for gambling debts? No! Never!

Margit was at once attacked by Farkas and Zoltan. They said that she was mercenary and without pity and, of course, as they too were deeply in debt, they felt that they could have been as magnanimous as they liked as any help for Akos would have to be paid for by Adam who, because of their insistence, was for once coming close to rebelling against his capable young wife. It was lucky for her that she was supported by Stanislo; and this settled the matter.

So they started to discuss where Akos could go. First, as a matter of course, they spoke of America. Then it was the turn of Java and, following that, of South Africa. But at each suggestion the same problem arose: what would he do when he arrived? Work as a shoe-shine boy? Get a job hoeing the earth on some plantation? The trouble was that he had no qualifications for earning his own living. Of course he could become a soldier, and indeed had been quite good at it when doing his voluntary service in the army; but where would he be needed?

It was this last suggestion that led to the decision that he should join the French Foreign Legion.

Akos agreed at once, and almost seemed pleased at the idea; but though at last everyone was of one opinion, no one knew how one went about it. What did one do? How did one get there?

Then someone thought of Tamas Laczok, he who had taken their father home after his attack at the ball. They had had a long talk with him after the old man had been found dead, and he had been the last of his acquaintance to see him alive. He had seemed full of good will and the Legion had been mentioned more than once when he had been telling them about his time in North Africa and how he had had to nurse sick soldiers in the desert. He would know what should be done, but who could find out for them without explaining why they wanted to know? The Alvinczy brothers refused at once. They would have nothing to do with making such embarrassing enquiries, not them! Neither would they lift a finger in such a matter; it would have to be someone else. Stanislo Gyeroffy also demurred, murmuring contemptuously, though in an elegant drawl: 'I really hardly know the man.'

The plan was on the point of being abandoned when Margit spoke up.

'I'll find out!' she said. By what means she did not reveal and the others did not ask. It was unlikely that she would have told them if they had. At most she might just have answered 'Somehow!', for she was a person of few words who did not take kindly to being cross-questioned about anything.

Margit had immediately thought of Balint Abady who was clever and discreet and who was on good terms with Tamas Laczok.

That very afternoon Balint took a horse-cab and was driven out to Bretfu. The coachman, who knew the area well, drove him to the foot of the hill that led to the village and stopped there because the horse would not have been able to manage the steep road that was now covered with melting snow.

'It's the little house you can see up there, your Lordship, the one below the vineyard,' said the coachman, pointing the way with his whip.

It was hard work trudging up the hill through mud and slush, and it was nearly a quarter of an hour later before Balint found himself in front of the house. It was a modest little building which must have been either a small summerhouse or else a room for pressing the grapes, before being converted into a one-room dwelling with a kitchen. Lamplight glowed through the window. Balint knocked and from inside a voice cried, '*Entrez!*'

Tamas Laczok was sitting on an upturned packing-case. He was in his shirtsleeves doing calculations beside a drawing board that was supported on two trestles. He welcomed Balint with a smile of pleasure saying, '*Quelle charmante visite, cher ami* – how kind of you to come to see me!' and he got up, cleared the only chair of his jacket, necktie and collar, threw them on the floor, gestured to Abady to sit down and, having guessed that the visit must have some purpose, at once asked, 'How can I be of service to you, my dear friend?'

Balint saw no reason to beat about the bush.

'How does one enlist in the Foreign Legion?' he asked.

His eyebrows slanting up even more dramatically than usual, Tamas winked at his visitor. Though he said nothing to show that he had guessed at once that Abady was enquiring on behalf of one of the Alvinczy boys, he answered in a matter-of-fact way as if it had been the most natural question in the world.

'The Foreign Legion? Oh, that's very simple!' And he at once gave Abady all the most important facts, namely that the candidate just presented himself at the recruiting office. No documents were necessary and no questions were asked. It was just like becoming a Carthusian friar. One could use any name one liked; the Legion did not care and indeed nearly all the men serving in it went under false names. There was a medical examination and once that was passed the candidate was offered a five-year contract. Promotion to corporal was fairly swift providing a man behaved himself, and it was by no means unknown for officers to be promoted from the ranks. After five years a man could leave the Legion or sign on for a further period.

'I know of several men who have quit after their years of service, bought a small farm out there in Algeria and now live happily at their ease. Of course the discipline is hard, very hard; but it has to be as the men are a pretty wild bunch, tough fellows, and rough too, though reliable comrades when the fighting gets grim and the patrols are ambushed. There is an iron tradition that no one lets down a comrade, ever. The climate's not too bad: it's healthy, even if it does get hot in the summer.'

As always Laczok spoke in French, and he went on to relate many things from his own experience when he had been building the railway in the high Atlas and when he and his men had been protected by the Legion's vigilance. Laczok had been an exceptionally perceptive observer. Suddenly he stopped reminiscing and said, 'But I haven't offered you anything! Wouldn't you like some coffee? I'm always ready for a cup!' and without waiting for a reply he leaned back his strong, pillar-like torso, and called out in Hungarian, 'Rara! Rara! Where the Devil are you, you little beast?' and, turning back to Abady, he explained, 'Her real name is Esmeralda, but I call her Rara for short. Perhaps it's a bit sugary, but you'll see it suits her!'

The door opened quietly behind him and a very young, very slim and very beautiful gypsy girl came into the room. She wore a red dress as bright as a fireman's tunic, which set off her coal-black hair. Her brown skin seemed almost to have a greenish glow and it was with pouting lips and a languorous glance filled with sensual invitation that, in a throaty voice that suggested that she was in fact offering herself, she asked, 'You wanted me?'

'Coffee! For both of us!'

'It's on the stove; I'll bring some straight away!'

She went noiselessly from the room and a few moments later returned just as silently. Her bare feet did not make the smallest sound on the floor, for she walked on tiptoe like a young deer; and she moved slowly just as if she were performing some ancient ritual dance to a melody only she could hear. As she put down the tray she looked again at Tamas's guest and, in her long eyes and in the smile on her now widely parted lips, the invitation was unmistakable.

If Count Tamas had noticed this he showed no sign but went on with his tales of the Legion. 'I should think it's probably a good moment to join, for they'll be wanting recruits just now; more and more of them from what my old friends write to me from time to time. I see from the Paris papers – though they always write in such guarded terms – that France has got great plans for Morocco too these days. You can always tell what the French mean when they start complaining about this and that and talking about the security of their borders and the necessity to safeguard their economic interests. It just means that one of these days they'll march in; and once there everyone else will be squeezed out! You mark my words!'

'But at the Algeciras Conference, and when the Franco-German agreement was signed two years ago, the French again confirmed their open-door policy as regards Morocco, just as they guaranteed the independence and authority of the Sultan. France's influence is surely limited to political matters.'

'Pouf! The French don't bother about little things like that! I'll bet you anything you like that something is about to break there; and all the more so since they've sent in Lyautey from Algeria. I knew him when he was a mere captain, and I can tell you he's a tough one!'

Old Tamas then went on to talk about North Africa and all its problems. He talked well because he knew his subject. No matter how complicated the issue Laczok understood it and knew the real facts. Abady listened fascinated as his host unravelled the involved politics of Algeria and Morocco with the same clarity as a few days earlier he had talked about Albania.

It was dark when Abady finally took his leave. Tamas accompanied him to the door, saying, 'Wait a moment! There's a little path round the side of the house. It'll get you down dry-shod,' and he called through to the kitchen, 'Lajko! Lajko! Come out here!'

A slender gypsy boy, about seventeen years old, came running out. His beard had hardly sprouted and he wore an assortment of discarded gentleman's clothes – a shabby smoking-jacket and a patched pair of striped trousers – and his feet were thrust into an old pair of tennis shoes. Under the jacket his chest was bare. And on his finely carved Egyptian features was a sly smile of mock humility.

'At your service?' It was a question.

'You can show this gentleman down the side path.'

The youth started off but, noticing that Balint was not following him, stopped a few paces away.

Laczok, seeing the surprise in Balint's face, gave a roar of cynical laughter.

'*Elle affirme que c'est son frère, mais je ne le crois pas* – she says he is her brother, but I don't believe it!'

He gave a hefty slap to Abady's shoulder, and then bade him goodbye.

Abady and the gypsy descended the hill, the lad leading the way. He had all the litheness and grace of a panther and the quick, neat movements of his nomadic forebears. After swiftly taking five or six paces he stopped and looked back and waited for Abady to catch up. For a moment his white eyeballs gleamed in the smooth dark face and then he turned and went on down as if barely able to curb his youthful impatience.

Abady descended the path at his own pace. The city's myriad lights glowed down in the valley and for a moment Abady found himself almost blinded by the arc-lights of the station at the foot of the hill. For a moment or two he paused to gaze at the beauty of the great spread of tiny lights in the dark night; and, as he stopped, he was thinking what a strange man Tamas Laczok was.

He knew so much, he was filled with esoteric knowledge, he had gazed at wide horizons and not been dazzled, and he was also a man of culture and refinement. But he had used none of it: he had just let it go to waste, burying himself here in a ramshackle cottage with a little gypsy whore, and yet he showed all the signs of being a happy man.

Balint thought of poor Gazsi Kadacsay, who had killed himself in despair because he could not acquire what Count Tamas had carelessly tossed away. He wondered if Gazsi's fate would have been different if he had managed to learn all that Tamas had learned; and would Laczok be so carefree and merry if, with all his knowledge, he had not abandoned his origins and turned his back on power and worldly success? Was it some inborn wisdom that had given him the strength to throw all that away, or would he have been just as happy if fate had not made him leave his own country and go away to learn about the world elsewhere? Would he have been as jovial and contented if he had merely stayed at home, living in idleness and easy ignorance?

Was a man formed by his experience or by his natural talents? Can a man only give up calmly what he is already sure of possessing, and never what he has vainly longed to acquire?

PART THREE

CHAPTER ONE

LATE IN THE afternoon of March 7th, 1912, there was an exceptionally large crowd of people milling about in the spacious reception rooms of the National Casino Club in Budapest. As well as the familiar group of card-players and all those so-called '*szkupcsina*' – the disgruntled old armchair politicians who were forever complaining – on this day there was an almost complete gathering of the ruling party's political leaders. They were all waiting for the return from Vienna of the Minister-President, Khuen-Hedervary, who had let it be known that he was bringing important news and wished everyone to be present so that he could discuss it with them in confidence.

In those days the Casino Club was always being used for such meetings because anyone who was a member could go in and out without anyone else wondering what they were doing there and, furthermore, since those who were not members were permitted to use one of the restaurant rooms on the ground floor, anyone could be seen coming in without the press guessing that something was up and broadcasting the news to the general public.

Everyone realized the news must be exceptionally important; it was known that Count Berchtold, Austria's foreign minister since the death of Aehrenthal a few months before, was also coming from Vienna and would see Khuen-Hedervary that night.

And very important it was – sudden, unexpected, serious and astonishing. It was also alarming and seemed fraught with danger. It was simply that at the previous day's audience, Franz-Josef had instructed Khuen-Hedervary to inform the political leaders of Hungary that after more than half a century on the throne he was seriously considering abdication. He had informed the Minister-President that ever since 1867 he had faithfully and honestly respected the agreement drawn up in that year between the governments of Austria and Hungary, that he had done everything he could to humour the leaders of Hungary, always promoting Hungarian interests and honouring that country's great families and now, or so it seemed to him, it was the descendants of those very people who had turned away from him and left it to him alone to preserve the terms of that agreement.

'In these circumstances,' the monarch had continued, 'we authorize you to explain confidentially to your colleagues that if the Party of 1867 now in power decides to ally themselves with those who wish to erode our most important governing powers, then we are ready to abdicate at once and hand the throne over to our successor!' He had then added, with conscious irony: 'Then they'll see what they are in for!'

The King's words were a direct reference to the proposal put forward by Ferenc Kossuth which, if accepted, would have put an end to the Commander-in-Chief's right to mobilize the reserves should the politicians' obstructive tactics prevent the annual recruiting law being passed in Parliament. This proposal, after much debate, had been accepted not only by Andrassy, but also, and most unexpectedly, by Tisza and by Khuen-Hedervary himself – in other words by the majority of the 1867 Party. The reason was that the opposition's obstruction of the passing of the defence estimates had already kept going since the previous July, and Kossuth had made it clear that acceptance of his terms was the price that had to be paid if the obstruction was to come to an end.

Tisza and Khuen-Hedervary had been almost alone in realizing that, in the present deteriorating situation in Europe, the primary consideration must be the building up of the armed forces. Tisza also did not think the diminution of the Commander-in-Chief's prerogatives – which in any case he had planned to bring about in due course – anything like as important as bringing to an end the stalemate in Parliament. For them both the overriding priority was to modernize the army.

Since the previous July the European situation had grown worse and worse.

The revolt in Albania had spread alarmingly. The rebels had been joined by several more tribes and even by officers from the Sultan's army. Everywhere Turks were being assassinated and the government in Istanbul had ordered up reinforcements to control the borders with Montenegro. Nikita had at once replied by mobilizing the Montenegrin reserves while at the same time cynically offering peace negotiations – this from the man who had aided the Albanian rebels with sanctuary and supplies of arms! In this he had not been alone, for it was known that aid also came, if clandestinely, from Italy, for many resident Albanians had re-crossed the Adriatic and joined their compatriots in fighting the Turks. No one believed that this was done without the connivance and active help of the government in Rome and indeed it was the first tangible sign of Italy's going her own way regardless of the official policy of her allies in the Triple Alliance, Austria-Hungary and Germany, whose Balkan policy was firmly based on maintaining the *status quo* of the Turkish empire.

All these developments were but a foretaste of what was to come, a curtain-raiser, as it were, to events elsewhere.

At Agadir in Morocco a few German citizens were subjected to some insignificant barbarity, whereupon Berlin despatched a destroyer, the 'Panther', to demand satisfaction and, if necessary, to exact retribution. Making a show of force with no preliminary negotiations was in itself sufficiently provocative, but matters were made worse when the Kaiser Wilhelm, who was given to such over-hasty actions, sent a telegram to the German commanding officer: '*Panther! Fass!* – Panther! Catch 'em!'

The European powers, who had between them settled Morocco's fate at the Algeciras Conference in 1906, protested loudly at this arrogance on Germany's part, especially when Berlin declared it a matter which concerned France and Germany alone. At once the French and English standpoints were made clear to the world; France protested strongly and London declared it stood firmly behind Paris. In a few days, tension mounted so high that war seemed inevitable and, even though Reuters announced that Great Britain had no wish to be involved, the Atlantic Fleet was put in readiness and a flotilla of torpedo-boats left Portland with sealed orders. Some saw all this as a God-given opportunity to destroy the German fleet whose recent build-up had been worrying England for some time. Had this been allowed to happen a general European war would have been inevitable.

As it happened the German chancellor, Bethman-Holweg, found himself forced to come to an agreement with the French. This was not easy, but after prolonged negotiations, during which the German demands grew progressively weaker, Bethman-Holweg was obliged to accept compensation in the form of a slice of the Congo which was riddled with yellow fever.

It was an ignominious ending to an enterprise which had started with such a high-handed flourish; but for all its comedy the affair had its serious side. Before the Agadir incident the open-door policy as regards Morocco had been generally accepted. Now it was clear that Germany had bought peace by abandoning a policy that was in everybody's interest. And this she had done by selling her commercial rights in Morocco in exchange for a dish of lentils, which is what her newly acquired colony in Africa was derisively named by the other powers. Germany's action in almost breaking the peace and then descending to diplomatic blackmail (even though it was clear to everyone that what she had given up in Morocco was far more valuable than what she received elsewhere) served as Bethman-Holweg's introduction to the stage of world politics – and it was also the first significant dent in Germany's prestige abroad.

The Moroccan crisis had lasted from July 5th, 1911 until the end of September in the same year, and coincided with the general mobilization in Montenegro. This marked the start, in Budapest, of the parliamentary obstruction of the Hungarian army estimates. On July 9th Asquith announced Britain's soli-darity with France, and on July 11th Kossuth declared that he would fight the Hungarian government's defence proposals with all the means in his power: and it was on the following day that he put into effect the obstructive tactics designed to prevent the modernization of the Hungarian army.

On July 26th the British fleet was put in a state of readiness and on the 30th Gyula Justh held a public meeting at which he brandished the slogan of universal suffrage as infinitely more important to Hungary than the nation's ability to defend itself. The rabble, roused by this irresponsible speechifying, streamed wildly down Rakoczy Street and was only halted at the corner of the Karolyi Ring. This occurred on the same afternoon that the British torpedo-boat flotilla left Portland Harbour for an 'unknown destination', and when the prospect of a European war had been at its most menacing.

And so it went on. Parallel to every event of world impor-tance was some manifestation of purely parochial interest in Budapest; and when the Agadir incident was closed and the revolt in Albania came to a temporary halt, then other sinister happenings disturbed the peace of Europe, many of them close to the borders of Hungary, matters so dangerous and so close to home that one would have thought someone in Budapest would have noticed.

The next move was once again in the Balkans, close to the Hungarian border.

The Franco-German agreement was signed on September 28th. Two days earlier two Italian fleets sailed from Syracuse, one to conquer Tripoli, the other to attack the Turkish empire.

Both of these moves were unexpected and came as a surprise to Vienna as to Berlin. It had been long recognized that France had agreed to Tripoli being in Italy's sphere of influence, even after that country had seized upon Tunis; but no one had thought of it as being anything more than a sop to Italian sensibilities, a sort of consolation-plaster to be applied to the Italian public's wounded heart, and of little importance as there were so few Italians living in that part of North Africa. And indeed few people had given it a thought for some time past.

Now, all of a sudden, Rome remembered she was short of colonies and declared war on the Sublime Porte. Of course, when Germany had seen fit to ignore the international agreements settled at Algeciras and took her own individual line at Agadir, a proceeding whose negotiated settlement effectively closed the old open-door to Morocco, she did irreparable harm to Italy's trading interests. At much the same time Aehrenthal's sudden announcement of the annexation of Bosnia-Herzegovina had encouraged Italy to enter, even if somewhat belatedly, the European powers' race to acquire colonies. And this she did, independently of her allies and, as Austria had done with Bosnia in 1908, keeping her intentions secret until the last minute. Once again those international agreements, on which the peace of Europe had so long depended, were ignored.

This had happened in October, but despite the inevitable international repercussions, in Budapest no one seemed to notice and in public life nothing was changed. Political argument and obstruction went on as before, with the political leaders all claiming to be acting in the nation's best interests. Public opinion remained unawakened to the implications of what was happening abroad; and though Apponyi asked the House to consider what would happen if the Turko-Italian conflict spread to the Balkans, in the very same session all that seemed to interest Mihaly Karolyi, one of the leading opponents of the government, was the possibility of obtaining cheap meat from the Argentine.

The Speaker, Berzeviczy, tried to arrange a meeting between the government and the opposition in the Karolyi palace ... but only three ministers turned up, and the negotiations and the obstruction continued for a whole month until Berzeviczy resigned. There was then a short truce so that the Budget could be passed, during which time matters of defence were put on the shelf until, three weeks later, they were brought up again only to be the object of renewed obstruction.

By this time it had become obvious that the '*Entente cordiale*' – Britain, France and Russia – which had brought Germany to her knees over the Moroccan question, would present a solid front whatever happened and that Italy's war in Tripolitania was being backed by Britain and France: the proof, if proof were needed, was the occupation by Britain of the Egyptian port of Solum.

And in Hungary all went on as before. As the world situation got worse and worse so the politicians in Budapest buried their heads deeper in the sand and went to war only with each other.

Franz-Josef's threat of abdication came like a thunderbolt from a clear sky. He had ruled so long, become so associated with the very idea of monarchy, that it seemed that the man himself, and only he, was in fact the institution. Perhaps some people realized that one day a change would come, but few could imagine what it would be like. In Hungary some of the political leaders such as Justh and his followers had, through the turncoat Kristoffy, maintained some sort of contact with the so-called 'workshop' of Franz-Josef's heir, the Archduke Franz-Ferdinand, at the Belvedere Palace in Vienna, but it must be admitted that this was mainly a matter of political tactics, one of the backstairs routes to power. Such men hoped that by exerting pressure on the Heir they might finally not only gain some of their vote-catching aims (such as, for instance, the introduction of universal suffrage) but also that this would enable them to ride into office; but they never really grasped that a change of ruler might also involve other changes too. Some there were, ambitious men who felt their talents had not been sufficiently appreciated, who offered themselves to the Belvedere with much the same desperation as a bankrupt foolishly spending his last penny on a lottery ticket expecting thereby to win a fortune! But it would have been difficult, among all the thousands of other politically-minded inhabitants of Budapest, to find one who had really considered either the effects of change or indeed that change might come at any time, maybe today, maybe tomorrow.

Now, suddenly, this horrid prospect was upon them; and it had appeared in its most unexpected form, the possible abdication of the monarch.

While the Minister-President conferred with his colleagues behind the closed doors of the Deak Room, and while Count Berchtold, accompanied by a small group of old friends, strolled with insouciant elegance through the galleries of the club, more and more people came thronging into the public rooms. In little groups they discussed the terrible news in hushed voices and, at the bottom of the stairs, the newspaper men waited for definite news, and cross-questioned each other to find out if anyone knew more than they did. The telephone never stopped ringing, sounding as loud as a fireman's bell in the general hush.

Everyone was upset and worried, for to most of them the Heir represented the Unknown. Only one thing was sure, and that was that Franz-Ferdinand hated the Hungarians. Only that was certain, everything else was a mere question-mark.

The government's supporters were filled with anxiety, but the opposition's reaction was one of anger. No one dared say openly what they felt, but the unspoken thought was there behind their words and what they felt was anger, anger with the old monarch who seemed to have stolen a march upon them all by being so ungentlemanly as to make such a threat at such a time. Why, it was as if two men had been playing a friendly game of chess – only it happened to be the game of government – when suddenly one of them got up and walked away!

Indeed it was all a little like chess where the accepted rules make sure that bishops only move diagonally, knights can jump a square or two, and pawns, while they can be taken from the side, can only move forwards and then only one pace at a time; and every move has only one aim, to checkmate the opponent's king. For as long as anyone could remember politics in Budapest had been like that. By strictly interpreting the House Rules, by reviving forgotten procedures, by shifting loyalty and by endless declarations of vote-catching slogans, the opposition had for more than ten years obstructed all progress, especially delaying the modernization of the army, until they thought they had got the king surrounded and defenceless. This was how they themselves saw the situation in 1912. Their reasoning was thus: who needs an army? The country? Not at all: only the king needed an army. Who needs a navy? Well, the king needed a navy; and if he wanted it all that much then he must be made to pay for it and pay for it by conceding the opposition's just demands. Of course he would give in because the pressure of world affairs would make it imperative for him. The worse the international situation became, the more they would insist on their demands being met, and they would squeeze the old sovereign until he would be forced to concede all they asked. Now, just as they had come to believe that this policy was working and that the government was preparing to surrender, what happens? The king announces that he is going to quit the game and let his successor take his place at the chessboard. It was a hard blow; and as unfair and as unsporting as the player who slams his fist down on the table. It was more: it was not the act of a gentleman.

Though that is what everyone thought, no one said it openly.

Fredi Wuelffenstein came as close as any to saying frankly what was in his mind. He was standing in the doorway of the Szechenyi Room holding forth to a group of younger men in the belief, not entirely justified, that they admired him. Noisily advancing the left-wing view, he said, 'We mustn't fall for this! The King is only bluffing. He just wants to scare us, which isn't at all what we might expect of him. Of course he won't abdicate! Never! Not he! It's bluff, nothing but bluff! He believes we'll all be so scared of what the Heir'll do that we'll just give in; but we won't. Anyhow, what would happen if Franz-Ferdinand did become King? All he could do would be to come to some arrangement with us. We wouldn't crown him if he didn't; and without a coronation there'd be no King! Even the Belvedere must accept that. It's one of Hungary's most sacred traditions . . .' and he went on, ever more loudly and brashly, and always repeating himself, as people do who have only a meagre vocabulary at their command. Each time he said the same thing again he beat his fist like a hammer as if this would serve to convince his audience.

Then Niki Kollonich intervened. At the last elections he had come into the house on the Popular Party ticket. He was just as prying, insolent and insincere a man as he had been a boy; and he loved to stir up trouble. Now, he asked mildly: 'Surely I remember you saying last autumn that we ought to pay court to the Heir, to His Highness the Archduke Franz-Ferdinand?'

Wuelffenstein nearly exploded with rage because what Niki had said was only too true. Not long before, through his sister the beautiful Countess Beredy, he had managed to wangle an invitation to shoot at the Archduke's place at More; and all that had happened had been that his host had completely ignored him, failed even to give him the time of day and indeed had not appeared even to notice his presence despite the smart English clothes he wore each day. This had continued for the whole three days of the shooting party – not a word, not even a glance. The only result of the whole expedition had been that back in Budapest, where the news of his presence in the enemy's camp had been widely trumpeted, poor Fredi now found himself an object of suspicion in his own party.

'I never said any such thing!' he shouted. 'All I said was that the Heir should be kept informed, that we should see that he knew what we wanted. Someone ought to tell him that we'll never give in, and that we won't yield an inch. He's got to know that without our co-operation the Crown gets nothing! That's what I said. Without us there'll be nothing, no army, nothing, just nothing!'

Niki then added, in admiring tones, 'Of course you told him that when you were shooting together, didn't you?'

'I've always said it, and to him too ... at least I would have done if the occasion had arisen ... but he doesn't impress me, I can tell you that! Nor anyone else either for that matter. And as for the Archduke, well, he has no say in the matter until he becomes King; and when that time comes he can only rule if we want him to!'

Even Fredi might not have argued so passionately, nor uttered such idiotic remarks, had he seen who was standing behind him.

It was Slawata, adviser to the Austrian Foreign Office and an intimate of Franz-Ferdinand. Behind his thick glasses his eyes seemed to gaze into the distance and the bland expression on his face gave away nothing of what he might be thinking. He stood there, apparently somewhat bored, as if he had simply strayed there by chance. After a moment or two he wandered off to see what he might overhear elsewhere.

At that moment Abady arrived at the club and almost collided with Slawata at the door. The latter at once brightened up as if thankful at last to meet someone he knew.

'*Komm! Ich muss mit dir reden!* – come with me, I want a word with you. At last I've found somebody I can talk to. Let's find a quiet spot!' And so saying he took Balint's arm and led him away.

For some time Balint had tried to avoid Jan Slawata's confidences, because Slawata frequently said things that offended Balint's patriotic feelings. Yet it was difficult to avoid meeting this old colleague – for they had both started their careers in the Ministry for Foreign Affairs in Vienna – and there was something about having worked in the Ballplatz that formed a bond between its alumni that often lasted a lifetime. So it was with Slawata and Abady. Whatever their differences there always remained this old link, which was something more than mere friendship for it was based less on mutual attraction and more on the fact that, diplomatically speaking, they spoke the same language. Usually Abady's reluctance to listen to Slawata's often tactless opinions had led to his avoiding the diplomat's company, but on this day he welcomed it, for he was anxious to hear something more authoritative than the gossip and rumour that were flooding the Casino at that moment.

'You can imagine,' said the friend and confidant of Franz-Ferdinand, 'the emotions produced by the Old Man's announcement. For years we have been waiting for our turn to come and now we are not even ready for it! Nothing is prepared, we have no definite programme and no men trained and ready to take over the reins of government. Of course His Highness knows what he wants, but the details still have to be worked out. The "workshop" is feverishly busy, but I can tell you it's chaos, absolute chaos! Personally I could wish for some other solution to this crisis ... we're simply not ready! I've been sent to see how the land lies, find out what people are thinking, judge everyone's reactions, their moods, what their reactions are ... It's not a nice job, and I don't like it one bit. And it's a dreadful responsibility. If anything goes wrong then I'll get the blame and His Highness, as you know, can be pretty ruthless. He doesn't play games, that one!'

'Well, I for one don't think there'll be any change,' said Abady. 'As I see it Khuen-Hedervary will resign and whoever succeeds will simply back down and withdraw the resolution. After all the government only adopted it as a means to stop all this obstruction.'

'That might be so had Tisza not accepted it too; but with him involved things are much more serious. The resolution is now his baby. Of course I now see what a mistake we made in telling our defence minister Auffenburg to protest to the Hungarian government. That's what has made Tisza so angry; you know how touchy he can be about anything that seems like an infringement of Hungary's independence. Anyhow we think Tisza has an ulterior motive in supporting the resolution: he wants to use it against us as soon as there is a change of ruler. The theory at the Belvedere is that Tisza believes that when this happens there won't be any more bargaining; just a clean break with the resolution remaining but with the obstructionists removed. If, when the Heir ascends the throne, he finds himself opposed by a majority in the Hungarian Parliament, then he'll find himself up against the Constitution. In our view Tisza is the true enemy, not those loud-mouthed demagogues in opposition. He is a far more serious opponent than the others, much stronger – a real hard Hungarian, that one!'

Slawata could not leave the subject of the dangers he saw in Tisza's surprising support of the resolution; neither could he conceal his deep anxiety. He was clearly worried by what Tisza might obtain in a private audience with Franz-Josef. Indeed he might even persuade the old monarch, who had always appreciated his brilliance and charm of manner, to give way, especially if he could convince Franz-Josef that Auffenberg's unfortunate intervention in Hungary's parliamentary affairs had been instigated by the Heir, which, of course, it had been. If Tisza was able to make it seem that the resolution was the logical outcome of Franz-Josef's own work, and was designed to protect the 1867 Compromise against the destructive plots of the Heir, then it was by no means unlikely that the monarch would withdraw his threat of abdication. 'And then,' went on Slawata, 'we shall really find ourselves in difficulties; and we've already got enough as it is.'

Balint had never seen Slawata so worried. He, who had never been anything but sure of himself, of the rightness of his view of things, of the ineluctable truth of his own judgement and the sureness of his political analysis, now seemed so hesitant and so unsure of himself that he was reduced to seeking advice. To

Balint it looked as if Slawata had at last grasped what an abyss yawned before the politician who had pronounced judgement on political affairs when he had no responsibility for their conduct, and was then forced to stand by what he had said.

The envoy of the Belvedere sighed deeply, took off his thick spectacles, wiped them on his handkerchief and replaced them on his nose; and Balint, who had long before noticed that Slawata always did this when he was about to say something important, turned to him expectantly just as the politician looked Balint full in the face and said, 'If there should be a change of monarch, would you consider the offer of a portfolio in the new government?'

This was quite unexpected, and a thin crease of anxiety appeared on Balint's forehead. What he already knew of the Heir's plans for the Dual Monarchy – and most of it had come from Slawata himself – was utterly opposed to Abady's most cherished belief in traditional values. He had been revolted by what Count Czernin had written some years before, when he had prophesied that Franz-Ferdinand would transform the loose conglomeration of independent countries that had formed the Habsburg empire into a huge monolithic authoritarian super-state with an all-powerful central government. This was just what the youthful Franz-Josef himself had once proposed long before he had accepted the 1867 Compromise. At that time Balint's own grandfather, Count Peter, had been nominated without his consent to the proposed new Upper House and had, scornfully, refused to have any part in a project which would have imposed Austrian authority throughout the Balkans; and even, eventually, to find his beloved Transylvania handed over as a dowry to whatever Habsburg princeling found himself nominated to the throne of Romania! Memories of what his grandfather had told him flooded through Balint's mind until his blood boiled with anger.

Even so he remained outwardly calm, and answered the question put to him with another.

'I would have to know first with whom I would have to serve; and, of course, what programme was envisaged.' Abady's voice was suddenly very cold.

'Kristoffy is the only man who has His Highness's confidence.'

'Kristoffy! Why, that's ridiculous! Apart from anything else there isn't a man in the country who'd consent to work with him!'

'Oh, but perhaps there is,' and Slawata smiled knowingly.

'We have reason to believe that Lukacs would ... and maybe even Justh.'

'Justh is a radical Independent and it was Kristoffy who destroyed that party when he was Minister of the Interior. They're deadly enemies! Nothing would make those two work together!'

'You perhaps do not know that they have been in secret contact for quite a time. They came together over the universal suffrage proposals, and those form the first part of the Heir's programme for Hungary. Other things will come later.'

'What "other things"?'

Franz-Ferdinand's confidential envoy barely hesitated before he uttered that old diplomats' familiar plea for secrecy, '*Unter uns, natürlich* – just between ourselves, of course!' and then started to explain:

The first step, he said, would be a manifesto from the ruler. The principal item would be the introduction of universal suffrage. The importance of national defence would be touched upon, as would the need slightly to modify the terms of the Compromise so as to put an end to all the current bickering. The existing Parliament would be asked only to pass the necessary legislation for the suffrage proposals and the defence estimates – both with validity for one year – and the government, which would have been in on the planning of this programme, would then prorogue Parliament as soon as these two measures had become law. Everything else, the coronation and the proclaiming and passing of the laws needed for bringing about the centralization of the Monarchy, would be the task of the next Parliament.

'In that case,' interrupted Balint, 'the first thing is to make sure that whatever proposals Kristoffy makes to the House are accepted by a decent majority. Frankly, I find that most unlikely.'

'Lukacs will bring over the radicals in the government party and Justh will be followed by the whole Independent clan. When that happens the People's Party would naturally join us too. All that would be left against us would be Tisza and his lot.'

'Just let us suppose all this happens. Do not forget that with this political grouping Justh would be the only leader with a majority; and can you imagine him voting for an increase in Austrian power and centralization, and not for his own programme based on the union of our two countries only through the person of the monarch who sits on both thrones? Justh will be careful to see that the suffrage proposals, and the redrawing of constituency boundaries, are all to his own party's advantage. And I'm sure that even if today he seems to agree to accept revision of the Compromise and the centralization of the Monarchy, even if he goes so far as to give in over the army proposals, he'll only do it with the secret reservation that the revised voting laws ensure the supremacy of his Independent Party. In the case that the future reforms have to be introduced by Justh, then the future ruler will find himself in a far greater predicament than Franz-Josef has ever done. And, even if this does not happen, any collaboration between Lukacs, Kristoffy and Justh is bound to fall apart at the first strain put upon it. What then?'

'Then we would bring in our own voting laws and proceed accordingly!'

'Do you really believe it would work? That you'd be able so easily to create a majority that would approve ...', and here Balint paused as he searched for some ironic phrase to clothe his real thoughts, '... would approve of what you have planned so neatly?'

'*Mein Gott* – my God!' replied Slawata forcefully. 'The Belvedere "workshop" certainly believes it possible. We count on Lukacs to carry at least half, possibly two-thirds, of the government party; Kristoffy the radicals – though it's true there are not many of them and those mostly intellectuals – and most of the minorities. So Justh would just have to join in, and the socialists with him. That's how Kristoffy sees it ... and also Milan Hodzsa.'

'Hodzsa? Is he part of all this too?'

'Of course! His Highness has much confidence in him.'

For a few moments there was silence between the two men. Then Abady spoke, and his manner was both serious and unusually dry.

'I find all this alarmingly adventuresome, and very dangerous, as much to the Archduke as to anyone else. The mere fact of a change of monarch constitutes a crisis. To add to it a general election, with all its attendant clash of chauvinist slogans and demagoguery, would be nothing less than madness. It would be sheer chaos, it couldn't be anything else. The monarch could never work with a Parliament opposed to all he stood for. The new ruler would find himself in a hopelessly false position, and helpless with it. There'd be no question today of imposing a repressive régime like that of Count Bach after 1848. The old

Emperor could only do it then because he had Russia behind
him and peace everywhere else. Today it would be unthinkable.
Anyhow it couldn't last and would soon end badly. Only chaos
would remain, with all the various parties at loggerheads, desperately jockeying for position. What a picture to show the world!
Especially now when we're already pretty near to chaos at home
and the Balkans are ready to flare up at any moment! What a time
to start provoking even more turmoil in the country!'

Slawata replied pensively, 'Well, it's the only thing against it.'

'It certainly is not! There are far deeper and more serious
matters at stake. The very stability of the Monarchy lies in its
respect for tradition. It rests on tradition and in turn is upheld by
it. The ties between the monarch and the different strata of
society and of the administration of the country are legion. The
ruler who ignores this, and starts to destroy these links and
replace them with something altogether less ancient, reputable
and respected, will destroy the foundation on which his kingdom
rests. A dictator thrown up by a revolution can do this because
he owes his pre-eminence to his popularity. A successful general
can do it because he is supported by his troops. But that sort of
power rarely outlives the man who creates it. Such a dictator can
try to make all men equal, and indeed he is wise to attempt it, if
only because such potent personal rule will always be more effective if it is imposed on a homogenous society than on one based
on a historic class structure, which is the historic rock on which
hereditary monarchy is built. Hereditary power is only possible
when it rules a society that is itself built up in layers whose traditional apex is the Crown. There is nothing logical in this. It is a
historical and emotional acceptance of an illogical fact; that is all.
The monarch who turns demagogue and who puts himself at the
head of popular revolutionary movements may fancy that he's
feathering his own nest, but what he's really doing is preparing
the way for a republic, or for the ruin of his country!'

Slawata smiled ironically as he said, 'All that is sheer Montes-
quieu – *esprit des lois!*'

'Of course! But it is no less true, however long ago it was
written. Anyway we are only guessing. All this is purely hypothe-
tical and I, for one, don't believe His Majesty has any intention
of abdicating . . . so all this talk is really about nothing, at least for
the moment. Khuen-Hedervary will resign and a new government will be formed which will reform the suffrage laws, which

in my opinion should have been done long ago. I hear that Justh is quite ready, at least for a year, to drop all that tiresome obstructionism, especially as regards the army estimates. So, if the army question is out of the way, the other reforms the Heir wants to see could well be presented without upsetting anyone.'

Slawata's reply took Balint by surprise.

'But we don't want anything while Franz-Josef is still on the throne. Indeed we'll make quite sure no real reform is possible. Perhaps some little concession here and there, but only if it proves unavoidable. His Highness wants to do it all after he succeeds to the throne, and until then he'll do everything in his power to prevent any changes. If Laszlo Lukacs becomes Minister-President, which seems likely, he'll forbid it outright!'

'Even if that means holding up the defence proposals?' marvelled Balint.

'Even that!'

'I just don't understand! Surely, in these critical times, the country's military readiness is vital to the Monarchy itself? Isn't that just what the Heir has been trying to achieve?'

'Of course, but not at that price! Just think,' the Heir's trusted adviser went on, 'when the Archduke succeeds to the throne the most important card he'll hold will be the introduction of general suffrage. And it must be he, and he alone, who gets the credit. If it is introduced now, before his time comes, he at once loses his trump card and with it the handle which will open the door to his other plans. Therefore nothing must be done now, nothing. Under no circumstances. Under no circumstances at all! Better for everything to stay as it is.'

Balint jumped up unable to conceal his anger.

'What insufferable egotism! Here is our country behind all the other powers in military preparedness. We are in the middle of an appalling international crisis, and our beloved Archduke is prepared for purely selfish reasons to hinder what is in his and the country's best interests!'

'No need to flare up like that!' said Slawata. 'After all the Old One can't live for ever . . . and perhaps in a month or two . . . ?'

'In a month or two you'll be able to embark on these dangerous adventures you speak of . . . is that it? I can see that nothing else is important to you now. All you want to do is to destroy what we already have – and the more brutally the better – only to replace it with some ill-thought-out and thoroughly nebulous super-monarchy. And that is why, as you yourself admitted, you can't find any supporters who are worth a tinker's cuss! The only men you'll find to support such a plan are those who have nothing to lose or those who fancy they'll benefit even if everything else crumbles.'

'I'm most disappointed that you should take it this way,' said Slawata morosely. Then he too got up. 'And I'm sorry, because in you I had hoped to find a colleague and sympathizer.'

'You have nothing to be sorry about! I should never ever have supported such a plan. Indeed, you have nothing to be sorry about ... *Servus!*'

'*Servus!*'

Balint turned away and left without offering his hand.

CHAPTER TWO

IN THE FOLLOWING weeks Balint often recalled his talk with Slawata. For the moment everything remained much the same as before. The government resigned but was re-formed almost as it had been after some three weeks of argument and, as a result, the resolution which had so provoked the ruler was dropped. Khuen-Hedervary agreed to continue in office so as to get matters cleared up but, after another three weeks of renewed and gleeful obstruction from the opposition, gave in his final resignation and withdrew from politics. So, in the middle of April, Laszlo Lukacs became Minister-President.

Officially his programme barely differed from that of his predecessor, but he had surreptitious negotiations with Justh even before he took office. It was much the same with other grandees of the opposition, but it was soon clear that such inter-party contacts were purely formal and had little significance.

Gossip about the news now became ever more confused and confusing, to the point where the most unlikely and impossible was everywhere believed. It would be declared as gospel truth that Lukacs and Justh, those dedicated left-wing reformers, were forming a right-wing lobby with – or without – the support of Tisza, their arch-enemy. There were even some developments which seemed to lend credence to this unlikely tale, such as when the followers of Kossuth sent a delegation to Vienna to protest that Auffenberg's message to the Budapest Parliament constituted an infringement of Hungarian sovereignty, only to find that the Austrian minister's action was defended by one Tivadar Batthyanyi who belonged to Justh's own inner circle. This represented a complete volte-face, and it was followed by others. Mihaly Karolyi, the president of the OMGE – the reactionary land-owners' agricultural association – who had always been a member of the Independent Party and who only two years before had been campaigning at Tisza's side on the suffrage issue, was now known to have switched allegiances and, as a radical, was acting as go-between between Justh and the heads of the government.

Though gossip was rampant, no one knew anything for certain; except, of course, that the atmosphere behind the scenes was becoming stormier and stormier while all the old obstruction went on as merrily as ever. Public interest in what was happening in Parliament was steadily being stifled, for all that anyone could find out from reading the newspapers was that the country's elected legislators either met in closed session or else were insisting upon voting only about trivialities. This was all too boring to be of any general interest.

During this time Abady only came to Budapest when it was necessary for his work for the Co-operatives. His mother had planned to return home at the end of April so as the weeks went by Balint spent much of his time travelling between Transylvania, Budapest and Abbazia, where Countess Roza still was.

Now, just when she was about to come home, something occurred to delay her. Her room at the Hungaria Hotel in the capital had already been reserved and her son daily expected to hear when she would arrive. The telegram came, but it was not what Balint was expecting. It read: 'CAN'T TRAVEL NOW. LETTER IN POST. MOTHER.'

Two days later the letter arrived. It proved to be a large hotel envelope with the address written by some hand Balint did not know instead of his mother's slanting spidery handwriting. Anxiously Balint tore it open to find two letters inside.

The larger one read:

'My dear boy,
'I am dictating these lines; but do not be disturbed as I am not seriously unwell. I have had a slight mishap in that when I woke

up this morning I found I could not use my right hand properly.
It is limp, rather as if it were asleep. As it did not get any better
during the morning, at midday I sent for a doctor – though you
know how much I dislike them. He has diagnosed circulation
trouble and says it will soon be better. He has ordered me to have
alcohol compresses and massage. It is all quite trivial, but I did not
feel like travelling in this rather helpless state. So I shall stay on
here for a couple of days, really only because it would be difficult in
the wagon-lit train compartment with only one hand working, and
it would be hard to dress and undress in the sleeper. You know how
I dislike being helped.

'Please don't worry. There is no need for you to think of
coming here.

'A thousand kisses.'

Countess Roza had dictated this letter to her old personal maid
Terka, who had herself written the second letter. In this she said:

'I am only writing this to your Lordship to let your Lordship know
that this is really so and that her Ladyship is not worse than she
says. I was rather scared this morning when I saw that she could
not use her arm, but there is nothing else wrong, your Lordship,
only this, and the doctor told me himself what he told her Ladyship,
that it will get better gradually. Please excuse the liberty in writing
to your Lordship, but I thought you would want to know.

'I kiss your Lordship's hands. Terka.'

Balint left for Abbazia the same day even though he had promised
Adrienne, who was going to Lausanne to visit her daughter at
the beginning of May, that he would meet her in Budapest and
go with her to Vienna, where they could spend a few days
together. He sent an express letter to Kolozsvar to explain why
he had had to abandon this plan, and left on the evening train.

He found his mother exactly as she had described herself. She
could move her hand and fingers a little, but had no strength in
them. Balint went to see the doctor on his own and the latter
told him: 'It is arteriosclerosis. She will get better, though it is
possible that she will never be quite the same as before. All the
same it must be taken seriously if only as a sign that there is a
tendency to apoplectic strokes. Some people are prone to this,
and there is really no avoiding action we can advise. Perhaps it
might benefit your mother to go to Bad Gastein in the summer.'

Countess Roza did her best to put on a show of crossness because her son had come when she had said it was not necessary; but it was obvious that she was really very pleased and happy. They spent sixteen more days together on the Quarnero coast.

The doctor's prognosis turned out to be correct. The old lady recovered the use of her hand, but even though she was soon able to write with it after a fashion, it was never quite the same as before.

During these days together Balint felt himself closer to his mother than he ever had been. It was as if a certain hardness in her was now dissolving. It may have been that in a hotel that regal arrogance was not so marked as at home at Denestornya where it never left her. There was nothing that Balint could put his finger on, nothing obvious, especially in the old lady's attitude to her son, but there was something gentler and softer about her, almost as if the trouble with her arm had given rise to a foreboding that had caused her, for the first time, to look into herself. Somehow Balint was aware of this. It was not just a suspicion, he knew it; and as a result he tried himself to be just that much warmer with her than before, only a little, just enough to please her, but not too much as he knew how much his mother detested anything that smacked of sentiment or effusiveness.

In the middle of May they started for home; and Balint, who thought that it must be about then that Adrienne would be returning from Lausanne, sent a telegram to tell her their plans.

The day they arrived in Budapest – though Balint had argued against it because such fashionable places were sure to be crowded at that time of year – they went to have tea at Gerbeaud's. Countess Roza insisted; Balint had noticed at Abbazia that his mother had recently shown a liking for being surrounded by people. It was an unexpected change in the old lady who had always avoided crowds, rarely went out to other people's houses and never went to restaurants or tea-rooms.

Now, all of a sudden, she seemed to want to be surrounded by people. It was as if the bustle and turmoil of everyday life brought her joy, as if what had happened in that hotel room by the sea had reminded her that her life was passing inexorably.

As they always did now Balint and his mother walked arm in arm.

Of course Gerbeaud's was very crowded. Every table was occupied and every chair taken, and in front of the long counter customers were standing two or three deep. Finally they found a place just beside the door, Countess Roza with her back to the wall and Balint on her right. They were so close to the doorway that many of the people crowding in at that fashionable hour brushed against their table.

Countess Roza did not mind at all. Smiling with good humour she sat there patiently until at long last her coffee topped with whipped cream was brought her. Then, slowly stirring it, she watched the mob flow to and fro as the throng of society women almost fell over each other as they fought their way in and out. The old lady's slightly protuberant grey eyes watched it all with amused tolerance, even though some of the customers were only inches from her chair.

It's amazing, thought Balint, as he bent forward to sip his tea. How she would have loathed all this only a month or so ago!

A tall young woman dressed in rust-coloured linen appeared in the doorway.

It was Adrienne.

She could hardly get through against the rush of those trying to get out, and had to stand by the door to let the crowd go by. She stood there, beside the door, with her back to where Countess Abady was sitting.

She was already standing patiently there when Balint looked up and of course instantly knew who it was.

Joy flooded through him ... and then fear of what would happen next. If Adrienne did not see them, even though she was so close, and so did not greet his mother, Countess Roza would assume that it was done on purpose. Also it was unthinkable that, finding themselves so close to each other, they could make do with a formal greeting. A few words, however trivial, would have to be exchanged, or it would be ruder than if they managed not to see each other at all. He knew that Adrienne would do whatever was necessary, but how would his mother react? After all she had hated Adrienne for years, and for a long time the two women had not met. Before that, if they had somehow encountered each other at a charity bazaar or in the house of mutual friends, Countess Roza would nod icily and turn away. What would she do now? It would be dreadful to have to stand by and see his mother, by her manner if not in so many words, insult and hurt the woman he loved.

All this flashed through his mind, and his heart constricted with pain.

And then the unexpected happened.

Roza Abady touched Adrienne's sleeve with her left hand and in gentle tones said, 'Why, Adrienne! Didn't you see me?'

The younger woman turned, startled by something so unexpected. For a moment she was lost for words, but she quickly recovered herself, greeted the old lady in her turn and lifted Countess Roza's hand to her lips. There was more in this spontaneous gesture than the mere politeness of a younger woman for an older, for in those days grown women kissed old ladies' hands only if they were close relations. In Adrienne's gesture gratitude was almost equally blended with humility. Then, across the table, she greeted Balint, who had risen when she turned towards them.

Countess Roza waved to Balint's empty chair and said, 'Won't you join us? We're rather squeezed, but do come and sit with us ... or are you with friends?'

'Thank you. I'd love to for a moment if I may. I just came in to get something.'

Adrienne spoke hesitantly in rather an embarrassed tone, but the old lady was completely calm and as cheerful as if nothing had ever come between them. She even seemed happy, and indeed she was happy because her desire to play the role of the gracious royal lady always surged up in her whenever she had a chance of giving, and especially when that gift would be unexpected and surprising, and appear to come from the great height of her queenly throne. In her happiness now there was also mingled a real element of goodness as well as a certain faint and forgiving irony for the obvious embarrassment of her son as well as that of Adrienne, though she was careful not to let any of this appear. She rambled on naturally – perhaps indeed almost too volubly – so as to help the others regain their equanimity, telling Adrienne all about Abbazia and how she had spent the winter there, and then asking for news of Adrienne's father, Akos Miloth, of her sister Margit, and even of her little girl Clemmie who she had heard was at school in Switzerland – so sensible to have her brought up there!

'I came here to buy her some chocolates,' said Adrienne, 'and

also some for the headmistress and her room-mother. I always
do, every time I come back, just to show how much I appreciate
them.'

Then, apparently without any reason, she added, 'I only just
arrived – on the five o'clock train this afternoon,' and Balint
wondered if she said this so as to show that she had known nothing of the Abadys' movements and so had not contrived this
meeting in collusion with him.

They exchanged a few more words and then Adrienne got up
and said goodbye, disappearing into the throng of busy shoppers
at the counter. A little later they saw her go out carrying three
parcels. As Adrienne passed near Countess Roza she bowed her
head gracefully to the old lady ... and in her eyes Balint could
catch the glint of tears.

A quarter of an hour later Balint took his mother back to her
hotel. They walked in silence and they did not speak, even when
they separated in the great hallway of the Hungaria, except
merely to confirm what they were doing that evening. Balint was
anxious to look in at the Casino to hear all the latest news. When
they said goodbye he kissed her hand but held it in his for a fraction longer than usual. Countess Abady patted her son's cheek
with her chubby little hand.

These two almost imperceptible gestures were all that was
needed to mark the gratitude of the son and the acknowledgement of reconciliation by the mother. It was enough for both of
them.

When Balint arrived the Casino was crowded. Storms were
brewing once again.

During the previous weeks Lukacs had been doing everything he could to get the army estimates passed with only a
year's validity. To get Justh's co-operation he had made two
different offers on the suffrage question. Both had been turned
down. Neither did he get very far elsewhere for Apponyi, in a
public speech, declared that neither he nor any of his followers
would even discuss what Lukacs was proposing, while Justh
let it be known that he found even the suffrage concessions
inadequate.

The chances of reaching general agreement were still further
reduced by a split in the Independent Party, for just when it
had appeared that an agreement with Justh was imminent, the

Kossuth-Apponyi group brought up an absurdly far-fetched set of nationalistic demands. Then, as Justh did not want to be made to appear less patriotic than the others, he in turn put forward some even more radical suggestions – and only Lukacs knew how his hands had been tied by his secret allegiance to the Heir's policies which left him with no room for manoeuvre. The Justh party now put forward ever more stubborn and revolutionary demands for reform in the mistaken belief that the Minister-President had the power to grant them. They had the means to obstruct the passing by Parliament of any measures with which they did not agree, and they used this power relentlessly. All that was done in the House in those days was endless voting on trivialities ... voting, voting ... closed sessions and more voting.

At this point Tisza once more emerged into the limelight.

Though it had not yet happened, it was everywhere believed that soon Navy, who had succeeded Berzeviczy as Speaker of the House, would resign and that Tisza would take his place.

This would mean a violation of the Rules of the House for only a few years before, in 1904, Tisza had himself been at the head of affairs.

Abady moved from group to group, saying nothing but listening to what everyone had to say. He only stayed about fifteen minutes listening to each discussion before moving on to the next; but everywhere he heard the same thing, hatred for Tisza, hatred and more hatred, hatred from every kind and shade of opinion in the opposition, hatred from faithful believers in the 1867 Compromise, hatred from the followers of Andrassy, from members of the People's Party and even from those unrepentant old politicians who still brandished the banner of 1848 and revolt against the Habsburgs. There was no difference anywhere.

On the other hand there was no such unanimity in the government's own ranks. Those few supporters of Tisza who were present kept their mouths firmly closed and stood about in frigid silence. The rest of Lukacs's supporters belonged to that familiar type of politician, inane and passive like so many who blindly follow where they think the majority are leading and who are only happy when betting on a certainty. Such men are dismayed by the hazardous and they were now restless and anxious, shaking their heads and vainly trying to reassure themselves by repeating to each other what they firmly believed to be words of ponderous

political wisdom. They were obviously scared, for they remembered what had happened in 1904, and the memory of the disastrous days that followed now made their very bones ache. They
tried to bolster up their courage by telling each other that Tisza's
force of will would overcome all difficulties and that it would be
done peaceably and with none of the violence of those other
days. The mere fact of having a strong man like Tisza controlling
the business of the House would be menace enough to keep the
trouble-makers in their place. Hedging their bets, as such politicians are wont to do, a number of them went round whispering
in the ears of anyone who would listen, especially their political
opponents, that should there be any repetition of violence in the
Chamber, they personally had never approved of such methods
and indeed went so far as to oppose them!

Balint found all this deeply disheartening. He thought of
Tisza, whom he greatly admired, risking his entire political
future faced with the deadly hatred of his opponents and backed
only by a mob as treacherous as the men he was trying to confront. The more he thought about this appalling situation the
more worried he became.

He had no doubt that the policy of forced votes would win
the day. If Tisza managed to by-pass the Rules of the House and
succeeded in getting the necessary legislation passed, he would
be applauded by the majority and, though the opposition might
rant and rave, that was all it would amount to. But afterwards?
What would come later? All Balint could see was that Tisza
would pile up such a mountain of hatred against himself that
he would find himself permanently consigned to a political no-
man's-land. What a tragedy if his powerful presence were to be
forever lost to Hungarian public life, especially if that loss came
about because he had been sold down the line by his own
followers, maybe even by this present government, or by its
successor, as soon as it might seem expedient to return to the rule
of law! Nothing would ever wash away that legacy of hatred, for
not only would the opposition do all it could to keep it alive but
the government's own supporters would do the same if only
to make sure that the most eligible candidate for the office of
Minister-President was squeezed out of the race. No one else
would suffer in the same way, but Tisza could find himself
excluded for life from any high office. Could it be coincidence,
Balint wondered, that this fate was reserved for the man Slawata

had declared to be the most serious obstacle to the Belvedere's adventurous plans?

But what other solution was there? At present effective government was impossible for, if the rule of law was to be respected, then this irresponsible handful of obstructionists could continue indefinitely to hold up implementation of everything the country so urgently needed. To break down this obstruction, the only course seemed to be to ignore those very rules which for centuries had guaranteed the freedom and integrity of the Hungarian Parliament. The pity was that it looked as if no one but Tisza would shoulder the responsibility for doing this and that he and he alone would afterwards be blamed. Was it not possible that some other courageous, hard-headed politician could be found? Someone not so important to the state, who would not be such a loss if he found himself cast out into the wilderness? That would at least be better; for the cynical truth is that the man who acts is blamed, not he who gave the order. The man on the platform gets the rotten eggs, the brains behind him are forgotten.

Balint thought he should speak to Tisza on the subject.

For a long time he wondered if he really should mix himself up in all this. Wouldn't Tisza think he was just pushing himself forward? But what he had thought made him so anxious that it seemed more important to pass it on to Tisza himself. The next morning he asked when he could see him and was given an appointment that afternoon.

Balint talked at length. He told the ex-Minister-President that he agreed with the need for bringing an end to the present impasse and that to by-pass the Rules of the House was perhaps the only way. He told the older man of the hatred for him that was already being shouted out loud and which would become far worse if he put his plan into execution. Taking into account Tisza's well-known puritan disregard of his own best interests, he said nothing about personal unpopularity and indeed emphasized what he honestly believed, that personal advantage must always give way to the nation's best interests. But, and he said this roughly lest it might be taken as an ill-judged attempt at flattery, there was another aspect to this matter which was of over-riding importance. The question was not whether Tisza would suffer personally by being cast out of political life, but whether the country would suffer by losing him. He was, said

Balint, the only man of sufficient stature and experience to stand up to the demagogues who surrounded him. Therefore a man so important to the future direction of the nation's affairs should not be expected to undertake, or indeed exposed to, a task that a lesser and more disposable politician could do just as well. Balint begged him not to accept the nomination for Speaker. Surely, he said, there must be someone among Tisza's followers who would be eager for the post and who would do everything that Tisza asked of him?

Tisza listened attentively. He never once interrupted the younger man, but he looked closely at him through the thick glasses which made his grey eyes seem so enormous.

When Balint finished he answered him point by point with circumstantial detail to reinforce what he was saying. He conceded that Abady was in many ways right in what he said and particularly that anyone who succeeded in bringing down the obstructionists was putting his head on the political block. But ... but ... over-riding all other considerations was the vital necessity of restoring order to Parliament. He did not deny what Balint had said about his own pre-eminent stature, it was so self-evident that to do so would have been a pose unworthy of him; and Tisza was no poseur. He knew that his country would probably have need of him in the future, but despite the risks he had decided that now it was for him to act. He alone had the prestige to carry it off and no one else could shoulder that particular burden. He would not regret it, even if it meant that afterwards he would have to abandon public life. It was necessary for the country; and the cause was worth the sacrifice.

'If I have to I will then go quietly into retirement.'

His reasoning was like a well-forged chain. There was not a single flaw, nor an unnecessary word. Every phrase was as solidly cast as bronze.

Tisza then got to his feet and as Balint was escorting him back to the corridor of the House he thanked the younger man for his good wishes in the most friendly terms. Then, tall, erect and broad-shouldered, he walked calmly to the head of the stairs and disappeared from Balint's sight.

Tisza was elected Speaker on May 22nd.

The socialists, who saw in this the death-knell of all their plans, at once announced a general strike. The factory workers turned out in force, joined up with the city rabble, and started over-turning trams and trucks so as to build barricades. The mob was heading for the Parliament building but was stopped by the police at the corner of Alkotmany Street. Stones were thrown at the police and a few pistol-shots were heard. Then the police fired back: six dead, 182 wounded.

While this was happening in the square outside, the legislators in the House were still voting for or against a host of uncon-sidered trifles.

Throughout the country it seemed as if a storm was brewing.

That was what each man felt and fancied he saw. Behind Tisza's back all sorts of surreptitious discussions were taking place. Secret messages passed between Laszlo Lukacs and the Independents and, though it never became known exactly what happened, it seemed likely that the Minister-President was still seeking a peaceful solution through agreement over the suffrage question. What was certain was that Kossuth and Justh believed that such an agreement, whether based on law or not, existed. Only that could explain why, on June 1st, Kossuth demanded to be heard in debate and offered, in the name of the Independent Party, to abandon all obstructionist activity if the number of those to receive the vote was increased by 120 per cent. Lukacs at first gave an evasive answer but on the following day he refused categorically to accept Kossuth's proposal. Some people thought then that he must have been influenced by fear of Tisza, but it is more likely that he had had to stall so as to have time to consult the Belvedere, and that the Heir refused his agreement because he had set his face against all radical reform until he succeeded to the throne.

The disappointment aroused a storm of indignation in the ranks of the Independent Party and their next meeting was held in an angry mood.

This was the situation which Balint found on his return to Budapest with his mother on June 4th. He had already realized that whatever he found going on in Parliament would be distaste-ful to him, for he had grown up with a belief in the sacredness of Hungary's constitution and respect for its traditions. It had been painful to read about recent events in the newspapers, but now, seeing it for himself, it was worse. All the same he had to be there, just as eight and a half years before, when the derisively-named 'Darabont' (or Bodyguard) government had sent soldiers into the House to enforce its will. Balint sensed that something of the sort might happen again, now that passions were even more inflamed than before and there had been shooting in the streets outside. If the same sort of thing occurred in the present session then Tisza was not the sort of man to cower before the guns of the military, and if he were bold enough to stand up to them then Balint felt it would be cowardly not to do the same.

The signs of the coming storm were all there when the session began. From the outset the opposition brought into play one of its oldest time-wasting tricks, the filibuster. A member whose ability to spin any point out for an unconscionable time demanded to be heard on a point of order concerning the Rules of the House. Traditionally such a demand must be given priority, and at least three-quarters of an hour or more could be satisfactorily wasted in this way. Tisza merely dismissed the request in the most summary fashion. Bedlam at once broke out on the left, with members drumming on the benches and demanding an immediate closed session.

From where Balint was seated he could see Tisza clearly. The newly-elected Speaker sat there motionless, waiting for the hubbub to subside. The sun glinted on his short greying hair and his eyes were hidden by his thick glasses which were like two shining discs placed just under his forehead. At last, when it was possible to be heard, he said in a serious tone, 'I must ask the honourable Members to abandon the course they have adopted, a course which is bringing our country to ruin.'

Undoubtedly he knew in advance that so mild a rebuke would be in vain and that his request would be greeted, as it was, with whistles, drumming on the benches, stamping and loud irreverent shouting. Tisza called for order, and again started to speak. His voice was solemn and his manner calm, and only when he quoted back at his political opponents some of their own words did he allow himself some ironic overtones.

'My duty,' he said, 'as guardian of order in this House, is to bring to a definite end all obstructive tactics and technical objections which, as Count Gyula Andrassy has said, can be forged into an effective weapon by a mere twenty ill-intentioned members, and which, Albert Apponyi has declared, constitute usurpation of the nation's age-old liberties ...' but he was not allowed to finish the sentence for his voice was drowned by the uproar his words had produced. Men jumped to their feet from the benches on the extreme left and howled their anger, then, above it all, Tisza somehow again made himself heard.

'I ask the House now if it accepts the Defence Estimate Bill or not? I wish for an answer: Yes or No?'

The majority of those present at once stood up to show their acceptance and Tisza declared the motion passed. The opposition was now powerless to do anything but continue to howl their fury, cursing and raging and hurling insults in every direction, insults which never reached their mark for the noise was such that no one could hear what they were shouting. While this was going on Tisza closed the session, got up and walked out as slowly and as calmly as if he were merely out for an afternoon stroll.

This all happened before midday.

Abady went to the House again for the afternoon session. It was barely half-past three when he looked into the Chamber and saw that the opposition was already there in force. They had heard that Tisza had ordered a police cordon and had been afraid that they would not be allowed into the building. And so it happened that, with only a few exceptions, all the seats on the left-wing benches were already occupied. Everyone there seemed happy, even merry, exchanging jokes and laughing as if they were expecting something exceptionally amusing to happen. Some had brought whistles, others bells; and they were busy showing each other what they had brought and gently trying them out. What fun we'll have, they muttered to each other; what jolly, jolly fun!

At four o'clock the government party took their seats and there was an ominous hush which lasted until Tisza rose to open the session. Then bedlam broke loose again with the sound of whistles blowing, bells ringing, voices shouting and crowing with manic laughter. No one could hear a word the Speaker uttered, though everyone could see his mouth open and shut. Then he stopped trying to speak, noted something with his pencil, rose and left the Chamber, all members of the government party trooping out after him. The noise-makers thought that they had won that round.

But not for long.

A moment or two later the red plush draperies over the door to the Chamber behind the left-wing benches were drawn aside and the Chief Usher entered with a paper in his hand. Behind him could be seen a high official of the Parliament in his gold-braided uniform, and behind him row after row of policemen.

From where Balint stood it was difficult to see exactly what happened next, but behind the dense phalanx of policemen there seemed to be some heated discussion, perhaps even a brawl.

What happened was this. Mihaly Karolyi, who found himself in the corridor just as it was filling up with policemen, pushed his way into the Chamber through the central door on the left, jumped up on to the writing desk of the first bench in front of him, stepped over the shoulders of those sitting there and ran, white shoes flashing and arms spread wide, along the bench-tops until he found himself in front of Justh. Then it seemed that he struck out at the nearest policeman with both fists – though it was impossible to see whether they reached their mark or not for at that moment expert arms caught him and lifted him in the air, and four stalwart policemen carried him bodily outside. He was the only one who physically attacked the police that day, though strangely enough his name never figured on the list of those who were arrested later.

The others merely adopted an attitude of passive resistance. When the man in gold braid touched them on the shoulder, they got up quietly and were escorted out by two policemen.

Abady left after the first of the obstructionist members had been ejected from the Chamber.

He had come to the session because he considered it his duty; and he remained until the police arrived because, though he knew that he would be deeply shocked by what was going to happen, he agreed that it was necessary. While all this was going on he just stood like one mesmerized, for though his innermost feelings were outraged and although he was horrified by what was happening, he could not tear his eyes away but felt impelled to stand there and watch the horror as it happened.

With a bitter taste in his mouth he stepped out into the corridor. It was empty, for Tisza had evidently given orders to his followers that on this day they should keep discreetly in the background and not wander about as they usually did. Even the ushers had disappeared.

Balint walked swiftly downstairs. In the hall on the ground floor a small group of ejected Members stood nonchalantly at one side surrounded by policemen; they were still there when

Balint returned from the cloakroom having collected his hat and stick.

Now they were crowding round the main entrance and Balint wondered what on earth they could be waiting for. Could it be checking of their papers, or were their captors expecting others to join them before they were all hurried away in one large group?

Abady was soon enlightened: the ejected members were having their photographs taken.

Eager newsmen were standing outside beside the pillars of the portico, and each group of three or four arrested men paused on the threshold as they came out, their guards flanking them, and moved on, only to have their place taken by the next group, as soon as all the cameras had clicked.

Soon it was the turn of Marton Kuthenvary, who had had more experience of newspaper men than most. He knew exactly what was needed and asked his escorting policemen to take him out into the sun before stopping for the picture-taking ritual. He wanted to be sure that the picture was a good one and knew that anything taken in the shadow of the portico might be too obscure for the 'victim' to be immediately identified.

The police, whose orders, it turned out, had been only to escort the recalcitrant Members to the door but no further, demurred, but Kuthenvary insisted, cunningly pointing out that the colonnade of the entrance was an integral part of the building and that they would not be infringing their orders if they came with him as far as the outer pillars. The argument was reinforced with a couple of good cigars, and the astute Kuthenvary got his way.

The published picture was one of the best. There the 'victim of tyranny' stands framed by agents of authority, the very picture of outraged, dignified righteousness. Since he was being forcibly removed from the building Kuthenvary had asked the policemen to hold both his arms as if pinioned and, even when the photographers were on the point of getting their distances right, he had stopped everything, crying 'Wait!' as he took off his hat and handed it to one of his attendants. This done, he had again struck a pose and said, 'All right, I'm ready now!'

The result was everything Kuthenvary could have wished. His flowing hair, cut to look like that of the great poet-patriot Petofi, waved dramatically in the wind and his tall figure looked at its most impressive between two little short men in uniform.

Balint reached the square just as the photograph was taken. Then Kuthenvary came down the steps.

'Hello! Balint, my dear fellow!' he called out. 'I'll send that to my constituents in Csik . . . a hundred copies . . . it'll be excellent propaganda, don't you think?'

From that afternoon the Parliament building was surrounded by a police cordon.

Nevertheless, three days later one of the excluded members, an obscure, little-known MP called Gyula Kovacs, managed somehow to climb in over a balcony, jump into the Chamber, fire three shots at Tisza and aim a fourth at himself.

Tisza was unhurt and remained standing calmly at his place. Seeing his assailant fall and assuming that he had killed himself, he continued what he was saying, adding in his precise everyday manner:

'This is just the doing of some poor miserable madman, who has himself anticipated his just punishment. We should all look upon his action, and his fate, with the compassion due to those who lose their wits.'

From that moment the opposition members did not even try to attend the House. They had a 'Manifesto of Protest' published in the papers; but it was received by the general public with lethargy and indifference.

The session was brought to an end as soon as some amendments had been made to the House Rules and some minor legislation passed, unanimously of course. Then followed the summer recess.

Balint did not wait for the official end of the session. He went home to Transylvania.

CHAPTER THREE

THE STEAM-SAW'S RHYTHMIC whirring could be heard all over the sawmill compound, through the mountains of sawdust, through the neat stacks of prepared planks which rose in high regular blocks beside the tar-covered roofs of the motor-shed, the canteen and the manager's offices, through the dense pine forests which covered the surrounding hillsides, and far down into the valley of the Retyicel at the head of which the Abady sawmill had been built. The timber-fenced compound was as large as a mountain village.

It was midday and the sun's bright rays were almost perpendicular. There was no shadow anywhere and on the smooth pillar-like trunks that had been stripped of their bark in the forest the sunlight glinted with a shimmering yellow glow. The newly cut planks could have been made of yellow-gold velvet and the piles of sawdust were like saffron-coloured snow ... and, as always wherever a steam-saw is in action, everything looked as clean as if it had just been scrubbed.

About half an hour before, Abady had ridden down from the ridge of the Fraszinet where he had been inspecting a new plantation in the forest. There, the forest-manager, Winkler, and the head forest guard, Andras Zutor (Honey), had walked the plantations with him. A few hundred yards away was the forest lodge of Szkrind where they would all eat before starting off for the mountain pass of Kucsulat. Balint's tent was already on its way with two other foresters – the *gornyiks* – and a supply of fresh horses because they would have a long way to go if they were to arrive that evening near to the source of the Beles which rose just below the southernmost part of the Abady forests on the slopes of the Ursoia. Balint was to start after the others, and with his fast horse he expected to catch them up about halfway; but in the meantime he had come down to the sawmill where he had to meet one of the directors of the Frankel enterprise to whom Balint was contracted to sell all his timber.

As Balint emerged from the labyrinth of woodpiles a young man appeared, somewhat stealthily, less than a hundred paces away where the compound almost touched the surrounding woodlands. It was Kula, whose full name was Lung Nyikulaj, the grandson of the old headman of the village of Pejkoja whose inhabitants Balint had for some time been trying to protect from the extortions of the local officials. He was a well-intentioned youth and for some time had been Abady's confidential informant.

Kula had hurried down from his village and disappeared across the willow-fringed stream marking the boundary of Pejkoja into the dense woodlands behind. He did not go directly to Meregyo, which was his ostensible objective, but had started from home saying that first he had to visit the canteen manager at Szkrind who wanted to buy some cheeses. From there he would go on to Meregyo to see the judge who had two horses for sale. All this was because everyone in the mountains knew everything about everyone else, and had he been seen at Szkrind without good reason, especially when he was supposed to be going to Meregyo, news of this unusual detour would have spread abroad just as if it had been reported in the newspapers. And nobody must get to hear that he had had a clandestine meeting with the *mariassa* – the lord – for, in that part of the mountains where all the peasants were of Romanian stock, a Hungarian landowner who was also an aristocrat was inevitably an object of suspicion.

Because of this, Honey Zutor and Kula had concocted the plan between them that the only way such a meeting could be kept secret was if it should take place, apparently by accident, in an alleyway between those towering blocks of wood where nobody would see them. The *mariassa* would stroll casually out from the side of the mill and Kula would come in from the other side. The day and exact time were settled in advance and, as at midday the Fraszinet ridge could be clearly seen from Pejkoja, all Kula had to do was to keep watch and set out as soon as he saw Balint leave the ridge. Everything had gone according to plan and Kula was already there waiting among the trees when Balint rode into the sawmill compound.

Young Kula was taking a great risk. What he had to tell Abady concerned the nefarious activities of Gaszton Simo, the Hungarian notary for the Gyurkuca district, whose unscrupulous dealings had caused much misery and hardship for the men of the mountains, and who saw to it that no one crossed him with impunity.

Among those who had suffered most were the people of Pejkoja. What Simo had done, and was still doing, was to give aid to the money-lenders so that they exacted extortionate rates of interest when the villagers had had a bad year and needed money to tide them over. Then when they could not repay the loans, he arranged foreclosures. In this he was partnered by the rascally Romanian *popa*, the parish priest of Gyurkuca. Some years before the worst of the money-lenders, one dark snow-bound night, had been brutally murdered, and his house, with all his papers, burnt to the ground. Despite this setback Simo had not ceased to plunder the ignorant peasants in the mountain villages, until most of the poor people of Pejkoja had been dispossessed of their land and had been forced to pay rent for what had formerly belonged to them. Abady had tried his best to protect them and had offered to take up their case himself and pay any legal costs, but the villagers had refused, partly because they did not trust the *mariassa*'s motives and partly out of fear of the priest. Even so Abady had tried to take the matter into his own hands and file a complaint against Simo, which, he had hoped, would lead to the notary being transferred elsewhere. This had failed because Simo's superiors in the county town had told Abady that he had no legal grounds on which action could be taken. So, until now, all his well-intentioned efforts had been in vain.

Most of this had happened more than six years before. Since then Abady had not let up in his search for evidence which would condemn the rascally notary, but so far he had not been able to find anyone among the men of the mountain who dared provide him with what he wanted.

Now it appeared that something else, nothing to do with the money-lending racket, had at last come to light.

For many years it had been the custom for the peasants to pay their taxes to the notary's office, a practice which Simo had always maintained was not an obligation on his part but merely a service he was glad to be able to provide. Recently there had begun to be trouble and several of the mountain farmers had received 'reminders' from the tax office that the last demands had not been paid. Simo told everyone concerned that this must be due to some clerical error and that he would take care of the matter for them. No one knew what he had done, but at least the threatened bailiffs did not appear. Now, suddenly, the situation got worse and in Pejkoja alone three men found themselves faced with having their belongings seized and auctioned if they did not immediately disgorge what they had already handed over to Simo. One of them was Kula's grandfather.

The proof of Simo's guilt was what he now handed to Abady. It consisted of a receipt signed by Simo, the order for seizure and sale from the bailiff's office, and a power of attorney for Balint on which old Juon aluj Maftye had put his mark.

The midday siren had just sounded when Balint bade farewell to his employees at the sawmill, mounted his dappled grey horse and trotted swiftly away. In half an hour he had arrived at the pass.

He had gone alone without a groom or forester, partly because he knew the mountains so well he did not need a guide, and partly because no mountain pony could have kept pace with his horse. He always did this when not on official business or out stalking, for the forests seemed to him at their most beautiful when he rode through them alone. So he would send the pack-horses on ahead and follow at his own speed.

On this day the ostensible reason for the expedition was to hunt wolves. Reports had been received from shepherds grazing their flocks on the clearings high on the Ursoia that wolves had been seen prowling at night and that they had already done much damage. It was true that this report was ten days old when it reached Balint in Kolozsvar and that wolves rarely stayed for long in any one district. Still, it was just possible that they might still be there and so Balint had thought it worth a try.

It was sheer chance that wolves had been reported on the Ursoia at that moment, but there was nothing haphazard about Balint's desire to spend a few nights alone in the mountains. If this pretext had not come his way he would have thought up something else . . . anything that could be used to camouflage his real reason for going there which was simply to meet Adrienne where they could be alone in a place they both loved.

They had planned a visit to the mountains long before, but every time they had talked of it, it had been as of some unrealizable dream, some bliss that the unknown future might hold for them; for until recently they could find no way of arranging it without news of their tryst in the mountains being everywhere noised abroad. Now, at the beginning of summer, an opportunity had suddenly and unexpectedly presented itself.

Since Margit Miloth had married Adam Alvinczy and moved to a small manor house her father owned at Magyar-Tohat, she had begun to poke her sharp little beak of a nose into the running of her father's estates. Old 'Rattle' Miloth, as he did about everything, complained loudly, shouting to all and sundry that he was being robbed by his own daughter; but Margit took no notice and arranged for her husband to look over all her father's holding explaining that Adam must have some occupation and that this was as useful as any. As a result she had discovered that Count Miloth owned some forestland high in the Upper Aranyos, not much, a mere 900 acres, mostly of apparently unprofitable mixed beech forest. Of course Adam had to go and inspect it and it proved to be quite a nice little forest with a lot of handsome

beech trees, which had little value up there, but there was also a
smallish stand of pine, most of it young, for the local peasants had
long ago taken to stealing any timber worth felling. This, Margit
decided, must be changed and the Miloth forests properly
guarded. It was, she declared, a wicked waste to abandon their
property like that, and if not properly guarded the next thing
would be that the young saplings would be stolen for sale as
Christmas trees. A forest lodge was built on her orders and an
experienced forest guard was engaged and installed there.

All this had happened the previous year.

At the beginning of May Margit's small son developed
whooping-cough and the doctor recommended that as soon as
he was well enough he should be taken to the mountains for a
change of air.

Margit had seen no reason to go to some expensive resort miles
away when they had their own little lodge at Albak which, at an
altitude of twelve hundred metres, was certainly high enough.
The little house there was clean and new, and it had a marvellous
view. They would be able to stay there for two or three weeks,
which would cost them nothing, breathing in mountain air that
was as clean and fresh as any in the high Alps.

And so it turned out that at the end of June Margit and her
son, together with the maid, who was also the child's nurse, and
the cook, moved to the lodge for two or three weeks. The forest
guard went to sleep in the stable, and a summer oven was built
close to the house. The lodge only had two rooms and a little
kitchen, but it was quite enough for the three women and the
child.

It was Margit's visit to the mountains which had made it possible at long last for Balint and Adrienne to make their dream
come true. Adrienne would go up to visit her sister for a few days
and then, saying that she wanted to go on directly to Almasko,
which would take her by way of the Beles and Banffy-Hunyad,
she could easily slip over to meet Balint on the Ursoia which was
near the source of the Beles and only some three hours' walk
from the Upper Aranyos. There she would be able to sleep in
Balint's tent, and the following day walk down through the Valko
woods to the government mill on the Szamos river where the
carriage from Almasko would be waiting for her.

They had just worked it all out when news came that wolves
had been seen on the Ursoia. This delighted Balint as it gave him

a perfect reason to go up the mountains and to go alone ... for it was still important that Adrienne's name should be protected from common gossip.

It was quite a distance to the high ridge of the Kaliniassa. They had to go up the valley of the Szamos and through the Valko estate lands, and even then there was another ridge to pass. It was dusk before Balint's little group arrived on the Ursoia and darkness had fallen by the time his tent had been erected. Then Honey Zutor and the *gornyiks* set off once again for the Kaliniassa with strict orders not to move from there or wander about in the forest until Balint came down himself. At the Kaliniassa there was a log cabin and a barn where the horses could be stalled, for after the news that wolves were in the area it was too dangerous to turn them loose to graze in the forest meadows. On the way wolf tracks had been seen, though it was impossible to say if they were new or a few days old.

When Balint was alone he dined by the light of a small lamp off the bread and bacon he had brought with him and then sat outside the opening. He did not light a fire, but just sat there quietly. It was a glorious starlit night with the countless stars of heaven shining brightly in the dark sky. He thought he had never seen so many, and the Milky Way was like a vast river of light, its darker patches like islands, that wound its way from one horizon to the other. The great constellations were like letters of fire in the sky and, in Balint's imagination, seemed to be making their way ever closer to him so as eventually to disclose some ageless secret message even to that worm-like creature that was man, the secret, perhaps, of life and death ... and of eternity ...

The distant horizons could still just be made out, especially where it seemed that some tiny reddish star could be glimpsed trembling through the tips of the sharp fang-like pines that covered the mountain ridges in front of him. Occasionally, and very far away, a dog could be heard barking in the valleys below. Then silence, only silence: but it was not the silence of an empty room, solitary and deadly; rather was it a living silence, a silence that pulsated with the life of the great forests.

Balint stayed where he was for a long time, alone outside his tent in the cold quiet night. His soul was filled with the beauty by which he was surrounded; and he fancied that he could almost hear Adrienne's light steps as if she were already hastening towards him along forest paths paved with stars. Though they would not be together until the following day it was as if their desire for each other throbbed in unison on the mountain ridges that lay between them.

Two days before Adrienne had arrived at Margit's little lodge. She was not the only guest. Pityu Kendy was already there and making himself extremely useful because, with the family there, there was too much work for the forest guard who found himself not only having to look after the two ponies, scythe the grass and bring it in for their fodder and bedding, but also to go down to Albak to fetch milk and poultry and Margit's letters. So Pityu was at once put to work cutting wood and splitting kindling for the fire, cleaning the horses' tack and also, which was far more important, pushing the perambulator along the mountain paths, seeing that it was first in the sun, then in the shade, and then in the sun again. Here in the mountains this was no longer women's work, for there were more stones than soil on the rough tracks round the lodge. Pityu did everything he was asked with joy in his heart, for since he had transferred his hopeless love for Adrienne into an even deeper devotion to Margit, he was in total bondage to her. It was a happy bondage because Margit never teased him, as her sister had done, or saddened him by seeming to flirt with other men, as Adrienne had, but just accepted his hopeless devotion and listened to his litanies of love with an almost motherly tenderness and sympathy. Sometimes she would scold him, taking him to task for his tendency to drink too much, but she always treated him as a human being worth scolding and not as some sort of toy, which was how Adrienne had treated all her admirers. And the more she scolded the happier he was, because it meant that at least she had some use for him even if it was only splitting logs. As a result Pityu was happy; and it did not matter to him that he had to sleep at the other end of the barn from the forest guard, nor that he had to wash at the well as he was not allowed in the house until the rooms had been cleaned.

Adrienne's coming did not make him any happier, for it was difficult for him to forget that, before Margit had married Adam Alvinczy, both men had vied with each other in their protestations of eternal love for her elder sister. Pityu was always embarrassed when he found himself in company with the two sisters together. He was afraid that Adrienne would laugh at him. He was afraid to open his mouth in front of her, afraid to remain silent, and afraid even to look at Margit lest his love for her should be too obvious. He felt very awkward.

It was a great relief to Pityu when, on the second day of Adrienne's stay, a little mountain pony arrived from the Szamos brought by a lad employed as a servant by one of the Gyurkuca farmers. The boy said that the pony had been hired down in the valley for some *doamna* – lady – so that on the following day she could ride down to the Beles where her carriage would be waiting.

A relief that Adrienne would be leaving? Yes, thought Pityu; but that night, lying in the darkness of the barn, the dismaying thought came to him that of course he would be expected to act as Adrienne's escort and so it would be most impolite of him if he did not at once offer to go with her.

What a disaster! Two precious days of his stay with Margit would be lost, for he certainly wouldn't be able to get back before the evening of the next day at the earliest. It was also a very long walk. Not so bad while they were going downhill, but afterwards, climbing up again – why, it would take at least six hours! Pityu was all too conscious that with his increasing girth and short fat legs he was no mountaineer. Moreover he would probably get lost; and even if he didn't he would be dog-tired by the time he got back. Worse than that was the realization that he would have to spend hours alone with a woman with whom for years he had fancied himself in love and to whom he had spoken only of love. What could he do now? What could he say to her? How should he behave? Should he try to justify his desertion in favour of her sister? It seemed to him that whatever he might say would only be an admission that all those sighs of love and years of adoration had been no more than moonshine and empty rhetoric!

Poor Pityu did not know which way to turn; and it weighed on him all the more that he did not want to admit to himself that neither the old love nor the new had ever been real, that it was all a pose, and a habit. When he and Adam made such a performance of being in love with Adrienne, they could console each other with mutual complaints about how cruel she was to them both. Even now, when the adoration had been transferred to Adam's wife Margit, he could still pour out his heart to Adam who was not in the least jealous any more than he had been when they both fancied themselves in love with her sister. If he were now to face up to reality he would have to admit to himself that none of it had ever been more than play-acting. Poor Pityu lay awake racked with the impossibility of finding any solution to his problems, and logical thought was not made any easier firstly because at the far end of the barn the forest guard Gligor was snoring loudly, and secondly, because though the straw bed was comfortable enough, the old blanket that covered him stank of stale sweat and there was an equally noisome smell from the boots of the boy from Gyurkuca that were hanging up to dry nearby.

It was so difficult to think straight in these uncomfortable surroundings that Pityu found himself repeatedly reaching under the drinking trough for the sizeable flask of old brandy that he had hidden there. It had had to be hidden because Margit had forbidden him to touch a drop while he was there; but it was his only comfort, and after several generous swigs he finally fell asleep – though still without finding any solution to his woes.

He was up at dawn. His first job was to rub down the newly arrived pony, brush it and prepare the animal just as he had been taught during his period of military service as a hussar. When Adrienne's bags were brought out from the house he fastened them with professional skill to the wooden saddle and then stood there, in hob-nailed boots and with a rucksack on his back, waiting for Margit and Adrienne to come out. Gligor, also dressed ready for a journey, and the boy from Gyurkuca, waited with him.

It was eight o'clock before the sisters came out of the house and walked over to where the pony was waiting.

Pityu at once offered to go with Adrienne. He begged her to accept his services, perhaps a shade too fervently for during the long wait he had paid several swift visits to the barn to get some Dutch courage from the clandestine brandy-flask.

Margit did not give Adrienne time to reply but answered swiftly, 'Certainly not! You're not leaving here!' Then she laughed and said, 'What an idea! Leaving two women alone without a man to protect them! It'll be quite enough if Gligor goes.'

'I don't need him either,' said Adrienne. 'The boy knows the road; he came up it only yesterday.'

But Pityu insisted. 'Impossible! Going alone through the forest with some lad you don't know! I can't allow it, I can't! I can't possibly let you go like that, I can't!' And, holding his beaky nose high in the air, he started gesticulating wildly.

Margit turned sharply towards him and said, 'What a way to talk! If I didn't know there was no liquor in the house anyone'd think you'd been drinking!'

Brought up short by such a suspicion Pityu stopped insisting at once, and from then on concentrated so hard on being careful that he hardly said another word.

The sisters said their goodbyes and Adrienne set off on foot along the ridge. The forester went first, followed by Adrienne and behind them the boy leading the pony.

Margit waited until they reached the second turning on the path and then called out after them, 'Addy! When you get to the top, send back Gligor if you don't need him any more. The post arrives today and I'd like him to go down to the village.'

'All right, I'll send him back,' called Adrienne, and the little band disappeared from view. Young Countess Alvinczy gazed after them for a moment or two, a tiny smile on her face. Then she turned abruptly to Pityu and said roughly, 'Well? What are you standing about here for? Take off that rucksack and split some wood. No lunch for anybody who doesn't work!'

Clumsily the young man started to take the bag off his back, and as he did so Margit looked hard and suspiciously at him.

Balint had been waiting since dawn at Piatra Talharilor – the Thieves' Stone – just where the Abady forests met the common-lands of Valko and the district of Ambak. The four towers of rock dominating the steep hilltop meadow gave the place its name.

He stood there watching the little road which started far away down by the bed of the Aranyos, wound its way along the ridge which marked the watershed between the valleys and, about two kilometres from where he stood, dipped suddenly down beside the edge of the sheep pastures and disappeared towards the upper stream of the Beles. With his binoculars he could see a long way.

Finally, at about ten o'clock, what he was waiting for appeared: there, in the far distance, was Adrienne riding the pony, and the lad from Gyurkuca was leading the way.

He left the rock and met them on the saddle of the ridge. After a brief greeting, Adrienne dismounted and Balint led the boy and the pony to the shepherds' hut at the bottom of the meadow and told him to wait there until they came to fetch him in the morn-ing. Then he came back to Adrienne and at once they started upwards on the mountain path which wound its way ever higher, round a dense stand of pines which covered the upper slopes, through labyrinths of huge rocks and scattered junipers, until they arrived at the summit of the Ursoia.

As they mounted ever higher so the landscape widened until they could see ridge after ridge of tree-covered hilltops. The bald slopes on the Albak side had long disappeared from view on the other side of the ridge and, from where they now stood, nothing could be seen but seemingly endless forest. Deep shadows marked the valleys between the peaks and everywhere else it was as if the mountains were covered by a dense coat of dark-green fur. There was little to be seen except the centuries-old primæval forest, the sharp tips of the treetops pushing ever upwards, jostling each other in their efforts to reach the sky. Upwards, always upwards. The steep slopes might have been etched with blue-green arrowheads so regular, so uniform that they were as unreal as a geometrical drawing or an embroidery pattern. In contrast, just below them, a green meadow could be seen beyond the sheep-pens until it too was bounded by the dark of the forests.

This meadow was a bright angry green on which the sun shone so brightly that silvery reflections danced over the virgin blades of grass, for here the shepherds had cleared the meadow, burning away any small trees, juniper bushes or shrubs leaving only the precious grazing for their animals. The meadow was like a carpet without a fault.

High above, where Balint and Adrienne had stopped, the ground was littered with stones and between them were dwarf pines, silky tassels of broom, and grey and lilac thistles in profusion.

It was hot, and as they went slowly onwards by the edge of a steep cliff Balint, carrying Adrienne's bag, went ahead to lead the way. Here the going was not easy for the path was often barely more than a foot wide and creased with the deep furrows made by the winter storms. Sometimes they displaced stones which rolled swiftly down the rocky slopes below, and sometimes they had to pick their way through steep twisted steps of granite. It took some time to reach the forest and, when they did so, entering the trees from the blinding light of the open mountain top, it was like stepping suddenly into night. After the shimmering heat of the Ursoia's stony summit, the cool heart of the forest was a welcome relief.

Covered in perspiration they sank down on a bed of moss.

'Oh, how hot I feel!' said Adrienne. 'Wouldn't it be wonderful if we could bathe!'

'There's a rubber tub in my tent; but I've not much water.'

'That doesn't matter as long as it's icy cold.'

After a few moments Balint, hesitatingly and slowly, as though for some reason he felt impelled to hide the desire he felt rising within him, said, 'If . . . if you don't mind the cold . . . and it really would be icy . . . there's something else we could do. There's a mountain pool not far from here, just fifteen or twenty minutes' walk, where one of our fast mountain streams is partially blocked. It has a sandy bottom.'

Adrienne opened her golden eyes wide.

'Here? In the forest . . . in daylight . . . ?'

'There'll be no one about.'

'No one?'

'No one! Just us . . . alone in the forest.'

They gazed deeply into each other's eyes. Adrienne's full lips slowly curved back and she lifted her chin and spread out her fingers as if she were counting with them. Then, very softly, she uttered just one word – 'Good' – very slowly; and her warm deep voice prolonged the word with sensuous languor.

The path they took was a mere deer track through the trees. Underfoot was deep moss as resilient as a sponge and their legs were brushed by the cranberry leaves that grew everywhere around them. They descended a steep slope beneath trees like giants, and here and there a ray of sunshine penetrated the thick foliage overhead, irradiating a tree-trunk until it glowed like the embers of a fire, or struck vivid green or red reflections from the leaves of burdock and the shy flowers of the forest. Otherwise all around them was in deep black shadow.

The air grew markedly moist, for though they could not yet glimpse the stream they were now very close and the sound of rushing water grew ever louder.

And then there it was before them.

They emerged out of the thick trees on to the bank of a size-able basin of water, almost circular, with steep banks dipping down to it that were so regular that they might have been carved by the hand of man himself. Here the cranberries tumbled in tropical profusion; and here and there could be glimpsed blue-bells, buttercups and pale green ethereal ferns. In the middle of the basin some rocks rose above the surface of the water, heavy black rocks, glistening with the water that flowed around and over their smooth polished surface. Around them were little flecks of foam left by the swift-flowing stream.

The basin had been formed by a natural obstruction in the stream's path and into this little pool the water cascaded over some other rocks some two and a half metres above its surface. Unusually the water fell not vertically but diagonally, hitting the side of other rocks that projected from the mountain side until it divided into countless little rivulets all casting upwards a spray as fine as powder.

The patches of foam glinted snow-white in the sun, but almost everything else was in deep shadow. The steamy vapour was steel-grey, the pond black as the rocks and, on the bank opposite, the sand was so covered in thick moss that it too seemed as black as the dense vault of the foliage of the maples overhead, which, with the faint blue tinge of the pines that surrounded them, closed off the sky like the roof of a tent.

'Stay where you are!' commanded Adrienne as she started to climb down.

Balint stretched himself out on the top of the bank some way above the surface of the water, and fell at once into a profound daydream, in which it seemed that around him was neither forest nor rocks, no rushing stream, no space and no distance. Everything was two-dimensional, with narrow rays of sunlight like ephemeral shafts of transparent gold-dust that glimmered faintly here and there, the only light in a world of shadow where thin clouds of greyish vapour floated weightless like a veil designed to disguise and soften the almost theatrical regularity of some lilac-coloured columns which were, in reality, the tree-trunks around him. Everything seemed unreal and insubstantial.

Now, at the base of this magic picture, there appeared concentric rings moving ever outwards on the smoked glass surface of the water and, in their centre, the vapour clouds swirled round the naked ivory-white limbs of the woman who was making her way to the centre of the pool, shoulders thrown back and alternately swinging her stretched-out arms behind her. Her hair seemed even darker than the surrounding rocks, or the moss and lichen and tree-trunks, and it too seemed to float like a cloud above her pale body. Where she walked the shallow pool grew gradually deeper so that, as she approached the waterfall, the foam which had at first just gathered only round her ankles, started to cling first to her thighs and then, as she was descending ever deeper into the water, mounting higher and higher over her body, to swirl in mounting confusion as if crazed by desire for what it touched and by what it was parted by and embraced.

She stood there like a vision of some figure of legend, of a wood nymph bathing herself in the wild deserted forest, perhaps even of the goddess of all forests, Artemis herself. She stretched her arms far above the black crown of her hair and, very slowly, started to turn towards him, the lacy foam sometimes reaching even to her chin as the rushing water swirled round the nipples of her breasts and concealing, but not entirely, the dark triangle of her womanhood. It was as if she were standing in a translucent case of shimmering glass.

One of the sun's rays fell just where she stood, and where the jet of water splashed fiercely over her shoulders it put up a spray that might have been composed of innumerable tiny diamonds. At that moment a small almost circular rainbow appeared in the air above her head and, as Balint watched entranced, it seemed to be being held high above her head in her own upstretched arms.

The way to Balint's tent was along a wide but abandoned forest road that wound its way through thickets of young trees. For most of the way they walked hand in hand, only separating for a moment from time to time where the young saplings had invaded the path and blocked their way or when they had to climb over a fallen tree.

They walked without speaking, instinctively feeling that it would have been a sacrilege to break the primæval silence which remained with them until they reached the tent. And even there, in the peace of their refuge, they barely said a word.

They ate a simple meal in the open space in front of the tent, sitting on the edge of the little meadow that lay between the trees and the edge of the cliffs from which the view seemed so immense.

It was like being high above the open sea; for the horizon, now itself only a vague outline in the haze of the afternoon's heat, seemed unattainably far away. Then for a long time they lay there in each other's arms, gazing at the sky above.

Huge tumbling clouds sailed lazily above them, sometimes seeming hardly to move at all.

Around them nothing moved, not even the air.

* * *

At the same time Margit and Pityu were also having their midday meal some miles away. The child had been fed earlier and was asleep in his pram not far from where they sat under the lodge's wooden portico.

Pityu was nervous and worried because Margit had been even cooler than usual towards him all morning. At first he had thought that she had been angry only because he had offered to accompany her sister, forgetting everything that he was supposed to do about the house. Accordingly he tried to make amends by taking his axe, going to the woods and felling three young beech trees, carrying them back to the house and cutting them up into firewood. It had been heavy work that had made him sweat and blistered his hands; and he had hoped that, seeing this, Margit would have uttered some consolatory words of appreciation. She had done nothing of the sort. Instead she had looked icily at what he was doing and then, announcing that she had some letters to write, disappeared into the house and only emerged at midday. It had been a bad omen and Pityu knew instinctively that there was going to be trouble.

He was not mistaken. Trouble indeed there was. When he had been chopping the wood with such zeal Margit had gone into the barn and found the hidden brandy-flask. She said nothing until they had finished their meal. Then she spoke her mind.

'You have broken your word to me. You promised you would not drink anything here; it was the only condition I made when you asked if you could come. This was vile of you and particularly base to me. Not only did you break your promise, but you also sneaked the brandy up here yourself. I would have been angry enough if you'd gone down to the village and got drunk there. Maybe I'd have forgiven you if you'd done it openly ... but, oh no! You tried to trick me in my own house. It was vile of you, and so you can pack up and be off ... this instant!'

Pityu tried his best to interrupt her, to no avail; and when she had finished he still tried to justify himself, to excuse himself and to make promises never to do it again. Young Margit remained unmoved and inflexible, and after Pityu had tried to stammer out his regret she interrupted him and called to Gligor the forester:

'This gentleman is going down to Albak. Saddle one of the ponies and put his bags on it!' And without another word she turned and went back into the house.

And so Pityu had to leave: he could do nothing else. At least she had not humiliated him by entrusting her letters to Gligor, and it was some consolation, indeed the only consolation, that when he was about to go she handed them to him, explaining which was to her father, which to her husband and which to the estate manager at Varjas, saying as she did so that she could rely on him to put them safely in the post at Torda and that they would thus arrive all the sooner. It wasn't much, but it was something!

So down the mountain road he plodded with a heavy heart, that rocky, steep path that only eight days before he had mounted in such happiness. Now he stumbled and tripped and was miserable, for clambering about in the mountains was not something he enjoyed at the best of times, and on this day it was worse than ever. Somehow he had never mastered walking with a heavy iron stick and now, with his hands raw from all that axe-work, the more he grasped it the more it felt as if he were picking burning coals from the fire. He had not minded the blisters when he thought he was being useful to her by cutting the wood, but now it was different. He had been turned out of Paradise, however modest it had been, and now every painful step took him further and further into the wilderness.

A strip of light appeared under the canvas door of the tent. It was dawn. Balint woke first and then Adrienne. One of them murmured, 'It's the dawn,' and then the other repeated, 'the dawn', and together, as if by a mutual impulse, they started to get up.

The pale light called them outside and there the air was cold, with the steely cold of the high mountains that stimulated and invigorated like a draft of cool champagne. They stood together, arms entwined, breathing in deeply.

Just above the far horizon a narrow strip of yellow light outlined long lilac-coloured clouds. The sky was violet and hanging in it was the sickle moon. As they watched the sky lightened to mauve and then to grey, and from grey to palest green, except high above them where it seemed to have no colour at all. The outlines of the mountains were etched strongly against the light sky but seemed paper-thin, those closest to them, those which were covered by the pine forest, jagged like the teeth of a saw, but the furthest away rounded, as if cut from metal discs. These were the great curves of the Magura of Gyalu, or the pyramids of the Triple Mountains and the flattened summit of the Dobrin.

But no matter how different these ranges were in reality they now all seemed the same, ridge after ridge of them, as harmonious as the rhythms of a great symphony, cutting into the sky like giant knife-blades projecting from earth.

Nearby, in the slight dawn breeze, the ink-black branches of young pines moved slightly to and fro; but everything was still in shadow, showing no sign of colour except in the sky, shadows, darker or paler, but still shadows as in a faded drawing in pen and wash.

The light increased, not steadily but seemingly in rhythmic steps that could almost be counted. A siskin started calling from a thicket of dwarf pines. Then from far away another responded, to be followed by the morning song of the blackbirds. A tiny titmouse was to be seen flitting from branch to branch, and then another, and another...

Silently watching, Balint and Adrienne stood at the edge of the cliffs waiting for the sun to rise. It was like being in a new world of which they were the first inhabitants, watching for the first dawn of Creation.

The long horizon blazed into red and gold, and long shafts of sunlight rose from the hilltops, racing across the sky until vapoury shreds of cloud, hitherto unseen, shone blood-red. Higher still other clouds appeared, in long strips like celestial ribbons, the highest and nearest edged with silver and those furthest away glowing orange, saffron and an incandescent green. It was as if behind the horizon some giant furnace was being stoked into flame and was pouring out streams of liquid metal.

Now the light seemed to rush upon them for, as if touched by a magic wand, the shadowy outlines of the mountains took on the colours of day, light blue in the far distance and nearer at hand a rich spectrum of different greens. A rosy enamel illumined the bluffs of rock, but still there were no shadows, only nature's own colours, and it seemed to the watchers that the whole world was waiting with a throbbing heart for the eternal mystery of sunrise.

Then the veil of clouds was shattered, torn apart and annihilated, and in its place the sun rose, triumphant, so bright that it could not be looked at. As they turned away the couple saw that at long last the growing sunlight cast its shadows on the earth, shadows that lay prostrate on the ground, at the foot of cliffs, trees and shrubs, as if in homage and gratitude for the renewal of life.

Homage and gratitude were what Balint and Adrienne felt too

as they stood, arms enlaced, at the edge of the cliffs. Almost as soon as the first ray of sun had touched the crown of the trees above them, they felt its warmth first on their heads, then downwards across their bodies to their feet until it was also there on the meadow-grass and the wild flowers and in the branches of the dwarf pines that surrounded them.

The birds now came to life, swarms of them, crested hoopoes on the tree-branches, blackbirds pecking on the floor of the meadow, and woodpeckers running up and down the tree-trunks. Below them a kingfisher darted from the depths of the valley and settled in a tree nearby. Somewhere a squirrel started its morning chatter.

For a long time they stood there, still motionless, alone as if they had been Adam and Eve, the first couple on earth, surrounded by the joyful chorus of the birds' morning song.

Entranced they stood there, gazing into the radiance that surrounded them and engulfed their world with transcendental beauty, a beauty so strong and intoxicating that they felt that at any moment it would, like a magnet, draw them ever upwards, soaring into the infinite.

Adrienne took a step forwards and in ecstasy spread her arms out towards the rising sun . . .

PART FOUR

CHAPTER ONE

SHORTLY AFTERWARDS A meeting was held at the local head-quarters of the Denestornya branch of the National Agricultural Association. The association's affairs were discussed first, and afterwards, as was the custom, the local officials of the Co-operative held their own meeting. They did so because both organizations' committees were made up of much the same people – the Protestant pastor, the chemist and ten or more local farmers. The meetings were held every other Sunday, after church. Arpad Pelikan was there in his dual capacity as manager of the Agricultural Association's storehouse and also as treasurer of the Co-operative. Two others were there, Abady's secretary Miklos Ganyi, who always attended if he was not away on some business of his employer; and young Aron Kozma, who represented the head offices in Budapest of both organizations. It was his responsibility to oversee all business transactions.

Kozma had been Abady's confidential adviser for some years and his right-hand man ever since Balint had started to interest himself in the formation of rural Co-operative societies in Transylvania. He was the perfect foil to Balint, for his practical knowledge and common sense complemented Abady's enthusiasm, which was all too apt to lead him into impractical adventures. As a result Balint had learned to entrust complete control to him, and so, whenever he turned up at Denestornya, the Co-operative meeting was hastily convened so that Kozma could be present when important decisions had to be made. On such occasions it was better that Balint should be absent because his impetuosity had already led him into some unfortunate scrapes.

One of these had recently occurred at Denestornya itself. An eighty-acre farm had come up for sale in the district and Balint had insisted on it being bought by the Co-operative to be split up and resold to the people of the village. There was nothing wrong with the idea and it would probably have worked well if the farmland had gone to those who could pay for it. This had been the intention of the local committee, but Balint, through the goodness of his own heart and blind trust in the goodness of everyone else's, had supported the claims of the poorest of those offering to buy the land. The result had been that some of the poorest farmers, though getting their little parcels of land and at once occupying them, either did not repay the purchase price at all or did so only in part. Had Balint not offered to pay for them, the Co-operative's committee would have been in trouble.

Similar things had happened elsewhere: there had been a foolhardy purchase of a harvesting machine at Haromszek and an ill-considered construction of a building for the Co-operative in a village in the district of Csik. These too had proved expensive adventures destructive of the idea of self-help and co-operation which was the basis of the whole educational movement.

When the meetings were over Kozma shook hands with the other committee members and started to walk back to the castle with Ganyi.

For the first part of their way they were accompanied by old Gergely Szakacs, Roza Abady's pensioned-off head groom whose house lay in that direction, and by Pelikan, who walked with them out of courtesy to the visitor from Budapest. They went on foot because Countess Abady did not like to have her horses put to on a Sunday unless it was necessary. The weather was beautiful, although it was already mid-November, a real Indian summer, and so no one minded walking despite the distance; and indeed it was quite a walk for the Agricultural Association's headquarters lay at the far end of the village which consisted of a single very long strung-out street. Most of the houses were lined up on the left of the mill-stream and, on the right, the land rose steeply to the hills. It was a good mile from the meeting place to the church beside the old manor house where Abady was waiting for them. This old mansion, though quite close to the castle itself, had been where Balint's grandfather, Count Peter, had lived. After the old man had died Countess Roza had allowed her rascally agent, the lawyer Azbej, to take up residence there, but when he had left some years before, Balint, whose work for the Co-operatives had vastly increased, had given over three rooms in the house for the movement's archives and secretariat.

As the four men walked down the long street they met many

of the village folk out walking. The village girls, arm in arm, all dressed in their Sunday finery, separated to make way for them and then joined up again as soon as they had passed, whispering to each other and giggling as country wenches always do.

All the young men were out too, strutting proudly together and occasionally tossing joking remarks in the girls' direction but not joining them, for that would come later in the afternoon when the dancing started. They lifted their caps respectfully to Kozma and his companions, as did the older men who stood chatting in front of the village hall. Kozma and the others, though deep in conversation, greeted everyone with equal courtesy.

They were discussing the meeting they had just attended and especially the bungled distribution of the recently purchased farmland.

Aron Kozma could not disguise how annoyed he had been, and how dismayed, when he had discovered how stupidly Abady had blundered by getting involved at all. It had been foolhardy, he said, and worse, it had done harm.

Countess Roza's old groom echoed Kozma's words.

'I said right at the beginning what a nonsense it was, but the young master is not one to listen to anyone else's words, however sensible. He just bangs on and storms his way into trouble, that one does! He's not cautious enough. It was a big mistake, a very big mistake in my opinion!'

For a little while Aron and old Gergely discussed what they both thought of Balint's credulity and of how he was so easily carried away by his own enthusiasm. Miklos Ganyi listened nervously until finally he felt impelled to interrupt. Then he spoke up most respectfully but still with determination.

'You gentlemen must excuse me, but ... in my opinion we should look at it differently. There are aspects which should not be forgotten. I don't think we should judge it quite as you gentlemen have been doing. Of course I admit that this business of the farm got out of hand; and also that Count Balint doesn't know enough about human nature. Perhaps it's just as well he doesn't. It may be for the better that he does let his sympathies run away with him from time to time. Yes, that has its good side too.'

'In what way?' inquired Kozma.

'Just think of it,' said Ganyi, his bony face suffused with enthusiasm. 'If Count Balint didn't always try to help everyone, where would our Co-operative be? It's only his enthusiasm and drive that gets so many people to work for him.'

He turned his thin brown face to Aron. His thick glasses glinted in the sun.

'Take me, for instance,' he went on. 'I was an assistant notary in Kis-Kukullo. I had six years' seniority and it wouldn't have been long before I'd have been a fully-fledged notary myself, if I'd stayed on. But Count Balint came to us one day and told us of his hopes and the great goal for which he was working ... and I left my job, my excellent little job, which would always somehow have given me a modest little income, and went to work for him. It wasn't so much what he said, for he's no great talker, but it was the faith behind it; you can almost feel the faith in him! And it's been the same for others too, lots of them.'

'He's right, you know,' said Arpad Pelikan, a short stocky man with a direct look. 'Indeed he is. I had a successful little store here; but when the Count wanted a manager for the Co-operative warehouse, I sold my shop and accepted the job. I would never had done it if I hadn't known that someone like Count Balint was behind it all. But I'm glad I did.'

'You're both right, of course. It's most interesting,' said Kozma, and he burst out laughing. 'I never thought about it like that before. Anyway, who am I to argue the point? Wasn't it the same for me? The Devil take me if I'd have worked for nothing if Count Balint hadn't talked me into it.' He paused, and then he added, smiling, 'And now, God help us, he's got hold of my young brother as well.'

Still talking of Balint they went on their way through the village.

As they walked they kicked up little scuffs of pale sand-coloured dust which rose like tiny pennant-like wisps at their heels until it was scattered by the wind.

When the morning service had ended and Kozma and Ganyi had set off from the church to attend their meeting at the other end of the village, Balint passed through the cemetery to the little door that led to the manor house. Every time he went that way, which was at least once a day, he thought about the old man and even fancied that Count Peter was there, waiting for him either among his beloved rose-bushes or else, further up, standing between the Doric columns of the portico. He could see him

even now, with his fine features, neatly trimmed pointed moustaches and silver hair, a sweet smile on his face and wisdom in
his eyes.

The place had been run down while the lawyer Azbej lived
there, but as soon as he moved out Balint had taken the neglected
garden in hand and planted new roses – standards along the path
and climbers to cover the front of the house – so that now the
place was nearly the same as he remembered it; not quite, for he
could not give the roses the same loving care as had his grandfather. Balint had also had the outside of the house restored as it
had been in Count Peter's day, so that the white walls and
columns, divested of Azbej's lurid repainting, were now just as
they had been. Inside it was different for, when the old man had
died, all his furniture had been removed and stored at the castle
for now, with one exception, it was not needed as the main
rooms of the house were only used as estate offices and for the
headquarters of the Co-operative. Only Count Peter's writing-
room had regained its old aspect with all his furniture replaced
as it had been. The walls were lined with bookcases made of
cherry-wood, of middle height and decorated with finely
wrought columns topped by Egyptian-looking heads of gilt and
greenish bronze with, at their base, gilded eagles' claws clutching
golden balls.

In this room everything was once again as it had been except
for the pictures – the watercolours by Barabas and the portrait of
Balint's great-grandmother by Isabey. Balint had taken them to
his own room in the angle-tower in the castle and there they had
remained, for Count Peter's workroom was now used only as
Balint's personal estate office.

The old desk stood in its original place in front of the windows
but Balint only used it when studying reports or signing papers,
for though its smooth leather top, black and polished and surrounded by a delicately wrought safety-rail, was an invitation to
work, the drawers below had been found to be locked when the
old gentleman had died and no one knew how to open them.
The keys to the side-drawers were, it was supposed, in the centre
drawer, but though the key to this was in its place and was the
right key – for it bore a tag in Count Peter's writing – and
although it turned quite easily, the drawer still did not open.
Balint was sure that somewhere there was a secret catch, but he
had never been able to find it. After many attempts he had finally

given up the struggle and indeed had been happy to do so for he felt instinctively that this drawer probably held some special memories, some long-dead secrets better left undisturbed. In any case he did not need those drawers, for near the door there stood a modern roll-top work table with its drawers of files, and this Balint used for his daily correspondence.

It was at his grandfather's old desk that Balint sat when Aron and Ganyi had gone to the meeting. His letters and a pile of newspapers had been put there for him and he at once took that day's paper and turned to the news from abroad. He had been doing this every morning for the past six weeks – ever since the Balkan War had started.

Every day the news was increasingly unexpected and confusing, and Balint read it all with growing anxiety. He was only too aware that the official policy of the Ballplatz was to maintain the *status quo*, but also that, on the contrary, the Heir himself planned to increase the direct rule of the Habsburgs and to extend it by enslaving the southern Slavs. The twists and turns revealed in the papers therefore baffled and confused him. That Russia wanted war was certain, for her power and influence were everywhere to be seen. But Vienna – what was her part in all this? Was Austria tacitly following her lead? Balint grew increasingly sure that somewhere, somehow, some fatal error was being compounded.

Austria-Hungary's foreign minister, whose authority and power could easily have put an end to the fighting, turned instead to subtle diplomacy and induced the other great powers, in apparent but deceptive harmony, merely to give a little rap on the knuckles to the heads of the warring Balkan states by letting them know that, whatever the result of the fighting, Vienna would never consent to any diminution in Turkish authority. This mild and ineffective warning was not issued until October 8th, 1912, by which time it should have been obvious to all that it would have no effect.

The only concession the great powers would allow, it seemed, was that Turkey must be induced to grant essential reforms in her administration of Macedonia. The news of this important climbdown also came too late: it arrived in Cetinje only on the afternoon of the day on which Nikita had already declared war on Turkey and sent his troops to invade her borders.

Balint could not conceive how all this muddle had been possible. It was not to be believed that Vienna had not known in

advance what was being plotted in Montenegro. Even if the
Ballplatz's own intelligence service had failed to pass on the
news, they could easily have been informed by merely reading
The Times, for the great London newspaper had published,
as early as the end of August, the full text of the Balkan Pact.
To imagine that, when Turkey had been defeated, anyone would
be able to induce the victorious armies to retreat behind the
ancient boundaries was an absurdity hard to credit. There must,
therefore, be some other explanation, and it could only be that
the central European powers took a Turkish victory for certain
and that Vienna was looking forward to the defeat of the Balkan
states. At any rate it was clear that this was the view of the Prussian
Marshal von der Goltz who had himself, a few years before,
planned the reorganization of the Turkish armies.

The Sublime Porte thanked the great powers for their interest
and promises of support, but clearly did not have much faith in
them; while the Balkan states paid no heed at all. Then the war
started and the Turks were chased from the field.

Barely ten days had passed before the Bulgarian army had
reached Adrianople and the Serbs, skirting the borders of Montenegro, had arrived at Uskub and entered Albania. They laid siege
to Scutari and were now nearing the Adriatic at Durazzo. The
Greeks were at Salonika. The race was on and it was no longer
a question of where the Turks would take up a stand but rather
which Turkish stronghold would fall first.

It was at this point that at last the Dual Monarchy seemed to
wake up to what was happening. Though indifferent to the fate
of Macedonia and Rumelia, that of Albania was a very different
matter. A Balkan Albania was not at all what Vienna could contemplate or permit, for it would be an intolerable invasion of
Austria's own interests if Serbian power was allowed so to extend
itself. Strong protests issued from the Ballplatz and also, though
in a lesser degree, from Italy who was alarmed at the prospect of
Serbian control of the eastern shores of the Adriatic.

The newspapers reported these disconcerting developments
with excited glee and, as Franz-Josef was at that moment in Budapest, his foreign minister Berchtold hurried there to be with him,
as did the Heir, Franz-Ferdinand, and Schemua, the head of the
Austrian general staff. The latter left on the following day for
Berlin, and three days later Conrad left for Bucharest with a personal letter, written in his own hand, from Franz-Josef to King

Carol. At the same moment a semi-official statement appeared which announced that Austria-Hungary, should it be necessary, would use force to ensure the independence of Albania. More was to follow.

A large portion of the Austro-Hungarian army was put on the alert and a million men were sent to the Russian border on the pretext of a trial mobilization.

Today there was even more disturbing news. At Mitrovica and Prizren in Serbia the Austro-Hungarian consulates had been invaded by the mob, Austrian flags torn down and the premises looted.

Balint sat at his desk staring moodily before him. The news of the previous few days had been alarming enough, but this was far worse, for an attack on any power's consulates, if it had been as reported, inevitably meant war, for no power, unless bent on *hara-kiri*, would let such a provocation pass.

He gazed out of the window with eyes hooded by anxiety.

Outside all was bathed in brilliant sunshine. The lawn which sloped down in front of the house was still as green as in summer but the leaves on the trees were already turning brown or reddish bronze. In front of the window a leaf, saffron-yellow with sharply serrated edges, floated in the slight breeze like the trembling flight of a giant butterfly.

It had come from the maple which grew at the corner of the house and for a while continued to float there, hesitating, balancing in the air, brightly lit by the autumn sun, until finally it fell to the ground to join, with an almost imperceptible rustle, its already fallen sisters. And, as it fell, another took its place before the window, held for a moment in the air until it too fell to the ground. Balint fancied for a moment that these dying leaves were conscious of their beauty as they prepared themselves for the death they knew would follow.

The garden was so peaceful that it was hard to believe that anywhere in the world there could exist hatred or war or destruction. It was as if such beauty must exist everywhere and as if peace must be universal.

Watching this Balint felt his heart constrict.

It was not only anxiety for his beloved country and for the fate of its simple people; something else worried him deeply. What was to become of his mother if war did break out?

Lately Countess Roza had been having sudden attacks of

dizziness. She had done her best to prevent anyone knowing, but Balint had divined her secret and was sure that something of the sort must have occurred the previous night, for in the morning she had sent him a message saying that she would not be going to church with him but intended to spend the morning in bed and to get up only at lunch time. There had to have been a serious reason for this, for Roza Abady, when at Denestornya, laid great store on being seen in her pew every Sunday morning. Balint had questioned her maid but the girl had not seemed to know anything and, though he had tried to see his mother himself, she had merely sent word that she wanted to sleep until midday and did not want to be disturbed.

Now all his thoughts were concentrated on what would become of her if there was a general mobilization and he had to go to war. If that happened he would certainly be away for several months, with no news of her and in a constant state of worry.

He was so agitated that he got up and walked about the room for a while before sitting down and taking up the newspapers again. He could find only one item that seemed even slightly reassuring. Sir Edward Grey had offered to mediate in the dispute and try to find a formula for restoring peace. That England was prepared to take this line seemed, at least, hopeful.

Then he turned to the home pages, but found nothing reassuring there.

Since Parliament had reassembled in mid-September, the loose coalition of the parties in opposition had changed its tactics. While most of its members had absented themselves from the summer debates, now they reappeared in force, for in their private meetings held in early autumn it had been all too clear that their policy of boycotting Parliament had passed almost unnoticed in the country. Something else would have to be tried. They were now again present in force, making provocative declarations which they read out with a lot of noise, scandalizing the more conservative members with noisy interruptions, blowing whistles and toy trumpets before again retiring *en masse*. Their well-publicized attitude was that all the sessions held since June 4th had been illegal and therefore invalid, and so there was nothing scandalous about their repeated clashes with whoever presided at the debates and with the parliamentary guards. On one occasion a large band entered the Chamber so tightly clasped together that they were able to occupy the floor of the House without the guards being able to reach those who should have been excluded. They stood there, between the ministers' seats and the stenographers' desks, from noon until the evening; and this heroic opposition lasted until eight p.m. when they decided to leave.

Later they tried something else. The guards had become more adept at keeping out those who were proscribed by the exclusion decrees, so the opposition cliques started to search for new ways round them. Someone found out that the kitchen staff could move freely in and out of the Parliament restaurant where no guards were posted. The plan was soon made: into the building by the kitchen entrance and up in the kitchen lift, which carried the paprika chicken and the veal fricassee to the restaurant floor close to the Chamber itself! What a surprise for everybody! There they'd be, and there they'd stay until in due course they were hustled out again, as they undoubtedly would be; but what did that matter when the great Tisza, to his shame and annoyance, would for once have been outwitted? The plan was put into action at once ... and failed. They were seen sneaking in, it seems, or perhaps one unwisely talkative member let out the secret which reached the officials in time. Whatever the reason, they were stopped before getting to their places, and the escapade was the talk of the day just when the Serb army was standing before Durazzo and the spectre of a world war was stalking the Danube basin and the foothills of the Carpathians.

At this same time other absurdities were being perpetrated in the Hungarian capital, and the newspapers lost no time in passing on the news to their readers.

The opposition leaders – Kossuth, Justh and Andrassy – seemed suddenly to become aware that all was not as it should be in the Balkans and felt they owed it to the people to make public their point of view. The opposition had to have a voice, they said; to make a stand, let their views be known. And in this they were, of course, right to recognize that they had gained nothing from their passivity and their refusal to attend debates. The general public had failed to appreciate the great moral lesson of their abstention and had not even realized that in this great dispute the opposition itself was really the injured party! It was, of course, the same realization that had brought them back into Parliament, which had prompted the renewed rash of obstructionist tactics, and led Zoltan Desy openly to attack Lukacs claiming that the

Minister-President was the 'world's biggest "Panamist"', though few people knew what he meant by the epithet except that it was rude. This had all been good clean fun and, they said, completely justifiable, even heroic ... until now, when the Balkan crisis seemed to deserve something more.

The opposition had to have a voice, they said; to take a stand, make a speech! Some cogent expression of opinion was necessary, something to show how original they were and how different from the government in power, how statesman-like, how much more intelligent and understanding!

It would not be enough merely to take part once more in the parliamentary debates on foreign affairs, and in any case if once they gave Tisza an opportunity to allow their members to speak it would be tantamount to recognizing his authority, to accepting his appointment as Speaker and his right to interpret the Rules of the House in his own way, all of which they had until now steadfastly refused to do. Why, someone might even interpret such a move as accepting the legality of Tisza's position, and that was unthinkable.

Instead they searched around to find another solution which, to them at least, appeared very droll and witty.

The opposition therefore proclaimed that 'Parliament' – their own self-styled Parliament, not the one that met in the official House – was the only true parliament and would hold its sessions in the ballroom of the Hotel Royal. There, they declared, the real Parliament would meet, complete with Speaker and Legal Authorities seated on a dais high above the members, a President, two Vice-Presidents and other necessary Officers of State.

The first member to speak was Albert Apponyi. In a speech redolent of sweet reason, he outlined recent political events in the capital and declared that all those gathered together that day in the hotel ballroom were the country's true representatives and that in their name, and that of the Hungarian nation, he saluted the heroic struggle of the Serbs, Greeks and Bulgarians. He talked about the right of all nations to determine their own affairs, and of the right to independence, and he therefore proposed that Hungary should make a noble gesture to those enslaved peoples and stretch out the 'hand of friendship' to Belgrade. This was the tenor of the motion he urged the delegates to accept.

Other speakers followed him. Among them Lovaszy and Lajos

Hollo went even further. Both had for some time been outspoken critics of Austria-Hungary's foreign policy. Now they
came out as outright partisans of Serbia, stating that Viennese
pretensions to the status of a world power were ridiculous and
based on nothing but foolish vanity. It was nothing to Hungary,
they said, how affairs in the Balkans were settled; and nothing
but folly to intervene in any way: it would be mere meddling in
other people's affairs. It was here that it was stated for the first
time, although still in somewhat veiled terms, that the alliance
with Germany was a harmful one and served only Germany's
interests. The general feeling that surged through all the
speeches, and which was expressed in vague terms of brotherly
sympathy for oppressed nations, was that the Hungarians were
loved throughout the Balkans while the Austrians were universally loathed. Apponyi's motion was accepted unanimously, and
everyone thought that by doing so they had made a 'heroic' protest against the pretensions of Vienna.

Balint put down his paper with a gesture of contempt, deeply
shocked by everything that he had read. This pseudo-Parliament
was crazy, he thought, and it was nothing short of sheer folly to
act so lightly when at any moment Hungary might be involved
in a war and the nation forced to fight for its very existence.

It was unbelievable, Balint reflected, that those so-called political leaders, Apponyi, Kossuth and Andrassy, could have been
so irresponsible as to permit such a declaration without realizing
what an effect it was bound to have abroad. It was tantamount to
an invitation to Russia to attack their beloved country, and it
would encourage all the petty Balkan states to underrate the
power of the Dual Monarchy and to scorn its warnings and
authority. And in Paris and St Petersburg it would look as if the
Austro-Hungarian empire was on the point of disintegration
with a revolution in Hungary as the first step. How was it possible
that none of them had paused to think of such consequences?

Balint got up again, went over to the window and opened it.
He stood there for a long time without moving and allowing the
cool air to circulate round him and calm him down.

Outside the dew still lay on that part of the grass that the sun
could not reach, and there, too, the unmelted hoarfrost lay like
milky glass. Elsewhere the lawn was dotted with fallen leaves,
coppery-red from the plane trees and butterfly-yellow from the
maple. The leaves were still falling, very slowly and floating in

the air like a light mist of golden smoke in front of the open window ... But Balint saw nothing of this. He merely stood there, staring sightlessly before him.

He came to himself only when the door opened and Aron Kozma and Ganyi entered the room. They gave him their report of the Co-operative meeting and told him that the book-keeping was in order and that they had found no faults in the society's management. Then Kozma outlined the present state of the problems attendant on the distribution of the newly acquired farmland, and said he was glad to report that the former muddles had been satisfactorily cleared up. Owing to the diligence of the more reliable members, the late-payers had been obliged to settle their debts and so the society was now in a position to repay the few thousand crowns that Abady had advanced. Kozma explained all this in great detail because he was anxious to make Balint understand how much trouble he had caused by his well-meaning but thoughtless intervention.

Balint nodded and seemed to be listening. Now and then he said something to show appreciation of what had been done, but though he was as polite and considerate as ever, his mind was not in it. All the time that Kozma was speaking Balint was still seeking to understand what lay behind that pseudo-parliamentarian debate that had so angered him.

Soon he believed that he had discovered what had led people who should have known better to act in that ridiculous way. It was nothing more than the almost universal belief of Hungarian politicians that their voices could only be heard inside their own country. Their whole conception of politics was based on this, and nobody for a moment believed that their actions and words were watched or heard by anyone abroad, not even Apponyi whose brother-in-law was ambassador in London and who presumably wrote home from time to time, nor Andrassy, whose father was close to Franz-Josef's intimate circle and who had for a while been a diplomat himself. In the heat of domestic passions it had never occurred to them to think of such matters as anything but the skirmishes of party politics which no one outside Hungary could for a moment understand or even be interested in. To these men the horizon extended no further than Vienna and outside this circle, this little Hungarian globe, there was nothing! The motion passed in the Hotel Royal's ballroom was not in reality meant even for the Balkan states, but only for the government in Budapest, or at best, for the monarch so that he might see how discontented its authors were.

The general public, which for centuries had had no interest in world affairs and had never even grasped the importance of the Balkan conflict, now showed no more interest in the opposition's motion, and in any case would never have believed that any reaction outside the country could have any more relevance than if it happened on the moon.

While these matters were passing through Balint's mind, he had been nodding approval of everything Kozma told him but in fact paying less and less attention to what was actually said. So now, when Kozma suggested that when they made their next tour together Balint should not only refrain from accepting any personal financial responsibility but should promise him never in any circumstances to do such a thing again, because such an action was the very negation of the idea of self-help and co-operation, Balint, who had heard only the last few words, at once replied, 'Of course I'll promise . . . of course, you're quite right!' and Kozma grinned at the secretary in triumph as if saying, 'You see how easily he can be convinced! He has even given his promise!'

It was now getting close to lunch time. They got up and were about to walk up to the castle when Balint realized that he had not even glanced at his mail. Accordingly he asked Kozma to go on to entertain his mother while he and the secretary went through the letters together. He would join them in a few minutes.

The first few letters dealt only with Co-operative business and so, after briefly scanning their contents, he handed them to Ganyi saying how they should be answered. The next letter was in a grey envelope and was from Honey Andras Zutor.

It concerned the notary Gaszton Simo and recounted how the young forester Kula had come to find him in the woods and had recounted that while he, Kula, had been at the market at Hunyad, the Romanian *popa* Timbus had gone to Pejkoja and threatened Kula's grandfather, old Juon aluj Maftye. Angrily he had asked the old man why he had gone so far as to denounce Simo for malpractice and how it was that he had dared to appoint a Kolozsvar lawyer to represent him. The old man had been badly scared and had told the priest that he had understood nothing of what was happening, that it was all in the hands of his grandson and that, as he was very infirm and could not read or write, he had merely signed whatever had been put before him. Old Juon had apparently said that he was guilty of nothing and that there was nothing of which he could be accused. The priest had then taken out some paper and tried to induce the old man to put his mark on it, but the grandfather, despite the priest's menaces, had resisted and had not signed. Kula now wrote that he feared the old man would not be able to hold out for long because he felt death approaching and Timbus had threatened him with eternal damnation. The young man did not know what was in the paper the priest wanted signed but thought it probably countermanded the lawyer's appointment, though of course it might have been something else, perhaps some appreciative statement about Gaszton Simo. The old man had not been told.

'. . . *and this is why I am writing to your Lordship,*' ended Honey's letter, which as usual was clear enough even if lacking in punctuation, '*because some big trouble may come of it Kula is frightened and sure that Timbus and Simo will certainly shake the old man and he said I saw Simo yesterday he is not an easy man to deal with and he may have been going to say something else but I looked hard at him and perhaps he thought I was going to hit him but it is certain that now he is in a good mood though only three weeks ago he talked about being fed up and wanting to move away but now he doesn't say this any more but quite different things . . .*'

Balint's face clouded. When he had left the mountains in August he had looked for a lawyer who spoke Romanian and who could not only plead old Juon's case at the tax office but who could also speak with the country people when the inspectors came to make their enquiries on the spot. It had not been easy to find the right man because everyone knew that Simo and the head County Sheriff were close friends and that therefore everyone in the Sheriff's office would move heaven and earth to protect their colleague. He had had to find someone who had no ties, either of family or friendship, with anyone in the Sheriff's office.

Finally one such had been found and the denunciation of Simo officially deposited with the authorities. As yet there had been no hearing and though an enquiry was bound to be held sooner or later, it was obviously in Simo's interest to do everything he could to postpone matters until he had had time to make the plaintiff withdraw. If he could achieve this then he would win the case.

It was not, however, only a case of clearing Simo's good name. If he were to be exonerated then it would be Simo himself who would have his hands on the steering-wheel. He could then file a complaint for malicious prosecution and the honest young Kula would find himself hounded and persecuted in his turn.

Balint grew ever more depressed at this terrible thought, for it would be a heavy responsibility if the young man should get into trouble because of his confidence in Balint. Looking up from Honey's letter Balint looked at Miklos Ganyi, sitting beside him at the desk. Through his thick black-rimmed spectacles Balint fancied he could see a look of compassion and an eagerness to be of help. It was as if Ganyi already knew what was worrying his employer, and it occurred to Balint that as the secretary had spent six years in a country notary's office he would be sure to know exactly how such enquiries were carried out and so perhaps would have a useful idea of what the consequences might be.

Turning to Ganyi he gave him a brief account of the affair and also told him that the accused was doing all he could to persuade the plaintiff to withdraw.

Ganyi listened attentively, his long bony face tilted sideways as was his habit when listening to something important.

'I have heard about this case,' he said, when Abady had finished. 'I had it from Winkler, the forest supervisor, when he was last here. Simo will certainly be dismissed if the case is proved. This is automatic in cases of tax fraud. However, if they can persuade the old man to declare that his grandson never explained what he was being induced to sign, and especially if he were to say that the receipt he produced had nothing to do with the tax demand but was for something quite different, there could then be some very serious results.'

Ganyi paused, and then went on: 'Since the old man cannot read or write then no retribution would fall on him; but the grandson could be made to seem responsible and could be accused of slander and of falsifying legal documents. For these crimes he might well be convicted ... and ... and perhaps not only him. Simo is quite capable of spreading his net further and indicting Andras Zutor as an instigator of the crime, and ...' – here Ganyi again hesitated before plucking up courage to say what was in his mind – '... and perhaps even your Lordship.'

'Really? Me too? Why?'

'Because it was your Lordship who recruited the lawyer and instructed him to proceed. Of course your Lordship's actions can easily be explained and defended for it would be clear that, no matter how the situation turns out, your Lordship acted in good faith and for the general good. It is unlikely that Simo would go as far as that, but your Lordship would certainly be subpoenaed as a witness and Simo would do all he could to drum up support in the press by posing as a martyr. You can be sure that the more trouble he can stir up the happier he'll be!'

'It would be ironic if Simo tried to act the sacrificial lamb! But what can we do? Go up and see old Juon?'

Ganyi's mouth opened until a glint of white teeth could be seen. Then, very slowly and with marked emphasis, he said, 'That I would not recommend. The old man is an essential witness and the accused would be sure to assert that a visit from your Lordship constituted an attempt to persuade the plaintiff to bear false witness. Such an assertion would only complicate matters. There is only one thing to do: explain to the grandson that it would be fatal to him personally if his grandfather were to withdraw. A watch must be kept on him, and this can easily be done, up there in the forests, without attracting anyone's attention.'

Balint stood up. He thought for a few moments and then put out his hand to Ganyi. 'Thank you for such excellent advice. I'll write to Zutor today.'

'Your Lordship should put nothing on paper. It'd be better not to write, for one never knows into what hands a letter may fall. Send for him and do it verbally; that would be better, far better!'

They went out, the secretary politely escorting his employer as far as the veranda steps. Then with a modest smile that pulled apart the line of his little black moustache, Ganyi added, 'Perhaps your Lordship would like to entrust this matter to me? With your permission I could explain everything to Zutor personally. I have had some experience in similar cases, and it might be better than if your Lordship . . . it would give me great pleasure.'

When Balint questioned his mother, Countess Abady merely said that she had been sleeping badly which was why she had decided to stay in bed that morning. She seemed in very good spirits and talked animatedly to Aron Kozma. She had put on the silk dress she kept for special occasions, perhaps because it was Sunday or perhaps it was because young Kozma was there, for his father had been a childhood playmate of hers, though she had not seen him for more than forty years. On this day she was at her most vivacious and, though her manner always held something of condescension in it, it was with all her old charm that she talked of horses and their breeding and of the hunts of long ago. Balint felt reassured.

After lunch he sent a telegram to Winkler at the forestry head-quarters on the Beles, telling him to send Zutor to Denestornya. Then, leaving Ganyi behind, he and Kozma got into his car and were driven away. That Zutor would find only his secretary there he did not mention. It was better that way.

As Balint got into his car Countess Roza came out on the balcony and continued to wave goodbye until the motor glided out of sight through the massive gateway in the castle's outer court.

Later Balint often thought of this moment and always in later years this was how he remembered her best, a diminutive figure standing very straight behind the carved stone balustrade, waving goodbye with her chubby little hand . . .

CHAPTER TWO

THE TOUR OF the Co-operative Centres in the south-eastern counties that Balint took with Aron Kozma lasted ten days. Their last stop was at Kis-Kukullo in a small village called Kis-Fuzes a mile or two from Dicso-Szentmarton.

All through the meeting, during the reading of reports and the checking of the books – and even more so during the voting which then followed – Balint and Kozma both noticed that everyone seemed to be in a great hurry to bring the meeting to a close. They whispered among themselves and glanced repeat-edly at the clock on the wall. When asked the question that everywhere else had loosed a flood of suggestions and endless discussion – 'Are there any complaints or special requests?' – everyone at once had said 'No, nothing! . . . Everything's fine! . . . Nothing at all! . . . no, nothing!' and looked eagerly towards the door.

Neither Abady nor Kozma could make out what could be

going on. They were both sure that there was no dark secret about the book-keeping that had to be kept from them, so they assumed that the village people were merely anxious to go somewhere else and were afraid that any prolongation of the Co-operative meeting might mean their missing the fun.

The general air of gloom and dismay that had seemed to mark the meeting vanished immediately when, about midday, Balint brought the discussion to an end and headed for his car. Then it was as if a heavy load had been lifted from everyone's shoulders and, wreathed in smiles and merrily shaking hands with the visitors, they escorted Balint and Kozma to their motor, happily closed the car doors upon them and waved goodbye with such enthusiasm it was as if they were calling out with one voice, 'Now it's time to go! Go! Go now!'

In the Kukullo valley the villages were so close together that it seemed that each one started where the last left off. The next on their route was Gyalfalva where the manor house belonged to Pityu Kendy. They reached it after a drive that took only a few minutes despite the fact that the road was crowded with pedestrians, many of them young men, girls and children and all of them from Kis-Fuzes, who were hurrying along as merrily as if they were on their way to a country market or a travelling circus.

The village street of Gyalfalva was no less crowded and everyone smiled and waved at the car's passengers, assuming, no doubt, that they were all bound for the same festive destination. Held up by this happy crowd Balint's car crept along until it was nearly opposite the entrance to Pityu's house. Here, in the curve of the wooden palisade that flanked the gates to the Kendy manor, the crowd was so thick that they were forced to a halt. The chauffeur sounded his horn and the crowd at once gave way, but not along the road, only towards the Kendy gates. The driver started to explain that they were on their way to Dicso only to be faced by Pityu Kendy himself, dressed in a leather jacket and fur cap, who ran to the car, and shook hands with Balint and Kozma, crying, 'You can't shame me by passing my door and not coming in!' and went on to explain what was happening.

What he said was far from clear. Today, he declared, was a great day, an important day, which was why he had invited so many people. In fact he had invited everyone he knew, including Balint and Kozma. Hadn't they had his letter, he asked, and then

answered himself saying that of course they had not been at
home, but that he had written. Balint enquired what it was all
about, and Pityu explained that it had all been in the letter. He
had, he said eagerly, condemned Brandy to death and today was
the great day when the Court would pronounce sentence; now,
in a quarter of an hour, the Court would be in session. They were
only waiting for Balint's arrival, and that was why he had been
at the gates, because he had heard they were in the district and
was on the look-out for them.

Brandy? Court? Pronounce sentence? Balint and Kozma were
still as much in the dark as if Pityu had never launched into his
breathless attempt at explanation. All the same it was now clearly
impossible to continue on their way without stopping, all the
more so because at that moment some of the other guests came
crowding out of the gates, among them the two young Laczoks
and Zoltan Alvinczy, who at once launched into further explanation telling all over again how Pityu had sentenced Brandy to
death, while from the steps of the portico inside old Uncle
Ambrus bellowed out, 'Stop fooling around out there and drive
that spittoon of yours in!'

Balint was in no mood for any sort of party, for his tour of the
village Co-operatives had been exceptionally exhausting,
involving as it had daily discussions lasting from morning till
night. By the time he had got to bed in the evening he had still
not had time to read the daily papers, and with the continuing
Balkan crisis to worry him – for though it had recently calmed
down somewhat, it was still menacing enough – all he wanted to
do now was to get home. The idea of this jolly celebration
appalled him; but it would have been churlish just to drive on
and, besides, Balint had no desire to cause offence.

And so, with his companions, Balint got out of the car and
walked up to the house.

The large dining-room in the centre of the house was packed
with guests. There were the three Kendys, old Daniel, Uncle
Ambrus and Joska; Farkas Alvinczy, Kamuthy, and several neighbours including Todorka Racz, all drinking cronies of Pityu's.

Everyone was in a happy party mood, which had been reinforced by copious draughts of wine and brandy. The dining-
table was littered with empty and half-empty glasses.

Everyone, too, knew what this feast was about, for Pityu had taken care to explain the joke in detail and in his letters of invitations he had slipped a paper listing the crimes for which Brandy was to be arraigned and sentenced. Pityu clearly thought it was all a huge joke, of which he was proud to be the instigator, and now, in typical Transylvanian fashion, all his guests were drinking and laughing and teasing each other and their host.

Soon the great moment arrived.

Pityu Kendy called out, 'Guards! Do your duty!'

The two young Laczoks, Dezso and Erno, stepped forward wearing ancient military shakos, which Pityu had found in some drawer, and hung around with rusted sabres and dilapidated sabretaches. Both men were short and stocky with markedly Tartar features. They were as alike as twins. Standing strictly at attention they made an impressive pair with their gold-fringed headgear, even though this was somewhat moth-eaten.

Then came the command, 'Bring the accused up before the house!'

The two Laczoks clattered away and the guests followed them out on to the long stone terrace in front of the house. There they settled down in a semi-circle, on chairs that the footman and maid brought out from the dining-room. The chairs wobbled a little on the uneven paving stones, but the guests were in no state to notice. The sun was shining, the lovely pale sun of the beginning of winter, and everyone was eager for the fun to begin.

As the gentry settled themselves in their chairs, two gypsy bands took up their positions, one on each side, holding their instruments at the ready, and the village folk crowded together on the lawn in front of the house, all in festive clothes, young and old alike, the girls in their most elaborate finery. Among them a swarm of children tumbled about, sometimes running up close to the terrace and having to be dragged back before they reached the terrace steps, for they were too young to know their place.

Balint saw that among the crowd were all the men who had seemed so eager to get away from the Co-operative meeting.

Everywhere there was an air of expectancy and excitement, especially down on the lawn for they all knew that later there was to be a barbecue in the farmyard, with quantities of wine and gypsy music.

Now the gentlemen gaolers brought up the accused. It was a large wooden five-litre wine jug and they were carrying it by two handles that looked like arms. The belly of the jug was painted with flowers of all colours and the dome-shaped lid represented a face with wide slanting eyes and a huge moustache made of some kind of fur.

The culprit was carried up with stiff formality, in a most soldier-like manner, and placed on a bench that a footman hastily slid under it.

The arrival was greeted with cheers and, strangely enough, squatting there on the bench between two guards, who stood erect with drawn swords, the accused had an air of knowing malice, seeming to challenge everyone present, guards, judges and spectators alike, with a look of pride in his own wickedness.

The trial started, not in the usual way for Pityu himself was to be prosecutor, witness and judge and also, as everyone could see, executioner too, for strapped to his waist was his officer's revolver in its leather holster.

Pityu rose to his feet and, to a flourish from the gypsy bands, waved in the air the prosecution's crime-sheet.

'You vile scoundrel!' cried Pityu, and after this unflattering start proceeded to enumerate the crimes of which Brandy was accused: that he made men unsteady on their feet, that he caused dreadful headache, that he made noses swollen and empurpled and, finally, made men drunk so swiftly that there was no joy in it.

After these generalities Pityu turned to more personal charges, himself appearing as chief witness.

'I shall now testify,' read out Pityu, 'how many crimes have been committed against myself, how many times you have muddled my brains while I have been at cards and made me stake my all on a single ace. Time and time again you have encouraged me in foolhardy bids so that I have lost money. More than that you have so fuddled my wits that I have insulted my friends to the point that I have had to fight duels with them, slashing away with sabres for no good reason. And each time I have begged to be left free of you and so commit no more idiocies. Right up to this very day you have kept up this evil course. This summer, when I was a guest in the high mountains, I was thrown out in shame because you had furtively crept back and insinuated yourself once again into my confidence. Well, that was the last drop, I mean your last drop, and you deserve the penalty of death! Does everyone agree?'

'Death! Death! Death to the horrid criminal!' cried the guests on the terrace; and from down below, amid guffaws of laughter, the crowd echoed, 'Death!'

'And so, you horrible scoundrel, you see your last hour has come. But, so that no one can say you had no chance to defend yourself, I now invite you to offer your excuses. If you have anything to say, speak now!'

Pityu's manner of shouting at the accused was so stern and convincing that everyone was struck dumb and waited expectantly for the jug to reply. They listened in vain.

Then Pityu spoke again. 'Nothing to say? All right. Then I will proceed to sentence. Brandy is hereby condemned to death by firing squad for the manifold crimes he has committed against honest Peter Kendy, who from henceforth will only drink wine!'

Great jubilation. Cheers, hand-clapping, hats thrown in the air and another flourish from the gypsy bands. Then above the hubbub came another shout from Pityu:

'To the scaffold with him!'

A procession formed up. First went the gypsy band from the village, immediately followed by Pityu's footman and valet pushing a small cart in which they had placed the condemned Brandy on a bed of straw. On each side walked the young Laczoks with drawn sabres and behind it, proudly erect, stalked Pityu, who in turn was followed by the chief guests, the gypsy band from the county town and the older generation of farmers. The boys and children ran forwards on both sides, eager to be first at the place of execution.

The procession rounded the house to the strains of a funeral march, and then wended its way up the sloping garden until it reached a giant oak tree standing close to the surrounding wall. This was the appointed place.

The music stopped and the jug was lifted up and placed against the tree-trunk. The spectators formed a semi-circle with the two Laczoks at each end. Pityu stepped forward until he was about five paces away from the condemned. Then he took out his revolver, released the safety-catch, and called out, 'Now I shall send your guilty soul to Hell!'

Uncle Ambrus, who, the older he got, liked less and less for anyone else to steal the limelight, tried to spoil the effect by muttering, 'What rubbish! How can a jug have a soul?'

Pityu laughed back, 'But it can . . . the spirit of cherries!' and fired straight at the wooden jug.

The force of the bullet made the jug wobble twice on its little wooden legs before falling forwards on its belly. From beneath it spread streams of red liquid which collected in little puddles between the massive roots of the old tree.

Everyone now crowded round Pityu, cheering and applauding him while the gypsy band struck up the well-known aria 'The intriguer is no more!' from the opera *Laszlo Hunyady*. Old Daniel Kendy, oblivious of everything else, shuffled up to the toppled wooden jug, crouched down slowly and painfully and dipped his fingers in the spreading crimson stream. Then he licked his fingers twice and, with the air of a great connoisseur, said quietly to himself:

'Kirsch! Kirsch! *Quel dommage* – what a pity! Such a noble kirsch!'

Accompanied by the town band, who were now playing a selection of joyful tunes, the guests walked slowly back to the house and crowded once more into the big dining-room. The villagers were taken round to the farmyard by the estate overseer and his assistants and there they found meat roasting on spits and cauldrons bubbling away. The local gypsies struck up and soon all the younger people were dancing. Wine flowed from a barrel that had been tapped in the entrance to the barn and they could all knock back as much as they wanted.

In the dining-room too there was a lavish collection of Rhenish and other fine wines, as well as an imposing array of locally produced wines, new and old, and all of them so potent that the executed Brandy would have hidden himself in shame. Soon the food was brought in, simple country food, filling but unsophisticated, cabbage with smoked pork, and sausages of many different varieties, for it was just after the first pig-killing of the winter. Everyone ate heartily and laughed and joked . . . and they all drank heavily.

In half an hour several of the guests were drunk, but none more so than the noble host himself who was by now quite cross-eyed.

Otherwise the tipsiest of the older men, as might have been expected, was old Daniel and, among the younger ones, a neighbouring landowner, Vince Himleos, an extremely polite young man whose widowed mother had impressed upon him what an honour it was to be invited by Count Peter Kendy and had made him promise to mind his manners and to introduce himself to everyone present, especially to the older men.

With this motherly advice ringing in his ears, he was obsessed with the thought that maybe he was not doing this properly. The more he drank the more convinced he became that perhaps he had not been doing all that he should; indeed, he decided, after much agonizing, that more was needed, something that would save him from the awful fault of not knowing how to behave in noble company.

Accordingly he got up and staggered to the head of the table where Farkas Alvinczy and Kamuthy were sitting, clicked his heels and announced:

'I am Himleos!'

'*Servus* – how do you do?' they both responded politely, as did Uncle Ambrus, who was sitting next to them, for no one in such company minded a man being drunk and not fully in control of himself.

Then poor Himleos, whose old Hungarian name meant 'pox-ridden', reached old Dani, clicked his heels again and said his name once more.

As the older man did not turn round and answer, probably because he had not heard him, young Vince introduced himself again, more loudly and then, seeing that he still got no response, touched old Daniel's shoulder and yelled in his ear, 'I am Himleos!' and put out his hand.

Old Dani still did not turn fully to face him but briefly looked him up and down and then peered into his proffered palm. Then, under Dani's red nose, a wicked smile spread across his face and, stuttering badly as he always did when drunk, he said very slowly, 'I hope you g–g–g–get well s–s–soon!' and, chuckling to himself, turned back to his glass.

Young Vince staggered at this insult as if he had been struck. Though mild and inoffensive by nature the one thing he would never have accepted, even when sober, was that someone should make fun of his ancient family name . . . and now he was drunk. He stepped back and swung back his arm to strike out. Luckily Uncle Ambrus sprang up in time to grasp him in a powerful bear-hug so that Himleos could do nothing more than scream out, 'Monstrous! I protest . . . protest . . . I protest!'

The gypsy musicians fell silent and many of the younger men,

Pityu among them, ran forward, surrounded the irate Himleos
and dragged him to the other end of the room where they all,
especially the two young Laczoks who knew him well, did their
best to hush him up and calm him by telling him about old
Dani. Others busied themselves with Daniel Kendy himself,
who now rose to his feet and, swaying as if caught in a gale,
started to bow repeatedly in every direction and, in elegant
French, stammer out:

'*A v-v-votre d-d-disposition . . . v-v-votre d-d-dis . . .*' but got no
further for he was grasped by several strong arms and carried out
into the garden, for it was well known what followed when Dani
was in drink and started to bow to everyone present.

Abady took advantage of the general confusion to leave the
room. With Kozma in tow he quickly found his chauffeur who
was waiting for them just outside the main gates.

They drove swiftly through the village, which was now completely deserted because every man, woman and child was up at
the Kendy manor house carousing and dancing to the gypsy
music.

Balint left with a bitter taste in his mouth for it had been some
time since he had attended drunken revels of that kind. At the
mock trial and execution he had laughed with the others at the
humour of it all, but now, as they drove through the darkening
afternoon, he looked back with concern and bitterness at the
waste of talent and energy that had been lavished on such a lark.
Now, he thought, they would talk of nothing else unless it was
equally trivial. It was as if none of those people could ever for a
moment be serious, even when the country was threatened by
something as potentially dangerous as the Balkan crisis. Not a
word had been uttered about that, not a single word. And it had
been the same all through Balint's tour, during which he had met
all sorts of people, officials and men of all different stations and
standing in towns, villages and country districts. And these were
people who professed, in their own fashion, an interest in politics
and world events . . .

Kozma sat beside him, silent and apparently so wrapped in
thought that Balint wondered if he was thinking the same.

On reaching Dicso-Szentmarton they drove straight to the
hotel where they had intended to spend the night before visiting
three more villages the next day; but Kozma had to continue the

tour alone. At the hotel a telegram was waiting for Balint which the porter explained had come from Denestornya at midday.

Balint's heart constricted with anxiety as he opened it and all his fears were confirmed for Countess Roza had suffered a stroke that morning.

Balint returned at once to the car, hardly pausing to say goodbye to Aron.

'Denestornya!' he said. 'As fast as you can!' and the car sped off into the coal-black night.

Days passed without change. Winter set in and soon it was Christmas, the first Christmas in four years that Balint and his mother had spent at Denestornya and not at Abbazia.

Outwardly the festivities were conducted as they always had been.

Roza Abady sat in the centre of the great hall on the first floor of the castle facing the stairs. The dining-table had been extended to its full length and on it had been placed a huge tree decorated with angels'-hair, paper garlands, golden stars and a host of tiny candles. All around it were stacked high piles of winter clothes which Countess Roza and her two housekeepers had been knitting during the previous twelve months. These were for the children in the village and would not be distributed until after church on the following day. They were displayed now because Countess Abady somehow felt they were not really Christmas gifts unless they had first been placed round the symbolic tree.

Also on the table were a quantity of parcels all labelled with a name. These were her gifts for everyone of her household staff and their families, and consisted of shawls, dress materials, warm vests, coats and jackets without sleeves . . . and a lot of children's boots.

As had been the custom throughout Countess Roza's time, each recipient came in from the staircase where they had been waiting, in a rigid order of precedence, the children accompanied by their parents. 'Enter the hall, bow to the Gracious Countess, receive your present, kiss her hand and then leave quickly so as to make room for those who are waiting!'

This immutable ceremony proceeded as it always had. The two housekeepers, Mrs Tothy and Mrs Baczo, stood on each side of their mistress, pushed forward the children when they had to, and handed up the appropriate presents. The butler stood by the door to see that the right people came in, and also that they went out again.

Only one thing was different – the role played by the countess herself. In previous years she had personally given out each present; now Balint did this instead, for the old lady's right side was paralysed.

This year, too, she no longer spoke a few friendly words to each of her dependants as they stood bowing before her. Now she just nodded to them, for she did not want them to hear the few almost unintelligible words that were all she could utter, and offered them her left hand to kiss for she could no longer raise her leaden right arm. Even so, she still sat upright with her back like a ramrod, propped up by cushions. Now she sat in the wheel-chair in which she had been propelled from her own rooms, for it would have been too awkward to lift her into the throne-like armchair she had always used before. The wheelchair had been pushed forwards just in front of the tree so that she had the light behind her, casting shadows so that no one should see her dis-torted face. To make quite sure of this she wore a lace bonnet that was tied with extra-wide ribbons. This helped to support her chin.

Countess Roza had ordered all these arrangements herself, explaining to her maid and to the housekeepers, in the babble of sound that only they had learned to understand, when they had dressed her for the feast. Even so her eyes sparkled angrily for a moment when she fancied they had not fully understood what she wanted, for to her it was of the utmost importance that nobody should be shocked by her appearance nor for a moment feel sorry for her; no one, not even her own faithful servants. While she was still living she must remain what she had always been, a great lady with her head held high, a sovereign queen in her own right, wrapped in indomitable pride like a robe of purple and ermine.

And so, outwardly at least, all was as it always had been on every Christmas Eve at Denestornya for the last forty years. But the myriad candles in the great chandeliers and in the sconces, and all those tiny flames that covered the tree and which were reflected in cascades of polished crystal, sparkled in vain. The Shadow of Death lurked in the immense hall and everyone who stepped inside that resplendent room could feel his presence.

Perhaps he was lurking in the gilded display cabinets or in the deep window embrasures, or even in the next room, in the darkness of the neighbouring drawing-room which could just be glimpsed through the tall glazed doors. Wherever he was he was there, waiting; and at any moment he might step forward. Even now, or in a few moments, there would be a faint tinkle from the glass doors and he would be there before them ... Everyone felt it: while coming forward, bowing and kissing their mistress's hand, they would send covert frightened glances to the far end of the hall where the white doorway and the black squares of glass hid something frightening and unknown.

There were few of Countess Roza's retainers who did not feel a wave of relief as they regained the great stone stairway and could steal away.

CHAPTER THREE

IN THE NEW YEAR, at the end of February, the affair which had led to the formal denunciation of Gaszton Simo by old Juon aluj Maftye, of Pejkoja in the mountains, took a new turn.

To recall what had led to this we should remember that in the spring of the previous year – 1912 – old Juon had received a tax demand which claimed the payment of some 286 crowns for arrears dating back to 1909. At this point he was not unduly worried. A year and a half before, he had received a similar reminder which had not been followed up since old Juon had at once complained to the local notary Gaszton Simo, to whom, when the demands had first come in, he had paid the tax money and from whom he had received a receipt. The notary had expressed himself outraged that the tax office should be in such a muddle and promised to go himself to the county offices in Banffy-Hunyad and see that the misunderstanding was cleared up. When no further demands had been delivered by the village policeman the old man assumed that Simo had been as good as his word. For eighteen months there was official silence until in that fateful spring of the previous year there had come a new demand for the same arrears, and in August this had been followed by an order for the seizure and sale of all Juon aluj Maftye's possessions.

At that time old Juon's affairs had been looked after by his grandson, Kula, who had at once taken the papers to Honey Andras Zutor, Abady's trusted chief forester, to ask his advice. In his turn Honey had reported the matter to Balint because he knew that for several years past his master, knowing how Simo had exploited the simple people in the mountain villages and extorted everything he could from them, had already once tried to have the notary removed from office. Now Balint had acted again. He had got young Kula to obtain from his grandfather a blank Power of Attorney, which had been delivered to Count Abady together with the notary's original receipt.

Balint had then found a lawyer in Kolozsvar who was willing to handle the matter, had the power of attorney vested in him, and arranged for Simo to be denounced for embezzlement and false pretences at the appropriate office of the Ministry of Finance. And so the matter took an official turn.

However, wheels grind slowly and the enquiry by the tax inspectors became more and more strung out. The ball was thrown from court to court – but each time only after another long delay. Five weeks would pass before a letter received any reply. Then the men in the Ministry wrote to the county tax office which passed the letter on to the Sheriff. The Sheriff eventually returned the papers to the tax office saying that it was their responsibility, not his. The tax authorities wrote once more to the provincial county office stating that this matter came under their jurisdiction, not that of the tax office, since there was nothing on Simo's receipt to say that it concerned anything to do with taxes. The finance office therefore disclaimed all responsibility in its turn, as in their opinion this was either a disciplinary matter for the county's administrators or else a case to be heard in the criminal courts. The papers were then sent once more to the County Sheriff to determine whose responsibility it all was. In the meantime Gaszton Simo offered himself for a disciplinary inspection, but cunningly sent this offer to the wrong office. He did not approach the Under-Sheriff as he should have, but instead approached the association of local notaries of which he himself was president.

The notaries' association refused Simo's request to be investigated saying that it had authority only in internal disciplinary matters, not in anything that concerned members of the public. At the same time they held a special meeting and unanimously passed a vote of confidence in Simo's probity: thereby making it clear to Balint that Simo had somehow manipulated the whole cadre of county notaries into taking his side.

This had been the situation at the beginning of March. Until then, though nothing definite had transpired, it had seemed as if Damocles's sword was suspended over Simo's head. But then matters took a very different turn.

Gaszton Simo himself filed a complaint for false accusation, denouncing in his turn old Juon's grandson, Kula, and accusing Honey Zutor not only of complicity but also of having instigated a plot against him.

For proof he offered a declaration from old Juon that his grandson had deceived him, that being unable to read or write he had had no idea that the paper on which Kula had forced him to put his mark had been a Power of Attorney, that he had only recently learned this and wished at once to disclaim any such intention, that the receipt from Simo that the boy had taken from him did not apply to anything to do with tax payments but only to an old debt that he had repaid and furthermore that he had never said anything against the notary Simo whom he held in the greatest esteem and respect. He ended by begging forgiveness, saying that his grandson had abused his trust, and that he was nothing but a simple helpless old man who had known nothing of what was happening.

It was a good document, well-written, clear and wonderfully precise. And not only precise but also very much to the point, for every accusation against the notary had been logically disposed of and refuted in advance. The declaration had been countersigned by two witnesses, Timbus, the parish priest of Gyurkuca, and one of the church-wardens. In a postscript the old man stated that he had dictated the declaration to the priest, and this too was countersigned by two witnesses, the same church-warden and the village school-teacher. Nothing could have been seen to be better nor more seemingly in order.

The news of Simo's counter-action reached Denestornya without delay in a letter from Kalman Nyiresy, the pensioned-off forestry director of the Abady estates, who wrote a fulsome and repetitious account of what had happened. It was clear from the letter what joy Nyiresy took in passing on the bad news, despite the terms of flattery and simulated homage in which it was phrased.

Nyiresy had never forgiven Balint for having enforced his retirement, even though he had been presented with a large house at Banffy-Hunyad with a garden that reached down to the river Koros, and a pension amounting to half his former salary. The reason was that for more than thirty years he had been able to lord it up in the mountains, doing no work but living well at his employer's expense. He still lived well at Banffy-Hunyad, giving parties and entertaining his friends as if he were a country gentleman. But this was nothing compared to his life up on the Beles where he had been overlord of sixteen thousand acres, where he could shoot what he liked, eat as much venison as he wished, fish for trout in and out of season, and use the meadows for his own grazing; for, until Balint himself took an interest, no one had ever asked him to account for his stewardship.

In sombre mood Balint read Nyiresy's letter. He was disgusted by it, for he could almost see the outrageous old man with his white beard, sitting at his desk and pulling at a long pipe, smiling wickedly under his huge tobacco-stained moustaches as he contemplated with what displeasure his former master would read what he had to tell. He was certain that the news came direct from Simo, for the two had been friends for many years; and indeed it was more than probable that they had composed the letter together, chuckling with joy as they poured out more wine and champagne and drank toasts to the notary's certain triumph.

Throwing down the letter Balint tried hard to banish this disagreeable picture from his mind lest it should cloud his judgement.

The Juon aluj Maftye affair had now become serious. That Simo had embezzled the old man's money was certain, and would remain so; but that the young Kula, with this new evidence, would be found guilty seemed equally certain. What else could the County Court do? And Zutor too might well suffer.

Balint knew that he could never let this happen. He could never sit idly by, doing nothing, while simple people who had trusted him and acted on his orders found themselves in trouble because of him. That was unthinkable.

And yet, what could he do?

There was only one thing, and that was to insist upon appearing as witness for the defence. In this way he could tell the whole truth and shoulder any blame that might come his way. If he went into the witness box he could tell the world everything he knew about the criminal alliance between Simo and the *popa* Timbus, and how for years they had extorted everything they could from the mountain people. It was true that he could prove nothing, but what did that matter? He would also make it clear that the denunciation of Simo had been his idea, and that he had organized it from the start. Let them condemn him if they wished. It did not matter so long as Kula and Zutor went free, for they had only acted on his orders.

It was an ugly and indeed dangerous situation, even though, as a Member of Parliament, he was immune from prosecution in the county courts. In such circumstances he would be allowed to resign his seat — and of course would himself insist on his release. Then a few weeks later he would find himself in the place of the accused. In the meantime what a picnic the scandal-press would have, dragging his name in the mud, vilifying the lazy aristocrat who had dared to slander the clean-living notary who worked so hard in his humble country post! Weeks and months of insult and shame would be his lot until the case was finally heard and then, if the Minister of Justice declared a 'non-suit' in recognition of his years of unselfish public service, which was by no means certain, he might avoid a prison sentence though nothing would wipe away the stain on his name.

None of this was as important as the fact that he must stand up for those who were only involved because of him.

Only one consoling thought came to him at this bitter moment. He need no longer worry about his mother's feelings, for the stroke had mercifully so incapacitated her that they could keep from her all knowledge of what was happening to her only son. She would not have to know how their good name was being besmirched.

But what if matters went so far that he was sent to prison, what would happen then? Could they keep that from her too? And, with a shudder, the wish arose in him that his mother should never live to see that dreadful day.

Two weeks went by, two weeks full of dismal foreboding, during which everyone at Denestornya, the secretary Ganyi, Peter the butler, the two housekeepers, Mrs Tothy and Mrs Baczo, and the other servants, even the retired stable manager, Gergely Szakacs, went about their work with worried faces. Everyone knew that the Simo affair had taken a sinister turn, though no one dared mention it.

Abady himself spoke of it only to Adrienne whom he used to visit from time to time in the evening at the Uzdy villa just outside Kolozsvar. Then, as they lay in each other's arms, he would talk over with her all the horrible possibilities of the forthcoming case. Adrienne had at once approved of everything he intended to do, saying that he really had no choice, even if it meant going to prison. They had talked over the case from every angle, but never found any other solution. Even so Balint returned from his visits to Adrienne with renewed hope for, despite the fact that everything seemed against him, Adrienne could never bring herself to believe that things would end badly. It was impossible, she said, impossible. It was a moral impossibility and so it just could not be! Faced with this intuitive certainty Balint somehow managed to keep up his own courage.

On the evening before the case was to be heard the principal actors were all in Banffy-Hunyad, even young Kula who was spending the night at the house of Honey Andras Zutor. Everyone would be taking the early train to Kolozsvar where the county courts were held.

Old Juon aluj Maftye did not come because the notary Simo, afraid that he might blurt out the truth under cross-examination, had arranged a medical certificate for him. The old man was glad to stay at home because he was worried about the paper that the priest had made him sign, and yet knew he would never dare to revoke it and state it had been forced out of him. The other accusers were there in force, Gaszton Simo and the *popa* Timbus, the witnesses to Juon aluj Maftye's disclaimer, and three others who had been brought in to bear witness to Kula's connection with Zutor. These last were spending two nights in a shed at Nyiresy's house so as to make sure they did not stray off somewhere else.

The priest Timbus and Gaszton Simo were dining merrily at Nyiresy's table along with Simo's chief protector, the Head Sheriff, the station-master and two lawyers, all important local notabilities and all good friends with Nyiresy and Simo. Beside them the *popa* was only small fry, but he was there as an essential witness at the following day's trial.

The wine was flowing and a gypsy band playing for all its

worth. The dinner had been lavish, as Simo had contributed a
roebuck and at least thirty trout that he said he had confiscated
from poachers.

'Luckily I caught them just at the right moment!' he said,
winking at the Head Sheriff who knew all his little tricks.

'What a rascal you are, Gaszton!' he laughed back, even
though these were things they never normally spoke about for
the Sheriff liked to preserve his dignity.

Nyiresy owned a vineyard near Ermellek and the strong wines
they were drinking came from there. It had not taken long before
tongues were loosened and now there was no longer any pretence of talking of the forthcoming trial with impartial earnest-
ness. Now they talked loudly and arrogantly, spicing their talk
with obscene jokes, and no one bothered to disguise his malice
or his hatred of Count Abady, for it was not only the host who
bore a grudge against Balint but all the others too. One or two
resented the meddlesome aristocrat and were jealous of him, but
most of them were only influenced by a feeling of solidarity with
Nyiresy whom they regarded as a good fellow who liked his cards
and wine and entertained them all so generously.

There were those who resented Balint because he had taken
the Abady forests in hand and put an end to their poaching his
game, but the main cause of their dislike was that they looked
upon him as a trouble-maker. This epithet, in their eyes, meant
anyone who made the lazy work, who pressed them into service
for the new Co-operatives, who was always having officious
messages sent to them from the county offices or the Prefect
demanding speedy action, whose meddling sent them on tiresome and exhausting journeys connected with infringements of
the forestry and game laws, and who was continually pressing for
the Land Registry Office to keep its records accurate and up to
date. In a word, he 'made trouble' – and now there was this
unnecessary affair of the notary Simo which had entailed endless
paperwork. Scribble. Scribble. Scribble.

It was this last which had enraged the Chief Judge, who liked
to think himself sovereign in such matters. So what happens, he
demanded? Along comes this young Count putting his nose in
affairs which do not concern him and who does not even live
here but in the county of Torda-Aranyos miles away.

This judge was known as a hard man who liked his own way
and before whom the whole county trembled. If he approved of

someone, they flourished; but woe betide the man who crossed him. And now there had appeared this meddlesome aristocrat who had somehow stumbled in from an adjoining county and who dared denounce one of his own trusted notaries. Further he had seen fit to denounce him in the capital, thereby by-passing the Judge's sacred authority. It was intolerable.

The host sat in the place of honour with his long-stemmed meerschaum pipe resting on the table-cloth in front of him. He was wreathed in smiles, delighted at the way everything seemed to be going. He did not say much but sat smiling under his huge tobacco-stained white moustaches. When he did speak thick clouds of smoke coiled upwards from his mouth as from the craters of Etna; but with him the poisonous gases were replaced by words of venom.

On his right sat the Chief Judge, who was a broad-faced, thick-set man with a clipped moustache and greying hair cut to a short bristle. A vertical wrinkle separated his eyebrows, which everyone knew was the mark of a stern man. He too spoke sel-dom, but when he did, first slowly removing the leathery stump of a chewed cigar from his mouth, everyone else fell silent out of respect for his undoubted authority. His grey eyes were like ice, and when he smiled and showed a glint of white teeth, it seemed to stem not from merriment but only an intention to bite.

Next to him was the station-master and, across the table, Simo's lawyer, Dr Todor Farkas, who was known in Banffy-Hunyad, though not to his face, as 'Dr That-is-to-say', as he used this phrase at every opportunity. Beside him was Simo and then another local lawyer, Balazs Toth. Finally there was the director of the Land Registry Office, then the Sheriff and the *popa* Gyula Timbus.

Of course they talked of nothing but the case and the news that Dr That-is-to-say had brought, namely that Abady himself had come forward as a witness for the defence. Simo's lawyer had heard the news that morning in Kolozsvar and now it was being eagerly mulled over. The news was so exciting, and so unexpected, that the gypsies played in vain. Nobody listened to a note.

Everyone had something to say, but Nyiresy summed up all their thoughts in one phrase: 'What the hell is that rotten bastard up to now?'

Only Simo found it disconcerting. He felt it would have been

better if the case had been heard without Abady, who was a
Member of Parliament, putting his oar in and interfering. What
the Devil did he want? It was extremely disquieting. Anything
could happen. He had always been against involving Abady . . .
and now? It was a bad business, he thought, but he was careful not
to show his anxiety but laughed broadly and roared out, 'Well, let
him appear! We'll push him around a bit!'

'I expect he just wants to pour some whitewash on that rascally
forester of his, Andras Zutor,' said Balazs Toth.

'It won't be easy . . . that is to say . . . Kula Lung was induced
to bear false witness either by Zutor or by the Count himself.
Nothing else is possible. Anyhow no one is going to believe that
an ignorant mountain lad could hire a lawyer in Kolozsvar all
on his own.' And Dr Farkas went on to declare that he for one
had always been sure that Abady was behind the whole thing:
'. . . that is to say . . . there is no doubt that the Count is the real
culprit. I was only in favour of leaving him out of the accusation
because he is a Member of Parliament and, if we were out to get
him, we'd have to wait ages while we had him unseated; and not
only that but, well, that is to say, our friend Gaszton always said
he wanted the case heard quickly. But there is nothing to worry
about, indeed it is all for the best . . . that is to say . . . tomorrow
I'll get him in a high old muddle when I question him. Then
either he'll have to deny everything, which will mean his friends
Kula and Zutor will be found guilty, or else it'll be clear to all to
see that he himself was behind it all, and then we'll indict him
too.' Dr That-is-to-say spoke with smug malice.

Huge puffs of smoke came from beneath Nyiresy's great
moustaches and he said, 'That's talking, that is! Send the Noble
Lord to gaol, eh? We'll all drink to that!' And he laughed loudly
as he raised his glass high and touched all the others within reach.
The gypsies, though not understanding what it was all about,
played a flourish.

General hubbub broke out and when it subsided a little the
Head Sheriff turned to Simo and, speaking very slowly, asked,
'You're sure that Abady doesn't have anything concrete, some
other paper, perhaps? It'd mean trouble if matters were to take
another turn, you know.'

'Of course not; what could he have?' said Simo quickly.

Then the lawyer interrupted, saying, 'It is quite impossible that
he should come up with something else, quite impossible . . .

that is to say . . . supposing – just supposing, mind you, not conceding – that the Count tried to bring in other facts, things that
had nothing to do with this case, the judge would refuse to hear
them. The law does not permit it. Our evidence is clear, and we
have written statements to prove it. These are quite straightforward. They cover the whole case and cannot be gainsaid.
I ought to know; after all I drafted them myself. Faced with our
evidence there can be no argument. In court tomorrow there
will only be one issue and that is the degree of responsibility of
the accused. Nothing else!'

'Why is that?' asked the station-master, just for something
to say.

'These are the facts. Juon Lung aluj Maftye has made a legally
valid declaration that he was misled by his grandson and that our
friend Gaszton Simo has always behaved most correctly towards
him. Therefore the author of the false accusation is Juon's grandson Kula. Now, what we wish to prove is that this Kula did not
himself think up the idea but was pushed into criminal behaviour
by Andras Zutor. Kula Lung, as the first accused, will certainly
be found guilty, and most probably Zutor as well . . . that is to say
. . . for Zutor was cognizant of, and indeed behind, everything
that Kula did. What sentence these two get, light or heavy, will
depend on whether we can show the Count to have inspired the
whole malicious proceeding. If we can, then Zutor's guilt will
be to some extent mitigated because he is the Count's employee,
as will Kula's to a lesser degree, and the court will not be slow to
appreciate the moral pressure that someone like the Count can
apply if he wishes. There is one possible outcome, but only if we
can get the Count to admit his part in the matter. Personally
I don't think we will, that is to say, Count Abady cannot be such
a fool as to fall into that little trap. But the alternative is much
more certain. Abady will, of course, try to show that Zutor is not
to blame. That is where I come in, that is to say, I know for a fact
that it was Abady who enlisted the defence lawyer and who gave
him old Juon's Power of Attorney. But I won't bring that up at
tomorrow's hearing: all I will do is force him to declare that he
had no part in the matter. It will be enough for the moment . . .
that is to say . . . Kula and Zutor will naturally be found guilty
and our friend Gaszton will immediately be vindicated, which is
the most important thing.'

'Well,' interrupted Nyiresy furiously, 'and what happens to

that high-born brat? Does he walk away free then? Nothing
more?'

Dr That-is-to-say leaned back in his chair and waved a finger
in the air with pompous self-righteousness. 'Didn't I say that was
where I came in? On the following day we will accuse Abady of
perjury, and won't that be a lovely thing to see? Eh?'

The host erupted in cheers and Simo's little shoe-button eyes
sparkled with glee.

Now the Chief Judge decided to intervene.

'I wouldn't go as far as that – not that I want to see him go
free, oh no! – but there are political considerations. If the two
accused are condemned that will be shame enough for our noble
Count. No one will ever speak to him again in those mountain
villages. He won't be able to stick his oar in any more or worry
about things which do not concern him. We'll be free of him
and that'll be enough. I'd hold on to that perjury charge for a
while. With that in our pockets we'll have got him where we
want him . . . for years to come; and if he ever again starts up his
little tricks we'll let him know what we've got on him.'

'You old rogue!' cried Nyiresy as he exploded with laughter
and slapped his neighbour on the back. 'Treat him like that pack
of notaries you've got, eh? First catch 'em out in some fault, and
then keep it dangling over their heads!'

Between the Judge's thin lips his teeth gleamed.

'Exactly. That has always been my method.'

'But you can't seriously want me to abandon my plan?' cried
Dr Farkas, outraged. 'Fail to catch Abady for perjury when he's
practically thrown himself into our clutches? Oh no! Nobody
can wish that!'

He was at once backed up by the other lawyer, Balazs Toth,
and so went on, 'Is that what you want? In my client's best
interests I forgo the pleasure of calling the Count as a witness,
even though I always knew what a God-given opportunity it
would be to start criminal proceedings which would have made
me famous . . . that is to say, how did Karoly Eotvos make his
name? With the Eszlar case! And Polonyi and other famous
lawyers? Always through some great criminal proceedings. I've
denied myself this until now because professional ethics make the
client's best interests paramount and I will always be faithful to
that. I will stick to that and get this Kula found guilty, but once
that's done, it's time to do myself some good. Why, even the

petition to Parliament to have Abady unseated so he can stand trial for perjury like anyone else – why, that will be advertisement enough. The press will be full of it! Then the case itself. Every word will be printed in the papers. There'll be reporters, interviews, a magnificent speech for the prosecution which will be printed in full . . . and at last the verdict. To bring an MP, who is also an aristocrat, to trial, sentence and prison, to stand before the world as the champion of honour and justice . . . ! I will never give that up, never! I'll see it through to the end . . . and the end will be magnificent!'

He was so worked up and shouted with so much enthusiasm and sublime ambition that everyone started to cheer and the Judge called across the table, 'All right, I don't mind! Put him in prison then. Put him in prison!'

CHAPTER FOUR

BALINT SPENT THE evening in his own rooms in Kolozsvar. He had arrived in the late afternoon and as soon as he got out of his car the hall porter told him that some man unknown to him had already called twice, asking for Count Abady, and had left a card.

It was just a little piece of cardboard on which was written *Koriolan Timbus*.

'He said, your Lordship, that it was very important and that he'd come again in the evening.'

Timbus? Surely it couldn't be the priest from Gyurkuca, for his name was Gyula. But if not, who could it be? Was it perhaps his son?

'What sort of a man was he? Young? Slim?'

'Yes, your Lordship, very skinny and didn't look at all well.'

Then it must be the priest's son, that fanatic young agitator with his head filled with irredentist pro-Romanian ideals. He was a sickly youth whom Balint had only seen twice; once lying on a couch at his father's house with hatred in his eyes, and then again at the railway station at Balazsfalva when he had surreptitiously handed some paper to the Romanian lawyer Timisan. It seemed most unlikely, thought Balint, that he would voluntarily come to see him, but then who else could it be?

'Very well then,' said Balint. 'Send him up when he comes.'

It would not really matter if the young man took up some of his time, for Balint had no plans to go out that evening.

Later, in his study, Balint paced up and down going over and over what he would say in court the following morning and how he would say it. Firstly it was necessary to put his thoughts in order and make a list of the points he wanted to make, saying what had prompted him to arrange for the notary to be denounced and making it quite clear that in his own mind he was working only for the public good. As he worked out what he would say he realized more and more how thin, from the legal point of view, was his evidence. It was more than possible that the court would not even listen to him, but if he was heard then it was at least certain that Kula and Zutor would go free. And then he'd have to bear the blame himself. That no longer mattered. He had to go through with it and accept whatever came his way. He could accept anything, even shame, ignominy and the destruction of his good name, rather than allow two men to be punished whose only fault was trusting him and carrying out his orders. The way ahead was clear; there was no way out.

He was so deep in these dismal thoughts that for a moment, when Timbus was announced, he had forgotten that he was expecting a visitor.

The door opened and a very thin, narrow-chested young man came in. A few sparse tufts of beard grew on his emaciated face and his long black hair stood up untamed and rebellious. Two red spots glowed on his cheekbones.

He came forward very slowly to where Abady was standing by his desk, and when he stood before him he bowed stiffly but ignored Balint's outstretched hand. Then he sat down in one of the chairs placed beside the desk.

Abady followed his example and then asked, 'What can I do for you?'

The young man cleared his throat twice, hesitated, and then in a rush of words like a sudden flood, he croaked out, 'I . . . I . . . came about tomorrow, about tomorrow's case . . . about the trial of Kula . . .'

'About the case?'

'Yes, the case. I've thought about it for a long time because what will happen all depends on me. Do you understand? On me, only on me!'

'I must confess I don't understand.'

'Yes. On me, only on me!'

Timbus's burning eyes were full of hatred, but they never left Balint's face and it was obvious that he was having a battle with himself and had to make up his mind about something before he could go on. Then suddenly it all came out in a torrent of words that seemingly tumbled over one another.

'Yes, on me, for I have the old man's disclaimer, written by that scoundrel Simo, and Simo's letter, the one he sent to my father. He wrote it to my father and my father tore it up and threw it away, but that was afterwards, after he came back from Pejkoja, from seeing Juon aluj Maftye. Then he threw it away, but I found it. I read it. I read them both and I wish I hadn't. Understand? And since then I can't sleep, because it is a dreadful thing. Do you understand? A dreadful evil thing.'

He stared at Abady with a look that might have been taken for menace. For a moment he paused and then he went on, 'Yes, a dreadful, evil thing. Do you understand me? My father on one side and on the other young Kula, a poor simple Romanian. And the truth? Either I betray my own father ... or I suppress the truth ... and you are on the side of the truth and so I have to save you, even you, of all people!'

He looked aggressively again at Abady and then added, almost to himself, 'I thought about it all night long, until dawn, but I can't do anything else. So I came.'

He reached in his inside pocket, took out a folded wad of paper and threw it on the desk.

'Here it is!'

By now Timbus was very short of breath and after panting out the last words he leaned back in his chair, exhausted.

Balint had listened carefully to what the young man had to say. Now he was filled with pity for him, for the internal battle which still raged within him sounded in every word he uttered with such passion and effort that Balint barely noticed his rude manner and obvious hostility.

'Well then? Read it! Why don't you read it, that's what I brought it for!' he shouted and, leaning forward, pushed the papers towards Balint with thin dry fingers as if they were garbage he was reluctant to touch.

Balint opened the packet.

Inside were two papers, one a long double sheet, the other a short private letter.

Both had been torn and screwed up and one of them was held together only by a centimetre or two that had remained untorn. At the top corner of the larger sheet were printed the name and professional address of Dr Todor Farkas and below were some hand-written words which started '*I, Juon Lung aluj Maftye, declare . . .*' It was the draft text of the declaration said to have been dictated by the old man to the priest in Pejkoja and was written in precise legal terms.

The smaller sheet was in Gaszton Simo's writing, and read:

'*. . . since you told me last week that old Juon has now been per-suaded to do what we want I am sending you a draft which I have had drawn up and which you must make the old man sign. Take this up to him in Pejkoja. Take with you also pen and paper and two witnesses we can trust. Leave these two outside and go in to see the old man alone. There you must write it down as if he had dictated it to you. Then put this draft in your pocket and call in the witnesses so that they can see that it was indeed there that you have written the paper. Then the old man must put his mark on it in their presence. You do not have to explain what this is all about* (this sentence was underlined twice). *We must be quick about this. I've had that good-for-nothing wretch of a grandson, Kula, called in for questioning about his army service. He'll be retained at the recruiting office for two days so you must hurry over to Pejkoja at dawn tomorrow and do exactly what I've told you. You won't regret it, I assure you. When you get home be sure to destroy the draft and this letter. I would have come myself and not written but my lumbago has come on again and I can't get out of bed. It doesn't matter much, but take care to burn these papers when you get home . . .*'

As he read these words Balint was filled with joy and relief. Salvation at the last moment, salvation from the mess he had got himself into. More, it meant that Kula and Zutor would be freed of all blame. All the worries of the past weeks fell away like a heavy weight taken from him. He looked up at Timbus and, filled with gratitude, he held out his hand, saying, 'I don't know how to thank you!'

The young man's reaction was the same as before: he just looked back as if he had never seen Balint's proffered hand. Then, venomously, he said, 'You needn't bother. I'll take no thanks from you, not from you!'

'And why not?' replied Balint smiling. 'The mere fact that you've done this today shows that good intentions will come together somehow and will always prove stronger than hatred ... even that hatred you so obviously feel for me.'

'That's just it! Try as I may I have to admit that for years you've tried to help my people. I've seen it for a long time. But why do you do it? What is behind it? What are you up to? It's all just some trick, I know.'

'Oh, come! You don't really believe that, do you?'

Timbus's face darkened. Speaking almost as if to himself, he said, 'N-no, but I wish I did!' Then he went on angrily, 'It is absurd, ridiculous. For a Hungarian lord to help our people, why it's the very opposite of all I've been taught to believe. It contradicts everything I've ever learned and what I want to believe, everything I've worked for, everything I believe to be true. It's absurd ... just absurd!'

'Not at all. Why, old Juon himself, Kula's grandfather, told me that there was a time when all the mountain people had the greatest faith and trust in *my* grandfather. You must have been told of this too. I myself remember, though I was only a child then, how often so many of your people came to him with their problems asking for his advice or getting him to settle their disputes. He acted as a sort of judge for them, and they always had faith in his judgement.'

'That's just what the old people say: but they're stupid, credulous. They understand nothing and they've forgotten that they were nothing but serfs, slaves who were forced to work and flogged if they didn't. And who exploited them? You did, you powerful Hungarian lords!'

'They were never slaves! All right, let's talk about the serfs. They themselves were all equal whether they were Romanian or Hungarian. They hung together, like everyone of the same station in life. It was the same all over Europe and no one then thought of it in racial or nationalistic terms. And it's pure legend that any landowner would exploit his own serfs. It would have been dead against his own best interests. What a landowner wanted was to have contented people working for him. In times of war the lords would fight with other lords and then they destroyed each other's lands, and your opponents' serfs would suffer too. But not your own, never!'

Timbus tried to answer Balint's words in a flood of exasperated argument, going over the whole hotly debated question of the ancient Dacians and their descendants, the Romanians, who had occupied that land since the times of the Romans. He quoted Sinka, Anonymus, Hasdeu and Xenophon. In broken phrases which poured out in confusion, new ones starting before the last was finished, he tried to evoke all those multifarious tomes of ancient political theory which had been written to prove what he had so eagerly absorbed, namely that a Latin civilization had flourished in Transylvania long before the arrival of the conquering Hungarian hordes. He spoke with such passion that he was soon shouting at his host.

He was stopped by a fit of coughing, a dreadful racking cough which seemed to break him in two, as he crouched in his chair with a handkerchief pressed to his mouth. It was a dry gasping fit which seemed to tear his lungs apart. When, at long last, it abated and he was able to straighten up again, he leaned back in his chair in total exhaustion.

Balint would have liked to reply that, long before the Hungarians arrived in the ancient province of Dacia, Transylvania had repeatedly been overrun by Goths, Vandals, Gepids, Avars and other barbarian tribes and a full six hundred years had passed between the time when the Emperor Aurelian withdrew his legions and the arrival of the Hungarians. And during these six hundred years the history of Transylvania had only been that of a highway whose path was trodden by countless nomads who came that way and then passed on. He would have liked to add that there existed no records and no traces of any indigenous culture, but he stopped himself because when Timbus dropped his handkerchief in his lap Balint saw that it was stained with blood, not just a drop or so but large spreading stains. Blood! The poor man was coughing blood, and Balint was stopped in his tracks by pity for the unhappy young fanatic.

'This is all very ancient history,' he said in a soothing voice. 'These things happened over a thousand years ago, so what good does it do to argue about it now? The truth is that only two peoples who are not Slav or Germanic live in the Danube basin now and those are the Romanians and the Hungarians; and they would do well to learn to live with each other. It is in the interest of both nations and we should never forget that. Of course mistakes have been made and are still being made, but it is surely the duty of every man of good faith to work for reconciliation. It will never be easy, because crimes have been committed and there are many wrongs to be righted. But all this hatred, this hatred that has built up over the centuries, must somehow be washed away. It must be!'

In the heat of his own conviction Balint managed to find many arguments he felt to be convincing. It was the first time he had tried to express in an organized way what he had long felt.

He ended by saying, 'I am sure that the time will come when all these past wrongs are forgotten and your people and mine will no longer be kept apart by hatred and resentment, but will live side by side together like brothers.'

Timbus, who had been listening in silence, now jumped up and shouted, 'Never! Never that! Never! Never!' He stood there trembling, with burning eyes.

'Why not?' answered Balint gently. 'To me it is a historic necessity. Our two peoples – and I ignore the Slavs and Germans – have no other true relations in this part of Europe. We must come together and trust each other if we don't both want to find ourselves the slaves of our neighbours. It must happen if we are to survive.'

'Maybe it's so . . . maybe!' muttered Timbus. 'Maybe . . . some day . . .' Then he raised his thin arms in the air, gesturing with those emaciated talons, his hands, and a high scream, full of hatred, broke from him, 'But first . . . first we'll pay you back tenfold . . . a hundredfold, and after that . . . No! Not even then . . . Never! Never!'

Reeling, he turned about, ran to the door, wrenched it open and disappeared slamming the door behind him.

Balint did not attend the court. After Simo's lawyer, Dr Todor Farkas, had thundered out his accusations against Kula and Zutor, Abady's lawyer got to his feet; but instead of addressing the court he merely went up to the presiding judge and, without comment, handed up Gaszton Simo's letter and the draft of old Juon's recantation. This brought the case to an end with shame to the accusers and complete vindication and acquittal for Kula and Zutor. When the judge read out his findings he addressed scathing words to Dr Farkas, reprimanding him for unforgivably unprofessional conduct in writing the draft at all, and then for his audacity in declaring to the court that it was dictated by old Juon with no help from anyone else. The intimidation of the old man was so obvious that little more had to be said. It was the end of Dr That-is-to-say's career. He managed somehow to avoid disciplinary action from the lawyers' association, but he never again appeared in any but unimportant and insignificant cases.

Simo was dismissed from his post at once. To save him from prison some influential relations somehow found the money to repay not only what he had embezzled from old Juon but also many other sums which came to light as soon as his dealings were investigated. He was then sent far away to Borod where he earned a meagre living as a humble scribe paid by the day. That was the end of his self-created little kingdom in the mountains.

An honest notary was now sent to Gyurkuca. He had been recommended by Balint, and his appointment was made so as to honour Count Abady and thus show the world that the past was now forgotten.

This was the work of the Chief Judge, who was a clever man.

CHAPTER FIVE

FROM THE DAY that Roza Abady has her stroke Balint hardly moved from Denestornya. If he had to go to Kolozsvar for an evening he would spend the night there but always returned early the following morning so as not to be too long away from his mother's bedside. The longest time he ever stayed away was the day and a half that he had to spend in town dealing with the affair of Gaszton Simo.

At this time he was completely preoccupied with his mother's illness.

Every day Countess Abady spent more and more time asleep. Even when she was awake she could rarely pay attention for more than half an hour to anything Balint came in to tell her. He would recount news of the horses, or the fallow deer, or, in early February, of the newly born lambs and litters of piglets – every day something different and always something cheerful and amusing, something funny or unexpected, a little joke at which his mother might smile and even occasionally give a little laugh. It always had to be good news or some minor success, but even so she tired fast, and then her attention faded and soon she would again close her eyes.

Balint went to see her just two or three times a day; at midday before luncheon, again in the afternoon when they would have tea together on the glazed-in upper veranda, and sometimes in the early evening when she had been lifted from her wheelchair and put to bed. A young doctor was kept in permanent attendance because had there been any emergency or change in her condition it would have taken too long to get the country physician to drive over from Gyeres. Since the beginning of January there were also two trained nurses, one for the day and the other to watch at night. The two housekeepers, Mrs Tothy and Mrs Baczo, hardly ever left their mistress's side, for only they could understand her occasional mumbled words. Besides, they knew her habits.

There was little for Balint to do. Indeed his mother seemed not always to notice when he came and went. She never sent for him or spoke about him and often it seemed that she would not notice if he had been absent for several days. All the same he did not dare go away as he was convinced that if he did something dreadful would happen, as when he had gone to the Szekler country in December.

During these long months he cut himself off from the world. All the Co-operative business was done by letter, and the Simo affair, serious and ominous as it had been, was the only thing to have dragged his thoughts away from his mother's condition.

Everything seemed unreal and remote. He even read the daily papers with the same indifference, only glancing superficially at what was reported each day, which at any other time would have interested him deeply.

The political situation in Budapest grew ever more fraught and potentially dangerous. Party hatred exploded into personal feuds and even Tisza found himself obliged to fight several duels with political opponents who had insulted him. It was always they who were wounded and retired, for Tisza was a better swordsman than most and always emerged unscathed.

Laszlo Lukacs was attacked even more frequently than Tisza. Zoltan Desy in a speech at a public banquet again unloosed the epithet 'the world's greatest Panamist', which everyone now knew to mean 'scoundrel' or 'unscrupulous crook', at which Lukacs, as Minister-President, took him to court. Whereupon Desy told the world that Lukacs, when Minister of Finance in 1910, had renewed a bank's salt-shipping contract in return for a donation of several million crowns to Lukacs's party funds, that he, Desy, knew all the gruesome details, and that this payment had financed Lukacs's election campaign. In turn Lukacs replied that the renewal of the bank's contract had in no way added to its profits, that the contribution to party funds had been from simple good will and political conviction and that furthermore he, Lukacs, never had, nor ever would have, profited by a single penny.

The publicity did no one any good, even though Lukacs's personal integrity had been confirmed when Desy lost the case.

But that was not the end of the affair.

The very day the verdict against Desy was proclaimed, Andrassy, Apponyi and Aladar Zichy endorsed everything Desy had said; and the scandal thus reached monumental proportions. Even the foreign press reported the matter in full, though no one at home seemed to pause for a moment to consider how Hungary's reputation abroad was being damaged. All these patriotic politicians seemed to think of was getting even with their opponents who had forced Parliament to accept the army estimates. Party passions obscured everything else.

From then on no one in the House would speak on any subject other than the salt-contract scandal. In vain did the government try to introduce a bill for wider suffrage. The waves of personal hatred and malice were so strong that no progress could be made. One day in March the opposition appeared in force in the Chamber, and Lovaszy, backed by some seventy or eighty supporters, shouted out 'Stop for a moment!' and in the brief silence that followed all those behind him started calling out 'Salt! Salt! Salt! Salt!' Of course Tisza suspended the session and ordered in the guards. These were at once rounded on by the rebellious members, who tried to wean the guards from their duty by explaining to them that their military oaths were not valid and did all they could to get them too to mutiny and disobey orders.

This was the first time that these so-called politicians, who made great play of their patriotic duty, tried to incite mutiny. It did not succeed.

Now they looked around for new allies and even went so far as to make common ground with the most left-wing of the Galilei Club, with whom they organized a big meeting in the Vigado. At this rally the public were regaled with the unusual sight of the otherwise reactionary Apponyi and Aladar Zichy sitting side by side with Jaszi and Kunfi who some years later were to play a leading part in the October Revolution and the Bolshevik regime which followed it. Everything was forgotten except party hatreds and opposition to the government.

At the same time as this was happening at home the situation abroad was growing ever more serious.

Diplomatic activity had never been so frenzied. In London a conference was convened to heal the wounds and lead to peace, but it was held in vain. Even though Turkey accepted most of the great powers' proposals, peace seemed as elusive as ever. The much-vaunted disinterestedness of the great powers was clearly shown for what it really was by their insistence on Turkey's ceding the Aegean Islands to their own jurisdiction – a concession that was immediately granted but which led only to the peace talks being abandoned. Adrianople remained under siege while Montenegro never paused for a moment in the shelling and encircling of Scutari, cynically disregarding the fact that the London Conference had just confirmed Albania's right of ownership.

What impertinence! said the great powers. This cannot be tolerated, they muttered indignantly: but six weeks went by until it was already the end of March before they managed to agree upon any practical action. A resolution was made summoning Nikita to explain himself. Nikita refused to appear. Then, at the beginning of April, the Allied fleets demonstrated before Antivari. Still Nikita refused either to budge or to restrain his army. Then an international blockade against tiny Montenegro was declared; but even this had no effect upon Nikita, who scornfully ignored it while his armies occupied Scutari.

And they stayed there, regardless of the menaces launched from the London Conference. Nikita must have had secret knowledge that Russia stood behind him despite her ambassador's public support for the sanctions agreed in London.

The Dual Monarchy now found herself forced to take the initiative. In London she declared that she could not tolerate the Montenegrin presence in Scutari and would therefore 'act independently'.

War, which had been coming nearer and nearer for two months, now stood before the door.

Balint read all this in the newspapers, but he was not as affected as he used to be; for his anxiety was personal and near at hand.

There was, firstly, his mother's uncertain condition, and then, for a while, the impending trial. Though this faded with the collapse of the prosecution, it did not alleviate Balint's anxiety. Indeed it rather increased it for now Balint had something else to worry about.

Only this was real to him: this and the beauty of Denestornya in spring.

By the middle of March the snow had vanished but for a few patches on the northern sides of the nearby hills. For a while some lingering traces of white remained on the banks of the streams but, when these disappeared, on the riverbanks and beside the paths, young grass started to shoot up and, in meadows which had lain asleep all winter, violets bloomed in their thousands.

One afternoon in early May Balint returned from a visit to the mares who had been put out at grass in the meadows near the castle until the summer grazing paddocks were ready for them.

On the steps of the main entrance he found the old butler Peter waiting to tell him that Countess Roza had been repeatedly asking for her son.

'Where is she? She isn't feeling any worse, is she?' he asked.

'Not at all, my Lord,' replied Peter. 'On the contrary she seems suddenly to be better. In fact her Ladyship is expecting you on the veranda. She has already asked for her tea.'

Balint ran up the stairs, passed through the billiard-room and there, on the glazed-in veranda, sat his mother in her wheelchair. At first he could not see her face, for she was sitting with her back to him, but as soon as he took his place on the sofa beside her he saw an unexpectedly joyful radiance in her eyes. When the old lady saw him sitting beside her she put out her left hand – the only one she could move – and took his in her own.

'Ah!' she said. 'Here you are! Here you are!' The words were not quite clear, indeed they sounded more like 'He-y-Ga!' though to Balint's ears they seemed clearer than for many months. Her still half-frozen face was irradiated with a happy smile.

'Where have you been? I've been waiting for you . . . waiting for you so long . . .' and her smile seemed to suggest that she had been awaiting him for years, since time immemorial.

Balint did not quite know what to make of this, for he had been with his mother two hours before, just after lunch. And not only that but for some weeks she had received him with such indifference that this sudden warmth made him wonder in surprise whether she had really recognized him at all. Whatever the reason for the change he was overjoyed and started to tell her about the mares grazing in the meadow and how the new grass was already growing lush and appetizing, with plenty of clover in it. Everything he told the old lady was happy and encouraging, and she would squeeze his hand and interrupt, saying, 'Oh, I am so happy, so happy!', while the repeated little pressures of her fingers seemed to pulsate to the rhythm of his words.

As he spoke the nurse Hedwig offered the old lady the special cup with a spout from which she could drink her coffee and buffalo's milk. Roza Abady allowed the spout to be put in her mouth and then, when she had drunk her fill, her lips to be wiped with a white napkin. On this day she let this be done for her without protest, though on all other days she had let them know that she hated to be helped and would herself hold the cup to her mouth with her left hand. Now she was using her left hand to hold Balint's and did not let it go for an instant. As soon as possible she turned towards Balint and gazed hard at his face as if she could never see too much of him. Soon, however, she started to tire, and then it was clear what had rejoiced her heart.

Countess Roza closed her eyes and leaned her head back against the pillow. Then, just before dozing off, she murmured, 'Tamas! I am so happy ... so happy that you came back! Tamas, my Tamas!' And she spoke quite clearly without even the hint of a slur.

For a moment Balint did not fully understand; but then it came to him – Roza Abady had thought that it was not he but his father Tamas who had sat beside her and held her hand; Tamas, who had died twenty-five years before, had come back; and that was what had made her so happy.

She did not sleep for long. In barely half an hour she was awake again.

Her first glance was at her son who had sat there without moving, his hand imprisoned in hers, all the time she had been asleep. Again she smiled at him.

Perhaps subconsciously recalling what Balint had been telling her before she drifted off to sleep, Countess Roza's first words were: 'Let's go ... to the stud-farm ... to the stud ... '

Balint did not at once understand what she was saying, so the old lady shook three times the hand she still held imprisoned in hers, repeating, 'To the stud . . . with you . . . the stud!' and when Balint tried to dissuade her some nervous energy so took possession of her that again she said: '. . . to the stud-farm . . . I want . . . with you . . . to see the mares . . .' and the veins stood out on her forehead.

The nurse ran to find the doctor, and when he came the three of them tried to calm her down and explain that it would be too tiring for her to visit the stud-farm straight away, too much for her. In the end they succeeded, possibly because by then she was too tired by her own eagerness to argue further, but it was only after they had promised that they would take her to see her beloved horses in the morning. Then she dozed off again.

The next day the country practitioner from Aranyos-Gyeres was called in early and the two doctors discussed whether they should allow the promised expedition. In the end they agreed that if the patient still wanted to go out she should be allowed to do so, for the weather was exceptionally fine and surely, if she were carried carefully downstairs and pushed gently along the smoothest paths, no harm could come of it. On the contrary it might help renew her will to live, that will which until the previous day's miraculous revival had so noticeably declined.

Balint was still somewhat anxious, but felt unable to forbid it; all the more so because the previous evening, when he had gone to visit his mother in bed, and early that morning when he had looked in to see how she was, he saw in her such happy expectation and joy that he did not have the heart to disappoint her.

With a contented smile she had welcomed him to her side; and each time she had again called him by his father's name. Filled with renewed joy she told her maids, in his presence, which dress and which bonnet she would wear that day . . . and what she chose was her finest.

As might have been expected the news had spread early that the old countess was going to visit the mares and so all the Denestornya employees gathered below the castle hill just where the great avenue of tall Hungarian oaks began.

The wheelchair was carried down the stairs by Simon Jäger and Balint. At the bottom of the steps that led up to the castle's main entrance old Gergely Szakacs was waiting to ask for the honour of wheeling his old mistress along the paths of the garden and park.

So a procession was formed.

Balint took his place to the left of the wheelchair, his hand still held by his mother's. On her right was the nurse Hedwig and behind Gergely Szakacs walked the two physicians and the second nurse. These were followed by Peter the butler, holding a big box of sugar-lumps, and Countess Roza's elderly maid Terka. Behind the group tottered the two housekeepers, Mrs Baczo and Mrs Tothy, overweight and struggling to keep up with the others. Breathless and flat-footed, these two were forced to give up before they were halfway to wherever their mistress was going.

On each side of the alley that ran between the great oak trees stood a line of the entire staff, indoor and outdoor, of the castle and estate of Denestornya. Everyone was there, even two of the park game-keepers who, hearing that there was a chance to catch a glimpse of their mistress, had come to be there with the others. All the men held their caps in their hands and saluted silently as Countess Roza's chair was pushed slowly past.

Sitting almost upright, her slipper-shod feet placed on the footrest as if it were a footstool, the old countess passed between the two lines of her employees like a queen on a slow-moving throne. Even now, old and ailing and very, very weak, she was still the ruler. She was wearing the same lace-trimmed bonnet that she had put on to hand out the presents the previous Christmas. The wide ribbon was tied tightly with a large bow beneath her chin – for she did not want anyone to see how distorted her features had become – and as she passed she inclined her head slightly to left and to right and did her best to smile.

And in fact she did smile, a smile irradiated with happiness and triumph ... for she was thinking that all these dear people had gathered there not only for her but also to greet that beloved husband who somehow had come home at last and who was now walking at her side, and holding her hand, as he had done so long ago when they were both young.

The procession went on its way until it reached the bank of the millstream. There Balint took the box of sugar from old Peter and, alone with his mother and the nurse, and of course Gergely Szakacs pushing the chair, they made their way along the path that led across the great meadow. The others all stayed behind at the end of the oak avenue, while Simon Jäger and the stable lads ran off towards the bridge over the river.

'Where are they going?' asked Countess Roza, smiling up at Balint.

'They're going to drive the mares over here.'

'Good! That's good!' the old lady agreed happily.

As they waited she looked to the right, towards a stand of tall poplars whose silver buds were just beginning to unfold, and to the undergrowth beneath them where the hawthorn bushes were covered with creamy white flowers. Then she turned her head to the left to look along the lines of lime trees and wide-spreading horse-chestnuts whose great trunks were outlined by the morning sun. From where they stood the view extended into the far distance, which was why the meadow was known as the Meadow of the Great View – and now Countess Roza, her slightly protruding eyes opened wide, gazed over the vast extent of her domains before again looking up at her son, and saying, as she squeezed his fingers in hers, 'You see how beautiful, how beautiful it all is . . . how beautiful!'

Balint could not reply. His eyes were full of tears and all he could do was to give her hand an answering squeeze.

Far in the distance the mares could now be seen coming towards them, galloping because the stable lads were cracking their whips behind them and this was something to which they were not accustomed. On they came, at a fast gallop, and only stopped about fifty paces away from the little group. There they stood, heads lifted high, with ears cocked as if asking who these people were who had strayed on to their meadow and wondering what was this strange little carriage they had never seen before. For a moment they stood in amazement, almost motionless, with nostrils distended . . . but only for a moment, for suddenly one of the older mares came forward and advanced towards Countess Roza. Then came another, and another, and then, again another, until it was clear that they had all recognized their beloved mistress and were hurrying to her side.

In a few moments her wheelchair was surrounded. So close they came that their soft muzzles searched her face and rested on her shoulder, asking for the familiar lump of sugar. Balint and Szakacs had a hard time keeping them in order, but Countess Abady was laughing happily, 'See? This is Csujtar . . . and Menyet . . . and here is Borostyan . . .' and with her left hand she gave them lump after lump of sugar. She gave and gave and gave; until at last her arm tired and fell into her lap. Then she closed her eyes and leaned back in the cushions murmuring, 'I'm so happy, so happy!'

She said it so softly that it was barely more than a breath. She did not move. Her head was inclined towards her shoulder.

'She's tired,' said the nurse. 'We should wait a little.'

Balint, helped by Gergely Szakacs, succeeded in driving the mares a little further away. Then they returned to his mother.

She was still in the same position, quite motionless, a smile upon her lips. For a few moments her son waited. Then he took her hand in his. It was already cold and she had no pulse. The two physicians hurried to her, but all they could do was to confirm that she had just died. The younger doctor suggested trying to resuscitate her by an injection, but Balint and the other doctor would not allow it, believing it a dreadful idea, just for a few hours, to bring the dying back from other shores only to suffer again before finally letting go. Why should they trouble her now, she who had died so beautifully and in such happiness?

Gently they lowered the chair's back. Then they raised the footrest until Countess Roza lay almost horizontally, her chin still supported by the bonnet's wide ribbon.

Slowly they started back.

Once again they passed under the great flower-laden trees where the birds were all singing their joy in this resplendent return of spring. Behind them the same procession re-formed, but it was now a funeral cortège.

Further back, just a few paces away, the whole stud followed, all of them, close to each other, their heads lowered as if in sorrow for the dead mistress who had loved them so much. It was as if they too wished to honour her last journey.

At the bridge over the millstream they were held back by the stable lads. Then one of them neighed. They remained there a long time.

PART FIVE

CHAPTER ONE

WHEN THE BALKAN war finally came to an end, Leopold
Berchtold, foreign minister of the Dual Monarchy, summoned
a delegation of both Houses of Parliament to meet him on
November 19th, 1913. The delegation included members of
both the government and the opposition parties in proportion to
their strength in the House.

In the previous year Berchtold had sent for a similar delegation
so as to give the representatives of the Hungarian Parliament a
résumé of the Ballplatz's view of the state of foreign affairs. This
had not been easy the year before; in the autumn of 1913 it was
even more difficult.

A year and a half had passed since Berchtold had first taken
charge of the Viennese Foreign Office, and in this time all his
efforts at diplomacy had ended in failure. When the Balkan War
had started Berchtold had been so confident of a Turkish victory
that he had then declared that, no matter what happened at the
front, the *status quo* in the Balkans would remain unchanged.
He had spoken recklessly, and too soon, for almost at once the
rebels in the Turkish provinces had chased the Ottoman armies
from the field, and so there had been no question, after such
dizzying triumphs, of ordering the victorious insurgents to withdraw behind their former frontiers. Berchtold had then found
himself in the unenviable position of having to go cap in hand
to the London Conference, defend his now untenable former
convictions and somehow save what he could from the debacle
he had failed to foresee. His task had been to evict Nikita from
Scutari and prevent the Serbs from obtaining such influence in
Albania that they would acquire the use of an Adriatic port. His
aims therefore had been entirely negative.

All this had formed the theme of Berchtold's address the previous year; and, because then the situation in the Balkans was still
far from being settled, and also because the Dual Monarchy's

relations with Russia had been particularly strained, he had managed to set forth his exposé without encountering undue criticism.

A year later the situation was very different. At the end of August the Bucharest peace treaty had been signed and so what had previously remained uncertain now had somehow to be explained away. As far as Austria-Hungary was concerned the profit-and-loss account showed a deficit, and Berchtold had the pitiful task of trying to make the best of it.

The truth was that the Dual Monarchy had everywhere been the loser, and furthermore the Balkan states had acted as if she did not exist. In May an agreement between Bulgaria and Romania had handed Silistria to the latter in return for Romania's neutrality during the hostilities; and it seemed that this must have been planned by a former secret agreement inspired by St Petersburg. Already, despite Romania being a party to the Threefold Agreement, Bulgaria, which with the help of the Ballplatz and Aerenthal had finally become independent of Turkish suzerainty three years before, had also annexed Rumelia. As soon as these moves were made relations between the different Balkan states became soured, for they all aspired to a share of the disintegrating Ottoman empire, and promptly quarrelled among themselves as to who should get what. Russia was asked to arbitrate, but when, encouraged once more by Vienna, Bulgaria refused to accept the Tsar's verdict, war again broke out. This time Russia encouraged the other Balkan states, now also including Romania, to turn against her disobedient former protégé Bulgaria.

The war was over in ten days.

On July 1st the Serbian army defeated the Bulgarians. On July 3rd the Romanian army marched south and by July 10th stood before Sofia. Meanwhile the Greeks chased the Bulgarians from the Aegean coast while the Turkish Enver Pasha advanced upon Adrianople, over which much blood had already been spilt, and reconquered it with almost no casualties.

In these ten days Austria-Hungary lost her last vestiges of respect in the Balkans. Something might have been saved, even at the last minute, if she had seen fit to intervene, but the Dual Monarchy made no move. This may have been wise, in that her intervention could well have provoked a war with Russia, but the real reason for this inactivity was that, after all the internal confusions which had obstructed the modernization of the army,

Austria-Hungary was then even more unprepared for war than she was to be in 1914.

So, though she could hardly have done anything else, the end result was that in the eyes of Europe these Balkan wars were lost, not by Turkey but by the Austro-Hungarian Monarchy.

Up to the last minute the Austrian Foreign Office did its best to camouflage the truth. Firstly the Ballplatz declared that, along with the other great powers, Austria reserved the right to approve the terms of the forthcoming peace treaty. It is probable that she imagined the London Conference would stand firmly behind her and thereby do something to save her good name. Unfortunately the great powers, including Germany, did nothing of the sort: they all approved the peace terms unreservedly.

This produced a new dilemma. Either Austria could pursue her aims unilaterally, which might lead her into war without the support of either Germany or Italy, or she had to renounce her claim to revise the peace terms in the way that best suited her. Faced with this impasse the Dual Monarchy withdrew from the London Conference.

From the beginning Austria had put herself in a false position. Her diplomacy was ill thought-out and badly prepared; and it showed the world how many cracks there were in the Threefold Alliance of Austria, Germany and Italy. Above all it antagonized Romania, who in the end received more from the Bucharest Agreement than she would have been allowed by St Petersburg only a few months previously. Austria's claim to have the right to approve the peace terms therefore seemed to the Romanians to be an attempt to limit their share of the spoils, though that had never been Berchtold's intention.

Romania's revenge was to come in the following year.

The main result of this feckless muddling was that from the moment Austria-Hungary withdrew from the London Conference, the world got on quite well without her. Vienna no longer had any say in Balkan affairs. The Turkish-Bulgarian treaty, and that between Turkey and Greece, had both been settled and signed without anyone even asking the opinion of Austria. It was as if the Dual Monarchy did not exist. She did make one more attempt to retrieve her lost prestige by issuing an ultimatum to Serbia that Albania's independence must be preserved; but the effect of this was lessened by the fact that it was also the policy of Italy and England – above all of England, who did not relish the possibility of having a Serbian (which meant Russian) fleet at large in the Mediterranean.

This was what Berchtold had somehow to explain to the delegation from Hungary. His presentation of the disagreeable facts was masterly.

Firstly he emphasized that Austria-Hungary's foreign policy was based on the need to preserve peace. He spoke of the 'harmony' which existed between the great powers, even including Russia – though he did admit that in the previous years there had been 'some small differences of opinion' which had later all been smoothed away. This had been a definite success for the Monarchy's diplomacy.

He then spoke appreciatively of the Ottoman Empire. It had proved its continued power and vitality by the re-taking of Adrianople from the vanquished Bulgarians. That the Sultan had also lost two great provinces was, in one way, advantageous to Turkey for she was thereby relieved of some of her most unruly subjects ... quite a happy result, in fact! It was, of course, true that when the war began Austria-Hungary's principal aim had been the maintenance of the *status quo*, but, as Berchtold's predecessor, Gyula Andrassy, had said as early as 1878, 'We mustn't prop up a crumbling house until the day it collapses.' So it was with the *status quo*. In this he took the same view as his great predecessor.

All this Berchtold told with great skill and authority. No one could have bettered his air of effortless superiority. His distinguished appearance, with high balding forehead, recalled a stylized figure from a magazine devoted to men's fashions. He spoke as from a great distance, so *de haut en bas* that he left no doubt in his hearers' minds that he belonged to the inner circle of the Vienna 'Olympus', that social group so exclusive that only a few of its members were not born to the purple.

Indeed his exposé was masterly.

He represented the independence of Albania as a triumph of Viennese diplomacy and, as evidence of this, he announced that Austria had already found a suitable king for that new and still untamed country. This was the Prince of Wied, who until recently had served in a Prussian guards regiment, the so-called Yellow Uhlans.

There was also another extraordinary success to be told: it was the cession of the island of Adakaleh to Hungary. This, he felt

sure, would please the Hungarians as it had figured so largely in
the classical Magyar novel *The Golden Man*.

With the account of these two great successes Berchtold
brought his address to an end. The meeting was then terminated
and all discussion postponed until the following day.

In this way the Austrian foreign minister had somehow extri-
cated himself from a most awkward position, though this, ultimately, was not because of the brilliance of his exposition, nor
because of little Adakaleh, but because the whole affair was at
once overshadowed by the unwise comportment of the opposition members of the Hungarian delegation who provoked a
scandal by raising the matter of Tisza's use of the parliamentary
guards in Budapest – this when discussion of all internal matters
was forbidden to them. It had long been agreed that the delegation could discuss only foreign affairs, matters concerning
the joint Austro-Hungarian army, and the general state of the
economy. The intervention was all the more unexpected
because it was those very members of the delegation who had
so defiantly affirmed that internal matters were taboo, who now
brought them up to the scandal of all those in the public rooms
of the palais in the Bankgasse where Berchtold had given his
address.

It was only after half the time allocated for the discussion had
been wasted in this way that the delegation was able to turn to
those foreign affairs which were, after all, the sole *raison d'être* of
the meeting.

Now, finally, Berchtold found himself asked some very awkward questions. Was it true, someone asked, that Germany had
abandoned the Dual Monarchy on the question of Austria's
claim to inspect and if necessary revise the terms of the Bucharest
peace treaty? Why, asked another, had Berchtold not spoken in
warmer terms of the role played by France?

This last question was raised by Mihaly Karolyi, who by then
had become the acknowledged leader of the Independent Party.
Karolyi praised the part played by Poincaré and asked why there
had been no criticism of the totally passive role played by the
Ballplatz throughout the whole Balkan crisis and the London
Conference which had followed. This attitude was not entirely
logical, coming from the representative of those who had
extended the hand of friendship to Serbia from the great height
of the pseudo-parliament in the Hotel Royal's ballroom: for how

could someone who saw no wrong in aggression emanating from Belgrade condemn the passivity of Vienna?

The presence of the delegation brought quite a number of Hungarians to the Austrian capital.

It was also the reason why Balint found himself there. He had been appointed in the autumn by Tisza who wished to reward him for having given up his non-party stand and joining the government party when Tisza took office.

Abady had thought about this for some time and the move had made things easier for him, especially in regard to his work for the Co-operatives. Now he no longer had to apply for an audience with the appropriate minister but could buttonhole him at any time in the party's private rooms. Balint's change of heart had had nothing to do with his political beliefs. It the past he had remained free of party allegiances only because of his innate distaste for any restraint on his freedom of action. Now he overcame this.

He had not come to Vienna from Budapest with the others, but from Switzerland where he had just spent a few days with Adrienne on the shores of Lac Léman near Nyon. From there Adrienne had gone on to Lausanne to visit her daughter while Balint returned to Vienna. In their little pension they had registered as man and wife – which in those days before passports posed no problems – and indeed this is what they now considered themselves.

That terrible unbreakable chain which had bound Adrienne to her incurably mad husband had shattered of its own accord in the autumn. On November 2nd Pal Uzdy died suddenly.

He had been in excellent health until the end of the summer and indeed, throughout the four years of his confinement, and though his mind had gradually grown ever more clouded, his physical condition had even improved. He had put on weight and there seemed to be no reason why he should not live for years, even possibly outliving his wife.

In the middle of September, however, his persecution-mania took a new turn. He said nothing to anyone, not even to Adrienne who visited him often, but he began to imagine that his medical adviser was trying to poison him. Normally it was to Adrienne that he would confide his innermost thoughts, but not this time. It was his keeper who began to notice a change in the

patient and soon diagnosed the trouble. Uzdy started by sniffing
at his food suspiciously, and then leaving most of it on the plate
until he was eating almost nothing. The doctor did his best to
persuade him to eat but though Uzdy pretended to agree, he
would tip the soup into the wash-basin and throw the meat and
vegetables into the lavatory pan. When this was discovered they
tried installing a little electric cooker in Uzdy's room so that he
himself could prepare the eggs that his keeper brought him telling
the sick man, though of course it was not true, that he had
smuggled them in from outside without the hospital people
knowing anything about it. He also brought him apples and pears
and a little silver knife with which to peel them himself. This
worked for a few days, but proved to be a failure when Uzdy,
from his window, caught sight of his keeper talking to the hated
doctor. From then on he refused to eat at all, and would soon
have died of starvation if Fate had not decided otherwise.

He grew very thin, barely more than skin and bones, and for
hours he would pace up and down his room without stopping.
Soon he could hardly keep himself upright, but reeled from side
to side grabbing hold of whatever piece of furniture he found
in his way. Though too weak to stay upright for more than a
moment without support, nothing would make him stop.

On the last day of October he slipped and struck his back
against the bedpost. The injury sparked off an attack of pleurisy
which soon affected his lungs. In three days he was dead.

He was buried at Varalmas, where his own mad father had
been interred. It was after this that Adrienne decided to visit her
daughter.

It was still necessary in those days to do nothing which might
cause tongues to wag and so Balint left before her, having
arranged that they should meet in Salzburg and only from there
go on to Switzerland together. They did this principally because
it would not have been thought seemly, despite the circumstances, for Adrienne to have travelled alone with a man during
the first weeks of mourning. They used the opportunity to talk
over their future together. Adrienne was insistent that they
should wait until the year's official mourning was at an end before
they married. This, she felt, was for the sake of her daughter who
would never afterwards wonder why her mother had not waited
for the customary period. Balint felt obliged to agree.

In spite of the reason for this voyage it turned out to be like a honeymoon. Here, for the first time, they were alone, with no fear of discovery or exposure, and happy in the knowledge that their future together was at long last assured.

Balint's only regret was that his mother had not lived to see how things had turned out. He knew that she would no longer have opposed his marriage to Adrienne but, on the contrary, would have rejoiced with him. He remembered how sweet and welcoming she had been to Adrienne that time they had so unexpectedly met at Gerbeaud's. He knew that his mother would have approved.

Balint had chosen a small pension on the edge of the lake. It had only twenty rooms and had been converted from the country retreat of some patrician family from Geneva who had had it built at the end of the eighteenth century and named it, after the fashion of those days, 'Monbijou'. The name had been kept, and suited it well. It was designed in the French manner, elegant and stylish, and typical of the sort of modest, but not too modest, retreat built by the wealthy of those days. The house faced the lake. In front of it a wide lawn sloped gently down to the water's side and it was backed by giant oak trees. Across the lake the mountains rose, a wild jumble of rocky crags above which, whenever the clouds parted, could be seen the snow-covered triangular peak of Mont Blanc. This seemed to float so high in the sky that it was difficult to imagine that it was anywhere attached to the earth.

There they stayed for eight days, eight days of quiet joy and happiness far removed from the impassioned fever of their first coming together in Venice when every minute of that month of frenzied love-making had to be made the most of as both of them feared that any one of those days might have been their last on earth. Then every dawn might have heralded a parting made final by death. Now all was different. They lived together beside the lake in calm intimacy . . . and in the happy promise that soon they would never again be parted.

They made all sorts of plans, reaching out many, many years ahead. They would have a quiet wedding with only two witnesses, no one else. Some modernization would have to be done at Denestornya; electricity installed and two new bathrooms, one for Adrienne and the other . . . the other for the future when their son, who had not been spoken of by them for a long time, not since Uzdy's madness, would then at long last have become a reality. This, they now felt, was sure; and the child would be the crown of their love, a descendant who would be the living proof of their enduring will to live.

CHAPTER TWO

AFTER THE MEETING Balint went to a concert given by the Vienna Philharmonic Orchestra to hear one of the Beethoven symphonies.

It was quite late when the concert was over and Balint hurried to get to Sacher's before midnight when the public dining-room closed.

He was too late. The lights had been turned out and all the table-cloths removed. Balint found himself somewhat put out for he did not know anywhere else where he could get a quiet meal without music. He turned back from the dining-room and had just entered the front hall when he met Peter and Niki Kollonich coming in.

'Have you come to get some food?' asked Balint. 'They've just closed here, so I've got to find somewhere else.'

'Come and join us then,' replied Peter. 'We've got a private room for supper. Kristof-Zalamery and I booked it in advance!'

'It's really very nice of you, but if it's with gypsy music and girls then I don't think it's for me tonight.'

They reassured him. No gypsies and no girls, except for one who would be coming later. She was La Pantera, a famous Spanish dancer who had been appearing at the Ronacher Theatre for the last two months and who had thrown the imperial capital into a fever.

Abady had already heard of her. She was, he knew, beautiful as well as being an accomplished dancer – but she had become even more famous for her diamonds which had been pictured in every illustrated paper in the world. This had been done many, many times, since La Pantera, or her manager, used these famous jewels for the dancer's publicity. Just in case interest in the diamonds should wane, they were stolen every five or six months – only to be recovered a week or ten days later. Each time this happened they could be written up again, with every detail lovingly described and the enormous value greatly exaggerated so as to tease the respectable reader.

Balint and his cousins were shown into the private room where they found only Fredi Wuelffenstein, who had been invited by Zalamery. Fredi, who was also a member of the delegation, was admiring his tall, slim figure in the wall mirror. With his padded shoulders, pale blond hair and the face of a white negro, it looked as if he had been trying to emulate the statesmanlike poise he had so admired in Berchtold that afternoon.

Then Stefi Szent-Gyorgyi came in and they all started to talk. At first Fredi tried hard to get them on to politics but this did not suit either Balint or the Kollonich brothers. First of all each one of them wanted to know why the others were in Vienna. Stefi, it seemed, was going to England to hunt, while Peter and Niki were on their way back to Hungary after a visit to Upper Austria where they had been invited for the pheasant-shooting. At first the talk was all about guns and horses and game-birds, but it was not long before they started to talk about La Pantera and Kristof Zalamery. They all knew that Kristof had fallen madly in love with the dancer the very first night she appeared; and since then the whole town had been talking about the fortune that he had been spending on her, and especially about the diamond dog-collar necklace that he had added to her famous collection. Every detail was known to the good people of Vienna. It had been bought at Klinkosch's in the Mehlmarkt and had cost sixty thousand crowns. It was also known that he was ferociously jealous and guarded her like a dragon, and so, though he liked to show her off, he never left her side.

'At this very moment he's waiting in his carriage at the stage door of the Ronacher. He'll stay there until she's changed and then,' said Peter, 'he'll bring her straight here thereby making sure she doesn't meet anyone else on the way!'

Niki laughed. 'What an ass that Kristof is! All that money spent on the girl and all that trouble keeping an eye on her ... and she cuckolds him every night!'

'That can't be possible! Why, he lives with her at the Imperial Hotel!'

'Oh yes, but they have separate rooms divided by a sitting-room. Kristof can stay with her only until three a.m. Then she sends him away saying she has to get her sleep if she's going to be able to dance properly the following night. That's when the others come in!'

'What rubbish you do talk!' said Peter, who was always upset

by his brother's love of making mischief. 'That's far too complicated. Why would anyone else be there, ready and waiting?
Where are they? In the corridor? In the hall? It's absurd: nothing
but the usual lying Viennese gossip!'

'Not a bit of it. La Pantera has a confidante, half-secretary,
half-procuress. She is older than the dancer and goes everywhere
with her. Everyone calls her "Contessa", probably because it
sounds well. Anyhow you strike your bargain with her, and you
wait in her room, which is next to La Pantera's, until the coast
is clear!'

'And how do you know all this?' asked his brother angrily.

'How do I know it? How? Everyone in Vienna knows it!'

'Everybody is . . . everybody is nobody.'

'Well, if you really want to know,' chuckled Niki, 'it's because
I did it only yesterday. It wasn't even very expensive, only five
hundred crowns. It was worth it just for the fun of it all. I rather
like making a fool of that good old Kristof!'

Abady felt slightly nauseated.

He got up to leave, but it was too late. Just at that moment the
door opened and Zalamery entered with the dancer upon his arm.

The man was built like a Hercules, though slightly balding
and beginning to run to fat. He was a heavy man and though
his dinner-jacket had been made by one of London's most
famous tailors and was a perfect fit, on Zalamery it looked as if
it had been rented from a stage costume shop. It was like this
with everything he did. He owned a large stable of racehorses
. . . but never won a race. His forests in Marmaros were endless . . . but he never shot a stag himself, though it was true that
his guests had some good sport. He was a good-hearted man,
but vain. He liked to be admired, and he liked to show off the
splendour of his possessions. This was why he felt impelled to
bring his mistress for his friends to see.

The woman was truly beautiful. She was tall and slim. Under
a helmet of raven-black hair her face was one of classical beauty
and her eyes sparkled under the thickest of black lashes. Her
hands, feet and legs were perfectly formed, but her glory was her
walk. She moved like one of the great cats, a puma or a jaguar,
who seemed always ready to pounce. It was presumably from this
quality that she had been named La Pantera, the leopard. Her
look was cold as ice, like that of a wild beast.

She wore a dress of dark blue silk with wide sleeves. It was tied at the waist by a sash of the same material and seemed to be half evening dress and half tea-gown. She wore only one piece of jewellery, the diamond collar that Kristof had given her. This was just to please the donor: the rest she only wore when she danced.

Introductions were made and she offered her hands for the men to kiss.

There was nothing to show that she even noticed Niki, and it is possible that she did not even remember him for it was obvious to Balint at least that she was not really interested in other people. To her everything was reduced to business, her dancing, her diamonds, her beauty and her fixed icy smile.

She talked coolly about all sorts of bland cosmopolitan subjects. Her manners were impeccable.

Saying that she was tired after the performance, she asked only for a glass of champagne and a little cold fish, nothing more.

'We won't be staying long, will we?' she asked Zalamery humbly, as if to underline to the other men that she regarded Kristof as her lord and master. She then told how she had a rehearsal at midday because she was preparing a new number, a Russian dance which was very difficult but which would be very beautiful. She would have to work hard at it, she said, because she was going to do it at St Petersburg in three weeks' time. It would be just right for a Russian audience, and she was sure they were going to love it.

And so she rattled on. Everything she said was impersonal, even mechanical, and Balint was sure that this was how she talked in every city she visited, with hundreds and hundreds of adoring men whose names she may never have learned and whose faces she forgot at once. Then she would move on to another capital and to other men. If she had not been so beautiful she would have been essentially boring. As it was her movements were so fluid and so alluring that to watch them was such a joy that no one noticed the banality of her conversation. Her hands, her fingers, her arms moved always in perfect harmony with the tilt of her head and the line of her shoulders. The picture seemed to have no flaw. It was as if a great artist had designed every pose she adopted.

Balint was wondering whether she had studied her effects, or whether they were natural and inborn, when across the room from him he saw an elderly woman come in and stand by the door of the apartment.

She was of middle height and rather thin. She wore a dress of smooth black silk. Her hair must once have been light brown but there remained now only a few strands of this colour: the rest was bluish silver and there was a great deal of it piled in two thick tresses into the form of a crown much in the style that can be seen in portraits of the Empress Elisabeth, Queen of Hungary. On each side of her face some tiny short curls framed her high slightly oriental cheekbones. It was an interesting face, pale and elegant, and its pallor was accentuated by a startling pair of black eyebrows that just met in the middle. Though obviously no longer young, she held herself very straight, and so distinguished was her bearing that beside her the splendid La Pantera might have been just a pretty chambermaid.

She greeted no one and did not seem to expect to be greeted herself. She was like a soldier, on duty and waiting for orders.

'*J'ai tout rassemblé, madame* – I've collected everything. Here they are, *il ne manque rien* – there is nothing missing,' and she passed her hand over the sizeable morocco-leather bag that hung from her arm. It was clear that she was speaking of the diamonds which were always in her charge. 'Do you need anything else?'

'No. Not now. You can go back to the hotel, Contessa ... No, wait a moment! Take this with you, please!' replied La Pantera. Then she turned to Zalamery and said: 'You won't mind if I take this off now, will you?' as she touched the diamond dog-collar he had given her.

'Would you undo it for me?' she asked and bent her lovely neck to Zalamery's broad chest.

It was not easy for him, and a few moments passed before his thick fingers managed to release the clasp.

While this was happening the Contessa stood quietly by without moving. Only her eyes moved as she looked round the table and Balint felt that they lingered for a moment when they came to him. It was almost as if she would have liked to look longer at him. He was attracted by her looks and by those light grey eyes set under the dark eyebrows. He felt he had somewhere seen that glance before, but it was only a fleeting impression and soon passed away.

Kristof handed the diamond collar to the Contessa. The lock of the leather bag clicked to; then she looked once more at Abady

and for a moment stared hard at him. Then she turned back to
the dancer and said, '*Bonne nuit, madame. Bonne nuit, messieurs,*'
and with a slight inclination of her head with its massive crown
of silver hair, she left the room.

Balint was not sure if he had imagined it, but it had seemed to
him that when the Contessa was saying goodbye to the men in
the room she was really only saying it to him. Who was she? Who
could she be? Had he ever seen her before?

All around him the conversation started up again, but Balint
could think of nothing but the woman who had just gone out.

A few moments later a waiter came in and handed a visiting
card to Abady. On it was printed the name 'Comtesse Julie
Ladossa' and on the other side had been written a few words in
Hungarian, '*Please come out for a moment*'. Julie Ladossa! She was
Laszlo Gyeroffy's mother!

He went out at once and found her sitting on one of the sofas
that lined the walls of the ante-room. The morocco-leather bag
was on her knees and resting on it were her hands, long narrow
aristocratic hands that were still beautiful even if lined with age.
They were an artist's hands, Laszlo's hands. Balint sat down
beside her.

'Please don't be offended that I asked you to come out. It is
such a long time since I talked to anyone from my own country.
I recognized you at once – you're so like your father – and so as
to be sure I asked the head waiter if it really was you.'

'What can I do for you?' asked Balint, but he found himself
too embarrassed by the encounter to go on. It would have been
absurd to greet Laszlo's mother with some polite formula like
'How do you do?' especially as he had met her acting as someone's servant, or was it worse than that?

He wondered what terrible times she had been through until
she had finally ended up like this.

It was true that she showed no signs of degradation, no traces
of the life she must have led unless, perhaps, it was to be seen in
a faint cynical turn at the corner of her mouth, a little bitter smile
that suggested that there was nothing and no one she did not
despise, least of all herself. A wilful, stubborn line rose where her
eyebrows met.

Then she was asking him all about Transylvania, about her old
acquaintances, about the Alvinczys, the Laczoks, whom she
referred to by their full names as if they were no relation to her

and as if they had not all been her childhood friends and play-mates. Obviously she wished to make it clear to him that she no longer belonged to that world, that she no longer deserved to and would not presume even to think so.

All this was said in a calm conversational and conventional manner as if they were talking about matters that did not really in any way concern them. After a while she fell silent.

Then in a deeper tone, very softly but with an underlying force of barely suppressed passion, she asked, 'How ... how is my son?'

It was difficult for Balint to find the right words with which to answer. If only she had still used the light, somewhat distant tones with which she had asked all her other questions he would prob-ably have told her the cruel truth quite openly. He would have said that her son had turned into a depraved drunkard and was bankrupt. He would have told her in the baldest terms – perhaps out of anger, or resentment, or the desire for revenge – that Laszlo's tragic life had begun that day in his early childhood when he had been deserted by his mother. But Julie Ladossa had spoken to him in that passionate voice, that voice which came from somewhere deep inside her soul; that voice in which could be heard the echo of many years of guilt and remorse, of more than two decades of sorrow and humble acknowledgement of her own fault, and in those half-strangled tones he had recog-nized the force of her living tragedy.

Therefore he hesitated before answering her questions and, when he did, he did so with compassion. He told the truth, but he did it gently. He did not conceal Laszlo's sad situation, how he had sold the house and land and now lived on a small pension in one of his former tenants' houses at Kozard. He said that he had been ill but that Balint believed that he was now a little better, though it was some time since he had seen his cousin who had now broken off all relations with everyone he had known in the past.

'He too!' she whispered. 'So it has happened to him too,' and she stared ahead of her.

They did not speak for some minutes. Then she got up, saying: 'From here we are going to St Petersburg. Then to Moscow, Odessa and Bucharest. We shall be in Budapest at the end of February ... If you happen to be there ... and wouldn't mind seeing me again ... you might perhaps have some news. I would be so grateful!'

'Of course! I'll see you with great pleasure!'

'We shall probably be at the Hungaria, but I'm not sure because the agent arranges everything like that.'

Balint thought that Julie Ladossa would now put out her hand and leave; but she just stood there, without speaking, though she obviously had something on her mind. Her eyes were fixed far, far away and the vertical line on her forehead seemed even more deeply etched than before. Then, speaking swiftly and urgently, she looked at Abady and said, 'Tell me! Tell me! Do you sometimes see Sandor Kendy, the one they call Crookface?'

'Of course. Not often, but when I'm in Kolozsvar he sometimes comes to town.'

A strange, unexpected and cruel smile played across her lips. Then she straightened up so abruptly that she might have suddenly grown several inches taller. From under her thick lashes there flashed a look of uncontrollable hatred. 'Well! If you see him again, tell him that we have met ... and also what I'm doing now!'

Now she did put out her hand, and then, from the door, she spoke again, 'Be sure to tell him that too ... that too ...' and she laughed as she went out, a laugh that to Balint seemed filled with cruelty.

Balint stayed where he was, rooted to the spot.

What had she said? Why on earth should she want that of him?

And why did she ask after Crookface only now and not when she had enquired after all her other old friends? Why this unexpected commission ... and, above all, why that demonic laughter?

How did it all fit together?

He tried to recall everything he had ever heard about Laszlo's mother. He had never heard any mention of Sandor Kendy when people had talked about Julie Ladossa. Neither her sister-in-law, Princess Kollonich, nor even Aunt Lizinka who never left any piece of evil gossip unsaid, had ever mentioned him. It was true that no one had ever told him with whom she had eloped and it seemed that no one really knew, for Aunt Lizinka told many different stories, at one time saying it was with a hussar who happened to be riding by, or a waiter, or a tightrope walker, but it was clear she was just improvising for she really knew nothing and her candidates for the culprit were always unknown men, never anyone they all knew like Sandor Kendy. Crookface was surely above suspicion.

This was how Balint's first thoughts took him; but then other memories came into his mind. There had been that evening he had spent at Crookface's manor at Kis-Keresztur where he had seen the portrait of a lovely young woman he had taken to be Crookface's deaf wife when young. It was quite a logical assumption because the picture had been exactly like Countess Kendy dressed for a costume ball, for her gown had been in the style of the eighties, old-fashioned now and covered with the frills of the past. He remembered that he had asked about this but had not been given an answer.

Now he also remembered that the picture seemed at one time to have been damaged. There had been signs of a repair to a diagonal gash that had once sliced the picture almost in two, right down to the little painted bouquets on the skirt. He had noticed it then but something in the gruff old man's manner had prevented him from asking about it. Many years before he had heard that when Julie Ladossa had bolted Mihaly Gyeroffy had slashed at her portrait and flung it out of the window. Could Crookface's picture have been that portrait? And if it was, how had it got to Keresztur? And why?

Had Kendy married that gentle deaf girl who was not of his class just because she was so like that other who had flung out of his life with a peal of demonic laughter some thirty years before?

These were all unconnected fragments from an untold story. For a moment Balint felt almost ashamed of himself, prying into matters that did not concern him. Let it all pass into oblivion, he said to himself. Let nobody know. One shouldn't rake up the past. If there was one thing in a man's life that should remain strictly private, and which was no concern of anyone else's, it was his innermost feelings. Those were one's own: to others they should be taboo.

He thought of his own love for Adrienne, a love that had now lasted ten years, and he was filled with happiness and gratitude. They had never misunderstood each other no matter what storms had afflicted their lives. Now it seemed they had reached port at last.

Until death do us part.

CHAPTER THREE

BALINT NEVER GAVE Julie Ladossa's message to Crookface
Kendy. In fact he had never intended to, but his conversation
with the 'Contessa' did have one other result.

When the former Countess Gyeroffy was asking him about
her son, Balint felt ashamed that he could tell her nothing
about Laszlo except for a few generalities and ashamed that he
had not thought about his cousin and childhood friend for many
months. It was true that this was not his fault but Laszlo's, who
had rebuffed every gesture made towards him. The latest rejection had come when Balint had sent him a telegram to let him
know that Countess Roza had just died and to offer to send
over a car so that Laszlo could attend the funeral. Laszlo had not
replied, not even with a message of condolence, nothing. Balint
had been so offended by this that at the time he had felt he would
never be able to forgive the cousin who had once been such a
close friend. Now, however, he decided to bury his resentment
and go over to see Laszlo and try once again to become friends
with him.

As soon as he got home to Denestornya he drove over to
Kozard. The weather, as so often in Transylvania at the beginning
of December, was sunny and mild.

He arrived about midday at the little house in which he knew
Laszlo was living. The door of wooden laths that led through the
crumbling fence was open. It looked as if it was never closed.
Balint walked straight into the house. The first room he entered
was the kitchen, and through this could be seen a room in total
disorder, an unmade plank bed at one side, a rough wooden table
nearby, a country cape of rough cloth hung on one wall and
under it lay an ancient pair of peasant's boots. None of this,
thought Balint, could have belonged to Laszlo, so he walked
through to the next room.

This was not much better, though the pinewood furniture had
at least been polished. It looked as if it had come originally from
one of the servants' rooms at the manor house. On the chest of
drawers lay a gun-case of ornate brass-bound leather engraved
with Laszlo's name inaccurately spelt 'Count Ladislas Gieroffy'.
This room had been tidied, the floor properly scoured and the
windows opened to let in the air.

Balint walked round the house hoping to find Laszlo sitting on the sunny side. He wasn't there. There was no one there. Then Balint saw that there was a girl standing at the far end of the garden, an adolescent girl who was washing laundry in the stream. He walked down to where she stood on the bank dipping the clothes in the water, soaping them and then scrubbing what she held on a little wooden board.

The girl was astonishingly lovely, so beautiful that Balint was lost for words when he finally came face to face with her. She had large doe-like eyes fringed by dark lashes and her long eyebrows were so fine they might have been painted on with a brush. Her face was a perfect oval and her skin both pale and rose-coloured. Her red lips were full, as red as blood, and she was as slim as a reed. The sleeves of her dress were turned up to the elbow and her smooth satiny arms were as rosy as her face and neck. Only her hands were roughened by hard work. She wore a kerchief tied round her head like all the peasants of that region, but her clothes had been made to be worn in the city, even if now they were worn and patched. Her apron was in rags and her bare feet were slipped into an old pair of ladies' button boots which would have reached to mid-calf if most of the buttons had not disappeared years before. No matter how old and dirty her clothes the girl was so beautiful that one forgot everything but that.

Balint greeted her and then said, 'I'm looking for Laszlo Gyeroffy. Do you know where I can find him?'

The girl looked at him with a scornful expression on her beautiful face.

'What do you want of him? Why are you looking for him?' she asked sullenly.

'I am his cousin, Balint Abady.'

The girl made a little curtsy, as good manners demanded.

'I am Regina Bischitz.' Then she added, 'My father owns the village shop.'

'Well, now we know each other,' said Balint with a light laugh, 'perhaps you could tell me where Laszlo is?'

Regina shrugged.

'He's not here. They took him to Szamos-Ujvar.'

'They took him?'

'Yes. That Fabian, he took him . . .' and grabbing a shirt that was both filthy and torn, she held it up for a moment before her and then plunged it into the stream, wrung it out and started to rub it with soap.

'Fabian? Who is this Fabian?'

'Ugh!' said the girl. 'He is a bad man, that Fabian! He always takes him with him . . . and there he makes him drink, and . . . and carouse . . . and it is so bad for him. He's a worthless scoundrel, that Fabian!'

'If I knew where he was at Szamos-Ujvar I'd drive in and find him.'

'You can't go there, not there! It's terrible!' cried Regina, and her eyes filled with tears. 'That Fabian, he takes him to see bad women, wicked women . . . that's how he's ruining him. The Count is so ill, so very ill and that's why . . . and he makes him drink and drink . . . and . . .'

She stopped without saying the last word but balled up her hand into a fist and made as if she were hitting someone with it. Then she picked up the shirt again and started to rub it with such fury that if it had been the hated Fabian it would have been as if she were doing her best to choke all life out of what she held in her hands.

She turned away from Balint and, as she did so, she bent forward and huge tears fell from her face like a rain of large diamonds on the wet cloth she was holding so fiercely.

There was a fallen tree-trunk facing the girl. Balint sat down on it and waited for quite a long time. Finally the girl finished her work and stood there panting in front of him. Then he asked again when Laszlo would be back.

'It's no use waiting for him,' said the girl. 'Even if he does come soon he'll be in a dreadful state, dreadful. He'll mess up the room again . . . and I scrubbed it this morning early. Oh, I can do it! I do everything, the washing-up, the scrubbing, the airing, everything!'

She seemed overcome with sorrow. Then she sat down on the edge of a little bench, with her back very straight and her head inclined, staring at nothing.

'Doesn't he have any other servant?'

'I am not his servant, I . . . I do it because I want to. I can't bear to see . . . to see a gentleman like the Count . . . such a great gentleman . . . to see him . . . so uncared-for . . .'

'Didn't he have an old man called Marton looking after him? What happened to him?'

The girl waved her hand in the air.

'He's useless. He just cooks and cleans the Count's boots, nothing else. He's gone off again now, probably to lay snares in the woods. It's the only thing that interests him. I do everything here because I can't bear to see the filth he'd live in if I didn't. No one knows I do it. It has to be in secret. I can only come when my father isn't around and can't see me leaving the shop. I can work here today because he's gone to Kolozsvar. Most times I can only do it at night, or very early in the morning, because if he catches me I get a beating.'

She stopped and again looked straight ahead of her.

The kerchief fell from her head and her long Titian hair fluttered in the slight breeze. Sitting on the bench she was like a statue with her firm breasts straining the thin cloth of her blouse. She was very beautiful, a rose of Sharon not yet fully open but no longer a bud. Tears brimmed under her long lashes and then again rolled down her cheeks.

'How old are you, child?' asked Balint, trying to distract her from whatever she was thinking.

'Fifteen,' she muttered, but still went on staring in front of her. Then suddenly she broke out in a wail of complaint, though Balint could not tell whether she had sensed the sympathy in him or whether she was so filled with sorrow that she could not keep it to herself.

She spoke in broken phrases, with no words directly connected.

From her poured the story of how, some five years before, when Laszlo had been confined to his bed with pneumonia, she had watched by his bedside and nursed him back to health. Since then she had done everything for him, even stealing brandy when his credit at her father's shop had been exhausted. Soap too, and paraffin.

She did everything. Always more and more, but always in vain, quite in vain.

'In vain? What do you mean, in vain?' asked Balint in astonishment.

'Just that! In vain. He doesn't speak to me ... except when I bring him brandy. Then he just says "You're a good little girl, Regina!" or "I'm glad you came, Regina!" But it's not praise for me. It's all he says, ever ... and it's only for the brandy, not for me.'

'Are you sure?'

'I'm sure all right. He accepts everything I do, but I never get a word of thanks. To him it's nothing more than his due, nothing out of the ordinary that I should clean for him, tidy him up when he's dead drunk, rub his arms and his legs with that horrid black ointment he has to have for that ... that trouble he caught in Szamos-Ujvar.'

Now, at last, she jumped up, full with rebellion. 'But me? Why, he doesn't even pat my cheek!'

Balint wanted to reassure her and said, 'I am sure that's only because he thinks you're still barely more than a child, Regina. He's probably very fond of you in his own way.'

'Do you really think so?' she asked eagerly as she sat down again. Then, a shy smile came into her face and she said, 'Yes, I suppose so, in his way. To him I'm just a sort of household pet who's useful to him. I am the only person he talks to. He tells me – oh, so much about his life ... and to me it is some little reward because he tells me about such wonderful things, and in such beautiful words.' For a moment she seemed lost in thought, and then added sadly, 'But since he's got so thin he doesn't talk much any more.'

Taken by surprise Abady said: 'He's got very thin? Since when?'

'Just in the last few weeks. Of course he hardly eats at all. It's hard for him to keep it down!'

Now Balint started to question the girl as to whether Laszlo was seeing a doctor and what were his symptoms? Did he, for example, have little patches of red on his cheekbones? Regina answered all his questions quite intelligently. The doctor, she said, came every week. The Count coughed a lot, but not more than before. Those red spots? Yes, they did appear if he had drunk a lot ... but otherwise? Maybe yes, at other times too.

Balint did not speak for a few moments. Then he said, 'We ought to get him into a sanatorium. I could see that he was taken good care of ... and he'd get trained nursing.'

'Take him away? Away from here?' cried Regina, distracted with fear, with terror lest they should take him away from her so that she would never see him again, never ever again. No, not that! Never that, her heart would break.

Regina now sensed that she had said too much and that she'd

somehow endangered the man who had become her only reason for living. Now, at once, she had to cover up the truth for otherwise they would take Laszlo away from her; and so the words poured out of her, swiftly trying to take the sting out of anything serious she might have said: the doctor had praised her nursing and said it was quite adequate, and not only the doctor from Iklod who saw Laszlo every week, but also the chief consultant from Szamos-Ujvar who came over from time to time; also there was somebody else who saw to it that the Count was properly looked after. Dr Simay he was called, the same man who sent her father twenty florins every week for Laszlo's food and who also paid the chemist's bills.

'Who is this Dr Simay?'

'He's a lawyer at Szamos-Ujvar. My father writes to him whenever ... whenever something is needed.'

'So he really is being properly looked after? All the time?'

'Oh, yes! Ever since he was ill with pneumonia,' insisted Regina.

Until then she had stuck fairly closely to the truth, but now she felt impelled to lie. Resolutely she then said, 'All the doctors think he's getting on very well and ... and soon will be quite himself again.'

Abady was surprised.

'But only just now you said he was losing weight and couldn't keep his food down and you were afraid he'd soon die?'

Regina smiled.

'Well, yes, I did say that, but I didn't really mean it like that.'

'Really?'

'Yes. I ... I ... was upset that he'd gone ... gone there again ... for that ... and so I said more than I meant. But it really isn't as bad as that, really it isn't.'

Young Regina played her chosen part so well that Balint believed her when she made out she had exaggerated everything out of jealousy and anger. Still, he did not want to leave without establishing some sort of contact with his old friend.

'Look, my dear,' he said as he took some money and a visiting card from his wallet, 'I won't wait for Laszlo this time, but I'm going to leave these two hundred crowns with you because I know I can trust you to use it for Laszlo if something happens and then you'll be able to buy whatever he needs. And here is my address. If he does take a turn for the worse, or if I can be of help in any way whatever, please send me a telegram at once. You will, won't you?'

'Of course!' she cried. 'Of course I will; at once. I'll send for you at once!' and, as she spoke the words, inwardly she swore to herself, Never! Never! Never! Just so that you can take him away from me? Never that! Never ever that!

They shook hands near the stream. Balint had barely turned away when she was already back at work at her washing. Nevertheless she glanced covertly back at him several times, fearing that he might change his mind and wait for his cousin after all.

If he did that he would certainly take him away from her, especially if Laszlo came back dead drunk, for then it would be obvious that everything she had said about his getting better had been a lie.

She looked many times in the direction of the road until the engine had been started and the car driven swiftly away towards Kolozsvar. Only then did she relax.

CHAPTER FOUR

THAT YEAR, FOR the first time, Balint spent Christmas alone, but he consoled himself by thinking that it would only be that once.

In the years to come Adrienne would be there; and, if God was kind, others too, more and more.

For the great household at Denestornya everything passed as it always had, with the same ceremonies as there had been during Countess Roza's lifetime. Nothing had changed: the tree was placed in the centre of the dining-table, around it heaps of presents on the white table-cloth that had been arranged, as before, by Mrs Tothy and Mrs Baczo. The old butler, Peter, stood by the door, as in every other year. There was one difference: Countess Roza's throne-like gilt chair was not in its usual place.

Instead Balint stood, slightly to one side just as if his mother had still been there, and handed out the presents to the women and children who came in one by one just as they always had. He wanted no break in the tradition so that next Christmas Adrienne would continue what Roza Abady had done all her life.

When everyone had left and most of the myriad candles in the chandeliers and in the sconces had been snuffed out, Balint stayed there for a long time. He walked from end to end of the immense hall, stopping before the display cabinets, gazing deeply at all the family treasures they contained and also at the objects on the tables that had been placed in the deep window embrasures. They all had their part in his past and that of the family. He looked at everything pensively, almost absent-mindedly. It was a strangely varied collection ranging from exquisite pieces of china from Meissen and Vienna to a huge ancient lock of rusty iron which had once fastened the castle's portcullis. There were also some things which were frankly cheap or ugly, but these were souvenirs of Countess Roza's youth and had been kept for the sentimental memories they evoked. There was a pottery figure of a girl whose skirt would oscillate if touched, a china pug with bulging eyes which had been given to his mother as a child and treasured by her ever since and so placed side by side with the precious cups of gold and silver and the pieces of fine porcelain – objects that had been handed down from generations of former Abadys.

Balint knew the history of each object: and he swore then that everything must always stay as it always had been.

After a long time he went down to the ground floor. There he put on a warm coat and went out into the dark night. Across the courtyard and down to the churchyard where a new Abady vault had been built up against the church when, at the end of the eighteenth century, there had been no more room in the crypt beneath the nave. Here were resting the remains of Balint's grandparents, of his father and, since the previous spring, also of his mother.

The vault was locked, but Balint had had no intention of going in. He only wanted to go as far as the door so as, symbolically, to tell Countess Roza that the Christmas Eve ceremony had been held and that he had done it, and always would do it, exactly as she had. He remained there only for a minute or two. Then he said a silent prayer and walked back up to the castle.

Time went slowly by. Adrienne came back from Lausanne rather later than she had planned because little Clemmie had had some recurrent bouts of fever and Adrienne had not wanted to leave until the girl had been thoroughly checked by the doctors. Finally they declared that there was no cause for anxiety, that this sort of thing often occurred with growing girls and soon would disappear of itself. Nothing to worry about, they said.

So Adrienne came home reassured.

There was a great deal to do as soon as she was back. She and Balint had many plans to make. With their architect they worked on the detailed plans of that part of the castle in which they were going to live. Discussions were held with contractors for installing running water and electric light, hitherto unknown at Denestornya despite the family's great means. Decisions had to be made about whether the necessary power should come from motor generators or from turbines driven by the mill. All sorts of new projects occupied them every day.

In the great world outside there was a lull, even in the Balkans. Only the Albanians were still in turmoil. Oddly enough they did not seem at all to appreciate the new Prussian guards officer king that the great powers had so carefully chosen for them. It was true that the excellent Prince of Wied was hardly known to his new subjects for in the last two months, ever since he had become King, he had barely set foot in his new country but had preferred to make a round of the courts of Europe, great and small, to offer thanks for his elevation to royal status. Wherever he went he was greatly admired. He was tall and slim and powerfully built and boasted a full set of white, if somewhat equine, teeth. Such a tour was an excellent opportunity to show off these physical advantages and make himself admired, for as a ruling monarch he was able always to stand in the middle of the room, thereby making sure that he was the centre of attention and that everyone would be able to see what a fine upstanding lad he was; and, as all the parties were given for him, all he had to do was to smile continuously with a benevolent, if not very intelligent, expression on his face.

And how was he repaid by those vile Albanians? Only two months out of the country and revolution broke out. Not only that but in January those ungrateful rebels announced that the Prince of Wied had been deposed and replaced by a man of their own choice – one Izzet Pasha. The great powers declared that this was beyond endurance and sent a fleet to demonstrate off Valona. At the same time they bade the Prince of Wied to hurry up and take possession of his throne. 'At once!' the new King cried; but then found that his country's new coat of arms was not ready.

He had ordered it to be prepared by some of the world's leading experts on heraldry, and naturally could not present himself
to his new subjects without it, for how could a man be a real king
if he had no proper heraldic insignia? Not only that but he had
to form a royal guard, and although he had issued a tempting
invitation to the adventure-hungry young aristocrats of Europe,
no one had yet come forward; and how could he set foot in his
kingdom without a guard? So he continued on his travels, always
smiling, and went to Rome, Berlin and London.

While the 'pacification' of Albania found no smooth path, the
solutions proposed in the Aegean proceeded without a hitch.
The islands of Imbros and Tenedos were given back to Turkey
while the rest were handed over to Greece. It was true that these
were still occupied by the English, but as this was said to be only a
temporary arrangement, it seemed that peace had been achieved
there too.

All the same there were a few signs that something disquieting
was moving under the surface, and this not only in the Balkans.
It was rumoured that a Russian secret agent, one Count Dobrinsky, was travelling about in disguise on the Hungarian side of the
Carpathians.

It seemed that he had already been in Ruthenia for some little
time and that his presence there had only become remarked
when, instead of the old-style little wooden chapels, there had
been erected many new churches built of stone in the Russian
manner with money from an unknown source. Wherever such
a new 'Russian' church appeared so at the same time did a portrait of the Tsar, Father of all the Russias. But Dobrinsky was not
only there to build propaganda churches, his real function, it was
reported, was to draw strategic maps of the passes over the Carpathians and to recruit a network of confidential informers, about
fifty of whom had been arrested and brought to trial at the end
of December.

This was the calm before the storm. It was the beginning of
1914.

Society in the Hungarian capital did not seem to be aware of
any of these things. Nor did Parliament. Nearly everyone was
interested only by whatever scandal came their way. Only Tisza
was doing everything he could to make up for lost time. Only
he saw how necessary this was. Even though it was so late in the
day he did all he could to bring peace to the controversy over

the status of the ethnic minorities in the kingdom. He alone, it seemed, realized how essential it was to get these troubles settled before some world crisis would test the country's mettle. He initiated talks with the influential Romanian politician Maniu – and was promptly attacked by Justh and other chauvinist demagogues for so doing. The county of Pest reacted stormily. The discussions went on for some six weeks, until, in the end, the Romanian 'national committee' rejected the Minister-President's overtures. Despite their refusal to co-operate Tisza declared that for his part he would be as good as his word and continue to hold out the hand of friendship whether it was grasped or not.

It was the last very late attempt to solve a problem that had dogged Hungarian politics for more than a decade. It was, perhaps, a trifle shop-soiled too, because of the irredentist pretensions of the Bucharest peace treaty. But Tisza, even if he had wanted to, could not then have offered more. His hands were tied, firstly by the fact that public opinion was against him and secondly because there were so few others in public life sufficiently clear-sighted to realize the seriousness of the international situation.

At the end of February Balint again found himself back in the Kalotaszeg. He had to go to Magyarokerek to deal with a most interesting situation that had developed there. After a series of abortive attempts a Co-operative society had been formed in the villages in the mountains where the only work was in forestry. This was not unlike the one or two similar societies which had already been formed in the Szekler country. Abady was anxious to persuade this new Co-operative to affiliate to his national movement. This was no easy task, especially in the bigger villages like Kalota-Szentkiraly, Valko and Gyero-Monostor who had all rejected the idea of affiliation. However, the people of Magyar-okerek were more flexible in their ideas and accepted Balint's proposition within a month of forming their Co-operative. Balint therefore felt himself bound to find them a forest, for though the villagers were honest, and full of good will and joy in their work, they had no money with which to pay for the standing timber on whatever land might be made available to them. This was the custom, but it was difficult to find a land-owner willing to forgo the profit on land which he had always regarded as there only for his personal profit.

Balint accordingly had decided to give them one of his own holdings which was separate from the other Abady forests. It was situated on the south side of the Kohegy on the boundaries of the county of Szekelyjo. Balint's idea was to allow the villagers to owe him the purchase price until they could start to make a profit from felling the adult trees. Accordingly he went there with his own forest manager, the engineer Winkler, and his secretary Miklos Ganyi, to advise the Co-operative on how to plan the felling and also how to run the new society.

It was pouring with rain when Balint's little party arrived. Everywhere was water and mud and their only consolation was that most of the snow had already disappeared from the mountains.

They walked the boundaries of the forest and checked that they were properly marked; and in the afternoon they sat down in the judge's house and saw that the contract was properly drawn up. At the same time they drew up a schedule of when the timber should be sold and what its price should be. Then they estimated how much would be left, when the land price had been paid and the cost of the labour settled, to form the society's capital. This last had been Abady's express wish and would be his gift.

When all these things had been settled and there only remained some minor details and the preparation of fine copies of the agreements – work which would take an hour at most and which could best be done by Winkler and Ganyi – Balint realized that he had time to call on Farkas Alvinczy, whom he had not seen for a long time.

Since old Count Adam Alvinczy had died and his sons divided up their diminished inheritance, Farkas had hardly stirred from Magyarokerek.

Balint had last seen him at Kis-Kukullo when he had found himself dragged in to attend Pityu's party to celebrate the trial and execution of Brandy. Even there Farkas's presence had been exceptional; and since then he had not stirred from home.

Balint had to climb a steep path to reach the Alvinczy manor house. It was perhaps just as well that it was already evening and that night was falling, for the state of dilapidation of the hand-some old house was not as obvious as it would have been by day. As it was one hardly noticed that the plaster was falling away in great patches and that one corner of the house was crumbling.

There were no servants to be seen but a light shone from one of the ground-floor windows. Balint stepped up on to the columned portico and opened the door.

Inside he saw Farkas Alvinczy, sitting at a large dining-table on which was spread a huge map lit by a single lamp. Farkas was leaning over the table and was apparently so deep in a book that lay beside the map that he did not notice Abady until he was standing in front of him.

'Why, Balint!' he cried. 'Whatever are you doing here?'

It was obvious that he was delighted to see his visitor, though his greeting was elegantly moderate and free of effusiveness. Balint was at once offered some refreshment, and it was no home-brewed beverage, but a choice of the best liqueurs.

'What would you prefer?' asked Farkas. 'Would you like Benedictine, Cointreau, Chartreuse, Maraschino di Zara? Or something else? I think I've got everything.'

Indeed all these elegant bottles stood nearby in a row on the sideboard.

'You know it's the only thing I spend money on now. Since I gave up the great world – and the high life of the capital – I just don't have the means any more. This is my only indulgence. For a man like myself . . . used to only the best . . . well . . .'

They touched glasses and sat down at the table. Balint explained what brought him up to the forests and then they talked of some of their mutual friends, of economics and the prospects for the next harvest. These subjects were soon exhausted, for it was obvious to Balint that none of this really interested his friend any more for Farkas treated it all with haughty contempt. With a dismissive wave of his hand and a mocking smile he said, 'None of this is very important; just little things for little people!'

After more somewhat desultory talk between them Farkas finally spoke of the map that covered the table and which had been carefully attached to it by metal clips. It represented the Indian Ocean, from Aden to the Malacca Straits. When Balint asked why he was studying this map Farkas for the first time became quite animated and eloquent.

'That is where I'm travelling at present! You see? Today my ship arrived here!'

'Your ship?'

'Yes, my ship. This is it!' and he pointed to a steel pen head which had been placed on the blue-coloured sea, pointing to Ceylon at the foot of the pink-coloured sub-continent of India. 'This pen here, that is my ship. Every day I push it forward the distance travelled in the previous twenty-four hours, according to this book. The day before yesterday we left Bombay, and tomorrow we shall arrive at Colombo.'

He told how he had travelled like this for the last two years. He had ordered accounts of voyages and the corresponding maps, and each day he read just as much as was covered by that day – no more, for that would be cheating. Like this it was just as if he were making the voyage himself. If the traveller wrote that he had spent five days at sea with nothing to relate, then Farkas waited five days before reading on or marking the map.

'But isn't that rather dull, making yourself wait five days?'

'Not at all! Time goes by. Sometimes faster than you'd imagine. I think about the sea and about my travelling companions. I dress for dinner in the evenings – you always do on a luxury liner, you know.'

He told Balint he was now a much-travelled man. The previous year he had rounded Cape Horn, visited Terra del Fuego and indeed 'done' South America. He had also been to the South Pole and back. It had been beautiful and most interesting even though it had been a shorter trip than he really liked.

'This one is very good. The weather's lovely and so far the sea has been quite calm!'

Balint looked hard at Alvinczy wondering if he was making fun of him and was just saying all this for a joke, but it was clear he meant everything he said and took it all very seriously. On Farkas's classical features, on that still beautiful if now slightly puffy face, there was an expression only of calm honesty. None of the young Alvinczys had ever shown any sign of a sense of humour and now it was obvious that the man was simply telling the truth. Looking at him Balint noticed how well-turned-out and soigné Farkas still was. He was freshly shaved, his hair had been brushed smooth; and he was wearing a well-cut double-breasted dark blue smoking jacket with gold buttons, just what an elegant man of fashion would wear while cruising the world's oceans.

'Where is your ship going?' asked Balint, so as to make him talk on.

'Tokyo. Then from Tokyo down to the Philippines and on the

return trip we shall call at Java and Sumatra. I need another map
for that part of the voyage, of course, but I've got it here all ready.
Would you like to see it?'

He was about to get up to fetch it when Miklos Ganyi
appeared at the door seemingly rather agitated.

'This urgent telegram was brought up from Hunyad by a
special messenger. He had to ride up. I'm sure it must be important or Zutor wouldn't have sent it on after us.'

'Please excuse me!' said Balint to Alvinczy as he opened the
envelope. It had been sent that day at midday and read:

'THE FOLLOWING TELEGRAM CAME TODAY FROM
SZAMOS KOZARD; THE COUNT IS VERY ILL. PLEASE
COME AT ONCE. REGINA.'

Balint jumped up. Laszlo! Laszlo, his Laszlo, was dying and was
perhaps already dead. He would have to start for Kozard at once.
Balint read out the message to Farkas and for a few moments they
discussed the sad news. Then Balint and Ganyi set off.

Alvinczy came with them only as far as the door. He said the
proper words of condolence: 'What a pity – a real shame – he
was such an old friend!' but one could tell that the news had not
really meant anything to him. As soon as the others had gone, he
turned on his heel and hastened back to his book and his map.

Balint caught the night express to Kolozsvar. There another
telegram was waiting for him. It came from Kozard and read:

'THE NOBLE COUNT LASZLO GYEROFFY WENT TO A
BETTER WORLD AT FOUR P.M. THIS AFTERNOON. I CON-
SIDER IT MY SACRED DUTY TO PROVIDE EVERYTHING
NECESSARY. PLACING AT YOUR LORDSHIP'S FEET MY
DEEPEST CONDOLENCES I REMAIN YOUR LORDSHIP'S
MOST HUMBLE SERVANT – AZBEJ.'

Early the next morning Balint left by car for Kozard. Before
leaving he remembered that La Pantera should have been in
Budapest since the previous Saturday and so Julie Ladossa would
be there too. So he sent a telegram to her at the Hotel Hungaria.

He reached Kozard just before eight o'clock.

Old Marton Balogh was sitting on the doorstep. He looked

old and worn and he just sat there looking glumly ahead of him. He did not get up when Balint came up, nor did he touch his cap; and when Abady questioned him, he merely pointed with his thumb to the room behind him and muttered, 'There, in the back-room. The young Jewess is with him,' and then went on staring into space.

Regina sat by the window at a table she had pushed there so as to make more space in the room for the moment when they would bring in the coffin. She had been alone with Laszlo when he died. She had shut his eyes, tied up his chin, washed the body and shaved his previous day's stubble. Now Laszlo was lying there covered with a sheet. His two pillows had been placed on the chest of drawers.

In front of the girl was some bedding – three towels and two blankets, some shirts, too, and handkerchiefs and socks. She was making a list so that everything could be accounted for, though to whom and why she had not thought. The important thing was that everything should be in order; and so there she was, stub of pencil in hand, making a list of the clothes in the pile in front of her.

Her red hair flamed in the light from the window.

She replied to all Balint's questions calmly and intelligently. Her large doe-like eyes seemed even larger as a result of her long vigil, but despite all her hard work she did not seem tired. Calmly she told what had happened.

Laszlo, she said, had just wasted away. Sometimes he had taken just half a glass of milk, but latterly not even that. He had not been in pain and recently had hardly even coughed. He had slept more and more, and in the last few days had only been awake for a few minutes at a time. He had slept quietly until the moment when he had turned to the wall and died.

'Why didn't you let me know earlier, as you promised?' asked Balint crossly.

Regina did not answer, but just looked at him with pouting lips. Then she said, 'Would you like to see him?'

They stepped over to the bed and she folded back the sheet.

It looked as if Laszlo were asleep; even though it was the sleep of death. To Balint, looking at his fine aquiline nose and long moustaches, it was strange to see him so calm, which he never had been in life. His waxen face was barely more than skin and bone but about his mouth there still seemed to linger a faint mocking smile, while those eyebrows which met in the middle were raised at the edges as if in contempt.

Abady somehow resented his unexpectedly strange expression and was relieved when Regina covered his face again.

'In this cupboard there is a lovely suit. He told me to put it on him when he was dead.'

Balint was startled.

'Did he know he was dying then?'

'No, not now, anyhow. He said it a long time ago.' She opened the cupboard and hanging there was an iron-grey morning coat, a double-breasted cream-coloured waistcoat and a pair of striped trousers. Under the suit was a pair of black and beige buttoned boots. 'He once said that though he'd sold everything else he ever possessed he would never sell this suit no matter how much he needed the money!'

Regina then took the suit out of the cupboard and laid it out neatly on the chair.

'They said yesterday evening, the men from Szamos-Ujvar, that they'd bring in the coffin at midday. He ought to be ready by then.'

Balint offered to help her.

They slit each piece of clothing down the back so that it would be easier to put on. As Regina was cutting the waistcoat a small blue card fell from the pocket. It was a tote ticket from some long-forgotten race meeting. Abady picked it up and saw that on it was printed the letter nine. It must have been a losing ticket for if it had won then surely Laszlo would have handed it in, despite the fact that it was only for quite a small sum, just ten crowns, no more. Balint wondered what to do about it. His first thought was to throw it away, but then it occurred to him that it might have had some special memory for Laszlo and that that was why he had kept it.

It was true that that ticket had meant something special to Laszlo, though it was doubtful whether he ever realized he still had it in the pocket of the suit he had never worn again after that day at the King's Cup race in Budapest when he had promised Klara Kollonich never again to gamble. In the grandstand he had said to her 'I promise!' and they had shaken hands on it. So as to mislead anyone who was standing near and might have heard these solemn words and seen the mysterious handshake and wondered what they signified, she had given him ten crowns and asked him to put them on a horse for her, just as if they had only been discussing a bet. He had put the money on Number Nine.

The bet had been lost ... and the girl too. Laszlo had broken his word to her and had gone on gambling. To him that ticket had been the symbol of the day the Fates had turned against him.

Abady knew nothing of this, but his instinct told him to put the blue ticket back in the pocket from which it had fallen.

Outside the house Bischitz saw the car and asked the chauffeur about his master. When he learned that it was Count Abady, who was rich and important and a close relation of the dead man, he at once began to wonder if he might be able to get him to pay for all the soap, paraffin and brandy that Regina had stolen from the shop. He knew he could not send in an account for these to Dr Simay, who was hard and severe and would only say that he was not responsible for what the shopkeeper's daughter might have pinched on the sly. Bischitz was not even sure that it had been Regina, for all he knew for certain was that he had missed some stock that he thought ought to have been there, and he could not even say how much had been taken. Still, he now thought, such a distinguished gentleman as Count Abady was certain to have a softer heart than the stern lawyer, for wasn't he even now inside the house and, as he had seen through the window, talking kindly to his daughter?

Accordingly he hastened back to the shop and started to make out a bill. Being an honest shopkeeper he was careful not to add anything extra – though he did round off the total – but added it all up more or less to what he thought had disappeared.

When Abady came out of the house just before midday Bischitz had already been waiting for him for some time. Hat in hand he introduced himself and, after a lengthy explanation, offered Balint his account. He never mentioned how many times he had slapped Regina when he fancied she had taken something, but spoke warmly of her as if she had done it all with his approval. He even managed to give the impression that he had encouraged her.

Balint was about to take the bill, which amounted to a few thousand crowns, when a carriage with jangling harness drove up from the north and stopped beside them. A short, stout man with greying hair stepped out. He was aged about sixty and wore a short imperial and thick glasses. Peering at Abady with the slightly squinting gaze of the short-sighted, he spoke directly to the shopkeeper.

'What sort of a bill is that?'

Bischitz started and then, rushing his words, he began to explain that there had been certain expenses which, merely out of discretion of course, he had not mentioned before for, still out of discretion of course, there had been some old debts of Count Laszlo's ... and some new ones ... and he hadn't wanted to trouble anyone with them.

There was nothing soft about the lawyer, for it was Dr Simay who had arrived, and he at once called the shopkeeper to order.

'I gave strict instructions that you were to give no credit. Further I forbade you to turn to anyone else in anything that concerned Count Gyeroffy's needs. Give that to me,' he ordered, 'and I will look it over.' He then went up to Abady and introduced himself, 'Dr Geza Simay, at your service.'

They shook hands and Balint then explained that he had come at once to provide whatever was necessary for Laszlo's funeral, and added that he had brought the necessary funds with him.

'That won't be necessary, my Lord,' replied Simay. 'I have already made all the arrangements. The announcements have been sent out from my office. The coffin will be here in half an hour and the service and interment will take place tomorrow morning at ten o'clock. The local pastor has already agreed to conduct the service.'

'But the costs? My cousin had no money, and the small annuity that he has been receiving from Azbej ceases with his death. I would never agree that the man who deprived Laszlo of everything should now wish to appear generous and pay for his funeral.'

Simay smiled.

'Azbej is paying for nothing, my Lord. There has been no annuity or anything else from him. Up until now it is I who have provided everything for Count Laszlo, and I shall settle these costs as well.'

'What? No annuity from Azbej? But I thought ... ? Well then, where did the money come from?'

Simay paused for a moment, as if he had just realized that perhaps he had said more than he should. Then, unperturbed and unhurried, he went on to tell something, if not all, of the truth.

'I used to look after all the late Mihaly Gyeroffy's affairs; so it was quite natural that I should see to his son's interests too.'

'So it was you who provided for Laszlo?'

'Not I myself. I merely arranged what had to be done,' said Simay hesitantly. 'I had my orders. It is the same with the funeral.'

'You had your orders?'

'Exactly. I am a lawyer, you know, and this had been part of my legal work.' Simay spoke somewhat dryly, and then, to cut short any further enquiry, he turned to Bischitz and said, 'The coffin will arrive at any moment. Please have a few strong men ready to carry it into the house!' To Abady he said: 'I hope your Lordship will now excuse me. I have to go up to the family vault,' and after a brief farewell hurried off up the hill towards the manor house.

Balint was surprised by what he had just heard and asked himself who then could it have been who had kept Laszlo from starvation. Could it have been his aunts? Surely not Agnes Gyeroffy, Princess Kollonich? Or her sister Countess Szent-Gyorgyi, the gentle Elise? That was more likely; and yet how could she have organized all this so quickly when she lived so far away at Jablanka, in the Slovakian province of Nyitra? It was possible, he supposed, that she had given her instructions in advance; and yet it seemed unlikely. It was all very mysterious.

There was nothing more for Balint to do at Kozard that morning so he got into his car and was driven back to Kolozsvar where he found a telegram waiting for him. It was from Julie Ladossa, saying that she would arrive by that evening express from Budapest.

So she really was coming!

Balint at once wondered if her arrival would make for any problems with the others who would be coming for the funeral. How would they behave towards the notorious former Countess Gyeroffy? Would they greet her correctly ... or cut her dead? That would be dreadful, no matter how justified. Balint now realized that it had been thoughtless of him to have sent off that telegram; but as he had he would now have to suffer the consequences. As to himself he decided at once that he would behave towards Julie Ladossa as if he knew nothing at all about her past. He would give her all the respect that was due to her as Laszlo's mother, just as if she had never abandoned the position to which she had been born. That, he decided, was the right thing to do.

He went to meet her at the station. The train was on time.

Holding herself as erect as the last time he had seen her she got down from the carriage with head held high. She was wearing the same black dress as she had that night in Vienna and Balint wondered if it was the only good dress she possessed. She held out her hand, explaining that she would have been there in the morning but that as they were staying at the Royal Hotel and not at the Hungaria she had not received the news at once.

She spoke calmly, in even natural tones. She showed no signs of sorrow or tearfulness. In fact there was no change in her manner, though Balint felt that if anything her face was even more expressionless than when they had last met. Was the vertical furrow on her forehead a shade more pronounced and her lips even more compressed, as if she was consciously clenching her jaws? It was so uncertain that Balint was not sure if it was really there or whether he had imagined it.

He took her to the Central Hotel and saw her to her room, saying that he would fetch her in his car at eight-thirty the following morning.

'Are you taking anyone else?' she asked.

'No. Only you, Aunt Julie.'

At that last word she turned her head away abruptly. Then, very quickly, she muttered, 'Goodnight!' and disappeared into her room.

Balint returned home on foot. As he went he was assailed by many memories of childhood and of his years at school when he and Laszlo had lodged together at the Theresianum in Vienna. His heart contracted with sorrow and he was so overcome that tears filled his eyes. He longed for Adrienne's comforting presence, but she had had to leave again for Lausanne some five days before as they had wired her that her daughter was ill again and that she should come to be with her. If Adrienne had been at home he could have gone straight to her and told her of his sadness, and she would have listened and understood and comforted him; but she was not there and he had no one to whom he could pour out what was in his heart.

He walked on until he reached the Abady town house, but when he reached the entrance he stopped, knowing that he would not sleep. Perhaps a long walk would help calm him, he thought, and so, even though a slight rain had started, he turned away and quite involuntarily headed for the Monostor road, towards the Uzdy villa. For a long time he stood there, by the bridge that led to the park, and then, after wandering for a while down the tree-lined alleys, he made his way back to the centre of the town. He had been walking for more than an hour and a half.

As he entered the market square he stopped, startled. A tall dark woman was standing on the sidewalk in front of the church. She just stood there without moving, apparently staring at the main entrance, lit up by one of the streetlights.

Balint had recognized her at once: it was Julie Ladossa.

Holding her voluminous coat tightly around her, she stood there like a figure of stone; and Balint wondered how long she had been there and if, like himself, she had been wandering about in the dark night ever since they had parted earlier that evening.

He turned swiftly away in case she should catch a glimpse of him and think that he was spying on her. Balint now took a turn through the streets of the old town and when he finally found himself in the passage beside the Town Hall which gave on to the market square, he looked again towards the church.

The dark shape was still there, just as before, motionless in the slight drizzle. Was she going to stay there all night?

The street in front of the little house at Kozard had been deserted when Balint had arrived the previous day: now it was thronged with people. All the village folk were standing there waiting.

The road was muddy, but the rain had stopped and so everyone could wait without getting wet.

The Bischitz husband and wife were there, dressed in all their finery as if for the Sabbath; and Fabian was strutting about giving orders in a stentorian voice. Old Marton was hovering disconsolate near the house. Only Regina was nowhere to be seen.

The entire Azbej family had turned up – Mrs Azbej, short, fat, full-bosomed, with several double chins; the Azbej children, short and dark, with eyes like tiny black plums, the image of their father; and the dishonest little lawyer himself, all self-importance, strutting about playing the host and receiving the eminent mourners as they arrived.

He had already welcomed the chief judge of the district and the doctor from Iklod and led them towards the ramshackle barn that stood in a corner of the manor house grounds.

That morning the coffin had been brought there and set up on a bier, according to Dr Simay's instructions. He had ordered it

so because there would not have been enough room for the
mourners to pay their last respects in Laszlo's little cottage. The
inside of the barn had been decorated, again on Simay's orders,
with branches of pine cut from the woods that Mihaly Gyeroffy
had planted but which now belonged to Azbej, as the little lawyer
did not fail to point out so as to show everyone what a generous
fellow he was.

When Abady arrived with Julie Ladossa, Azbej hurried forward on his short legs to greet them, bowing obsequiously, the
image of grief-stricken sorrow, even though he had no idea who
the lady was that Balint had brought with him. 'Such a blow!
Such a terrible blow!' he whispered with his tiny mouth, holding
his hat in one hand and with the other repeatedly wiping his eyes
with a huge handkerchief. Backing before them with more bows
and protestations of devotion to the deceased noble Count, he
led them to the barn. They could see little more of him than the
top of his round bristling pate of black hair.

At the door two gendarmes in full-dress uniform stood at
attention. They were there not only for good form but because
the coffin had not yet been closed. Its lid was leaning against the
barn wall. The Chief Judge and the doctor stood together by
the hedge smoking and nearby were the dark-clad employees
of the funeral director.

Only Dr Simay was inside the barn. He had had the chairs from
Laszlo's house brought there and placed in a line in front of the
open coffin. He was sitting on one of them.

When Balint and Julie Ladossa came in he stood up and
went to greet them. Suddenly he stopped in his tracks and with
both hands touched his glasses as if he could not believe what
he saw. Julie Ladossa stopped too. For a few moments they
stared at each other, then Simay bowed coldly. She nodded in
acknowledgement.

Now they stepped forward to the bier, Abady and the
unknown lady to one side and Dr Simay to the other. He stood
there for a moment at the head of the coffin and then, with a
hard glance at Julie Ladossa, suddenly grabbed the shroud and
disclosed the body.

There was something vengeful in the quick movement as if to
say 'See, this is your doing! This is what became of the son you
abandoned!'

Julie Ladossa did not move. She looked for a long time at the prematurely aged man with the thin wasted face and parchment-like skin and grey hair at his temples. It was the face of an Egyptian mummy, but who was he? Could it be the same being she had remembered through so many long self-accusing nights, only as a baby, as a three-year-old, a growing boy who still kept the round rosy features of babyhood? She had had to imagine him as a youth, counting the years so as to guess what the growing man had looked like . . . but this, this skeletal corpse, with a razor-sharp aquiline nose and long moustaches, dressed in a morning coat and starched collar and patent-leather shoes? There were no memories which tied him to her. In his petrified calm he was as strange to her as some unknown inanimate object.

She tried to force herself to kiss his face, but she couldn't do it; so she made the sign of the cross with her finger on the dead man's forehead and then stepped back beside Balint who had previously placed his wreath at the foot of the bier.

From outside came the sound of a powerful car. It was Dodo Gyalakuthy. She was followed by Mrs Bogdan Lazar from Dezsmer. Both of them brought wreaths which they placed beside Balint's, and both of them said a short prayer beside the coffin. And to them too the dead man was a stranger, seeming to bear no resemblance to the Laszlo with whom they had both been in love. Then they took their seats beside Julie Ladossa and waited.

Someone came forward and covered up the body with the shroud which was made of silk with a wide border of lace.

The Provost of the county arrived, with two deacons, an altar-boy and six singers. The officiating priest wore a black and silver cope, and the others similar funeral vestments. The service began.

Dies iræ, dies illa. The traditional requiem hymn sounded as beautiful as ever. Then the Provost circled the coffin twice, sprinkling it with holy water, followed by the incense, wafted from a thurible of massive gilt metal.

'How thoughtful of you to have arranged such a worthy service!' whispered Julie Ladossa to Balint.

'It wasn't me,' he replied. 'Perhaps it was our good aunt Szent-Gyorgyi. I really don't know who did it. Geza Simay took care of everything. He had his orders but he wouldn't say who from.'

Hearing this Julie Ladossa sat up even straighter, and it seemed to Balint that something of a secret joy flashed briefly in her eyes . . . why, he wondered?

* * *

The wreaths were taken up and the coffin placed on a wooden stretcher which was lifted on to the shoulders of eight men who then carried it outside, where the priest and the deacons were waiting, crosses held high, to lead the procession to the Gyer-offy vault.

Balint offered his arm to Laszlo's mother, but she shrank back. 'Up there? To the vault? No! No! I won't go there ...!' she whispered. Balint could hardly catch what she said, but her face was set and there was terror in her eyes. Balint answered, also in a whisper, 'Wait for me in Laszlo's house then. I'll be back soon.'

The procession formed up and started on its way, the people from the village crowding round behind. Julie Ladossa waited until they had all gone, and then turned and walked away.

At Laszlo's little house the door at the left of the porch was half open, so she went straight in. In the corner by the stove, hunched up like some wounded animal and crouching on the floor, a young girl was sobbing. It was Regina.

She had collapsed there in the morning when they had carried out the coffin. Until then she had been sad but had remained calm. She had busied herself by seeing that everything was in its proper place, by seeing that Laszlo's bedding in the coffin was neatly folded as it should be, by putting a cushion beneath his head so that he should lie as comfortably as possible, and then she had smoothed his clothes and adjusted his tie. All this time she felt he still belonged to her. Through the night she had watched by the coffin, sitting next to him on the floor and he was still hers, just as he had been when wasting away before her eyes. For her he remained forever her Fairy Prince, that noble, resplendent Prince of her dreams in whom she had always believed and whom she worshipped. Until that morning.

But when the funeral director's men had come in and started to carry out the coffin she realized for the first time that they were going to take him away from her, take away for ever the man she loved, whom she had loved ever since her childhood, whom she had served and nursed and worshipped with every fibre in her being, heedless of misery and humiliation, heedless of all the obstacles put in her way, for he had always been hers, only hers. Until this last awful moment. It was terrible for her that now these strangers should come in and tear from her every joy and dream for which Laszlo had stood, even deprive her of that pain she had always felt in loving him. She grasped the coffin firmly, defying them to take it from her, fighting so that they shouldn't rob her of what was rightfully hers, only hers.

The men pushed her roughly away and she fell in the corner by the stove. It was as if she had been broken in two. Her head was between her knees and her arms folded tightly above it. All that could be seen of her was her thin body in its torn cotton dress and the flaming red hair that tumbled over her shoulders.

Julie Ladossa was taken by surprise to find this adolescent girl crouched there alone in the almost empty room.

She went over to her, lifted her carefully up and sat her on the bed beside her despite the girl's resistance. Now this resistance stopped and Regina collapsed into Julie's lap, once again overcome by a frenzied weeping. Soon the hot rebellious sobbing faded into a more peaceful released sorrow.

Then Laszlo's mother's tears also began to flow.

They sat there together for a long time, the older woman rigidly upright, the young girl lying softly in her lap. Julie Ladossa's hand gently stroked Regina's hair, smoothly, gently, continuously stroking, stroking . . . eternally stroking . . .

At last the woman spoke, just one phrase, in a low voice: 'Did you love him?'

'Desperately,' whispered the girl. 'Desperately, desperately!' Then she got up and put her arms round the sad unknown lady who sat beside her, and kissed her. And so they remained, kissing each other's cheeks with their arms enlaced, the lady in the silken dress and the forlorn girl in her rags.

Together they mourned Laszlo, the mother who had forsaken him and the little girl who had remained faithful unto death.

The bells had just chimed midday when Balint came to find Julie Ladossa and take her back to Kolozsvar.

Her eyes were opened wide as if she were seeing visions. The wrinkles round her mouth seemed even deeper than before.

They had barely passed the Hubertus clubhouse when Julie Ladossa was already asking, 'What times do the trains leave?'

'There are three. One leaves soon, at half-past one; the next at six o'clock, and at eleven there is the night express. You can get a sleeper on that.'

'I'd like to catch the first if it's possible.'

They got to the station in time.

'Thank you ... for everything! Thank you very much ...!'
she said as she stopped at a second-class carriage. Then she shook
hands quickly and got in hurriedly as if pursued.

Balint was walking up and down in his room, thinking about
Laszlo and of all those past memories that his death had brought
back and which had now been buried with him, when his valet
came in. It was about five o'clock.

'Someone has come from the Central Hotel with something
for your Lordship. Shall I ask him to come in?'

'Of course.'

A messenger entered with a long package wrapped in tissue
paper.

'This was brought from one of the flower-shops for Countess
Ladossa, my Lord; but she left no address and so the manager told
me to bring it round here to your Lordship.'

'Thank you,' said Balint. 'Put it down over there, will you?'
and handed the man a tip.

Flowers? Someone had sent flowers to Julie Ladossa?

He opened the parcel to see if there was any card enclosed so
that he could return the gift to the sender.

There was nothing; only five beautiful old-fashioned roses,
pale golden-yellow Maréchal Niel. There was no name, no card.
Balint had no idea what to do with them. It would have been
useless to send them on to Budapest for they would be dead long
before they arrived, indeed they were already fully open and
starting to wilt.

He carried them over to a table in the corner, meaning to find
a vase for them. As he did so a few petals fell to the ground.

It was hardly worthwhile putting them in water.

PART SIX

CHAPTER ONE

Gornergrat, 3,300 metres above sea level.

ON A NARROW ridge of granite there stood a small hotel built of wood on stone foundations. A broad terrace stretched across the front of the building, looking over a deep abyss. All around there was perpetual snow and, directly beneath, glaciers. Beyond these was a further immense valley shaped like a giant cauldron, so deep that from above it seemed almost unreal and the occasional houses as small as grains of rice. Beyond the cauldron was a wall of mountains over which towered the Matterhorn, a solitary peak which shot high in the air with an almost perpendicular rock-face culminating in a narrow granite spike so sharp that it was like some giant claw reaching out to the sky above.

The hotel could only be reached by cable-car. Balint had arrived at midday, called there by Adrienne who had chosen this place because, in the middle of July, there would be few other guests, for in those days tourists only came to such high altitudes in August. And also because it was little more than an hour's drive from Montana where was the sanatorium to which her daughter had been taken when she became ill at school. Adrienne had been there since February.

Balint spent his time wondering why she had sent for him and what it was she wanted to tell him. Her telegram had included the words '*there are decisive matters we must discuss . . .*'

His heart had constricted. What did she mean by the cold formal phrase 'decisive matters'? What could there be that she was not able to write in a letter, that she had to tell him herself? What sort of danger could be threatening them now? In her last letter Adrienne had written that her daughter had suffered a lung hæmorrhage. It had been a short letter, and then there had been nothing for two weeks, though before that she had written nearly every day.

Then, five days ago before had come this telegram with every detail of their meeting carefully planned.

For what seemed an eternity Balint waited alone for Adrienne to arrive, alone with dismal thoughts and nagging distress and foreboding.

He must have walked up and down the terrace at least fifty times before he was able to pull himself together and force himself to think about other things. Otherwise I shall go crazy, he said to himself.

There were plenty of other matters to worry about.

At the end of June the Heir had been assassinated at Sarajevo, in a double tragedy which had taken the life not only of Franz-Ferdinand but also of his wife, the only being he had ever loved and probably the only person who had ever loved him. At the news of his death the Hungarian people had breathed more easily, for they all knew he was no lover of their country and no one, as yet, had imagined that his murder might lead to war. In this their feeling was reinforced by the general indifference with which the Heir's death had been greeted in Vienna itself. He had even been buried with far less ceremony than his rank would normally have demanded and Balint had been one of the few politicians in Budapest who judged that this was a grave error, for if Austria-Hungary was to maintain her position as a great power it should at once have realized that the assassination had been the direct result of a Serbian conspiracy hatched in Belgrade and should have been treated as such. To those farsighted few the future seemed full of foreboding.

The prospects were indeed dark. Any military retaliation would inevitably explode into war, that war that had already twice seemed inevitable; once in 1908 after the annexation of Bosnia-Herzegovina and then again, in the previous year, when the Balkan conflict had started.

There seemed to be only one hope. A royal prince had been brutally murdered and it was unlikely that any European monarch would wish to side with those who had killed the heir to a brother kingdom.

If the Ballplatz were to be sufficiently adroit to exploit this aspect of the crisis and demand satisfaction without raising the spectre of official Serbian complicity, if it were possible to do this without giving rise to the assumption that Austria was seeking an excuse to invade and annex Serbia, then perhaps war might be avoided.

This was not impossible. With skilful diplomacy it might just be achieved, but the crucial question still remained – was this what Berchtold really wanted and was he sufficiently able to bring it off? So far his handling of the Balkan problem did not give rise to hope. Maybe he could do it . . . maybe . . . ?

It had never seemed that he wanted war, and indeed until now he had managed to avoid it, even if only by dint of shameful concessions. Would it be the same now?

But if he failed, what then? What would be the fate of Hungary, unprepared as she was, with an antiquated army and a leadership composed only of those who had always been bitterly opposed even to discussing anything that concerned the defence of the nation?

Balint tried to force himself to think only about such matters, to drown his personal worries in analysing the world's problems; but he failed. Subconsciously he could not shake off a sense of some deep personal tragedy and his heart seemed to beat at the back of his throat.

Adrienne did not arrive until after four o'clock.

'Forgive me,' she said. 'I couldn't start when I wanted to. Clemmie was so restless that I had to wait until she calmed down.'

She was very pale. There were dark shadows under her eyes, and she was worn out after a succession of sleepless nights. She had lost weight and the skin was stretched tight over her cheekbones. Her chin seemed sharper, perhaps because she was so much thinner, perhaps because of what she had decided she must tell him. She seemed unusually solemn, and her manner was distant.

They sat down facing each other at one of the tables on the terrace.

'What is it . . . what is it you have to tell me?' asked Balint hesitantly. He felt so self-conscious that he could hardly get out the words.

Adrienne's eyes opened wide and her golden irises gazed straight at Balint. After a few moments' silence she started to speak, very slowly: 'We can never get married! I have to take back my promise.'

'But that is ridiculous!' he cried, almost jumping out of his seat.

'Wait a minute! You must let me explain.'

'Explain? How can you explain such a thing?'

'Be patient with me, Balint . . . and please don't interrupt, it's difficult enough without that!'

Clemmie, she said, had been brought up to the sanatorium at Montana after her first hæmorrhage. She had needed careful round-the-clock nursing and had to be watched every minute of the day and kept to a strict régime of meals and rest-times and lying in the sun. It had not been easy for the little girl was wilful and rebellious and would not listen to anyone except her mother. The doctors and nurses alone could do nothing with her if her mother was not there beside them. It seemed that the girl had confidence only in her. At first she had even been suspicious of Adrienne, but as her condition had improved so had her trust in her mother.

After a while it had seemed that the child was getting better. She had put on weight and her recurrent fevers had diminished and they had even said that maybe soon she would be able to come down to a milder climate. Then came a second hæmorrhage. A new lesion had opened on the other side of the lung. This was usually fatal and Adrienne had been told that if she left the sanatorium the child would be dead in a few weeks. It would be by staying where she was and strictly obeying the doctors' orders that her life could be prolonged. If she did that then she might live for a few years – perhaps five or six, perhaps ten or even twelve – but no more. That was the verdict of the specialist, and everything that Adrienne had read told her the same thing. And even this would only be if she stayed in the high mountains with the most expert nursing.

'So you see what the situation is. I have to make a choice and it is only natural that I should choose to stay with my child.'

'But there's no reason why we shouldn't marry? Why should all this stand in our way? I'd stay up here with you if I had to.'

Adrienne interrupted him.

'You know that is absurd!' she said. 'For you to give up everything, all your work, your home, everything that you have created and live for . . . just to live up here moving from one sanatorium to another. It's impossible! I wouldn't accept it! I couldn't!'

'Why not, if I wanted it?

'No! Never! Not that!'

Adrienne now started speaking more softly, and as she did so she reached across the table and took Balint's hand in hers.

'Look,' she said. 'There are other things too, things we have
to think about if we marry and live together here. We'd still have
the same awful worry, always fearing what we both crave for,
what our bodies crave for! I could never go on like that! Could
I give birth to your child here? Here, surrounded by all these
consumptives?'

Balint bowed his head without saying anything. For a while
he gazed out over the valley. Then he turned to her and said, very
slowly: 'How can this sacrifice make any sense? You say she only
has a few years; so what does it matter if it is five or six, or ten,
or twelve? If there is no hope of her ever getting better, if sooner
or later – it may sound heartless but I have to say it – if there is
no chance of recovery why do we have to destroy ourselves when
there is no hope? It would all be in vain. If that is to be her fate,
does it matter if it's sooner or later?'

'Don't think I haven't thought about it, though it's a dreadful
thing for a mother to do. Oh, yes! The thought came, though
I wish it hadn't ... but it's impossible! How could I leave her
here knowing that I'd be responsible for her death? For she will
die soon if I go away, if I abandon her ... and just think, think!
If we were to have children of our own we'd never be free of
the memory of what we'd done. Every time we looked at our
children, every time we kissed and caressed them, I'd remember
that it had been for them that I'd forsaken this fatherless child and
left her here to die alone. No! No! No! The horror of it!'

For some time they sat there without speaking, both with their
own sombre thoughts. Finally Balint broke the silence between
them.

'You would throw away your happiness for someone who
doesn't love you and never has loved you?'

'It's true,' she replied softly, almost as if she were ashamed of
admitting it. 'It's true enough, but I have to do it, it is my duty.
You see, I know that she's clinging to me now because she
believes that only I can help her.' Now Adrienne raised her voice
until she was almost shouting at him. 'What else can I do? Every
night she clutches at me and cries, "You won't let me die, will
you? You won't let me die?" I have to stay with her. What else
can I do?'

Balint stood up and walked over to the balustrade of the terrace
and leaned on it looking into the distance. After a moment
Adrienne joined him there. For a long time they just stood side

by side without speaking. The daylight faded into evening and soon the valley below was in complete darkness. Only the mountain tops were still lit by the dying sun. Now and again one of them would say something, a few disjointed words that were little more than punctuation to what they left unsaid.

Then Balint said: 'Why should we separate now? Why do we have to decide? Why now? Something will come up ... we can wait.'

Much later Adrienne murmured: 'I will always fight for what we want, in every way I'll do everything I can,' and fell silent again. After a long time she said: 'It may be a very long time. With proper care she may live for ten years.' Several minutes later she murmured: 'To wait so long? We've waited so many years already; and I am so tired.'

'I'll wait for ever! Until the time ...'

For a long time they did not speak. It was now quite dark and a few stars appeared in the sky.

'I'll have to go back soon. I'm afraid she'll be waiting for me, that she won't sleep until I come. And she has to sleep a lot. It's important for her ... I have to go!'

But she did not move and Balint realized that she still had something to tell him, something that was even more painful for her than what had already been said. She was a long, long time making up her mind to speak and, when she did, it was very softly as if she were talking to herself, though none the less determined:

'We are no longer young enough to make plans for the future. You are thirty-six, I will soon be thirty-four. Time passes; and you cannot wait for a long, long time,' she said with renewed emphasis. Then she paused again before saying: 'It would add to my grief if I knew I had forced this waiting on you ... made you so ... so ... lonely. That is why I have to know you are free and ... and not thinking any more about me.'

Balint did not answer but hid his face in his hands. The night grew colder as they stood there silently together.

All around them the snow-clad peaks glimmered softly in the light of a crescent moon. Below them, as far as they could see, stretched the frozen clefts of a great glacier. There was nothing to see but ice and snow, only ice and snow, a petrified world where there could be no life. Ice everywhere, like the frozen inferno of Dante's seventh hell. Even the sky seemed carved from ice, clean, majestic . . . and implacable . . . and even the stars held no mercy.

In front rose the ink-black outline of the Matterhorn, seeming more than ever like a claw, Satan's claw, reaching for the Heavens. The great peak was no longer a natural pyramid of rock but rather some fatal razor-sharp milestone threatening death to the sky above – a milestone that pointed to the end of the world.

The next evening Balint left the express at Salzburg. Later he had no memory of the journey. He had bought a ticket for Budapest, but on impulse got out at Salzburg instead.

He felt he could not possibly go home to Hungary. In Budapest he would meet so many people he knew; and it would be the same in Transylvania. And if he went to Denestornya he would everywhere be reminded of so many fruitless plans and of all those hopes and dreams which had come to nothing. People would greet him and talk to him, and he would be forced to reply hiding his hurt behind a face of stone and pretending that he was still interested by the farce of everyday life. He decided he wanted to see no one and speak to no one; for all he now desired was to hide, to creep into some concealed corner and die.

He left the train and had himself driven to some small anonymous hotel near the station where he could be alone without the risk of seeing anyone he knew.

He did not count the days but passed his time sitting aimlessly at his hotel window hardly hearing the trains that rumbled past, neither the goods trains that shunted to and fro, nor the slow-moving passenger trains that sometimes stayed half an hour or so at the station before moving leisurely on, nor even the fast expresses that hurtled into the nearby station, brakes screaming with senseless haste, and then almost at once clattering over the points as they hastened away. At dusk the lamps started to glow, little points of white or red light, some of which moved and vanished and then returned and some which remained constantly in place. Whistles shrilled and shrieked, some short and some long drawn-out, until it seemed as if the very engines were crying out in pain.

At night Balint would go for long walks partly so as to escape from the four walls of his dismal little room and partly to tire himself out so that perhaps when he returned he would be able to sleep, to sleep as if he were already dead.

* * *

One afternoon, as he was sitting at his window staring at nothing, he gradually became aware of some unusual activity below; newsboys were rushing down the street excitedly calling out:

'*Extraausgabe – Ultimatum zurückgewiesen!* – Extra! Extra! Ultimatum rejected!' Passers-by were stopping and buying and then gathering in groups to discuss what they read. Balint could not imagine what had happened and so hurried down and bought a paper himself. He read the news quickly. Serbia had rejected an ultimatum from Vienna and the Austrian ambassador, Giessl, had already left Belgrade.

War! This could only mean war!

He could not stay a moment longer; so he packed hurriedly and took the first train out.

Home! He had to get home!

CHAPTER TWO

THE RAIL TRAFFIC was so dense that it took two days for Balint to get to Budapest. He arrived at three in the afternoon.

The capital was in a fever of excitement. As yet there had been only partial mobilization, just enough to overrun Serbia.

'At last!' people said. 'Now we'll teach that rabble a lesson!' Everyone was saying the same thing; the porters in the hotels, the shopkeepers, and even the newspapers. It seemed as if all the world had awoken from some enchanted sleep and in consequence was in high good humour. At the Casino Club it was the same, and some of the younger members were already strutting about in the gold braid of the Hussar uniform or the red and blue of the Lancers. 'We'll teach 'em!' they cried.

All at once the air was filled with heroism and glory, and politics were forgotten. All those petty issues, which formerly had aroused such bitter hatreds, had been blown away by the winds of war.

Balint took refuge in the library. There he read all the papers of the last few days, both the national and international news, so as to learn what had happened between the sending of the ultimatum and its rejection. Then he went to the party headquarters which overlooked the boulevard at the corner of

Dohany Street and the Karoly Ring, where he would learn the most recent news. Above all he wanted to see Tisza himself and ask how it was that they had got to that point, what preparations had been made and what he believed would be the result. Above all he wanted to know whether, if war did come, it could be limited to Serbia, or whether Russia was expected to intervene thereby starting a general European conflagration.

There was an immense crowd at the party headquarters, more than Balint had ever seen there before, filling all the rooms and as animated and merry as if drunk on champagne.

Most were discussing the fact that a big pro-war demonstration was shortly due to arrive before the building to cheer the party leader Tisza. Any minute now they should be there, enthusiastically shouting for war. This was wonderful, for all at once the government party had become popular again after always previously having been scornfully labelled the 'lackeys of Turkey', or 'foreign slaves', or 'Vienna's paid gaolers', which for years had been the epithets lavished on them by the Coalition press. Now, at last, they were allowed to be full-blooded patriotic Hungarians!

The doors on to the balcony were open and many people stood there watching for the march down the Karoly Ring of all those who were on their way to acclaim the government, while those inside kept on asking if the demonstration was yet in sight.

Suddenly the cry arose: 'Here they come! They're turning the corner of the boulevard. Where is Tisza? They'll be here any minute! Tisza! Where is Tisza?'

The Minister-President was sitting on a low chair in the hall, smoking a cigar and looking as remote and introspective as ever. He barely said a word to all those close associates who swarmed round him.

'They're coming now, they're coming!' And indeed down the boulevard there poured a huge concourse of people who filled the street and the pavements in line after line that stretched right across between the houses on each side. They came with military precision, carrying banners and singing the national anthem, thousands of voices raised high as they marched steadily forward.

In front of the party headquarters they stopped; and, from above, it was a most impressive sight. The great wide boulevard from Deak Square to Emperor Wilhelm Street was black with people. They were so many that no one could count them, but there must have been twenty or thirty thousand, perhaps more.

All that could be seen of the dense crowd was a sea of hats and waving banners. Somewhere below the balcony someone started calling out, but there was so much noise that the words could not be heard. Then came a mighty roar: 'Tisza! Hurrah for Tisza! Tisza and the War!'

The cry rang out from as far away as Deak Square and minutes passed as 'Tisza and the War!' reverberated from tens of thousands of throats.

Then someone started to make a speech from the balcony and, though he was cheered while speaking, and after he had finished, it was soon obvious that this was not enough. The people wanted Tisza, the Minister-President himself; and no one else would satisfy them.

'Tisza! Tisza! We want Tisza!' the crowd chanted from below.

Some men rushed in from the balcony. 'They want you. They want you to speak to them,' they cried. 'What a day! They're calling for you! They want you to speak to them. At last! At last!'

But Tisza made no move. He sent someone else in his stead.

Another speech was made; and another; and then several others and even one from a side balcony to show all those who could not find a place in front of the main balcony that their war-fever too was appreciated. This went on for some time, but though the people listened they were not satisfied. They had come for Tisza and they meant to hear him, only him, no one else would satisfy them. Again came the roar: 'Tisza! Tisza!' they shouted insistently, angrily.

Gabor Daniel, Pekar and several others ran back to Tisza.

'You have to speak to them! They only want to hear you!' they cried. For a long time they argued and insisted, distressed and upset by their leader's stubborn refusal to move.

Further away some of his followers did not hide their resentment, muttering to each other that his stubbornness was impossible to understand. How could he, who for years had been the most hated man in Hungary, refuse to appear when everything had been changed and the mob was calling hysterically for him? Now they wanted to cheer him – and he wanted none of it! Now of all times, when it was so important. And they whispered to each other: 'This is sheer masochism! He's happy only when they hate him!' The whole party was indignant.

They could not have known that Tisza was opposed to the war. No one knew, except only those who had attended the

King's Council meetings. On the day that the ultimatum had been decided, Tisza had at once resigned. He had remained in office only because ordered to by the monarch himself. He had resigned because he had thought that by doing so he would be able to modify the harsh terms of the ultimatum; but when he had found that his struggle would be in vain and that he would never be able to bring Berchtold and Conrad to his way of thinking, he had decided to stay as he knew that he alone was strong enough to hold the country together at such a critical time. At the express wish of the King he had agreed to keep his opposition secret, principally because he knew that Hungary's new-found unity would be shattered if it was known what he really felt. So he accepted responsibility for a war he had fought hard to prevent. Out of a sense of duty he had accepted a task he loathed, the task of organizing a war knowing well what it would mean. He accepted it in silence, a silence that lasted until his death. And he never changed his opinion, even though it was hidden from the world. In his public speeches he spoke only of effort, duty and self-sacrifice; but he never tried to justify the conflict.

Tisza's real views only became known years after his death when the secret files in Vienna were made public. At the time therefore the resentment of the party's rank and file at their leader's refusal to speak was only to be expected.

There was nothing to be done. They had to let the crowd go, explaining, with a lie, that the Minister-President wasn't there, that he had had to be absent on some urgent business.

Morose and disappointed the great crowd melted away. Many of the party members also went home. Darkness fell and few people were left in the party headquarters.

Balint, who had been every bit as irritated by Tisza's intransigence as the others, saw that the number of those surrounding him had diminished and decided he would try to speak to him. He started to move across the hall, but halfway across he caught sight of Tisza's face and stopped in his tracks.

There the man sat, in a deep armchair, not speaking to anyone, with a dark expression on his face and teeth clenched. What a tragic face the man had! Abady was startled and he sensed at once that there must have been some deep compulsion to explain why he had refused to speak, why he had rejected all appeals from his followers, why he could not allow himself to go out and make a speech and allow himself to be cheered – at least not that, never that!

Balint knew he could not intrude, so he turned away and went home. But he never forgot the moment when he had seen him there, sitting in silence in the deep armchair with his legs crossed, his thick-lensed glasses making his eyes seem so much larger, a bitter crease on his forehead and even more bitter lines reaching down each side of his face. He had sat there motionless, staring ahead of him as if all he could see was the fate of his country. Silent. Chewing a cigar.

Balint stayed only a day or two in Budapest, just long enough to buy a uniform and some other equipment he would need, and clear up some unfinished business in the head office of the Co-operative Movement before enlisting in the army.

Then he left for Kolozsvar.

In Transylvania too everyone was happy and full of confidence, even though by then it had become clear that their real enemy was Russia, while France and England had both declared war on Austria's ally Germany. It was also fairly sure that their other ally, Italy, could not be relied upon and that Romania would remain neutral. Nevertheless euphoria was in the air and among the gayest were the young men, all reserve officers, who were eagerly preparing to rejoin their regiments. Only the women were anxious, the mothers and sisters.

Balint found a number of his old friends who were making the most of their last days carousing with gypsy music and revelling in the joys of saying farewell. At that moment life was suddenly freer – and the girls more complaisant. Some of the men were still dressed in everyday clothes, but most were already sporting their uniforms.

He saw the Laczok boys and young Zoltan Miloth, Adrienne's brother. There also were Pityu Kendy, Joska Kendy, Aron Kozma with three of his cousins, Isti Kamuthy, Adam Alvinczy and his young brother, and even the eldest Alvinczy, Farkas, who had abandoned his vicarious travels and, though it was now rather tight for him, had donned his old sky-blue hussar's tunic.

In Monostor Street Balint met the kind Ida Kendy, Countess Laczok, who had come in from Var-Siklod to see that her sons were well provided with a host of things they would not need, scarves to keep out the cold and other oddments so that they would not get wet at the front. She was out shopping when Balint met her and though filled with anxiety she did her best to hide it and smiled gaily when Balint greeted her.

The smile faded as soon as she looked closely at him. 'Have you been ill?' she asked. 'You look so pale!'

Balint parried the question and they walked on together. This was when he encountered the three Alvinczys. Those tall, fair, good-looking and broad-shouldered young men were walking along arm-in-arm and keeping step, their heels tapping in true military fashion and spurs clinking as they went. They kissed Aunt Ida's hand and shook Abady's and talked loudly in high good humour.

Farkas gave Abady several hearty claps on the shoulder, as befitted a military man, for there was now no trace of the world-weary melancholic that Balint had last seen at Magyarokerek. Now he was all merry and extrovert. The Alvinczy brothers were as happy and confident of success as if they were just setting off for a ball. 'We'll be back by Christmas!' they cried, for had not the German Emperor said the same and he, of all people, should know. 'It's carnival time!' they shouted. 'Hurrah! Hurrah! The hussars are coming!'

'Seeing you three,' smiled Aunt Ida, 'anyone'd believe we'll beat the Russians in no time!'

'We three?' replied Farkas. 'We won't only be three. We've just had news from Fiume that Akos has escaped from the Foreign Legion. He ran off the moment he heard about the war and gets here the day after tomorrow. Then there'll be four of us!'

Balint and Countess Laczok were fascinated by the news and at once asked how it had happened and how they had heard. The brothers did not know very much. It seemed that Akos had arrived at Fiume on one of the Austria-Lloyd steamers. At Casablanca he had swum halfway across the harbour, discreetly boarded a ship and stowed away until after she had sailed. Then he had worked his passage as a stoker. At Fiume he had been arrested as he had no papers, but the Governor of Fiume, who had known Farkas Alvinczy when he had been in Parliament, had believed Akos's story and wired to Farkas for confirmation. So all was well.

Standing at strict attention the brothers said their goodbyes and clattered off as if they had been soldiers all their lives.

* * *

Abady said goodbye to Aunt Ida when they reached a shop she wanted to visit.

He had just turned homewards when Aurel Timisan spoke to him: 'Well, well, my Lord! And what do you think of this turn of events?' There was a mocking tone in his voice and a smile lurked behind his thick white moustache.

Balint did not care for the undoubted irony in the question and so answered only with some mild generality. Then he asked: 'Tell me, why did the Romanian minority, through your new parliamentary lobby, refuse Tisza's overtures? As a first step to national co-operation it seemed to me a most remarkable move for the government to have made.'

'A first step? We're a long way from that now! We, my dear Count, are realists. Before the Balkan War, even before the peace, we might have considered it. But now? That is all history now, and all around us the old Monarchy is breaking up!' He waved two fingers lightly in the air, and went on: 'Today the Heir to the throne, the only man who might have brought us together, is dead. Perhaps he . . . ?'

'I'll never believe that. His ideas were crazy. A Triple Monarchy? Habsburg imperialism taking in all the southern Slavs as far as Salonika? Why, Franz-Ferdinand's programme was sheer fantasy!'

'Perhaps. I don't deny it; but there was an idea there,' replied the old Timisan pensively. Then, with a flash of sincerity, he said: 'Fate has a macabre sense of humour, has she not? Our poor Archduke was murdered by the Slavs whom he loved and wanted to make great; and now the Hungarians, whom he hated, are making war to avenge him. It is amusing, is it not? Really very funny indeed!'

Balint found the old revolutionary's mocking smile insupportable. They parted, and Balint went home.

CHAPTER THREE

BALINT ARRIVED AT Denestornya in the afternoon. Two of the stable lads had already received their army papers, as had eight farm workers, a '*darabont*' – man of all work – the blacksmith and three of the under-gardeners and, most serious of all, Miklos

Ganyi, his right-hand man. There was a great deal to do for all these had somehow to be replaced, and all arrangements must be made before Balint himself left to rejoin his regiment at Varad on the following day.

On his desk was a registered letter from Vienna. The envelope bore the elegant gold circle emblem of the foreign ministry. It was from Slawata, now head of his department. It was dated August 4th and informed Abady that Slawata had arranged for him to be seconded to the General Staff as liaison officer for the Ministry of Foreign Affairs. He was asked to go at once to Vienna where his duties would be explained to him.

Balint was sure that Slawata had done this out of good will for an old friend thinking that he could thereby save him from service in the front line. It also showed that Slawata at least was happy about the way things were going, because he went on to take Balint into his confidence, telling him '*Berchtold hat die Sache brilliant gemacht* – Berchtold has managed everything brilliantly,' and he went on to explain exactly where this brilliance lay. He had purposely, wrote Slawata, not shown the text of the ultimatum to Austria's allies; neither to Berlin lest they should pass it on to Rome, nor to Rome since they would have shown it at once to London and Paris! Even if it had got no further than Vienna there would have been cabinet meetings and discussions and the wording would have been changed and toned down. They would have ruled out the demand for compensation which would ensure '*Die endgültige Abrechnung* – the final reckoning . . .' In this way Berchtold had so arranged it all that no one could stop him.

Italy, of course, went on Slawata, had already abandoned her former friends, but then Austria had not taken her into account for several years past; but the German foreign minister, Bethman-Hollweg, good fellow that he was, had swallowed it all without a word! '*Wir haben den Kerl überrumpelt!* – we caught the fellow unawares!'

Balint was horrified by the casual tone of everything Slawata wrote. He supposed that it was possible that this was not exactly what he thought but that, as a career diplomat, he was merely applauding the adroitness with which Berchtold had out-manoeuvred his allies.

Later on another sentence struck him. '*Conrad war auch famos* – Conrad, too, was splendid!' for it was he who had broken down

the opposition of the Emperor himself. What had happened was
that Conrad, as Chief of the Austrian general staff, had told
Franz-Josef that the Serbs had already forced the crossing of the
Sava river. It had not been true, but it had been the only way to
get the monarch's signature.

Balint read this letter sitting at his grandfather's desk in Count
Peter's old manor.

He was overcome with anger and the deepest sorrow. So
between them Berchtold and Conrad had forced the country
into war! And they had chosen this moment to do so! Balint
could not conceive how they could have shouldered such an
awful responsibility, even if one admitted that sooner or later war
would have been inevitable.

As for Russia, she had been preparing for war for a long time
and so, even if hostilities did not start at once, they were inevitable in the next year or so. The great show-down could not be
postponed more than three years at most; but to provoke it now,
when the Dual Monarchy was at a severe disadvantage, seemed
to Balint to be sheer folly. Surely it would have been better to
wait, for the situation was so fluid that things might well have
improved. It was always possible that Russian and English
interests in Asia might conflict; while, in Africa, English, French
and Italian aims could well be so opposed that any alliance
between those nations would be gravely threatened. There were
sinister stirrings in Ireland that might pre-occupy the British.
Given time anything could occur to diminish the encircling
threat to Germany and Austria.

But they had chosen this moment when everyone was their
enemy!

Balint sat for a long time before the window. Then he sat up and
shook himself. He had not come there to waste time in gloomy
thoughts but to put his affairs in order before he had to leave.

He picked up a telegram-form, addressed it to Slawata, and
wrote:

'DANK. KANN UNMOGLICH KOMMEN. HABE MICH BEI
REGIMENT GEMELDET — THANK YOU. UNABLE TO COME
NOW. AM RECALLED TO MY REGIMENT.'

He had joined the Vilos hussars and was expected at regimental
headquarters for posting to the front. Of course he could save his

skin by accepting some important job on the general staff, but why should he worry about his own life? After all it wasn't worth anything any more – a bullet would be better . . .

This thought was uppermost in his mind as he started to work with Ganyi. Together they went over all the files and arranged matters so that the Co-operatives could carry on despite their absence. He decided to burn all his private papers, and sent word up to the castle to light a fire in the tower room for this purpose.

Ganyi took his leave, and Balint was about to follow him out when he again started thinking about what the war might bring. Unlike everyone else he was convinced that it would last for a long time and that it was bound to be lost. He had not said this to anyone because he did not want to undermine their warlike enthusiasm, but he had thought this from the very beginning. It was possible that the Russians might well get as far as Denestornya, and, if they did, then everything would be destroyed and he would be far away if he were not already dead.

His eyes now fell on his grandfather's desk, and he thought that he really should open it and know what was in it before an invading enemy hacked it to pieces. What sacrilege, thought Balint, that this simple old piece of furniture which held so many memories of his childhood might be thoughtlessly destroyed. He felt for the key and fitted it into the lock. Then the unexpected happened. The key turned easily and the lock clicked. This had never happened when he had tried it before, but perhaps now he had unknowingly been more adroit. He pulled the drawer out and looked inside. A strange old scent assailed him, a scent made up of tobacco in an old wooden box, and sealing-wax long turned to resin.

Then he took up the other keys and opened the side drawers. There he found all sorts of little mementos – a golden amber mouthpiece for a pipe, a fine whetstone that Peter Abady must have brought from England, a green leather case with six handsome razors, one for each day of the week; and a little wreath carved from lime-wood which Balint remembered his father showing him and explaining that it was the work of Ferenc Deak himself who had given it to him many years before. Its history was engraved on the base.

There were so many things, now of no possible use.

In the left-hand drawer he found the pair of satin slippers that he also recalled having seen when he was a boy. They were heel-less and the soles were paper-thin. Narrow ribbons were attached to them and they were so small that their owner must have had feet as delicate as wafers. Now, as Balint picked them up, he fancied he saw his grandfather turning them over, showing him the wear on the soles, smiling, and saying 'Look! See how much that little charmer danced!'

Under the shoes was a thick envelope, quite small, only about three inches wide, wrapped in yellowing paper, tied with string and sealed at every flap with black wax. On it was written '*To be burned after my death*'. Above the words was a cross and the date: 1837. The writing was Count Peter's.

They must be letters, a woman's letters, for their edges could be felt through the paper covering. Inside could be felt something else, which seemed to be a little oval frame with a glass front. Balint felt sure it must be the miniature of the letter-writer. Now he recalled what his grandfather's old school-friend, the actor Minya Gal, had told him. Though it had been ten years before, he remembered it well. In guarded terms the old man had told the story of Peter Abady's first love, of a tragic passion that had been shattered by an enforced parting, and how after it his grandfather went off on his travels and no one had heard from him for nearly three years.

It had been an ancient romance whose relics were imprisoned in that carefully fastened envelope, and one that had no doubt ended in a death, which was perhaps what the cross had signified.

It was lucky that he had managed at last to open the drawer for now Balint would be able to ensure that the old count's long-kept secret could be kept from the prying eyes of strangers. He would see to it that his grandfather's wish was respected. Putting the slippers in his pocket he gathered up the packet of letters and the few documents of his own that he wanted to destroy and made his way up to the castle.

He decided to wait until the evening when the fire would be burning well.

The windows were open and outside it was dark. Balint's lamp was set down far from the draught and where he sat all light seemed to come from the fire.

First Balint threw all his own writings into the flames and, when these were blazing up, he threw on top the slippers and his grandfather's envelope, which did not seem to want to catch fire but only just smouldered at the edges. Taking up the poker he tried to push a hole in the envelope so that air would get in. The flames caught, ran along the string and the envelope opened of itself. A tiny coloured miniature slipped out and fell into the embers below. The glass shattered, the metal frame curled up in the heat and in the few seconds before it was consumed by fire he could see the face of a charming young woman who seemed to be smiling up at him.

Balint sat by the fireplace for a long time. He waited until everything had been reduced to ashes, until there was no trace left of the throbbing of two young hearts almost a century before nor of their secret love and hidden tragedy. The likeness of his grandfather still hung on the wall of the small sitting-room – an early Barabas in an Empire frame – but that of the other had just been burnt and it had smiled at him before crumbling to ashes.

The next morning he woke early; it was the last morning he would spend in his ancestral home for a long time, perhaps for ever.

He went to say goodbye to his favourite animals, firstly to the horses out at grass in the hillside pastures, then to the young stallions and then to the mares in their separate paddocks in the park. To each he gave some sugar as a token of his farewell and became very moved by the affection of his old hunters, and especially when Honeydew, Gazsi Kadacsay's thoroughbred, came up and rubbed his face with her soft velvety muzzle.

He made the round of the gardens and then walked up to the summerhouse on the hill above the castle. From there he toured the kitchen gardens and the orchards.

Finally he returned to the house and went into almost every room in that vast building, including his mother's apartments, which had been left unchanged since her death. Everywhere he went, he stopped in front of all of the treasures of art and ancient pieces of furniture, and, above all, stared hard at the many family portraits. In the billiard-room were hung great-grandfathers and great-great-grandfathers in their wigs and powdered hair, great-grandmothers holding tiny bunches of flowers or a little mirror in their delicate tapering fingers. There were also many of more distant relations, young and old, and some of children, boys little more than toddlers, clad in silken skirts but already sporting Hungarian fur hats.

He went the round of the mirror-fronted bookcases in the library and locked up two of them that had been left open so that the magic circle of looking-glass in that round tower room should remain unbroken.

From the billiard-room he passed into the great first-floor dining-hall. Through five of the tall windows the sun shone blindingly bright on the polished wooden floor and glinted on the gilded surface of the showcases and the ormolu feet of the Chinese lacquer cabinets that stood by the walls. The contrasting shadows in the ceiling threw the baroque carved plaster into high relief. Balint stopped in front of one of the pair of copper samovars that stood on the wide serving-tables and caressed it lovingly. Then he gently stroked the little white porcelain figure of one of his great-great-uncles in Hungarian gala dress. He looked into the showcases with their heterogeneous collection of many little objects, greeted the china pug and the dancing girl, and then went on through the blue salon to the yellow drawing-room; and everywhere he went he murmured a soft farewell, to the four *famille verte* K'ang Hsi plates that had been set in gilded bronze in the seventeenth century, to the clusters of glass grapes in the early Murano chandeliers, to the sets of Delft vases and above all to the full-size portrait of Denes Abady, painted by Mytens in the green and gold uniform of the King's Master of Horse; and then to those of his immediate forebears, his father and mother and grandmother, that gazed at him from every wall.

And all the time he said goodbye to many childhood memories. It was on the sharp corner of this table that he had banged his head when only five years old and he had stood just there when his mother had swiftly pressed a silver coin to his forehead. It was on the corner of that carpet that he had tripped, upset the lamp and nearly caused a fire. Here, in this armchair, his grandfather had always sat, with crossed legs, when he came to lunch at the castle every Wednesday. Balint had sat on the floor at his feet and played with his tin soldiers, and from there he had first noticed that Count Peter wore soft half-boots under his trousers and how amazed he had been by the sight, not then knowing that it had been the fashion until the first half of the nineteenth century.

He opened a door at the far end of the room. It led to a small staircase and, beyond this, to the wing that he had started to modernize in the spring. The work had been well under way until he had had it stopped by telegram from Salzburg. He stopped there, feeling he could not bear ever again to see those rooms where he would have lived with Adrienne, to gaze upon anything associated with those dreams of happiness, the spacious bedroom, the day and night nurseries for those heirs of his body that would now never be born.

Resolutely, but with a sombre air, he turned and walked quickly away, back through the drawing-rooms and the dining-hall. Then he descended the wide stone stairs, with their rococo stucco ceiling and ancient faded Gobelins tapestries. It was a stairway fit for kings.

He went down very slowly, keeping very carefully to the very centre of the carpet; step after step, solemnly and slowly until he arrived in the dark gloom of the entrance hall, stone-faced, like a man entering his own tomb.

Early in the afternoon Balint's car drove the full circle of the horseshoe-shaped entrance court with its enclosing walls topped by baroque stone statues, and rumbled swiftly through the arched gateway.

He was driven so fast that in ten minutes they had reached the main road, but there they had to slow down, for the highway was crowded with people from Torda and wagons loaded with bales of hay. They too were on their way to the railway station at Aranyos-Gyeres.

From time to time the throng was so thick that the car had to be stopped. Everyone on the road was a reservist who had been called to the colours. They were mostly in groups of between fifty and sixty men, but sometimes they were much larger, perhaps of more than a hundred. They marched in military fashion, four to a row, and on each side of the road stood women and girls crying as they waited to see their menfolk, husbands, sons and lovers, on their way to the station. Among them were some old men looking for the last time at their grandsons. Some of the young men carried bundles or trunks, others had piled their luggage on little one-horse carts.

At the head of each group there marched gypsy bands and men carrying banners. Some of the newly mobilized soldiers carried flasks of country brandy, others danced gaily in front of the bands singing as they went. But no one had drunk too much, and indeed most of the men had a dignified, serious mien, soberly doing with good-natured calm what they knew to be expected of them.

Balint had put on his uniform, and every time he passed one of these groups they would break out into enthusiastic cheering.

'Hurrah for the war!' they cried. 'Hurrah for the war!'

Some of them recognized him, and then they called out: 'Hurrah for Abady!' and again 'Hurrah for the war!' They all felt full of courage, and were gay and confident: only the women sobbed quietly and dabbed at their eyes.

Balint saluted every band, his heart constricting with pain each time he did so; but he could only acknowledge their greetings and be touched by their simple confidence. He could not echo their cheers, but sat upright with his hand to his cap as he drove past group after group.

It was difficult to get through Torda, for there was an immense crowd in the market-place selecting mountain ponies – pretty little animals, mostly dapple-greys with tiny hard hooves, hardy and willing, crossed with Arab blood. They were needed to draw the machine guns and man the mountain batteries on the Bosnian front. What marvellous animals, thought Balint, and not one will return. They'll all perish, every one.

When he finally got through the town the sun was already low in the sky.

The car raced up to the Dobodo Pass. Here they had to stop again for at the junction with the main road there came all the people from Torda-Turia and Szentmarton, with banners and music like the others. Now there were many more women as well as old people and children, who Balint thought had probably come because they knew they could have a rest at Torda before finally saying goodbye to their men.

Balint got out and sat at the edge of the road looking down the valley of the Aranyos river. It was bathed in sunshine and when he took up his binoculars he found he could even see the bend of the Maros far away. There he could just glimpse a small stand of pine trees, dark indigo-blue in the pale-blue distance.

It was the garden at Maros-Szilvas, which had once been the property of Dinora Malhuysen. As a very young man he had often ridden over to visit her, usually at night. What a long time ago it had been – almost twenty years! He wondered what had become of her, what Fate had held in store for poor little Dinora?

To his right, beyond the shining ribbon of the Aranyos, on the edge of the Keresztes-Mezo lowlands, lay Denestornya.

The hill on which the castle stood was covered with trees and shrubs. Here and there could be seen parts of the long walls and something seemed to be glistening in the reflected sunshine. Balint wondered if it was part of the western façade, perhaps the glazing on the upper veranda, but he could not be sure and even thought that it might be only his imagination. The green patina of the conical copper roofs of the corner towers was plain to see, and these, no matter from what distance they could be glimpsed, gave a clear impression of the size of the vast building. It was like a great stone peninsula jutting out from the wave-crests of the surrounding trees. The long walls spread out in beauty, and the thin white strip to the right formed by the enclosure of the horseshoe court, and the little rectangle of the church half hidden among the confused roofs of the village seemed strangely small between the massive proportions of the castle and of his grandfather's manor house nearby.

Balint again bade farewell to all that lay before him, to the beauty by which he had been surrounded since his childhood, and to all those dreams which had come to such a sad end.

By now those merry bands of eager young men had passed on their way. Gone were the farm carts and baggage. Balint was alone. He returned to the car and drove on.

The road descended steeply into the valley, which was now in deep shadow. He crossed a bridge and then there came a sharp bend.

Here too he was assailed by memories, for it was just there that two years before, on returning to Denestornya, full of happiness after the evening when he had seen Adrienne again at the performance of *Madam Butterfly* at Kolozsvar, he had met Gazsi Kadacsay. Once again he fancied he could see Gazsi as he cantered towards him on his well-fed little pony. Poor Gazsi! His house was not visible from there, that house where his unhappy friend had killed himself from despair at his wasted life and because the culture for which he had yearned had seemed forever beyond his reach.

Banishing such thoughts, he drove on, determined not to waste time regretting the past.

When he reached the foothills of the Felek the car was again delayed because the road was everywhere encumbered by droves

of white oxen and bullocks on their way to the slaughterhouse
where they would be killed to feed the army.

He drove on slowly, for he often had to stop because the road
was so crowded. About a hundred yards from the next pass the
engine boiled – white steam spurting out of the radiator. As there
was no water to be had nearby the chauffeur went back down
the road to find a well. Balint walked on up to the summit to wait
there until rejoined by the car.

In front of him lay a wonderful landscape in the centre of
which was Kolozsvar. To the right the Szamos curved away until,
at Apahida, it disappeared to the north. On his left lay the valley
of Gyalu and beyond it a range of snow-capped mountains.

Behind him the sun went down below the horizon. But there
was still light enough to see what lay before him.

He leaned against the stone wall by the road, still consciously
bidding farewell to all he saw.

Not far away below there was a butter-yellow building beside
the Monostor Road. It was the Uzdy villa, and beside it Balint
could make out the break in the palings of the garden, just where
lay the little gate to the bridge through which, in happier times,
he had so often passed on his way to visit Adrienne.

Not far away was the green-tiled roof of the asylum where Pal
Uzdy had died and, a little to the right, was the theatre from
which he had fled so precipitously on finding Adrienne in the
next box on the night of the opera. There too was the hill of
the Harzongard where he had walked with Adrienne in the first
spring of their ten years of love for each other.

All his life lay before him, his whole past, everything. Even
Kozard, where Laszlo lay buried. He wanted to say farewell to
him too, and he searched the distance through his binoculars for
a sight of the manor house at Kozard and the Gyeroffy family
vault just above it. It lay at the most northerly point of the Szamos
valley; and there it was, a tiny patch of white, a little triangle on
the left bank.

A deep bitterness came over him as he stood there alone, high
above the world he had known and which was now doomed to
perish.

In his mind's eye he saw too the whole generation to which
he belonged, that generation, still young, which had grown up
in that long period of peace that had followed the troubled years
before 1867. It was the men of his generation that had come after

those years of reform and who were the successors of such men as Deak, Eotvos, Miko, and Andrassy, who had lived through the nightmare of the revolution and the repression which followed, who had learned from their tribulations and who had known how to meet troubles with calm and moderation.

But this generation, Balint's own, had drifted farther and farther away from the practical wisdom of their forebears. Reality had been gradually replaced by self-deception, conceit and sheer wrong-headed obstinacy.

Everyone was guilty, all the upper strata of Hungarian society.

He saw before him the entire class of great landowners, spoilt by an arrogance that had led them to neglect the good management of their estates, preferring to vie for pompous offices of state and political advantage. He saw the professors of history, who thought only of the revolutionary struggle against the Habsburg domination and who denigrated those who would have encouraged the Hungarian people to self-knowledge and hard work, with the result that the minds of the young had been filled only with illusory ideals and chauvinistic slogans. From the turn of the century his generation had been fed with self-congratulatory theories which had so misled it that any criticism was at once dismissed as unpatriotic.

He saw before him the magnates and noble families who thought only of social prominence, who forgot their European affiliations and threw the weight of their great fortunes and moral influence behind all that nationalistic nonsense of which they did not believe a word and which, in consequence, had poisoned the nation's politics.

All this he saw before him, just as if he were looking back from beyond the grave.

Now this beloved country would perish, and with it most of his generation. It would perish with this meaningless war; for until now those rousing battle-cries had only meant a call to wars of words and speechifying and argument; and the repeated exhortations to hold out to the last man had only meant not to speak until the end of a debate, and were far from the true murderous reality.

Now this land would perish, and with it that deluded generation that had given importance only to theories, phrases and formulae, that had ignored all reality, that had chased like children after the *fata morgana* of mirage and illusion, that had turned away from everything on which their strength was based, that denied the vital importance of power and self-criticism and national unity.

One virtue alone remained: the will to fight.

And that too would prove in vain.

The town below was now in darkness. Night had fallen.

Only the sky in the west flamed with life.

Long shreds of cloud floated high; ash-coloured strips with shining tassels touched the far horizon. Around and beneath them fire, everywhere fire. The whole world beyond the horizon seemed to be in flames. On the line of the horizon itself the colour was blood-red, rising in the blinding heat of tongues of fire, fiery tears along its whole length as if the whole universe wept burning ash into an ocean of blood. Below the red inferno of the sky were etched heavy, dark-lilac-coloured mountain peaks, their hard-edged contours merging into some endless monolith; they were the mountains of Gyalu and the Magura and, behind them, the mighty Vlegyassa itself.

Vast stony ridges that slanted upwards to the sky.

Giant coffins, a people's tombstones.

In motionless majesty they stood there beneath a world in flames.

The car arrived.

Balint started the descent from the summit.

THE END

Bonczhida, May 20th, 1940

ABOUT THE TRANSLATORS

PATRICK THURSFIELD and KATALIN BÁNFFY-JELEN are the translators of *The Transylvanian Trilogy* (*They Were Counted*, *They Were Found Wanting*, *They Were Divided*, winner of the Weidenfeld Translation Prize 2002), and *The Phoenix Land*, also by Miklós Bánffy.

Not to scale

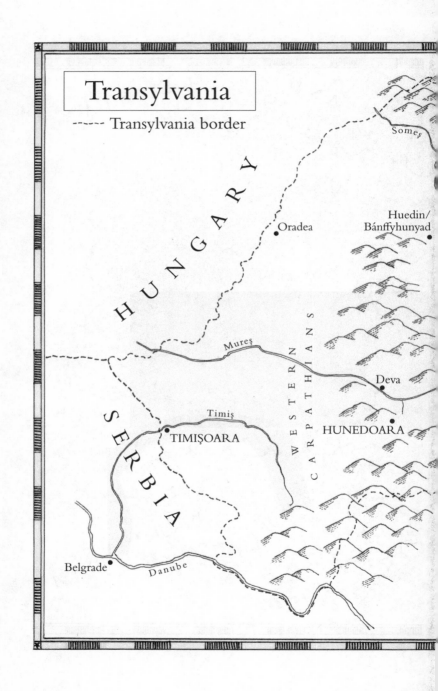

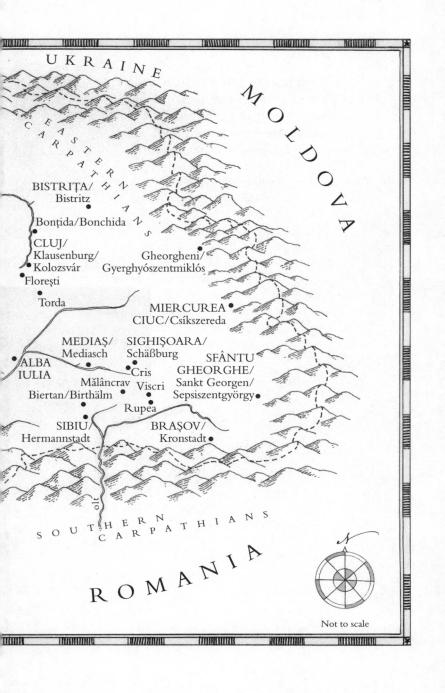

This book is set in BEMBO which was cut
by the punch-cutter Francesco Griffo
for the Venetian printer-publisher
Aldus Manutius in early 1495
and first used in a pamphlet
by a young scholar
named Pietro
Bembo.